MW01027669

Also by Robert Coover

Short Fiction

Pricksongs & Descants

In Bed One Night & Other Brief Encounters

A Night at the Movies

Plays

A Theological Position

Novels

The Origin of the Brunists

The Universal Baseball Association, J. Henry Waugh, Prop.

The Public Burning

A Political Fable

Spanking the Maid

Gerald's Party

Whatever Happened to Gloomy Gus of the Chicago Bears?

Pinocchio in Venice

a novel

JOHN'S WIFE

ROBERT COOVER

Scribner Paperback Fiction

PUBLISHED BY SIMON & SCHUSTER

SCRIBNER PAPERBACK FICTION
Simon & Schuster Inc.
Rockefeller Center
1230 Avenue of the Americas
New York, NY 10020

This book is a work of fiction. Names, characters, places, and incidents either are products of the author's imagination or are used fictitiously. Any resemblance to actual events or locales or persons, living or dead, is entirely coincidental.

First Scribner Paperback Fiction edition 1997
SCRIBNER PAPERBACK FICTION *and design are trademarks of Simon & Schuster Inc.*

Designed by Elina D. Nudelman

Manufactured in the United States of America

1 3 5 7 9 10 8 6 4 2

The Library of Congress has cataloged the Simon & Schuster edition as follows:
Coover, Robert.
John's wife / Robert Coover
p. cm.
I. Title.
PS3553.O633J6 1996
813'.54—dc20 95-49600

CIP
ISBN 0-684-81841-8
0-684-83043-4 (Pbk)

Portions of John's Wife *first appeared in* Conjunctions. *The author is grateful to Miriam and Toby Olson for the use of their Cape Cod home during a crucial stage of the writing of this book. Thanks, also, to Brown University and Deutscher Academischer Austauschdienst.*

For Angela Carter, whose infamous illusionist Doctor Hoffman believed, like Ovid, that "the world exists only as a medium for our desires," and that "Nothing . . . is ever completed; it only changes."

And for Ovid:

"Those two, with so much else in common, were models
for me, masters, examples to follow, and now my justification."

—TRISTIA, BOOK II

. . . Once, there was a man named John. John had money, family, power, good health, high regard, many friends. Though he worked hard for these things, he actually found it difficult not to succeed; though not easily satisfied, he was often satisfied, a man whose considerable resources matched his considerable desires. A fortunate man, John. He was a builder by trade: where he walked, the earth changed, because he wished it so, and, like as not, his wishes all came true. Closed doors opened to him and obstacles fell. His enthusiasms were legendary. He ate and drank heartily but not to excess, played a tough but jocular game of golf, roamed the world on extended business trips, collected guns and cars and exotic fishing tackle, had the pleasure of many women, flew airplanes, contemplated running for Congress just for the sport of it. In spite of all that happened to his wife and friends, John lived happily ever after, as though this were somehow his destiny and his due.

Floyd, less favored, worked for John. He managed John's Main Street hardware business, envied John's power, having none of his own, and coveted John's wife. "Covet" was Floyd's word, out of his respect for the Bible, and because he knew what an evil man he was. It embarrassed Floyd to speak of religion outside of Sunday school and at the bowling alley he swore his soul away to the dark powers with every split or spare he blew, but Floyd had come to this quiet prairie town on the run from a thieving and hell-raising past and had got the church between him and the forces—both vindictive and tempting—that pursued him, and so far it had served him well. He was thankful and taught the Bible to John's children at Sunday school, his voice trembling as he ticked off the Ten Commandments, potent with consequence. Floyd bowled in the winter leagues, toured distant national parks with his wife Edna in the summers, and ran the best hardware store for miles around. Their nearest friend in town was old Stu the car dealer, the only person here they felt at home with, though they saw less of him after his first wife died. They never had a falling out, though, as Otis later claimed.

Now, Gordon was also attracted to John's wife, though not quite in the same way as Floyd. "Covet" was not his word, nor exactly his inclination. What engaged Gordon's attention were her fleeting glances and her subtle movements, somehow never quite complete. She seemed always to be at rest and not at rest at the same time. There was a stillness, a stateliness about her that gave her a kind of monumental grace—yet his photos of her, whether in the studio or out on the streets, never seemed quite able to capture this, no two alike, their infinite variety suggesting an elusive mystery that tested him and drew him on. Gordon sold film, albums, frames, and cameras in his photo shop, developed the snaps of others, took passport and wedding and news photos, and was locally famous for his studio portraits, but before all else, he was an artist. And John's wife, whom he associated with the intrinsic indwelling truth of the town, its very suchness, so to speak, was—though she was not entirely aware of this—his principal subject. He longed to do a complete study of her, in all her public and private aspects. John's wife stepping out of her car (he had this one). John's wife trying on a hat. John's wife dreaming. John's wife teeing off, walking her dog (this, too), combing her daughter's hair, combing her own hair, scratching an itch. He'd called her in the titles of his collection by many names but never her own—"Andromeda," "Eunomia," "Muse," "Princess," "Echo" (suggested to him by a story his friend Ellsworth had once told), "Beauty," "Woman," "Model," "Desire," "She"—but all of these names provoked private stirrings in him that he felt to be in conflict with his higher artistic aspirations, so in the end he chose the more professional and impersonal practice of considering his photos of her as subsets of his traditional studio family portraits and thence referred to her simply as "John's Wife." As in "John's Wife Taking Communion" (now in his collection). "John's Wife Pregnant" (missed it). "John's Wife Emerging from the Morning Mist" (not yet). He wished to tour her as Floyd might a national park, to explore her intimately, exhaustively, hour by hour, inch by inch—John's wife on the telephone, John's wife at a PTA meeting, on a swing, at the movies, John's wife writing a letter, John's wife examining her underwear, John's wife in the supermarket, at the doctor's office, at a dance, in the rain, in ecstasy, in doubt—until there was nothing left to see. It might be said that Gordon—whose passion was to capture the private gesture, the hidden surface, the vanishing secrets of the race, freeing them from time's ceaseless violence—coveted stasis.

Something like this could be said of Otis as well, though Otis was no photographer. He had bought a camera once, but had felt clumsy with the thing in his hand, cheated by the little paper pictures: his wife had fattened, his children grown to brats, these lost shapes meant nothing to him. Otis was a man of the present, it was the community, here and now, that held his interest. This community Otis saw as a closed system, no less fixed by custom and routine than by its boundaries on the map, a clocklike mechanism if not perfect in its parts and movements, then at least perfectly adequate. Nothing upset him more than disruptions to the pattern of the daily round. He thought people should go out of town to get drunk, and stay out until they were sober. Parties were for Saturday nights; noise on other nights made Otis nervous. He distrusted all intrusions, all changes, strangers, big ideas: why mess with a good thing? Even unseasonable weather disconcerted him. John's grand projects did, admire him though he might. Newsman Ellsworth's wacky getup, kids dragracing over the humpback bridge out by Settler's Woods or out at the malls, that spooky photographer with his secret albums, loitering strangers and cars with out-of-state plates. Otis thought of himself as a kind of guardian warrior, one eye on the periphery, one eye on the center. At the center lived John's wife, whom he loved.

Floyd, Gordon, Otis, then: all with this in common. And others, too: Kevin, for example, later known as Patch, his eye on her shifting hips and stiffened elbow, or the embittered Nerd with the hallowed garter in his pocket, dreamy Ellsworth and scheming Rex, her pastor Reverend ("Let it happen") Lenny, wistful old Alf with his finger up her, Fish and Turtle ("Got the hots," said Fish, and Turtle blushed and grinned and got them, too)—what male in town was *not*, one way or another, fascinated by John's wife? John was not. An irony. Or perhaps this is often the case. John was a busy man who liked to make money, see the world, have a good time while it lasted, and as for women, he used them as freely and unreflectively as he did men. And with much less hope of making money off them, though he often did. He supposed they had their problems, who did not? But he had a big construction firm to run, lands to master, malls and suburbs to build, as well as Barnaby's old lumberyard, a chain of stores, an airport and a budding cargo line, money in several national and local businesses and industries, everything from computer games and action toys to alarm systems and armaments, he had properties and ambitions (on his shortlist: a racetrack and a baseball team) and an appetite big as the prairie, and when he thought of his wife and children, he thought of them mainly as political and social assets, which he estimated once a year by means of Trevor's tax returns and Gordon's family portraits. Anyway, he disbelieved in love, at least between people. What John loved, as he told Nevada while doing a loop and roll at a thousand feet that made her wet her pants with excitement and terror, were the days of his life.

Gordon, gesture's hunter, would have understood John's view of love, though he didn't know of it. As John loved life, Gordon loved form. People, intrinsically grotesque, were beautiful only (as he had put it many years ago, shocking his friend Ellsworth, who could not understand the photos he was taking of his mother) as shapes frozen in space. Beyond his photographs, life was disintegration and madness, a meaningless frenzied blur. Birth, death, labor, love: he looked, blinked, and out of his acid baths came a piece of time. Chosen by him, held by him. Forever his, while the world outside dissolved into obscene confusion, vaguely remembered, if at all. Some subjects—a child with its finger in its nose, a dead body, an empty swimming pool, crumpled metal, an intimate scar, reflections in a window—drew him toward a kind of interpretive engagement, in which the photographic forms seemed to hold on to something not visible on the surface of his print. Others (which he thought of as somehow nobler)—John's wife, for example, uninhabited vistas, slanted light on bared flesh—released him from these worldly illusions into the freedom of pure but sensuous abstraction. Such moments, such photos, he could contemplate forever.

One day, Waldo and Lorraine walked into Gordon's studio to order portraits of their two boys, and lying flat on the glass counter was a blowup of John's wife, taken from a group shot at a country club dance. Lorraine, who distrusted John's wife in the same way that she distrusted the heroines of all the novels she'd read, cast a suspicious glance at Gordon: who was this picture for? Couldn't be for John, what did he care for photographs, much less of his wife? Lorraine's husband Waldo said: "Hey! What a swell picture of John's wife!" She could have strangled him. Fat Gordon flushed and pushed the photo aside: Lorraine saw this and wondered if there was some kind of hanky-panky going on. She had heard about some of this clown's other photos. Lorraine had had a dream about him once in which he seemed to exist in or as a dirty puddle on the floor, and she'd awakened with the realization that there was something sinister about the photographer that generally went unrecognized. Waldo continued to beam happily, noticing nothing. Lorraine had married the most popular guy in college, but he was a complete corkhead, an imbecilic party boy—what she and the other girls used to call a windup talking dildo. John had brought her husband here as his Assistant VP, but, with his brain, he was more like an Assistant BB. Empty Wallets, they called him. When John asked her why she gave Waldo such a hard time, she'd replied: "Marry a prick with ears and soon all you've got left are the ears." John had grinned his grin and she'd felt her spine lock up. "Haw," said Waldo now as Gordon's wife Pauline came in with her blouse half-buttoned and her hair uncombed, and while Waldo ogled the little frump, Gordon said: "Where the heck's my schedule-book, Pauline?" She didn't know.

Why would Lorraine suspect hanky-panky where John's wife was concerned? Probably, her best friend Marge would say, because Lorraine was a constitutionally suspicious woman, made all the more so by her vulgar, butt-slapping, two-timing husband, and because, being a relative newcomer in town, Lorraine didn't know John's wife all that well. Marge could have told her: suspect John if you like, hanky-panky was that man's middle name (she would have been telling Lorraine nothing new), but not his wife. It would be like suspecting that the cornflowers in John's wife's garden got up at night and went out chasing bees. Marge had grown up here, a year behind John in school, a year ahead of his wife, and in an isolated little prairie town like this one they were all like siblings. They'd gone to birthday parties together, church picnics, field trips, highschool and country club dances. They were in National Honor Society together, they'd exchanged valentines and May baskets, played hide-and-seek, colored Easter eggs in each other's kitchens, raced bicycles and had fights, popped one another's blackheads. The world had changed over the years since then and everything in it, but not John's wife, poor thing. Everybody's favorite Homecoming Queen. Period. Marge felt pity for her, but at the same time hated her for being pitiable, just as she despised John but admired him for having the power to be despicable. Marge and John had fought since grade school, were still fighting, most recently over the brutal razing of the city park to build another of John's tasteless eyesores, this time a concrete civic center and swimming pool, and most of the time John, more ruthless than she, and richer, too, had beat her, beat her badly. She'd never let that stop her, she had gone on standing up to him all her life, fighting back through defeat after defeat. Just as she was about to do again, so he'd better get ready. It was the only thing a man like that could respect, and truth to tell, Marge wanted that, John's respect, and knew that she deserved it.

The trouble was, she went about it backassward, and with an ass as ugly as hers, this was a big mistake, or anyway that was Lorraine's husband Waldo's opinion. Marge was a tedious busybody ("pissy-potty" was how Waldo pronounced it, never softly), a piece of cold "pushy" with an old axe to battle, a butt like a stop sign, and for tits nothing but knuckled nipples, hard as brass. It was her husband Trevor (Triv was Waldo's name for him, short for Trivial Trev) who wore the panties in that family, Waldo always said. He called Marge Herr Marge, sometimes Hairy Marge or Butch, Mad Marge when she had her dander up, which was most of the time when Waldo was around, he gave her little peace. Nor she him, it was disgust at first sight. When he and Lollie first came to town some years ago, thanks to his good old college pal and true-blue fraternity brother, Long John, Waldo had got paired up with Marge in a mixed-twosomes tourney at the club, and not only had she outscored him, he'd been too crocked on the back nine to do anything but slash wildly at his approach shots, or even, what the hell, to see the goddamn greens he was supposedly aiming at, and so had blown their chances for the trophy, which she was apparently used to winning.

Most of the time, she'd had to help him find his ball, which seemed always to be miles away from where he'd last seen it, and in ever worsening circumstances, which for some reason tickled his funnybone. "Hoo-boy! Gone again! Go fetch, Marge!" The one time when he found it before she did, he stood on it, drinking from his pocket flask, and let her keep looking until she was frothing at the mouth, his stifled laughter pumping out an obstreperous rat-a-tat, itself not unlike stifled laughter, from the other end of his wind machine. Herr Marge didn't think it was at all funny when he finally "discovered" the ball underneath his alligator golf shoe ("So that's what it was! Sumbitch! Thought my corns was acting up!"), but Waldo was having a terrific time. On the last hole, he just couldn't sink his putt, the goddamned green kept tipping and yawing on him, so after six or seven goofy tries, one from between his legs with the handle of the putter, the business end hooked in the fly of his checkered lavender golf pants, he just laid back and swatted the little booger out of sight, maxing out on that hole as a kind of fitting climax to a wonderful day. His partner, determinedly lining up her own putt, was muttering bitterly about his obnoxious drunken behavior, his boring vulgarity, and his basic inability to play this game, so he tossed down another ball, turned sober long enough to keep the green steady under his feet, and with a clean crisp stroke caromed his ball into hers, croquet-style, while she was still bent over it, sending it off into a sand trap, a brilliant shot that was widely admired at the nineteenth hole afterwards by just about everyone except Mad Marge and his own unloving wife Lorraine, who dragged him away, the mean old grouch, before he'd reaped his full rewards.

Well, they were new in town that summer and wholly dependent on the beneficence of good brother John, whose wife was close to that woman, or said to be, so Waldo's wife had her reasons for jerking the reins, but as to love, it was true, there was none of it in her heart, for—even though she had once guided her life by it, due, she now believed, to bad reading habits—Lorraine, like Gordon and John, disbelieved in love. A sales hook for the entertainment racket, meaningful as "lite" on diet foods, that was her opinion. Waldo, who had had few reading habits, good or bad, still did believe in love, even if he couldn't say what it was. He knew, though, it could get you in trouble, and if it could, would. This view of love as an irresistible but chastising force would have been shared by many in town—by Veronica, for example, another schoolchum of John's wife and much chastised by that emotion to which she nevertheless wistfully clung—or by Otis, upholder of order, for whom love was more or less the same thing as grace, though one could sometimes make you hot and foolish, while the other usually did not—or by Beatrice, the preacher's wife, who believed that all love came from the Creator, like her husband Lennox said on Sunday mornings, but that the Lord sometimes moved in mysteriously distressing ways. As now, for example: how was it possible, dear God, her present plight? Kate the town librarian, referring to this sweet-joy/wild-woe power of love to overwhelm, delight, and then undo, liked to say that humankind's apprehensions of the divine and of the diabolical were equally love's delusions, while goodness, truth, and beauty, without love, were fantasies, idle fictions of a mind turned in on itself and meaningful as chicken scratchings. That is to say, Kate, assenting but without illusions, also believed, much loved herself so long as she lived, in love. As did Dutch the motelkeeper, who nightly watched what he called meat fever erupt and die beyond his magic mirrors but scrupulously kept his distance from a force he thought of as anything but benign. And likewise Alf, he of the inquiring finger, for whom love was, unreasonably, reason's sedative, else best understood as a chemical reaction to certain neural stimuli, sometimes locally pleasurable, generally overrated. His nurse Columbia sympathized with this latter opinion, though more or less, with but one exception, in the abstract, but did not trust her widowered colleague's pose of bemused detachment, especially with John's wife in the stirrups. For Clarissa, it was just great, love was. "Intense" was her word for it. Like, wow. But for her granddad, Barnaby the builder, it only led to despair, pinning you to the earth and gnawing your heart out, without letting you die. If one could stop loving, there would be peace and death. Barnaby being yet another who, inconsolably, loved John's wife.

Ah well, love: a profound subject. Back in his mayoral days, giving the traditional bandstand speech at the climax of the annual Pioneers Day parade one hot summer, John's wife still just a schoolkid then, Barnaby's old lawyer friend Maynard, thumbs hooked in the sleeveholes of his vest, speculated that it was love that had made and mapped the town: the original pioneers' love of adventure that brought them out here, the settlers' love of the land that caused them to stay and put down roots, the love of the early town planners for order and progress and the entrepreneurial spirit, those qualities that caused this great town center to rise so gloriously where nothing larger than teepees had ever been seen before, and the love of all those present for justice and prosperity and the good life and for one another. And also for God, he was quick to add. He evoked the time when the only sounds you would hear in these streets would be the clip-clop of horses in the dirt and mud, the lazy drone of bees and locusts, the clink of chopped ice in the lemonade pitchers and the creaking of porch swings, and he said that these were the sounds of love. He spoke of the town as their common mother, the town limits as her loving embrace, and he compared the crisscross grid of the streets to the quilting of a mattress on which, he said, we were all one big loving family, causing his sister Opal, John's mother, to pick up her paper fan and wave it in front of her face, perhaps finding this one metaphor too many and wishing to remind her brother it was time to have the preacher bless them all and sit down. This Maynard was the father of John's garter-clutching cousin Maynard Junior, sometimes known as the Mange or the Nerd, for whom love was a singular obsession, otherwise a kind of dirty joke, and he in turn in time became the father of Maynard III, also called Turtle, who thought love was for wimps until his buddy Fish gave him a couple of new ideas a few weeks ago, which were exciting but not very clear.

Old silver-tongued Grandpa Maynard might still be around, but the city park and its quaint gazebo-like bandstand where he flaunted his rhetoric were forever gone, just a dimming memory now like the now-dimming ex-mayor's fondly remembered clinks, creaks, and clip-clops, public speaking of the all-community sort being performed in more recent times inside the new civic center or else, until John created Peapatch Park, on temporary staging erected in the asphalt parking lot outside, depending on the weather and the occasion. This starkly modern new edifice, named in honor of old Barnaby the builder and built by his son-in-law, was generally held to be, though controversial, the town's major new construction of the decade, perhaps (some said) of the century, its most popular architectural innovation being its Olympic-sized swimming pool with retractable roof, famous throughout the state and written up in all the metropolitan Sunday papers. You could always count on John to make things happen. His old football, wrestling, and track coach Snuffy, one of the city councilmen most responsible for pushing the project through all its legal and political obstacles (always some soreheads opposed to progress), became, with John's blessing, the unopposed candidate for the mayoralty and was himself a public speaker of some renown, plain-talking but inspirational in his gruff straight-from-the-shoulder cut-the-crap way. Old Snuffy, as the townsfolk liked to put it, knew how to kick butt. Starting with his own teams. More than one young wiseass in this town had got used in practice as a live tackling dummy until the message got through that when Snuffy talked about giving your all for the team, son, he meant *all*. Ever do two hundred push-ups with a foot in your back? In the mud? In full uniform? *After* a game? About love, though, this inveterate bachelor had little to say. He was better on grit and hustle and hanging tough. Had Snuffy known women in his time? Sure, plenty. And all kinds, too, from two-bit to fancy. But love, which he believed in like everybody else, was never a head-to-head body slam with some woman, or man or boy either, it was more abstract than that, more like an ideal form, to speak in the philosophizing manner, as in "I love this game!" or "Body contact! I love it!" To love was to play hard, and to be loved was to win.

God-fearing Floyd, who managed John's downtown hardware store and was a lifelong expert on butt kicking, mostly from the receiving end, had a more down-to-earth, one-on-one notion of what love was, having once loved his own wife Edna, and that was how he knew that what he now felt for John's wife was covetousness. He did not want to give himself to her, did not want to embrace her, care for her, adore her, live with her. He did not even want to make love to her. He wanted to throw her down on her fantastic ass and fuck the bejesus out of her. Praise the Lord, this had not yet happened. "Thou shalt not!" he roared at the giggling brats in Sunday school, his voice quaking with the conflict in his heart. He often imagined taking her right there, among the choir robes, something about the glossy feel of them, the range of murky body odors, the cheap lockerroom challenge of the church's damp back chambers with their unpainted cement walls, cold tile floors. Or else over a counter of carpet tacks, flare nuts, and auger bits down at the store on Main Street. On top of the lead float in the Pioneers Day parade. On the fancy lime green toilet in John's house between bridge hands (the toilet in Floyd's house was white with a pink terrycloth seat cover and a loose handle). Or, shoot, why not trump her right on the cardtable itself, frigging grand slam! Maybe his feelings toward John were mixed up in these stormy desires. Whenever the four of them played bridge or had dinner together, which was about once every three or four months, depending on John's sullen sense of duty (Floyd sensed this and it embittered him), Floyd contrived to sit so as to have his knee pressed against John's wife's knee. This recklessness: was it just another effort to emulate John?

John was a man often emulated, Floyd was not alone in this. Some men emulated his style, others his vocabulary, some his aggressiveness or his laugh. Alf emulated his golf swing, not that it did him any good, old Stu the car dealer his jokes and Hard Yard his derring-do, Lennox his cool acceptance of the way things were. When Lennox told his wife Beatrice, his children, his students, his congregation, and most of all himself, "Let it happen," he was emulating John. For John's old highschool coach Snuffy, entering politics, it was not so much the boy's fierce team loyalties that he emulated (these Snuffy shared and who knows but engendered) as his strategic use of them in others. In short, it was John's smarts he sought to emulate, just as for Dutch it was his friend's killer instincts, and for Marge's husband Trevor, aka Trivial Trev, his employer's respect for numbers, for statistics. "There's no such thing as money, Trev," John used to tell him, his reading spectacles halfway down his broken nose making him look mockingly professorial, "only the counting of it." Trevor also emulated John's attention to detail, his caution with money, his staying power, but he may have been misreading John, seeing what he wanted to see. As all do. Lorraine's corkhead husband Waldo emulated everything about John, some even thought he was making fun of John, but in actuality Waldo thought John was emulating *him*. Perhaps Waldo was right, partly right anyway, they had been buddies since college, it was a question of which came first, as Waldo liked to say: the chigger or the leg. Though they had often shared women in the past, Waldo even emulated John's attitude toward John's wife: utter disinterest. Anything else would have seemed like incest to him.

Otis, who emulated John's quiet force, something he had picked up from John back when they had played football here together, had been in love with John's wife since high school, though she was surely unaware of it. He had never gone out with her, hardly dreamed of it (in this respect, there was no emulating John, not for Otis), had rarely even spoken to her, but they had met a couple of times at highschool parties, and one night at one of them she had taught him how to dance. He could still see, as though in a dream, their four feet shuffling about below them, crisscrossing on the shiny hardwood floor of the school gym, their toes bumping, could still feel her soft hand on the back of his neck as she led him about. Though he was now married with four children and never danced, the warm proximity and generosity of her young body that night in the highschool gym was still his best and most magical knowledge of womanhood. Whenever Otis, self-styled guardian warrior, thought of the Virgin Mary, he thought of John's wife.

Whenever Pauline the photographer's wife thought of Otis, she thought of the way he cried the first time she sucked him off. She thought he should play James Cagney in the movies. Whenever she thought of Otis's cleft-chinned highschool football coach Snuffy, she thought of a cartoon character in a dirty comicbook who wore his impotence on his face. Not surprising that her husband Gordon's campaign poster headshot of the squinty old geezer with the sausage nose had attracted so much graffiti. Whenever she thought of her husband, she thought of some kind of fat robot with a big glass eye and an exploding forehead. Once he had got the floodlamps so close to her thighs, he had burned them. This shot (what did he think he'd see?) had not turned out. Whenever Pauline thought of the three brothers from the drugstore, Harvard, Yale, and Cornell, she thought of a story about eating and bedding down she'd been told in the first grade. Would her life have been different had she been born with golden locks? It was not a question Pauline would ever have asked. Here's another: What is love? If pressed, she'd probably have said that it was something that ran over you like a devil train or a wild mule, knocking down all the walls, for that was pretty much what she thought of whenever she thought of love. Whenever Pauline thought of John's friend Waldo, she thought of a guy in a carnival who invited people in to see the loving couple two feet tall. His wife punched the tickets. With her teeth. Whenever she thought of John, she thought of a young magician (though he was no longer young) with his shadowed face ablaze at the edges with unnatural fire and his pants stuffed full of writhing copperheads. What a night that was. Or must have been: it was like a dream or an old movie. Whenever she thought of John's wife, she thought of her dead sister coming to her in a nightmare: she was taller than the doorframe, ten years old, wore a ragged white nightdress, and her breasts were dripping blood.

Why did Otis cry when Pauline sucked him off that first time? Otis was a hard man, one of the hardest around. And Pauline was in her day the sweetest cocksucker in high school, maybe the best the town had ever had. A cynic might suppose it was because John had married the girl that hard man loved. A romantic might say there was something wrong with him. Otis knew better than either: he cried, he knew, for the loss of his freedom. He had taken this experience into his life, and now it would never let him go. He knew, even before he came, lying there in the back of the old panel truck in the Country Tavern parking lot, his knotted-up ass beginning to slap the cold metal floor, that there would be many nights in the years to come when he would need Pauline's mouth again, when he would roam the streets in a fever, unable to work, unable to go home to his wife and children, unable even to think clearly. As for John marrying the girl he loved, well, she was from a good family in town, Otis from a poor one, if you could even call it a family, and he was younger than she was, he couldn't blame her for failing to notice him, for marrying a guy who had everything like John, which anyway happened when he was far away at war, and in fact he wished them both well. He became, though at some distance, their friend and protector. John could leave home at any time and know that his wife would be safe. Yet, often, more often even than for Pauline's warm wet mouth around his cock, Otis the lawman longed for the touch of John's wife's hand on the back of his neck again.

Thus, the men of the town revealed themselves through their longings, Otis, Maynard, Floyd, and all the others. Women, too, Lorraine, Marge, Veronica, Beatrice, but in a different way: they were holding something together out here in this vast emptiness, themselves perhaps. The men were more audacious, risked more in their fantasies, as though they perceived this as a birthright. Death was the province of the women, and wisdom, and paradox—garbage left them by the men perhaps, but useful to them as they plotted out the terms of their survival after the cataclysm. Men ventured, but women prepared the field, spreading their skirts out over what ground they could hold (Lollie's image; her friend Marge, whom Waldo called Mad Marge, rarely wore skirts, saw it differently). The attention of John's wife, however momentary and enigmatic, was one of the laurels the town's men competed for, while the women, contrarily, often felt threatened by John's wife, yet protected by her at the same time. Lorraine, having lost much, sometimes felt she hated her, yet had to admit she needed her as she needed Waldo's idiocy: one had to live with these strange forces. John's wife often called forth these ambivalent responses from the women around her. Trevor's wife Marge envied John's wife, pitied her. Little Clarissa felt a kind of sentimental rage toward her, Opal a jealous affection, Lumby an erotic disgust. Old Stu's wife Daphne loved her, more than anyone in the world really, but she could have expressed this better if John's wife were dead. Floyd's wife Edna watched her as one watched a cloud: perhaps it would rain; it didn't matter.

Daphne watched everything these days as one watched a cloud. Seeing and not seeing. John's wife was her best friend, had been, maybe still was, who could say? Things were pretty vague. Her memories, too, about as cloudy as the rest of it, thanks to Amazing Grace, but she could still recall sitting in the cold concrete stands of a university football game with John, drinking whiskey from a pocket flask. He had invited her up for a Thanksgiving weekend and she had brought her best friend from high school along, John fixing her up with one of his fraternity brothers. Daphne and John were under a blanket and he had his free hand in her pants and she felt very good. As she felt now, with her own hand in her pants, lacking any available other: funny how entangled the present was with the past, hard to tell them apart sometimes. Daphne's friend was there at the game that day with a comedian named Val or Vern, whatever happened to that guy, he had a missing molar he could whistle through and he sang like a tinny prewar radio crooner, you could even hear the static. How vivid it all was! She should write this up for Elsie's newspaper: "I Remember." The guy's favorite number was "When the Red, Red Robin Comes Bob, Bob, Bobbin' Along," and while he warbled away, John thrummed her clitoris like a tuning fork. Magic. Like another dimension. It was cold. The sky was blue. The team they were cheering won. Later, in some other memory, might have been the same weekend, more likely not (Christmas? Easter? some time that stank of festering happiness), her best friend had her head on John's shoulder in the front seat of John's new silver Mustang, while Daphne was getting mauled on the cramped bucket seats on the floor in the back by a guy with a flat-top haircut and a boil on his nose, feeling not so good. Sort of like, she thought then, thought now, sniffing her fingers, a runner in a relay race, passing on the baton, not because she was ready to let go of it—not Daphne, hell's bells, are you kidding? give me that sucker!—but because she was supposed to. No wonder she'd been maid of honor at their wedding.

A remarkable event, that wedding, the best the town had seen in years and nothing like it in the nearly two decades since. As one might expect, of course, when Mitch's son married the builder's daughter, so dazzlingly beautiful on the day, people said the sight of her made their eyes smart. Her mother, too, was a looker in her day, as many present were reminded when the bride glided into view, though there was a mischievous fiery-eyed edge to Audrey's darker beauty that her gentle and radiant daughter, beloved by all who knew her as Audrey was not, did not possess. The church was wall-to-wall that memorable day with political bigwigs from the state capital and visiting business cronies of the two family patriarchs, together with all the schoolfriends of the bride, including a penpal all the way from Paris, France, a complementary pack of John's fraternity brothers down from the university, whooping it up like puppies, Waldo among them, still unmarried then, a multitude of family, friends, and employees, and a great congregation of ordinary townsfolk, young and old, enthralled witnesses to this grand and extravagant event, so full, it seemed, of meaning for them all. Kate the librarian, a thoughtful soul, remarked to her friend Harriet on the occasion (Harriet had just expressed her disappointment that Oxford's and Kate's son Yale was not after all the groom, adding with a regretful sigh that the more things change, the more they stay the same, and this wedding just proved it) that, yes, great ingatherings of this kind did indeed confirm the community's traditional view of itself, but confirmation was also a kind of transformation: this town, unchanging, would never be the same again. On the day, few would have read any but auspicious omens in such an oracle. Daphne, as the maid of honor, was paired with John's handsome fraternity brother Bruce, his best man: lucky sidekicks, everyone thought, headed for a Hollywood ending. Daphne thought so, too, and it might have happened, were it not, she supposed, for the penpal, and had Daphne behaved herself, too much perhaps to ask. Instead, it was John's cousin Maynard Junior who, aching rather for the leg that wore it, caught the bridal garter and paid the piper, a day he remembered as the morning after the last day of his life. Full of regret, Maynard. But years, wives, lives later: he still had the garter.

Daphne's fourth and most recent husband, old Stu, golfing buddy of the groom's father, supplier of Ford trucks to the bride's, and so an honored guest at the wedding, remembered it as a day of destiny, helped along in this remembering, never good at it by himself, by one of Gordon's strangely prophetic photographs, the yellowed eighteen-year-old clipping of which from *The Town Crier* he kept as long as he lived, framed, on his office desk down at the car lot: "LET HIM EAT CAKE!" it said. "MAID OF HONOR NOURISHES WEDDING GUEST." That was at the reception, whiskey by then having eased his allergic reaction to the airless church, or anyhow made his suffering seem more remote. It was a real cattleyard in that church, to put a plain word on it, a perfumed crowd so thick you couldn't breathe, and where there weren't people there were flowers, heaps of them everywhere, so piled up the brick walls seemed to fall away behind them, a delight to the eye maybe but not to Stu's tender passages: he had to load up on the antihistamines to keep from wrecking the service with his explosive country-boy sneezing, and even so spent half the ceremony with his head ducked, his wife Winnie, his wife back then, tut-tutting scornfully at his side while down in his lap he quaked and wheezed like an old hounddog with a bone in his throat. There were more flowers at the reception, too, bombing him afresh with their fragrant rot, Audrey must have bought out the whole damned county, but ice-cold whiskey now as well to wash down the antihistamines and scour out the rust—a dangerous chemistry maybe, but by then Stu badly needed both and cared not a goose's fart for the consequences nor for tedious Winnie's whiny scolding, ever the backseat driver. Crowds like these were typically just so many potential car buyers for Stu, and he had imagined, as he always did, moving at least half his inventory in such a happy free-spending pack-up—mostly upmarket Lincoln-and-Merc trade at that, a real high-class sale barn—but he couldn't even see their goddamn faces. When he did finally make a pitch he found himself pushing a four-wheel-drive farm truck on the little girl from France who seemed to think he was telling her a naughty joke. She was peering up at him, all smiles, waiting for the punchline, so he shifted gears, leaned close, and rumbled melodically in her frail papery ear: "Hinky-dinky, par-lee-*ffoo!*" He winked, roared his big laugh, punched her softly in the shoulder, and thinking, well, the French they are a funny race, drifted off into the noisy blur, looking for the self-service pump: and the next thing he knew, Daphne's hand was on the throttle and her tongue was in his ear.

Gordon had taken the photo now sitting on the old car dealer's desk, but Ellsworth had cropped and capped it for his weekly newspaper, Stu and Daph in, their partners out. This was not the tongue-in-the-ear teaser, but her cake-in-the-kisser boffo, though Ellsworth had caught both acts. Who hadn't? Daphne was pretty manic in those days, hard not to notice, and old Stu, sitting beside her, so drunk his weepy red eyes were crossed, had been an easy target. Earlier that day, or maybe it was later, as she stretched for the bridal bouquet, her strapless bodice had pulled away and, instead of covering herself, Daphne had, whooping like a raffle-winner, grabbed the bouquet and held it to her face, her bare breasts bugging out over the fallen cups on either side of the clutched stems like startled cartoon eyes—another of Gordon's photos, one that failed to make *The Town Crier*'s historic spread of course, though it remained to this day a backshop favorite, even though the model herself had, as one might say, outgrown it. The wedding had excited Ellsworth as had little else in his four years back here, and he had front-paged it two weeks running, both before and after, with two inside photo pages in the second week's issue, he being yet another in this town with a special affection for John's wife, more than that really if truth be known, but motivated as well by his newsman's nose: this joining of the local fortunes made for a terrific story, he felt, just when the town most needed one. The entire area at the time was in something of a recession, lying dormant, waiting for something to come along and wake it up, and the wedding was like a fresh breath of life, a real pickup for everyone. Literally, as it turned out: for it was announced at the reception, like a gift from the good fairies, that the state highway commission had decided to route its four-lane north-south link to the new cross-country interstate highway—a sympathetic mating, as it were (Ellsworth's thought)—past the edge of town, ensuring its continued prosperity. They all drank to the wedding couple's health and to their own, Ellsworth climaxing the occasion with the recital, by way of a toast to the bride, of his newest poem, later to be published in *The Town Crier:*

> It may have been the *Knave of Hearts*
>   Who stole the tarts away,
> But after all had played their parts
>   'Twas *Beauty* stole the day!

Though this poem was a great success, both in performance and in print, Gordon disdained it. Indeed, it saddened him. Ellsworth was full of himself, proud of his worldly travels and his quirky bohemian ways, but it was Gordon who had kept alive, though he no longer painted, their youthful artistic principles. They had been pals since the days of toy soldiers and model airplanes, Ellsworth great with the stories that dramatized their play, creating trajectory, Gordon a stickler for the detail that gave it its intensity, its *body*, as it were. Gordon could not remember when they "grew up," if ever they did, it was more like their playing simply ripened into something more profound somehow, all by itself, as though what was serious about it was there all along, down inside, just waiting to be revealed, but however it happened, they found themselves suddenly so much *older* than anyone around them, even the grown-ups, and certainly light-years beyond their classmates, fashion freaks and sexual athletes maybe, but mentally still in diapers, penned up like driveling toddlers in the world's frivolous illusions. What Ellsworth liked to call "the show," a coining from their feverish years. Ellsworth was careful with his words then, respecting their shape and gravity. "*The show I know,*" he wrote in one of his rhyming aphorisms, they were just highschool sophomores at the time, reading passionately, painting and writing, showing each other their best and worst efforts, laying plans deep into the night for their escape together, "*the real I feel.*" The poet and the artist: they were inseparable. Until Ellsworth went off into the world to become famous and live the wandering minstrel's life, leaving Gordon behind to care for his invalid mother. Couldn't do that with a paintbrush, not in this town. He took up photography.

They were a pair, all right, Gordo and Elsie, as some folks called them, flamboyant but shy at the same time, always out in the middle of things but never part of them—they hardly seemed like real people at times—but one accepted them as one accepted a nervous tic or a sixth toe, as much part of the body politic in their loony way as John and his wife, and here as sure as warts, as Officer Otis liked to say, to stay. Okay, a bit off the wall maybe—Ellsworth in his cape and beret and long black hair hanging threadily from his bald patch, Gordon bobbing and waddling like a sweaty circus animal in his mute goggle-eyed search for the right angle—but harmless: they never gave Otis any trouble, except for the way they poked their noses into everything, and they had always treated him with respect even though he was a lot younger than they were. Otis had barely begun high school when he first started turning up in the pages of *The Town Crier* as a freshman lineman on probably the best football team the school had ever had, the one that John captained, and for the Thanksgiving game he even got interviewed and Coach Snuffy introduced him as "a battling bulwark" and old fat Gordon took his photograph. Even Otis's old man was impressed and came to a game after that. Looking back, he now knew that that was the first year of that newspaper's existence, Ellsworth having just come back to town, but at the time Otis had had the feeling it was history itself and had been there forever, even before God, and that he was stepping out of nowhere into its pages, into its light, like one chosen, one touched by a sudden grace. There were more photographs and more interviews in the years that followed, but the coverage became more ordinary, or felt that way—of course the team without John and the rest of that great class of seniors was more ordinary, too: the light had dimmed. But had not gone out: the reporter and his photographer recorded his team captaincy, his graduation, his Purple Heart and then his marriage when he got out, his appointment to the force, his children, his investigations and arrests, his promotions, his attendance at civic functions, his league bowling scores. They missed a few things—like his fucking of the photographer's wife, for example—but Otis understood as well as did Ellsworth that some things were properly historical and some were not. Not all the photographer's photos, for example, had made the pages of *The Town Crier*, nor should they, and some perhaps, including those Pauline had been telling Otis about, squirreled away at the back of the studio, should never have been taken.

These photographs that lay concealed from public view in over two hundred carefully maintained and catalogued albums shelved in the back room were, Gordon knew, his greatest achievements, but in the way that all artists are misunderstood (the ironies neither escaped him nor embittered him), what he was best known for in town were his commercial studio portraits. In the spring there were school class, club, and team photos, then graduation, first communions, and weddings in June, the Pioneers Day costumes, birthdays and anniversaries and new babies all year round, Christmas card family portraits in the autumn, club and company year-end galas to follow. There was hardly a household in town without at least one of his photographs, the only thing on most of their walls, buffets, or pianos resembling original art, and all the record most had of family history. Of course, Gordon was good at them as at everything else in what others called his job: they were sharply focused, majestically lit, elegantly composed, ultimately flattering. They were even, for occasions so inherently formal, unusually expressive, something one might not have expected, knowing Gordon, a notoriously timid and solitary man, severe even and cold. Weird, some said. No "Hey there sourpuss watch the little say cheese birdie" from Gordon. But no matter how banal the occasion, he was determined to get each composition just right and his broad pantomimic gestures as he tacked and bobbed behind his lights and camera, demonstrating the attitudes he wished his subjects to assume as they posed there on his little curtained stage, always brought a kind of theatrical gaiety to the otherwise awkward occasion. They loved him suddenly, not knowing why, nor did he understand this either, but it was the love one felt (Pauline understood this) for a clown, and it showed in their faces.

The photographer's circussy style was not lost on John's young son Mikey, who used it for one of his famous wordless monodramas at his parents' annual Pioneers Day barbecue the summer of the civic center controversy, an awkward occasion for Trevor whose wife Marge was leading the opposition to the building of the annoying thing, having even managed that very week to get a temporary restraining order (soon to be overturned, of course, no stopping John) to prevent the plowing up of the city park, and who, even at the barbecue, had trouble keeping her mouth shut. Well, nothing new there. Trevor was John's personal accountant and a corporation officer, Marge the town's most intransigent gadfly, there'd been embarrassing parties like this before. Fortunately John was a tolerant man with a good sense of humor, maybe he even got a kick out of Marge's quixotic activism, they'd been at it since grade school after all, and—until now anyway—she'd not put Trevor's business relationship with John at any serious risk. Trevor sipped his spring water and knocked on what he hoped was wood: John was about ninety percent of all the business relationships he had. Little Mikey had roped a pillow around his tummy, buttoned on one of his father's trenchcoats, its tails dragging the ground, and rigged a fanciful camera out of a video cassette, toilet paper tubes, plastic dishware from a child's tea set, and a penlight which his sister Clarissa complained he'd stolen from her bedroom. Now he bobbed and waddled through the lawn party, taking everyone's photo by switching the penlight on and off, organizing "family portraits" with broad ludicrous gestures, and, whenever she hove into sight, chasing his mother about with his peculiar apparatus, click-click-clicking away as though demonically possessed. Not everyone got the point of Mikey's act, especially this last part, even if they knew who was being mocked, but Trevor knew, he'd seen the photographer up to his tricks before. The first time, he'd been sitting in the Sixth Street Cafe on a crisp autumn day with a client, a farmer for whom he was setting up an improved health insurance policy with term life attached, when the photographer had come galumphing past the plateglass window, apparently on his way into the cafe. Suddenly, he'd pulled up short, his lashless eyes bulging, and then had hurried in his walrussy way across the street to the newspaper office and printshop and had ducked inside, reappearing behind the window over there a few seconds later, now hidden behind a camera with a long gleaming lens. He'd seemed to be aiming straight at Trevor, which had made him pull back a bit into the shadows, mildly alarmed. But then the true target of Gordon's photographic attentions had come by, walking her dog. The dog had caught the food odors from the cafe and brought her to an abrupt stop, blocking Trevor's view of the window across the street. When she had passed, the window was empty. Since then, more than once, he'd seen the fat photographer in timid clandestine pursuit, and in turn, inexplicably amused, had begun quietly to pursue the pursuer.

Here is one of Gordon's photos on the same theme, though not the one John's personal accountant saw being taken: A slender woman in a white tennis costume, having emerged from the driver's seat of a Lincoln Town Car, is leaning back in to retrieve something from the front seat, her purse perhaps. The car is parked among many others in a vast blacktop lot in the middle of a modern shopping mall, and indeed the photo seems to have been taken from inside another car parked not far away. Has she surprised two young vandals? Dressed in studded leather jackets, printed tee shirts, and torn jeans, they seem to be fleeing from the far side of the Town Car as though to escape capture. Or, more likely, confinement: one of the two girls has her arm extended behind her as though she might have just pushed the backseat door shut, even as she rushes away. In the background, near the mock-arcade entrance to the mall with its automatic glass doors and rows of nested wire shopping carts, young out-of-focus dressalikes can be seen in studied poses—slouching, smoking, waving—vaguely reminiscent of smalltown photographs from generations past. Slanted sunlight falls on the driver's white tennis shorts, creating a kind of blurry nimbus or halo around her hips (the impression is that of having been stared at too hard and long), a seeming photographic flaw that was perhaps, through darkroom manipulation, intentional.

Clarissa, one of the secondary subjects in Gordon's parking lot photo of the radiant tennis shorts (part of a continuing series), was not at all happy with her stupid little brother's impersonation of the town photographer that afternoon at her daddy's annual summer barbecue, refusing to take part with the other kids in his pseudo family portraits and determined to find some way of sabotaging the little showboat. It was especially disgusting the way Mikey went scuttling after their mom with that dumb thingamajig every time she came outside—why did everyone think it was so funny? When Clarissa complained that he was going to use up her penlight batteries, they all just laughed. Even Uncle Bruce, who had flown in just for the day and on whom both she and Jennifer had a tremendous crush that summer, seemed amused by the little sicko, it was unbelievable. Uncle Bruce was not really her uncle, as she had to keep reminding Jennifer all the time, Jennifer wanting Bruce all for herself and accusing Clarissa of what she called incestual madness. He and her father had both been in the same fraternity at college, and her father had told Clarissa years and years ago that since he called him "brother Bruce," she could call him uncle. Of course, Jen's father had also been in their fraternity, but that was different. Clarissa had dibs. Uncle Bruce was very sexy for an older man and tons of fun and Clarissa had made him promise a long time ago that when she grew up he would marry her, and she still meant it whether he did or not: she'd had it engraved in secret code on her love-slave ankle bracelet just to prove it. So, when Uncle Bruce not only let Mikey drag him into one of his ridiculous imitation studio photos, and one making fun maybe of her own family at that, but even with a big laugh and a hug pulled Jennifer along with him to be his pretend wife (Jen was really eating it up: come on! this was her best friend?), it was too much. She went looking for Jennifer's nerdy brother Fish, found him hiding in the garage, sucking on a snitched can of beer. "Hey, Creep, where are those firecrackers you told me you brought?"

These annual Pioneers Day barbecues were part of a year-round parade of social affairs lavishly hosted by John and his wife, including everything from bridge foursomes, cocktail parties, and stag poker nights to bowl game gatherings, formal dinners, and kids' birthday parties, a festal sequence that gave incident and body to the evanescent flow, configuring the town's present as Ellsworth's weekly paper and Gordon's family portraits recomposed and fixed the past. The Christmas season did not really begin until their annual open house, the presidents' midwinter birthdays gave way to John's between, and their backyard barbecues were famous throughout the state, such wealth and power gathering there on those long summer days as to tickle all the senses: one could smell it suddenly in the rich sweet smoke, see it in the rugged smile of the handsome host, striding through the fresh-mown grass in his tooled boots and brushed denims, taste it on the quickened palate, hear it in the squat tumblers of golden whiskey wherein ice tinkled like pockets full of fairy coins. Brother Bruce, rare guest and ever rarer, called them milestones to oblivion, but was always cheerful when he said so, often donning the chef's apron and pitching in, entertaining Clarissa with elephant jokes and funny riddles, showing Mikey magic tricks. Out-of-towners like Bruce were frequent guests, business cronies and college friends, clients, investors, politicians, all those who peopled John's wider world beyond, dropping into town to join the local cast of characters as though from out the clouds, sometimes literally so by way of John's airport, manifestations incarnate of the community's global connections and beaming witnesses to its calendric revels, as celebrated at the home of John and his wife, that consummate hostess. As Waldo, another of John's fraternity brothers and at the time his Assistant Vice President in Charge of Sales, put it that afternoon while John's funny kid was into his fat photogoofer number, clinking glasses in a toast to the pioneer spirit of exploration and new discoveries with a beautiful young woman whose name he couldn't remember (didn't matter, at this point in a party all young women were beautiful and had the same name): "Only thing wrong with John's parties, baby, is that, like life itself, they're fucking beautiful but they're too fucking short." He threw his arm around the woman and raised his glass to Mikey and hollered "Haw!" as the kid passed by, pointing his crazy gizmo at them, and the way her head bounced off his shoulder he definitely had the impression that she was at least as drunk as he was or else stoned, which meant she was quite possibly as much in love with him at that moment as he was with her, whoever the hell she was. "You gotta move fast, know what I mean? or before you can even get your ass into the swing of things, shit, baby, the show's over."

As it was, alas, for Kate the librarian, who, had she still been alive at the time of little Mikey's miming of the town photographer at John's Pioneers Day barbecue that summer, might have remarked on the way that parody and performance focus the attention in a way that the everyday realities of existence cannot. "One drifts through daily life as in a dream," she once remarked to her friend Harriet, also, sad to say, deceased, "waking up only when things turn nightmarish, otherwise being carried along on a free association of images, faintly erotic maybe, faintly fearful, all of it blurring into a half-remembered past that's more like an imaginary space than some aspect of time." She had made this remark while sitting with Harriet and John's mother Opal on a bench in the old city park, not yet razed back then, and Opal remembered it to this day for precisely the reason that it did seem to parody the very moment in which they sat, dappled by the sunlight filtering through the leafy branches above as though sprinkled by that gold dust they sometimes used in the movies to indicate a magical moment isolated from the implacable flow of time. Since Opal was not one much given to such flights of fancy, she supposed the image had popped into her head because of Harriet's earlier remark that "Sometimes I feel more alive at the movies or in the middle of a good novel than I do on the streets of this damned town." Harriet had had a romantic past, she was probably just feeling restless as she often did, her restlessness making her the insatiable moviegoer and devourer of popular novels that she was. Kate now went on to say that while all novels lied about the past, simply by being things whose pages turned in sequence, life, as kept more loosely in the memory, was not a random shuffle either, but more like a subtle interweaving of mysteriously linked moments whose buried significance in effect defined the rememberer. Poor dear Kate, ever the one for the mind-boggling aphorism. She once, while at one of John's parties, described them as "cyclic rituals whose purpose was to deny the incorruptible innocence of time," though what Kate meant by that Opal could not even guess. Opal thought of her son's parties as themselves altogether innocent, not to say generous and spontaneous and celebrative, and she always looked forward to them, but she did understand how much more went on at them than any one person could know, each person's experience of such tangly gatherings being so different from all the others, until someone like little Mikey came along to give them all something at the center to share, even if that something was so frivolous as the playacting of a child.

For Reverend Lenny, another witness of Mikey's masque that afternoon in John's backyard, nothing in the world was frivolous, least of all a child's enactment of the adult world, or else it all was, which he also accepted of course as a strong possibility. Lenny, yet another member of John's old college fraternity present that day and better known to his brothers up at State as Knucksie, sometimes Ob-knucks or Noxious to the pledges he mastered in those long-gone days, mostly happy, give or take a toga party and beer bust or two he'd rather not think about, and rarely did, had come here with his family—his wife Beatrice and their children Philip, Jennifer, and Zoe—nearly a decade ago, thanks to brother John's timely intervention, and, though not without some adjustment difficulties and unremitting ambivalence and self-doubt, Lennox had over the years come to accept his new vocation as a moral and spiritual leader of the community, and indeed to embrace it. When he first arrived and took up his new mission among, except for John, these total strangers, nothing was easy, but what was hardest were the Sunday sermons. It was like writing term papers all over again, something Lennox had always hated and rarely managed to accomplish without a little help from his friends. Now, suddenly, he had to do one every week, no friends at hand, and for a while he fell back pretty heavily on stuff he stole out of books. Eventually, though, once he discovered that no one was grading him, or even for the most part listening, it became his favorite task.

His own special thing, as his wife Beatrice (who strode past now in her fringed leather jacket, pleated skirt, and bright red boots, bearing a large plastic bowl of potato salad like the Holy Grail: she blinked at him as though in wonderment and smiled) liked to say. What amazed him was how everything worked; God—or the gods, any would do, Reverend Lenny was not a fundamentalist—was wonderful. Lennox found he could take any experience, news item, anecdote, whatever, abstract its essence (the fun part), link it metaphorically to some general aspect of the human condition (always plenty of opportunity for pathos, humor, compassion, rue), weave in any images that freely came to mind, toss in a Biblical passage or two (Second John, for example: "And now I beg you, lady, not as though I were writing you a new commandment, but the one we have had from the beginning, that we love one another . . . for he who abides in the doctrine of Christ has both the Father and the Son": that one was so brilliant it had caused John's lawyer cousin's wife to faint dead away), speak with conviction, gravity, and intensity, and shazam! another brilliant spellbinding supersermon. So much fun was it, he soon found himself testing God's limits, as it were, by attempting to convert the most unlikely material—a golf game, rock lyrics, a visit to the barbershop or a bellyflop at the country club pool, Saturday morning TV cartoons, dirty jokes, shopping at the malls, even the holes in doughnuts or the repairing of a clogged stool in the church basement—into Sunday morning classics of spiritual uplift and moral wisdom. Certainly *he* was uplifted if no one else was. It was nearly as good as turning on (and he had used that, too, only lightly veiled: John had winked at him from the front of the congregation). So, while John's son was aping the town photographer at his parents' Pioneers Day garden party, Lennox was doing what he always did at such events: gathering images. He had decided it was time to take advantage of the hot topic of the day and preach on the doctrinal meaning of a "civic center": What was it and why was it (in theory) so significant to us all? What did it mean that the beloved park with all its natural Edenic beauty had to be sacrificed so that that center of our civility could be, not found, but fashioned? He envisioned a link to the great themes of the settling of this nation, the New Jerusalem dream and all that, and thus (his wife's costume suddenly delighted him) to this weekend's celebrations: hey, genius, right on! He watched John's little boy with his taped-junk "camera," bobbing about frenetically with a kind of despairing enthusiasm, a hopeful anguish, and thought: a paradigm for our piteous effort to focus upon the real, to find that center. What *was* the real, and why was it so elusive? As though in reply, John's wife passed in her knee-length shorts and crisp cotton shirt, all eyes in the backyard upon her, and Lennox thought: whatever it is, it has substance. Form. Body. And bodily parts. For God so loved the world that he eschewed mere abstractions. But to accept the fleshly real (he was watching his old fraternity brother, once known as Loose Bruce, put his arms around his little pubescent daughter, Jennifer's face flushed with puppy love) was to accept pain and (his son Philip—or his wife's, anyway—and John's daughter Clarissa came out of the garage together, looking guilty) paradox. Irony. Was that not, in point of fact, the very message of the Cross? Yes, it was taking shape, the main themes were all there. All it lacked was a little spark and pop, a final kicker, a quote from the Good Book maybe, something with which to say: "This, my friends, this, *this* is real!"

When the firecrackers went off behind John's screwy kid, Maynard II, he, whose wife had swooned during the preacher's sermon, was just thinking about his cousin's power and how, maybe, with old Barnaby's help, he was about to trounce that contemptible cocksucker at last, so he was both startled (dropped his goddamned paper plate of barbecue right down the front of his pants) and at the same time felt somehow confirmed in his hopes, as though that sudden explosive racket was in celebration (a sympathetic glance at his pants from John's wife, looking down upon him from the back deck, added to his feeling of triumph; although, ever the languishing fool for love, he wished for more, she did send one of the kitchen help out with a wet towel) of his ineluctable and unprecedented win. Yet another fucking illusion, as he was to find out soon enough, but at the time that summer it looked like a sure thing, so when wild applause followed the fireworks, Maynard embraced it as though it were for him, gave a whoop himself and winked across the lawn at his wife Veronica, who dropped her jaw and returned him a sneering hawk-nosed what-the-hell's-the-matter-with-you-scumbag? look. A joy to be around, that girl. Should have sobered Maynard up, but it didn't. He was feeling too damned cocky. Old Barnaby, pissed at the way his son-in-law had fucked him over and in a fit over the civic center outrage (and it *was* an outrage), had come to Maynard's law firm with a sweet plan, well-funded, and Maynard had put the final touches to it, it was beautiful. John's ass was grass, he was sure of it. Not that that would be the end of it. His cuz was tough in the clinches and could play mean and dirty. You could sometimes take a point off him, but it was hard to win the game, Maynard knew that. When they were kids, their families used to do Thanksgivings together, and in and around the ritual gut-stuffing they'd get up all-day Monopoly games, which John always won, even if in the end he had to use strong-arm tactics. Everyone cheated of course, but it was Maynard who always got caught. One day John spied him palming an extra house onto Marvin Gardens and decided to call a kangaroo court. It was one of Maynard's earliest and most enduring lessons in the way the law worked. He was introduced into the dock as "greasy Mayo Nerd" and his defense was met with wet Bronx cheers, especially from the younger shits, getting back at him with John's protection. He was found guilty of course and his fine was that he had to wear his clothes backward and make a loud vomiting noise every time someone mentioned mincemeat pie. Aunt Opal, John's mother, had brought the mincemeat pie that year so he took a terrific cuffing from his old man the first time he made that noise, John always getting someone else to do the dirty work for him. Maynard's dad was the mayor back then and quick with his law-and-order swats across the side of his head, Maynard was always scared of him. Now the rheumy-eyed old fart was his law partner and pretty much did as he was told.

The real reason that day for the burst of enthusiastic lawn-wide applause, which whooping Maynard in his willing self-delusion accepted as celebration of his own imminent victory, was the spectacular conclusion to little Mikey's mimed performance, a bit of improvisational showmanship that even Lorraine, once a serious student of such matters and no fan of John's youngest brat (the little weirdo clearly had a serious oedipal problem, for one thing), had to admire. Lorraine, whose dopey husband Waldo, he of the corked head and wayward prick, was one of those who did John's dirty work nowadays in his grown-up Monopoly games, had, like the lawyer Maynard, been thinking other thoughts when the firecrackers went off: to wit, where have all the flowers gone? How had Sweet Lorraine, the fraternity world's favorite party girl and teacher's petted pet of the English department, got transformed into this shapeless old bag drinking beer from a can in the backyard of a hick town bullyboy, standing in crushed buns and dogshit and wondering what griefs the dolts she was living with had in store for her next? Her helpmeet Waldo was drunkenly hustling one of the local housewives while the bimbo's husband snarled nearby, Lollie's halfwit sons were getting dragged around by John's boy like trained bears, and she herself, watching John's wife temporarily distract attention from her own son's popular dumb show (the kid's act was easy, that crazy photographer *was* a clown, and like all clowns, no joke) simply by passing by, felt near to tears. Damn it, it wasn't fair! They'd promised her a happy ending! Whereupon, Mikey's bitchy big sister Clarissa snuck up behind him while he was concentrating on trying to balance his goofy apparatus on a tripod made of three golfclubs and lit a tin bucket full of firecrackers at his feet. Everyone jumped when they went off, even Lorraine who had seen it coming, everyone except Mikey, who merely pointed his "camera" in different directions and pushed the penlight button as though each pop were the taking of a shot. He dropped the contraption to his side when the explosions stopped, then slowly lifted it again as though guessing there must be more to come, or maybe he peeked. He pivoted, pointed the toilet-roll tube lens at his shocked sister, and—*POP! POP!*—snapped her turning on her heel in frustration and rage and stomping away. It was a sensation. Lorraine felt, just for a moment (much worse was to happen, she knew that), reconciled to the goddamned world once more, and even laughed and applauded with the others as the little photographer-clown took his waddling exit by chasing his mother up onto the deck and into the house again.

Beatrice's perspective on this Pioneers Day barbecue in John's backyard, not sharing Lorraine's chronic vexation, was that smalltown life out here on the prairie was pretty crazy (a couple of years later it would be her turn back here, no hosts but the children—what curious times lay ahead!—to be, popping her own cracker, the star attraction), but what the heck, God was good and a generous know-it-all who cared for the little sparrow even, so, as her husband would say, chirp chirp, Trix, let it all happen. After the fireworks (where did John get those things? it was fun but was it legal? or did it, John being who he was, even matter? not to Trixie did it), Lenny was looking positively beatific, and that made Beatrice, who was cheerful by nature, even more cheerful, for in truth she worshiped her goofy husband, only wishing that he, like she, might have some notion of what worship might be. She would watch him in the pulpit on Sunday mornings, delivering his famous sermons, everybody talked about them, and she would know, even if no one else did, that he was just pretending, like with everything else. He pretended to be a preacher, a father, a friend, a lover, the cosmos as unreal to him as a B movie, but he was a good pretender, so what difference did it make? Well, one. Beatrice felt certain that Lenny'd never had, though he'd pretended to, a really great orgasm, and this made her feel somehow inadequate and caused her to wonder sometimes what it was they really shared. Beatrice believed, with all her heart, in the mystical power of the orgasm, it was what linked you to everything else in the whole universe, and she surrendered to it wherever and whenever it came upon her just as a saint would do when God called, for that was exactly how she saw it, and no matter what it might cost her, sometimes quite a lot. But saints suffered, too, didn't they? Just look at Jesus: he had it about as rough as it could get, but in the end he ascended, an experience Beatrice herself had enjoyed, it was great. As a little girl, she got off all the time on Jesus, just thinking about him and his spacey life, so weird and beautiful, and she still could and did, though she no longer needed him or anybody else, she was directly wired now, she could turn ecstasy on like flipping a light switch, and maybe it was just as well that cool Lenny was there to switch it off when she'd been gone too long and lovingly bring her home again.

Her mother's freaky ways embarrassed Jennifer, but intrigued her, too: grown-up life might not be as boring as it mostly seemed in this nowhere place. Everything was so desperately flat and common here, you knew just what was going to happen every minute—even out at the malls and the pool, the only halfway exciting places around, you could guess what people were going to say as soon as they opened their mouths, it was like they were all in a play or something, just reading their lines, it was very depressing—but it didn't need to be that way, and her unpredictable mother was at least, spooky as she was, a case in point. Bruce was another and a more reassuring one than her mixed-up mom. He flew in and out at will, this town having no claim on him, nor any other either, he was as free as the wind like everyone should be, like Jennifer would be when she got out of here, she could hardly wait. Bruce seemed to know and do or have done everything, he was very wild and very wise at the same time, and yet somehow tragic, too, like those beautiful guys in the movies who always died young, though Bruce would not die young, he was already too old for that, and a good thing, too, because Jennifer loved him madly and wanted him around when she was ready to escape this dump, before or after she finished high school, she really didn't care, what was all that junk good for anyway? Bruce had lots of lovers, Jennifer knew that, but unlike her best friend Clarissa who, when she wanted something, wanted all or nothing, Jennifer did not mind sharing. Clarissa was a real problem. Bruce was a college friend of both their fathers, Clarissa having always called him Uncle Bruce, though they weren't related, which Jennifer thought was childish, especially now after she'd got her period, but for Clarissa it was a way of trying to own him somehow, and teasing her about it only tended to make it worse. She and Clarissa were the closest of friends, they went everywhere together, planned to leave here together, too—bosom pals, they once joked when they went to buy their first bras together, and in truth, no joke, they were—but because of Clarissa's possessive attitude, Bruce stood between them. That afternoon at the barbecue, for example, when she and Bruce posed for Clarissa's little brother's make-believe camera and Bruce was hugging her in a way that sent a tingling all the way to her toes, she knew it was making Clarissa mad as all get-out and Jennifer was sorry about that, but she just couldn't help it. She could only hope he wouldn't let go, it was magic.

John's friend Bruce, who so willingly joined in little Mikey's play that day, was perhaps the only person out there who did not know who was being caricatured, and so missed half the point, or more, but then no one got it all, not even Trevor who knew what no others present knew but who had never, it being against his wife Marge's principles, posed for a family portrait, much nuance thus lost on him as well, this being, as Gordon himself would say, the fate of all art, even of the amateur backyard variety: to become, stripped of nuance, a caricature of itself. Gordon's wife Pauline, who knew what Trevor knew but was not so curious about it (that lady was the main attraction around here, why shouldn't Gordon take her picture?), but who was not present in John's backyard on that day, or on any other day for that matter, would not have known what nuance was, though she would have enjoyed the little boy's portrait of her portraitist husband as clown and taken it in whole, feeling flattered that something of her private world had been so publicly noticed. But then: had Pauline fallen in love with a clown? No, nor, whatever others might think, married one either, though that was another story. Love was for heroes, giants, and wizards, of whom she'd had some in her mouth maybe, between her breasts even, and up her Sodom-and-Gomorrah, as Daddy Duwayne called it, but none in her life, that strange thing that went on outside the holes in her body. When it came to romance, that old true-love lottery, Pauline had drawn the short straw: suck *that*, kid! as her fairy godfather was wont to put it in his pedagogical sessions on the floor of their filthy trailer. Where, many years ago, in the scattered iconography ripped from stolen magazines that aroused her crazy tutor's red-eyed zeal, she had glimpsed a way out. She was nineteen when she finally approached old Gordon and asked him to help her. She knew him only by his shop window with all the glitzy photographs of make-believe families and fairytale weddings, his moony face in the dim shadows behind it, but she assumed he had a swollen spunk-sack that needed relief like any other man and they could strike a deal. Her best years were over, had been since her sixteenth birthday, she knew that—reality-training was one deprivation Pauline had not suffered—but she felt she had one last chance to make her fortune, or the nearest thing to it she could ever hope for, before she turned twenty and it was all over. Her body was ripe enough if a bit beat up (you could brush that out) and she had no pride, but she needed a photographer and Gordon was the only one in town. So she put her best summery dress on over nothing, hid behind the sunglasses a boy had bought her the year before at the Pioneers Day fair, all the wages she had got on that occasion, and screwing up her courage, pushed in, jangling bells, and announced she wanted her picture taken. "Hey, Pauline! Whatcha doin?!" someone yelped as though goosed. It was that little highschool boy Corny. She hadn't noticed there were other people in there. Her sunglasses maybe. Or just too nervous. Corny was with his dad, who was wearing his crisp white jacket from the drugstore, shiny black pens periscoping out of the breast pocket like secret cameras. And there was a girl there, too, thin and pale, dressed mostly in black, with her hair in tight dark ringlets around her parchmenty ears and funny little teeth in her smiling mouth like rows of tiny white corn kernels. She didn't look all that well. "This is Pauline, Dad! From school! We're getting passport photos, Pauline—Dad's sending me to Paris! For graduation!" Big surprise. Corny's heart-shaped face under its wispy blond cap was pink as a valentine, poor boy. His father stared at her through his thick lenses as though examining her through a microscope, gripping the lapels of his white jacket in a pose she recognized from the family photo in the window out front. Pauline stared back, but wished now she had her underwear on. The bells over the door still seemed to be ringing, but they probably weren't. "So, uh, how's it goin', Pauline, for gosh sake? Where ya been?"

Where Cornell had been the night before, made manifest by his tin-whistle squeak and telltale flush—and, had anyone noticed, the little hickey on her neck—was with Pauline. Tears of farewell before being sent off to Paris, declarations of love, and all that. He supposed his father did not know, a supposition only partly correct: prophylactics had gone missing at the drugstore over the past year, a pattern made familiar in their own time by Oxford's other two sons. Discovering this had brought tears to his eyes: Ah, little Corny . . . He was the baby of the family and had seemed till now as though spellbound by childhood: finishing high school and still reading comicbooks, playing with games and toys. Oxford, worried about him, had thought this graduation trip to Europe might somehow work a sea change—might disenchant the boy, so to speak—and he'd trusted the strange frail woman beside him as his dear departed Yale once did, yet feared for poor Cornell and for himself: he had lost so much and this was his last son, Paris was so far away, he could not bear more sadness. He had peered searchingly at the bold girl standing there before them in that gloomy photo shop with her sunglasses on and her toes pointed in—what had Corny called her? Pauline?—but though ready to grasp at any straw, he'd found nothing that might give him hope. A certain wide-browed full-lipped generosity maybe, nothing more. She was probably just using Corny, as so many others did. Of course the light was bad, his eyesight weak, his concentration undermined by grief, he might have missed something. No rash prejudgments. He'd keep the drawer of condom packets replenished and see what happened.

What happened, or seemed to happen—all this was a decade and a half ago—was that Corny, mortified by his public denial of Pauline, went to Paris that summer without seeing her again, and when, after chastening adventures quite different from those his father had envisioned for him, he returned, Pauline was no longer available. He entered university, though not the one that he'd been named for, as a pharmacy student, and some four years later fulfilled at last his father's lifelong dream, though yet again not in the way he had imagined. Oxford, a staunch rationalist in a town where such a faith was held by few, was such a devotee of the great institutions of higher learning that he had named his children after four of them—Harvard, Yale, Columbia, and Cornell—hoping each might go then where appointed. None did. Only Yale came close, attending Princeton, and then to study French, not pharmacy. It was Cornell finally who, if only up at State, pursued at least (a promise to his mother Kate, the town librarian, then gravely ill) his father's trade, renewing Oxford's faded hopes that a son might yet return, solace and companion to his autumn years, to carry on what he had here established. These hopes were dashed a few months later when his mother killed herself and Corny suddenly took on Harvie's errant ways, let the scraggly hairs on his face grow down, burned his library card, dropped out, and in that paradoxical idiom of the times, "turned on," but then were unexpectedly revived once more when, without advertisement, the boy shaved all but his upper lip and wed a sober northern girl named Gretchen, a pharmacy major more industrious than brilliant maybe, but fully aware of her limitations, which included a withered leg and myopia as severe as Oxford's. Though Corny dreamed perhaps of grander things, Gretchen brought him home.

Gretchen in innocence once had dreamed her leg was whole, or could be made so, but came to accept instead, finding a father-in-law she'd never dreamed to have, an orthopedic correction and partial interest in a pharmacy one day to be made a whole one in a way her leg could never be. She was a satisfied woman who never showed this with a smile, except sometimes alone with her sister-in-law Lumby, her public face one of pained intensity like that of a long-distance runner about to hit the wall: the goal in sight but dreadful hazards on the route. When, a few years later, John built his newest mall out by the highway, he offered them bright spacious quarters there, which excited Cornell, restless in the dull downtown, duller by the day, but which Oxford feared as a threat to his own dreams of continuity and meaning. As the expense of such a move and broad expansion would have required a partnership with John, Gretchen unhesitatingly sided with her father-in-law and against her whining husband, putting her lame foot down resolutely like the banging of a wooden gavel, and thus began, shaped by frustrated dreams, that family's slow decline.

In such manner the entire town might be said to have been shaped, its streets laid out by what, though against all probability, might yet be, its daily dialogue sustained by what had not, as though it might have done, come true—though John, again, was an exception. He got always, as if a rule unto himself, more or less what he dreamt of. Perhaps John dreamt wiser dreams, asking from others only what he knew they could give, or taking from them only what he knew they could not refuse him: a kind of magic formula by which John prospered and took his considerable pleasure. Buildings, parks, whole neighborhoods disappeared, and in their place rose banks and malls and housing clusters with lawns where grass had never grown, and simply because John willed it so and other wills were weaker. He endured trials, true, the intrafamilial battle over his new downtown civic center and swimming pool being but the latest, but he relished these trials, as he once had relished the goalline plunge and the raised bar, contests that quickened him, full of risk and body contact, bruising sometimes, exhausting, but never fatal, or almost never, and concluded always, win or lose, with celebrations—celebrations often at John's expense, for John was also, as all were witness, a generous man, free of rancor and loyal to a fault. Friends from boyhood, school, teams, companies or clubs were friends for life—ask Dutch, a pal since Little League, Loose Bruce or Lennox from fraternity, his old coach

Snuffy, Waldo, Otis, Kevin, Trev, they owed him much—and women, too, enjoying John's beneficence and care long after having given so little, unless they erred and thought it much. Women loved John, most of them did, though he never asked for this, not even from his wife, demanding only a fair exchange, love poor coin, he believed, in such transactions.

Not all women understood this well, and so suffered injured hearts and bouts of self-abasement when their own love declarations were not matched by John or seemingly even heard. Thus, Lollie, as she was known in those days: self-styled sorority archetype, fun-loving, smart, and virgin, parting her thighs at last with elegant simplicity one night down in the games and chapter room of John's fraternity while a party raged above, her heart racing, her mind a new erogenous zone stroked with prospects and announcements, love bubbling up on her lips like water pumped from a well, from which John appreciatively drank his fill, groaning, "Yes, yes!," suddenly configuring thereby her shapeless life with narrative thrust and plot and conversion to the future perfect—or so she thought until the heartless knave turned up at the sorority house a few evenings later to pick up one of the younger girls for an all-night pool party and, bumping into a startled Lollie, laughingly gave her a hug that iced her spine. Never thawed. Still couldn't touch her goddamn toes.

Well, the first time, it had its pleasures, it had its bite, not easily forgotten, nor easily retold. Ellsworth's "I Remember" column had been running in the town newspaper for years, yet no such tale had surfaced there, though Harriet's frank account of her wartime experiences as an army nurse in Britain did not exclude her bombshelter snuggle with a handsome surgeon whose name she never knew until they met and married eight months later. The meeting took place over an amputation, the wedding in a vicar's cottage beside a bombed-out church. Legendary times, those romantic war years, envied by most, their own rites celebrated in less glamorous circumstances, even when in marriage beds, more often in car seats and cheap motels, school toilets and darkened rec rooms, listening not for the buzzing hum of approaching aircraft or the whistle of the fateful bomb, but for a creak on the stairs, approaching bushwhackers, authority's freezing knock or opened door. The sound in Daphne's ears when it happened was the whine of a mosquito, that and the rusty squeak of cot springs beneath the bare mattress whereon she struggled. There were smells of leaf rot and sawdust and stale beer and old tennis shoes. The guy with her had her arms pinned behind her with one hand and was ripping her panties off with the other while she pitched and kicked, and what she was thinking while she tried to fight him off (she still remembered this) was that, if he got her panties down, that damned mosquito was going to bite her on her bare butt. And it did, too. Edna heard water dripping that first time, trucks grinding by, Opal her brother's whisper not to tell, Harvard a prostitute's wry complaints, the sniggering of his pals outside the door. What teenaged Lenny heard was the congregation on the floor above singing "O Zion, Haste Thy Mission High Fulfilling," as his geography teacher and friend of his mother took him inside her on top of the stainless steel worktable down in the church kitchen, whimpering, "Oh, yes, sweet Jesus! sweet Jesus!," while for Pauline it was her Daddy Duwayne in his cidery jacket, unbuckling his old jeans and rumbling, "C'mere now, you little harlot, let's see what we can do about knockin' down that wicked ole wall of Jericho!" She was seven years old and thought that Cherry-Go might be an icecream flavor.

Ronnie, like old Alf and Harriet, actually heard humming aircraft and exploding bombs, Cherry-Going, as it were, to the sounds of war, but this happened, long after the real war, out at the old drive-in movie theater where later the interstate link cut through, erasing, so to speak, the scene of the crime. It was following a highschool football game and she still had her cheerleading clothes on, which made it both easier and harder. Easier because there were almost no preliminaries to be got through, harder because the underpants were tight and made of heavy lined material like a swimming suit, so there was no going in past the legband, like some guys had tried to do before with flimsier stuff there. Veronica had made up her mind to go all the way some time before, but most of the boys she was going out with seemed to know even less about it than she did, though they'd never admit it, and she just couldn't trust them. Then, suddenly, the perfect opportunity arose, so quickly it almost took her breath away, when John, home from college, turned up unexpectedly at a weekend football game and, after coming over to josh around with Coach Snuffy and the boys at halftime, turned and asked her what she was doing later on. Ronnie had gone out with him once before, long ago, but he was too fast for her then. Now she was ready, or thought she was, and she said, "I don't know, you got any good ideas?" It should have been wonderful. It wasn't. She bled and bled, she just couldn't stop. She always was unlucky. Up on the screen, they were cursing and yelling and stabbing each other with bayonets, but at the time she didn't see the humor in this. Neither did John, who was really mad about what she had done and was still doing to the backseat of his father's car. He jammed his underpants and hers between her legs and drove her home, dropped her off, she sobbing her apologies, at the curb. As she waddled up the walk, she heard the car door slam and, glancing back, saw him coming up the walk behind her. He was smiling: was he laughing at her? Maybe he wanted his underpants back. Confused and frightened and sick with shame, she threw them at him and ran away, as best she could run, hands between her legs, and left him standing back there like that guy in the movies, alone on a battlefield of corpses. She cried for three days after. Bled more, too, had to see the doctor. She hated sex then, though later she got used to it. Whereupon worse things happened.

Others might have had similar tales to tell—Trixie, for example, now known as Beatrice, the preacher's wife, or poor ill-fated Marie-Claire, the Paris penpal, even perhaps (who knows?) John's wife—but Nevada, a generation younger, was not one of these. Nevada was a career woman, skillful, charming, industrious, worldly wise, discreet. She had met John a year or so ago while working in a private plane and boat show in Denver, a gig she'd picked up for a mouthful of cum in Houston. John was there with an associate from Chicago, shopping for a little hedgehopper of his own, as he called it, but he was scouting companies, too, a man, she judged, of vision and expanding fortunes, well worth a deeper acquaintance. His wife? An abstraction, absent, not yet a nuisance. Like all the women at the show, Nevada had a prepared resume with her, which she showed to John in bed that night over a restorative whiskey, while a pornographic film played silently on the hotel TV, solemn and unheeded as a church service. The resume indicated that she was unmarried, could type and had some familiarity with word processors, enjoyed travel, and was accustomed to flexible workhours. When John asked her about her ambitions, she smiled, pressed the sweating whiskey glass against a perky young breast, just under the erecting nipple at the lip as though to milk it, or to let it dip its beak to drink, and said she hoped to get into personnel management. He was impressed (his generous laughter told her so) and took her on, remarking that her first assignment was a bit of stiff committee work: to wit, taking the starch out of an incorrigibly hardheaded standing member.

John bought a plane in Denver that week, not his first, and a company, too, together with Bruce, a joint venture—again, not their first. It was Bruce perhaps to whom John felt the closest ties. From the time they met up at State, pledge brothers at the fraternity their freshman year, they held most things in common, including money, clothes, textbooks, and women. They even sat exams for one another, laughing their way through business management, education's biggest joke, partnered each other for bridge, cross-country drives, and tennis, cocaptained the golf team their senior year, drinking together from the trophies they won. Bruce best man at his postgraduation wedding, John bestmanned Bruce's then in turn, at least the first of them, this one with a woman John had shared with Bruce for a time, filling in when Bruce had other thighs or hands to spread. If Bruce had had John's wife, John would not have begrudged him this, though if he'd had her he would in any case not have remembered it, for though, like John, he had a head for names, figures, products, profit margins, even radio frequencies and phone numbers, when it came to glory 'oles, as he reverentially called them, they were all the same to Bruce, love them as he did. No, to wallow in the memory of a great fuck was for Bruce little better than self-abuse, a kind of impotence really. Every day was a great fuck, potentially anyhow, or you shot yourself, and John, though less radically, shared Bruce's views in this. In business, too, views and money often shared, Bruce again the long-shot gambler, plunging into entertainment and oil futures, heavy arms and high-risk third world ventures, steady John amassing his portfolio around transport, banking, and property development, partnering each other when their interests or holdings crossed, as they often did. Bruce had taught John how to fly and they had bought a rustic fishing cabin up at the lakes together, laid down a landing strip, went there over the years to fish, shoot ducks and geese in season, take women not their wives, Bruce frequently the provider, though John, too, had gifts to bring from time to time, Nevada but a recent example, joint venture of another kidney. Their cabin became what Bruce, through all his schemes, adventures, wives, and sprees, thought of as home, quite unlike John in this, the basic difference between them being that John was a builder, Loose Bruce was not.

John the builder had added a simple but elegant A-frame lounge of cedar and glass to the fishing cabin, with a big fireplace at one end and views through the trees out over the lake, had improved the septic system, installed an oil-fueled generator, and put in showers and sauna and extra bedrooms, but the furnishings were plain and functional, the decorations few, the general aroma of the place that of pine, mud, and men. Once the airstrip was down, John had blocked off the main entry road with trees and boulders, though he'd left a lesser-known back route open for the man with snowplow and mower he'd hired to keep the airstrip cleared. The first time Dutch saw the place, flown up there by John in a late-summer fishing party (no women on these hometown group occasions, often as not no Bruce either), he was reminded immediately of the clubhouse they'd built as highschool seniors on his old man's property at the edge of Settler's Woods. He divined at once therefore the full range of activities the cabin had been designed—or redesigned—for, and was not surprised to find a bidet in one of the bathrooms, which John shrugged off as a fancy of the previous owner. Even the cabin's lone piece of art, a splotched and ripped-up canvas, hanging in shreds like something spilling from an open fly (people were crazy, what they paid money for these days), was not unlike their clubhouse's tattered pinups clipped or torn from old magazines. For most of the men in the fishing party, if not for Dutch, it was a time up here for escaping their women and the prescripted town-bound lives those women had made for them, a time for virile reflection in the wild to which they all felt they'd been born, but from which somehow mysteriously expelled, a time to shoot and hook and kill and to eat the killed and, unnagged, drink their fill, a time to tell stories not elsewhere tellable and to test one another in all the half-forgotten ways of old. Thus, pissing, shooting, angling, and drinking contests, all-night high-stakes poker, manhood-challenging wisecracks and shower baiting. Again, Dutch thought, so like the days of the "getaway," as they'd called their old clubhouse (and as Dutch now called his motel bar, located on the clubhouse site), except that women, still a novelty, were more important to them then, a female body, most often human, frequently the arena for their manly competitions. John, unrivaled cherry-picker with his own vast resources, was a rare participant in those gangshags of old—or "club sandwiches," as they were called back then—though when caught up in one, as at the climax of his own stag party, an event arranged by Dutch as a wedding gift to his former Little League battery mate, he never shied from joining in, firm and upright clubman that he always was.

Bruce, best man when John, constructing story, married the builder's daughter, was also at the stag party the night before, a reassuring event for Bruce, faced with the disturbing prospect of John's seemingly straight-faced plunge into the wedded condition and the consequent loss of his one true companion in this ludicrous shithole of a world. Bruce, a city boy, albeit less of urb than sub, approached this remote hog wallow that day with trepidation, a stranger to its hobnail country ways, except so far as John had acridly portrayed them on their college drinking bouts, visions dancing in his booze-bruised head of desensitized TV zombies dangerously adrift on potholed junker-lined streets, of blue laws, Bible Belters, and bottle flies, and of ersatz icecream parlors crawling with pimply beauty queens and noisome brats. When asked what was the principal activity of his hometown, John had once replied: "Ass scratching. Two-handed." John had given the real world up for this? Well, John had added: "Like every other place I know," it's true. It was Bruce's world still strewn with antique values. A "diseased romantic," John had called him once, or someone had and John had laughed, Bruce, too, admitting it was so, and adding that it was a glory 'ole that had corrupted him—cuntamination, he called it—the first he ever knew: "Birth robbed me, buddy, of my fetal hopes and innocence, it's been downhill ever since I slid that fucking tube." Arrival was by rented car, John's airport not yet built back then of course, a numbing passage through vast treeless fields and desolate commercial strips as alien to human life as anything Bruce's grim misgivings might have led him to imagine. Yes, the worst he'd feared was true. But then, a small creek once crossed over, the humpback bridge nearly pitching him through the roof when he hit it, a little wooded patch rose up on the far shore as if conjured from the weedy soil, and on the other side of that the town appeared and showed a bit of grace: smooth tree-shaded streets with wide-porched houses sitting landscaped lawns, brightly bordered with the seasonal flower show, this followed by a cool green park leading to the town center where young women smiled at him as he passed by, the streets here lined with Lincolns, Caddies, and a Mercedes-Benz or two that put his scrap of rented tin to happy shame. The Pioneer Hotel was a musty relic with frayed linens and prewar plumbing, but all the gang were there, the antediluvian bar and lobby dust astir with their sudden booming talk and laughter. A few bolts of aged sourmash poured by brother Waldo and an afternoon round of golf on what turned out to be inventive sunswept fairways and well-kept greens revived Bruce wholly, and after the obligatory rehearsal dinner, enlivened by brother Beans rising to toast the bride's family with his fly vividly agape, the stag party that followed restored his faith in the human comedy and in his old boonfellow John, wired though he may have been.

That park Bruce passed, no longer there, once hosted Sunday Sousa bands, political campaigners, homemade carnivals, and horseshoes tournaments, as well as the famous Pioneers Day pageants, at one of which, a child still, princesslike in white organdy and lace, John's wife had starred as The Spirit of Enterprise. This pageant, third and last to be penned by school bard Ellsworth, graduating senior about to flee these rustic precincts for what he called the center stage, was a centennial paean to creation, prairie-style, and so eulogized the century's builders, not least old Barnaby, wee Enterprise's very father, whose beloved city park now served as his encomium's mise-en-scène and shaded him where he proudly sat. In time, his son-in-law's civic center, newest proof of initiative's power to transform, would concretely rise in Barnaby's name where John's wife once performed, its all-weather Olympic pool become her bikini'd daughter's rock-scripted stage for performances of a more speculative sort, but on that long-ago day the old park seemed ageless, eternal, some sort of sacred site, mother to them all, even the oldtimers forgetting for the moment that it had not always been there, but Barnaby had built it. How sweet his daughter was that day as she recited, in Ellsworth's accents, Ellsworth's lines about the builder's Olympian power to sow his seed upon e'en the thornéd and rocky waysides of the world and see whole cities rise defiantly like living parables of imagination's potency, untrammeled reason's finest crops!

> Here in Reason's beauteous grove we stand,
> Its glory being: *'Twas made by human hand!*

Though most that leafy sunswept day applauded, enchanted by the pretty child, angelically aglow in the dappled light, and moved by the tears in her father's eyes (a rich man, yes, a pillar and a patron, but old-shoe common, one of us), some grumbled that that oddball boy who wrote the thing had courted blasphemy with his foolishness, messing with the Good Book like that, then had compounded his sin by the use of an innocent child for his impieties' transmission. They were not far from wrong, though only Gordon, privy to the throes of composition, knew to what extent his irreverent friend had with his Olympish wordplays mocked the town: the seed of the city fathers, whom Ellsworth slyly, in a rhyme with "creators," compared to "master painters," not so much sown as spilled, this town, he said to Gordon, a hand-job made by, of all trades, the jack-ofs. Not for me, twiddle-dee! Kiss my bum, twiddle-dum! This grinningly declaimed while sprawled in the nude, wearing a top hat and smoking a long cigar, Gordon at the easel, frustrated with the impossible translation of light on flesh into oily smears on canvas-board, saddened by his boyhood friend's announced departure, and musing the while on the aesthetic ugliness of the dark lumpy dangle between men's legs, as though something that should be inside had grotesquely fallen out, Gordon's an abstract ideal of pure unblemished form, wartless, headless, hairless, truth expressed best when least expressed (the poet's line, though it was Gordon who, in other words, first said it). Because he was leaving town forever, Ellsworth allowed his friend to photograph his poses that the paintings might someday (they both believed in art) get done, these taken with a borrowed camera, Gordon's first essays on film, including one of a laughing Ellsworth dressed only in his highschool drum major's hat, looking back over his bony white shoulder, baton raised on high, other hand hidden, but somewhere between his hairy legs: See ya later, master painter!

Of course, he returned, the silly man, though not with tail between his legs, where it belonged, as most had hoped, but cocky still and weird as ever, only a monkish bald spot on his crown marking his seven years away, no other signs of the misfortunes which all felt must befall so unrepentant a wiseass in the world. Well, concealed perhaps, the bruises, for return at least he did, and after nose-thumbing farewells that had seemed irrevocable, all ties severed, bridges burnt. So what brought him back? Filial duty, Ellsworth would explain with a flick of a wrist as though brushing away a fly, that and the need, he would add with a weary condescending smile from beneath his jaunty black beret, for a quiet out-of-the-way place to finish his novel-in-progress. As for the alleged novel, who could say, but it was true that his enfeebled father, though he'd bitterly disowned his eccentric son, could no longer run the old family printshop alone, it was Ellsworth saved it, perhaps not beyond redemption after all. This certainly was Barnaby's view, had been all along. Barnaby was close to that family, Ellsworth's parents his parents' friends and his in turn, he'd known the strange boy since his awkward birth twenty years too late and had half-adopted him when the gawky child's aged mother died, and so it was Barnaby who, remembering the little hand-drawn and -lettered newspapers the boy would entertain his infant daughter with, had located him and, with offers to back a weekly newspaper if Ellsworth would print and edit it, brought him home again. And thus began *The Town Crier,* successor to *The Daily Patriot,* which had died in Ellsworth's absence, nothing but an oral record left of all the time between, the which and more Ellsworth now collected—grist, it was suspected, for his novel-if-a-novel's mill—in his guest column "I Remember."

"Quiet! This place? Is old Elsie kidding?" Daphne had hooted when her best friend told her what that longhaired geek, a relative of sorts and once upon a time her friend's babysitter, had said that summer he first came back. She'd blown a bubble with her gum, sucked it in, and snapped it with her bright white teeth: Oh, what a smile she had back then! Everybody said so! "Honey, this town is jumping!" This was out at the country club pool, it was the summer before their sophomore year in high school, and Daphne was ready for anything and everything, though she had only the dimmest notion, got mostly from the movies and the hit parade, what everything might be. That is to say, as she put it years later on the telephone to her best friend (still wed to John, though Daphne by then was, as she liked to put it, under her fourth), she knew everything in those days about sexual intercourse, but nothing at all about fucking. She had a crush that summer on the lifeguard at the pool, an older guy named Dean, Lean Dean, already in college, a boy with beautiful bronzed muscles and a blonde crewcut and cute blue shorts that showed his bulge, which moved, she knew, when she walked by, she'd seen this and he'd winked at her. In those days swimsuits showed less skin, at least in this town, but midriffs were anyway never Daphne's strong suit, what she had most abundantly looked good in what she wore, good enough that the guys all stopped to stare or joke, the simps, as she climbed up wet out of the pool, popping her knockers in place, or strode out on the diving board, tugging at the leg-seams where they'd crept up her bouncing cheeks, feeling their eyes pasted on her behind like little sequins with electric charges, her nipples so hard with the rub of their gaze sometimes they felt like rayguns about to fire and blow them all away. Oh boy. She hung around the pool whenever her folks would let her, and one evening near the end of the season Dean drove her home in his pickup truck, stopping off near the humpback bridge at the edge of Settler's Woods to feel her up, and then apologize, and that was that. "I don't care," she'd whispered, but probably not loud enough. She came to care but that was a few months later, Settler's Woods by then in autumn colors and creepy with musty shadows and the smell of rot, the guy she was with a senior footballer they all called Colt, a guy she was going steady with, so to speak, who'd kissed her uncupped tits and had had his hand between her legs, excitements she was still getting used to and not too sure about. Now he said he had something to show her and he took her out to a one-room tarpaper house at the back of Settler's Woods she'd never seen before, some kind of clubhouse, she learned later, that the senior boys had built. She hung back, but Colt grabbed hold of her wrist and pulled her in. "C'mon, Daph, don't be a party pooper," he laughed. "What party?" she asked, but too late, they were already inside and the bolt was thrown. A mosquito whined. I Remember.

That clubhouse, built by John and his friends, all seniors that year, on a stubbly piece of land owned by Dutch's old man at the back edge of the woods outside of town, was the first thing John put up that stayed a while. It was still there five years later at the time of his wedding and did not come down, though by then abandoned and the floor rotted out, until Dutch's new motel got built out there some five or six years further on. As with all John's constructions, function, not craft or style or beauty, determined its design: one comfortably sized room with bare wooden floors and walls, low pitched roof, a door made from a tabletop and three framed windows, unpaned but screened and wooden-shuttered (chair seats did the job) to let the breezes through, no plumbing or electrics but a junkyard coal stove for the winter, and furnished with a kitchen table under a hanging Coleman lantern for playing cards, half a dozen folding chairs, an old leatherette sofa with the springs poking out, a single bed and cotton mattress, car blankets and ashtrays tossed around to make it feel like home, a flyswatter, a spike with toilet paper beside the door, and saucy calendar pin-ups, baseball pennants, girls' panties, an American flag, and photos clipped from sun-worshiper magazines tacked up on the walls. Though John, having more options, used it less than most, its principle appealed to him: people were multifaceted creatures needing a variety of discrete spaces to fulfill themselves. In short, one house was not enough. Not for the living. Or, as he put it to Waldo and Bruce and the others out at the Country Tavern the night before his marriage, accepting Harvie's newest round of iced gin, Dutch's of cold beer, and describing the place they were headed next: "We just wanted a getaway somewhere, a place we could be ourselves. Of course, we were ourselves wherever we went, but this was different, the getaway was a kind of sanctuary, you know, like a chapel or a basketball court or a whorehouse, a place where—" "Where anything can happen," proposed Harvie, clinking gin jiggers with him, while around him his friends slowly bobbed and rotated, as though on a carousel. "No, not . . . not anything." He felt utterly lucid and totally bombed out of his mind at the same time, not used to gin clearly, if gin was clearly what it was. "It's more like a kind of theater set where the script is different, but what you do there is fucking scripted, just the same. Like a, you know, a church service." What was he saying? Where was he? "All right then, Father Dutch," grinned his best man Bruce, tossing back his gin and rising unsteadily, "goddamn it, let us pray!"

Prayer for Pauline had always been associated with a zealous assault on all her orifices, that being Daddy Duwayne's zinger-wielding mode of sermonizing, and so what transpired that night before John was wived was not without for Pauline its spiritual overtones, its aura of a sacred service, or else a diabolical one, made more so by the strange magical things happening to her mind or in it, the vivid things she saw, not seen since, and almost, her grown-up imagination failing her, beyond recall. Even the funky old-mattress smell of that shape-shifting cabin (she went looking after, could never find it, came to believe it never was) brought back to her her mad daddy's religious exercises on the trailer floor, though thankfully free on this occasion of the whippings her daddy always laid on, even as he mounted her, to, as he put it, beat the devil out. No beatings, nothing worse than the ritual baptism (though this was much later, another age really, after the magic had faded, and it happened in a ditch), just a surrender so total she seemed not to have a self any longer, all that she was, absorbed into a transcendent otherness that penetrated her utterly and lifted her out of herself into something as vast as the night sky and as intimate as pain and sweat. She was fourteen years old then and her breasts were full and firm and, though she could be sure of little else after, she knew that her yearning heart, which lay nestled between them like a baby bird, was passionately stroked that night by that cosmic otherness and that, as its personification reared majestically above her, his hair was on fire with eerie curling flames, strange-colored, like luminous serpents from another world.

Dutch, from beneath this six-ring circus, had a similar view, through the girl's unwashed hair, of his tit-fucking buddy's flaming head, but though stoned, he knew it merely to be the haloing effect of the gas lantern overhead. Dutch harbored no illusions. Things were what they were. There was no magic. Not even in Harvie's hallucinogens. Life and the mechanics of life were the same thing. He liked to keep his distance, keep his eye on it. At that moment he was lying on his back on the mattressed kitchen table with his dick up the ass of a young girl, ceremonial proxy (he knew, they all knew) for the bride-to-be, but he would just as soon have had someone else where he was and be watching it all from an easy chair. Wouldn't have all this fucking weight pressing down on him, for one thing, or be rubbing testimonials with a freaking Hard Yard between the girl's quivering thighs and thus between his own as well, risking a multidirectional scattershot shower of cum from all the others. Well, anything for old John. This stag night's entertainment, just climaxing, was Dutch's personal wedding gift to his old battery mate, that and the special wedding party rate at the downtown Pioneer Hotel, owned by Dutch's old man. Dutch and John went back to childhood when Dutch caught John in Little League. They'd been through school together and a lot more besides. The hotel went back much further of course, but not, as some thought, to pioneer days, though some kind of hostelry may have been appended to the livery stable that once occupied the spot, according to an archive photo. The Railway Saloon stood there during the days when a spur was laid to town, but both were gone now, and some time after the Great War the Pioneer Hotel was built in anticipation of a boom that never happened, not in these parts. Dutch's granddad picked it up at a bankruptcy auction, ran it as a bar and roominghouse until a new war gave it life again, the linens dating from that brief revival. John's wedding party was its last hurrah. A few years later when the old man died, the two pals struck a deal and John tore it down and built a bank and office block there, Dutch moving out to catch the highway trade with his new motel.

Floyd stayed out there when he first hit town. The motel had just been built, you could smell the fresh-laid cinderblocks and the carpet glue. Booked in for a night, stayed for three weeks, then moved into town, hitting a bit of luck rare in his life, so rare he was never able to say for sure after whether it had been good or bad. Floyd, on the mend from mean times, had in desperation grabbed up several sales jobs, peddling a versatile cheapjack line that ranged from coolers and cosmetics to brushes, Bibles, and magical potions for men afflicted with baldness and loss of vigor. He stopped in at the local hardware store to push his range of screwdriver sets and do-it-yourself rockingchair kits, which he'd had a bit of luck with in these independent backwater operations, often starved for a gimmick to beat the chains, but now all too few and far between. There was a tall broad-shouldered guy in there with his sleeves rolled up who looked skeptically down his slightly broken nose at Floyd, picked up one of the screwdrivers, and bent it double with his bare hands. "This stuff's junk," he said. "Hell, I know it," Floyd acknowledged with a shrug, glancing around. "I do believe in the do-it-yourself line, though, and I don't see enough of that in here. You should ought to have an auto parts section, too. You're away behind the times." The guy studied him a moment. He looked like he might be about to take a swing, so Floyd turned to go, figuring on maybe a bowl of chili and a piece of pie at the cheap cafe next door, but the guy stopped him. "Wait a minute. You want regular work? My manager just quit. I'm looking for somebody to run this store." Floyd paused, loath to get pushed around, especially by a young shit, still wet behind the ears, but startled by the offer and the amazing timing and needing the job. He didn't even know how he was going to pay his overnight motel bill. "I got a job. But I'll think on it." "I haven't got time to fuck around, friend. I mean right now. On with the overalls or out the goddamn door." Floyd sighed, gazed round the dusty old store, peeled off his checkered jacket. "Let me see if they're my size." John covered his motel bill for three weeks while he looked for a house. He called his wife Edna who didn't believe him until he sent her a bus ticket to help him join in the house search. She was so happy once she got to town, she asked for it for the first time in a decade. It made Floyd's heart swell and fill his chest to see her all flushed and eager like that, she almost looked a girl again.

Dutch saw her, too. Not much to see, but he was testing out his two-way mirrors still, and the salesman gave her quite a ride, enough to get off on anyway while waiting for a better show. Of which plenty to come, to spend a phrase. He'd seen it all, Dutch had, over the dozen years since then, a seamless flow: Marriage nights, adulteries, group gropes. Old guys taking virgin blood. Young kids fumbling. Child sex, dog sex, toilet sex, you name it. Rapes and whippings, faggots and dykes. Gangbangs. Incest. But mostly forlorn meat-beaters, all alone. Melancholy places, highway motels. A lot of fucking solitary sadness, as Dutch knew well. Some used fancy gadgetry, especially the women, others anything at hand. Dutch liked the improvisors best, left stuff around for them like bait to use, but learned more from the others. Sometimes he wanted to reach out and pat a quivering unknuckling ass, say well done, knowing then how God must feel, having to keep his distance, else spoil the show. Couldn't even use the spectacle as a turn-on for a fuck or bring a buddy in for laughs, as in the old days at the Palace Theater, that'd be the end of it. He used to think that what God went for, if there was a God, was all the stories, why else would He keep watching, but now he thought there were no stories, only one: this ceaseless show and he/He who watched it. Or maybe Dutch had the wrong seat in the house. For stories, he eventually came to believe, somehow always had to do with numbers, numbers and sequence, and maybe this was God's game, too, having started maybe with one and two and set them humping, but having long since gone on from there, Dutch in his innocence sitting still in the kiddie rows with his useless dick in his hands like a fishing pole, the real stories having all moved elsewhere. The only other who knew about the Back Room mirrors was John, having installed them for Dutch when he built the place, compensation for his lost Palace. Saved a couple of seats from the old moviehouse, too, and the banner that hung in the lobby: "Where the Movies Are Still the Movies." John got no delight in ogling what he couldn't get his organ into, but sometimes used the room when opening and closing deals, lodging clients and adversaries there, his interest not in bottoms but in bottom lines, and so closer to the notion Dutch had of story, or maybe the notion's inspiration. John rarely dropped by himself, just let Dutch tape the conferences and calls.

Which was how John found out about his father-in-law's attempt a year or so ago at the time of their civic center squabble to wrest his construction firm away, the thankless old fossil. Could have wiped John out. It would never have happened if Audrey were still alive, she the smart one in that pair, and loyal to John who'd helped her double their retirement fortune with his genius for investment, a fortune funding now Barnaby's callous raid. Behind the wedding vows all those years before lay other contracts, silent shifts of wealth and property, unseen by most but sending ripples of rumor and anticipation through the town as in election years or before state championships or raffle draws. John's ancestors had come to town as harness makers and blacksmiths, his great-great-grandfather a manufacturer of horse troughs and owner of the town's first hardware store, or at least that was the legend. Paint and wallpaper had soon been added, a real estate agency and a sheet metal company, and his father Mitch had got into heating, refrigeration, and air-conditioning, landing lucrative wartime contracts through his political connections, even though almost everything had to be subcontracted out. Mitch had plowed his profits back into minerals, banks, and land, cheap farmland mostly, bought at mortgagors' auctions and become prime sites when they put the highway through. Mitch had kept the land and investments but given John the family businesses to use as tokens in his nuptial dealings with the builder, a simple exchange that gave the boy a quarter of the new amalgamated construction firm and related enterprises, his wife's power-of-attorney forms effectively making it a half. When Audrey died, they each, thanks to a will John had helped her to draft, had thirds, and John, then in his thirties and chafing at the bit, set about easing his grieving father-in-law into an early and hopefully distant retirement. Old Barnaby was a builder famous for his solid constructions, most of the best houses in town had been built by him, but he was slow and too expensive, such craftsmanship was for the rich, a limited market in such a town as this, and out of step with the throwaway times. John understood the common need, wanted to build not houses but whole developments, his own an art of most for least, quick, cheap, and functional, disdaining the vain illusions of perpetuity, a view which Barnaby understood but poorly, so causing them endless friction. And then, just when John had overreached himself in his civic center and newest mall constructions and faced a cash-flow crunch, there came an irresistible offer from an unexpected source: an upstate client of his sorehead cousin Maynard, an industrial and commercial paving company, looking for a merger. Their other chips included an insulation and roofing company, a small tile manufacturer, and a line in septic tanks and cesspools, as well as real estate; they wanted only thirty percent of the final package and were offering a three hundred grand cash investment to close the deal. It seemed too good to be true. "They think you're hot," said Maynard with a sour shrug, which John found he could only half believe. As they approached the signing stage and the negotiators came to town, John offered them free lodging at Dutch's motel, joined Dutch in the old movie seats in the Back Room for once to watch the show, see who turned up and what got said. He figured there had to be a card they hadn't shown yet. He hadn't expected it, though, to be his father-in-law.

Maynard II, who had helped old Barnaby cook up the deal to get his company back, stolen from him by John, was not, it's true, a happy man. It was he who'd caught the garter at the famous wedding when John's fraternity brother shied from it, mindful not of its alleged foretellings but of the sweet warm leg from which it came; he who, having finally two years later, third time lucky, passed the bar, had then, feeling magnaminous, wed the gatherer of the bride's bouquet, public boobs, bad rep, and all, a marriage that had lasted less than a year, though it had seemed a century or two longer than that; and he who, with one exception, loathed all women only slightly less than he loathed all men, that exception not being the thriftless screamer who was his present legal mate and mother of his only son. It might be said that Maynard had courted John's wife all the six years before her marriage, her four in high school and two beyond, though as Maynard had no gift at courting, only he could have known that was what he was doing. Certainly she could have had no inkling, though she must have noticed he was always there, humble and serviceable as a pencil sharpener or a cafeteria tray. One day, the happiest of his life perhaps, she turned to him suddenly, the great distance between them dissolving for a moment as her gaze uncharacteristically penetrated his, and said (he'd just rethreaded and tightened the chain on her bicycle): "Maynard"—she always called him Maynard, even in casual haste, never "Nerd" or "Junior" as the others did—"Maynard, you're really very sweet." Or at least that was what she seemed to say, he could not be sure, his ears were ringing so. He thought for a moment then she was going to kiss him, a thought that nearly made him let go in his corduroys, but she only squeezed his hand (a hand that for some time after went unwashed) and then, as though without transition, she was gone again, their torrid romance ended when not yet begun. She married in due time his cross-cousin John, a ruthless cocksman who'd systematically cracked half the hymens in high school, as though he'd bought or won the rights to them, what did he need another for? The heartless egotistical hardballing sonuvabitch, how could he help but hate him?

Thus, though most men admired John, a model for all men, there were many among them who also feared him some, and even those who, resenting him for his usurpations, mistrustful of his success and power, would have been glad to see him fall, feeling the relief of a balance struck, as when gangsters or presidents die, or wars disturb the dull interminable peace.

But not Waldo. No, Jesus, he'd be dead without that beautiful bastard, John was all that stood between Waldo and the awful abyss, a mighty rock in a weary land, may he live and prosper to the end of time. Waldo was not from this town. He and John had been drinking buddies at college. Waldo had brought John into the fraternity, had protected him from most of the pledge horseshit, seen to it that John succeeded him in the chapter presidency. Those were the days, oh man, playing ball, boozing, screwing sorority girls, then all-night bridge and poker till the break of dawn, he and Long John and Knucks and Beans and Brains and old Loose Bruce, a fuck-off's golden age. Waldo, in love with those times, couldn't leave them, was still raising hell and drifting drunkenly through a series of worsening sales jobs, dragging Lollie and the kids about, when he ran into John at a home builders show in Chicago and overnight became an Assistant Vice President in Charge of Sales for a number of John's enterprises. Now about all he did was preside over John's local paint and wallpaper business and run an errand now and then, like the one that helped to nail wicked old Barn, but he knew, whatever happened, shit, old John, good brother, would take care of him.

John's fraternal succor both rankled Waldo's wife Lorraine and reconciled her in some small part to her wretched fate: how had a class act like herself—once voted "Most Likely to Marry a Millionaire," a B-plus lit major, and a hotshot on the tennis courts—ended up a desexed overweight smalltown hausfrau chained to a shopping basket, three of the world's most unabashed underachievers, and a prehistoric Ford stationwagon off Stu's used-car lot, suffering from crankcase drip and a fatal skin disease? She should have left the sodden deadbeat she'd wed—madly, after a wild party—years ago, before she met him in fact, but not only were there the two kids to think about, tedious little louts though they were, the truth was, her lot once cast, her options were few. Alimony would have been zip in those shiftless years adrift, jobs she could have tolerated or even applied for were few, and the mirror on the wall told her plain she'd been condemned to a brief bloom: one pollination and the "Here's Lollie!" show was over, nothing but bracken and stinkweeds after, only a drunk in a dark room could ever again get up a semi-tumescent interest. Which was how she got knocked up the second time, not even sure Waldo knew who he was with when, like a bushel of old winter apples, he fell on her, scattering himself mushily in all directions. So she was relieved to have someone come to their rescue, even if, as rescues went, it was a pretty half-assed affair, regretting only that that someone had to be the callous sonuvabitch who took the only maidenhead she ever had. Not that she missed it—what the hell, let it go, good riddance, it was just getting in her way anyhow—but she really didn't want ever to see the capricious bastard again, much less live in the same goddamned town with him. Made her feel vulnerable and exposed, as though she'd stepped out naked from behind the doctor's screen and found herself and her sagging ass on Main Street. She still didn't know where to look when they were in the same room together, and in mixed-doubles foursomes on the golf course, it cost her a stroke each time John glanced her way or handed her a tee for one she'd splintered. Did he get a charge out of that? Probably, who knows. She sometimes had the weird feeling that John had brought to this town, not Waldo, but her, and no doubt others like her as well, not out of any sense of caring for an old flame (that was flattering herself), and not just to make her eat shit and feel the fool either, though she wouldn't put it past him, but just because, a smalltowner to the bone, he'd started up these stories and wanted to keep them all around him, see how they all came out.

Beatrice would have been startled by Lorraine's insight, had she known of it, so similar was it to one of her own. For her husband Lennox, too, whom Waldo called Knucks and the townsfolk Reverend Lenny, had by John been raised from the dead, brought here, and restored to a station of eminence and dignity not his since his days as fraternity chaplain and pledge master, and she, too, thought she might have been the secret beneficiary of John's unexpected brotherly love—his midlife atonement, as it were, for the dissolute excesses of his youth. For which, at least as they affected her, traumatic as it had all been at the time, she forgave him. Lennox's feelings, she knew, were more ambivalent, as they always were, part of his character really, a trait that sometimes approximated moral weakness, though now in his new pastoral career, he had learned to dissemble a certain steadfastness in his convictions, an appearance—most of the time—of equanimity and resolve, and so was held by his congregation in general good repute. They saw him, she believed, as a good man, honest and forthright, gentle in his chastisements, understanding at hospital bedsides and burials, artistic in his church services, if perhaps a bit vague and overly intellectual, and they saw her as the good man's wife and helpmeet, his organist and choir director and mother of his three children. Most of which was nearly true.

Floyd, who taught Sunday school in Reverend Lenny's church, thought of him as a candy-ass and a prevaricator, a pulpit flimflammer not to be trusted, sinful in not hating sin enough. The silly prat probably didn't even know what it was. Did Floyd know? Too well. Still had nightmares, blood on his hands. This town, the church, the hardware store: a wall Floyd was throwing up between himself and his past. He was still tough as the nails he sold, old Floyd was, but now he was tough for the Lord. He and Edna had been in town a couple of years already and felt like locals when the new preacher turned up, some old college bud of John's, people said, just like that seedy bozo Waldo, who came wallowing in the year after, tongue out and wagging his broad behind, and whose only serious job, as far as Floyd could tell, was to sub for John from time to time on the compulsory bridge nights, the female knee then under the table as alluring as a bend in a rusty drainpipe. These people all made Floyd feel old. And vulnerable. John was taking over the family construction company in those years, encouraged by his mother-in-law, not yet dead then but soon to be, and Floyd saw less and less of him, cut from the party invite lists, ignored at the old family hardware store while bigger things got done. Even Stu and they had drifted apart what with poor old Winnie dead and gone, these were lonely times for him and Edna, potluck suppers at the church, the bowling league, and TV quiz shows mostly what they had here of social life. Sometimes Floyd felt like taking a big hammer and smashing every cussed thing in sight. Even that wall he was so painstakingly building. He wanted to shove his fingers deep into the bloodred-rimmed fingerholes of his personalized bowling ball and roll a strike of such terrific force that nothing, nothing, was left standing after.

Intimations of covetous Floyd's hidden yearnings reached young Clarissa and her friends through his Sunday school lessons, in which he seemed to take special delight—his thin wide lips twitching then in a scary kind of grin that the other kids, who called him Old Hoot 'n' Holler, often made fun of—in describing the tortures of hell and the terrific ways God smote his enemies and the day Jesus suddenly blew his cool and almost wackily set about "cleansing the temple," as the Bible said, or supposedly said, a story which Clarissa tended to take personally, since she associated her dad with the temple, and probably rightly so, too. That man managed one of her father's stores, and it was like he was working for her dad and against him at the same time. Still, you couldn't take him seriously. Clarissa and her friends mostly regarded Old Hoot's ravings as just so much overexcited horsedookie frankly, even her best friend Jennifer, whose own dad was the preacher and had told her it ain't necessarily so, and the older boys at the church called him a dumb cracker who ought to go join the holy rollers, what was he doing in a serious church like this one anyway? There were exceptions, her something-cousin Little Maynard, for example, or Turtle, as he was now called: he was all eyes and ears, a disciple born and bred, so turned on by all the blood and gore he seemed almost to look forward to God wasting the earth and sending them all screaming into the pits of hell. He was always trying to scare her little brother Mikey and the younger kids with his weirdo ideas, and once when they were smaller Clarissa had even caught him tying Mikey and Jennifer's baby sister Zoe down and pinching them with barbecue tongs, which he said were the devil's pincers. They had a fight then, and she called him the name all the other kids were calling him, even though back then she didn't like to use bad language, and because she was bigger than he was, she was able to give him a good slapping and take the tongs away from him and untie the two little ones, who then surprised her in a way she was never able to understand by siding with him against her.

They didn't really do anything, they just pushed at her and yelled at her to stop hitting him, all of them bawling like babies now and calling her names, so she left them in disgust, wondering why she had ever bothered to try to help in the first place. A lesson learned.

Little Maynard was the firstborn of twice-wed Maynard II and Veronica, proudly named Maynard III, proudly but thoughtlessly, for it is a bad enough thing to be called the Nerd, much worse to be Nerd the Turd. It had started already in the second grade. Little, as his folks called him, didn't even get the joke at first, and he certainly couldn't figure out where it all came from, it being the sort of thing his dad never wanted to talk about, blowing his stack whenever he was asked, even swatting Little once across the back of the head. Hard. Finally it was his mom who let it all out one day when she was fed up with his dad, one of the many days, she was fed up with him most of the time, and she always let the whole world know about it. So, that was when he found out that back when his own mom and dad were still in junior high, and Grandpa Maynard had just got elected mayor of the town, everyone at school had started calling his dad Mayor Nerd. Okay, ha ha, very funny, but come on, that was centuries ago, how did the guys in his class know that? Little figured it must have something to do with Clarissa and Mikey, who were Uncle John's kids, Uncle John being one of his dad's worst enemies and so probably the person who had started it all in the first place. Clarissa was mean and sneaky enough to do something like that to Little, she was always bullying him, he hated her and had often found himself wishing that Jesus or somebody would order him to take her pants down and spank the daylights out of her, and although Mikey was a spooky little twit who kept to himself pretty much and hardly ever said anything at all, Little didn't trust him. He didn't trust much of anybody actually, it was more like a general principle, something his dad had taught him early on, about the only exception being his friend Fish, one of the preacher's kids, Zoe's and Jennifer's big brother. Fish was older than he was, already in high school, and knew just about everything, at least the things Little wanted to know. The first thing he taught him was his weekly paper route when Little took it over, but even that first day they soon got to talking about lots of other things, starting with baseball and God, but pretty soon moving on to more interesting stuff. Things that happened on the paper route, for example. Fish was a good explainer. Then one day Fish heard one of the other kids calling him Turd while they were playing video games out at the mall ("Quit hogging the fricking machine, Turd!" is what the dumb jerk said), and Fish just grabbed him by the back of the neck and said: "What did I hear you say? I think I heard you say, ah, 'Turtle,' is that right?" "Yeah, yeah! Ow! Turtle!" the kid squeaked and they all laughed nervously, and after that they mostly called him Turtle, though some of them still said it with a *d.* It was like some kind of joke they were all in on, but that was okay, he was in on it, too. So everything was cool. It was Fish and Turtle from then on. And it was Fish who told him about collecting for the *Crier* at the big house of Turtle's Uncle John one Saturday morning and finding his aunt there all alone. Just out of the bath. Fish said. Naked. Stark naked. You should have seen.

Naked flesh: ever a sight to see, with all its glowing surfaces, its creases and dimples and hairy bits, and especially when generally withheld from view. As was the case with most in town past the crawling age, at least in public between the sexes, John's wife no exception. Many had imagined her *au naturel,* as Ellsworth, showing off, once put it in *The Town Crier* when describing the orthodontist's scandalous daughter at a famous Pioneers Day parade ("how natural," is how most folks thought that naughty phrase got spoken, the naughty girl herself long gone from here), but though few would miss the chance, few had actually seen John's wife starkly so. Young Fish's brag, if overheard, would have aroused doubt in most, envy in many, rage in a few perhaps and/or anxiety or mad desire, but certainly in all quarters a great curiosity. For Gordon, who longed to photograph John's wife exhaustively, it would have added another shot for his projected study: "John's Wife (Wet) Draped in Falling Towel." He had not thought of this one, not yet, though he had envisioned her, before his lens, on a barren hilltop, dressed in a gauzy stuff like mist, gently pivoting on one foot, glancing around, her hair caught by a breeze, her far hip lifting slightly, her trailing hand waist-high, a mysterious shadow between her thighs: "John's Wife Turning Through Diaphanous Wisps." And also, more akin to the paperboy's uncorroborated report, standing naked ("John's Wife . . .") in the rain, face uplifted, arms outstretched, feet together, her body streaming and glistening in the downpour, diamonds of light in her pubic hair. This one he had practiced with his wife Pauline, and the results, free as he was to play with angles, lenses, filters, and exposures, were professional enough, quite admirable in some respects, but there was no magic in them. No *radiance.* Not even in his blowups of the diamonds of light.

"Radiance" was a word often used when speaking of John's wife, though what was meant by it, few could say. "Radiant" was how her parents Barnaby and

Audrey described her as a baby when astark, delighting in the little creature, excessively so perhaps, she being the only one they ever had, though others, too, privileged back then to behold her entire, John's folks Mitch and Opal among them, often remarked that the precious child truly "glowed with health." She was still "dazzling" (see the testimonials in her highschool yearbooks) as she blossomed into the well-dressed woman whom John undressed, starkly, to his great delight, but whom others glimpsed in similar state along the way, or thought they did, Gordon's friend Ellsworth, for example, who babysat her and dressed her up (and down) for the make-believe games they played. "Babes in the Woods." "Sleeping Beauty." "Narcissus and Echo." "Alice Through the Looking-Glass." And games that Ellsworth made up from scratch, like "Dreaming Awake" and "The Artist and His Model." "Narcissus and Echo" was a particular favorite of both of them, copycat play that was lots of fun, followed by a kind of hide-and-seek. Ellsworth would hunch over his own reflection—in a rain puddle, a paddling pool, a hubcap, kettle bottom, or snow shovel, most often just a handmirror at his feet—while she "vanished," leaving her clothes behind, the playacting ones she wore on top. While she was looking for a hiding place, Ellsworth, his gaze fixed upon the pale acne'd image of himself (sometimes, cheating, he'd tip the mirror to see, between his legs, the dress-up clothes come off), would call out to her in phrases stolen from *Ancient Mythologies* and she would shout back at him the last words that he said—"Won't anyone come play with me?" "Play with me!" "Why can't I see you?" "See you!" "Don't be such a nincompoop!" "Poop!" "Where have you gone?" "Gone!"—until she had finally hidden, and then she would be silent and he would go looking for her, tickling her when he found her. But not too hard. Just a little. The tickling was not her favorite part. Nor, though he liked it, his. After that, they'd get dressed up and do it again, though sometimes, just to be fair, he'd be Echo. Of course, this was a long time ago, when Ellsworth was even younger than Fish was now.

Fish, whose proper name was Philip, Fish being the name his baby sister Jennifer gave him when they were both just toddlers, was the oldest of three children and the only son of Beatrice and Reverend Lenny, though when he was born his parents were still known mostly as Trixie and Knucks. That is to say, he was certainly Beatrice's oldest, she never able to say for sure, after what happened that night at the fraternity house toga party, that Lennox was the father, in fact probably he wasn't, though of course she told him he was, and he seemed to accept that and married her willingly when she asked him to, being a good man at heart, whatever he believed. "Why not?" he said. "Let it happen." A good man, but also, truth to tell, a weak man, with a talent for trouble, trouble she had had to share over the years, and as for what he believed, that was always pretty vague, whatever the subject, rather too vague for a man of the cloth, as she often remarked, though always with understanding and forbearance. Needful virtues in their trying years adrift. When Philip was born and Lenny had graduated, thanks to a fraternity brother named Brains who wrote three of his final papers for him, she and Lenny had left the baby with her mother and taken a little honeymoon, a spiritual holiday, as Lenny called it, irony being one of his redeeming qualities. He had signed up for a dozen or more credit cards and they had gone on an international spree, living like royalty all over the world until the credit limits were all used up and the collection agencies came after them. Not much those blue-suited bullies could do. All she and Lenny had left when they got back was an old car hidden in her mother's garage and the baby. The bullies found and took the car. Carted it off on a truck bed, Lenny having sold the wheels. Well, she and Lenny had had a wonderful time, quite literally the time of their lives, and they felt no guilt about the credit card companies, it was their fault for giving them all that credit in the first place, right? But now what? In college, Lenny had majored in philosophy and religious studies, and jobs in these fields were scarce, especially now that he had more or less lost his credibility as a moral exemplar, at least in the eyes of the establishment. About the best they could find were part-time jobs in charity organizations, working with the underprivileged and the handicapped, Beatrice sometimes able to give music and dancing lessons or, until she got pregnant with Jennifer—who was more likely Lenny's, most likely of the three—to play the piano in bars and restaurants. Finally, like a miracle, Lennox landed a job teaching religious studies at a small liberal arts college, hard up for cheap staff and willing to overlook his minor misdemeanors. In fact, the times were such, his credit card–burning had a certain heroic luster: down with the system, yay. The teaching went well, the students seemed to love him, and he even managed, at Beatrice's insistence, to get ordained in his spare time. Beatrice helped the students put on an underground satirical revue, they experimented with the drugs that were popular at that time, little Zoe was born. If it had not been for that unfortunate incident with one of Lenny's hysterical freshman students they might be there still. When he got fired, Lennox seemed to lose all his self-esteem and stayed stoned almost all the time. Luckily, Beatrice had been a zealous sender of Christmas cards, so over the years, throughout their travels and travails, they had stayed in touch with John. It was not exactly Christmastime, but she got in touch again. It was good timing. For all his faults, she thought, God bless John.

Reverend Lenny, ever more ambivalent than his wife, would have to agree and, of course, disagree. Even about the timing, for as it happened, when they first came to town a decade ago, their arrival coincided with the violent death of Stu's first wife Winnie, Lenny's first service here—or anywhere—therefore a funeral, a discouraging omen, and besides, Lenny knew nothing at all about funerals, having always, on principle, avoided them. Even his own father's he had skipped out on. So, to gear up for this newest trial and because he feared it was expected of him, he decided to pay a pastoral visit, hat in hand, to the bereaved, hoping that if they had to pray, they could pray in silence. He had found the old boy on his knees, all right, but only because he couldn't stand up. He was pie-eyed, nose bandaged, tongue loose in his mouth as a bell-clapper, and his pants looked like they'd been used for a floor-mop in a men's room. He offered Lenny a drink on condition that he'd pour two, having lost his bottle grip, and Lenny decided it was probably the Christian thing to do, his own throat parched moreover with all his day's—week's, month's—hypocritical posturings, he badly needed one. Time passed, during which old Stu tried to sell him a car (credit no problem), sang a song about honkytonk women, confessed to murder, and told him what he said was a true story about a nun, eventually canonized, who had a second rectum where her other business ought to be. The worst thing was that Lenny found himself laughing like a heathen, another bottle, at least one, having been opened in the meantime. Actually that was probably the second worst thing. The worst thing was that he realized he couldn't walk, he was alone in a darkening kitchen with a confessed murderer, and there was a committee of ladies from the church at the front door, bearing gifts of food, John's wife among them. There was the honorable and manly way to behave on such occasions, and there was the despicable tail-between-the-legs sneak-thief way. He chose as always the latter, snatching up his hat and Bible and clattering on his hands and knees into the bedroom and under the bed, where he awoke four hours later, his nose full of dust balls and his erstwhile host snoring overhead like a pneumatic drill. He crept out, thinking about his wife and the terrific story he would have to make up, and found himself face-to-face with a woman, stretched out on the bed beside the brain-dead widower, fully dressed, even to a hat and black veil, and resting a bottle on her belly. "Hey, Preacher, good to see you back among the living," she slurred throatily this side of the raucous snores, the bottle doing a little dance as she spoke. She wore the veil tossed back like a ballplayer with his cap on backwards. "Whaddaya say we take a little communion, hunh?" She winked broadly, raising her knees and spreading them, her green eyes crossing, then refocusing. "If you do, honey, I'll tell you where your shoes are."

Serving on church committees, consoling those who had lost loved ones, and providing sustenance to those in need were but a few of John's wife's volunteer civic and religious activities in town. She was also a member of the BPW, Ladies' Aid, the Parent-Teacher Association, and the Literary Society, which met each month in the town library, except in the summer, less often since the longtime town librarian had died. She rarely missed a school play, attending even those in which friends' children performed. When old Snuffy retired after nearly thirty years of highschool teaching and coaching to take up a managerial post out at John's airport, it was she who presented him at halftime of the homecoming game with the honorary "Coach of the Century" trophy from his players and ex-players, which read simply: DIG IN, SON. Many in town might pass unnoticed for weeks on end, old Snuffy himself, for example, or others like the drugstore simpleton, tethered to his pinball machines and video games, or his sister Columbia, sullenly overweight and whited out by her nursing uniform, or timid Trevor, housebound Edna, and most old folks much of the time, sad to say, but not John's wife. She was at the inaugural meeting of the town cleanup campaign, and when they stenciled KEEP OUR TOWN BEAUTIFUL on all the trashcans in town, she helped cut the stencils, and people said hers were the neatest. She collected door-to-door each year for the Community Chest and the March of Dimes, sang in the church choir, and though she rarely sought or held office, was treasurer for two years of the Pioneers Day parade committee. She was always in the parade itself, on one float or another or perched on the backseat of one of the lead convertibles, usually dressed in a beautiful pioneer costume, her presence as indispensable as a definiendum's to a definition (something Kate the librarian once said, though not even Ellsworth could repeat it after). When the decorating of the city fire hydrants was in fashion, she painted one a vivid emerald green, trimmed in metallic gold, which many said was an expression of her true personality, hidden beneath her modest, somewhat dry and formal surface, and others said showed a lack of a sense of humor. Ellsworth recalled that these were the colors of the dress a princess wore in a story he had read to her as a child and Maynard that this was how her highschool bicycle was painted, each deriving his own private meaning from his recollection, which may or may not have been accurate. Gordon's photos of the hydrant and its painter added nothing to his knowledge, though a swatch of glitter on her bluejeaned thigh did haunt for a time his darkroom nights. Waldo's wife Lorraine, who interpreted all the painted fireplugs as condom fantasies (hers she'd painted like a one-eyed toothless Martian in a tux, though lame Gretchen won first prize with a winsome portrait of her white-jacketed father-in-law), felt a twinge of jealousy when she saw John's wife's hydrant, but Barnaby felt only sorrow, perceiving his daughter's deep malaise.

By the time Gretchen won the hydrant-painting competition, her husband Cornell, though the father of her six children, including triplets born just three months before the contest, much to Grandpa's great delight (thus the beaming smile on the fireplug's cartoon face), was little more than a peripheral nuisance to the family, which centered now around the thickly bespectacled lady from the north with the anguished grimace and the withered leg. Lumby loved her, Oxford did, as did all her babies of course (and there were more to come), and so did even, from a distance, her brother-in-law Harvie, grateful that his lonely sister had found true companionship at last, and so, with brotherly gratitude, loving the beloved. And Corny, who spent his mind-bombed days behind pinball machines and pornographic magazines, loved her, too, as best he could in his woeful way, having less than all his marbles, as was often said—a strange boy stranger yet as man: his thinning hair uncombed, his eyes unfocused, the hairs of his blond moustache hanging down over his pink mouth like a kind of wispy curtain, nothing but nonsense heard from behind it. With cause, of course, were his marbles lost and scattered, as all who knew his Paris story knew, but that boy was born to strangeness, not all there from the get-go, and in more marbly ways than one, as his sister Lumby would say, speaking euphemistically, she unable to figure out, given his little problem, just how the little sperm machine got the job done, so to speak. Though get it done he clearly did, his bride's fecundity, even at this early stage in her parturient career, already notorious in the town and soon to become a local legend.

One who was not surprised by the frequent ripening of the crippled drugstore lady's womb was Pauline, who had seen Corny's little problem, as his sister called it, from a different perspective. Though she and Corny had been in high school at the same time, just a class or two apart, Pauline had always thought of him as light-years younger, not only because she felt so much older than almost all the boys she knew, but because Corny was such a backward little shrimp, hanging out mostly with gradeschool children right up into her senior year in highschool, which was when she began noticing him staring at her from across the room with that confused wall-eyed look of puppydog desire she had seen drift across the faces of successive generations of boys like the special effects in werewolf movies. She had known by all her five senses his two brothers before him, Harvie, the one they called Hard Yard, being off only by an inch or two, and Yale, who was so sweet, and she supposed, by the looks he was giving her, she would eventually know their little brother in like manner as well. This came to pass, though not without a great deal of hesitation on Corny's part, a lot of time-wasting teasing and pretended hostility and disinterest and silly snickering in the corridors, before he finally turned up at the trailer park on his bicycle one twilit summer evening with two of his little friends, asking if she would like to go riding with them. Luckily, her Daddy Duwayne was not around, he would have eaten them alive. She asked them how much money they had and what they wanted. The idea of needing money had apparently not occurred to them: nothing but small change among the three of them. But what they wanted was small change, too: they merely wanted (after a long list of false wants was got through, starting with the supposed fun of a bike ride) to see. So she took them around behind the trailer and dropped her jeans and underpants, raised her tee shirt. Their frozen, pop-eyed, red-faced, grimacing expressions were so comic-book–like they made her laugh. "You can touch if you want," she said, feeling generous. Corny held back but the others poked about gingerly like little kids trying to guess the contents of wrapped Christmas presents, and eventually Corny, timidly, joined in. Even body hair seemed strange to them, though one said squeakily he had seen his mother's and it was just like that, as though this were some kind of brag. She chased them off finally with threats of her violent daddy's imminent return, but they were back almost every week after that, with more money now and with more boldness in their explorations. They made her bend over and touch her toes, squat, lie down and spread her legs, roll over, get up on her knees and elbows, lie on her side with one knee in the air, press up on her shoulders with her knees by her ears, as they squeezed and patted and palpated and dipped their fingers in wherever they could. Then one evening, just for fun, she told them it was their turn, they had to take their clothes off now and show her. They went rigid with fear, and when she reached for one of their belt buckles, they ran off, leaving her giggling in her own puddle of cast-off clothes and feeling about a hundred years old. But then, later, Corny came back alone and, though he had seemingly lost his power to speak, he indicated by his undone belt buckle that she was to undress him and so she did, remarking to herself, as she took what she found down there into that cavity which had made her locally famous and by which she logged what simple memory she kept of that half of the town's population, how much more interesting it was, even for an incurious person such as herself, to know mankind in all its variety than to surrender, like John's wife, say, to the experience of one alone, no matter how beautiful.

Pauline's loving embrace of the world's variety was not unlike that, if not of his wife, of John himself, though whereas Pauline was fundamentally interested in men's zingers, as she often called them—a childish corruption of Daddy Duwayne's "old sinner," which, because it perversely pleased him, stuck—John was fundamentally uninterested in any zinger but his own, and in that only with respect to where, variously, he might safely and pleasurably put it. To be fair, it could be said that John did therefore share Pauline's fundamental preference for a variety of sexual partners, but John's love of the world's novelty did not end there, nor was it even fundamentally sexual unless all human activities might be reduced to displacements for sexual ones, as some believed—Alf, for example, or Dutch, or Lorraine in her more bookish highbrow moments, more and more infrequent as the years rolled on. Moreover, even in the matter of sexual partners, there was a catholicity in Pauline's taste which John, obeying some unstated aesthetic, did not espouse, to his discredit perhaps from a democratic point of view; but then, the democratic point of view was never one that appealed to John very much, though he paid lip service to it and found it profitable. John felt at one with the universe and the universe was not democratic, it was an uninhibited exhibition of colliding forces, of which a bruising game of football was only the barest echo, but an echo at least, which was why he loved it, and the less refereeing the better, a good fuck likewise. Democracy was a sad little human defense mechanism for the inherently powerless against the powerful, a pipe dream and a failure for the most part, instigated by fear and perpetuated by pissants like his cousin Maynard. Or that butch buttinski Marge. It sought to diffuse, curb, and redistribute power, but it did not, as John knew full well and to his daily increase, succeed. It was a joke. Like that variation on the old "put out or get out" line about the guy (old Stu always liked to hear John tell this one) in the beat-up Ford pickup who stops for a girl walking down a lonely country road crying, she explaining through her tears how she'd been taken out into the woods by a guy in a Lincoln Continental (it was a Cadillac when John had first heard it) who had presented her with that cruel and infamous choice, which of course to her was no choice at all. The guy in the truck tells her to hop in, he'll take her to town, and they go bouncing and jolting and rattling down the road until finally the girl asks to be let out. "Right now, mister, I mean it!" she yells above the clatter. "I'd rather be raped any day in a Lincoln, than get jerked off in a goddamn Ford!"

Stu himself liked to tell this joke when John was not around, occasionally substituting a Chevy or a Toyota for the Ford, though for some reason the joke had a way of stalling out on him when he did that. Another joke he liked to tell, one of his favorites, was the one about the oldtimer who, hollering out, "Mind if I play through, boys?," goes skipping past the young fellows on the golf course, whacking out his long straight drives, then drinks them all under the table back at the clubhouse after, prompting one of them to ask: "Whoo! You still in such fine whack in everything you do, old man?" "Aw, hell no," he confesses, lighting up a nine-inch stogie. "Old age is a bitch, son. Take last night, for example. Woke my little darlin' up about midnight and asked her how about it, and she says: 'How about what? You just had it at ten o'clock and eleven o'clock, you old goat!' That's the trouble, see—goddamn *memory's* goin'!" Stu's little darlin' was Daphne, and although she was a newer model, she was already, like her loving hubby and the principal heroes of his jokes, a pretty heavy guzzler, had been since their cheatin' days, as Stu liked to call them, it was partly what brought them together, that and her ability to rouse back then his anesthetized pecker. Until recently, Stu was about the only one who ever saw the dear girl sober, and then he was usually soused to the eyeballs himself, which was just as well, since it could be a pretty demoralizing experience, being around Daphne when she didn't have a healthy toot on, something more common of late, sad to say, have to remember to fire that young mechanic. Stu and Daphne laced their breakfast juice with gin every morning (Daphne called the drink "Amazing Grace," Stu his day's choke start) and sometimes never got around to supper at all. During weekdays Stu had his Ford-Mercury car lot to keep him busy, Daphne her phonecalls, but there was always a bottle reassuringly to hand for each of them, a comfortable old habit that helped to make their evenings mellow if not altogether coherent or easy to recollect after. Goddamn memory, as Stu would rumble with a grin, elbow sliding on the bar, trying to remember what it was he had to remember to do.

Daphne, once briefly John's little darlin', had also been, more or less at the same time, John's wife's best friend and so maid of honor at her wedding, the day that her present ginwinner reckoned as Day One of the romance that brought him back from the living dead, though years were to transpire before she could get around to that little bit of prestidigitation, having to get fucked over first by a passing parade of other nameless pricks, so she was nearly thirty when she started solacing old Stu, he not yet a widower but soon to be. The first thing she ever did for him was to help him back up when he fell off his barstool, a favor he returned more than once, they were made for each other. Not, however, that she supposed so at John's wedding ten years earlier, when, sick of the old redneck's drooling half-witticisms at her side while she was trying, with an infuriating lack of success, to get the best man's fickle attention, she whopped old Stu in the chops with a piece of cake, an event now part of the family legend. That still didn't shut the relentless sonuvabitch up, and when, as a mimed punchline to some slurred dumb-ass hillbilly joke, he poked his long florid nose in her cleavage, yuk-yukking in his plate after, she coolly dipped her hand in the soupy bowl of strawberries and cream, turned, and licking his weedy ear to distract him, grabbed him in the crotch, leaving a vivid handprint that he apparently, falling in love (so he told her years later), never noticed, though everyone else did, not least that old warhorse he was married to: his colorful forced exit was admired by all, Daphne's lone triumph of the day. Centuries later, she still thought of John's wife as her best friend, and though what with her daily excursions into oblivion it could hardly be said that, besides old Stu, Daphne had any real friends anymore, in a way it remained true, because when Daphne went into orbit she often got into long gossipy telephone chats with John's wife, just like in the old days, the only difference being that now John's wife was not always on the other end of the line.

Though most of the townsfolk who knew her would have agreed that Stu's first wife, whom Daphne called a warhorse when not worse, must have been pretty hard to live with, not everyone would have blamed Winnie, that blowhard crapulous car dealer of hers being no bargain either (Stu would cheerfully admit this with a crooked grin, blinking his pale reddish lashes as though amazed at the wisdom of it, then tell the one about the old fleabag who swallowed a razor blade), and few, even among those who loved her least and laughed most at the jokes about her, would have painted her so blackly as did Stu and Daphne, who seemed sometimes almost to be trying to ward off her lingering presence by ridicule and invective even a decade after she was dead. Trevor's wife Marge in particular was quick to leap to Winnie's defense, both before and after the deplorable accident out at the old humpback bridge (an accident that changed Otis's life, at least for a time), speaking of her as an essentially noble and principled woman, driven to a kind of impotent rage by the town's antiquated and oppressive mores, of which her husband Stu was the perfect bonehead sexist exemplar. A woman of culture who had married a hick and a boor. Of course, Marge was said to be something of a dragon herself, and Winnie was her aunt. Ellsworth's account of Winnie's "tragic untimely death" in *The Town Crier* spoke of "her many cultural, civic, and religious activities" and of "this great inestimable loss to the community," but in truth he hardly knew the woman, or her husband either for that matter, being a nondriver, nor a golfer either, it was a jaded cliché-ridden obituary, could have been about anybody. More than announcing a woman's accidental death, it announced that something had died in him. Obits of course were a newsman's ceaseless charge. Sooner or later, all, all pass away and, passing, exact their column inches no less than their graveyard footage. Ellsworth kept a file cabinet stuffed with bios ready to be plucked for print when a citizen fell, but truth to tell he was never ready when it actually happened, as surprised by others' deaths as he would one day be by his own. That file cabinet, once his refuge, now made his heart sink when his eye fell on it and caused him to doubt the folly of his having cast himself as the town historian, he who could gather all the stuff of stories but could no longer find any story in the stuff, an apostle of the word fallen from grace, a deserter trapped in the trenches. More than anything it was the mind-numbing volume of mazy detail, the surfeit of story, life's disorderly overabundance not death's neat closure, that defeated him. That filing cabinet had no rear panel: it opened out upon infinity. When he reached into one of its crammed drawers he was reaching toward the abyss, and so toward madness. At the time of Winnie's death, he had been back in this town for a dozen years and his fortieth birthday, no matter which way he turned, was staring him baldly in the face. Probably his best line in the obit in fact was when he compared her death to that of an infant: "Her life, at forty, barely begun, was, like innocence abused, abruptly and cruelly ended when . . . " Ellsworth decided to dig out his old novel-in-progress, which he was now calling *The Artist and His Model,* and start working on it again.

Few in town had the dimmest notion as to what Ellsworth was talking about in that obituary, though most thought it grand. That at least was the opinion of Floyd's wife Edna, she being another who got on passably with the deceased when she was still alive. When Edna and Floyd first moved to town, Winnie and Stu were their nearest friends, the only ones they had that first year really, most folks polite and kind to them in a Christian sort of way, but more like how people treated coloreds nowadays than truly come-on-over, kick-your-shoes-off friendly; Floyd felt it too, saying sometimes it made him almost homesick for truck stops and motels. They had just moved into their first rented house, everything still a sorry sight, no curtains on the windows yet and mice in the stove, when Winnie drove by to invite them over for supper that first time. Except for a cocktail party at John's house which was more like an arrest than an invitation and where even the hired help made them feel unwashed, it was their first invitation out in donkey ears, since back when Floyd first hit the road really and started up all his troubles—Edna in her excitement found herself all dressed up about two hours before and having to use the clattery old toilet with its stained bowl and chipped wooden seat every ten minutes or so, leaving the door open because there was no light in there, Floyd teasing her and saying: "Hell, he's seen my old heap, he just wants to sell us a car, that's all." But he was pleased and excited, too. Because true or not, it didn't matter. It meant that for the first time since they could hardly remember they were part of something more than just each other, which sometimes honestly wasn't all that much, it was almost like getting born again. And Floyd was right, that man *did* try to sell him a car, didn't just try, he succeeded, but not without some fun about it, and in friendly accents that took Edna down-home again and almost made her cry for feeling so lost and uprooted. Stu poured some whiskey for him and Floyd after supper, put on some Cajun fiddle music, told some jokes, including one about a rich Texan he said he once knew who was so big he wouldn't fit in his coffin until they gave the corpse an enema, and then they were able to bury him in a shoebox and had room for his boots as well, which made Edna, who had been constipated ever since she got here (she was bothered somehow by all those motel mirrors), giggle so hard she nearly fell off her chair, Floyd remarking as he sucked a cube that it sounded like the damn guy he was working for, setting her off all the more, God help, even Winnie joining the silly laughter now, and then Stu said he ought to give a Ford product a try. Floyd, winking at Edna, just excusing herself to go use the bathroom for a while, said he only drove General Motors cars on the road, having an old soldier's respect for rank, but all right, he'd try a used car from him, about five years old, say, and if the results were satisfying, he'd be back later for a trade-in. Which was how they got their deep purple Mercury. Truth to tell, it wasn't all that grand a car, they hardly drove it away but it needed a new clutch and the brakes relined, but they went on after that, buying all their cars from Stu, even after poor Winnie got killed in a wreck a couple of years later, it seemed like they owed old Stu that much, no matter that his young new wife never had them over anymore.

Edna's husband Floyd had managed John's downtown hardware store ever since then, and though he was good at it and made John a pile of money—money John spent on cars and guns and airplanes, and on pussy too no doubt, his wife on clothes, jewelry, and fancy fittings for their big ranch-style house, the one John built—Floyd always had the notion that John was only tolerating him. He should have got promoted out of this junkshop years ago, but he seemed stuck for good and all, like a rusty peg, right where he was at. It was Floyd whose introduction of the do-it-yourself line had completely turned the old museum around, but when John had set up a big new warehouse-style DIY store out at the new mall he had hired another guy to manage it, telling Floyd, after having effectively just pulled the plug on him, that he couldn't afford to let the Main Street store go down the tubes and needed him there to keep the doors open. Since then, with hard work, smart buying, and a new Hobby Corner line, he had somehow managed to break even, probably mostly on account of his salary was so all-fired low, but in spite of that John had been on his back most of the time. He'd pop in unannounced, complain about the bookshelf kits that weren't moving or kick at some of the crud littering the aisles or run a grim-faced check on the cash register, snapping at him that he wasn't doing enough to stop petty theft and why wasn't the goddamn garden stuff out, it was already the end of February. There was a time, back before the Bible, when Floyd would have stuck a man for talking to him like that. Still could, of course. Eye for an eye, self-defense, and all that, he had his rights, but he was more a New Testament man these days than Old. Or maybe it wasn't just the Bible, maybe it was something about John himself that held him back. There was the day, for example, when, without any explanation, John had walked into the store, grabbed up an ax, and swung it flat-side against a pillar. Nothing had happened, so he had swung it again and again, ferociously, as like to bring the store down, until finally the handle had cracked. Then he had wanted to know why the hell Floyd was buying such cheap goods for the store. Floyd had been pretty amazed by this act, not to say a little terrified, and he'd felt like a sap for weeks, until finally one day he'd overheard John's old college bud Waldo at the cafe next door telling a story about John trying to pry open a can with one of those axes on a hunting trip and having to take a lot of razzing from the boys he was with when the handle snapped. Floyd was so anxious to please John, so fearful of a rebuke, that sometimes it made him feel like a damned fairy. Which was partly why he coveted John's wife, why he wanted to cuckold him, and not just cuckold him, but split his fricking old lady wide open, so the next time John visited that place, if ever he still did, the peckerhead would know a real man had been there before him. Whenever he imagined himself doing this, however, she was not really there. It was more like punching a hole in the universe.

This was a strange thing about John's wife: a thereness that was not there. She always seemed to be at the very heart of things in town, an endearing and ubiquitous presence, yet few of the town's citizens, if asked, could have described her, even as she passed before their eyes, or said what made her tick, or if they could or thought they could, would have found few or none who would agree. Coveted object, elusive mystery, beloved ideal, hated rival, princess, saint, or social asset, John's wife elicited opinions and emotions as varied and numerous as the townsfolk themselves, her unknowability being finally all they could agree upon, and even then with reservations, for some said she was so much herself that she was simply unapproachable ("unreadable," as Lorraine liked to put it), others that the trouble was that she had no personality at all, so there was nothing to be known. Even fundamental matters were in dispute, her age, the tenor of her voice, the sizes that she wore. Take her eyes, for example. When a woman in New Orleans asked John one night their color, John didn't know. Nor could Alf, who knew her inside out, have said, though he probably had it written down somewhere. They weren't alone. Otis, who tended to look away when he talked to her, would have said her eyes were blue, the color of the Virgin's, though Marge thought them brown, like mud, and Daphne green, the color of her own. Barnaby knew their color, but knew them as the eyes of an innocent child, peering up at him from his knee, and Ellsworth, too, recalling with such clarity the little girl he'd once big-brothered, sometimes found it difficult to see the married woman before his eyes. Indeed, most supposed her younger than she really was, and of those who knew her then some claimed she hadn't changed since highschool, even though she no longer seriously resembled her senior yearbook photo (nor did she at the time, they pointed out, one of the town photographer's rare failures, as he himself would have, somewhat nonplused, acknowledged). Contrarily, Clarissa thought her ancient and completely out of touch.

Of course, anyone over eighteen was ancient in Clarissa's eyes. She had her favorites among those beyond the pale—her new highschool biology teacher, Granny Opal, the lead guitar of Blue Metal Studs, her daddy (by whom, for Clarissa, the sun rose and set), and especially Uncle Bruce—but her mother these days was not among them. She didn't exactly do anything, but she just kept getting in the way, even when she was nowhere in sight. Oh, she loved her, you couldn't help but love your mother, she supposed, but life was both incredibly exciting and incredibly boring, and her mother was part of the boring bit. Even just the *idea* of her mother was. Destined, she felt certain, like the beautiful faraway lady she had been named after, for a tragic fate, Clarissa wanted to taste it all before it was too late, the world for her was like an awesome carnival full of dynamite surprises with bright lights and screams and laughs and wild killer rides, like in one of her favorite videos, and she had an appetite for it that wouldn't quit, but when her mother came around, or just came to mind, it all went away, like someone shut the music off, making her feel edgy and restless and completely exhausted at the same time. Her mother didn't seem to affect Mikey that way, but Mikey was different and still a baby—he had only *just* stopped wetting the bed and he still liked to dress up and put on his silly wordless plays.

Clarissa's parents' second honeymoon in beautiful faraway Paris had been full of dynamite surprises, too, not least, though not then known, the conception, after nearly three years of trying, of their first child, and thus their daughter's name, a tribute to their wonder-working hostess and to her gaiety and bravery and charm, and not, as Clarissa might have fancied—the events a part of her prehistory and their chronology confused—to Marie-Claire's seeming propensity for romantic disaster. The invitation, proffered at the wedding three years before, had been to her parents' palatial home in La Muette at the edge of the Bois de Boulogne, and the first surprise, upon arrival, was that Marie-Claire had become an artist and had had what she called a "blow-off" with her parents, whom she described, flinging her thin hands about, then choking herself and bugging her eyes, as tyrannical and stiflingly bourgeois, and she had left home, moving into a kind of artist's garret in an unspoiled corner of the Latin Quarter above an Algerian cafe, a cellar cabaret, and the site of an open-air market. This rooftop space—all higgledy-piggledy with a hundred stacked and leaning canvases in its one large many-angled room, sketches and clippings taped to the water-stained walls under its coven ceilings, the toilet on the far side of the refrigerator and the claw-footed bathtub under the front window next to the sofa bed—she lent to them, moving out to stay with friends, but turning up each day to be their guide and companion. Thus, for ten days, the very center of the city was theirs, the towers of Notre Dame visible over the tiled roofs of the ancient district from their bathtub, the boats and bookstalls on the Seine a few steps from their street door. And the nights, too, were theirs, after their festive brasserie suppers with Marie-Claire, and perhaps it was the wine or the feeling of recklessness and danger and improvisation or the spicy air of couscous on the street below, the harsh music, or the delicious dislocation, the oddity of living in a kind of unwalled efficiency bathroom high above a medieval congestion all but unimaginable to them just a week before, back home in their neat brick house that Barnaby had built, that brought on such arousal, or more likely it was all of these things, together with, John had to admit it, the erotic presence of Marie-Claire, dressed mostly in wispy bits of widowy black (though the dreadful news did not come until the next-to-last day), but whatever the cause or causes, he seemed to be hot as a firecracker all the time, a veritable walking hard-on, in and out of the soft sweet saddle at every opportunity, and with an energy and urgency that took him back to his days as a highschool athlete. And Clarissa—whose eyes, like John's, were gray, and so no clue to the disputed color of her mother's—was the consequence of this gloriously bohemian adventure. One of them anyway.

Eye color he seemed not to have noted down, but as to Clarissa's mother's disputed age, Trevor the accountant could tell it to the day, knew too her social and medical history, as well as that of most of the people related to her. Yet, as though knowing these things so well made the rest more unknowable, when he tried to think of her, all he could see was an abstract point on the abstract graph of his insurance actuarial tables. Of course, most people in town occupied similar featureless points in Trevor's imagination, but none so exclusively, nor were their points so, well, so restless, so inclined to go adrift. Aware that his tendency to reduce all life stories to statistical data was a flaw of sorts, and one moreover that might cause offense, Trevor would set off to, say, a gathering at the country club, determined to greet her as a fellow human creature, to comment perhaps, with his customary tact and caution, upon her dress or her good health, and to concentrate upon some particular of her person which he might later recall as peculiarly hers. Shyness limited his close attention to her upper reaches, her nose perhaps, her ear and ring, her throat at his most daring, but stare as he might her image would not stick. At home he would draw out his charts and, after careful computations, locate her point, all he had left for all his effort, and—inevitably—would find it moved. As though his stare had altered her life expectancy, or his, at least, of hers. This indeterminacy made no sense. John's wife was unknowable perhaps, but she was also unchanging, the very image of constancy, at least in this town. She was, abidingly, what she was. So what did it mean that he could not fix the fixed? Trevor felt he had been given a privileged glimpse of something, but he did not know of what. Only that, whatever it was, it was, well, disconcerting. He had tried, obliquely, to speak of this to his wife Marge, who had known John's wife since childhood, and had found himself clumsily rambling on about her mother Audrey's premature death and what that might signify, the relative statistical risks of attractive and unattractive women, the wealth factor in the prolonging or shortening of life, and the hazards of being anywhere near the center of a community's focus, little of which was to the point, Marge cutting him off finally with: "Oh, she's all right. But what do you think about John?" "John?"

What Trevor thought about John he could not, on that occasion, say, but what John thought about his schoolchum Marge was that she was a horsey, aggressive meddler, a knee-jerk belligerent, cold and flaky as canned tuna. He admired her competitiveness, especially out on the course, she was the perennial women's club champion, but she was too impatient to be fun to play with, striding leggily down the fairway ahead of everyone, head bulled forward, furious with frivolous delay, which, for most people out there, was the whole point of the game. She set a lot of people's teeth on edge, had done since a kid. Waldo, who ran John's paint and wallpaper business and was frivolity personified, despised the woman, calling her, though rarely to her face, Butch and Sarge and

Herr Marge, and referring to her prissy linen-suited husband Trevor (whom he called Triv) as "that little Dutchman with his finger in the dyke." One night at the club, in front of everybody, Waldo told Kevin the bartender not to put any of those boxy pieces of ice with holes in their bottoms in his drink, because he'd had enough of those for one day. Marge had outplayed him once again that afternoon in a mixed-doubles foursome, snorting scornfully whenever he misjudged an approach shot or blew a putt, and asking him on the sixteenth, after he'd failed to get out of a sandtrap in spite of three mighty but impotent swings, if he'd like her to bring him a little bucket and shovel. His icy wisecrack later back at the clubhouse got him half a laugh, but cost him his night out, his wife Lollie doing her usual drag-bigmouth-Waldo-home act after that. John appreciated Waldo's feelings, but, except when Marge interfered with his construction projects, was himself more discreet. She was his wife's friend, for one thing, but more than that: Marge was a mobilizer, presiding over just about every club and charity in town, always collecting for one damned thing or another, a woman for whom no task was too daunting, no neighborhood too strange, no door exempt from the good cause's knock; she would be useful to him if he ever ran for Congress.

Though such an alliance might indeed have been negotiable, in spite of all the wars they had waged from the playground on, John's forced politeness in truth wounded Marge more than any dumb salesman's nasty cuts. She felt ill understood by John, though not surprised by this, John's grasp of character being purely pragmatic and about as subtle as his taste in women, which ran, as far as she could tell, to busty party girls and ambitious little roundheeled gum-snappers. She felt sorry for his wife, her friend since grade school, but was angered by her, too, for letting herself be used so, and for letting John live a life so little challenged, exaggerating his power when she should have been testing it, honing it, making it count for something, instead of letting him wreck the town with it. Marge felt her own womanly powers wasted by such waste, but what could she do? His wife was the closest she could get to him except in a fight. Though she'd towered over most of the highschool boys in town, runts still at that age, Marge in her college days had been merely tall, a lean handsome blonde, as she thought of herself, a little long in the legs maybe, a bit flat and broad in the hips and bony in the chest, but trim and fit, bright, engaged, a political force on a campus where women typically weren't, a terrific conversationalist, more guys should have been interested. But somehow she always turned them off. She knew why. They felt threatened. It was her power, but she couldn't switch it off, so it was also her weakness. Only Trev was not turned off, though turned on was not exactly what he was either.

Waldo's wife Lorraine had a theory about Marge. Marge was maybe her best friend in town, in spite of Waldo's constant sabotage and Marge's bossy ways. They played golf and tennis together, Lorraine served on Marge's many committees and espoused her causes, showed up at her club meetings, cut the weed habit with her help, listened sympathetically to her harsh views on men, they had a lot in common and Lorraine felt she knew her well. Knew what made her melt a bit, what bored her, what drove her up the wall. She could tell almost to the hour, for example, when Marge's period came on, though for that matter so could just about anyone else, Marge suffering periods powerful and sudden as a maddened mare's. Her appetites were like that, too, hunger hitting her like a blow to the midriff, thirst suddenly taking her voice away, making her hands shake as she grabbed up the iced tea. The two had met while up at State together, though were not real friends there. Lollie, over the protests of many of her sorority sisters, had tried to pledge the ungainly girl after getting beat out by her for president of the Pep Club, but Marge had turned her down flat, letting her know at the time what she thought of the Geek Societies, as she called them, they'd had a pretty nasty scrap over it. Lollie, snubbed and sore, had not returned Marge's waves and halloos thereafter, until Marge, running for student council president against a fraternity man, came by to seek the sorority's support. And against all odds, got it, too, and Lollie's renewed admiration as well, having mixed feelings by that time about fraternity men herself. But their real friendship had begun, a partial consolation for Lorraine, when fate unkindly brought her to this godforsaken town. Without Marge, she would have gone crazy here, and maybe vice versa, too. So Lorraine knew her well. And her theory about her was that, although inside her crusty shell a sensuous woman lay dormant, in spite of her long marriage to Trevor and all her tough brave talk, Marge was still a virgin.

The night Lorraine dragged Waldo home from the club for insulting Mad Marge with his half-iced ass-cube crack was neither the first nor the last time she'd taken him by the scruff and made him look a pussywhipped fool, but though it burned his butt and made him want to hit the road, never to see the ugly uptight bitch again, he knew he couldn't get by without her. She managed the finances, fed them all, kept the house in order and the cars repaired, shepherded the kids about, covered for all his fuckups and weathered his suicidal binges, she was a goddamn saint in her way. But like most saints she tended to take the fun out of everything. And what the hell else was there? Good thing she wasn't with him the first time he came to this town to usher at Long John's wedding. He and Lollie were more or less engaged already, screwing implying that in those ancient purblind times, but he came alone, knowing all the brothers would be here, wanting the freedom of that. Anyway, Lollie never cared much for John. It was only for a weekend, but shit, man, it was one helluva great party. What he could remember of it. A kind of grand faretheewool to college daze. They'd all met up the day before the wedding at the old Pioneer Hotel. Majestic old place, full of polished wood and etched glass and crystal chandeliers, gone now, a piece of history. The long bar in the Old Wagon Wheel Cocktail Lounge was made of ancient weathered railway ties, most beautiful goddamn piece of furniture he ever saw. Dutch now had it out in his motel bar, the Getaway, but it didn't look the same there, cut down and crowded in. Waldo had arrived and propped himself at it like the castle warden and called for a bottle of the best fucking sourmash in the house and the party had begun. By noon the place was packed. Political and business pals of the fathers of the bride and groom were also there, an older generation, but they could hold their own, and they seemed to love being around the college boys and did a lot of the setting up. Food was ordered up, but he couldn't remember if he ate any of it or not, didn't matter, he was feeling great, young and powerful and ready for anything that happened. Lots did. First, though, they hit the course for a round of golf, bottles in the bags and ice and mix in the carts, and though he seemed to recall slashing around in the rough quite a bit, he ended up with a decent score and they took some coins off the old boys, maybe somebody fudged. After that there was the wedding rehearsal, good for plenty of laughs, then a big feast back at the hotel, jester Beans doing his famous open-fly gag during the toasts, and finally the real party began. Old Dutch had rigged it all. Maybe the best goddamn blowout he was ever at. Or maybe not, but he sure as hell hadn't seen its equal since. It was like a piece of theater, each new act better than the last. Ended at dawn with him and Hard Yard and Loose Bruce, what was left of the Dirty Six, serenading the bride on old Barnaby's lawn like battle-weary but triumphant cocks crowing the fucking sun up. Beautiful! Oh my Christ, where did it all go?

Daphne, the maid of honor at that historic wedding, was available after the rehearsal dinner and ready for anything that happened, too, open flies not excluded, but she had less luck that night than Waldo. The boys, it seemed, had other things to do. She had been paired—by wedding protocol, but also, she'd felt, as a kind of so-long-kid gift from John—with the best man, a handsome smoothie from John's fraternity named Bruce, obviously loaded, an altogether consoling consolation prize, had the prize been hers. But juicy Brucie, polite and attentive though he was, had his eye on another. Daphne was the bride's best and oldest friend, she knew absolutely everything about her, or supposed she did, but she never was able to figure out where the hell that French penpal came from. Probably the two of them had met on one of those trips Audrey, always full of fancypants improvement schemes for her daughter, had taken her on. Whatever, from wherever, Marie-Claire was a veritable apparition, she had all the guys gaga, Breast Man Brucie-boy among them, it was like they'd never seen a girl before. Ringlets and baby teeth and big dark eyes—hey, she was cute, but not that cute. Maybe it was her goddamned accent. Or maybe she knew some French tricks American girls were not privy to. Later that night, abandoned by the guys and bored with each other, Daphne and Ronnie and some of the girls decided to crash the stag party out at the Country Tavern, or at least to go have a peek and see what lurid depravity the unsociable assholes were up to. It was a pretty depressing scene: a porno flick running on all by itself in a darkened corner, a dozen or so fagged-out yo-yos playing cards or pool or throwing it down sullenly at the bar, one of her ex-steadies out cold, wearing nothing but an ashtray for a codpiece, sad songs on the antique jukebox. Some party. Daphne would have gone in there and livened it up for them, but neither Bruce nor John was there, this lot was dead and gone, beyond reprieve. She figured the rest of the guys were with, damn her eyes, the penpal.

The groomsman officially paired with the French bridesmaid at John's wedding (though he was not in the Country Tavern that night Daphne and her friends peeked in either, nor was he with Marie-Claire) was Harvard, oldest son of Oxford the druggist and his librarian wife Kate, brother to Yale, Columbia, and Cornell, and known as Harvie in the family, Hard Yard to intimates, of whom John, with whom he'd cocaptained the highschool track team their senior year, was one. Harvard, a shy, gentle, and dutiful fellow, a good athlete in spite of what Coach Snuffy called his "handicap" ("Tie a knot in that nasty thing, son, before you catch it on the bar going over and damage the equipment!") and pride of the showerroom but not quite the scholar his father had hoped for, was a chemistry major at a West Coast surfers' college at the time of the wedding, showing few signs of graduating soon, if ever, but demonstrating a talent, widely esteemed among scientists, for experimentation, a talent that contributed spectacularly to the revels of the final night of his friend John's bachelorhood, revels that in turn, maturing into revelation as yard, mind, and soul all came and came together, changed Harvie's life forever, John's ass theatrically marked by this sudden transformation. Thus, it might be said that Harvie, unlike most people in this town, created, as though in obedience to the slogan on an old calendar down at his father's drugstore, "A Better Life Through Chemistry," his own destiny. Years later, returning here for his mother's funeral, for whose sake he wore a suit instead of a dress, he told his baby brother Cornell that "out there" it doesn't matter what you've got but how you use it. In a small town like this everybody is always measuring. Out there, there are too many, measuring makes no sense. This generous message was meant to console and uplift little Corny, though it probably missed its mark.

Harvie's baby brother was at that time a biology student up at State, not a very good one, but by then the only member of the family still in school, their sister Columbia having dropped out to be near her cancer-stricken mother in her final months and seemingly destined, now a doctor's practical nurse, never to return. Cornell would not last long either. In fact, though he would return to college after his mother's funeral, he would never, no matter how his father pleaded, scolded, reasoned, wept, attend another class. He became a haggard, unkempt quadrangle hangabout, notorious only for his monosyllabic mewlings, his runny nose and spotted pants, the latter something of a campus legend, likened unto an aerial map of a free-fire zone, a mess of curdled gravy, the abode of the damned, a laminated spunk husks exhibit, the rag used to clean out the cafeteria food trays (itself known as "Grandma's diaper"), Flocculus Rex, a poison puffball bed, the chitinous scutum of something unspeakably inhuman (an alien resident perhaps of that ghastly fork if not the freaked-out host himself), trampled cowflop, the Milky Way, a spermatazoic Field of Armageddon, and, simply, a zippered scumbag. Poor unwashed unlaundered Corny, who went to Paris to become a man and saw such a thing as to make manhood no place to go and boyhood no place he could return to. "Ondress me," she said, and then, when, in a magical trance (he was thinking of a certain set of four strange comicbooks, thereafter discontinued, that he owned), he did, she said: "Merci, mon petit! Now ronn down to ze delicatesse be-low and breeng for us a bott-ell of Beaujolais nouveau, and we weell make l'amour nouveau, ze new true love of ze heart and blood!" Oh boy. Sounded great. He left her standing there, eyes wide open, looking startled with wanting, thin legs apart and both hands between them, kneading and wringing what was there as though trying to tear it out and give it to him, and ran down the four dark flights of stairs and out into the spicy street, his heart fluttering in his chest like a trapped moth in a glass jar, explosions already erupting stickily between his own skinny thighs. With his clumsy highschool French, it took Corny too long a while, racing from shop to shop and bar to bar, to come to understand that, on Midsummer's Eve, Beaujolais nouveau was not something he was likely to find. Well. He paused, staring bleakly at a swarthy rat-faced shopkeeper, as the truth sank in. Such cruel teasing was nothing new in Corny's life. Usually he merely turned away from it. But in this nightmarish place, so far from home, where could he go? The smirking shopkeeper seemed to be recommending, in his threatening foreign tongue, another wine with the word "Love" in its name. This confused Corny and made his face hot, but, hastily, he bought it and, homesick now for his friend Pauline, and for his faithful games and toys which never deceived him, turned his steps back toward Marie-Claire's studio, fearing further humiliations, but keeping faint hopes alive—why not? as his father would say, it's perfectly reasonable—for a pleasant surprise.

Pauline had been with Corny not long before he left for Paris, though she had known Marie-Claire's fiancé Yale as well, and Harvie, too, each in their own time. All the girls loved Yale's zinger, it was just right, but his brothers' were more like things you might see in a circus sideshow, and for opposite reasons. Harvard's was the one best known around town, a giant thing, ghostly white, almost scary, with all its veins showing like Invisible Man. Because of it, all the kids called him Hard Yard, which was ironic, not because of its length, but because it was almost always limply adangle, half stiff at best until that stag party the night before John's wedding, which Pauline also attended. Corny's, contrarily, was like a tiny twig with only one testicle beneath it no bigger than a schoolyard aggie, but though it didn't look like a real zinger, more like a plastic toy one, it was rigid as a fork tine all the time and popped and popped off all the time, as his trousers, even back then in high school and his mother Kate still alive to wash them, attested. After nine or ten quick ones one night, Pauline begged him to stop or he might hurt himself, and Corny only looked puzzled and, guiding her hand to the tip of it, spurted again. And then—thup!—again, each time firing well past her hip. Cornell liked most to have her reach under her thigh and squeeze his testicle, if she could find it, as, sometimes three or four times in quick succession, almost like hiccups, he spilled his seed in her, or more precisely into his rubber, stolen from his dad's drugstore. These rubbers, of course, did not stay on, Pauline had to wear them like a kind of inner lining. Pushing them in there made her feel pretty silly, but fecund Gretchen later proved the wisdom of it, and feeling silly in boy-girl stuff was one thing that never bothered Pauline much. Everything changed that summer for both of them and many years would pass before they would become good friends again, though when it happened it would seem quite natural, even if by then nothing else did, but Pauline would never forget the last time she and Corny were together that summer. It was the night before Pauline went to Gordon's studio to ask him to take her photograph for the men's magazines. Cornell had come to the trailer with tears running down his smooth pink cheeks to tell her he was going to Paris and would not be seeing her again soon. "I love you," he stammered, coming all over her bluejeans. No one had ever said that to Pauline before, nor would she soon hear it said again, and it left her feeling bewildered and, oddly, a bit sad. It made her think of her sister, the one Daddy Duwayne, looking down at his shoes, said ran away to find her mother.

"I love you": so simple for some to say (for Daphne, it was as common as an expletive), so awkward for many, such as Otis, Snuffy, Marge, and Mitch, while for others—John, for example—so irrelevant, an artifice serving as a kind of functional code in songs and movies, sometimes useful in his lover-as-fool jokes though rarely as a punchline. When his fraternity brother Waldo, lover-as-fool personified, said "I love you," it was no joke, he truly meant it, no matter who was with him, even if he'd won her in a raffle in the dark, because that was what love was, blind and brief and all that. Lorraine had heard him say it many times, sometimes even to her, and she knew that he meant it and that his meaning it meant nothing, the phrase having passed her own lips but once, then never more. It was often like that: if left unsaid too long the tongue felt clumsied by it. When, that same summer that Corny went to Paris, Harriet was dying, her husband Alf, grieving at her bedside, realized he hadn't said it since the war years. It seemed to make sense back then, less now, though he found a way of saying it again before she died, pleasing her, he felt, by enclosing it, like John, in story: "Hey, do you remember when . . . ?" John's mother Opal, having like Alf lost the words somewhere, found them again when her grandchildren came along, but discovered within the phrase a heart-wrenching sorrow she'd not noticed before. When she told her friend Kate about this at Harriet's funeral, which was shortly after Clarissa was born, what Kate said was: "Grief for ourselves is what makes love for others possible. And grievous. Wise love loves only the unchanging. But to love only the changeless and the eternal, Opal, is to love with a cold heart." It was not exactly to a thing eternal that warmhearted Veronica avowed her love, though Second John could not be said to have changed much since first she said it, and grief, she'd be quick to agree, was part of it. Clarissa, now grown but untaught as yet in grief, had practiced the line over and over, but had yet to find its right moment, though she had in mind a target for it. She and her friend Jennifer often argued about the right time to say it, before or after, Clarissa usually insisting upon it as a statement of intent, otherwise it was just a corny way to say thank you, Jen wanting to know how you could really be *sure* until afterwards, wasn't it more like a question before, and so a kind of tease? It was something that the Model said in Ellsworth's novel-in-progress (if you'd have asked her the question Jennifer asked, she'd have replied: before or after what?), but not the Artist, who felt the integrity and purity of his art threatened by such irrational declarations: her saying so made his vision blur and his hands shake, such that weeks passed (in fictional time) before he felt he could attempt another drawing of her, and then only from behind her shoulder.

For Jennifer's father, "I love you" was a call from earth to his tripping Trixie, guiding her home again. Though drugs were off the menu since their move into the manse, Beatrice still sometimes, involuntarily, revisited trips from the past, and though these episodes were never (so she said) an unpleasant experience, and could even be, as best she could remember, spiritually enlightening, they were not held by this community of skeptical prairie folk to be in any serious sense visionary, and so complicated at times Reverend Lenny's ministerial career, even while enlivening his sermons. He would find her, for example, sprawled out in her socks and underpants on the cold linoleum floor of the church basement, her head pillowed perhaps (thanks to some good Christian) by her own cast-off clothing or the cushion from the piano stool, her eyes focused on some distant unnamed galaxy beyond the perforated plasterboard ceiling. He would kneel down beside her, put his mouth by her ear, and whisper to her his incantation of love as though sending a radio signal out into the cosmos, meanwhile thinking: How can I use this on Sunday morning? Thus, his famous "Sleeping Beauty" sermon: God awakening us with his love from life's deep sleep. And his sermon on the efficacy of prayer: learning to whisper "I love you" into God's cosmic ear. Sometimes it helped to reach inside her panties and stroke her there, pulling her back to this world by activitating her own magnetic field, as it were, and when she awoke, not knowing how she had got where she was, she would often say that his voice was like a call beyond a distant door, which his fingers were slowly opening. Lenny hadn't figured out yet how to get finger-fucking into one of his sermons, but he knew it could be done. God was great.

Maynard Junior had said "I love you" in his head over and over, but like Lorraine, out loud only once in his life, and that time to a urinal. This was back at the time of his cousin John's wedding. His dad was the mayor in those days, and he was then known to the locals as Mayo or Mayor Nerd, and more commonly, as simply the Nerd. Three years away in pre-law at Duke had not changed this. The Nerd was a man, in this town, icono-cized and so condemned. As one of John's groomsmen, Maynard felt obliged to paste a smile on his face that weekend and go along with everything like a good sport, even though he felt wrenched apart inside with fury, bitterness, and grief. During dessert at the rehearsal dinner down at the old Pioneer Hotel, someone made a lighthearted remark about the marriage bed, and the horrific image of his loathsome hairy-assed cousin assaulting the angelic thighs of his beloved, which he had managed to keep repressed all evening, rose suddenly and brought the night's banquet up with it—he barely had time to lurch away from the table and hurl himself into the men's room before it all roared out of him like a last violent goodbye. *"I love you!"* he bellowed as he geysered forth, though it was doubtful that the others heard anything but "woof" or "barf." "The Nerd has very tender sensibilities," someone was explaining to a roomful of laughter as he returned (even the bride had a smile on her precious face), and his weak damp-eyed rejoinder was, "That's right, happens to me every time some damn fool gets married." The party moved from the banquet room into the hotel bar where the drinks were on Uncle Mitch and the bawdy songs and stupid jokes courtesy of John's drunken frat-rat brothers, the older men and even some of their wives joining in for a while, though most of the ladies under-stood they were no longer all that welcome. Though Maynard felt, not for the first or last time in his life, like the last frail bastion of sanity in a sickeningly mad world, he joined in as best he could and even contributed a verse to "Roll Your Leg Over" that won him a round of applause, redemption of sorts, though she who mattered was no longer there to witness it:

> Here's to my cousin John, the man getting hitched!
> One helluva goddamn son-of-a-Mitch!
>
> Oh, roll your leg over, roll your leg over . . . !

As the evening wore on, most of the old folks dropped off and, on a signal from Dutch, the men remaining grabbed up all the unemptied bottles and moved on out to a tavern and pool hall at the edge of town, where Dutch had set up poker tables, a bandstand with instruments for those who wanted to jam, and a screen and projector, for which he had rented a dozen old blue movies, or maybe he owned them. The jokes gradually got coarser, the noise louder, the stakes higher, the air thicker, the singing more like shouting. Two guys stripped down and got into a wrestling match, another started playing the drums and cymbals with his penis, the piano with his ass. All Maynard wanted was to go home, and when Dutch and John and a couple of the others tried to sneak away, just as some of the rest were proposing a farting contest, he tried to join them. They obviously didn't want him along, the clubby bastards, but he insisted, his voice rising to an urgent squawk—he wasn't going to get fucking left behind! He was nearly crying, and others out there were getting curious about what was going on, so finally, pissed off, they shushed him and gave in. He wished afterwards they hadn't.

About the same time that helluva goddamn son-of-a-Mitch was slipping out of the Country Tavern with five of his pals for what they were calling "a prayer meeting," his helluva goddamn father, fresh black stogie in his jowls, was drifting smugly, if somewhat boozily, out of the old Pioneer Hotel, having conducted a little communion service of his own, closing down the bar in there while closing a deal with some of his capitol pals, in town for tomorrow's wedding, a deal that would route the new proposed highway across some twenty miles of his own land holdings, opening up hundreds of acres out there for development—this area was growing by leaps and bounds, and God bless the bounder who leapt first, amen. Mitch foresaw that the rest of his life would be spent in this enterprise and those that would follow naturally thereupon, and he was proud of it. What were the fucking pioneers themselves, after all, but early land developers? He was taking his place in the great national epic, and he felt like a goddamned hero, a saint, a giant among pygmies. He was feeling "high," as the young folks liked to say nowadays (and he wasn't so old himself, goddamn it), high and dry, too much so certainly to turn in just yet. His wife Opal was home already, driven there earlier by the bride's parents, as were most of the locals past the age of twenty-five or so, and the younger ones were all out at the Country Tavern or else at parties of their own, so the prospect facing this giant among pygmies, standing legs apart out there on the sidewalk in front of the darkening Pioneer Hotel and weaving just a bit, was one of solitude and impenetrable shadows and deep tranquillity. In short, no fun at all. It was at moments like this that Mitch missed the big city. Always somewhere to go, something to do, someone to get to know, in a Biblical manner of speaking. Nothing doing here even if something *was* doing: to wit, his old maxims about taking your trade out of town, sowing wild oats in distant fields, keeping hair pie off the local menu, and so on, all of which Mitch equated with family values, which he vigorously championed and rigorously (more or less rigorously) adhered to, as he planned to now, unsteady though he was. He considered taking a quiet midnight stroll in the park, still lit up across the way with its old-fashioned postlamps, get his feet back under him, as it were, but he remembered he was carrying a lot of weekend cash in his pocket. This was the sort of town where you could park your car (it was John's little souped-up silver Mustang awaiting him, he saw, John had taken the Continental for the night) with the motor running, leave your house wide open when you left town for a week, drop your wallet in the street and get it back intact, always had been since it first got settled over a hundred years ago, but times were changing, and there were a lot of strangers in town now. Besides, he might interrupt something over there, a kiddy orgy under the bandstand or crazed drug addicts in the bushes, he'd heard rumors. That was why they were beefing up the police force. Ever since they had found what they said was an illegal substance in the car of those kids who got killed playing chicken on the highway out by the trailer park. It was a fucking shame the way families were falling apart these days, failing their responsibilities, Mitch thought, unlocking the Mustang and stumbling a bit as he struggled with the door. Couldn't remember walking over to the car, but here he was. He took a deep pull on his cigar, blew smoke up at the flickering streetlamp overhead, getting his bearings, then lowered himself inside. Fucking bucket seats. Got one leg in all right, had problems with the second one. Whoo, felt like he was grappling with some kind of prehistoric beast ("Bucking fuck-it seats!" he said out loud to the night crowding around him, hoping to make it back away a bit), or else he'd grown the leg of an elephant, and he suffered a sudden pang of longing for his beautiful old prewar Packard, the one with the running board. He could crawl in and out of that fantastic machine when he was so drunk he couldn't walk, and whether or not the goddamned thing was standing still. The trouble today, he thought, as he dragged the rest of him in out of the menacing night at last, hauled the door shut with an echoey whump (that reassuring running board on his old Packard had somehow reminded him once more of family values), and then fumbled, grunting, for the keys which he'd dropped on the floor, was that there was too much self-centeredness, not enough thought for the other guy, and especially the young. What the hell was happening to this country? If Mitch had his way, every time a kid got in trouble, he'd clap his old man's ass in jail until it was sorted out. Teach the egocentric sonuvabitch a little goddamned civic virtue. Something Mitch (there they were—but where was the cigar? Jesus) would never have to face: his boy was a fucking prince. Had a wild hair or two, of course, wouldn't be Mitch's son if he didn't, but John was a great kid, straight as they come. And now, hell (he found the cigar, scuffed at the sparks on the floor with the clutched keys, planted the dead stub back in his jowls, straightened up confusedly: felt like he'd fallen down a well somewhere), the boy was getting married, hard to believe. It was like things were speeding up somehow, how did we get here so fucking fast? Next thing you knew, he'd be a grandfather, and then . . . shit . . . But not yet. Not yet, goddamn it. Mitch turned the ignition, revved up from a gentle purr to a low growl, and pulled out into the lonely night, jaws clamped defiantly around the cigar. Not yet! He was glad to see John marry, of course (that's right, dumbo, turn on the damned lights), and a good choice, lovely girl, Audrey's kid, Homecoming Queen and all that, and he believed marriage would help John understand him better, help him appreciate his old dad's steadfast whaddayacallit, forgive him his trespasses. So, yes, he was in a celebrative mood all round, Mitch was, and he realized that, in this mood (he was thinking about Audrey, the old prewar Packard-vintage model, so wild and beautiful—and now they were to be in-laws, who could have foreseen such a thing?), he was headed out toward the stag party at the Country Tavern. Now, he knew the last thing those young studs wanted was some old fucker hanging around, looking over their shoulders, he'd been the first to point that out to his peers when the lads took off from the hotel hours earlier, he had no intention of going out there, hell no, won't go, and yet, here he was, the nose of the silvery beast (he tapped the accelerator and felt it spring forward with a throaty snarl) pointed unerringly toward that place like a well-trained birddog with a bone-on and getting up speed. Well, what the heck, wouldn't hurt to drop in for a beer, unload a joke or two, let them know he was one of the boys at heart, a good guy they could count on in the clutches, then buy them a final round and, duty beckoning the lonely hero, roar off, chin up, into the melancholic night.

Ellsworth had not, except for a general mention of the "weekend festivities," reported on that stag party in his newspaper, *The Town Crier,* though he knew about it, or some of it anyway. It was not for reasons of taste that he omitted it from his coverage of the wedding, otherwise extensive if not in fact exhaustive—no, what did he care about such matters, he who had snubbed his nose at propriety all his life? Nor was it a factor that the father of the bride was his patron; the record must be kept, as Barnaby himself would say, no fudging, my boy, on that. The point was, Ellsworth was interested only in recording significant history, and *a*-historicity was the very raison d'être, he knew, of stag parties, and indeed of all such carnivalesque activities. It was his duty as the town chronicler to bear witness, not to mere surface excitements, but to history's deeper design. Or so he told himself back in those early days, his file cabinets still as orderly then as a genre plot, more folders in them than documents and reassuringly comprehensive, like a local map of time. So, though Gordon for reasons of his own was rather keen on following through on the night's more irregular activities, Ellsworth was satisfied (comedians excluded) with the formal wide-angle lens photographs of the rehearsal dinner, paid and posed for by the parents of the betrothed, and after these had been taken he led a reluctant Gordon back to his studio to discuss the photo coverage of the wedding itself on the morrow and to carry on with the conversation they had begun as boys some twenty years before. Gordon's growing fascination with the irrational, the erotic, the sensational, the morbid bordered, Ellsworth felt, on pornography, and caused him to doubt his friend's continued commitment to those higher artistic principles they had once so passionately held in common, and which Gordon still claimed, all evidence to the contrary, allegiance to. There was, for example, the bizarre series of pictures Gordon was taking at this time of his dying mother, no longer compos mentis or even continent, confined now to her old iron bed in one of the dismal little back rooms above the shop. Perhaps, like all men, Gordon was blind to his own transformations. Ellsworth suspected that photography itself, not in his judgment an art form at all, might be the efficient cause of this relapse, the effortless voyeuristic eye replacing the critical eye of the creative artist, who must construct, out of the void of a blank canvas, over and over again, ever afresh, his own space, forms, patterns of light and color, unaided by the easy accident of an opened lens.

Pauline, who knew everything there was to know about ahistoricity, being a longtime native of those unlighted regions, also had cause to wonder about her husband's artistic principles, not to mention the soundness of his mind, though this was sometime later, his mother whom she never knew passed on by then, her daddy jailed, John's wedding ancient history, her own more recent but even more forgotten. Pauline, it should be said, was not a curious person. Teachers had often noted this with some dismay on her report cards. It was something Daddy Duwayne, ever her most influential mentor, had broken her of early on. Narcissistic men sometimes found this characteristic lessened their erotic enjoyment when with her, but most found it comforting. Being incurious, Pauline supposed all others, except maybe teachers, were as well, and it was not until little Corny and his friends started using her like an animated pop-up picture book that it occurred to her she might have something to offer to those wanting to see but not use, and willing to pay for it besides, and if she could not thereby wholly escape her ahistorical condition, she might, if fortune smiled, escape at least the trailer park. Had she not been by nature or by education so incurious, that first photo session, after Gordon had shooed Corny and his father and that poor little French girl out of the studio and locked the door, might right then have made her think twice about returning for another, but Pauline had long since grown accustomed to the eccentricities of the aroused male, and so not only came back for further sittings, so-called (sitting being what he rarely let her do), but in time moved in above the studio and, after the ruckus with Daddy Duwayne, married the photographer. By then, of course, she had given up on the glittering kingdom of the centerfold, just a childish fantasy anyway, she supposed, and had come to accept as her lot in life these safe dusty rooms overlooking Main Street, wherein she was, if not transported, at least more or less content. Gordon's photos of her were much too unusual for the men's magazines, needless to say—he kept trying to turn her into something other than what she was—nor would he have sent them there even had they been suitable. His photos of her, as with many others, were not for general viewing, but were kept in large thick albums in locked cabinets at the back of the shop. Others might have been curious about these albums, but Pauline of course was not. Though, like all artists, he was a bit peculiar, her husband, though he sometimes hurt her, rarely had much to say, and had a crazy way of staring, he had nevertheless taken good care of her and was, she believed, essentially a good man or anyway benign—at least that was how she felt up to the time that poor lady was killed at the humpback bridge and Gordon, obsessed with the accident and exhausted from overwork, uncharacteristically left some of his secret albums out and open where she could not help but see. One lot in particular gave her goosebumps. She decided to tell Otis about them the next time she saw him.

This was not to be for some time, as it turned out, due to a religious experience suffered by the town's police chief. After Duwayne's arrest some four years before, Otis, not yet the chief, had picked Pauline up at the photo studio in his squad car and driven her out to the trailer park to ask her some questions about what he had found there in the course of his investigations. Though Pauline told it without emotion, it was a pretty sordid story of rape, child-battering, incest, torture, and all manner of filthy and unnatural sexual acts, all mixed up with her father's mad evangelical harangues—sordid but also quite exciting: the next thing Otis knew he was getting sucked off again, and this time he didn't cry. After that, he and Pauline visited the trailer more or less regularly. He picked up more of the story, ashamed that it was such a turn-on, and over time a kind of friendship grew up between them. Otis would ask her to show him exactly what it was her father did to her, she would get him to play the part of the father, though of course he would never really hurt her, and they would end up on the floor a little later in a sweaty cuddle, he telling her by then about his own boyhood, his troubles at home after his old lady walked out on them, the black moods his old man went through until finally he blew his stupid brains out, and then about his own marriage, too early probably, right out of the army, didn't even know what it was all about before the kids started coming, but mostly about his job and about life down at the station, where he hoped to be promoted soon. She was a good listener, never asked questions, but remembered all the things he told her, making them seem important. She got married, he gave her and the photographer a nice present, his wife had more children that her husband photographed, the promotion came through, they went on meeting out at the trailer. It was like a second life they could visit from time to time, and so the months and years went by. But then one day he stepped out of the trailer, still buttoning up, and there was John's wife. He was momentarily blinded as though suffering some kind of holy vision, his ears started to pop and ring, and he found himself, crazily, reaching for his revolver. Somehow, instinctively, he managed to slam the door shut behind him, hoping Pauline took the hint, and as his vision cleared he saw that John's wife was not alone, but with some sort of committee of housewives. He still couldn't hear what they were saying, but enough leaked through to suggest it had something to do with the town beautification program. The trailer park was an eyesore and they wanted to do something about it. He stood there with his circuits blown, nodding stupidly, a speechless imbecile trying to look serious, hoping only that his fly was done up but afraid to look. One of the women, squinting suspiciously, took a sharp look for him, then cast her skeptical gaze up at his face, seeming to peer straight through him and on into the trailer behind. This was the wife of the Ford-Mercury dealer. One night later she was dead. Grotesquely. Upside-down, blood leaking from her ears. But still staring. And the day after that, Otis arranged for a long weekend and went on religious retreat, promising the Virgin never to see Pauline again.

Here is one of Gordon's photographs of what Otis saw that night out at the bridge: Viewed in silhouetted profile through a shattered side door window against bright spotlights beamed down from the road above and bouncing off the trickling creek in which the crushed automobile lies, a head, partly submerged, dangles upside down from a broken neck, wearing the shallow creek water across its forehead like a flatcap or a mortar board. Headlamps pierce the night like a blind stare and, in the center of the photo, one high wheel provides a visual echo of the rainbow-arched bridge rising bleakly, upper right, into the dense dark sky above. On the left, a squat figure, also in silhouette and featureless except for thick spectacles ablaze with reflected light, descends the slope from the road above like some sort of otherworldly beast of prey, hunched over and knees bent as if about to pounce, while higher up in the center of the picture, near the foot of the concrete bridge, a scarecrowlike personage, well-lit and seen from the rear, slumps contortively, legs bandied and long arms draped over the shoulders of two white-jacketed helpers, his head fallen forward and out of view, so giving the impression of a headless man with loose airy limbs fluttering in the night breeze. This photograph, now in one of Gordon's shelved backshop albums, is labeled simply "W-37," suggesting that what is important is not the identity of the persons in the photograph or their stories or any conceivable meaning that might be attached to the events displayed, but rather simply the composition itself: Time, a fraction of it, frozen into an aesthetically compelling pattern, and all there is to know. This austere view, however, is undermined by the photograph itself, for in it there is another figure, uniformed and proxy for the absent viewer, gazing out upon the scene from a position just below the foot of the bridge with a look of profound perplexity, his billed cap tipped back, seeming almost to turn his head from character to character in his effort to interpret what he sees before him. To locate, or to confirm, its meaning. Even the photographer seems part of the policeman's intense study, which engages us as it engages him. Something is being revealed. What is it?

"Honey, you can be the first to congratulate me," Daphne was telling her best friend on the telephone the next morning, that day that Otis made his sacred vow. "I'm engaged again." Her friend did not seem terribly impressed by this news. Of course, Daphne had been engaged half a dozen times at least over the last ten years, married thrice, it was not the sort of news that made the world shake. Still, Daphne had more to tell, just wait until she heard it all. Her last husband was Nikko, the pro out at the country club. That one didn't last a year, but it wasn't her fault, Nikko had vamoosed with that little fifteen-year-old exhibitionist, daughter of the town's orthodontist, after the little fanny twitcher, already notorious for swimming topless at the country club pool, had scandalized the entire community by turning up at the Pioneers Day parade as an Indian princess dressed in nothing but beads and psychedelic body paint. When Nikko blew town, John brought in young Kevin, the present club pro and barkeep, prodigal son of a business crony, with whom Daphne enjoyed a brief consolatory if hazy fling. Probably John's wife thought that's who she was going to marry now. "No, not Kevin, sweetie, that's been over for ages. Listen, Kevin's approach shots are clever and he's fun in the rough, so to speak, but the boy's drives are short and choppy and he can never keep his eye on the ball, if you follow me. Pulls the flag too soon, too. No, I've been seeing—well, now don't tell anyone, sugar, it wouldn't look right, not yet, but let me put it this way, your old chum is going to be driving nothing but T-birds and Lincolns from now on. That's right. Well, he's old, I know, but that only makes him all the more appreciative, and believe me, appreciation is something I could use more of just now. I'll be honest, when that shithead Nikko left me for that little highschool kid, I realized suddenly that my ass was at least ten years out of date—I mean, god-*damn* it, honey, I'm not *cute* anymore. You've been lucky, it's been harder for me. And besides—this is just between us girls, but as someone who's got pretty high standards you'll appreciate this—Old Stu's hung like a horse. I kid you not. It's a real old country-boy dong, the kind they tell jokes about. Admittedly it doesn't have a lot of starch in it—mostly it just lies there, curled up like an old hounddog in front of the fire, as Stu says—but I've made it get up on its hind legs and do a few tricks, and old Stu's so grateful he cries, and then I cry, too, and I realize if it's not love as I'd always imagined it, what the hell, it's love just the same. So you're going to have to stand up there with me and the preacher one more time, can you bear it? Honest to God, sugar, I don't know what we'd do without you around here. And at least that cute fraternity-boy preacher's new, so we'll be able to tell this batch of wedding photos from the last ones, right? I think I'll wear burgundy red this time, it's the color of the Thunderbird Stu's giving me. We have to wait for the funeral of course, but—what? Winnie? Winnie got killed last night, hadn't you heard? Out at the humpback bridge. Sorry, I thought you knew . . ."

Alf had happened to be on call that night that Winnie died, and the ambulance swung round to pick him up on the way to the wreck. He was not as sober as he should have been, but under the circumstances it hardly mattered. Old Stu had, anyone could see at a glance, joined him in widowerhood, and, unscathed except for a scratch across his nose, was himself able to walk away. Or would have been if he had been sober enough to walk at all. Winnie had probably been killed on impact, though the anger and alarm on her face suggested she had seen it coming. The police officer, examining the road, could find no skid marks: "Must have rammed that fucker at full throttle," he muttered, looking a bit rattled, seeming not to want to get near the wreck itself. They had hit the side of the bridge on Winnie's side, but may have already been rolling, ending up wheels high in the creek below, so it wasn't easy getting them out. There were a few drunks from the tavern down the road, come to lend a hand, but they all seemed a bit disoriented by it all, staggering around bleakly in muddy circles, in and out of the beams of the headlights piercing the damp night eerily, and the photographer, something of a nutcase anyway, was preoccupied with getting it all on record just as it had happened, so it was pretty much left up to Alf and his drivers to pull Stu and Winnie out of there. While they were struggling, knee-deep in weedy water, with the Mercury's crushed doors, a strange-looking bespectacled woman with an exaggerated limp came down into the ditch and gave them a hand. She had apparently just been driving by. She was strong and efficient and especially useful in helping them work the dead body out through the smashed window so she could be stretchered off, though the man she was with, evidently having no stomach for such labors, remained in their car up at the side of the road, staring straight ahead and clutching the steering wheel with both hands. When Alf accompanied the young woman back to the car, thanking her for helping out, he saw that the man was his nurse's brother Cornell, Oxford's youngest boy, and he knew then that this woman was his new bride. Her first night in town probably. One she would no doubt long remember.

Alf's nurse Columbia would not have been surprised at this display, that Gretchen was a real take-charge girl, that was definitely the impression she had brought back from the wedding, though it was not her immediate one. Her first impression had been that Gretchen was ill-tempered and pushy, stomping around aggressively in her orthopedic boot as if she were hammering nails, a haughty and sharp-tongued shrew who was abusive to Corny and quarrelsome with strangers and, on top of it, blind as a mole, which in some ways she unfortunately resembled. Not a good start. But her bad humor, Lumby soon learned, was mostly her brother's fault as usual. Gretchen had arranged a whole series of appointments with doctors and labs and county clerks and photographers and justices of the peace and what all, and Corny had wandered off to play a pinball machine somewhere and had missed them all, meaning everything had got thrown off by a day, the lesser things just abandoned. Luckily it was only a civil marriage and they had no big honeymoon plans (though *those* reservations had to be changed, too), but still, Columbia could understand how her baby brother, who had also somehow managed to misplace the rings (they found them finally in the lining of his tatty jacket, bought for a quarter off the Salvation Army racks—the rings, of course, Gretchen herself had purchased), could exasperate a person. Certainly he had tested his own family's patience over the past few years with his indolent numskull ways, ever since that awful highschool graduation trip to Paris. When Corny had announced the wedding to them in a phonecall a few days before, startling everyone, her father assumed the stupid boy must have got some damned hippie pregnant. Lumby didn't think so. She had played doctors with Corny once upon a time, and so had some idea what his problems were. On the other hand, she could not imagine who *would* marry the little dummy, and so drove up to the ceremony feeling nearly as skeptical as her father did. She was the only member of the family to attend, acting as one of the witnesses, Harvie being totally out of touch, her father too depressed to go. Her father was depressed all the time back then, it was a kind of endless soapbox routine and frankly getting a bit much to take. It was like he thought he was the only one who missed Yale and Mom. Lumby was mad that he wouldn't go up there with her, and she let him know how she felt about it—what kind of father *was* he, for pete's sake?—but given the sort of wedding that it was, it was probably just as well. He and Corny would have just got into another whining match, and her father, half blind himself, would not have noticed what a real find Gretchen was, and so, like the man who wasted the only wishes he ever got, might have turned her off before she could ever come here and work her magic on them all.

Oxford's failing in truth was not in wasting wishes, but in having no clear second wish when the only wish he ever wished did not come true. Oxford was a reasonable man, and his sole desire was simply that the world be at least as reasonable as he was, a certain recipe for despair as just about anyone in town could have told him, and as often did close friends like Alf, closer when they both were suddenly left alone and then more often, too: "Human reason is an evolutionary deformity, my friend, an aberrant mutation, a miserable freak. Don't trust it. The life force itself is savage and mindless. Ruthless. Like a trapped beast. Believe me, I witness its stupid cruelty every day. And in its ruthlessness, it engenders monsters, human reason just one of its grotesque miscreations. Just thinking about it, Oxford, is enough to make you shit your britches. The brain thinking about itself: better than a damned enema." This said by the old gynecologist, emergency room surgeon, and general practitioner over hot bitter coffee in the Sixth Street Cafe, peering out the window at a dirty rain splashing the cracked blacktop in the empty center of a decentered town. A pause. A rueful sigh. "The only consolation is that monsters, cast off by the force that made them, usually self-destruct. Sooner or later." Oxford had no reply. He could only gaze out through his tears upon the horror, somewhat fuzzy because of his myopia. Alf's and Oxford's wives, Harriet and Kate, friends in life, had paired themselves in untimely death as well, perishing of lingering diseases of the inner organs two years apart (though Oxford's Kate had cut her suffering short with an overdose of sleeping pills, taken from the store), a double loss to the community and a reminder to all of the brevity of life's fitful fever, as Ellsworth put it, in a rhyme with "forever grieve her," in his special *Town Crier* eulogy to Kate as the longtime city librarian. Perhaps it was this morbid reminder that had caused Alf that particular day, two years of grieving fever welling up behind his own eyes, to leave his finger inside John's wife a contemplative moment longer than he needed to, or that made Marge cry when she saw the wrecking ball bring down the old Pioneer Hotel which she had never even entered except when obliged, as at John's wedding, for example, or that inspired Nikko the golf pro to abandon his wife Daphne a few weeks later and run off with the orthodontist's uninhibited teenage daughter, or that prompted young Cornell to drop completely out of sight for a year and more, further sorrowing his heartbroken father, left now with so little. Poor Oxford. His wife was dead, two of his sons had turned into wildly irresponsible crackbrains, utterly unrecognizable even to those who loved them, the third, the one with the most promise, had been senselessly killed in a distant war, and he himself was reduced to living alone with his churlish daughter, a fat and rather stupid girl who had tried but failed both pre-med and pharmacy, and had ended up working now as a practical nurse for Alf, largely thanks to her father having asked this of his old colleague as a personal favor, so the downtown pharmacist had reason, his noble and rational dreams of a noble and rational world come to such ruin, to feel a bit crushed in the spirit. Cornell had been his last fond hope, his most bitter disappointment, and so he saw nothing to cheer about when his mad son surfaced suddenly a year or two after his mother's burial to announce his impending marriage to the staggering half-blind creature described shortly thereafter by his daughter on the telephone. The woman sounded like the very emblem of that deformity Oxford's dream of reason had become. She will be the death of me, or anyway of my sanity, he thought, weeping as he often did in those dark days, when he hung up. He was wrong about this, however. As he admitted to his friend Alf over a sunny midmorning feast of blueberry pancakes and vanilla icecream many years later, his tears long dried and two of his eight grandchildren in the double stroller at his side, Gretchen was in truth the real son he no longer had.

Gretchen's fecundity amazed the town. A patriarchal future was not the vision most had had, lacking Pauline's privy knowledge, when autographing little Corny's high school yearbook. Maybe Gretchen's myopia helped, some said, to find what others could not see or even say for sure was there. Or was it, others asked, that trip to Paris with Yale's old flame that made the child child-maker? Drew him out, in a manner of speaking? They say the toilet was in the living room of that strange bohemian garret, and the bathtub was the artist's sofa, naughtily aimed mirrors everywhere, where could innocence hide in a place like that? Maybe Corny learned a little French after all, in other words, before the lights went out. It was possible, but if so, there was little sign of it on his return, his heart-shaped face with its gaping stare and unwiped mucus streaks reminding some of crackled porcelain, others of a dead child, too long unburied. An odd boy, made odder still, that was the judgment, so when the babies started to drop by twos and threes, it caught the whole town by surprise (old Stu, elbow sliding on the country club bar, said he'd asked the lady druggist if she got three every time, and what she'd said, he said, was, "Oh no, sometimes we don't get none at all!"), not least his family, though they soon got used to it. For all her minute playroom examinations and later health ed and anatomy courses and her career in a doctor's office, after all, Columbia never had figured out exactly how males worked (Gretchen promised to show her), and as for Oxford, that reasonable man, he had been wrong about so many things it did not surprise him to be wrong about another. Columbia, being a nurse, or nearly, to a sometimes gynecologist, was a great help through all the pregnancies, giving Gretchen her shots and sometimes a back massage, even once an enema, and accompanying her, since she worked there, through all her visits to the doctor and often to the lab for her scans and blood tests. During the backrubs, Gretchen would tell her about all the problems she was having with her wacky husband, how sometimes he was all over her like a rabbit and other times she couldn't get near him, he'd hide under the bed or in the closet, or else out in the alley behind the drugstore, prowling around like he was looking for his lost wits. Corny seemed to get it in his head from time to time that he wasn't really married to Gretchen, that it was all a trick of some kind, or else he'd fallen asleep and couldn't wake up, he was a real lunatic. Columbia of course was always very sympathetic, having had to put up with her demented little brother all her life, and she said she thought it all had something to do with that crazy trip to Paris, and Gretchen agreed. Gretchen said sometimes it was like there were two Cornys. And neither of them worth a bent penny, Lumby would add, and they'd both giggle, and sometimes hold hands.

Cornell's hostess in Paris, on a highschool graduation trip arranged by his father, was his big brother Yale's French sweetheart Marie-Claire, penpal of John's wife and bridesmaid at her wedding, the one Daphne thought seducing Bruce. Had the horny maid of honor had her eyes on anyone all that day but the best man, however, she would have seen the gazes Yale and Marie-Claire were exchanging during rehearsal and at the dinner after, would have noticed that they'd stayed behind while the others drifted toward the bar, Yale there more as the bride's pal than the groom's and so easily forgotten when it came time to play stags and hens. Yale was the serious one in that family, both parents' admitted favorite—but no hard feelings, he was also Harvie's favorite and the younger kids', too, a boy born to love and be loved as well. Greatest thing, as is often said, Yale had it. Daphne's classmates had voted him both Most Popular Boy *and* Most Likely to Succeed, two accolades rarely paired, not even John in his day had been so honored. By the time he met Marie-Claire—and forget the bridal bouquet and the garter next day, this was that wedding's one true (to quote one of their love letters later on) full-blown romance—Yale was halfway through Princeton, majoring then in chemistry and what was coming to be known as computer science, but soon to switch to French, foreseeing a life that would take him far from these parts forever, correct in this, as it turned out, though not in the way he had imagined. The plan, elaborated in their long weekly, sometimes daily, love letters, which each wrote in the other's tongue, delightfully cross-pollinating and scrambling their endearments, double ententendres' meanings doubly doubled, was for Yale to finish his degree and then find a teaching or translating job in Paris where they could live together, which folks back home, lovingly envious, thought of as the French way of doing things. With the diploma in his hands, he already had the airline ticket in his pocket, a graduation gift from his family, sent him in a packet from the drugstore Oxford labeled a "prescription for peace and joy," to which his mother Kate appended one of her succinct aphorisms: "Love is the source code!"—but before he could join Marie-Claire he got drafted, was made an officer, went off to a war that was not a war, and loved by those he led with love, got shot on patrol in that part of him that had once memorized the conjugations of *être* and *foutre* and devised on the computer a pioneer on-line concordance for the collected works of Mallarmé and Baudelaire, who, the shocked and grieving community learned from *The Town Crier,* were French literary personages, known best as poets, contemporaries of this town's early settlers, few of whom by contrast could even write.

It was during a routine business call home while on his second honeymoon in Paris that John learned of Yale's fall on the field of battle, so it fell to him to break the tragic news to their hostess Marie-Claire, an awkward situation, made worse by hainqui-dainqui's recent mischief, but John handled it with his usual panache, as the natives there would say, and proved that he was a man, as his mother Opal often asserted, not without compassion. Although, true, few who knew him would have described John so, in this matter John himself would have agreed with his mother: he was, he had no doubt of it, a compassionate man. Except when he was in a tough ballgame. Which of course was just about all the time, since that was mainly how he defined life. Compassion was the most natural thing in the world but you could rarely get down to it, that's how he felt. Too much of life's rough-and-tumble in the way most of the time, and a good thing, too, else he'd be bored silly. Compassion, in effect, was what was left over when the game was easy: a generous party, a timely job or a business tip, a tax-deductible gift. It was a bonus at Christmastime for his employees, even if he planned to fire them. A visit to the bedside of a guy you'd hit, flowers for the wedding of a rejected lover. Sometimes just a thoughtful phonecall, or a slap on the butt. Three rooms and bath in a retirement community was what stricken Barnaby got, Oxford an offer to save his pharmacy which he foolishly rejected, Lenny a piano for the church basement that Beatrice had asked for, Snuffy new team uniforms, then an airport job, and later, in politics, John's endorsement. Waldo got business trips when Lollie was too hard on him, Lollie the chance to partner John sometimes in mixed-doubles foursomes. He suffered nights of bridge with his hardware man and his simple wife, even to Mad Marge threw a cookie now and then, though usually by way of her husband's insurance business, and to Harvie he once sent a marabou stole to show he cared and understood, compassionate man that he was.

"Compassion? He calls that shit compassion?" his cousin Maynard would have snorted bitterly had he known John's thoughts, though of course he didn't. Couldn't. He had trouble enough reading his own dark mind, forget the minds of others. And the Nerd, or Backdoor Mange, as his ex-wife Daphne sometimes called him, was not the sort of person John or anyone else would ever confide in, except for Veronica of course, who did, and wed him, then suffered ever after having her past flung back at her like those custard pies they throw in the movies. Sympathy was not in Maynard's vocabulary, compassion wasn't, nor in his heart either. Love was, but narrowly so, so narrowly only he knew it was lodged there. Like a rock, a deeply imbedded stone that his thoughts tripped over, losing coherence, and that sometimes turned red-hot and caused his senses to fail him and his body to shake as though with a fever and his organs to expel their contents. It was strange, he did not understand it, never could, thought of it as something completely crazy, but he could not shift it out of there, it was as much a part of him as his stubby dong, his hairy flat feet, his five o'clock shadow. So instead of kicking at it, he tried to polish it, but everything he did, always for her or for his love for her and his need to be near her, went wrong somehow, whether it was marrying her best friends to be closer to her or producing a kid to companion hers or trying to protect her and her father from John's cruel depredations or just keeping up the pretense of a social life (he *hated* the social life) so as to see her from time to time (only *she* could polish what he could not): all failed. His love was dumb and blind and taught him nothing: he was, classically, its hapless fool. And now, since her father's foiled raid, though he'd only done it for her: anathema. The great deceiver, cast as, he was, and so cast out wholly. He could not even speak to her anymore nor look her way when she passed by. If ever she still did, it was as though they existed in different worlds. Compassion? Hey, save it for the Nerd, whose pain was deep and, save for a frayed garter in his pocket, utterly without balm.

Certainly no solace from his same-named son, a rival of sorts who also had his eye on John's wife, or hoped to soon; according to his best pal Fish, it went with the paper route. Love was not in Little's vocabulary either, not yet anyway, though it was growing—his vocabulary, that is (other things, too, as he excitedly showed to Fish)—growing by lips and buns, as you might say, laps and bums, mostly filling up as it was at this time with words for bodily parts and what you did with them. Fish, as always, was his master in this, and not just in the naming but also in more practical instruction, the preacher's son being a talented artist in his own right and also having access to certain books and magazines in his father's collection that he said were attempts to depict what *really* got God mad at Sodom and Gomorrah. Nowadays, according to his dad, God was more understanding, humans were only humans, after all, so what the heck, let it happen. Fish often had interesting things to say, not just about girls and what made them tick ("—and tuck," Fish would always add and pump his fist), but also about God and cars and drugs and computer games and what happened to you when you died, lots of things. He taught Little how to skateboard, how to roll a joint and smoke it, how to tell real rock from pop music (which he called "poop music"), how to play poker and chess and do tricks with matches, how to sneak into the swimming pool without paying, and how to tell if a girl was a virgin or not. He promised to show him how to drive when he got his own license and gave Turtle to understand that all his worldly wisdom was at his young friend's beck and call. A born teacher, he was. The only thing Turtle couldn't understand about Fish was that he had *his* eye on Turtle's bitchy cousin Clarissa, a total pain in the neck if ever there was one, though it was true, she was more Fish's age, and she did seem, in her tight jeans and torn shirt or in her string bikini at the new pool, as Fish put it, "hot to twot." Or something like that. He'd seen her naked, or almost naked, Fish said, and when Turtle asked him if she was a virgin, he said he hadn't been able to test her out yet, but he thought she was. Fish's sister Jen was her best friend and so she hung out at the manse a lot, sleeping over sometimes, the two of them listening to music, girl-talking, drinking diet pop or sometimes beers, smoking dope when Fish's folks weren't around, and often on hot days when they were high, or even sometimes when they weren't, they liked to goof around in their underwear. The reason Fish thought Clarissa was still a virgin was because he heard her complaining about it to Jen in her bedroom one night while he was watching them through the keyhole. He said she said she couldn't wait to do it. It? Fish told him. Turtle also had to admit he didn't know exactly what a keyhole was, not if you could see through it, but when Fish showed him one (their manse was much older than Turtle's house, and more interesting in lots of ways) he could see how it might be useful.

Clarissa knew that Jennifer's creepy goggle-eyed big brother was lurking outside the door that night, as he did most nights she stayed over. She didn't know how a girl as cool as Jennifer could even have a jerky brother like that, but then who was she to talk, what with the retard she was stuck with? At least Philip wasn't still wetting the bed. "Oh yes, he is," Jennifer giggled. "Every night! Only with different stuff!" Clarissa thought Philip, better known at school as Fish, had got his nickname from his stupid bug-eyed buck-toothed look, but when Jennifer told her that she'd given him that nickname when she was a baby, he'd had it forever, Clarissa was not surprised. People grow into their names, she believed that, just as she was growing into hers. "Marie-Claire once had a lover she walked like a dog," she told Jennifer, always a good listener. They were lying around in their underwear, listening to some new CDs. "With a leash and a chain and everything. She took him to the park and made him do tricks for her and spanked him in public with a rolled-up newspaper." She had to fill in some of the details, but the main points of the story were all true, she'd overheard her daddy tell it. Up in an airplane with Uncle Bruce. "Well, one night he went wild and started frothing at the mouth and he attacked her and tried to bite her in her, you know, between the legs. Hard!" "Boy! Talk about getting eaten out!" "It wasn't funny, Jen! He was trying to kill her, but Marie-Claire strangled him with her legs until he quit. After that, she wouldn't let him be her dog anymore, but he never got over it. All the rest of his life he walked around on all fours, until one day a car hit him." Jennifer thought it was a great story and said she'd turn all her lovers into aardvarks because of how long their tongues were, a fact she'd picked up from a silly poem in a children's book. Jennifer seemed obsessed about tongues lately. "Or else Bambi's father," she sighed dreamily, running her fingers inside her briefs. Philip wandered in then, trying to look bored. "Mom's coming home soon with Zoe," he said. Clarissa didn't mind other people's moms, just her own. Whom she seemed to see less and less of these days, so it wasn't too bad. Her mother was useful, but deep down Clarissa wished she'd go away and leave her alone. And take dumb Mikey with her. She pulled down her bra cup to poke at her nipple as though she might have a mosquito bite there, then peered up at Philip to watch him redden. She tried to think of what Marie-Claire might say, and then she thought of it: "You look like a fish out of water," she said. "Why don't you flop on out of here, Popeye, and go suck air someplace else?" And as Jennifer spluttered with laughter and hugged her thighs, he ducked out. This was the woman Clarissa was growing up to be. Because of her name. It was—she had just recently learned the word for it—her destiny. Knowing what was coming, what was *really* coming, was pretty scary, but it gave her an edge. She liked it. Whatever she did, it would come out the same, so there was nothing she couldn't do. No one could intimidate her, not even teachers or her parents' friends or the parents of her own. Certainly not the local police goons: during the bust at the mall, she'd collected everybody's stash, walked it coolly right through the assault lines. She owned the school corridors and lunchroom, was queen-elect of the mall rats and pool punks, would meet any dare. At the new downtown civic center pool that her daddy built, she hung around all day in a string bikini that drove the guys bananas. But if they tried to touch her, she'd scratch their eyes out. Not too close, Creep. Danger, High Voltage. This is what love was. It was great. Totally intense.

Gordon had photos of the new pool, the old one as well and the one at the country club, but no bikini shots. Not even of Pauline. He did have a black-and-white picture of Clarissa's mother, taken years ago at the country club pool, but in a modest one-piece swimsuit, tied at the neck and open at the back, not a bikini. Cheesecake, as it was called when he was a boy, was not Gordon's fancy, not his artistic métier. Intimacy was. Sensuous intensity. Intimations of timelessness. And purity of line. In the photo of John's wife, one of his favorites in an ongoing sequence begun nearly a quarter of a century ago, she is pulling herself up out of the pool near the low diving board, her bare back to the camera, one foot up on the concrete ledge, the other still in the water. Her hair is hidden inside a rubber bathing cap. Perhaps only Gordon would know who the swimmer was, but this very anonymity of his subject gratified him: an intricate arrangement of soft rounded glistening shapes, pure and clean and ultimately nonobjective, unnameable, set against a severe geometry. Blowups of isolated fragments of this photo shared these qualities and recalled for him his earliest painterly pursuits, his speculative juxtapositions of hard and soft, line and texture, edge and surface. The pale dimpled membrane of the bathing cap, backgrounded by dark hedges and the chainlink fence at the pool's outer border, provided impressions, when enlarged, of erotic moonscapes, set against an ominous cosmic grid, just as the potentially prurient and distracting crotch region, barely visible above the waterline and here at full stretch, lent itself with ease to tastefully harmonious studies in textural contrast, of which he had successfully attempted several. Gordon's favorite area of the photo, however, was the bare back, and especially the glowing expanse of tensed wet flesh from braced right shoulder to lower left rib. He had explored this section inch by inch through long, infinitely pleasurable darkroom nights, emerging with a series of finished prints as near to his artistic ideals as any he had been able to achieve with a camera. In most of his pool photos, however, old and new, at least those mounted in his "Uninhabited Vistas" albums with their panoramic views of abandoned fields, empty parking lots, derelict drive-in movie theaters, windowed reflections of blank skies, and desolate dawn streets dampened with rain, there are no swimmers, and often as not there is no water either.

In another country club photograph, taken more recently, John's wife, wearing a pale silk blouse later that evening to be dampened with gin, is receiving a lesson from the young golf pro on the proper way to grip a seven-iron. Her instructor is standing behind her, reaching around with both hands on hers and peering over her shoulder at the golf club she is holding, or at least down in that general direction. To get this shot, roughly three-quarters frontal, the photographer placed himself inside the caddy shack, just down the hill a hundred yards or so, and used a telephoto lens while focusing through an open window. Well, "placed himself" was perhaps misleading. He hid himself there. It was a surprisingly swift and covert maneuver. Trevor, watching discreetly from within the clubhouse lounge, almost missed it, remarking to himself, and not for the first time, that for a big man, outwardly clumsy, the photographer could move nimbly enough when he wanted to. Gordon, not a member, was a rare visitor to the club, here on this occasion ostensibly to photograph the new fleet of electric carts for the weekly newspaper, the old caddy shack now serving primarily as a garage for these vehicles, and his presence was odd enough that it caught Trevor's attention, especially with John's wife in the vicinity. So, with his own wife still out on the course somewhere, Trevor amused himself by keeping his eye on ("tailing" was the word, was it not?) the furtive cameraman. What possessed him to do this? Was it the same compulsion that gripped the photographer? Trevor didn't think so, though they did hold in common the desire to see without being seen, and he thought Gordon might be struggling with something like his own wandering actuarial graph point. The difference between their quests was that between object and subject, outer and inner, visible behavior and hidden motive. There was something baldly suggestive about the way muscular young Kevin in his burgundy red golf shirt and yellow pants was embracing John's wife from the rear, but Trevor doubted that Gordon saw in Kevin anything more than a visual irritant, an obstruction to an unimpeded view of the main target of his camera lens. Or anyway, this would be in accord with the general artistic principles expressed by Gordon in a *Town Crier* interview with his friend Ellsworth some years ago, principles and ideals that appealed to Trevor, for whom beauty and number were essentially synonymous, even as he doubted those ideals' validity. Or even their possibility. It was that doubt now, he believed, that compelled him to shadow the photographer, as though the photographer were offering himself up as an arena for the display of the paradoxical inner drama of a necessarily conflicted soul in pursuit of an impossible ideal. Surface eruptions were inevitable, and Trevor, his own inner drama developing apace, would be their witness.

Curiously, there was, though he had no knowledge of Trevor's pursuits and little enough of his friend Gordon's, a character much like this in Ellsworth's current novel-in-progress, *The Artist and His Model:* a mysterious unnamed personage, known simply at this point as the Stalker. Ellsworth had not invited him in, he had intruded upon the text unbidden. He was, so far, albeit deeply disturbing, no more than a minor figure, having made appearances only in one brief scene (which could get cut), a few unconnected fragments (in one, he asks the disconcerting question: How much does the child know?) and a handful of loose marginal notes, but he already posed a profound menace, not merely to the other characters in the novel (to wit, the Artist, his Model), but to the original plot as well, threatening it now with a total restructuring. Ellsworth had been seriously engaged with this book for over a decade, ever since words had failed him in the obituary of the car dealer's wife, killed in an accident, and at one stage he had well over thirty pages which he considered "polished." He had even had them set on the backshop linotype so as to contemplate them in printed form. Yes, they were fine. More than fine: classic. Then the Stalker crept in and, just by lurking obscurely at the edges, erased nearly half of them, and the twenty pages or so that remained, even if unchanged, no longer remotely resembled the twenty pages or so he had originally written. What did it mean, for example, to say that "The Artist, pondering the relationship between formal idealism and geometrical optics as he touched pen to paper, recognized that the triangle formed by his penpoint, the Model, sitting ten yards away, and his inner eye was in fact an equilateral one, but that when his stroke was untrue, or ink was spilled, or the Model started picking her nose, as she was doing now, it was not the equilaterality that was affected, but the triangle's planeness," when, suddenly, there was this other pair of eyes skulking about somewhere in the neighborhood? A debacle, as the great masters would say, but what could he do about it? When the Stalker first appeared and half his novel decomposed before his very eyes, Ellsworth panicked and, using all his authorial powers, forcibly threw the intruder out, restored the lost pages, and then added a few more (a productive period, though it proved illusory) as a kind of security fence around what he mistakenly thought of as his own private property, but all (he could have predicted this) to no avail. The Stalker was still there, inside the fence, which, far from keeping him out, served to encourage his interlopings, opening new pathways for him to explore, while yet hiding him from view. His Artist-character's remark, responding to the naiveté of his overly admiring Model, that "artists do not 'make' art, my dear, but are made *by* it," which Ellsworth had rejected as being overly melodramatic, now came back, in the person of the ineradicable Stalker, to haunt him.

Over the recent years, while a haunted Ellsworth, unbeknownst to the public at large, wrestled daily with a novel-once-in-progress now seriously imperiled by the Stalker's trespass, a few discerning readers (his friend Gordon, for example) might have noticed a gradual decline in the quality of *The Town Crier*, but most in town, like the Artist's admiring Model in the novel, were so in awe of anyone who could put two words together and spell them right that they found their old hometown rag, as they called it, not only as delightful as ever, but actually improving. In part, this was the Stalker's doing, for Ellsworth, increasingly engrossed in his narrative dilemmas, had come to rely more and more upon other contributors to keep the weekly newspaper going, and they in turn had each their own fans, most especially their own immediate families. Thus, the highschool journalism students, in addition to their traditional scholastic and athletic reporting, now provided regular book, movie, and music reviews (which amused their elders, even as they shook their heads at the dubious tastes of this new and noisy generation: *The Teen Choir,* some wryly called the paper now), the Chamber of Commerce secretary turned in a weekly business notes column called "You Can Bank On It!," the meaning of life was explored, mostly by members of the Ministerial Association, in a back-page box entitled "Afterthoughts," and just about everybody, sooner or later, wrote up something for the popular guest column, "I Remember." Some of these recollections were quite frivolous, such as those having to do with past fashions, dead pets or prewar prices, vanished landmarks, grandma's favorite recipes, and Halloween pranks in the days of outdoor privies, but others, such as Veronica's description of overcoming asthma to become a highschool cheerleader, or Otis's as-told-to account of learning about his father's self-inflicted death while lying wounded in a jungle hospital, or the nurse Columbia's loving tribute to her dead brother Yale, were deeply moving and often clipped and kept by the townsfolk. Tributes to those who had passed away were a common theme of course in the "I Remember" column—the librarian Kate's elegant remembrance, for example, only shortly before her own death, of her friend Harriet, the doctor's wife, whom she called "one of those great humane readers, impatient with grandeur and pretense, who profoundly transform the simplest work, utterly and for all time, merely by the act of reading it with an open heart," or John's wife's simple tribute to her Parisian friend, who on her visits to the town had won the hearts of all who knew her, or the editor Ellsworth's own sentimental memorial to the long-suffering mother of his good friend Gordon the photographer—but there was room for the other emotions, too, everything from humor to horror. Beatrice the preacher's wife recalled that day, just after they'd arrived in town, when she locked herself out of the manse by mistake with little Zoe inside and yelling her head off while her husband Lennox with the only other key was out making pastoral calls, so zealous in those early days that he didn't come home until ten at night, and then without the car which he had apparently left somewhere that he couldn't remember. "It was a real trip," she said in her typed draft, which the editor altered to "a real experience." She also said that what most impressed her about the place was that it was "a flat town, good for pushing babies around in," and that it was so friendly that "God Himself would feel right at home here just like we do." Trevor, the accountant and insurance broker, on the other hand, told of the horrific day he came upon the crushed body of the little six-year-old boy, killed on his bicycle by an unknown hit-and-run driver in a back alley behind the accountant's offices. Trevor, as he explained in his graphic yet delicate "I Remember" column, was so traumatized by the experience that he lost the sight of one eye for a time, as though the eye could not bear to see what it was seeing, Alf explaining that what he had had was a sort of minor stroke and that it might eventually clear up, allowing him to drive again. As, over time, happened. Trevor had offered a personal five-thousand-dollar reward (he reaffirmed this offer in his "I Remember" column) for any information leading to the arrest of the guilty driver, but so far this had not been collected.

Floyd could top that one, but when asked, said no. Floyd now managed John's downtown hardware store, but he was not from this town and no one in town knew much about his life before he came here, or thought much about it either. A traveling salesman who blew in out of nowhere, they knew that, an ignorant redneck with some familiarity with the Bible (the kids called him Old Hoot) and a marked reluctance to talk about his past, but once John had hired him, they all accepted him as he was (not much) and mostly forgot about him except when they needed a new door lock or toilet plunger or a lug wrench. But traveling, before he got here, was mostly what Floyd had done all his life, some of it selling, some trucking, a lot of it running from the law, the only settled times being those when they'd caught up with him and clapped his iniquitous ass into one prison or another, which was where he'd picked up his Bible knowledge and honed his cardplaying, the bowling came natural. Edna had been his girl in high school before they both dropped out, and she'd stuck with him through all the bad times, though not even she knew all he'd done. The things he'd been caught at, sure, the thieving and hell-raising they'd charged him with in one town or another when he didn't get out fast enough, but not everything. Some things nobody knew. There was the woman trucker who lured him on her CB radio to that lonely highway pullover, for example, the filthy drunken whore. Had a wart on her eyelid and a tuft of black hair on her chin. The old fleabag wanted fifty bucks for a quick ride. Got a quicker one than she counted on. She still turned up in Floyd's nightmares, wart and all, and sent him to his knees beside the bed in fervent prayer. It wasn't so much the sticking, he'd killed others, God save his shit-soaked soul, but the way he cut her up so badly and the places he dicked her after. I Remember. There were others, too, and none of them pretty—that fat cowboy with the false dentures who waved him over to help with a flat tire on his camper, then offered him a blowjob, for example, or the rich bitch in Santa Fe with the hairless tattooed pussy who wanted to hire him to knock off her husband, or that snot-nosed longhaired kid with rings in his ears he picked up outside Cheyenne, who made the mistake of saying he didn't think God existed, but if He did He was an asshole, that swoll-up shit-for-brains got it good. And that was the worst of it. Floyd repented of his sins but kept reliving them, knowing that for all his praying and promising, there was no meanness that had happened that couldn't happen again, and same way all over. It scared the bejabbers out of him but also somehow gave him the juice to get from day to day, and that was worrisome, too. What no one knew, except Edna maybe, was how damned vulnerable he felt, how closely the dark powers dogged his heels. John had saved his life with this hardware job, but if he ever got let go or the store got shut down, Floyd strictly hoped somebody would kill him before he walked out that fricking door.

That store Floyd managed probably should have been closed long ago or at least moved out to one of the malls, but it had been in the family a long time, always on that same corner of Sixth and Main, literally the cornerstone—or cornerstore—of the family legend, so John was reluctant, history sparing what history had abandoned, to shut it down, at least so long as his father was alive, and Mitch, though he had turned over most of the local day-to-day operations to his son and had announced his retirement more than once, showed no intention of cashing his chips in soon, on the contrary. Mitch's wartime profits had made him the largest landowner in the county and an influential business leader throughout the state, he was a major player in the area and felt that staying in the game was what kept him in the pink and his golf score down. He did not want to get in John's way, though, so, complying with the old wild oats dictum, once his to lay on John, he moved his financial dealings away from home and out into the national and international markets, crossing paths with his boy only when it came to a profitable exploitation of his local landholdings. John was just a kid, still in his mid-twenties when they worked up their first big project together, a neighborhood mall on the road out to the golf course, the town's first. Barnaby was still very much in the picture then, so it was a shopping center solid as Main Street and appealingly brick-cottagey, built in a semicircle around a parking lot with a fountain in the center and potted bushes lining the border, but it was soon found to be, as John had chafingly predicted, woefully inadequate. John called it a misuse of light and space, meaning he wanted more blacktop and more glass and less superfluous detail. The bushes blocked the display windows, the fountain (long since paved over) collected excrement and graffiti as wishing wells caught coins and used up valuable parking space, the heavy brickwork inhibited turnover renovations and the personal expression of the shopkeepers, and Barnaby's ban on marquees and neon and rooftop signs, Mitch's son felt, was like banning popcorn in the movie theaters. Worst of all was the lack of expansive unobstructed brightly lit shop floorspace, America's no-tricks answer to all the mirrored Versailles of the world, a mistake that John, riding over his father-in-law's muttered objections, put right on all his future shopping centers, but one never resolved in that first mall, now limited to arts and crafts boutiques, beauty parlors, and home video outlets. Barnaby's latest fiasco, his attempted raid on the family company, Mitch found repugnant and in fact completely loony, as though Audrey's death might have knocked Barn off his rocker, but, father to one, longtime business crony of the other, he did understand what divided John and his father-in-law, at least while the old curmudgeon was not yet himself so cruelly divided. John's first constructions had been high school and college theater sets: fantasy structures thrown up and knocked down in a day, and sufficient unto it, as the saying went, constructions Barnaby would never even acknowledge as such. Barnaby's first was his own home, a classic pictured to this day in books on twentieth-century American architecture, books John scoffed at as the purblind trivia of academic twinkies who wouldn't know which end of the hammer to pick up.

Clarissa, diminutive queen of the mall rats and the pool punks, would have loved her grandfather's description of her daddy's constructions as "fantasy structures." Especially the malls. Pure magic. They were, always had been ever since she was little. Like fairy kingdoms, sun palaces. They let her run wild in them back then and she could do no wrong and everybody smiled at her and gave her treats and presents, it was very exhilarating. Her daddy used to bring circus acts and musicians and famous comedians to the malls to draw the crowds, and there were always coin-operated machines to ride or play and free badges and balloons from the stores and special decorations for every season with Valentine redhots and chocolate Easter bunnies and Fourth of July fireworks and Halloween masks and corn candies and Christmas Santas. When she was only five years old she was a model in a spring swimsuit show out there, and she never forgot how they laughed and cheered, especially her daddy with his dazzling eyes lit up, when, in the middle of her routine, she tucked one arm in and, with a smile like the ones she'd seen on television, let the shoulder strap fall to her elbow. It was electric. Then her daddy built the new mall with the big food court in it and that became her favorite. Still was, even though there was an even fancier one now out by the highway. All the big kids started hanging out there in the food court, and lots of intense things were going on, grown-up things, though in the beginning she didn't know exactly what. Just that they seemed too important to miss. And now, for the first time, she was no longer allowed to run free, she always had to be with her mother or Granny Opal, the only grandmother she had left, so that just proved it. Something was happening. Luckily, there was a video games arcade right next to the taco bar and she could always get them to take her and Jennifer there (they were best friends now and both curious as cats), and then go for a coffee and leave them alone. It helped when her granddad had his stroke, because the retirement home was out near the mall and Granny Opal or her mother, whichever one was with them, often slipped away then to pay him a visit. Anyway, Clarissa was in high school now and too old to be chaperoned, and she said so in no uncertain terms. This was her *real* life and it wasn't fair to let her miss it. Jen, who was a preacher's kid, loved it at the malls just as much as Clarissa did; her word for it was "spiritual." She said she thought there was something phony about church and Sunday school with their blowhard Moseses and dead Jesuses, the malls were where God was going to show Himself (or Herself) if anywhere at all. You could just *feel* it. She and Jen figured out most things out there—the dare-me shoplifting, the ripped-off stuff for sale, the alcohol snuck into the rootbeers and milkshakes, the secret pot smoking and the funny pills and the furtive dealing, what was going down at the far end of the parking lot when people paired up and went out there for a while, all that—and they started dressing in printed album-cover tee shirts and leather jackets and chains and torn designer jeans so as to fit in better. Jen even got herself a nose ring, though she never wore it back home at the manse, she said it really freaked her mother. Clarissa was not so sure about this. Jennifer's mom used to be a hippie, and she was still spaced out a lot of the time. Which could be fun, she now knew. There was a lot of cigarette smoking going on out at the mall, too, of course, it seemed like everyone had the deathweed habit, but Clarissa didn't go that far. It was the one completely serious thing her father had ever said to her: "Clarissa, please. Promise me. Don't." And she had promised, and she'd never break her promise either, though she took it for granted if it wasn't tobacco, it was okay. Her dad loved her, but he was no square.

Opal felt uncomfortable leaving her granddaughter and her little friend by themselves, dressed so provocatively, in that loud unseemly place, but she felt even more uncomfortable sitting there alone among all those ill-behaved children, so she often, whenever obliged to take Clarissa to the mall, fulfilled a second obligation, this one to her daughter-in-law, by visiting the child's father, poor devastated Barnaby, at the retirement home, though it was hard to say in the end which experience was more repellent. The mall certainly was unbearably noisy and the air in the open restaurant area where the only chairs were was saturated with the fumes of fried fat and sticky sugars and cigarette smoke and a sour-milk smell that reminded her of sick babies. Outside there were no park areas or sidewalks or benches, or inside either, no place just to sit, but even if there were she would have felt conspicuous plopping herself down in the middle of all that mindless bustle. So, really, she had no choice, and anyway she did not really fear for her granddaughter, it was a public area, after all, dozens of people passing through every minute, and they all knew John's daughter when they saw her, what could possibly happen? The town had changed dramatically, almost unrecognizably, since Opal was a girl here, but in some ways her son's shopping malls, as Kate had pointed out to her when she was still alive, were a throwback to the village past of their youth, or perhaps even earlier. More anonymous maybe and off-center, but they were simple communal gathering places for scattered populations the way the old farm towns were (said Kate), this one among them, a place for barter and exchange, for the transmission of news and ideas, for ceremony and for courting and for friendly competition. When Opal, whose love for her son clashed with her distaste for his malls (if a throwback, certainly a parodic one), had objected that what was missing was that there were no churches out there, Kate had replied: "No imported old world churches maybe, but holy places just the same, Opal, good old national temples with the sacred stuff of glorious enterprise heaped up at the altars and shopping baskets as communion trays and beeping cash registers like the ringing of church bells, moral lessons provided by merchant-priests and their security guard–sextons. And there are all the fastfood chapels for ritual feasting, inviolable in content as kosher or Eucharist, and the cinemas for divine spectacle and iconic representation, with multiple screens for the different denominations, and mannequin angels and God's omnipresent Muzak voice and the final benediction straight down from heaven of the accepted credit card and even, or maybe above all, the vast apocalyptic barrenness of the parking lots: go visit those prophetic fields on a Sunday morning sometime, Opal, if you want a true"—and here she employed the very word that the preacher's daughter (virtually unknown to Kate at the time, little Jennifer being a less than devoted user of the municipal library), was to use many years later, riding home from the mall, all ecstatic in her adolescent way, in Opal's car—"'spiritual' experience." Ah, dear impossible wicked Kate, who never ever went to the malls herself, how she missed her! And Harriet, too, the doctor's wife, so many good friends gone! Even poor Audrey, difficult as she could be, Opal missed her, too, all her friends were slipping away, soon she'd be all alone. And now Audrey's Barnaby as well, not much better off than dead; she visited him as often as she could, but he didn't even seem to know who she was most of the time, it was very sad. It was while returning from just such a visit one day, Barnaby having mistaken her on this occasion for his dead wife, breaking into a violent tantrum and accusing her of betrayal and stupidity, some sort of division problem Audrey had got wrong or something, you could only make out about half of it, that Opal found the shopping mall surrounded by police cars with their blue lights flashing. She was in one of John's cars that day, so they waved her through. She felt dreadfully guilty, though whether on account of Barnaby's accusation or because of her abandonment of Clarissa or on behalf of her son whose mall was being so dramatically besieged, she couldn't say. But when Clarissa saw her, she came dancing over as though nothing were happening, carrying a big plastic bag from Jeans City with what looked like a box of shoes and Jennifer's folded-up jacket inside, Jennifer now wearing a man's white shirt, knotted at the waist, over her printed tee shirt which on this day, as Opal remembered all too clearly, showed four naked men holding musical instruments in shockingly obscene positions. And she the minister's daughter! These children today, Opal would never understand them. It was like there were no rules, no boundaries at all. And yet they seemed as innocent as ever. Clarissa, squealing something about finding "these really crazy walkers," leaned in and gave her a big hug and kiss, just like she used to do when she was little, but hadn't done in so many years Opal had forgotten what it felt like, and then insisted on skipping over to the police chief to show him her purchases. He waved her away with a weary smile, while continuing the conversation he was having on the walkie-talkie held at his mouth. Jennifer meanwhile, in the backseat, had a frozen smile on her face that made her look more dead than alive. Maybe she'd eaten something she shouldn't have. All the way home, Clarissa kept wanting to know about Opal's own adolescence, which Opal found flattering until Clarissa asked her: "When was the first time, Granny Opal, when you did it, you know, with a man, and what was it like back then?" "The first time was with your grandfather, of course," she lied, feeling suddenly less flattered. "And it was just as it should have been." The little rascal. When, a day or so later, Opal asked about the shoes, Clarissa shrugged and said they were the wrong size, she'd taken them back.

Opal's occasional visits to Barnaby were among the few that shattered man now received, Alf being about the only person outside of immediate family who still looked in regularly upon the old master builder since the stroke that had ripped away the main connections. His patient now lived alone in a three-room unit in the "professionally assisted" retirement center his son-in-law had built, a morose and defeated man, severed from his simplest habits, his speech difficult to comprehend even when he was coherent, which most often he was not, so far as Alf could tell. The old fellow wept a lot, especially whenever his daughter was mentioned. He spoke of John's wife as if she had been taken away and no longer existed, even though, on different days than Alf, she paid him weekly visits, according to the log in the main lobby. Barn sometimes wept over his wife Audrey, too, reenacting her deathbed scene, if that was what it was, but at other times he did not even remember who she was. He rarely remembered who Alf was, confusing him with old friends and relatives long dead, when acknowledging him at all. Others, still living, did drop by from time to time, at least early on, but the awkwardness of the exchange, its often bitter and bizarre nature, discouraged them. Barnaby had gone into deep retreat, making his visitors feel like intruders, disturbers of his misery's sour peace, so most stopped coming, sent notes instead which Barnaby left unopened. Alf supposed at first that depression over Audrey's death had fused the poor man's circuits, but in time he came to understand that it had more to do with some final desperate conflict with John, real or imagined, who could say. Something maybe about the new civic center. Difficult as things were between Barnaby and his son-in-law over the years, they might never have reached such a crisis, Alf now figured, tuning in as best he could, had it not been for John's paving over of the city park. Probably looked like outright treachery. Barnaby had drawn up the park plans while he was still in the army back during the war, and as soon as he got out he had razed the old wooden buildings that stood there, rolled the terrain out for the landscapers, personally planted the first tree and put the gingerbread on the bandstand, doing it all at cost or less, part of his vision of a builder's place in his community, and now suddenly there was his son-in-law, moving his bulldozers in. Had to upset him, and maybe all the more so that his name was attached to it. John's project was popular enough: a low-budget preformed concrete structure with an auditorium, gymnasium, Olympic-sized swimming pool with retractable roof (much ballyhooed, but more like a car sunroof, once in place), and ample parking space, which most people saw as a means of revitalizing the decaying town center, turning it into a kind of Main Street mall. John's old highschool coach and airport manager, now a councilman, had rallied city hall support, John's father had helped the city get partial funding for it from the state, and downtown businessmen had put up a substantial part of the rest, using the *Town Crier* column header as a fund-gathering slogan: "You Can Bank On It!" As for the park, John's argument was that it had become little more than an outsized litter basket, too expensive to keep safe and clean, and a breeding ground for crime and drugs. These days, nature lovers—and he (though armed) was one—went out of town for their rustic pleasures; the tired old park, ravaged by Dutch elm disease and a farm for vermin, was an anachronism. Saved them all money, too: the park land, he pointed out, was free.

There were plenty who disagreed. Committees were formed up to try to save the park, there were door-to-door campaigns, petitions for a referendum. Marge, needless to say, though Lorraine did, was mad as a wet hen. Lollie's helpmeet Waldo thereupon started calling her a "wet Hun" and dropped out of the club golf tournament that summer in protest against her constant bellyaching, which he said was polluting the course with acid pain, and also his heinie. Marge had her small successes, but Barnaby, at the time clear-sighted still, saw clearly the futility of this homely town-meetinghall approach: John had the mayor and the city council in his back pocket, plus the full weight of state and national government behind him, probably even majority support in town, and the park *had* been allowed to fall into a state of serious disrepair—part of John's strategy, Barnaby supposed. Had to credit the boy's wile. First, he destroys the town center with his junky outlying malls, then he puts the squeeze on that center's ruined faithful to buy themselves something back, cutting himself a handsome profit each direction. So ruthless was he, Barnaby actually began to fear for his daughter for whom, until then, he had only, John being the sort of husband that he was, felt sorry. Of course, there was nothing wrong with a civic center—hell, Barnaby would happily have built one twice as beautiful for half the money John was asking—but why, he wanted to know, did the town's only park have to be sacrificed for it? Too few objected, and they objectors more by reflex than by rage. Even Ellsworth, who should have known better, homespun tree-loving eulogies aside, seemed unable to resist the appeal of John's grand but fraudulent architectural drawings, which he published regularly in *The Town Crier,* fanciful as illustrations in children's books. There was only one way to stop him, Barnaby came to feel, and that was somehow to wrest his old company back from John, something only he and, with Audrey gone, he alone could do. Wouldn't be easy. It would mean risking everything he had. Might even alienate his daughter, an almost unbearable thought, she being all he had left in this world save his builder's pride. But he glimpsed a way, lonely and heroic though it was. One last grand adventure, come what may: he saw a path and took it. Well. A catastrophe, of course, worse than ever he could have guessed.

Ruined. Made the villain of a plot no longer his. Humiliated in front of his own daughter. Stripped of everything he had. Though he never figured out how or why. Betrayal probably. Didn't matter. When it was over, half of him was crushed and embittered, the other half was dead.

Dutch, would-be emulator of John's killer instincts, though only half so sure a shot, looked on admiringly as his ex-battery mate and fellow hunter gunned down his own in-law, toying with the hapless dodderer before finishing him off as one might shoot away the knees of a dumbstruck moose so as to create a moving target. Shot him down, then gutted him, cleaned him out. Many in town suspected betrayal, meaning Maynard, but Dutch knew better, having sat with John in his motel Back Room sucking a beer while on the other side of the mirrors poor old Barnaby with Maynard's slick collusion spread the hand they'd hoped to play. Dutch, as always slow to pick up on the story stuff of numbers, was a bit baffled at the time, understanding the conspiracy's dynamics but not the details, until the whipped and humbled Nerd, deftly pressed one afternoon at the motel bar, filled him in, at least enough to outline the plot by which the old man had hoped to retake the firm he had lost by an ill-writ will. Audrey's doing. After the wedding, the construction business, enlarged by the assets John brought in, was still, as Barnaby thought, three-fourths in the family, jointly owned by himself, his wife, his daughter, plus her husband John, a quarter each. In effect, though, it was a troublesomely fifty-fifty partnership between the two men, Barnaby the senior partner and a bully of a sort, full of antique certainties, John forced to bide his time. Audrey, meanwhile, anticipating as most wives do a prolonged widowhood, with John's advice so revised the family will as to change the shares to thirds on the death of any member, business a nuisance to her once Barnaby was gone and trusting her much-loved son-in-law to further gild her golden years, sparing her the details. And thus, when unexpectedly she popped off first instead, Barnaby was left with the short straw, a minor shareholder in the enterprise he had with his own hands created and by which he felt his life defined, now suddenly overruled by John at every turn, turns taken often and without remorse or pity, though always with a smile. Embittered, exasperated, but unbeaten ("It was the civic center that broke his water," Nerd told Dutch over an unhappy happy hour martini, "worse than rape, he said, the town like some kind of woman to him, to do that to the city park . . ."), Barnaby, abetted by Maynard, devised a scheme to recapture what he'd lost.

The deal was this: Through a dummy put in place by Maynard, Barnaby bought up controlling interest in another smaller building firm, an upstate industrial and commercial paving business with other attractive holdings, at least on paper, staking on this bold maneuver almost all he had, much more to be sure than that down-at-the-heels outfit, soon to be John's by default, was worth. Then, Barnaby still screened from view, Maynard approached John with a merger proposal, asking for forty-five percent of the new corporation, but "negotiating" easily down to thirty, giving John the illusion of continued control but Barnaby actually majority stock, once the masks came off. John still seemed reluctant, or else distracted, short on cash, he hinted, problems to be solved, so Maynard coaxed Barnaby into sweetening the pot with an investment offer: three hundred thousand dollars was the figure they came up with. Too much maybe, looked too eager. Probably what made John suspicious, though just how that wily fuckhead read their elaborately veiled stratagems as easily as the goddamn funny pages, Maynard would never figure out. John's wife might have helped him somehow, Barnaby being a sentimental old coot who talked too much, but she didn't seem quite in the picture, not these days anyway. Probably, as Maynard put it to Dutch out at the Getaway Bar and Grill that wet and gloomy end of day, remembering all the Monopoly games he had lost as a kid, it was just genius, intuition, John's fucking gambler's luck, and Dutch with a grunt agreed. "Or else there was a leak somewhere." "Mm. Speaking of which," Dutch rumbled, tweaking his crotch and sliding down off his stool. "Have another one on the house while I'm gone." He nodded at his barkeep as he sidled away, and the woman down at the other end of the bar stubbed out her smoke and said: "Thanks, honey, don't mind if I do." Maynard's bibulous and bilious ex. She often came in this time of day to wait for her husband Stu to drop in from the car lot and join her for a friendly drink or two before their serious swilling began, main reason Maynard didn't stop in here more often. "Hey, Daph," he greeted her, hunched over his glass, tearing the wet napkin under it with the pointed end of his plastic swizzle stick, "what's your ass go for these days down at the used-cunt lot?" "More than you're worth, scumbag." "Hunh. You mean it's overpriced like all the other junk your old man peddles." "Hey, you want me to punch that fatmouth sonuvabitch?" asked some swarthy young guy in greasy workclothes, sitting over in the shadows with a bottle of beer in his mitts. Maynard hadn't noticed him there before, didn't know who he was, though he'd seen him around town from time to time of late. One of his cousin's underpaid throwaway workers probably. "Nah, you better not, sweetie," Daphne said, lighting up again, blowing smoke out through her flared nostrils like rocket launchers. "That's the Nerd. Swing at him, you just get yourself all splattered in shit." "Jesus, what a nice fuckin' town this is," the guy muttered, and slumped back into the shadows, sucking at his beer.

This was Rex. He'd blown into town a year or so earlier with Nevada, and it was true, as Maynard supposed, he'd worked for John for a time, sitting in as an apprentice joiner with John's construction company, then driving a truck for the lumberyard for a while. John had taken a liking to him, or so it seemed, soon moving him out to his private airport as a kind of janitor and handyman, not the worst gig Rex had ever had. John met a lot of women out at that airport, Nevada among them, and Rex had the idea he staffed the place with trusties who kept their traps shut about his fucking around. Okay by him. Though he was no pimp, Rex was cool about Nevada's operations, she had what she had, her own bod her ax, and she did what she could with it, professional as a dentist or a computer programmer, he respected that and helped her unwind when she came back from one of her hustles, all stained and rumpled and wired from the tension of it. She needed him then, or said she did, and so she took him along with her wherever she went, and he needed that, needed the needing, it got him up like nothing else did, except maybe a wailing horn, and made more bearable what he'd come to call the daily grunt, stealing the line from somewhere, a tabloid or a music mag probably, the least of his thefts. So being in the neighborhood when an old guy nearly twice his age was punching out his woman didn't bother him, far from it—go to it, kid, pump the sucker dry, then come on home and lay your weary little chassis next to mine—no, what burned Rex's ass was the way John yelled at him one day when he caught him tinkering around inside one of his private planes. Wasn't even trying to steal anything, just trying to see how the fucking thing worked, trying to improve himself, as you might say, no call for John to get on his high horse like that, bawling him out and swatting at him with a rolled-up operator's manual when he crawled down out of there, like you'd do to a dog that had just shat on your rug. Right in front of old Snuffy the schnozz, Rex's windbag boss, and a bunch of the other dudes, grinning like fucking monkeys with grease guns up their butts. So then Rex did steal something after all: he copped some keys. And gave John the finger, went off to work as a mechanic in Stu's Ford garage, where he soon found himself servicing more than the old juicehead's cars.

That airport was John's own special baby, literally his pride and joy, loved more than his offspring, no surprise he was touchy about it. It was the first thing he ever built on his own without Barnaby interfering, just a cleared sod strip on a piece of his dad's land at first, not far from the new highway then being built, an arc of corrugated roofing tin added to an old collapsing barn for a hangar and a couple of construction trailers parked about, but as beautiful as anything he'd ever made before or since. Bruce had taken him up for the first time in his own Piper Cherokee a year or so before and, in midair, had handed him the controls, and John had experienced a rush unlike anything he'd ever felt before. This was on a visit to his old friend and fraternity brother up in the city, ostensibly a business trip, their first weekend together since John's recent wedding, and though Bruce had laid on a lot of entertainments, including a crazy party at the mansion of a young porno entrepreneur, featuring a glass-walled bar below pool level with naked nymphets swimming by, a hot new British band out on the terrace, and a contortionist in the upstairs lounge who could lie on her back, put her knees by her ears, and finger a tune on a flute blown by her ass while smoking a cigarette with her cunt, nothing could top that morning in the air. By the time of Bruce's first marriage a few months later, John had his first plane, a Skyhawk bought secondhand with Bruce's advice, Bruce joking that since he'd bought a secondhand bride with John's advice, their consultancy fees canceled each other out, and so John and his wife were able to fly up to the wedding, Audrey and Barnaby fit to be tied of course, their only daughter put at such risk, John telling them not to worry, he'd stay out of the war zone. He wanted to fly all the way to Paris for their second honeymoon not long after that, but Audrey nixed it, buying him off with money for an electricity generator for the airstrip and a proper hangar with a paved apron. Over the years, she herself began to fly with him, and liked it, even took some lessons before she died, though she continued to beg John to leave her daughter on the ground.

Gordon had one photo of John's wife taken at the airport, long ago, a chance opportunity. He'd thought, on the day, he'd got more, but when the developing was done, one was all he had. He had gone out there on a routine *Crier* assignment from Ellsworth to get shots of the new generator and the laying of the concrete foundations for the hangar being built, John agreeing to meet him there at noon to show him about. Ellsworth was giving him a lot of work for little pay in those days, but he was an old friend and Gordon did not complain. Must have been mid-February or so, the fields barren, but the day bright enough and not too cold. Not much to shoot at, even for a man who favored bleak abstractions, the new airport just another ugly scratch in a much-scarred landscape, but the occasion turned out to be a family event of sorts, Barnaby the only in-law missing, Mitch with a chewed-up unlit black cigar in his jowls, strolling about with his thumbs in his belt, admiring the premises, Opal and Audrey hovering maternally around John's wife, heavy then with her first child, and Gordon was able to convince them that a kind of family portrait out there in front of John's plane was in order. John's wife protested shyly, placing her hands lightly on her belly as though restraining a balloon about to fly away (Gordon, to his deep regret, did not get this photo, his unloaded camera hanging heavily at his side), but all the grandparents-to-be laughed her protests away, insisting they'd never seen her more beautiful. Indeed, she was almost childlike in her beauty, Gordon thought, though perhaps he was only seeing in her the beautiful child he once knew and, back in those days as a tagalong at the games his schoolpal Ellsworth played with her, drew. Once, somewhat frivolously, with a pregnant tummy, a secret sketch. There was a young man helping John with the hangar construction, a greasy-haired beer-bellied fellow famous for his Saturday night binges called Norbert or Norman, who got drafted not long after, went into the army engineers and stayed in, never looked back, gone like so many from this town for good, and together he and John rolled the plane out of the old hangar, which was little more than a tin canopy attached to an ancient gray barn whose roof was caving in (piece of history, that barn, gone three weeks later), and moved it over beside the new hangar-to-be's freshly spread concrete floor, still too wet to walk on. (Audrey had got them all to leave their handprints in the fresh cement, another photo Gordon had missed, having arrived too late, though he did photograph the handprint, the one he believed to be hers, many times over.) Gordon set about lining them up beneath one sleek white wing, worried a bit about the possible glare from the slanting sun off the shiny fuselage and trying to coax John's wife out from behind the others. He'd just got something like the pose he wanted when the whole session was interrupted by another airplane swooping by, a racier model, wagging its strutless wings, then circling around for a landing, everyone in John's party laughing and running out onto the packed-dirt airstrip to meet it, Gordon left with no one to photograph except the greasy-haired assistant, who stood alone beside the tail smirking stupidly. The new arrival, stepping dashingly out of his plane with a fistful of champagne bottles and a picnic basket, was one of John's rowdy university friends, Gordon recognized him from the wedding. He also had a woman with him who, unlike John's wife, wanted to be, front and center, in every photo Gordon tried to take, such that in the one photo he managed to get of John and his wife, there she was, throwing her arms around John and kicking one leg back, flapper-style, John's wife a shadowy blur, vaguely smiling, behind her. Later, John and his friend went up for a spin with the young woman, John's expectant wife declining, at the rather sharp bidding of her mother, the invitation to join them, giving Gordon hope that he might have her alone to his lens at last. But while, at their whooping insistence, he was photographing the three young people clambering up into the plane, the friend's hand playfully cupping the woman's behind, her mouth in a theatrical O, eyebrows bobbing and eyes crossed, the other two laughing back over their shoulders and waving champagne bottles at Gordon, the rest of the party made their exit: all he saw when he turned around was Mitch's car pulling up off the dirt shoulder onto the road into town. Well. His camera was loaded. He photographed the barn. The handprints in the wet cement.

In the end, Ellsworth printed one of the barn photos: "UNSIGHTLY LANDMARK TO VANISH SOON." But in the photo it was not unsightly. Gordon's lens had so intimately caressed the structure's ancient decrepitude one felt a compelling attachment to it, as though only now, in the fullest realization of its potential for rot and purposelessness, had it achieved its true beauty, its true meaning. The ruined barn lay, agonizing, against the white sky, Ellsworth realized with horror and fascination, like a dying body on a bed, like Gordon's own mother, her mind long gone, empty as the loft of that dusty old barn, dying alone in her room above the photo shop that early spring under the steady morose gaze of Gordon's cameras and lamps, the very reason Ellsworth was trying to keep his friend busy and out of the studio so much of the time. Ellsworth did not understand these photos Gordon was taking of his mother, now little more than a pathetic defecating vegetable. Gordon's father had died in the war, she had raised him, had been all Gordon had of family. "Didn't you love her?" he would ask. He remembered how, timidly, she would interrupt their play with cold milk and a tray of cookies, freshly baked. "Of course I loved her. I still do." Gordon was photographing the poor addled creature, head to foot, back to front, over and over again through the months and days of her progressive decline, contorting her shriveled limbs into bizarre attitudes as though in bitter mockery of the classic poses (he insisted no mockery of any kind was intended), but focusing mostly on her collapsing face, her gaping mouth, her blankly staring eyes. Ellsworth had sat through one of these sessions, but only one, he could take no more. The theme of the day seemed to be armpits. His own, as he watched his ponderous friend, eye locked to viewfinder, bear relentlessly down, felt moldy and perishable. The woman was diapered and her legs were covered with a sheet, so at least he didn't have to look at the bottom part, what he saw was sickening enough. Her breathing was shallow and raspy, punctuated by little snorts and grunts, but apparently unrelated to the awkward posturings her son was subjecting her to, just little mechanical tics and tocs, like the creaks and knocks one heard in an old house. Or an old barn. Ellsworth proudly eschewed the moral position in art and life alike, especially around Gordon, so he could not openly say what was truly disturbing him, could not even admit it wholly to himself, and instead deflected his acute distress into an argument about artistic principles. This, damn it, was not beautiful. "Maybe not," shrugged Gordon, framing armpit, chin, and nostrils, one shrunken breast, "but it might be. And if it can't be, then beauty can't be either. That's all. Now do me a favor, Ell, and hold her arm up beside her cheek like this, see—come on, just take hold of the wrist here and hold it straight up, so that—Ell—? Where are you going?"

These photos, taken some time before she had met her photographer husband, were among those Pauline showed to Otis many years later, long after her own first modeling experience and Duwayne's ruckus and arrest and her marriage, long after their periodic visits to the old trailer that followed over the years like a strange recurrent dream, interrupted finally by the death of the car dealer's wife and Otis's solemn promise to the Virgin, a promise he managed to keep for over three years, and then did not really break, not at first anyway, he and Pauline becoming friends again but only that, meeting for coffee now and then, enjoying relaxed comfortable chats like an old couple who had got used to each other. Otis was vaguely tempted at times maybe, his cock stirring faintly inside his stiff gray gabardines as though it had a memory of its own, a wayward thought it was trying fitfully to express, but he was able to keep things under control, and anyway Pauline, pushing thirty, was not quite the looker she used to be, especially in the midmorning glare coming through the plateglass window of the old Sixth Street Cafe, where they usually sat. No, he now saw Pauline from time to time, but he could still look the Virgin in the eye. Pauline had told him a lot of stories during these talks, some pretty disturbing ones, given the kind of life she'd had, poor kid, one in particular about the night before John's wedding, back when Otis was away at war, that Otis didn't know whether he should believe or not, and she had mentioned the photos several times before Otis finally realized that there was something about them that frightened her, a woman not easily frightened, and that he should maybe have a look. So, one morning when Gordon was busy all day at the high school taking senior class portraits, Pauline led Otis into the back of the shop and opened up the locked cabinets. There were hundreds of albums back there, an amazing sight (of course, he was a dogged fellow, her husband, turning up everywhere with his shoulderbag of fancy gear and rolls upon rolls of film, and he'd been at it for a quarter of a century, after all), but she went straight for the ones she wanted him to see. The pornographic photographs of the naked old lady Pauline showed him were pretty disgusting, all right, especially when Otis realized that the old thing was still more or less alive and must have been posing for that fruitcake, or been made to, but they were not, by themselves, what had upset Pauline. Pauline had told him about Gordon's early photo sessions with her, how she had explained what she wanted but how Gordon didn't seem to hear, how he wouldn't even let her take her clothes off at first, but insisted on shooting nothing but her face, and how she had to admit later he had found a kind of quizzical beauty on a face she had never been all that proud of, but then how he had slowly begun to undress her, literally ripping her summer frock off strip by strip at first, as though unwrapping a present or peeling an apple (what she was worried about at the time, she said, was how she was going to get home after, and what Daddy Duwayne would say when he saw her), making her put some underwear on when he reached that part—she had come without any, but he had found an old yellowed bra somewhere, a petticoat, and some of those thick silky panties from the war years you sometimes saw at a rummage sale—and then working these things off her, inch by inch, photographing every step of the strip from every angle, favoring the close-up of course, yet never touching her, just *pah-click, pah-click, pah-click* with that camera until she had begun to feel something crawling over her, a real physical presence of some kind sliding over her body, exciting in a way, but scary too, and then how he had begun posing her on a bed in a room upstairs in all these odd positions, getting around at last, or so she thought, to those photos she had come asking him for in the first place, yet somehow not as sexy as she had hoped, weird even sometimes, like when he shot up into her nostrils or focused on her feet or on her Sodom-and-Gomorrah or her armpits. Now she showed Otis those photos, mostly huge blowups that turned her body into a kind of vast rolling landscape, gigantic in scale yet minute in its details, distant and dreamy as desert dunes yet intimate as a pubic freckle, a wet nipple, an anal pucker. And the point was, they were, many of them, exact positional replicas of his photos of the old lady. It was spooky. It was as though, you know, as though . . . But Otis by now was only half listening. He could not get his eyes off the giant enlargements of Pauline's intimate parts. It was like some kind of magical voyage. He felt transported back to his childhood, until this moment all but forgotten, and to the stories of Merlin and Buck Rogers from the comicbooks, Sinbad and Plastic Man. So, when Pauline unzipped him, Otis knew he'd have to let the Virgin down . . .

Here, meanwhile, are some other photos from Gordon's albums, taken over the decades of his career as the town photographer: (1) On the sidewalk in front of the wide plateglass window of a simple one-story stucco structure filling the space between two older two-story buildings, one of brick, the other covered with imitation stone siding, a woman turns back to watch her leashed dog, a terrier of some sort, sniff at the sidewalk sandwich board announcing a turkey meatloaf and "cheese spuds" special, together with ("Hey Sweet Stuff!") homemade green apple pie with a cinnamon crust "all la Mode." The rainbowed lettering on the plateglass window reads SIXTH STREET CAFE, and there are two or three indistinct faces behind the window looking out, one wearing a baseball cap. Posters in one corner of the window announce the junior class play and the highschool football schedule. The woman, slender, young, or probably young, is dressed in light wool slacks, turtleneck sweater, and an open anorak, and is watched by an older square-headed man in droopy white overalls with a clipboard in his hands, who stands with his back to the camera at the right of the picture, near the hood of an old Ford pickup parked at the curb; he seems to be taking inventory of the items in the window of the hardware store beside the cafe. A sign above the handle of the cafe door between them, clearly legible, says GIMME A PUSH, I LOVE IT! The glass of this door has been cracked and taped. The building on the left of the picture, the one with the artificial siding, has a sign in its window that says CLOSING DOWN SALE! EVERYTHING MUST GO!, but this sign may have been there for some time; the building itself looks long since abandoned, casting an eerie shadowy emptiness on that side of the picture toward which the woman and dog are proceeding. The photo would appear to have been taken with an ordinary 50mm lens from across the empty oil-stained street, perhaps through a window. (2) A dark shallow puddle in what looks like an alleyway pothole reflects the corner of a brick wall or building and a creosoted pole, probably a light pole. In the stripe of pale light between these two imaged objects, rising (or falling) in their reflections like canyon walls, the surface of the puddle is broken by the tips of three larger stones, barren islands in the puddle's dead flat sea. Bits of litter—cigarette butts, a bottle cap, gum or candy wrappers—lie scattered randomly about the rocky shores of this miniature sea like unplanned settlements, or their ancient remains, for nothing here seems alive. The only object in the photograph out of scale with this modeler's perspective is the twisted bicycle wheel, its spokes broken and bent, only partly seen at one edge of the picture. It is vaguely abrasive, an irritant, like one idea rubbing up against another. It suggests that there is another picture, incompatible with this one, lying outside the one being seen; it suggests that there is *always* another picture lying outside the one being seen, that the incompatibility is irresolvable. (3) In a supermarket, a woman, possibly the same woman seen with the dog in the previous photo, though with longer hair now and dressed in pedal pushers and a sleeveless flowered blouse, squats to eye level with a small boy. Together they hold a tin can of something. Perhaps she is giving it to the boy to put into the shopping cart overhead. Or perhaps the boy has taken it off the shelf and she is putting it back. Her hair falls loosely over her back and bare upper arms, revealing more by seeming to conceal, just as her summer clothes, decorously loose-fitting, conceal as they seem to reveal: even where the heel of her shoe digs into one cheek of her buttocks, for example, there is no hint of the flesh beneath the cloth. The near aisle, the woman and the boy, the shelves behind them, the aisles beyond, all seem to be on much the same plane, suggesting the use of a telephoto lens. Into which the small boy is, wide-eyed but without expression, staring. (4) A heavy man in a plaid shirt and workpants sits on a straightback wooden chair in what seems to be the timbered inside of a rude garage or workshed. There are rough-hewn shelves overhead on which sit a row of gallon paint cans, most showing thick dull drips down the sides, though some with fresh spatterings, and next to them are crusted bottles of turpentine, small cans of stains and varnishes, a galvanized bucket half-concealing an old license plate pinned up behind it, and at the edge of the frame, a grimy dried-out fruit jar with the wooden handles of paintbrushes sticking out like black rabbit ears. The wooden wall beneath is damply stained as though a can of dark paint had been thrown at it. An old truck tire hangs there, draped by the twisted coils of a rubber garden hose, so long hooked on that spot above it that it comes to a sharply creased *V* over its nail. The man holds a double-barreled shotgun between his legs with unmistakable suggestiveness, stock between his knees, thumbed triggers at the crotch, barrels in his mouth. The top of his head is gone, though bits of it can still be seen on the underside of the shelves above and on the wall and elsewhere. The license plate with its meaningless sequence of letters and numbers seems to serve or to wish to serve as a kind of title for this photograph, but the title of the thick album in which it is archived is "The Environment of Violent Departure." (5) The front of the photographer's own shop, seen from the front corner, has been stove in by a panel truck belonging to the town paint and wallpaper store, according to the printing on the side. The truck, rearing up on its back wheels like a springing animal, is about halfway into the shop, and glass and photos and other odds and ends lie scattered about like bomb debris, but the driver's seat is empty. A short stout policeman in shirtsleeves, suspenders, and gabardine twill trousers tucked into polished boots, back to the camera, ponders the mess with hands on hips, the closely shaved roll of fat on the back of his neck, under the cap, faintly flushed as though with exertion. The two top-floor windows have been shattered as well, and in one of them a young woman stands, gazing placidly down upon the policeman, her hands at her blouse buttons. The two windows are browed with decorative lintels and so give the whole building, with its crenellated parapet, hinged sign in the middle, and gaping mouth below, the look of a startled human face, obscenely assaulted.

Mad Daddy Duwayne. Just went berserk that day Pauline moved out of the trailer and into the photographer's flat above his shop. He turned up in the street outside, red-eyed and bristling with weapons like a maniacal one-man assault team, and started blasting away, as though the building itself was something alive he was trying to kill. Sometimes he howled like an animal, sometimes like a preacher, bellowing then about the Whore of Babylon and God's great rod of wrath and the desecration of the temple, by which he probably meant the farewell message she had left scrawled on the toilet wall of the old trailer, and about the Day of Rapture (which he always pronounced as "Rupture") coming to cleanse the earth of false prophets and graven images and other dreadful abominations, otherwise just bellowing. Of course, Pauline had heard it all before, especially about the rod of wrath and the black stinking pits of hairy hell, Daddy Duwayne's theological specialties. She was alone in the building, Gordon having locked her in for safety's sake when he went off to photograph the funeral of the doctor's wife, and after her crazed daddy drove her away from the second-floor windows with his glass-splattering gunfire, spitting out his rabid thou-shalt-nots like foaming swearwords, she just went into the back bedroom where Gordon had been taking her picture, shut the door, and lay down on the old iron bed up there. She closed her eyes and listened to Daddy Duwayne carry on down in the street like it was the soundtrack from some old TV movie playing somewhere else, a trick she used to use in the trailer park to distance herself from his bruising exhortations. Sooner or later, she knew, he'd be in to get her and drag her out and then whip her down the street all the way home like he always did whenever she tried to run away. And she didn't think the photographer would come to take her back either; nobody ever stood up to Daddy Duwayne, he was too crazy. The bare mattress she was lying on had a kind of stale antiseptic smell, strange to her but not unpleasant. A lot nicer anyway than the trailer's garbagey old-socks stink with its infested floormat for a bed and its damp reeking toilet, small as a coffin, where he sometimes locked her up while he went out to spirit up the dead, as he called getting drunk. There was a long silence then, just like those times in the toilet. The shooting stopped. The shouting. Her hopes were not raised by this. She had learned long ago to distrust such peaceful pauses. She waited for the door to open and the bad part to begin. Instead there was a tremendous explosion and the whole building shook like maybe her daddy was right about it being the Day of Rupture after all, and she didn't know if she fell off the bed or leapt off, but she found herself on the floor on all fours, gaping at the door which had popped open by itself and expecting anything to come through it, maybe Jesus himself, or even worse. Nothing did. There was just the slow settling of plaster dust all around. She heard sirens. By the time she had crept through the broken glass to the front window and peeked out, they were carrying Daddy Duwayne away from the smashed-up panel truck on a stretcher. Out cold but under guard. He hadn't seriously hurt himself, as it turned out, but once they got ahold of him, they never let him go, so she couldn't help but have a soft spot in her heart for Otis after that. Daddy Duwayne got charged with a whole catalogue of crimes, just about all the Commandments getting mentioned, and all of which he was guilty of many times over, except maybe the charge on this occasion of attempted murder, which was a little unfair. Her daddy knew how to shoot. If he had seriously wanted to kill something, he would have.

Veronica was minding John's paint and wallpaper store that day, most everyone else in town having gone off to the funeral of poor Harriet whom she hardly knew. Not one for funerals anyway, really. Old Alf, Harriet's husband, she knew better; he'd done her a favor once. She sent him a nice card, expressing her deepest sympathy, but was happy to oblige when John asked her to watch the store. Veronica had returned home a year earlier after the failure of her first marriage, needing, for therapy as much as money, some kind of job, and John's wife, a former highschool classmate, had helped her get on at the paint store, in those days still downtown, she remembering that Veronica had once wanted to be an interior decorator, or perhaps it was Veronica who had reminded her of that. They had never been all that close, since Veronica never got along with her best friend Daphne, still didn't, but she didn't mind using what little influence she had because, anyway, she felt, John owed her one, that whole family did. Life had not been kind to Veronica. Braces, migraines, anemia, tonsilitis, asthma, she'd had it all as a kid. Then, once she got to high school, things were a little better, she was a cheerleader and a member of the choral society and popular enough, everybody calling her Ronnie back then, but though she was generous with her person (too generous, she always thought), she didn't believe in going all the way, not yet, she was too idealistic, and so she got a P.T. reputation, ridiculed the more, the more she gave. Daphne, especially, was cruel to her, and one day at the country club pool, in front of all the boys, asked her if she thought orgasms were more fun to have alone or in company, and Veronica, who wasn't really sure at that time what an orgasm was exactly (though when she did find out, she realized she had been having them all along, no big deal), could only turn red and stammer out something stupid about believing that was something one didn't talk about in public. "Aha! Just as I thought!" laughed Daphne and all the boys started laughing with her. "Alone!" And then, finally, when she did start going all the way, the worst possible thing happened, and that was when she got Alf to do that favor, if a favor was really what it was, she still had nightmares about it (or him: she had named the thing as though thereby to put it to eternal rest, but rest it, or he, would not), and worried, to the extent that she believed in such things, that she might have condemned herself to everlasting hell. She was scared after that, and ran into marriage the first offer that came along, an older guy she met in college and hardly knew before they were suddenly man and wife, and again she was too idealistic, but he wasn't, and when she couldn't take any more, she came back home and hired Maynard and his father and got a divorce, which dragged on and was very messy and depressing and left her feeling old and used up when it was over. But, never say die, she joined the choir at church and the Literary Society at the library and got a job at the paint and wallpaper store and started going out some with Maynard, who had just recently graduated from law school, but already looked forty. Maynard had also gone through a wretched first marriage and divorce, and like Veronica, had suffered from name-calling and undeserved ridicule all his life, and he probably hated Daphne, whom he called his old ball-breaker, even more than she did, so at least they had something in common. Just the same, even though she sympathized with him, he was in many ways still the Nerd he had always been, at least everybody in town seemed to think so, the only difference being that he now had a permanent five o'clock shadow, and so, whenever he brought up the subject of marriage, always seeming to have some kind of nasty grimace on his face, like it was a dirty joke or something, she always said she wasn't ready. That was until the day that crazy man came crashing into the store just as she had started to doze off, making her fall off her chair and nearly swallow her tongue. She couldn't see anything for a moment—blinded with panic was what she was, she suddenly knew what that meant—and when finally her focus came back again, there he was, pointing a gun at her face and demanding the keys to the panel truck outside. She had no idea where they were, so he started shooting at all the cans of paint. She was crying and praying and trying not to have an asthma attack, not knowing what to do and hating John for leaving her in a mess like this, not for the first time. Finally, in desperation, she opened up the cash register to give him all the money, and there were the keys. When he was gone, she decided, collapsed to the floor under a dripping paint can, where they found her later, somewhat out of touch and spackled all over with Provincial Blue, that maybe the working world was not for her after all, and two months later, when she'd got her breath back, she and Maynard were married.

"Ronnie and the Nerd! Perfect! Hell on earth! I can't think of any two assholes who deserve it more!" was what Daphne, on the telephone with her best friend and, as usual, doing most of the talking, said of the engagement news. Daphne had once been married to Maynard, it had lasted less than a year, a miserable time spent away at law school in a grad student flat, far from home, drunk most of the time or fucking around helplessly while that drudge hit—and hit and hit—the books. Later she would marry Nikko the golf pro, the one who ran away a few months later with the orthodontist's teenage daughter in her psychedelic warpaint, and after that it would be old Stu the car dealer, whom Daphne generously called Old Stud, at least for a while. But back at the time of Harriet's death and Duwayne's deranged assault on the paint store, Daphne's "current steady," as she called her second husband when she wasn't calling him Eric the Ready, the Rude, or the Rod, was the town's new surgeon and resident oncologist, caught by her before he'd even got his bags unpacked. "Speaking of which, honey—assholes, I mean—I hope Ronnie's isn't as tight as it used to be, it's in for some heavy drilling. Mange likes the back door, you know. Did I ever tell you about his enema routines? Talk about sloppy sex! Peeyoo!" The person on the other end of the line, the mother of a one-year-old by then (which had aroused strong but ambivalent feelings in Daphne, who longed to have children only so long as she did not have to be a mother), was probably not interested in this intelligence, there was some other reason Daphne had called her, but for the moment it had flown her mind, which in truth caged very little, even when soberer than she was now. "Still, it was about the only time old misery-guts ever let himself go, so to speak. That's not Eric's problem. You couldn't ask for a more relaxed guy, so relaxed he's asleep most of the time. Honest to God, I greet him in nothing but a dab of perfume when he comes home from the hospital, and all he does is give me this sweet sad smile and fold up like dropped pants. Hey, I know they're working him too hard out there, but they're not working *that* part of him, are they? Well, let's face it, they probably are, it's the only answer, isn't it? He's out there taking the temperature of all those hotpants nurses all day, dipsticking himself to exhaustion, poor boy, nothing left for his house calls. They do the scoring, I get the snoring. So what's a girl gonna do? Well, Colt was back in town a couple of weeks ago, that bastard, you know, for his aunt Harriet's funeral. This is just between you and me, honey, not a word now—but Eric had the duty that day, so Colt and I skipped the burial part afterwards and went to have a drink together at the downtown hotel where he was staying. We sat there at that old wooden bar, not saying much, feeling nostalgic about that old place now that they say it's going to be torn down, and while we were in that mood, he suggested we go to his room and get laid just for old times' sake. What—?! Old times was a goddamned *rape,* for Christ's sake, was he crazy? That's what I told him. Still, forgive and forget, water under the britches and all that, right?

Besides, he was looking pretty good, now that his hair was long. And he did say he was sorry, he was just a dumb little shit back then who didn't know any better, he said, so I asked him what it was worth to him, now that he was a grown-up shit. He kind of sneered and said, 'You doing it for money now, Daph?' and I said, 'No, come on, you prick, you abused the hell out of me when I was just an innocent kid and now you come back here and I'm a happily married woman and you think you can just have me for a shot of gin or two? How cheap do you think I am?' He studied me for a moment, and then he grinned and said, 'Okay, how much?' I didn't blink an eye, honey. I just grinned right back at him and said: 'A thousand bucks, sweetie. In cash. It'll buy me my cherry back.' I clinked his glass with mine, he stared at me for a minute, then he shrugged, winked, went off to the bank. And let me tell you. The sonuvabitch got his money's worth. So did I. I'd forgotten it could be so good. Not since—well . . . Never mind." She was about to say, not since the red, red robin came bob, bob, bobbin', but having almost no friends left in this town, decided against it, a rare moment of prudence. "When it was over, I gave him half his money back. No kidding. Sheer gratitude. It was in small bills, so he flung it onto the bed and we fucked on that, pardon the French, it was like being a kid again and rolling around in autumn leaves. Except you don't get dust up your nose. Oh, speaking of the French—hello? are you there, honey? yes?" Daphne asked, recalling at last the reason she had phoned. "That was terrible news about your friend, Marie-what's-her-name, so sudden and all. I'm really sorry. No, really. I noticed she was looking a little green around the gills when she was visiting here last month, but who would have guessed, hunh? It's crazy! What a world! How is John taking it? I mean, they'd got pretty close, hadn't they? Speaking loosely, I mean, her love of flying, and all that. Well, hell, good old unflappable John, straight up as always, no doubt. What do you suppose it was that made her do it? Still carrying the torch for Yale, you think? Or . . . ? Hello—?"

News of the sudden violent death of the French penpal, the one who had upstaged and jinxed Daphne at the wedding four years before, reached town by way of Oxford's boy Cornell, back home from his educational graduation trip abroad in a state bordering on severe shell shock, such that the news itself was rather minimal and had to be imagined, or as

Ellsworth, whose task it was to accomplish this feat week after week for the readers of *The Town Crier* would say, recreated. Selectively recreated, for there was news, intriguing as it might be in oral form, that did not suit the printed pages of the town's weekly newspaper, the widely rumored events out at the Country Tavern during Marie-Claire's visit to town the month before just one example, an episode referred to only obliquely in her obituary a few weeks later when Ellsworth wrote that the deceased was known for her "passionate zest for life and happiness, so typical of the natives of that great enlightened nation, and not always understood by simpler, more straightforward prairie folk." That got him in a bit of trouble with the locals actually, but Ellsworth brushed it aside in his usual lofty manner, remarking to his friend Gordon, who had mentioned some of the complaints he had heard, that, suffocating as he was in the bloated provincial crassitude of this bumpkin town, he felt obliged to put the needle in from time to time, simply to survive. Ellsworth's sympathies were perhaps affected by the fact that he was at this time hoping to season his own existence with a touch of French zest, his ancient dreams of the bohemian life having been revived that summer when his photographer friend suddenly took in a live model, a pretty little uninhibited gamine from the trailer camp. Ellsworth, foreseeing the delightful possibility of an old-fashioned beaux-arts ménage à trois, as Marie-Claire herself might have put it, once again took to wearing his beret and a kerchief tied round his neck (it was still too hot for the cape) and began paying regular visits to Gordon's studio, having assisted in previous photo sessions and, for the sake of art and friendship, offering to do so again. Gordon, however, was less generous with Pauline than he had been with his mother, may she rest in peace, and did not seem enthusiastic about Ellsworth's suggested new arrangements, which caused a certain distance to grow up between the two men for a time, though Gordon did show Ellsworth a few of his photos of the girl and asked him to witness his marriage to her the following year. About all Ellsworth got out of the whole affair was a paragraph for his novel-in-progress (at that time, several years before the crisis provoked by the death of the car dealer's wife, a novel with only one character and as yet untitled, though perhaps to be called *The Artist's Ordeal*), an aesthetic meditation on the teleology of models, which he read aloud at a meeting of the Literary Society at the public library (only John's wife understood in the least his artistic intentions, he read for her alone) and then abandoned, the larger project as well, and not for the first time. At times, Ellsworth stepped forth onto the international stage to accept the world's accolades for his innovatively designed yet classically structured masterpiece of creative fiction, and at other times he recognized that he had only managed to write about fourteen pages and probably only three of those were keepers, and gave it up. His journalistic recreation of the final hours of the French artist-friend of John and his wife, his primary sources being either incoherent or inaccessible, he also abandoned, limiting himself in the end to a brief obituary which remarked on the "shock and sorrow that rippled throughout our community when the tragic news, like a thrown stone, fell upon it," and an "I Remember" column supplied graciously by John's wife and published a few months later.

The suicide of Marie-Claire surprised many in town, perhaps even his wife, but not John. Marie-Claire was not strung together for a long life, John knew, something was bound to snap. He knew, too, he had had a part in it, he and hinky-dinky, but as usual John, whom some blessed and some did not, had no regrets. It would be like regretting the way the cosmos worked. If anything, he felt a vague sense of relief. Sex with Marie-Claire was like grappling with a wild thing: there could not be two survivors, something had to die. And, finally, John being who he was, it was her turn. Which was Bruce's take on it as well, she having become their paradigmatic heroine of all such stories. One of Marie-Claire's lovers, a young art student she'd known prior to Yale, had thrown himself under the Metro before her very eyes, and she had driven a married man, a friend of her father's, completely mad. A psychiatrist, if the story could be entirely believed, not always the case, for even melodrama Marie-Claire melodramatized. These were the ones he knew about, no doubt there were other casualties in Marie-Claire's passion wars, not including the ones he and Bruce had made up. Even Yale's death, apparently so remote, seemed to John linked somehow to the way love and death got fused in that crazy furnace inside her, and indeed Yale's last letters, sent from the combat zone, hinted at his own awareness of such a connection. He spoke not of "death's embrace," but of "embracing death," as though it were some sort of compulsion (though his imperfect French might have been at fault here), and he described his army patrol's search-and-destroy missions into the jungle's "perilously erotic hot green thighs" as "lustful plunges into sweet extinction." Of course, Yale always did relish the double entendre, all that may have been, even if a bit dark, just a joke. As was hinky-dinky at first. Apparently, at their wedding reception, the old Ford dealer had recited some verses from "Mademoiselle from Armentières" to Marie-Claire. Probably his idea of being friendly to a foreign visitor. All she could remember, as she told John and his wife one night in a Paris bistro during their second honeymoon three years later (they had just come from watching a troupe of "Troglodytes" perform a "*Scène d'amour*" in the airless underground cabaret beneath their garret flat), was something about four wheels and a truck—John could easily supply the missing rhyme—and the refrain line which, she said, had been puzzling her ever since. "Wut ees hainqui-dainqui?" she asked, smiling her mischievous smile. "Ees like hainqui-painqui?" "It's the same thing," laughed John, squeezing his wife's hand beside him, "only you use your dinky, not your pinky." Two days later, his wife went shopping for presents for their two sets of parents back home, planning to meet Marie-Claire at a gallery cafe in Saint-Germain-des-Prés for lunch, and an hour before that luncheon date, Marie-Claire turned up at the garret, where John, in his briefs, was shaving at the paint-stained sink. This in itself was not unusual. Marie-Claire often turned up, unannounced, at odd moments. Whenever she did, she always seemed to need to use the facilities, squatting quickly there behind the refrigerator, chattering gaily all the while over the splash of her pee, her head peeking out around the refrigerator door, telling them about things that had happened to her on the way over, a bit earthy, yet quite delicate, too, something John knew he could never carry off, he was very impressed. On this occasion, however, she stepped up behind him at the sink, ran her hands into his briefs as though crawling into the cellar, and, her smoldering dark eyes reflected in the scalloped mirror over his bare shoulder, whispered: "I am so lonely, dear Zhahn. Yell, he ees so far. May you help me? I am so much needing ze . . . ze hainqui-dainqui . . . *Parlez-vous?*" And so it became a kind of gentle joke between them, and a kind of bond, and when the news came through a couple of days later about Yale's death in action, that bond was, in tears and frenzy, hotly yet somehow mournfully sealed, and thus Marie-Claire's unhappy fate as well, forging thereby in John's mind an indelible link between horror and compassion, compassion and horror.

Things were quiet in town that early summer, so many years ago, of the second honeymoon in Paris, almost like in the old days, for the place seemed to have a way of slowing down when John and his wife were gone. Or maybe it was just the warm season, school out, business slow, a time for taking it easy. And it wasn't completely lifeless. The two cinemas, the Palace downtown and the

Night Sky drive-in, both destined soon to disappear, still drew good crowds, the country club links and pool were busy, likewise the gun club and the driving range, beer sales were up, youngsters gathered as always at the bus station pinball machines, there was Little League baseball and softball for the fathers and the highway was slowly getting built, you couldn't say nothing was happening. The town was growing, too, or so they said. But it was just quieter somehow, Opal thought, more easygoing, gentler, more like times past when this town was all there was and could set its own pace, and except for the turnover of births and deaths, the people within it were always the same. The war had changed all that, and then airplanes, TV, the new highways, the atom bomb, her restless son had. But the TVs, with the networks into their summer reruns and full of little else but depressing war news anyway, were mostly turned off now, the new war itself was far away, the streets and skies were quiet, her son and his young wife were on the other side of an ocean: it felt . . . it felt like those lazy summer days, not so long ago, when John was away at camp, Mitch frequently off at the same time on some trip or another, fishing or business or politics, and she was free to drift quietly for a couple of weeks through a life of her own, read a book from the library maybe, clean out John's bedroom, sun awhile on a park bench as she was doing now, have lunch with friends (she was waiting for Kate and Harriet) and nothing she had to rush home for, nothing she had to *think* about. These last three years since the wedding had not been easy for Opal, adjusting to the life of an older in-law. Her son, toughened into manhood, was still recognizably her son, yet she felt increasingly estranged from him, and even from her memories of him as a boy, and that made her feel edgy all the time. She was fond of Barnaby's daughter, always had been, steady as they come, that child, but she seemed to know her less well now than she had before the marriage. Fond of Barnaby, too, though as for Audrey, the less said the better. Certainly, give her credit, Audrey had adjusted to in-lawhood better than Opal had, she and John couldn't be cozier. Free with her money, that always made a big impression on John, free with her flattery, too. Audrey seemed to share in the young couple's lives as though it was the most natural thing in the world. Opal always felt intrusive if she stopped by to visit them, uncaring if she didn't, she never knew what to do. And always when she visited, she couldn't put her finger on it, but always she sensed there was something missing in that house. John's room maybe. That house had been Barnaby's house, still was really, she could feel her son's discomfort there, so meanwhile, Mitch ridiculing her for it, she kept John's old room at her house just as he'd last lived in it, not having any other use for it anyway. She sighed, distressed that she was spoiling this nice day with such thoughts (though she had once written an "I Remember" column for Ellsworth's paper about the park, which she had always loved, saying that it was a place where one could bring one's heavy thoughts and leave them behind, like an old newspaper left on a bench), and nodded politely at the young police officer who had tipped his hat at her, passing by on the park path. One of John's schoolfriends probably. Oh yes, the one whose father . . . A disturbed family, as was true of so many of the poor. One wondered if it was wise to make policemen out of them. She started to point out to him the obscenity of the cast-off man's sheath lying like a squashed grubworm by the steps of the bandstand, but thought better of it. He might think it vulgar of her to know what it was. On the other hand, as uninhibited as the young were nowadays, it might have been part of a public performance, she would just reveal, once again, what an old fuddy-duddy she was. It was true, she was, and she was proud of it. It wasn't that she thought that people shouldn't use such things, only that they shouldn't display them rudely. She had always been a permissive mother, had she not, yet she had insisted always on a certain public decency. How can we bear one another without it? When Oxford, who sold those items openly in his drugstore, had proclaimed loudly one night out at the country club that dispensers of the things ought to be as common as gumball machines, she had responded that she had been pleased to notice that gumball machines were in fact disappearing and that soon therefore she might be able to agree with him, a reply that had earned her general approval, and even John seemed favorably amused. It was hard to tell what his wife thought, but of course that was always the case. She saw Harriet, all alone, coming down the leafy path from the direction of the library, where Kate worked. She didn't look well. The rumors, alas, were probably true. Harriet and Alf had had three children, all of whom had long since flown the coop, at least Opal could be grateful that John had decided to make his life here at home. There were grandchildren, too, their latest photos an obligatory lunchtime ritual. Maybe that, she thought, not for the first time, was what was missing in her son's house: three years and still waiting. Harriet seemed paler than usual and, as she drew nearer, Opal saw that she was crying. Oh dear. Opal rose in alarm and anticipation, smoothing down her skirt, mustering that reassuring stoic reserve for which she was, justly, so well known and appreciated.

Harriet, bringing the news, had heard about Yale's distant death in the jungle from her husband Alf, he having been called out to attend to poor Kate, who had collapsed on receiving the notice. Oxford, too, though he fussed confusedly over his wife, seemed utterly stricken, and little Cornell sat in a corner staring mutely, unwiped snot running down his quivering upper lip like liquid glue. Only Columbia, home from university where she was studying pre-med, had had the presence of mind to call Alf and then use a little basic first aid for treating shock victims, feet up and all that, both parents submitting to her ministrations as though in a trance. After everyone else had been taken care of and the body had been brought back from the war zone and the memorial service held, Lumby fell into something of a melancholic stupor herself, though no one noticed by then or took it seriously, no one except her teachers at college who flunked her out of pre-med. But she couldn't keep her eyes on the page, couldn't even sit through an exam without her mind drifting off. Yale had been her favorite, maybe the only human male in the world she had truly loved and admired, and the world just seemed emptied out when he was gone, not worth the effort. When her mother asked her what was wrong, she said nothing seemed real anymore, she couldn't believe in it, it was like everybody was just pretending. All life's an artifice, her mother said. We are born into the stories made by others, we tinker a bit with the details, and then we die. She said this so sadly it made Lumby cry, and then that made her angry. Her mother never did really get over what happened to Yale, she just slowly declined over time, becoming ever more silent, until she died three years later, shortening her suffering at the end with a bottle of sleeping tablets from the drugstore, a withdrawal and departure that Lumby, needing her, could never quite forgive her for. Before that, however, there was one brief moment when the family pulled itself together to receive Yale's French sweetheart Marie-Claire when she paid a return visit to the town a year after his death, staying with John and his wife, who was an old friend, and also coincidentally Yale's girlfriend once upon a time. Lumby's parents treated Marie-Claire like a daughter that week, hosting quiet, somewhat dreary dinners, taking her out to visit Yale's grave, going through all of Yale's belongings with her, presenting her with many mementos of him, and returning her letters to her. She received these things gratefully, tearfully even, trembling all over, yet left them behind when she went home, taking Cornell with her like something she'd won at the carnival but didn't want; they had to bundle Yale's effects up and mail them to her. She was not there to receive them. Lost forever, those things. Nearly lost her stupid little brother Corny in the bargain.

Paying her respects at Yale's tomb was not the only purpose of Marie-Claire's visit to town that year. She was also returning her friends' second honeymoon trip to Paris of the year before and attending her little godchild's christening (godmotherhood not really a part of that Protestant ceremony, but on the subject of religion John and his wife were generously broadminded and worked it in), which had been especially arranged for her arrival. The baby, named Clarissa in honor of Marie-Claire, was a restless child who kept the household up all night ("She is, what you say, a girl-party, no?" said Marie-Claire with pride), and all day, too, as though afraid that she might miss something if she closed her little eyes. When Marie-Claire, touring John's airport, asked him what they would have called the baby had it been a boy, he jokingly replied, little Hankie, thank-ee. Though reminiscent still of the homemade dirt strips of aviation's early days, John's airport had been expanding. Over the year, getting friends to pitch in, and with money from his mother-in-law, John had been able to install a generator out there, build a new hangar, and clear enough land to extend his runway to nearly six thousand feet, about half of it paved. The paved length was all he needed for his little single-engine four-seater, of course, but he was already thinking far ahead to the time when jets and cargo planes would land here and he might even have a feeder airline of his own, or at least be operating some kind of air taxi service, linking his town to the great urban centers, which, from up on high, seemed to shimmer on the curved horizon like untapped treasure troves, spoils for the airborne adventurer. From up there, he could see, too, displayed like a briefing chart, how his town down below would grow, and in which direction, which properties he should buy, which sell, and where he should build his malls and housing developments. These revelations his wife missed out on mostly, grounded by her mother as she was, the doctor's prenatal seconding of the motion, after the difficult birth, still in place as well. The way things turned out, John probably should have left Marie-Claire on the ground, too, but though John enjoyed women in every imaginable way, what he loved most at that youthful time in his life was getting blown at the controls a couple of thousand feet up in the sky, and Marie-Claire had a kind of crazy explosive voracity, as he had discovered already last year in Paris, which not only turned her small delicate mouth with its pebbly rows of teeth and muscular tongue into something between a hydraulic pump and an automatic carwash gone amok, but which seemed to possess her entire body, causing her to tremble violently from head to foot and, whimpering like an animal at the door, even as her mouth with its flickering tongue raced madly up and down his shaft, to clutch and claw at his flesh as though trying to dig her way inside. Of course, fucking Marie-Claire was, if sometimes a bit like throwing yourself off a cliff, an even greater treat, but this was not Paris and at home on the ground that late spring, everyone supposedly mourning Yale, he was trying, with only partial success, to keep his distance from this wildly unpredictable girl, so susceptible to contagious sorrows, and up in the air fucking was impossible.

Or so he thought. It was his new troubleshooter Nevada more than a decade later who finally taught him otherwise, though she was more an athlete than an inflamed and impetuous lover. By then John had bought and sold a fleet of planes (though he still had the little Skyhawk and even took it up now and then for old times' sake), and the airport itself, now incorporated into the town and eligible for federal funding, had municipal electricity and water, its own septic system, parallel runways big enough for executive jets and small pressurized turboprops, a modest terminal and office building with toilets, payphones, and food and drink dispensing machines, a crew of mechanics and cargo handlers and a fulltime manager (his old football coach), parking lots for both planes and cars, fuel pumps and storage tanks, well-equipped hangars and repair sheds and warehouses, and new runway landing lights like glowing sapphires that could be activated from the air with a radio signal in the same way as automatic garage doors, a little parlor trick that always delighted the women when they found themselves caught out after dark, still dangerously high up off the ground, a trick that Marie-Claire, who would have loved it, did not live, poor girl, to see. Well, a sad story, but Marie-Claire was a lady of sad stories, excess and abandon the flame to her mothy passions, as Bruce once said of her when John told him of his Paris adventures. Not so their Nevada. Nevada was tough, smart, beautiful, efficient, cool. And spectacularly talented. There was no position she could not or would not assume, many of which neither Bruce nor John had ever enjoyed before, and she had a vagina clever as a trained circus animal. Bruce called it the "evil beaver," and loved it at least as much as did John, who first sent her to him as a kind of comic valentine, telling him to go take a flying fuck. Out of this world! As John said after one of their weekend cabin revels, it was as though she were what he had been looking for all along, and Bruce thought so, too, even though John was speaking as a compassionate pragmatist, Bruce more from the nihilistic point of view.

Of course, she blew her cool that first time up, but lots of women must have peed themselves in John's planes, probably he got a charge out of it. Certainly he liked to get them scared, she could see that right away in the sensuous menace of his crooked grin, it was a way of softening them up for what he wanted out of them, which was not just sky-high head, she sensed, but also a kind of quivering compliance, and scared was one emotion Nevada did not have to fake up there, that first time anyway. After a loop or a roll or two, most women, leaking helplessly from every orifice, probably went grabbing for his joystick like a security blanket. Any straw in a whirlwind, as they say. "Wow! What a trip!" she groaned as, her heart still pounding, she wiped her mouth against his strong lined throat and nuzzled in the graying hair behind his ear, wondering, somewhat lightheadedly as he took one hand off the controls long enough to give her soggy thatch a grateful squeeze, where her wet panties, flung from the window like a captured battle flag or a candy wrapper, might have landed. John had just told her a moment before, his free hand clenched in her hair then and his hips beginning to buck, that what he loved most in this world were the days of his life, and Nevada, glad merely that she was going to see another, now thought she rather liked the days of his life, too. "My turn," she whispered, stroking him stiff again. "If you can manage it," he laughed, somewhat surprised, and to show what a clever girl she was, she did a dexterous split across his lap, burying that magnetic pole of his, and, switching her torso from left to right without losing him or interfering with his piloting, corkscrewed him, as it were, thus providing him, as he dropped creamily (she seemed to hover for a moment, weightless, tingling all over), then pulled up fiercely, climactically, into her as her augmented mass bore explosively down on him, with the line with which he'd later send her up to Bruce. He loved it, loved her, she felt, he said he'd never known anyone quite like her, and she began to see how John might be different from the rest, how he might be pointing her toward something new, dizzyingly new, and how Rex might soon become a nuisance. Not to mention, of course, John's wife.

When Nevada told Rex about the scare she got and what John had said up there about loving the days of his life, Rex said: "That's his privilege, baby. He's a rich fucker. His days don't cost him anything. How can you help but love your life if every day's like winning the lottery?" Rex, who loved Nevada in his bluesy downbeat way and so had his own notions about what love was, had started out here in town working for John, like most people did, but he had got fed up with the bullying sonuvabitch and so blew that shit off and now he worked for Stu, repairing cars at the old boy's Ford-Mercury garage, working from a fake-book and a good right hand. No green in it. Nevada pulled down a lot more than he did, and sweated less doing it. But it kept him from wigging out, alone in a motel room or a lousy bar. Rex still wasn't thirty, but one thing he had learned: making money was the easiest fucking thing in the world, but you had to have some to get some, and when it had come to handing out the stakes, he'd got left out, simple as that. Man, he really hated fat cats like John and his wife, not because they were loaded, but because they didn't even know why it was they had it so good. He fixed their cars for them, all right, but in more ways than one. He'd put a new fanbelt on for them, but loosen a wheel or drain the brakes. He'd grind their valves, then leave the rocker gasket off, watching all the time for an angle, a gimmick, his break, access to a piece of the action. He hated Stu, too, but the old fart was a harmless boozer who spent most of his time dozing or telling his tedious cracker jokes, generally steering clear of the service area, so Rex got along all right with him. It was during one of Stu's dumb jokes one day that Rex looked up and found himself staring, from under her Town Car, straight up John's wife's skirt. She was patiently tuned in to Stu's bull, her back to Rex, and neither of them noticed him down there, so he had a good long look. He couldn't say afterwards exactly what it was he saw, it was like staring at the Milky Way through a telescope that wasn't quite in focus, but it made him feel like he was getting something for nothing, a piece of John's goods, so to speak, and it got him so hot, he had to reach under and pull himself off to keep from howling or going for the pot and jumping her where she stood. That'd give old Stu a punchline he'd—*ungh!*—never forget, he thought as he came, exploding powerfully into his greasy overalls. He opened his eyes again, still holding himself, still coming probably, feeling loose and dreamy, wanting another look, one he could remember, but she was gone. His mouth was dry. He felt deflated. Like a loser again. Cheated and robbed. He took his screwdriver and punched a hole in her muffler, thinking: So that honcho motherfucker loves the days of his life. Terrific. Me, I just get through them. And he spat drily and punched another hole.

Though he seemed not to notice, Stu was aware all along of Rex's hatred, thought of it as a sick streak in the boy, a transmission failure of a sort, knew also Rex was stealing him blind, but somehow, in spite of all this, Rex's malice, his paranoia, horniness, thievery, Stu felt some kind of kinship with the lad, and generally let him do what he wanted. Even lent a helping hand, often as not, though it made him feel a little like his block was cracked. Sometimes, just to let Rex know he wasn't completely stupid, Stu would try to catch him in some mischief or other. He'd leave a tenspot on a counter or a workbench, say, then demand to know what had happened to it when it disappeared. The kid would scowl at him, act like he was dealing with a crazy man, and Stu would have to reverse gears, back down, no longer sure whether he'd put the ten bucks there or only intended to. Same with the other stuff that went missing: Maybe it wasn't there in the first place, or vanished years ago. Couldn't say. Goddamn memory. Strangest maybe was the way he kept throwing that black-hearted whelp and his little darlin' together. He knew Daphne had the hots for the young scamp, the way she dressed and teased and showed her backseat every chance she got. Broke old Stu's heart to see them carrying on, but weirdly it gave him a charge, too, as though by giving Daph the keys to the inner office and leaving the lot on some invented errand or other, or letting Rex give her a ride to the Getaway, he were getting a stalled car moving again. Maybe, somehow, he was reliving his cheatin' days through the tacky little hotrod, whom he hated and feared, yet felt close as a father to. Stu had this ambivalent relationship with about everybody in town. He thought John was a great guy, for example, top of the line, but he didn't really like him. He did like John's wife, liked her a lot, hell, he'd do anything in the world for that girl, yet at the same time he felt he couldn't care less about her. For the most part, this relationship was mutual: everybody in town loved old Stu, their hearts went out to him, yet they all considered him a worthless old drunk who might as well be dead. He was everybody's friend, but nobody knew him.

Maybe Stu's ambivalent attitude toward Rex's malice had something to do with his notion that as far as life expectancy went, bad luck was good, good bad, a notion Alf heard him trying to explain in the country club bar one night (an unusual night, as it turned out) to Trevor, the insurance salesman, meaning to put him straight, he drawled, about what was wrong with his damfool actuarial tables, meaningless as a used-car price tag. There were others standing around, too, or perched on barstools, most of them having long since stopped listening to the garrulous old lush, though he still had the polite attention of John's wife beside him, always patient with the foolishness of others. Stu had just sold a Cougar and an Explorer XLT that day and so his rear axle was really dragging tonight, he said, since he thought of car sales as additions on the way to his own funeral: each man was given to sell so many cars in his life, and then: *pfft!* "Get ready to tow me to the junkyard, ole buddy," he growled, clutching his chest and rolling his eyes as though it were one of his punchlines, "I feel another sale comin' on!" And Trevor wheewheed in that silly sniggering way he had, covering his mouthful of bad teeth with his ring-studded left hand. Daphne, relatively sober and out of her usual baggy sweatsuit with the dirty seat and into a pink party dress for a change, told Stu to shut up, he was depressing everybody, and Stu sobered up for a second and gave her a look Alf hadn't seen on his face since before Winnie died. Then he grinned his gap-toothed country-boy grin and, wrapping his drinking arm around John's wife, asked her if she'd heard the one about the old boy here in town who'd died a few years back of diarrhea but his widow insisted they write "gonorrhea" as the cause on his inspection sticker. "Well, ole Doc here he wouldn't have none of that, y'know, bein' the—*hee ha!*—lawr-abidin' sort and knowin' the difference between them two 'rhears' and maybe even how to spell the little suckers, on accounta him havin' a college diploma and all, and he reminds her that ain't exactly the—*haw haw!*—gospel truth. 'Aw, hellfire, I know it,' she—*whoof! wharr!*—says, 'but I'd—*hoo!*—I'd rather folks—*yarff! hee! harr!*—folks remembered the old clunker as a—*heef!*—as a—*whoo!*—'" And, wheezing and snorting helplessly, he dropped his drink down John's wife's bosom and fell off his stool. Alf helped Daphne drag Stu out to his car and pour him in, and as he propped him up in the front seat, pushed the lock button on the door, and (Stu was muttering something incomprehensible about a fucked-up transmission) closed it, he thought: It's silly to keep people like Stu alive. Alf felt ashamed for his own part in it. The old fellow, drooling, slid back against the door and batted his freckled head on the window. Stu's wife Daphne, staring out at the little red pennant flapping over the eighteenth hole, now floodlit, said: "It's a goddamn mess," and Alf thought so, too. When he went back into the bar, vaguely uneasy about letting Daphne drive Stu home, he found John's wife holding her silk blouse in her fingertips, away from her breasts, flapping it about as though to shake the gin out. There were a lot of jokes, or what passed for jokes, about the tonic virtues of gin, the new improved flavor of mother's milk, and so on, and when they asked Alf his medical opinion, he sniffed and said that they *smelled* like martinis, okay, but he'd never seen them served in cups that big before. Trevor giggled like a moron at that one, and his wife Marge said: "Well, the party's getting a little rough!" Marge's cups wouldn't hold a martini's olive.

How much, his little darlin' Daphne wondered, driving foggily home that night, did Stu know about her and Rex? Plenty, probably. Hard to say, though, if it mattered. Maybe it even gave the old coot a peculiar pleasure to star in one of his own jokes. Made him a kind of living legend. "There was this old farmer, doncha know, who took him a young bride, a hot-wired little sports job who just couldn't get enough juicin' and left the old yokel too pooped out from so much time down in the Red River Valley to get his chores done out in the back acres. Ffoo! Fuckin' spread goin' to hell in a hangbasket and him, too, see. So directly he went and took on this young hired hand . . ." Did old Stu take notice when she stood over the horny boy while the kid was down in the pit, offering him the view she'd seen him gobbling up from the other women who came out there to get their oil changed and their motors tuned? Was he watching when she squatted down, knees spread, while sexy Rexy was on his back under a car, to kid around with him about needing a valve job or getting her own underbody greased? And if he did, if he was, did he care? Daphne had slipped into the somewhat boozy habit over the recent years of wearing a floppy fat-hiding sweatsuit wherever she went, gave her the illusion of being an athlete by day and it cushioned her and served for peejays when she fell over at night. Now, though, she was back into skirts again, not the old ones, of course, which no longer fit, had to buy a whole new closetful of the damned things, new underpants, too, with ribbons and peekaboo crotches and cute little messages the randy mechanic could read. Which he did, at first by long eye-filling gazes, hand on his connecting rod, later by braille, as you might say, which led her to crack back, when he alluded, somewhat cynically, to the mystery of her being attracted to a guy like him: "Mystery? Hell, honey, I'm an open book!" As the boy laughed his snarling laugh and nibbled at her clit, Daphne lit up and, blowing smoke at the motel room mirrors, thought about the long stupid shaggy-dog joke she and Stu had been playing out for so many years. Some of it right here in these rooms when warhorse Winnie was still around, though it really went back much farther than that, back to her best friend's wedding reception and her mythical handful of strawberries and cream, old Stu's "day of destiny," as he called it, half her goddamned life. Maybe it was time for the punchline. "Fuck me, sweetie pie," she whispered, stubbing out the smoke and squinting appraisingly at the tense mirrored buttocks of the creature hunched over her like a powerful predator gnawing at a carcass. "Fuck me hard!"

Veronica had been a witness to Daphne's attention-grabbing act with the strawberries that day of John's wedding, a day that for Veronica was also, as it was for Stu, a day of destiny, but like all such days in her life, a dark one. She was still haunted by the consequences, it made her shudder to think about it. Or him. Gave her migraines for a week. Ronnie, as she was known back then to her classmates, Daphne being one of them, had always been intimidated by that brash, promiscuous, and unpredictable girl, a girl who always seemed to have so much more fun than Ronnie did, even when she did such awful things, things Ronnie could not bring herself to do, and then did anyway. It was a no-win situation. When she resisted Daphne she got ridiculed, and when she tried to keep up with her she got in trouble. Like that night before the famous wedding when Daphne subverted the hen party and led an assault mission out to the Country Tavern to invade the stags. Ronnie had argued against the idea, which she thought of as dangerous though didn't say so. What she said was, let the boys be, they won't like it. Daphne said the boys didn't know what they liked until they saw it, and if Ronnie was chickenshit she could stay behind. So, naturally, she had to go, feeling she had a certain reputation to defend since that night at the drive-in with John which everybody seemed to know about, but first they argued about it for a while. There were others who had their doubts like Ronnie and a couple of them went home. Finally, when they did get out there, the party was pretty much over; certainly that guy Daphne had had her eye on all day was gone, and so was John. Daphne blamed Ronnie for that, said if she hadn't been such an uptight pain in the patoot, they'd have got out here sooner and maybe had some fun tonight. Then they all got back in their cars and gunned it out of there, leaving her behind; Ronnie had to walk home all alone, kicking herself all the way, hating Daphne, but hating her own timidity, too. Now and then lights would appear on the road behind her, guys coming back from the tavern, no doubt, and she would have to hide down in a ditch or behind trees or bushes, not knowing how to explain herself out there and afraid of what they might do if they found her alone, drunk as they were. Sometimes she felt like just letting them do whatever they wanted, what did it matter, and she only half hid as they passed by, but no one stopped. Not until she reached town, a few blocks from Main Street. A car pulled over. A silvery Ford Mustang, looking like a ghost in the moonlight: Veronica recognized it, and her heart skipped a beat as the door opened to her. When she saw who the driver was, she realized she was about to do something Daphne would never have dared to do. A first. Though it would be hard to brag about it. Happened in another town. Something about wild oats, he said. She got home a little before dawn. And a few weeks later, she had to go see Alf, tears in her eyes, and ask him for that dreadful favor, he stubbornly reluctant (it was a big crime then, he had a lot to lose, she knew that) until she told him who the father was.

Ronnie had tears in her eyes again that night, years later, when her nemesis's slobbering hubby, drunk as a dog, spilled his drink down John's wife's front in the country club bar, but this time they were tears of laughter. That it should happen to *her!* It was too funny! Everyone in the club was laughing, everyone except the father of the child Veronica finally did have, who was about to barf. Happened to Maynard from time to time. His "tender sensibilities," as someone had cracked so many years ago, same cause then as now. A form of mourning, as he thought of it. He took a deep breath and held it, staring hard at the kid behind the bar, who was trying to act cool, wiping glasses, moving bottles around, but whose wide-eyed gaze was locked on the wet blouse. Whose wasn't, but suffering Maynard's? John's linen-suited accountant Trevor was sniggering in his hiccuppy way while he stared at it, lard-ass Waldo was hee-hawing, John's old man was grinning and grinding away at his cigar the way Maynard, back in school, used to chew rubber bands. Beside him, Maynard's wife tittered and snorted like the witless beak-nosed twit she was, pushing her own cups forward, no doubt secretly jealous of the attention John's wife was getting. Veronica was the material form Maynard's bottomless misery had finally taken, the objective embodiment of his own self-loathing which it pleased him to strike out at from time to time, to slap and pummel and bury in curses, trying to purge himself of that which could not be purged, but giving him relief at least during the blind moments of his rage. The first wave of nausea passed (he was startled to notice Waldo's wife Lorraine staring at him as though alarmed and he quickly looked away, that stupid cow, was he that transparent?), but then old Alf, coming back in from mailing Stu and Daphne home, jokingly poked his bent snout at her cleavage and sniffed, and the sickness returned, forcing Maynard, desperately clutching the frayed garter in his pocket, to swallow hard, then bolt down his own martini, hoping only it would not come right back up. His eyes watered and for a moment John's wife was just a formless blur, not quite there. He blinked and brought her back, suddenly frightened about the risky moves (this was just before all the shit came down, when Maynard the eternally damned still thought he was going to whip his hateful cousin's ass at last) that he and Barnaby were making. He was doing it for her sake, hers and her father's, and John sure as hell deserved the pasting they were about to give him, but what would be *her* take on it? Well, she would be hurt, of course, that was unavoidable, but could she come to understand the issues at stake, the principles involved? In his fantasies, orphaned by the brawl between husband and father, she would turn to him for guidance and consolation (over and over, she had fallen, weeping, into Maynard's gentle and caring embrace), but did she have even the foggiest notion of what John had done to her father? It might look like sheer madness to her. Well, they'd all know soon enough, it was fast coming to a head. John had invited them all over to dinner on the weekend to announce the merger. Barnaby would be there, John's parents, his own dad, John's accountant, people from the bank. There was no turning back. Maynard set his empty glass down on the bar as though to end a sentence, just as John's depraved college buddy Bruce, a frequent hangabout in town of late, tucked his cigarette in the corner of his smirking lips, took the bar rag away from Kevin, and turned to John's wife to help her wipe her blouse—Maynard headed for the men's room, hoping his urgent stride would get him there in time.

Kevin, who doubled as country club pro and barkeep, was keeping a close eye on events that night, after what had happened earlier in the day. John's wife had always been a mystery to him, more so now. Kevin had come to town a dozen years ago, just out of university and one boozily happy but ineffectual year in the backwaters of the pro circuit; he'd meant to move on, get back in the competition, never did. His father, an upstate political friend of John's and a business colleague, had got him the job here, his predecessor having flown the coop that summer with a wild teenybopper, we should all be so lucky. The place sounded like more fun than it was, but given his prospects he might have ended up in scummier holes. He managed the club, gave lessons, ran the bar and the pro shop, entered a few smalltime tournaments just to keep his hand in and his name in circulation. Long hours, but they paid him for them. Women were easy enough to come by, everything from highschool kids to their grandmothers, he got in at least seventy-two holes of golf a week, the food and booze were free, and there was a lot of loose change lying around, so not a bad life. Giving lessons could be a drag, but it was extra money, and it was sometimes a way of making out. He found that women often liked him to help them with their grip and swing by standing behind them and reaching around to take hold of their hands on the club, one thing sooner or later then leading to another. And that was why he was watching John's wife closely that night that Stu gave her knockers a gin bath. She'd had a lesson with him that day and had seemed puzzled when he'd tried to correct her open grip. Almost without thinking about it, he had stepped behind her and reached round to cover her hands with his, and as he pressed up, almost ritually, against her soft buttocks in their pink and green Bermuda shorts, he was overtaken suddenly by a delicious sensation unlike any he'd ever felt before, not exactly sexual though it gave him a hard-on that nearly ripped his fly apart, more like the silky feeling he sometimes got when lying with a woman and staring at a starry sky. Then, just as suddenly, how could he explain it, she didn't seem to be there. He was holding only the club. He let go of it in alarm: and there she was, going into her swing. And so tonight, a night at the club like any other, the noise, the corny jokes, the usual barbs, John's wife the center of attention as she always was, Kev was just into his third scotch and beginning to relax—and then, suddenly, there was the spilled drink. Did she seem to dim slightly, to slip from view as the gin splashed down her front? Kevin reared up straight, grabbed a glass to wipe. No, there she was, plain as day, he was just imagining things. Maybe even trying to. Probably he ought to take it easy on the hootch. When John's pilot pal snatched up the bar rag and dabbed at her boobs, no problem, they bounced like anyone else's, and Kevin felt reassured.

John's accountant Trevor had an opportunity that night to take a steady contemplative look at John's wife's breasts and, with a little more courage, might even have been able to dab at them with a cocktail napkin, too, like John's happy-go-lucky friend, just in the spirit of the fun of course, and maybe that would have helped or maybe it wouldn't have, but as it was, by the time they got home, he could no longer remember what it was he had seen, could not even be sure Alf's rude remark about cup size was in any way descriptive. Vanished, yet again. If he let his mind drift, without concentrating, the expression on her face would come floating back: a kind of smile, or not a smile exactly, more like placid consent, or else a mild annoyance, politely contained. But the more he thought about it, of course, the less anything was there. Earlier in the day, he had seen the photographer take her picture during a golf lesson with the young pro, a picture he would very much like to see now, but he didn't know how to ask for it. Perhaps he could do a study on golfing styles and life expectancy. He got out his graphs and charts while Marge was getting ready for bed and attempted to locate her point again. No use. It just wouldn't stick. Too many variables or something. He recalled the old car dealer's system of calculations and knew there to be a certain truth hidden in them: did this truth apply to John's wife? He thought about her good fortune, her beauty, her wealth, her family, her seeming happiness, her sound health (he had seen the lab test results from her last physical, had perhaps a clearer image in his head of her blood and urine than he had of the expression on her face that night, thought sometimes he could even hear the beat of her heart inside the x-rayed chest or feel the squishy viscous dampness of the smear), and it occurred to him that all these assets were as equivocal as the "Negatives" on the lab test results: they revealed only absences, fixed nothing, contributed to the enigma of her existence rather than helping to resolve it. Marge was already snoring, sleep overtaking her with the same brute force that thirst or hunger always did. He knew about Marge's life expectancy: she would live long and vigorously, but death would one day take her by the throat and ravage her mercilessly as though itself seized by a violent passion.

What were snoring Marge's dreams? She claimed to have none, sleep for her a complete blackout, a departure into nonexistence, every waking a resurrection. For dreams, if she missed them (she didn't), she had her friend Lorraine's to wallow in, Lorraine a host to vivid nocturnal theater of the most elaborate sort and, while evasive on the subject of her waking life, a prolix reteller of her dreamtime adventures, often as not with a revelatory tag. Thus, the night that Stu spilled his drink down John's wife's front at the country club bar, she dreamt that she and Marge were in a breast shop trying on different sizes and models and joking about the bizarre value men in their foolishness placed on the silly things. John was there, and he told them it wasn't the breasts that were important but the nipples, and with that they got serious about their selection. There were all kinds, heaped up in wooden trays. John tried to make Marge wear a pair that looked like golfballs, but she fought him off. Yet ended up with them, just the same, dazzlingly white and marked only with a crimson dot (they came in a package of three, not two, but the third had been used and had a deep dirty gash). Lorraine fancied ones that looked like little eyeballs with lids that closed (she somehow had the idea that if she could flutter her lashes from her breasts, she told Marge, she'd have more luck), but somebody stole them. Who? Everyone was laughing, so she was pretty sure it was Waldo. "The sonuvabitch is having an affair, or is about to," is what she said the next day to Marge, which was not unlike prophesying the rising of the sun maybe, but Lorraine knew with a certainty now, because of the dream, that it was true. A pattern exposed by purloined nipples. John's wife was in the dream, too, but Lorraine couldn't see her, or at least couldn't describe her that next day to Marge. "Maybe she owned the place," she said with a shrug. What Lorraine didn't tell Marge, not yet anyway, needing more time to think about it, was why Maynard had startled her so the night before, when all eyes were on John's wife and her soaked blouse. Clear as a bell, amid the laughter and the joking and the scraping of chairs and barstools, she had heard it, like a cry of pain: "*I love you!*" She'd glanced around in alarm and knew as soon as she saw him that it was Maynard who'd cried out. But his lips were pressed together, his scowling face with its dark jowls was devoid of any hint of that tender emotion, and there were no signs anyone else in the room had heard it. She was sure of it, though. And the feeling she'd had about John's wife just then, at least as she remembered it the next day, was exactly the feeling she had about her later in the dream.

Lorraine was right of course, dream prophecy or no, about Waldo's infidelity, though she may have underestimated its extent. In truth, he was fucking around at every opportunity and the opportunities were far from few. Clarissa's view of her father's malls as magic spaces was one Waldo, had he known of it, would have shared. Since John had moved the home decoration business out to the new big one, Waldo was having a rousing great time, working some of the same turf Clarissa did, though at a different mall. He could have done with a more intimate business maybe than paint and wallpaper, but Waldo could work bedroom fabrics and bathroom fixtures like others worked novelties and lingerie, and there were always the food courts and the movie lobbies and the corridor outside his place of business which faced a bank of phones and a ladies' room. Much of the traffic was off the highway, it was like meeting in an airport terminal, but his targets were less the transient crowds than the mall's own working staff, a lot of them drifters themselves, migrant labor from out of town, just passing through. He'd hired a lot of them, with or without the telltale bruises on the inner arms that made them more vulnerable, and fucked not a few. He'd had some bad times, some of these gals being pretty tough cookies and a far cry from the sorority debs of the golden age, but mostly good times, hard, clean, invigorating, and without complicating residue. Quickies he took to a little office behind the stock room, a Vice Presidential perk (thanks, good brother John), but for true love he used Dutch's motel, his old pal there having given him a key to use, asking only that he call ahead to be sure the room was free. It made Waldo proud to live in a place where folks went out of their way for you, just because they knew and respected you. Smalltown life: shit, you couldn't beat it with a stick.

Dutch, who shared Waldo's appreciation of smalltown life, was grateful to the paint-and-wallpaper man for taking up some of the slack at the motel with his impromptu midday affairs when otherwise business was slow, and when the room, even when curtained, was still pretty well lit. Like a clear stream on a gray day. Dutch now owned a piece of the new luxury motel up near the Interstate and had money in a number of John's enterprises, including his cargo operations, but his little motel at the edge of Settler's Woods with its Getaway Bar and Grill and secret Back Room was his real home and where you could usually find him any hour of any day when he wasn't fishing. Dutch of course preferred his performers young, highschool fumblers and nervous virgins festooned with zits, cocky college kids excitedly bringing home their newly acquired expertise, but this was prime-time pageantry mostly. For daytime shows you had to take what you could get. True, there was something drearily predictable about Waldo's scores, but for Dutch, a movieseat connoisseur by now of meat fever's finer points, there were never ever two exactly alike, and Waldo himself was always open to any kind of goofiness and generous with the money that perked these women up, losers mostly, or at least that helped them go along with Waldo's games, which, depending on how much he'd had to drink, could be a bit rough but never mean. The most memorable of recent vintage was the woman with the colored dice tattooed between her tits and what looked like the Second Coming all over her butt (Dutch, silently, pleaded with Waldo to bring the woman over to the mirror to show him the sights, but no such luck), who told Waldo, in between humps, if he gave her a hundred-dollar bill she'd turn a trick he'd never seen before. Waldo, grinning expectantly, got one out. She rolled it up carefully, holding it up for him to see, then, spreading her legs wide to give him, and Dutch, too, a good view, slowly inserted it into her gash, pushing it deeper and deeper until it disappeared. Then she invited Waldo to try to get it out of there without using his hands. This was the sort of challenge the old sportsman relished, especially whilst recharging, and laughing his donkey laugh, he went after it with mouth, tongue, nose, cock, even his toes. "Give up?" "Naw!" He tried some of the gadgets that Dutch left lying around in that room ("No hands!" the woman giggled, the dice bouncing on her chest), but finally it was the simplest tool that worked: his own breast-pocket toothbrush clenched between his teeth. He worked the brush end in past the rolled-up bill and slowly eased it out of there. He unrolled it and what he found was a single dollar bill. "Haw!" he snorted in amazement and went fishing with his hands, causing the woman to whoop and squeal, but that C-note was gone for good. To Waldo's credit: to his delight. He gave that apocalyptic high roller a good fucking after and tucked another hundred up her gully to match. Witnessing Waldo having a poke was, admittedly, about as much fun most of the time as watching slugs fuck, but Dutch admired the guy's gutsy persistence, his bighearted determination to get it up, and up again. Too many wimps in this town got turned into grumpy house pets too fast, and as for their women, if they were having it off with other men more like men, this was not, for the most part, happening at Dutch's motel, though there were entertaining exceptions, Daphne and her young well-hung mechanic most recently. Irregular showtimes, but most often between lunch and happy hour. Daphne's ass had, to put it kindly, matured over the years, but then so had everyone else's, Dutch's included, he did not begrudge her this, especially given the exhibition the two of them were staging for him now. They went at it like animals, ravenous and wild, and Dutch, too, watching them from the Back Room, would often find himself up on his feet and pumping away like a madman, having to bite his tongue to keep from letting out a whoop when he popped his cork. And it was after one of these sheet-ripping furniture-wrecking sessions one afternoon that Dutch suffered a jolt of déjà vu that took him back a decade or more to the days when his motel was new, when old Stu's Winnie was still alive and Stu and Daphne were going at it in this same room. It was Daphne who brought it up then, too, if he remembered rightly. Now, Daph and her grease monkey were stretched out smoking and Dutch had just zipped up and turned to leave the Back Room, go check on things at the bar, when, over his shoulder and on the other side of the mirror, he heard Daphne say: "Hey, lover. Listen. What are we going to do about the old man?"

Déjà vu, as Ellsworth could have told anyone who wanted to know, was French for "already seen," and was properly used to describe that uncanny but illusory experience of feeling that something that was happening for the first time had actually happened before. It was in this sense that he had used it in his novel-in-progress when the Artist, leading his Model down to a riverbank and perching her on a stone there, has the sensation suddenly, as the Model leans forward to peer down into the gently flowing river, that he has witnessed this entire scene before, perhaps in a dream or a vision, but certainly at some psychic level profounder yet less concrete than the literal prospect that confronts him now. Alas, this was another scene largely obliterated by the Stalker: only the barren stone remained like an unoccupied pedestal, or something hard fallen into reality, inexplicably, out of a dream. Dreams and déjà vu often seemed to go together. The preacher's wife Beatrice tripping or Lorraine in the middle of her histrionic nighttime theater often felt that they somehow "recognized" the scenes they were in, as though from another life, just as Floyd, slicing the throat of the redhaired faggot outside Wichita, had the uncanny feeling, and not for the first time in such matters, that it had all happened before, as if in a crazy dream he'd had. Or, weirdly, was still having. What caused Veronica to faint in church when Reverend Lenny quoted from the Second Letter of John the Elder to the Elect Lady and Her Children, if it was not this sort of déjà vu? When Opal remarked to Kate, back before the librarian died, that sometimes she felt like she'd dreamt her whole life before living it (she'd only meant to suggest how simple and predictable it all was), her friend had frightened her by replying: "You probably have some childhood story you don't want to tell me, Opal . . ." That Kate. She'd also told Opal once that falling in love in a dream and then meeting that love in real life, an example of déjà vu often reported, if seldom believed, should not be regarded as an uncanny experience at all, and that those who did so held to an outdated, mechanistically passive theory of perception. "The percept is, always, a creation," she said, or something like that. Over Opal's head, really, and when she said so, Kate said: "We see what we want to see." "Oh yes." When Clarissa and Jennifer asked Uncle Bruce if he believed it was possible to fall in love in a dream, he said it was the only way he had ever fallen in love, all the women he had loved and even some of those he had married he had met first in dreams, and it was just a matter of recognizing them when they turned up later. In fact, he was still waiting for some of his dream loves to show up in the real world. Then a wink their way: or grow up.

That dreamlike "I've been here before" feeling that occasionally overwhelms travelers to strange realms was one that, with all its force, struck young Turtle, alias Maynard III, alias Little, alias Nerd the Turd (at the moment he felt most like Little), when he found himself at last face-to-face, so to speak, with that which he was certain he had never seen before, and by a route unavailable to him until just recently: a keyhole. He supposed there were a lot of houses in town with keyholes you could see through, but the houses his parents always lived in were too new, and maybe that was why they were so unhappy. Ever since his best buddy Fish pointed them out to him, Turtle had been peering through all the keyholes he could find, but mostly at the manse where he hoped he might see Jennifer in her underwear or Zoe taking a pee or something; there weren't any girls in his own house either, just his old mom. Usually he did this when Fish was not around, because it seemed to make Fish mad for reasons Turtle could not understand, not after he'd told him about keyholes in the first place. For all the time he spent stooped over and squinting through them, though, it seemed that all he was going to get out of it was a bad reputation around the manse, since he'd seen nothing, but they'd all seen him (Jennifer snuck up from behind one day and gave him a terrific kick that made him wham his eyebrow into the doorknob, and she called him a turdy nerd and a jerkoff and a sick little weirdo, it was as bad as what his mom was calling his dad these days, and about all he could do, and it wasn't much, was stick his tongue out at her and silently wish her pitched straight into hell on the end of a hot fork), but then one day there it was, like a magic show. It was the first thing he saw as he bent down to peek and at first he didn't even know what it was until he finally recognized the big fat legs sticking out on both sides of it. Wow. It—she—was lying out flat on a bed with her knees over the side, completely naked except for a pair of bright red boots with paired horses' heads burned into the sides as though with branding irons, and her eyes were wide open, but it was like she was asleep. By now, he was inside the room (that was how he could tell about her eyes), but he didn't remember opening the door and coming in and he was pretty sure the door was still shut behind him. She didn't seem to mind that he was there or maybe she didn't even see him, so he leaned down to get a closer look and this was when he had that powerful sense of having been here before though he knew he hadn't. Maybe it reminded him of something he had seen at the state park where they had all those funny rock formations and tall skinny caves. It was dark and damp-smelling and hairy all around, which made it seem secretive and hidden, but the thing itself, as best he could tell where the inside began and the outside ended, was soft and pink and puffy with a little lidded bump on top which he knew the name of from the books Fish had shown him but which felt different than he expected when he touched it. Under the bump, it seemed to become paler and paler in color the more toward the middle you got, almost like, deep inside, at, like, floor level, there was a light on. As Turtle knelt down as to a keyhole to see what he could see, he suddenly remembered old man Floyd hooting out in Sunday school: "If your right eye causes you to sin, pluck it out and throw it away!" Yikes. So he changed his position and, pushing her heavy legs apart so as to get in closer, peeked in with his left.

While the experiences of Little, Floyd, or Ellsworth's Artist were classic examples of déjà vu, the term was also often used, more loosely, to take note of cyclical or repetitive behavior or occurrences, or to describe one's sudden awareness of the similarity of events distant from one another in time. This was the sort of déjà vu Dutch was experiencing when he heard Daphne deliver a line much like one he'd heard a decade or so earlier but had since forgotten, a line with dramatic consequences then, perhaps again now. Or that which Nevada felt a short time later when, looking into the boyish face of a new sexual partner, she thought she found traces of an old love there. It was the sort of déjà vu that the police chief Otis suffered on that earlier occasion when dead Winnie's expression behind the shattered windshield of the wrecked car recalled one he had been confronted with the day before when she was still alive, an experience that, for a while anyway, changed his life. It might well describe that initial shock that Pauline felt that same day when, her husband preoccupied with his photos of the wreck, she saw those pictures in his secret albums that he'd taken of his mother years before: déjà vu. Even Alf, much less superstitious or susceptible to emotional reactions than either Otis or Pauline, experienced something not unlike déjà vu that night of the wreck when, somewhat drunkenly, he was helping his driver haul old Stu out through the sprung door on the driver's side and worrying how the hell they were going to extricate the pinned and crushed body of Winnie from the other side. Everyone else out there at the humpback bridge that night was wandering around in a state that reminded Alf of shell-shocked war victims, and when that dwarfish clubfooted woman, later known to him as Cornell's new wife Gretchen, came stumbling down the side of the ditch to help, he had sudden total recall of a battle scene during the war when a limping gnomelike creature, apparently out there scavenging from the dead, took time out from corpse robbing to help Alf dig a survivor out from under fallen debris, and afterwards he could not remember if that battle scene had ever taken place or if it was something he had seen in a movie or read about or only imagined. As for Gretchen's husband Cornell, gripping the steering wheel of his car up on the road that night of the wreck as though suffering a sudden seizure, whether or not he was experiencing anything like déjà vu at that moment, as his alarmed expression might have suggested, will never be known. Certainly the confused young man would have had no idea what the strange phrase meant, having repressed what little of that unfriendly language he learned in school after his postgraduation trip to Paris, retaining only a single French word, picked up over there on that awesome occasion, a word he never learned the meaning of, though forget it he never could. Returning with his bottle of wine that last night, though not the one she had in her perversity sent him out to find, he discovered that Marie-Claire had sprayed it gaudily on her studio wall: HINK. Probably there was meant to be another letter afterwards, but Marie-Claire's paint ran out, so to speak. There was just a long red swath down to the floor where Marie-Claire lay, her naked body, cooling, whiter than one of her fresh unpainted canvases. All now slashed to ribbons, the painted ones as well.

One of these slashed paintings, the only one known to have survived the artist (big money alone rescued this one from her tight-lipped parents' conflagration), found its way eventually to a back corner of John's and Bruce's fishing cabin, where Bruce was able to study it at his leisure, and his impression, after taking it down from the wall and folding its tatters back into place, was that it had not been slashed randomly: there was a pattern to the violence, as to the painting that preceded it. The original image on the canvas had been produced by the flinging of paint, from a can perhaps, or a loaded brush, maybe just by fistfuls (two parallel smudged fingerprints in a patch of green suggested this, a swipe at the ground itself as though to scar it), but there were powerful intimations in these blots and streaks and splotches of a life-crazed universe, utterly mad and made more so by the erotic urge, suggested by the vibrant untempered colors and their sensuous but frenzied encounters on the raw canvas, itself pale as bloodless flesh. The instrument Marie-Claire had used to rip up this cosmorama had been razor sharp, and she had blitzed it from the outside in, circling round in her offensive as though to entrap her prey before annihilating it. Her slashing, then, for all its daffy passion, appeared as a kind of hopeful, rational, and moral act, a defiant assault upon the heedless force that disturbed the universe at its core, seeding it with impossible dreams, and that deluded and destroyed its bearers incarnate. Of which, Bruce one: Marie-Claire had clearly been a kindred spirit, a pity he never knew her. He'd nearly had that pleasure. John had called him a few weeks before she died, asking him to come down and take her off his hands. She had returned to John's town, it seemed, to pay respects at her ex-soldierboy's tomb and attend the christening of her goddaughter, and, these pious rites accomplished, had progressed to more ecstatic ones, John the object now of her devotions. And thus his call to Bruce, committed at that moment, regrettably, to a high-risk Caribbean business deal and unable to rush to his old pal's rescue, delightful though that task appeared. Clothing had become a nuisance that week to Marie-Claire, an encumbrance to be cast off that the spirit might soar (the skin would have to go, too, of course, Bruce foresaw that in his kindredness), and since the spirit might launch itself abruptly from any street corner or market aisle, taking her out anywhere was risky, while keeping her at home made home a wacky and sometimes dangerous place, John's wife recovering still from the difficult birth, so somewhat remote and difficult even to focus upon (even more so nowadays for reasons Bruce did not understand) in the presence of that vivid dark-ringleted beauty, wet from the bath, say, dancing wildly through the house while singing "Mademoiselle from Armentières" in a schoolgirl's sweet and vulnerable voice, and dressed only in bright silk scarves (the famous Marie-Claire palette) knotted round her thighs and throat. John, seeking escape and release as well, made the mistake of taking this manic creature up in his private skymobile: a glorious feast (quoth John), but she painted the landscape below with her flimsy things and might have flung her flimsy self out at that hard canvas as well had not John, his ardor cooled and flying one-handed, restrained her with a desperate fingerlock deep within her nether canals. He'd had to sneak her home that afternoon in greasy airport coveralls, plotting the while her quick return to Paris.

Accomplished, but not before further indiscretions, the most spectacular being the night the uninhibited young mam'selle danced bare-assed and -foot on broken glass out at the Country Tavern at the edge of Settler's Woods, giving those old boys out there a vision that the next day they'd only half-believe, she having run away from John's house in anger after receiving no encouraging reply to her demand, issued in their master bedroom where John was just stepping into pajamas and his wife was feeding the insatiable baby: "*Wut ees happen to ze hainqui-dainqui—?!*" The young rookie cop on the beat that night was Otis, recently returned war hero and onetime Tavern regular, and fortunately, when called out ("Get your ass out here, Otis! On the double! She's smashing up the fucking place!"), he recognized the freaky girl from previous sightings around town and called up John, who called in Alf, who sedated her on a beer-stained table out there with a shot in her tight little fanny, Otis remarking to himself as he helped hold the wild thing down that this was the same table on which he'd carved the confession of his secret love many years before. Still in high school then, football over for the year, beer season begun. Yes, there it was, near the edge, much scarred over now with other hatchmarks and obscenities (a comically bespectacled cock-and-balls, for example, borrowing the *V* for one egg and poking erectly through the O of *LOVE)* and the accumulative hammerings of fists and bottles, and darkened with grease and beer and spit and sweat, but visible still and in fact grown more distinctive with age, he'd scored it deep. He hoped John, gripping the mad quivering girl on the other side, didn't see it, though he wouldn't know who'd cut it there even if he did. Could have been anyone, Otis had no monopoly on his love, any more than he had a monopoly on his religion or his patriotism, much as they may have defined him. And he was glad it was there, glad he'd done it, even if it was the sort of crime against property he was now paid to punish. He felt that for once in his life, he'd made a statement, definitive and true, a pledge of sorts that would ever guide him, and all the better only he could read it.

The interlacing of caricaturesque cock with Otis's solemn declaration on the tavern table, rediscovered by the young police officer the night of Marie-Claire's demented dance, had been accomplished four years earlier during the stag party the night before John's wedding, Otis then away at war, the innovative artist one of John's visiting fraternity brothers, known to all as Beans. The caricature, given away by the horn-rimmed specs: that of his best mate Brains, not, alas, in attendance at this historic occasion, being summer-scholared off to Oxford, thence no doubt to worlds beyond that bonehead Beans would never know, and so, sad times ahead. That anyway was Beans's doleful mood the night he ravished Otis's chaste troth on the tavern table with his own loving tribute to his friend. As Bruce to John, so Beans to Brains, pals inseparable, or so it had seemed to Beans until that fateful night. Or morning: the hour was uncertain. Beans sat in a stupor so thick it had evidently stopped his watch as well. Music played still on the old relic of a jukebox, a twangy stuff that scratched at Beans's inner ear with the persistence of a gnawing rodent, while drunken cardplayers growled and snorted fitfully in a cigar haze nearby, and on the far wall blue movies flickered silently, bare botties humping away with the dull regularity of waves breaking on a rocky beach. On a drizzly day. Staring at them, Beans thought: nothing ever changes. The old bump and grind: all there is, and all there'll ever be. Over by the ancient upright piano, a naked ex-wrestler, bruised and grimy, snored peacefully, his privates lidded with an overturned ashtray.

Someone had tied his big toe to the tripodded cymbals: that hope that springs eternal going for one last moment of whoopee. Too late. It had been a glorious day full of song and laughter and world-class inebriants—in the hotel bar, on the golf course, at the wedding rehearsal and the dinner after (where Beans had stolen the show, he wished old Brains had been there to see it), and then out here at the Country Tavern, where, among his many feats of elocutionary prowess and athletic skill, he'd won with customary style the farting contest—but now the party was over. His fraternity brothers were all gone, and most everyone else as well. Did he see them go? Couldn't remember. It was like they were here, and then they weren't here. Like old Brains himself: it almost seemed like he never was. Beans was alone at table with his Swiss Army knife and a bucket of stale beer and a sorrowful heart, his future—dull, lonely, and utterly predictable—spread out before him like those rolling landscapes of cleft flesh on the far wall: pale fugitive routes to a black and bottomless pit.

It was the announcement of the farting contest, at which Beans was soon to excel, that finally drove an appalled and long-suffering Maynard out of the Country Tavern that night, but had he known the consequences of that hasty retreat, he would have been glad to stay and blow the fucking Ninth Symphony out his ass, and throw in the "Hallelujah Chorus" for an encore. He'd hated every minute of the night as he was to hate every minute of the wedding day to follow, and all he wanted at the time was to get the hell out of there and go home. So when he got in the way of John and his asshole buddies trying to sneak out of the place and insisted they take him along, he'd thought he was just catching a ride into town. He was so goddamned upset he was nearly bawling, so they'd finally given in, not out of charity or palhood, but so as not to draw attention to themselves, the chickenshits. And that was how Maynard, condemned to Nerdhood and member all his life of little else, became a member of the Dirty Six and, in the end, maybe the dirtiest of the bunch. Certainly the stupidest. How had he let it happen? If he hadn't been keeping his distance from his insufferable cousin all night he might have noticed how weird they were all acting, and shown a bit more caution. Harvie the druggist's son had apparently concocted some kind of hallucinogenic brew they'd been throwing down and they'd all blown their fucking gourds. When they tried to force some of the crap on Maynard on the way to the clubhouse, he pretended to drink it but didn't. Later, though, when they'd pulled his pants down and got him between the legs of the girl, they'd shot it up his ass like an enema, using an old mosquito spray gun that hung on the wall out there and a lot of brute force. The gangbang was one thing, a helluva way to lose your cherry, but worse was to happen. For one thing, although everything suddenly had become lucidly clear to Maynard as though he'd just been given a total vision of the way the whole goddamned world worked, he found he'd lost control of his emotions. When he felt like crying or screaming, he heard himself laughing like a freaking maniac. When Harvie, testing the limits of the young kid's womb with his impossible broompole during their climactic six-on-one (Maynard was in her right hand), leaned down deliriously in mid-orgasm toward John's hairy ass, bucking away in front of his face, and took an ecstatic bite, Maynard, in horror and revulsion, let out an ecstatic yahoo of his own and blew jism all over what might be called the trysting place, coming for the first time really all night, though in truth it hurt like hell and gave him the peculiar impression for a moment that he was vomiting between his eyes. He loathed his cousin with all his heart, but when, over the little glassy-eyed guttersnipe's exhausted body, greasy with sweat and cum, Dutch proposed a toast, in all fucking seriousness, to John's bride of the morrow, Maynard found himself falling between John's bare arms and weeping like a baby with loving gratitude. Gratitude—?! It was terrible. And the worse it was, the more he seemed to be enjoying himself. He was overswept by a mortifying shame, being a man who never let himself go in public, but hated it when he had to put his clothes back on, singing them all an Indian war-song while dancing around buck-naked, wearing his shorts on his head like a chieftain's feathers. They had to wrestle him back into his clothes just as they'd wrestled him out of them. At Dutch's insistence, they took up a collection to pay the little tramp, whom they'd just learned was only fourteen years old, though she looked too out of it to care one way or the other about money. Dutch started it by tossing two twenties and a ten down on her bare belly, John raised him twenty on her glistening pubes, Dutch matched him up her privates with a grin. That got everyone into it, and in the end they all emptied out their pockets on or in her anatomy, which seemed to be rolling and heaving like a storm-tossed sea. Maynard was only carrying about fifteen or so, but he threw in everything he had, slapping it down in the sticky place between her undulating breasts where John had been as though spreading a royal flush. He felt like he was being robbed and, god, it was wonderful. Sheer bliss. John cut out then with heartfelt well wishes and blown kisses from all and Dutch said he'd take the little jailbait home to the trailer park; he asked Maynard to come along: she was dead meat and he'd need help. Nothing Maynard wanted more than to spring his wretched ass out of that reeling hellhole, but he couldn't move. Couldn't leave his old pals Harvie and what's-his-name and the other guy, could he? Christ, Dutch! Have a fucking heart! He was taking his clothes off again, but he had tears in his eyes. "Hey, buddy," Dutch whispered in his ear, one heavy arm wrapped around his shoulder as though clapping him in irons, "the best is yet to come! C'mon, now, let go your dick and give me a hand."

The dress Pauline wore to John's bachelor party, torn and stained though it was after, lasted her all through high school; nowadays, her clothes didn't seem to last her a week. She had been carhopping at a rootbeer drive-in that spring (Daddy Duwayne turned up sometime before Memorial Day, drunk and dangerous, and lost her her job), so when the fat boy invited her to the party, she used up all she'd saved to buy a sleeveless princess dress, a see-through bra, and new panties with a little lace fringe all round. She didn't have enough left over for new shoes or tights, so she had to go in her old school shoes and socks, the ones with the school colors at the tops. These, one shoe, and the dress were all she got home with, the dress in bad shape already and even worse after Daddy Duwayne got done with her, but she mended it and washed it and went on wearing it right up until the time she moved into Gordon's studio—in fact, it was still in the trailer when she and Otis went there after Daddy Duwayne's arrest, only Daddy Duwayne had hung it up in the toilet and shot it full of holes. For three or four years after that, she and Otis were close friends and visited the trailer together a lot, until something happened, she never figured out what (when she went to the police station and asked him, Otis turned red and wouldn't even look at her and said in his barking way that "that case was solved," or something like that), and they didn't become really good friends again for several years. In the meantime, though, the city cleaned up the trailer park and condemned Daddy Duwayne's trailer and hauled it away, and Otis got them to give her compensation for it, which she appreciated, since Gordon was nice to her but never gave her any money to spend. She bought some new designer jeans, a quilted anorak, some pretty blouses and a beaded vest, new pantyhose and underwear, a slinky sweater, a pair of ankle boots and some wedgies, popular back then, and three new dresses, including one with screenprint reproductions of the World's Fair, which was her favorite, and she was still wearing almost all these things seven or eight years later—really, right up until the last couple of weeks, when suddenly nothing seemed to fit anymore, not even the boots. Well, age was catching up with her, she supposed, you can't stay in kid sizes forever, and she made a trip out to one of the malls to buy a few new things, using money from the cash register that Gordon never missed. She'd hardly got used to her new clothes, however, when they no longer seemed to fit either. She split the new pantyhose trying to get them on, the jeans seemed to have shrunk before they'd even been washed, she couldn't get the nice sloppy sweater with silver tears and glitter on over her head, and her new full skirt suddenly wasn't full anymore. So, in pinned skirt, bedroom slippers, and one of Gordon's cardigans, she went hurrying out there again. As she passed through the food court with its delicious smells, she felt a terrible urge to stop for pancakes or a hamburger or maybe several, but she was afraid if she did she might not make it to the fashion shops in time. The safety pin popped on the skirt even as she ran past the video arcade. She not only needed new clothes, she needed them right away.

Clarissa, Jennifer, and Nevada were sitting at a table near the taco bar when Pauline went galumphing by, but only Nevada noticed her, the girls too absorbed with Uncle Bruce's beautiful girlfriend, whom both supposed to be at least a famous model and maybe even a singer or a movie star. It was amazing running into her out here, and they were both flattered that Nevada recognized them and actually took time to sit down with them and have a smoke and a diet cola with a lemon slice in it. This was hardly Hollywood or the Riviera, and Clarissa suddenly felt embarrassed about this place that she and Jennifer loved so, but when she tried to apologize for it, Nevada waved at her own smoke and said very emphatically, "Your father's a great builder," and that made it all right again. Clarissa knew that everyone sitting around them was watching them, and she wished her dad had not made her promise not to take up cigarettes because she felt it would be really cool now to share one with Nevada. When Clarissa asked if Uncle Bruce was in town, Nevada exhaled with pursed lips, smiled, and said: "Well, he's been in . . . and out . . ." When she smiled, you realized she wasn't quite so young after all, but the little lines that appeared, Clarissa thought, made her more beautiful than ever in a kind of wicked and knowing way. It was how Marie-Claire must have looked. She could see why Uncle Bruce would be crazy about her, at least for a while, but she wasn't at all jealous, or anyway not very. Jennifer was the real problem. When Nevada asked her where her mother was, Clarissa said she was pretty busy these days and didn't seem to be around much (busy at what? Clarissa didn't know), maybe she was on a trip somewhere, and Jen said, "My mom's always on a trip somewhere," which made Nevada smile again. Clarissa started to say that Granny Opal, who had brought them out here, had gone to the nursing home to visit her granddad who'd had a stroke, but thought better of it in the nick of time, and instead, pushing her hands into her leather jacket, she asked: "Did Uncle Bruce fly here in his own plane?" "Yes, we both did. He has a new one, you know, a jet. A real dream. Would you two like to go up with us sometime?" "Oh yes!" they both exclaimed at once, and Nevada smiled again, but this time more at Jennifer than at Clarissa, and this gave Clarissa a very unpleasant feeling. What was worse, she could see Granny Opal coming through the door at the far end with that dippy old-lady smile on her face, which for some reason made her want to hit Jennifer. Maybe Bruce's girlfriend saw her, too, or saw it all in Clarissa's face, because she stubbed out her smoke, tossed some money on the table (way too much, it was very flamboyant and showed the kinds of places she was used to), and rising in a very smart way that was almost like from a TV commercial, said: "Hey, it's been cool, team. I like this place. It's funky and real." Was she making fun? It didn't seem like it. Certainly Nevada seemed very sincere when she smiled down at them and added: "I'll catch you here again sometime soon."

It disturbed Opal to see the two children sitting with that older woman with the mask-like face who worked for John (when Opal asked her son one day what the woman did, he said she was his troubleshooter, and Opal wondered then: what trouble?), especially when the woman got up and left hurriedly without looking back as though sensing that Opal was approaching the table—what did it mean? what was going on?—but Opal was disturbed by so many things of late, this particular disturbance seemed relatively insignificant and was quickly shelved in a back corner of her mind: little Clarissa was a clever child and could take care of herself. Opal was less assured of her own ability to do so: she felt bewildered, apprehensive, and alone. She had just been visiting Barnaby who as usual mistook her for Audrey, and Opal, for one disorienting moment, had found herself answering back as though she were indeed Barnaby's dead wife, defending her in her own voice, as it were, from Barnaby's befuddled harangue. Then, that peculiar goggle-eyed photographer had lumbered into the room uninvited and started taking pictures of poor old Barnaby, standing there scratching his neck, unshaven and dentures removed, dribbling a bit, head cocked awkwardly to one side, bathrobe gaping and the fly of his boxer shorts, too, and Opal, finding this rude intrusion an insult to the old gentleman's dignity, had upbraided the photographer smartly and sent him backpedaling out the door, again behaving more like Audrey than herself. She had felt certain she had done the right thing, but such outbursts were so rare for her, she had felt faint afterwards, her heart palpitating and her hands shaking, and she had had to sit down suddenly, while Barnaby, cursing her and the rest of the world, staggered off to the bathroom, dragging one leg like an accusation. What was worse, Opal had seen something inside the gaping robe that made her believe Barnaby might be contemplating taking his own life, and she didn't know what to do about it, or whom to tell. The truth was, at this time in her life, Opal no longer had anyone she could confide in. Her grandchildren, though still dearer to her than her own life, had begun to distance themselves from her; her husband Mitch, having become very important up at the state capitol, was rarely in town anymore, much less at home; her best friends were all passed away; her brother Maynard, with whom she had never been close anyway, was slipping into senility; the young preacher, whom she had also run into at the retirement home, making his pastoral rounds, seemed to her to be on cloud nine most of the time (something Audrey always used to say) and of no use as a source of sane counsel; and even her son and his wife were rarely to be seen, seeming each to be living a life at some remove from her own—even when they were in the same room together, it was as though they existed on different planes, able to pass right through one another without touching. If she spoke up and said, "I believe Barnaby may be thinking about killing himself," who would listen? She was invisible. Perhaps Barnaby felt the same way. He was very angry about something, and no one was paying any attention. It seemed to have to do with business. He believed Audrey had done something that had destroyed his company. But of course it wasn't destroyed, it was ticking along very nicely, thank you, one reason Opal saw so little of her son these days. So maybe it was something that had happened years and years ago, if at all. Barnaby took business too seriously. As if he should be worrying about such things now, poor man! It was what had brought on his stroke, as best Opal could tell, she having been at that sad dinner when the old fellow collapsed. There had been some sort of bad news phoned in—Opal, distracted by little Mikey who had come into the dining room to show her his disappearing lipstick trick, not even trying to understand it—and down he'd gone. A shock to everyone. She herself had not been able to move, and later remembered what her friend Kate had said about the moment she got the news of her son Yale's death: "'Time stood still.' That hackneyed line from cheap novels. I suddenly understood it, Opal. Everything stopped. Cold. It was the freezing form that anguish takes in the human heart and mind, turning everything, even time, to stone." When the ambulance came to take Barnaby away, Opal had found herself in the kitchen, washing dishes, though John and his wife had more than enough domestic help, and talking out loud about the strange but beautiful accidents families were. Was John's wife standing there with her? She seemed to be. "He'll be all right," Opal had said, but perhaps only to her invisible self. And now, here he was, the shattered old man, consumed by rage and resentment, and much of it directed against his own son-in-law, in spite of all that John was doing for him, finding the best doctors, watching over his business, naming the new civic center after him (the dedication ceremony one of the few wholly happy events in Opal's life of late), and providing generously for him now when he was no longer able to provide for himself. It was tragic, really. Opal hoped her own mind would be clearer when the time came for John to take care of her, so that she could let him know how appreciative she was. It was scary to think about. But it might not be the worst thing that had happened to her. She'd be free from her frettings, for one thing, which now, in her solitude, were quite getting her down. And even if she might not be able to understand it all perfectly, she and her son would be close again, for the first time really since he was a little boy.

Who was that tedious old woman who had just left him? Barnaby couldn't remember, didn't really care. Thought for a moment it was Audrey and he started taking his frustration out on her, but the words didn't come out right. And then he knew it wasn't Audrey, Audrey was dead, and he shut up, feeling like a fool. Or two fools, more like it, he seemed to have two brains working at once, and neither of them worth a bent nail. What was on his mind, or minds, when he first got out of hospital, was how to kill himself. Whatever he attempted, they'd try to stop him, he knew that, and though it wasn't his intention, trying to outwit them probably helped keep his broken cookie from crumbling altogether, at least for a while. John had already arranged for his incarceration in this "assisted living" complex, as it was euphemistically called, and it was well-furnished but in John's style, which is to say, as impersonal as a chain hotel suite. Barnaby told them with what words he could find and get out that he wanted some of his own things, and he insisted on being taken to his old home to sort through his stuff by himself. This was not easy. Nothing worked right. It took him hours to open and close a drawer. They wanted to help, or so they said. He had to throw tantrums to chase them away and let him be. Bad luck on the hunting rifle, they'd already found it. But not his handgun. Bit of an antique, but it still fired, and it was loaded. He smuggled it out in a shoebox which he hid at the back of the closet of a senile old granny who lived down the corridor, knowing they'd search his own place, and they did. Only trouble was, he forgot where he hid it, even for a time forgot that he *had* hidden it, demanded to be taken back to his old home again, and when he couldn't find it anywhere, thought they'd confiscated that, too. But hadn't he just seen it? It was all confusing. Then, on a more or less sleepless night at four in the morning, he suddenly remembered and he went staggering down the hall, dragging his dead leg behind him, and got it. The old lady was wide awake in there, sitting propped up in bed. He nodded at her, but she just stared dimly. It was a long painful shuffle back to his room, seemed like miles, but he finally made it and prepared to shoot himself. Trouble was, he didn't want to leave without saying goodbye to his daughter. He wanted to warn her about what was happening and to tell her he loved her. He'd tried writing this out before, but his writing was illegible. Even he couldn't read it right after he'd written it. The next time she visited him, he'd tell her, and then he'd shoot himself. If she ever did visit him again. It had been ages. Not, as best he could remember, remembering not being what he now did best, since those ruthless civic center dedication ceremonies, when she'd turned toward him for a moment and looked him straight in the eyes, and he'd felt then like his heart was cracking just like his brain had done. Meanwhile, he hid the gun under some old letters and photos in a desk drawer and then realized, even before he'd pushed the drawer shut, that he had almost forgotten already where he'd put it. So he spent the rest of that morning stitching a kind of holster made out of a thick sock into the inside of his lounging robe, under the armpit where it was less obvious, forcing his old builder's hands to do what, clumsied by a sundered brain, they didn't know how to do anymore.

An impersonation of his cloven grandfather was the centerpiece of one of little Mikey's wordless plays, one of the more awesome nights in John's house, of which Lorraine had seen a few when John's wide-eyed deadpan boy took centerstage. Not all those present understood what he was doing, but those like Lollie who did, did not know whether to laugh or scream. He'd put on the old man's famous barn-red hardhat, a toybox acquisition since the stroke, and with wooden blocks had nimbly built with Barnaby's stubborn caution a fanciful village, intricate and solid. He'd taken measurements and stroked his chin and ordered up a toy earthmover to shift a block an inch and scratched his neck and perched a pediment on high and pulled his ear and smiled the old builder's dry manly smile to see what he had done. Trixie's little girl, meanwhile, stood by with kerchiefed hair and John's wife's nubbly autumn sweater falling to her ankles, an admiring gap-toothed smile pasted flatly on her freckled face, the object of her mimicry missing the performance. Where was she? Preoccupied maybe with caterers in the kitchen. Lorraine felt like something was slipping away, but she couldn't put her finger on it. It wasn't John. He passed through, big as ever, clapping backs and squeezing hands, harvesting congratulations for the recent acquisitions which had inspired the night's festivities, a company party of sorts in honor of the expanding empire. He seemed distantly amused by his son's show, watching it with one eye only, until he was dragged away by his father Mitch, who, back turned on his odd little namesake, gruffly asked him for another drink. Lorraine's own kid came in then with a golf club, John's visored golf cap down round his doggy ears, and Trixie's girl, smile stuck on her face still like a sign on a door, stepped back. Lorraine, too, glimpsing the horror of what was yet to come: she stepped back, her own face rigidly rictus-gaped as though aping little Zoe. As her boy teed up and Mikey/Barnaby, looking like he'd got his sneaker caught under a railway tie with the night express bearing down, sought frantically to wall round his town with alphabet blocks, many at the party laughed and cheered and Waldo ("Don't *do* that!" Lorraine was rasping, heart stopped, voice snagged in her throat: "You'll *break* something!") yelled out: "*Chin down and elbow straight, son! That's it! Now swat that sucker!*" He did, grinning under the golf cap like a moronic pinhead, a blow that sent blocks splattering every which direction, causing the guests to whoop and duck, Waldo hollering "*Fore!*" and falling backwards on the sofa where John's mother Opal in all her prissy dignity sat, insouciant as the storm's dead eye, even as that dumb clunk crashed hooting down on her. A terrifying clatter as the blocks flew, but, miraculously, nothing seemed to be broken after. Except the little builder. He rose from the rubble, his hardhat cockeyed, stumbling confusedly like one of those malfunctioning movie monsters, dragging his dead foot like a sack of concrete, one arm seemingly shriveled, the clawlike hand trembling at his belt, his face so contorted that one half somehow hung lower than the other. Mikey opened one side of his mouth and, faintly, spoke the only word he spoke all night. Most present probably heard only an animal-like grunt, but spellbound Lorraine knew what word it was: Goodbye. Marge had told her all about it. Including the part her husband Waldo, that indispensable Asst. Veep for

Sales (which Lorraine pronounced, "asswipe for sale"), had played in bringing the old fellow down. "Haw! Ain't that cute!" that corkhead snorted now, lifting himself off Opal's lap with a stupid wink and grin, as John's boy slowly took his crippled twitching exit, applause polite but widely scattered, most witnesses frozen where they stood like Lollie. Little Zoe, meanwhile, was nowhere to be seen, her part not so much a walk-on, it seemed, as a walk-off.

Little Zoe's big brother Philip missed his sister's turn, putting on a show of his own at about the same time in the downstairs toilet at the back of the house, very embarrassing. And now he had a story to tell, not about his performance (forget that), but about how it happened he was in there in the first place and what happened afterwards, a weird story but nobody he could trust enough to tell it to, now that Turtle and his family were no longer invited to this house and Turtle anyway nowhere to be found, the dumb kid's touchy parents just barking at him when Philip dropped by asking for him. Had they locked him in his room? Wouldn't be the first time, Turtle's dad could get pretty mean. Zoe said she'd heard he'd run away. Fish couldn't blame him if he had, he'd thought about it plenty of times himself, but he was surprised and, if it was true, a little hurt that Turtle hadn't asked him along. Not that he'd have gone. No? So what was keeping such a big fish here in this little puddle? Well, in a word, Clarissa. Philip couldn't help himself, he lusted after her sweet bod day and night. It was hopeless, she hated him, but then, he had the consoling impression she hated everybody, everybody but herself, he wasn't the only recipient of Ms. P. T. Big Head's icy jabs. But someday she'd need him, or need someone, and he'd be there at her elbow, and then she'd love him for the good and faithful soldier that he was. This was the centerpiece of his intensest fantasies: repentant Clarissa melting in his arms. Meanwhile, though: whatever he could get wherever he could find it, young or old, of which in this town no shortage, or such was the story he told. The truth was a bit different, sorry to say, for though he laid claim to at least a dozen girls from school, all of whom had conveniently graduated or moved elsewhere, and had lots of stories about older broads in town whose lawns he'd mowed or sidewalks shoveled, Fish in point of fact had yet to score and wondered if he was the only guy his age in the Western world whose hand was all he knew of that great mystery. Such a mystery was not even on his mind, though, when that ugly old fart with the meaty honker walked in on him in the john a few minutes ago and started upbraiding him for weakening all his manly faculties with self-abuse. That dickhead was running for mayor? What a town.

All Fish was trying to do at the time was pee through a hard-on. So how come he had a hard-on? For starters, because he always had one, or anyhow almost always, the main exceptions being in gym class showers, on trips to the dentist, and during his old man's Sunday sermons. But also in this instance because of, one, Clarissa's underwear drawer (he'd been pawing around in there while everyone else had headed into the living room to catch the kiddy mime show) and, two, Clarissa's mom, who had smiled at him when he stepped out of Clarissa's room with his hands deep in his pockets before she disappeared into the bathroom. That smile: it was weird, she'd never even looked at him before, his occasional brags notwithstanding. But now, wow . . . He'd waited there in the hall for a while, all alone, holding the hot pole between his legs as though, not to raise it, but to plant it, and when time passed and she did not come out he took a chance, walked over, and tried the door. It opened. As he entered, trying to seem casual while unzipping his pants (oops, sorry, didn't know anyone was in here), he realized that his mouth was hanging open, something he always tried to stop himself from doing, since he knew it was not his most flattering expression. He closed it and the door, blinked: the room was empty. He glanced into the shower stall, the towel cupboard, did a slow three-sixty: how had he missed her? Well. Not the first time opportunity had slipped away as though it never existed. His pants were open, his rod poking partway out: he decided he might as well go ahead and do what he'd pretended to come in here to do. In case, he found himself thinking, he needed an alibi. Which is when the old fart who was running for mayor blundered in, glowered at what he was holding, and laid into him for betraying his own body, sapping its vital juices and turning red corpuscles white. "You'll be old and dead before your time, son. Now put that little stick away before you break it, go wash your hands, and get your damned sissified butt outa here!" Fish was only too glad to oblige. Jesus. Didn't bother to wash his hands either, just ducked his head and shot out of there, headed for the twilit backyard, pausing only long enough in the empty kitchen to glance back at the toilet door in time to see Clarissa's mom come out of it, she smiling at him when she noticed him gawping there. Which was the strange yet true story he had to tell, but couldn't, the middle of it being the difficult part to explain. He saw Jennifer and Clarissa back in the shadows of the rose garden gazebo, also giving little Mikey's dumbshow a miss. He could tell by the way they were hunched over they were doing lines of coke. He approached them hopefully, trying to remember to keep his jaw closed, even though he knew they didn't want him around and would only insult him. But what could he do? Could he help it if he was madly in love with the little fast-track queen of the mall rats? "Hey," he said, drifting up. "Hey, it's the Creep," said his ladylove. "Get lost, asshole."

The Creep's mother, also Jennifer's and little Zoe's, once known as Trixie the go-go dancer and now as Beatrice the preacher's wife, had arrived at that party straight from church choir practice, feeling exhilarated. The singing had been unusually harmonious that afternoon, as though God had got inside them all and made his presence felt, an experience that always had an agreeably erotic effect on Beatrice. After everyone had left, many to get dressed for John's party, Beatrice, wishing to prolong this sweet musical communion, had stayed on to practice the organ for a while, letting the sacred melodies flow through her and into the organ pipes like the pumping of God's blood, feeling at one with herself and with the universe. And with the organ, she becoming its adjunct, the instrument's instrument, the pedals and keys her feet's and fingers' very reason for being, their raisin-something, as a teacher, one of her many teachers, once put it, and the same could be said for score and eyes, bench and bottom, music and mind—all of a piece, like some kind of magic! How happy she was! She'd never played better! Or been played better! As the music throbbed through her expanded body, her heart beating, her pipes resonating, in time to the turning of the spheres, tears of gratitude and intense well-being came to her eyes—and were still there, in the corners of her eyes, giving them an appealing twinkle, when she arrived at John's party just before sundown, still a bit breathless and full of nameless joy. John squeezed her hand with both of his when she came in, gave her a hug; her husband smiled at her from across the room; her smallest child, dressed in a sweater miles too big for her, one of Mikey's mother's, came to ask for her help in tying a kerchief in her hair; someone brought her a glass of bubbly wine. It was as though Beatrice had foreseen all of this before she entered the house, perhaps during choir practice or while playing the organ, and it was all very beautiful. Her husband was beautiful, John's house was beautiful, her friends were beautiful, her daughter was beautiful as she stepped into the luminous center of everyone's attention. Beatrice loved this town, these people, this moment in her life. Things weren't perfect, but Beatrice hoped they'd never change, not at least until she got to heaven. But of course they were already changing. That's how the world was, you couldn't stop it, harmony was unnatural to it, constancy was. A sudden presentiment of disaster sent a shiver down

Beatrice's spine and deep into that core of her which till now had been the seat of such holy ecstasy. She set her glass down, her eyes beginning to mist over. Her daughter had faded from sight somehow, even as she was watching her, her husband, too, though she was not. Something violent and irreversible was about to happen. Or had already happened but was about to be made manifest. Beatrice couldn't see it, blind to everything at that moment except her own panic and despair (where was John's wife?), but she could feel it. "Yipes!" she yelped when the blocks flew, and shrinking back, reached down with both hands to touch her tummy. Oh no, she thought. It can't be. I'm pregnant again.

Beatrice's apprehension of change, both imminent and immanent, was shared by many at that time, even at that moment, but not by all in town, lulled as they were by the walls around them, the immutable routines their lives were locked in, the regularity of their bowel movements. Even among those who acknowledged what Ellsworth called in his fortieth-birthday poem "the ever-whirling Wheel of Change" (which he sought "in vain to rearrange"), a poem published in *The Town Crier* a bit too close upon the automobile death of old Stu's first wife Winnie and Stu's snap remarriage to escape a dark joke or two at the time, many would have argued that change, too, was unchangeable, that like the heavenly bodies, it, too, had its enduring rhythms and routines, such that the very party at which Beatrice suffered her sudden perception of permutation-in-progress was itself a predesigned shaper and container of that change, and in its way unchangeable, in the way that the face of a clock, while never recording the same time twice, remained itself always the same. For some, this was terrifying, for others reassuring, just as these festivities, by which John and his wife solemnized for the town duration's ticks and tocks, were for some a grim challenge, and for others a welcome release, tedium's reprieve if not its remedy, and for not a few a taste of what might be but wasn't. Waldo lived for John's blowouts, whatever the hell they were or weren't, Lennox surrendered to them with a passive smile admirers called beatific, Marge wished them over before they ever began, feeling herself dragged into a smug self-congratulating sacrament she didn't believe in. John's parties worried Otis the town guardian some, head counter and clock watcher that he was, amused Audrey in her time, provoked whimsical aphorisms from Kate ("The collective effervescence of these gatherings," the late lamented librarian once remarked, "is like that of cheap champagne—it goes straight to your head, dissolving moral boundaries and separating self from body neat as an alchemical reaction, then awakens you, bloated and headachy, to an earthbound morning utterly without consolation . . ."), and whetted Veronica's acquisitive appetites, those appetites that enraged her breadwinner Maynard so. What Veronica saw in John's house, she sought to replicate in her own, even to the color of the bath towels and toilet paper, and by doing so thought of herself as a woman of taste. Well, no further worries for Maynard on that score: he and Ronnie had been permanently struck from the guest list since the recent company scandal, and had new things to fret and fume about: the wrecking of Maynard's career in town since Barnaby's stroke, for which he'd been largely blamed, their ostracization down on Main Street and out at the club, the disappearance of their son Little who had apparently run away from home when the scandal broke (Maynard, when gripped by his recurrent paranoia, could not escape the suspicion that his hard-assed cousin, in retribution, might have had the boy kidnapped), the bitterness dividing them as their social life withered and left them facing only one another. For Floyd the hardware man, who loathed every minute of John's parties but hated it more when not invited, more and more the case with the passing years, they provided a stage for his imagined dramas of retribution, involving often as not some violation of the willing or unwilling hostess: on top of the rec room piano or the buffet-laden dining table, for example, or out on the croquet pitch in the middle of the Pioneers Day barbecue, her limbs pinned by wickets, steaks sizzling and beercaps popping. Is it the Christmas open house to which this year they had not been invited? Floyd saw himself unwrapping her beneath the decorated eight-foot tree with all the rip-it-off impatience of a kid on Christmas morning, then, the little brass bells overhead ringing acclamatorily—are you watching, John?—pumping sperm into her like great gouts of eggnog. Fantasies about banging John's wife often enhanced Floyd's nights with Edna, bringing a little fire and brimstone to their homespun copulations—at least at the outset, before Edna gave herself away with an airy rumble as she always did and reminded him where he was: his wife always belched when she fornicated, as though it gave her indigestion. Or cured her of it. Once, he had loved this: her vulnerability. Now it was just a part of her like her fallen arches or the fuzz on her upper lip; her chenille bedspreads, the paintings of flowers and dogs she hung on her plain papered walls.

Of course, taste like John and his wife had, that cost money: what chance did Edna have, really? Edna's painted dogs cost five dollars each, frames included, John's Early American portraits and cowboy pictures thousands. Nevertheless, though she greatly admired John's house, and in fact considered it the most beautiful house she'd ever been in, more beautiful even than the ones they showed in all the magazines in the doctor's office, Edna (perhaps unique in this respect) did not envy John's wife and would not have liked to live in her house. Veronica might drive her husband to bankruptcy trying to duplicate it and Marge might be so embittered by all that inaccessible beauty that she had to punish herself with a kind of spiteful austerity, but not Edna. Edna was a simple woman who liked simple practical things, and John's house was just too grand, too intimidating. She and Floyd would go to a cocktail party there or a company get-together such as the one in which their little boy put on that funny little show with his hardhat and building blocks, or maybe to wander down through all that sprawling multileveled space to the oak-paneled rec room with its upright piano and drum set and hi-fi, its antique barroom spittoons and standing ashtrays and modern Greek throw rugs, to watch (Edna by now feeling oddly transported to one of those tunnel-of-love carnival rides) home movies or a football game, or perhaps to play bridge for an evening up on the main level in front of the monumental open-hearth fireplace with its old Dutch tiles and heavy brass implements, and she'd come out feeling six inches smaller. "What're you fidgeting about?" Floyd would ask her on the way home. "I don't rightly know, Floyd. My girdle feels like it's gone loose on me or something." Sometimes Edna had the impression that John's wife felt the same way about the house she did, that it made her feel lost and sad and small, and she understood (though not in the same sarcastic way) Marge's cruel remark that John's wife went well with the gold carpets: she *did* sometimes seem to melt right into them. In a manner of speaking, of course. Or, well, not entirely in a manner of speaking: one night playing bridge, for example, Edna had looked up from laying down her dummy hand (she'd just carried John's wife's opening bid to four hearts and was a trifle unsure about it) and John's wife was not there. Or seemed not to be. Maybe she's went to the bathroom, Edna had thought, and had glanced in that direction, but when she'd looked back, John's wife was smartly finessing the king of hearts with a jack from the board. Edna had mentioned this to Floyd afterwards, but all he'd said was: "She was lucky to make it, you overbid the hand." Maybe I should ought to have my spectacles checked, she'd thought, not knowing that Marge herself had had something like the selfsame experience, though at dinner, not at bridge.

Marge had missed Mikey's sundered-grandpa skit, boycotting, over her husband Trevor's soft but stubborn protest, that heartless victory whoop-up, the preliminaries for which, however, she *had* witnessed at the most painful dinner party she had ever attended, a ceremonial gathering called to celebrate the same loaves and fishes, one might say, though that first time not for real. A setup. She'd been, they'd all been. John's parents Mitch and Opal were there, old Barnaby, looking a bit flushed and distracted, the bank president and his wife, Maynard and Veronica, Maynard's parents, she and Trevor, a baker's dozen. John had an offer, he'd said, that he wanted them all to consider. Thus, Trevor's invitation as company accountant—or so she had thought at the time, wondering only what new environmental disaster John might now be hatching, and why wasn't his Vicious President in Charge of Salaciousness there, she could have used Lorraine's company. Later, though, she understood it all quite differently, understood that she, not Trevor, was the one John wanted present, she who'd joined Barnaby in his battle to save the town park, succeeding for a while, to John's great annoyance, with her house-to-house petition drive, but unable in the end to buck city hall and the power of a bottomless purse. A target by ricochet, so to speak. There was a famous story about John from his childhood. His parents had given him his first BB gun for his eighth birthday and he had spent the following summer shooting starlings out of the trees and sparrows out of the bushes. True to form, he had even managed to turn play to profit, earning a dime a dead bird for knocking the pigeons off the roof of the flour mill, still in operation back then. His favorite game was to try to kill two sparrows with one shot, which he sometimes managed to do by popping them when they came together to mate. His nasty little pals always saw something hilarious in that. One day he bet a bunch of them he could kill two turtledoves, perched on a backyard clothesline, with one BB. Impossible of course, so they all took him up on it, wagering everything from camp-knife holsters and bike locks to baseball cards and bottlecap collections. Whereupon he nicked one of them, executed it in a manner Marge was later, to her unending horror, to witness, and with his jackknife dug out the spent pellet, put it back in his gun, and sat back waiting for the dead dove's mate to return. "Hey! Not fair!" the other boys all complained, but they laughed, too, at John's outwitting them yet again, and then, reminded that they hadn't lost the bet yet, John still had to hit the second one and with a flattened pellet at that, they stuck around to see if he could do it.

And no doubt hoped he would. They could say they were there. Which was when Marge turned up, only seven herself, but already on fire with her loathing of the local barbarians. When she saw what John had done and was about to do, she tried to stop him, but the other boys held her back, cursing her in their vulgar infantile way and clapping their filthy hands over her mouth when the widowed dove settled forlornly back on the wire and John took aim. All she could do was twist away and scream at the bird, but the stupid thing just sat there, asking to get hit, a crazy suicidal passivity she came to see over time as a peculiarity of most victims. John fired and the bird dropped, fluttering confusedly, to the ground, so they all let go of her and ran over to watch the end of this little life-and-death entertainment. The poor creature seemed to be trying to swim away from them, desperately flopping along ahead of its killers as they charged down upon it, shrieking out their monosyllabic ejaculations, like a company of battle-crazed comicbook soldiers. They caught up to it in a garage driveway, circling round, blocking its escape. John poked at it meditatively with his BB gun, then put his foot over its head, hesitating for a moment as though to feel the beat of its life under the sole of his sneaker. Marge begged him to let it go, it was only wounded, she could take it home and make it well again, and he smiled at her in a generous and friendly way and said, well, he'd be glad to, but then he'd lose his bet, wouldn't he? And while he was smiling like that and giving every appearance of being reasonable and considering her appeal and the essential rightness of it, he shifted his weight onto the bird's head. At that dreadful dinner party, she was thinking about this moment, not about the sickening little crunching noise like the cracking of a dried nut or the blood squishing out under John's sneaker, nor even about the way the other boys howled at her to see her cry so, but about that warm considerate smile on John's face as his foot came down, a smile he was wearing that night as he interrupted a rather stupid argument they'd all got into on the abortion issue, conventional hausfrau Veronica suddenly disturbingly shrill on the topic but as incoherent as usual, to tell them all about the extraordinary business opportunity he had been offered from a company upstate specializing in paving, roofing, and septic tanks, a merger of sorts which seemingly left their own partnership intact and gave them, along with a wide portfolio of valuable new assets, a substantial cash bonus to boot. "Almost too good to believe!" he said with that terrifying smile on his face, and then a maid came in to say that John had a phone call. He took it there in the dining room, switching on the speakerphone so all could hear. "You know the probe you asked me to run into that little construction outfit up north, John? Well, hang on to your fucking sombrero, ole buddy, I got a lalapaloozer for you!" It was Lorraine's husband Waldo. The obnoxious lunkhead apparently wasn't as thick as he'd always seemed. He knew more about the proposed deal than seemed humanly possible. Maynard blanched, then reddened, then went white again as the report came through. His father and John's mother exchanged alarmed glances, Mitch bit clean through his cigar. Old Barnaby started, then slumped gray and shaken in his chair, a sponge for the terrible miasma of defeat and despair that had invaded the room like a gas attack. "The old judas is trying to snatch your goddamn company, John! Mange can give you the dingy details, since the shifty scumbag probably thought most of 'em up, but, in a word, the treacherous old buzzard is out to ruin you! You and his own daughter! Can you fucking believe it? Stealing every damned thing she's got! Hello? John? You there?" Slowly Barnaby rose. It was almost as though something had got him by the nape and was lifting him, dead weight, from where he sat. He leaned blearily toward his daughter to utter his faint word of farewell (did she even hear it? She seemed almost to dim as a light might do, and for a strange moment, Marge could not even be sure she was there, the word more real than she was), then pushed away from the table, and turned toward the door. Which was further than he got.

It was not until Maynard's unexpected backhand swat on the drive home afterwards that Veronica—who had simply remarked, as she'd remarked at table, that opposing abortion on grounds of family values was not only dumb but self-contradictory—began to have some intimation of the true consequences of that fateful dinner party. "*You stupid woman!*" her husband had cried as he belted her, catching her in the solar plexus, just beneath the seatbelt, and knocking her wind out. "Weren't you *listening*, for Chrissake? Don't you know what's happened?" There were tears running down his cheeks. "You mean about Barnaby?" she gasped and he hit her again and then banged his head over and over against the steering wheel. "*Be careful!*" "We've just been fucking *had*, you dumb bitch! We're ruined! *It's all over!*" She tried to grab the wheel, but he slapped her hands away and screamed: "*Fuck off! If I want to kill myself, I'll kill myself!*" Hysterical as he was, they were lucky to get home in one piece, if lucky was the right word. The piece they got home with was not all that great. It was true, Veronica hadn't really understood what John was going on about, business never did make much sense to her, even paint and wallpaper was over her head, nor had she paid much attention to that irritating phone call that John took at table, which she'd thought was plain bad manners, she'd been too upset about other things, had been really since they'd gotten dressed to go, when Maynard had glanced at her in her slip and asked her with a mean smirk if she was pregnant again, an insensitive remark at any time, but though he could not have known why (she'd told Maynard a lot about her past life back in their courting days, a big mistake, he clubbed her with it all the time, but not, thank heavens, about Second John), all the more so given the company she had to face that night at dinner. As she'd done before, of course, playing the shy discreet maiden who'd forgotten everything, aren't we all just friends, but what she'd done so long ago had been preying on her of late, making her feel haunted, like in that old expression about being haunted by your past. She was. How could one not be in a town like this, everyone's lives so intertangled, no way to get rid of anything, it all just kept looping round again, casting shadows on top of shadows, giving hidden meanings to everything that happened by day, turning dreams into nightmares by night. Partly her fault, she had to admit: in her loneliness before her second marriage and sometimes after, she had tried to imagine what might have happened had she not done what she did, and so had for a while brought a fantasy to life, and though she'd long since banished it from her daytime imagination, it still hung around in her dreams like a kind of leprous cowled mendicant, asking for what she could not give it. But if it was partly her fault, it was mostly this town's. If she'd got out of here, as she had intended, it would have all been ancient history by now, but that was not the life she got given. How could she have known back there on that night in the musty out-of-town motel cabin, just a scared obliging kid (she remembered crying silently, all scrunched up in a dark corner of that little metal shower stall afterwards, he'd sent her in there "to wash herself," as he had put it, and then had brusquely stuck his head in and, chewing on a dead cigar, scrubbed her genitals for her, then slapped her on the butt as if she were a pal), that middle age would find her so consequentially in such company, pretending that the world began last week. Life was really strange, such a terrible gulf between inner and outer, she didn't know if she could go on living it this way. How did John's wife do it? And then, as though to prod her crisis onto centerstage, she got seated at dinner between them, father and son, John falsely cheerful and ingratiating, almost as though he were teasing her, leading her on, old Mitch grinding away at one of his nauseating cigars before and after the meal and ignoring her throughout, as though she were somehow beneath his notice. Finally she just blurted it out, she couldn't help herself: "What do you think of the abortion issue?" Her husband snapped her a look meant to shut her up: what the hell are you trying to do, it said, don't spoil things! She did not appreciate his nasty look one bit, but at the same time she *was* sorry, it wasn't what she'd meant to say at all, nor how she'd meant to say it, why was she always so clumsy? "It's not an issue, it's a crime," John's father declared bluntly to the rest of the table but not to her, as though to put an end to this silly matter by merely speaking, and her dribbling father-in-law nodded his senile approval. The bank president said, "I suppose there must be exceptions," and Mitch barked back: "None that I know of. People have to be responsible for their actions." Marge dutifully took up the cudgels, but without much enthusiasm, she seemed unusually circumspect tonight, as Ronnie no doubt should have been; it was, to Ronnie's surprise, John who laughed and said: "Of course anyone who wants an abortion should have one. Why not? Women can do whatever the hell they want with their bodies, who's to tell them otherwise?" "Well, their husbands for one," growled his father, "their parents if they're not yet women, their religious counselors if they are, and the laws of the land if they're heathens!" He pursed his lips and tongued the mashed cigar across his mouth from one cheek to the other as though turning on or off some switch. "It's a question of family values, son, family values versus social anarchy!" "But that's stupid!" Veronica exclaimed, emboldened by John's complicit wink. "Most people who want or need—" "Most women, you mean, my dear," interrupted Mitch condescendingly, turning to her at last, aiming the cigar obscenely at her face, and she thought: I'm going to tell it now. All of it. It's time to let it out. Either that or she was going to cry. "Most women who want or need abortions and most men who want or need the women to have them either have no families in the first place or are trying to *save* the ones they have!" "Nonsense." "But what would *you* do if you'd made some girl pregnant and she—" "Now see here!" Mitch bristled angrily. "What are you trying to suggest?" "You've never had to have one," Maynard butted in, trying to cut her off, "so what do you care?" And just as she was about to tell him, tell them all, John rose and with a smile, the same smile he had on his face that night after the drive-in movie all those years ago, said he had an important announcement to make.

That chilling grin of John's. Once seen, not forgotten. Bruce had been through scores of scrapes and trials with the man—national tournaments and final exams, disciplinary boards, hard-ass negotiations, business crises, high-stake poker nights that turned nasty, dangerous storms, barroom rumbles, and worse (the day Bruce's old Piper Cherokee stalled out on them while buzzing the penthouse sundecks up in the city one blinding afternoon, for example)—and so had had ample opportunity over the years to witness it, but the most memorable occasion for Bruce was one morning during a fishing trip together up at a remote roadless place a day's flight and boat trip north of their cabin, when John, while taking a crap, got set upon by an angry grizzly. Bruce had gone down to the river to wash out their skillet after breakfasting on their dawn catch, and on the way back to camp, detouring round to their chosen dumping ground for his own soil-blessing rituals of the virgin day, he had come upon John and the bear doing a little double shuffle, slowly circling one another like sparring partners, John with his pants around his ankles and tracking through his own shit, the two of them just a few feet apart and the bear closing in. John had made a fundamental living-in-the-wild mistake, having left his weapons back up at the tent, but Bruce had not. He knelt, lay the skillet quietly in the undergrowth, raised the rifle to his shoulder—but then, even though the bear was now close enough to take a swipe at John, Bruce hesitated, captivated suddenly by John's intense concentration and incongruous smile as, in a half-crouch, hands out but elbows in and bent and gaze locked on his adversary's navel, he continued his shackled, bare-assed chassé around the grizzly as though not he but the animal was this death-dance's intended prey. As Bruce in utter fascination watched them through his rifle sights, he realized, somewhat to his horror, that however much he cherished his friendship with John, there was something else, something perverse, that he cherished more, and it had more to do with John's smile than with John himself. The first time he told this story to a bunch of the boys from John's hometown up at the cabin, he found John staring at him with that same smile iced on his face, and he knew that the story divided them and that it was also a kind of bond. The fat motelkeeper wanted to know if he shot the bear. Bruce wouldn't say.

John's troubleshooter Nevada (call what they had in their pants trouble, call what she did with the things shooting) had also, one chilly night after ass-slapping sex on the bear rug up at the cabin with the log fire dying, heard Bruce tell that story, but she took it as a simple confession of Bruce's ambivalence toward his friend. Bruce was smarter, richer, handsomer, more cultured and more daring than John, willing to work the most dangerous of trades, even leaner, longer where it counted, and taller, but John, somehow, always had the edge on him. It was hard to explain, impossible to describe, but there was something about John, something like the aura that accompanies the heroes in folktales and popular novels (it was Bruce himself who once said, seemingly without bitterness, that "if John's a story, then I'm an anecdote . . ."), that set him apart from all rivals, his terrifying grin a part of that, she'd seen it, too. When Nevada tried to find a phrase for that quality he had, all she could come up with was "John knows." It was, more than John himself, what Nevada loved, maybe the only thing she'd ever helplessly and unconditionally loved in her entire life. And whatever it was, it meant that, no matter what wit, wealth, power, or pluck he displayed, Bruce was always, in the presence of John, number two, and number two, as any schoolkid knows, is just another name for shit. Still, being around John improved Bruce's loving, and when she balled the two of them at once, it was Bruce who was usually the better performer of the two, John maybe holding something back on such ("joint-joint," as Bruce called them) occasions. Bruce, when in John's company, was passionate and generous and self-deprecatingly funny, with an ever-reliable erection no matter how conventional or how bizarre the scene, or whose the "glory 'oles," or how much dope he'd done—able to satisfy, that is, even when not satisfied himself—but when John was not around, Bruce was more conflicted, his dissatisfactions rising to the surface then, making him quirky, difficult, impetuous, sometimes even morose and impotent. At such times he often turned to bondage and ritualized cruelty as ways to quicken his jaded spirit; he was never really sadistic, but rather perversely playful, and therefore, Nevada believed, all the more dangerous, her response to which was always professional but never keen. The truth was, for all the tricks she knew, Nevada liked it plain and simple. What most aroused Bruce nowadays (and maybe this was always true: Nevada had also heard his droll account of John's wedding-eve stag party all those years ago) was the abuse of childish innocence, and more or less by default, it had fallen to Nevada's troubleshooting lot to become, with some success (children easier to come by of course than genuine innocence) a kind of procuress. Which was what she was doing out here in kiddyland at this sleazy podunk mall where the air reeked of grease, pot, and burnt sugar, and the deep electronic beat that thrummed volcanically beneath the ugly high-pitched racket was more like a living menace than music. She made sure there were no parents or grandparents around (a photographer:

she waited till he passed), then made her move. The two girls sensed her coming and looked up, smiling, glassy-eyed with their puppylove crushes. They were cute. Well. Too bad. It was going to hurt. But it was going to be fun.

Gordon, feverishly pressing his shutter button, could not believe his fortune, and for it he had to thank his wife Pauline and her peculiar condition which had sent him, yet again, on a shopping trip to the mall. In the lot outside, he had spotted the parked Lincoln, and so had grabbed his camera bag out of the trunk, an old habit. In the food court, John's young daughter was sitting with a friend, both in leather in spite of the summery weather, but their chauffeur was nowhere to be seen. It had to be John's wife who had driven the girls out here this time, Gordon figured, for he had just seen John's mother buying her little grandson an icecream cone downtown at the Sixth Street Cafe, and in fact had taken their photograph, something Ellsworth might use to fill space in *The Town Crier* during his annual summer slump, more serious this year than most. Ellsworth had apparently lost interest in this town and its inhabitants, his old boyhood pal Gordon included, and had in recent weeks become more eccentric and abstracted than ever, absenting himself from the streets and turning darkly inward as though harboring some secret grief or rancor. It was as though (and Gordon had been predicting this all along) he had lost his way. Gordon had not lost his. He now patrolled the corridors of this sprawling mall, steadfastly persevering in what had been his lifelong artistic pursuit, his camera hastily reloaded with a fresh cassette dug from the fast-film pocket of his bag and his finger on the button, but as usual of late, he must have missed her. Even when their paths crossed nowadays, for some reason they did not cross. As at the nursing home, for example: according to the log, they had both, more than once, been out there at the same time, yet somehow he had never caught so much as a glimpse of her, hover around stricken old Barnaby's door though he might. He supposed that was where she had gone now and thought to chase after, but decided his chances might be better if he waited for her return to the mall. Perhaps, in so public a place, he figured, it would be harder for her to slip from sight, but he did not know why he thought that. Meanwhile, there was the shopping to do. Pauline was outgrowing all her clothes, even the new ones that fit yesterday, and she was now largely confined to the rooms above the studio, wrapped in sheets and tablecloths. Gordon was fascinated by what was happening to her body and was photographing it exhaustively, front to back, top to bottom, reluctant though his incurious wife was in her new enormity to expose herself to his lens. But she needed him now and this was the price he exacted. She could not even squeeze into the bathtub any longer, but had to stand in it while he washed (and photographed) her, her immense pale flanks, when soaped up, like a sweating mare's, her belly a vast trembling panorama of gleaming slopes and gulleys. There was little hope of finding any feminine apparel that would still fit her, but the fat men's stores were at the opposite end of the mall from the fast-food section and Gordon was afraid of missing John's wife, having missed her so often of late. So, skipping the jeans, leather, and fashion boutiques with their improbable half-sizes, he took a chance on a more conservative ladies' wear emporium, still within view of Clarissa's table, that seemed to cater more humanely to all ages and sizes of women. When the salesclerk asked him what in particular he was looking for, Gordon replied, glancing back over his shoulder (some woman had joined the two girls, was it—!? no . . .), that he didn't care what article it was so long as it was for a person somewhat larger than himself, anything would do, this was an emergency. The sales clerk smiled enigmatically, then brought him some clothing for pregnant women. Most items were cut too small in the chest and shoulders but there was a nightshirt that might cover her top half, so he asked to try it on for size. The saleswoman gave him a very peculiar look, glancing suspiciously at his camera bag (he didn't even try to explain himself, what good would it do), but dutifully led him back to one of the changing rooms. He had stripped off his jacket and pulled the nightdress on over his shirt and was just about to step out into the light to judge the length and fullness when he saw her and ducked back into his cubicle, started fumbling with his cameras. He couldn't believe it! It was like a wish come true! She was in front of the full-length mirror, pivoting from side to side, trying on a belted crêpe de chine dress with a bow at the neck. He found that if he pressed his lens up flush against the gap between the louvered doors of the changing booth, he could see quite well and ran less risk of being seen. In his first shot of her, his finger trembling on the button, she was presenting her body in profile to the mirror, hands pressed flat to her tummy. Beautiful! She turned her other side to the mirror, caressed the silky skirt down over her hips: *puh-click!* She faced the mirror, hands behind her, palms out, resting on her bottom, breasts jutting—*puh-click!*—then undid the bow—*click!*—and opened the dress at the throat, spreading it back to her shoulders: *puh-click! puh-click!* She turned toward Gordon (he winced), but continued to look back over her shoulder at the mirror, and he fired again and again, eye becoming one now with the viewfinder window. He had never seen her with such startling clarity! He felt, oddly, like a visionary. He photographed her as she undid the belt and stood facing the mirror, hands on hips, then turned the little collar up and peeked over it, folded the hem up a couple of inches, checked the price on the tag at the side. As she returned to the changing room across from Gordon's, he shrank back for fear of being noticed: the little louvered doors only went down to the knees. Luckily, there was a spare tubular chair in his cubicle: he set it near the door and perched his bulk upon it. When next he peered out through his viewfinder, she was back in front of the mirror, dressed in a knee-length white linen tunic with big pockets and a military collar, that snapped up the front like a coat. As he clicked away, she swung back and forth, making the linen balloon and flutter around her body, opened and closed the collar, shoved her hands deep in the pockets, unsnapped the tunic at the bottom and thrust her bare thigh forward. Already, Gordon was titling his photos: "John's Wife Striding Through Diaphanous Clouds of White Linen." "John's Wife, Mirrored, Bares Her Clavicle." When she returned to her booth, she pulled on a matching pair of white linen slacks under the tunic, and as she emerged, still tugging them up over her hips, Gordon was nearly blinded by the sight of the little lace fringe across the top of her briefs. He realized that his professionalism was being tested, his objective artistic principles were on the line, and he settled down, breathing heavily, to concentrate on f-stops, focus, and framing. As best he could. His heart was banging away like a jackhammer and his cramped body, asquat on the wobbly chair, was sodden with sweat. She was now, without closing her cubicle door, removing the tunic and replacing it (a glimpse of that precious back! it was his—*puh-click! puh-click!*—forever!) with a kind of long-tailed cotton twill shirt, which she again tried out before the mirror. Then, in front of the mirror, the pants came off (he photographed the reflected white puddle at her reflected feet, the luminous shadow between her reflected thighs as she stooped, limpidly reflected, to pick them up: and even her stoop was elegant, not a stiff bend from the waist, broad behind in the air like a billboard like most of the women in this town, but a kind of balanced genuflection, like a runner kneeling to her starting pads) and she had a bare-legged look at herself—and Gordon had a look at herself and herself again—in the shirt alone. She was literally aglow. Back in the booth, the shirt came off as the door swung closed (did he get that one? he wasn't sure) and Gordon frantically rewound, fumbled for fresh film. But before he could reload, a glance through the louvered door told him she was gone. He leaned out the door just in time to see her leave the shop (was it she?) and fell hugely off his chair. By now he had the attention of everyone in the shop. What did it matter? He'd never be back here again, and this was, he knew, one of his life's great achievements, let them think what they liked. Serious art was always misunderstood. He snatched up his jacket and camera bag, throwing everything into it, and, head ducked, went bulling out, only to be met by the salesclerk at the exit into the corridor: "Sir—?!" Ah. He was still wearing the nightshirt. "Oh yes, I'll take it." No time for credit cards, he paid in cash, probably too much, he didn't care, keep the change, he was out of there.

Far from losing his way, as his friend Gordon supposed, Ellsworth had found it (dark inward turnings are not always what they seem), and thanks in large part to the nefarious Stalker. This unwelcome intruder had, more than a year ago, crossing some impossible barrier and against the author's determined will, invaded his novel-in-progress, *The Artist and His Model,* threatening to destroy it from within, merely by lingering, leeringly, in the shadows at its periphery, seen and not seen, like some incipient but irresistible malignancy. Ellsworth's courageous efforts to banish the trespasser (he *was* the author, was he not?) were not only ineffectual, they actually seemed to augment the Stalker's sinister powers, confirming his presence here once and for all and emboldening his ruthless encroachments. Collapse set in for several months as Ellsworth watched his novel disintegrate before his very eyes, his Artist's wise and eloquent quest for Beauty (this was the work's tragic theme: the noble pursuit of the unattainable ideal) turned to hollow self-parody in the presence of the derisory Stalker. The Artist seemed somehow aware of the Stalker's hovering contempt and grew increasingly querulous and impatient, tearing up what he had not yet begun, which confused his Model, who only wished to please, and brought tears to her eyes, which, on his seeing, caused him too to weep. "Stop! Don't cry," she pleaded, sobbing. "Why are you crying?" And gazing then, tearfully, into the child's tearful eyes, he (the author now, not the Artist) perceived that the theme of his work had changed: the Artist's arrogant quest for absolute Beauty had given way to a new understanding of the essential innocence of Art, an innocence embodied in this child and now in peril. Whereupon he (the Artist, of course, not the author) turned to face the Stalker. For weeks, then, Ellsworth had been struggling with this confrontation, finding it much more difficult than he could have imagined, but knowing that only by battling through would he rescue his life's work. No wonder Gordon had found him distant and moody. The Stalker, far from fleeing the Artist's bold challenge, had welcomed it, and indeed it was he who spoke most often, the Artist frequently reduced to a grave contemplative silence, perceiving that the defense of innocence was more the task of heart than mind, yet could not succeed by heart alone. He said: "Argument is useless. Art knows nothing, which is its power." "Nonsense," scoffed the Stalker. "Art, like your meaningless little aphorism, is an idle parlor trick, its so-called power nonexistent, once you escape the stifling oppression of the parlor." "It is you who have brought the parlor to the forest," said the Artist, and he took the Model's little hand and led her back to the abandoned rock beside the riverbank, posing her there as he had done once before in pre-Stalker times, experiencing once again the dreamlike quality of the scene as he composed it. He leaned her forward so that she rested more on her hands and thighs than on her backside, and he twisted her hair into a loose braid that fell over her far shoulder, revealing the inquisitive delicacy of her profiled face, the poignant vulnerability of her slender throat. "Art is the expression of Nature's exquisite insouciance," he said, setting up his easel. "No kidding!" someone sniggered in his ear. "So, tell me, why is the insouciant little tootsie in the exquisite altogether?" He spun about, but there was no one near. Far away, on a crest bereft of trees, a shadowy figure stood masquerading as—what? a devil, satyr, fiendish critic? "Because Art is pure," the Artist replied at full throat, "and begs no concealment or disguise." "So you say," laughed the voice in his ear, "but I find her maidenly flesh cushions, poised unconcealed above the stone there like the cloven earth rising behind the barren moon, a pure delight, if you'll pardon my saying so, and so, I think, do you." "Art, when pure, *is* delightful," responded the Artist, refusing to be baited, and with his charcoal blocked in the principal areas of light and darkness, moved, as always, by luminosity's contrast to its surrounding absence, the pluck of it, the audacity. The soft radiant curve of the child's back against the dense forest on the far bank alone made his heart ache with something like remorse. He thought (it was perhaps at this moment that Gordon stopped in at the plant to ask if Ellsworth would like a photographic essay of the town's flower gardens this summer and got such a brusque inattentive reply): Innocence is like the morning dew: it vanishes as soon as light is cast upon it. "Ah, well done there!" laughed the voice of the Stalker, as though peering at his canvas from behind his ear, the Stalker himself, up on the barren crest, dancing lewdly his faunlike dance. "See how you've captured the flushed glow of her juicy little buns, and the comic opposition of the shadowy gap between them, spreading naughtily like a dimpled grin! Ho ho! What a genius!" "Who's there?" the Model asked, breaking her pose and looking round. "No one," the Artist snapped, regretting his lie as soon as spoken, but suddenly afraid that the boundaries violated by the Stalker were but the first to fall. He reset her pose, but before he had returned to his easel, she had turned again to peer back over her shoulder. "Is someone there?" she called, and the Stalker replied: "Someone there!" "It's just an echo," said the Artist irritably, hearing, far away, the infuriating laughter of his adversary, itself echoing and reechoing as it died away. "Now resume your position, please!" But the child could not. Her foot had moved, her thigh was raised, her shoulder turned, her ear was cocked, her gaze restless. She seemed curious, annoyed, excited, amused, apprehensive, all at once. Her love and respect for him were unconditional, he knew that, yet her limbs would not stay where he directed them. "No, tuck your foot under here," he insisted, showing her where he meant, "then lean forward onto your hands, that's it—no, *no!*" He seized her thigh in both his hands and pulled it toward him, his sudden fervent grasp surprising them both. Except to take her hand or to push and prod a bit to set a pose, the Artist had rarely touched his Model. In fact, perhaps, he hadn't really known he could. He stared now at his broad long-fingered hands and what they—yes, so ardently—encircled. Her childish flesh was firm yet resilient, silky smooth, luminous, cool to the touch yet pulsing with a hidden warmth, and palpably without history. He slid one finger along a pale blue vein on the inside of her thigh, thinking: Art, even when idealized, participates in the Real. But it is the vein, not the blood, the container, not the contained, the design, not the flux. Or, perhaps, it is the finger *on* the vein . . . He relaxed his grip but did not release it, allowing his hands to encompass the child's tender thigh without quite grasping it (she was watching now, not his hands, but his eyes), the surfaces of their respective flesh in unbroken contact with one another, but only as a whisper is in contact with the ear, providing him with a direct heart-stopping apprehension of the radical sensuousness of all Beauty, and he knew then that he had not yet begun to be a true Artist, nor would he be one until he could approach his canvases with the same desire and the same restraint as he now held yet did not hold—as he now, in a word, *be*-held—his Model's soft young thigh. Was that the Stalker laughing? No, it was Ellsworth! He was leaping about in his study above the printshop like the Stalker doing his taunting satyric dance, whooping and laughing and yelling all at once! He blew kisses at the Stalker: his savior!

All around him, heaps and heaps of paper, scrawled on and typed on and scrawled on again: his novel! Underway at last! It really was! "I am a writer! I really am a writer!"

Old Stu the car dealer's little tootsie (otherwise known as his little peach among the lemons), who would have agreed with Ellsworth's Artist about the radical sensuousness of beauty (and/or the beauty of radical sensuousness) and also about the self-consuming allure of the unattainable ideal (e.g., why did she have cock on her mind all the time, it was driving her crazy), and who certainly was not lacking in pluck and audacity, was also—while dancing about naked after her morning bath with her hand between her legs and enjoying a snort (not the day's first) of Amazing Grace—celebrating a creative turning point in her life: to wit, imminent liberation from the impotent old lush who was her legal mate in exchange for a gorgeous and obedient hunk who was the very embodiment of animal lust with an ever-ready giggle stick that would put a studhorse to shame, without at the same time liberating herself from the old soon-to-be-(alas)-late lush's considerable wealth. Stu had taken all the risks for her a decade ago, and now Rex, who'd be by for her soon (in full sunlight, not caring who saw, the brazen boy) was doing the same again for her, she must have something after all. Yes, that old red red robin was throbbin' and bobbin' once again (must remember to give her best friend a call later and cheer her up), and so was she, her voluptuous parts—her still-youthful bosom, the cheeks of her abundant ass which her loverboy called "her funky rock-and-roll fin-tailed fanny," her trimmed-down but still plush and velvety belly—rising and falling massively with each gladsome bounce and making her feel very much inside her body, her body *as* body, which she now loved more than she'd ever loved it. The doorbell rang—why didn't the sweetie just come on in?—and Daphne went, lighting the trip fantastic (a joke from the motel, where they'd arranged all the lamps in the room around the bed like theater spotlights to set their bodies ablaze as they fucked, stoned, in front of the mirrors), to the door to let him in. Only it wasn't Rex, it was some kid, vaguely familiar but not quite placeable in the lacy midmorning haze of Amazing Grace. He stood there gaping at her, eyes half-crossed and hangdog jaw adroop, as though she were some sort of otherworldly apparition, reminding her of looks she used to get back in her highschool days, long past, some sweet, some not, and when she asked him what he wanted, all she could make out through his spellbound stammer was something about mowing her sidewalks. Wait a minute. Wasn't this Reverend Lenny's oldest kid? Daphne grinned, staring down at the rise in his pants. Like father, like son, as it said in the Bible, though as she recalled it was the father who had all the fun in that story and the son who took the licking. "All right, all right," she said, pushing the door open and stepping back, "but come on in, honey, don't make me stand out here in front of all the neighbors!" Which was how it was that, one thing leading to another in the usual ash-hauling way, she was lying asprawl on her unmade bed with the bareassed boy kneeling, tallow-faced, between her thighs, clearly scared shitless but glassy-eyed with rampant desire, when Rex turned up, not bothering to knock or ring the bell, as she had anticipated in the first place. "Well, well, what the fuck have we here?" bellowed the grease-stained mechanic, grabbing the thunderstruck kid (whose name, she had learned in one of his few audible declarations, was Philip) by the back of his shirt and raising him a couple of inches off the bed. "The naughty boy was trying to rape me, Rex," Daphne said languidly, and put her hand between her legs again. "No shit," said Rex. "Hell, I've torn motherfuckers' cocks out by the root and made them eat them for less than that." Daphne grinned. The boy's little bird had shriveled so, Rex would have a hard time finding it, much less getting a grip on it. His eyes were beginning to roll back as though he might be about to faint. "It's the preacher's kid," she said, feeling very hot and not wanting to put this off much longer. "Why don't we just make him pray for forgiveness of his sins?" Rex grinned down at her. God, he was beautiful! He pushed the terrified boy face down on the bed between her knees and yanked off his stylishly ragged jeans, which were still tangled around his ankles, then, after whipping the belt out, used the jeans to tie the kid's ankles to the foot of the bed. He grabbed young Philip by the scruff, still wielding the belt, and propped him up on his knees again, set his dingy white underpants on top of his head like a nun's bonnet. "All right, you know the chant to the Lord's Prayer, jive-ass?" The kid nodded bleakly, his eyes tearing under the limp waistband of his shorts. "Well, then, give me a lick, my man! Take it away!" "Our . . . our Father . . ." "*Louder!* Lemme hear you *blow!*" "Our Father—" "*Louder, damn you!*" roared Rex with a wink at her over the kid's shoulder and he laid the belt across the boy's backside with a resounding whop that sent him with a yelp face-first into the bedding between Daphne's legs again. "*I said louder, I mean louder! Drive it!*" Rex thundered, hauling the boy back up on his knees again. "Our . . . our . . . our . . ." And Rex cracked his butt again. Jesus, she was sopping wet, this was one of the best fucks she'd ever had and it hadn't even begun yet. "P-please," the kid whimpered. "I-I only—a j-job—" "You got a job, you miserable piece of pimpled ratshit! It's your break, you dig? Now, come on! I want you to wail! *Punch it out!*" In seeming fury, Rex took another mighty backswing, the leather whooshing fearsomely through the air above her, making her gasp, and a sudden spurt of pee rainbowed out between the boy's legs and trickled warmly down her knees. "Now, look what you've made him do!" Daphne whooped, and Rex grinned, pushing the kid's face into his own pee and snapping the belt smartly across his upraised fanny one more time for good measure, before stripping off his own greasy overalls: "Fucking goofball! What you call third stream! But he better keep ringing the changes on that tune, loud and clear, or the cat'll pay for his goddamned clams with a shredded ass!" Nothing on under the overalls: Rex said he liked the rough feel of the denim on his bare body, helped him keep his edge when everything else was bringing him down. Not down now. Lo and behold! The sight of that glorious love-cannon brought tears of joy and gratitude to Daphne's eyes: to get her bell rung like this at her age! Where did he come from? Hell, who cared? The important thing was not to wake up. "On earth as it is in heaven!" the kid was squawking through his tears. "Fuckin' A!" laughed Rex. "And you better pinch that piccolo tight, junior! Anyone pisses on me, he's a dead man!" Surely, the poor boy got an eyeful. She lost complete control of herself, they tore the bed up. Rex, stretching it out, so timed his climax as to coincide with one repetition or another of "Thy Kingdom come," but Daphne had been coming since they began, maybe before, she'd never been so transported, so inutterably possessed. "Amen, amen, amen, goddamn it, *amen!*" she gasped when Rex exploded in her, her whole body coming in wave after wave from her ears to her toes. Holy shit, what a miraculous fuck. On and on. "Deep down, I realize," she groaned (she would tell her best friend this, or anyway her best friend's answering machine, that girl having gone into a deep fade of late, all but lost to sight), still gripping with both hands her sweet lover's powerful ass, hallowed be its name, one of her legs curled over the back of his hairy one and toes stroking the skinny thigh of their supplicating witness, "I'm a very religious woman." Her foot, creeping up the boy's leg (she was feeling passionately motherly in her newfound piety), now found something there. She stroked it with her big toe, taking its measure, while writing her ineffable name, over and over, with her long painted nails on Rex's firm glossy cheeks, which she knew from long devotion to be paler than the rest of him, creamy in color and hairless, except for a little black tuft at the bottom of his spine like the stub of a recessive tail. "Take a look at his wee-wee, Rex! Stiff as a pencil! What'll we do with it?" "I don't know," said Rex, rolling off to the floor, the terrible abyss within her yawning for a moment as he pulled the plug. This was terrible. She needed it more now than she did ten minutes ago. Rex untied the boy, who was still timorously Our Fathering though no longer shouting. "But I think it's bigger than both of us, Daph. Let's share this scene with the neighbors." And before you could say "Thy will be done," young Philip was out in the front yard draped over the cute little sign with the brass-framed license plate that said DAPHNE AND STU with the company motto underneath, and his jeans and underpants were up on the porch roof, Rex himself, throughout all this neighborly sharing, in the devil-may-care altogether. (Had she asked him, while thrashing about: What about Stu? She had. And what, staggered among his own breathless grunts and snorts and in and around the squeaky "as we forgive others" and the "give us this days" of their little deacon, he'd said was: "Don't worry about it, baby. Just go out and buy yourself something cool to wear at the funeral.")

By the time Jennifer reached the mall with Clarissa for their date with Nevada, who was becoming one of their best friends, it seemed like everyone in town knew about her brother's exhibition of himself and at least half of them claimed to have seen the show in living color; his scrawny butt was famous and she had to deal with a lot of tiresome wisecracks about it, which she did with as much of her customary good humor as she could manage, under the circumstances. Just how it had all happened was not very clear, but there were a lot of rumors, some of them pretty wild, the jerk might actually get some mileage out of this in the long run, though for the moment he'd run for cover. In a way it had been a break for Jennifer because her mom, who was now big as a barn and more spaced out than ever, had earlier talked her into taking Zoe to the mall for the afternoon, but then her dad had agreed that Zoe shouldn't be exposed to all the inevitable dirty talk out there aimed at their own family, so she'd got out of it. One glance at her baby sister and Nevada might have withdrawn her invitation to Jen to go flying with Bruce the next day and Clarissa would have been able to go all by herself, something that would have really got up Jen's nose. So thanks to the Creep for that if for little else in her life. (Already Clarissa was calling him the Croup; wouldn't she!) Not to complain: Nevada had made her day, which otherwise had been turning pretty weird, what with her airhead mother and her brother and all the rest that was happening. Just coming out here to the mall, for example. Clarissa's mom had brought them, instead of her grandmother doing it, which was unusual by itself nowadays, but it got more unusual. Clarissa had been painting Jen's nails with a new black vampire polish so she hadn't been paying much attention, but she had a funny feeling when they pulled into the parking lot that there was no one driving the car. Just a feeling: when she looked up, Clarissa's mother was still there. But then, when they got out of the car, Jen turned back to look and she wasn't. The car was empty, so was the parking lot all around. She tried to say something about this to Clarissa, but Clarissa was too pumped to listen: "Come on, Jen, for pete's sake! Stop ruining things! We'll be late!" Jennifer saw that this business with Bruce and Nevada was putting a strain on their friendship, and she was sorry about that, but now that it was happening, there was nothing to do but let it, just like her dad always said. Of course they weren't late. They had to wait almost an hour, an hour filled mostly with explicit accounts of Philip up on the Ford dealer's roof with his pants off and the dumb jokes that went with it. At least it helped Clarissa relax, so they were in a pretty good mood when Nevada finally arrived and told them that Bruce was definitely flying in from Florida the next day to give them the ride he'd promised. Nevada had seemed especially interested that Jen was coming along, as though the whole thing depended on her, which brought Clarissa's fangs out again, but only for a moment because then Nevada turned her whole attention to Clarissa for a while, and said she loved the nail polish, whose idea was it, and so on, though once she winked quickly at Jennifer, making her feel suddenly ten years more grown up. About that time they all saw that fat photographer streaking through the mall with some kind of frilly nightshirt on over his street clothes. Nevada laughed and said: "Do you think he's stealing it?" "That's just old Gordo," Clarissa said dismissively. "He's pretty squirrely." "This whole town is," Jen said, then took a chance: "I only hope I get out of it before it drives me nuts, too." And Nevada smiled.

When Trevor saw Gordon come careening out of the ladies'-wear shop like a foundering old tanker, blowing steam and wearing a pink nightie as regalia, he went immediately to a payphone in the restrooms corridor of the mall and called the police to leave an anonymous complaint together with the name of the shop where they could get confirmation of this bizarre behavior. He did not know why he did this. He did not even know why he was out here. He had been having a late lunch in the Sixth Street Cafe, his usual, a cup of soup (beef noodle today) and a chicken salad sandwich on whole wheat, with a slice of lemon meringue pie for dessert, no coffee, and he was still thinking about his wife

Marge's latest insurrectionary venture and what problems it might cause him with John, when John's mother came in with her little grandson to buy him a chocolate icecream cone, followed almost immediately by Gordon and his camera, and they posed for pictures which Gordon said were for the newspaper, the chef, who was also the owner, coming out from the kitchen to get in them. Gordon had seemed to be in a hurry when he popped in, his mind elsewhere, but the moment he began the photo-taking session, frivolous though the occasion was, he became completely absorbed in his work and Trevor found himself becoming equally absorbed watching him. Gordon shifted his big hips about fluidly, searching out the best light, the right angle, moved a table and chairs, pulled down a sign taped to the counter near the cash register, took lightmeter readings with and without flash, switched lenses and filters, all in a matter of seconds, and before the icecream was even being scooped, he was already snapping away, bobbing, leaning, rearing, crouching, and it slowly dawned on Trevor that Gordon was not photographing the people at all, he probably didn't even see them: his focus was on the cone, passing from hand to hand and hand to mouth. Where it went, his lens went, and as it did, Gordon asked the little boy where his sister was. Opal said she thought she was out at the mall, "Mikey, how did you get chocolate on your nose?," and before she could scrub it away with a licked paper napkin, Gordon, without apology, was gone. The pie came, a house specialty, the meringue almost four inches high and light as air, but Trevor only poked at it. He was still thinking about the photographer, his amazing intensity, and the thought that came to him then, which he did not understand at all, or even quite believe to be true (there was the pie in front of him, for example), but which remained with him for all the rest of that day, was: *I have never known delight*. He knew of course where Gordon had gone, he'd made the same calculations Gordon had. Trevor paid his check, received an inquiry about his appetite, and went to pick up his car in the lot behind the bank building. He took his time, driving cautiously as he always did. At the mall, he spied John's daughter at a table with a couple of friends, but did not find Gordon until he came flying out of the ladies'-apparel store in his pink gown, though Trevor had peeked in there earlier as he made his rounds. Alarmed, almost as though in self-defense, then, he put in that panicky call to the police, regretting it as soon as he had done it, he hadn't even disguised his voice properly. This was not the first time, he had reported Gordon twice before, but those times only for fun. One day when, from his office window in the bank building, he had seen

Gordon sidle swiftly into the card shop and travel agency across the street and, from behind the scenic posters of beaches and hill towns, aim his telephoto lens at the bank door (Trevor knew why of course: John's wife's car was parked at the curb below), he called, also anonymously ("a worried bank customer"), to report the "suspicious behavior" of a person "lurking secretively" near the bank entrance, last seen peeking out from inside the travel agents' across the way. He was still giggling about it that night, it was the first time he'd ever done anything like that, and when Marge asked him what was so funny he fumbled for a moment in confusion and then said that John had taken out another half million of insurance and he was still feeling giddy. Then there was the even funnier time he'd called the police and in a high-pitched voice accused the photographer of sneaking around outside the women's changing room at the civic center swimming pool, a complete fabrication, since Trevor himself had never even seen the pool in operation, his only visit to it being before the dedication ceremony when the retractable roof was being demonstrated. Though he had thought of that call as only a kind of practical joke, he nevertheless felt more or less justified because of things he'd seen the photographer up to elsewhere, and he told himself it was even possible he'd guessed at a truth. Not likely, though. Gordon was not an ordinary voyeur, any more than Trevor was. It could even be said that he and Gordon were both searching for the same thing, Gordon more directly, fully aware of what he was doing and why, Trevor more speculatively, but more prudently. Though he had begun this little game as a mere lark, Trevor had come to believe that if he took it seriously enough, something, he didn't know what, would be revealed. It was as though Gordon and his camera were leading him, unwittingly, to buried treasure, and if he reported him mischievously to the police now and then it was only to remind himself that it was just a game, a harmless amusement. It was different today, though. He was frightened, he didn't know why. Was it because of Gordon's mad lumbering flight through the crowded mall, the disturbing impropriety of it, or had he suddenly become appalled at his own improper fascination with such madness? He ducked into the men's room after the call, afraid of being seen near a telephone (had anyone recognized him?), and was shocked when he peered in a mirror and saw the panic in his face, his rumpled clothing. And was that a floccule of meringue on his lapel? Trevor was known for his cool aplomb, his tidy dispassionate composure—something was terribly wrong! "The trouble is," he said to himself, dabbing at the sweat on his brow (he had sweat on his brow?), "you don't know who you are." "Who does?" asked some voice in one of the stalls, and Trevor, now thoroughly flustered, fled again.

The insurrectionary venture that troubled Trevor feared was his wife Marge's decision to challenge Snuffy, the popular ex–highschool football coach, airport manager, and can-do councilman, for mayor, not because she didn't like Snuffy (she certainly didn't), but because she could not let John's handpicked candidate run unopposed. Was this a democracy or one bully's fiefdom? She was afraid she already knew the answer to that, but even knowing it, she could not accept it, and she planned to run, not against Snuffy so much, he was just a proxy anyway, but against her old classmate and nemesis, the number one honcho himself. It would necessarily be a grassroots affair, she had no money for it, she'd have to confront all that wealth and power with a few volunteers (she had been trying to enlist Lollie's help, but the woman seemed strangely aloof these days; she hoped her cretinous husband hadn't finally turned her head), handmade posters and flyers, an exhaustive door-to-door campaign, tough talk, and an attention-grabbing platform, including a call for radical electoral reform. So far she'd kept everything under wraps, only Trevor knew, and he wasn't all that excited about it. As she expected: Trev was an accountant and this enterprise looked to fall pretty much in the loss column, she understood that; in the end John would find some way to clobber her, and Trevor, who needed John, knew it. Probably she told her husband just so he could brace himself, though she could have used a little moral support. Trev was an older grad student up at State when they met, a teaching assistant for Marge's Econ 101 class. She'd invited him to a civil rights rally and they had developed a kind of activist paldom, though Trev wasn't even political. Probably just lonely. That was all right. So was she. Just why marriage should have followed the way a street march follows a resolution was not that clear to either of them, but they had got used to and respected one another, discovering that they were about the only persons they didn't argue with, and the alternatives were few. Or rather: nil. No regrets. They were helpmeets in the true sense of the word, and now that she was finally launching her campaign, she knew he'd be at her side, no matter what his misgivings. She wanted maximum impact when she did announce formally, and she was doing that now with a concise but forceful and passionate position paper, the exact wording of which she had just finished drafting, to be published in this week's edition of *The Town Crier*. She was determined that this was not going to be a negative campaign, but she was pointing out that her opponent had a lifelong reputation for dealing ruthlessly and arbitrarily with those who were younger and less powerful than he and had frequently shown alarming evidence of undemocratic gender-biased attitudes. There were other rumors about the old coach's behavior that today would open him up to charges of sexual harassment, and she would not be disappointed if those rumors should come out as the campaign proceeded, and perhaps even be substantiated, though she herself of course would never bring them up. She had wanted something that would give the announcement of her candidacy a bit of a kick-start, so she had gone out earlier to see Barnaby at the retirement center to try to obtain his endorsement, but no help there. He seemed to think she was his bath lady, and he started yelling at her incoherently, something about his dead wife doing it, and probably telling her to get the hell out, which anyway she did. So she had called Trevor to tell him what she was doing and then delivered the document that would change her life and that perhaps of the entire town as well (she could *beat* that meathead!) to the newspaper office—which, oddly, was closed, no signs of life inside: she had to push it through the slot in the bottom panel of the door, her sense of drama offended, and angry that already, as she took her first dramatic step into bigtime electoral politics, she was being made to stoop instead of stride. Her fateful turn taken, she stood up, took a deep breath, looked around at the disappointingly empty sidewalks, and headed for the club where she could work off her tensions with a round or two of golf, have a quiet drink and supper with Trevor, lighten him up a bit (when she finally did see him, he seemed to be taking it much worse than she'd thought), and get ready for all hell to break loose tomorrow.

Kevin, the golf pro and manager of the country club, saw the dweeby linen-suited accountant come into the bar late that afternoon, looking a bit wigged out (he went straight for the gin instead of his usual mineral water at that time of day), but he paid him little attention, there was too much else to do, the new season was in full swing, first club tournament just two weeks away, his own urgent staffing problems were as yet unresolved (he'd appealed to the board, there was plenty of money for more help, what were they being so chintzy about), the greens and fairways were in shitty shape after the spring drought, the buttbrain groundskeepers handing him some crap about the water pressure being too low for the sprinklers to work properly, one of the local wives he'd been jamming was giving him a hard time since he'd tried to call it off, the new cook was threatening to quit (three in the last six weeks), one of the coolers was on the blink, also the pool filtering system, there were lights out over the east parking lot, potholes in the access road, dogshit in the sandtraps at the tenth and twelfth greens, Kevin hardly had time for that limp noodle, not even a golfer, more like a golf widower, husband of maybe the best all-round player at the club, her only weakness being her impatience around the edges of the greens. Her impatience generally: a pain in the hunkies. She was due in soon, old Marge—or Sarge, as some called her when not calling her worse—always one of the first ones back in, no matter when she went out. She just played through everybody like a bulldozer through butter: make way, you zombies. Big beef, Marge. This was one wife out here Kevin had not planted and would not. The crowds began to arrive, he was still shifting the beers into the working cooler from the dead one when they started pouring in, some clopping in off the course like old nags entering the feedbarn, others, as Trevor had done (he was over by the picture window now, staring blankly out on the dimming sky), joining them from town, full of all the usual asinine jokes and urgent demands. When John got back to town, Kevin would have a private chat with him about the workload out here. John always had a solution, and he didn't need the goddamned board to get things done. Kevin missed him when he wasn't around, the place always seemed a bit seedy without him. His wife had been out earlier in the day, or she probably had been, Kevin wasn't taking any bets on that lady's whereabouts anymore, or her ifabouts either, didn't even like to think about it and mostly didn't, but he was pretty sure he saw her, heading to the lockerrooms. He hadn't seen her since, but only John's wife could wear a gold lamé top over emerald-green slacks like that and look casual doing it. Another local hausfrau Kevin had not staked and would not, he knew, though would that he could. Just brushing up against her was magic. At the bar, the story of the day was about the bareassed preacher's kid crawling up onto Stu and Daphne's roof to retrieve his pants, and everybody had their own account of how those articles got up there in the first place. Some of them were pretty wonderful, and Kevin found himself loosening up a bit as the evening wore on, a tumblerful of iced single malt helping somewhat as well. Most of the stories had old Stu coming home from the car lot and finding Daphne in bed with the kid, throwing the pants on the roof himself, usually with some one-liner from Stu directed at Daphne or the kid. One version: "This time, son, you gotta crawl up there to get your britches back. Next time you'll have to crawl up there to get your balls back." Others said that Stu had tanned his ass before sending him up there, which accounted for the spectacular glow, or sent one of his mechanics over to do that bit of routine rear end realignment for him (that was another rumor: the brazen young mechanic), but others said they heard the kid threw them up there himself, a dare or something, or maybe just showing off: he'd also climbed up on the sign out in the front yard and started whacking off in full view, or so someone claimed who said they saw him. PKs: the same everywhere. An old regular out here named Alf said he didn't know about the monkey business on the sign, but that the kid, feeling cocky, had tossed his own bluejeans up there himself before going on inside was what he'd heard, too. Said it was like a kind of signal flag, you know, like raising the old blue peter, which meant his ship was ready to sail and let the world know it. Kevin had been ready to believe half the stories being told, but he figured the deadpan doctor, known for his hoard of ancient anecdotes, was pulling one out of the hat here. Alf was a hopeless old bent-backed duffer who approached the ball in a slouch, swinging from the elbows and carrying his neck out in front of his shoulders like a turkey buzzard, but he was hell to beat with a putter. "Old Stu came home and said *he'd* give him a blue peter, goddamn it, if he caught him around here again! He didn't mind him taking his wife for a spin with his little banger, but he'd be damned if he'd let him have free advertising!" There was also the more plausible rumor that Stu and Daphne had actually hired the kid to enrich their sex life, Stu himself was known to tell a lot of jokes on the subject, while someone who'd had a beer with Stu out at the Getaway this afternoon said Stu had claimed that it wasn't what it seemed, the kid was innocent, only came by to mow the lawn, it was just another prank of Winnie's ghost which even Kevin had heard Stu say was haunting him nowadays. "Knucksie's kid? Innocent?" old Waldo snorted, already half-bombed. "Naw, haw! Gimme a break, fellas! That boy's been cuttin' scrub all over town, he's a menace to virtue everywhere! But Daph was too smart for the rowdy little jackrabbit. When he tried to jump her, she told him first he'd have to put his pants on the roof, that was the only way not to have babies, and then when he'd got them up there, she told him old Stu had got wind of it and was on his way home with a bodyshop mallet to work his chassis over, but if he got his butt up there on the roof in a hurry and put those pants to use, she'd tell Stu she'd hired him to polish the shingles!" Well, while they were all laughing to beat hell at that one, who should come in but Stu and Daphne themselves, both shitfaced, hardly able to walk, Stu asking what's the joke. The sudden silence was earsplitting, but Waldo, not losing a beat, boomed out: "Haw! Look who's here! Hey, you hear what happened to old Stu?" People were choking on their drinks, Kevin included, ready to fall through the floor, and Waldo's better half grabbed his sleeve to yank him out of there, but the paint salesman winked with half his face and said: "Well, he was out in the sticks a coupla nights ago, miles from nowhere, and his car broke down, goddamn tin buckets they sell nowadays, can't trust 'em, and so, you know, he needed a place to stay overnight. But the rube at the only farmhouse in sight said, sorry, mister, all he had was two beds, one for him and his wife and the other one for his daughter. That's all right, says Stu, I'm harmless, my dingus got shot off in the war. I'm dreadful sorry to hear it, says the rube, okay, you can sleep with my daughter." By now, everybody was relaxed back into their drinks once again, laughing more than the joke was worth, most of them having heard it before, the old nine-inch stub gag, but so relieved to have Waldo cover for them everything seemed funny. But then, while everyone was still falling about stupidly after the punchline, Waldo turned to Stu and asked: "So what's this I hear about you sellin' fresh hotcakes off your roof, ole buddy?" Stu grinned blankly, pretending not to know what Waldo was talking about, started telling some tired old joke of his own about a pretzel salesman, Daphne meanwhile keeping her mouth shut through it all. Not at all like Daphne, most people were beginning to get the picture. The two of them threw down a couple of stiff ones and staggered out early, the cluster at the bar by then having pretty much scattered. And then, later, as Kevin more or less anticipated, some woman came in and said she'd found some green pants with a gold top hanging in the lockerroom, she'd have kept them for herself if she could have got into them, whose were they?

Nevada lay smoking that night in the brazen young mechanic's rustic one-room cabin in a prehistoric motel cluster halfway into the next county on what used to be the main road through here before the interstate link got built and all the action slid to the west and the dinosaurs died out. John was off on a business trip somewhere, Bruce due in tomorrow, but had left no messages, they both were together maybe, probably not. Cool jazz played on Rex's old hi-fi system (the CD player she'd given him sat, gathering yellow prairie dust, on a kitchenette shelf), punctuated from time to time by a dull metallic clang as Rex's elbows hit the rusty sides of the ancient shower stall. Paranoia drove Rex this far from where his daily bread got earned or otherwise acquired, his qualms about humanity in general augmented by his more particular mistrust of hicktown collusion, hypocrisy, and stupidity, and by, above all, his deep misgivings about

John, misgivings nettled by seething rancor (Rex forgave no trespasses), something they could not talk too much about, since John was Nevada's principal ticket, and had come to mean more to her than that really, and Rex knew it. Made his heart heavy, she knew, but he never complained, needing her, as was mutual. John kept a suite out at the new luxury motel on the interstate where he could come and go without notice, and Nevada stayed out there when in town, but whenever, as now, she was tensed up and had to mellow out, she came here. Rex gave her soothing body massages, a skill he'd picked up in one of his previous careers, and they had sex that was long, satisfying, and blissfully unpretentious. Sometimes they jogged together, or worked out a light set or two, and there was always some quality dope to do and stories to exchange from their respective workplaces. Tonight, for example, after a funny story about a kid she suspected might be little Jennifer's brother, Rex had shown her the contract he'd got the car dealer's wife to sign, to be postdated later, which gave Rex half the dealership and sole ownership of the service department, but which, by description, obliged him to marry the woman first. "She's an old pig, I know, and drunk more than not, but she's got what I want. You're drifting away from me, baby, I can't help that, but I want to be ready to do right by you when the show closes down and you come back to me." She'd started to protest, thought better of it, agreed instead that she was indeed feeling somewhat adrift but had no clear idea, as he seemed to, which way the wind was blowing (she felt unlinked with John away and as though jobless, somehow endangered), and then had asked him how they were going to get the husband out of the picture. "I've worked it out," was all he'd say, his reticence causing her some unease, since mostly he told her what was on his mind. Now, when he came out of the shower and sat on the bed, handing her the towel to dry his back, she told him about the operations she was running for John's pal Bruce, including their plans to take John's daughter and her little friend from the mall for a skyride in Bruce's jet tomorrow, providing that soldier of fortune got back from his Caribbean fun and games and the girls could escape their babysitters. Just a preliminary step; next move more serious, and nothing she could do really to stop it. She might, no choice of her own, be moving on. "Bruce is a cool guy but, deep down, something of a psycho. It's like he's always walking along the edge of a cliff and can't think of one good reason not to step off except for something like plain old animal hunger: he still wants more than he wants not to want. But if his appetite ever fails him, so long, brother, he's gone." Actually, she thought Bruce and Rex were a lot alike, but she knew Rex would resent her saying so, since it was always the old apples and oranges argument with Rex whenever it came to rich folks and poor. "That makes him an easy spender with other people's lives, too," she added, reaching around to towel Rex's drum-tight abs, "life itself probably being the thing he has the least respect for. He thinks life was some kind of fundamental mistake the universe made back when it orgasmed and the less of it the better." Rex got up to change the record, choosing something a bit more progressive and so more to his tastes, but not so far out as to chafe her gentled spirit. She lay back on the bed, gazing at his well-toned lats, firm butt, and dark muscular thighs, thinking: Bruce was right about one thing. Life was not, as some poetical types liked to claim, a dream, but being rooted in dreams (and dead ones at that) and more like them than not, if you were crazy enough to live life out, you might as well be crazy enough to live it as though it *were* a dream. It eased the suffering, and nothing more meaningless in a meaningless world than to suffer for nada. A spin on things, she noted, that gave you a lot of license. Rex rolled a fresh spliff and lit it, passed it down; she took a deep toke, then coiled smoke rings out at his semitumescent cock. "Straighten that muscle up," she said, "and we'll have a game of quoits."

The bed was for some in town a playground, as it was for newcomers Rex and Nevada when not a platform for their business ventures; it was a platform of sorts for Gordon the photographer as well, an artistic prop like a chair, a bathtub, the street, while for his friend Ellsworth it was more like a patch of meadow in the tangled forest of his creative imagination (the Artist had his hand on the Model's thigh again, lecturing the sardonic Stalker, hovering, unseen, nearby, on the higher morality of aesthetic truth); for many, like oldtimers Marge or Otis, the bed was simply a place to get some shut-eye; but for some it was nothing short of the rack, sheer hell on sheets. Try telling Veronica, for example, that sex was fun. It had a certain tickle, all right, but it was more like terminal athlete's foot. Or hemorrhoids, more aptly, given her dearly beloved's brutish fancies. For whom, the middle Maynard, no joy either. More like prosecuting a tough case, proving he could still do it, even if he hated it. Contrarily, Gretchen and Columbia, who were otherwise finding the town a bit shaky for them of late, were having a grand time there, playing with vibrators, ointments, penis extenders, and condoms, ribbed or pimpled, some even with ears and noses and little Martian antennae on them, which Gretchen had ordered through catalogues that arrived at the pharmacy and which kept them giggling throughout their evening recreation time, which was strictly limited, since they were both working women. Not that it was all just idle frolic, it was also quite educational, Columbia learning at last how men really worked when she took her turn strapping on a clear plastic penis with its inner anatomy showing through in bright colors and had a go for herself. For Alf, nurse Lumby's dyspeptic boss and deliverer of Gretchen's brood (an unusual case: he had to break her hymen to get the first ones out), a bed was where most people went to die, he attended them there and watched them go, his own true heart among them, and living alone now, he often avoided his own, wandering the streets at night or dropping off on the living room couch during consolingly banal TV reruns, pap against the dread. Even when Harriet was alive and they were still copulating (it was fun, they'd got a kick out of it for a while, in spite of their overawareness of its mechanics, but came quickly to think of it as kid stuff, and after the babies were born, turned to it only when in goofier moods, most often drunk or with others), they preferred any private place, in or out of the house, to the dreary bed, Harriet even more blunt than Alf about "crawling into the coffin" at night. "I'm pooped, I'm dead," she'd say, leaving a party. "I'm going to go put the meat in the cooler before it goes off." At a foreign-made piece of erotic fluff in the old Palace Theater one night, during a soft-focus view from the ceiling of lovers on a bed, the old army nurse had provoked an auditoriumful of irritable shushing by remarking, too loudly, that whenever she looked down on a bed like that, all she could think about was torn limbs, Alf adding laconically to turn the shushes to self-conscious laughter that he couldn't be sure because of the fuzzy camera work, but he thought the actress (fuzzy camera work was his problem now: hard as he stared at his finger—there was a message on its tip, he knew, something about a patient: what was it?—he couldn't bring it into focus) had a thyroid problem and recommended she get a checkup. Kate, who was there that night with Oxford, sitting beside them, and who in general had a benign view of beds (though, in the end, when it came, she refused to retire to one), pointed out that the white-sheeted bed viewed at that angle was a kind of screen-within-a-screen and that consequently the coupled lovers were not merely actors in a movie and thus nothing more than the ghostly illusions of a flickering light, but they were actors *playing* actors, and so had doubly lost their substance, as though to say that love itself was such an emptying out of emptiness, Oxford replying: "Or such a luminous density of layered sensations," all of which was making the younger crowd in the theater wish these old farts, long past a good time, would shut up and stop spoiling it for others. Dutch had booked that film, the bed as theater being his own preferred use of that ubiquitous piece of furniture: gave him his jollies without aggravation or anxieties and no strings after. He missed the old Palace with its big screen and high ceilings, appreciating in his own way the remark Waldo had made recently during one of his motel junkie-fucks that the beds he kept crawling into seemed to be drifting farther and farther away from the center as though that center were somehow getting lost, fading from view, the emaciated kid with him replying that she didn't know there ever was a center. "Sounds like you're on some kinda guilt trip, man." "Naw . . . haw!" For Floyd the hardware man, the bed was also a theater of sorts. He liked to take John's wife there, grab her by the hair, tie her to the bedposts, and whip her with his red suspenders, which he called his "cat." Then she'd moan and toss her head about and beg him to make love to her or kill her, she couldn't stand the passion welling up in her. He'd let her kiss and suck at his johnnie, chastising her all the while with his whistling cat. Then she'd belch, and he'd do what he could to have some kind of orgasm, and get off. He tried to imagine whipping Edna with his suspenders, but it seemed incredibly silly.

Why did Edna belch whenever she engaged in what a boy once called, inviting her to one, a mattress dance? She couldn't rightly say, it just came like that when she did, if coming was what she truly did (for Edna, it was more like being very nervous about something, and then suddenly, blissfully, not being nervous anymore: she always popped straight off afterwards without so much as a blink), but it probably had something to do with her stepmother's stern admonition that burping was the most wicked thing a body could do: just letting go like that, they lord, not giving a care. Maybe she was really talking about letting go out the other end, not being able to bring herself to say the word for that, but ever since, whenever Edna felt crazily reckless, like when a person had his thing in her, for example, up came the burps. Her stepmother also told her, on her wedding day, "I don't know how you're gonna cotton to what comes next, Edna, but wither you love it nor hate it, it won't last long. When the lollygagging's over, then love—if there sincerely be any—will come at you looking like something else again. If you recognize it and show you're grateful for it, however contrary it is from what you're customed to, then you'll have love in all ways passable in this world of the mortal body, but if you get bitter about what you've lost, and losing is mostly what you'll know, then, sure as you're born to die, Edna, love'll just dry up, and you'll be left standing nekkid in the cold without nothing to keep your heart from freezing up and cracking on the spot." Her stepmom did have a way with words. That "cracked heart" notion, which was associated in her mind with one winter so fearsome cold the windowpanes splintered, still caused Edna shortness of breath and made her press her hand to her breast to cozy it whenever she recalled it to mind. As to Edna's views on beds, they were of a strictly practical sort, having to do with price and sturdiness of construction, the firmness of the innersprings, and how easy it was to keep the headboards clean and change the linens, which on Edna's bed were mostly plain cotton (one color percale set for holidays), neatly covered with washable spreads and blankets, and always made up, first thing after breakfast. Fixing the bed up proper every morning was not just a housewifely habit. It was what most helped Edna to get on with each day, what with all the troubles Floyd got into through the years, the peculiar ways he had sometimes, not always nice, the loneliness she felt in this town, and the strange things happening in it of late. Strange things? Well, for example, there was the night their old friend Stu called, must have been about two in the morning, hadn't heard from him in a month of Sundays, and he was blubbering something about seeing Winnie's ghost. Of course, he was so besotted you couldn't hardly understand him, maybe he was just trying to tell one of his jokes, and he surely didn't remember it next day when Floyd took the car in to have the brakes relined, probably just an old drunk's nightmare, Floyd said, but it was mighty peculiar all the same. And then they say that little boy who's missing ran away, afraid of something terrible, but his parents won't even admit he's gone, like they know more than they can tell, or done something wrong they can't admit to, she heard folks gabbing about it at the checkout line in the supermarket. And had anyone seen the photographer's wife lately? someone asked. Edna hadn't and so did not know what that was about, though the expression on people's faces suggested that this was probably a story which went back aways, before hers and Floyd's time here, and so rightly belonged to them but not to her, and so she wouldn't know what to ask. Anyways, she was no gossip, though whether because of principles or shyness, she could not directly say, but if she were, she would have asked them, well, and what about John's wife? Since that vexing night at the bridge table,

Edna had seen her only once, setting with her children at church, wearing a red hat. But then she wasn't setting with her children. She was singing in the choir. And no hat on neither. Edna thought she must have winked off for a moment without taking notice. She recognized that she was staring and from the choir John's wife was staring back. Right smack into her eyes. First time she'd ever done that when she wasn't just doling charity. Edna ducked her head and prayed for guidance, too flustered to look again. After the service, she stood around outside until Floyd got too antsy, but she never saw her come out and she hadn't seen her since. Was she gone out of town? Or . . . or something else? It perplexed her deeply, like all the rest happening here of late, but Edna reckoned there were some things in this world she wasn't meant to understand; she made the bed. She tucked the corners of the sheets and blankets neatly, fluffed the pillows, laid the pretty chenille spread with its pale blue tassels, and placed embroidered pillows on top of the sleeping ones, and when she was done, it was like a pretty little box with the lid on, her answer to her stepmother's worries about "letting go." Edna never burped in public.

That was one of Beans's famous numbers. Good old Beans! Haw! Especially at the dinner table. You could count on him ripping one on nights (strange things going on in town? Waldo hadn't noticed; strangest thing he'd seen was a greasy lug wrench tangled in black silk panties at the foot of the motel bed he used sometimes; he had passed it on to old Stu a night or so ago at the country club, asking if he could use it, and Stu said, sure he could, it was his, and they both elbowed each other and had a big laugh: you dirty dog!) when the fraternity had special guests like a rich alumnus or the dean of women, most often just when someone was about to make a speech, Waldo himself a frequent victim: "Now, brothers, we should all feel free to say exactly what we think." *Wurrrr-RRP!* It was that or else honking his nose in a filthy rag if not the tablecloth itself or letting a thunderous fart, Beans won all the farting contests, too. The Wind Machine. Foghorn. Beans hated all ceremony—"People not acting like people," he'd say, eructating consummately for emphasis—and his vulgar gestures, which he called "elocutionary," were all meant, quite simply, to let the hot air out. Waldo sometimes imitated him, even to this day, much to the annoyance of Lorraine, who now crawled into bed beside him, and often as not to that purpose. Beans was a funny guy. He was adept at falling down stairs or off chairs, often grabbing, as though desperately, at some girl's skirt as he fell, and he carried stickers around with him saying things like EAT ME and BACK OFF!

I JUST CUT THE CHEESE! to slap on the backs of professors, BMOCs, and housemothers. He always kept a shirt at the bottom of the laundry basket for anyone who came in asking to borrow one for a big date, and he sometimes wore it himself to crowded classes or sorority parties, you couldn't get within a mile of him. At an all-university symposium, hosted by the dean of students, on the topic of what his fraternity brothers knew as tomcatting and the rest of the world called rape, Beans turned up with a couple of old prosthetic limbs (or maybe they came off an amputeed mannequin) tucked into a sleeve and a pantleg, his limbs doubled away inside his clothes, and when some gangly man-eater started railing madly against what she called geeks and frat-brats, Beans leaned toward the audience and made an impassioned confession, colorfully detailed, of all his sins against womankind (back at the house, it became known as "Brother Beans's Hymenbuster Address"), concluding with a promise to clap his offending organ in red-hot irons if it did not mind its p's, q's, and arse when appearing in public. "Just the same, hot stuff," he added, turning to the rabid fraternophobe (could this have been Marge? Waldo wasn't sure, but she was up there at State at the same time, politically gadflying as usual, though he didn't know her then, not his field; which was, in a word, partying; in turn, not Marge's), "I'd give an arm and a leg to get into your pants!" Whereupon, he ripped his leg out from his trousers, his arm from his shirt, and tossed them across the stage at the woman who looked like she was about to shit a brick from purple rage and terror. Applause, laughter, boos, and for beamish Beans another semester on probation, which he understood as his natural lot, prospering therein. At the reception party before John's wedding, Beans got up and proposed a toast to the families of the bride and groom with his fly gaping, one of his favorite gags and always good for laughs, because even if you were in on it, the fun then was watching the others trying to decide where to look or how to get him to sit down. "Now, I want to be completely open about my true feelings here," he would slur drunkenly, bending forward so as to spread the zippered doors more widely agape. "We are always so buttoned up about how we feel about one another. What's there to hide? Nothing! Or almost nothing. So tonight, and especially for all you ladies, I'm going to reveal something I've never revealed before . . ." He was a riot out at the stag party, too, a one-man band, using all his appendages, even his prick and his nose and not excluding his butt, for percussion, himself as a wind instrument, or, rather, a whole wind section. Waldo could hardly wait to see what stunt he'd pull at the wedding itself, but, best he could remember, he never showed up. Too hungover maybe, or maybe John, for his own sake, or his bride's, had him stowed away somewhere. Dear old Brother Beans. Hadn't seen him since. Loved that sucker once. Now it was like he never was. Feeling sentimental, Waldo rolled over on his side and, nighty-nighting Lollie, popped a three-stage cracker in memory of his long-lost fraternity brother and of bygone days. Life, my love: funniest, saddest circus in town.

Funny maybe. Sad certainly. But off the wall sometimes as well, her own freak show exhibit one. What more Lorraine knew about strange goings-on than did her corkhead hubby was that people were having trouble these days keeping John's bride, so long in the middle of things here, within their field of vision. She sort of was there, like always, and she sort of wasn't. At least that was what Lollie was picking up around town—picking up, that is, as in picking up a radio station when spinning the dial or punching the scan button. No one was *talking* about John's wife's tendency these days to come and go without actually coming or going, almost as though to mention it might bring bad luck, some sort of taboo or something, but they were thinking a lot about her and it, and of late, ever since that weird night at the club when Maynard had barked out his love inside her head, Lorraine had found herself, though she didn't know why and on the whole didn't like it, increasingly privy to their unspoken speculations. Which at first she'd thought *were* being spoken, making the mistake of asking, "What? Beg your pardon?" and getting sharp squinty gazes in return, irritable thought-motes sifting through that were anything but generous toward her person. Not that she was served much better when she kept her mouth shut. Some things you just didn't want to know. That line about wishing to see ourselves as others see us was a crock of shit. So fearful was Lorraine of what her last best friend Marge might really think of her, in fact, she'd been avoiding her recently, even though Marge had called her twice now to tell her she was making a very big decision and she needed—*please!*—Lorraine's help, but she did run into her milquetoast husband out at the country club one afternoon when Marge was out on the course, and learned, tuning in while he stared absently out at the practice green, that, one, watching John's wife walk her clubs to the first tee a while ago, Trevor had been able to see only isolated bodily parts shifting along, never the whole person, and, two, her point on his "action aerialgraphs" (had Lorraine heard him right?) had vanished altogether, whatever that meant. Stopping in at the little downtown drugstore for her summer supply of antifungal cream and foot powder, Band-Aids, calamine and sunburn lotion, antibiotic ointment, bug spray, antacids, moisturizing cream, and an over-the-counter hemorrhoid treatment that Lorraine hoped the crippled pharmacist in there with the Coke-bottle lenses who always looked like she had a cob up her ass would think was for Waldo (she did), she overheard, so to speak, an account of how someone (had to be John's wife from what she could "see" of her) came in earlier, stepped up onto the old penny weighing machine Oxford had installed in there half a century ago, and then, more or less abruptly, wasn't there anymore—but the machine still registered her weight as though she were. This was supposedly similar to something that had happened when she "lumbered into the doctor's office"(?) a few days ago. Certainly old Alf seemed worried about her (there was a squishy tactile image that meant nothing to Lollie, though it made her shudder when she flashed on it, or it on her, a night ago out at the club), the police chief did, the woman's hairdresser, her odd son's teacher likewise. Beatrice had a story about her from church choir practice (Lorraine could hear her thin and thinning voice, but could not see her, not quite aware that this was also Beatrice's own sensation), though it only leaked in fragments through Trixie's overwhelming preoccupation these days with the unfathomable mystery of her pregnancy, which Lorraine gathered was more than mere uncertainty about who the father might be. And so on around town, Veronica, Daphne, even John's mother, a pattern emerging, fading, reassembling itself, much like the subject of that pattern herself. But what to make of it? Lollie didn't know, knew even less what to make of this newfound gift of hers, call it that, more like a collapse of some part of her immune system, in truth, and capable, she knew, of driving her batty. Did she truly want to know about Brother Beans's obnoxious performance at a stag party eighteen years ago? No, she did not. Her boys had got into a fight at bedtime and, breaking it up, she'd discovered she knew everything that was boiling up in their hateful little minds, including their intimate loathing of her just at that moment, thanks a lot, guys. Too much. Peace, please. And, so beseeching, Lollie had quietly slipped into bed beside her dreamless spouse, who, having saluted her fulsomely from beneath his big tent, now snored peacefully beside her (nothing but utter darkness there when she turned in—damn him for his unearned peace of mind!), wishing she'd brought some matches to bed with her so that she might light up one of his salutes and give his butt something to think about even if he remained impenetrable between the eats.

Fire! The forest is on fire! Oh my God! *All is lost!* Where's my–? No, no, the Artist (author) was just dreaming, it's all right, calm down, get a drink of water. Ellsworth staggered from cot to sink and ran the cold tap full blast as though to douse the still vivid flames, his heart pounding. It was so *real!* The Artist, too, terrified, his heart pounding, lying there on the riverbank where he's thrown himself: he plunges his head in the water (the whole damned forest was ablaze!), thinking: The Stalker's not the truly dangerous one. I am. He stroked his face. In the dull silvered mirror over the sink, Ellsworth saw the suffering writer, eyes hollow and cheeks unshaven, thready hair unwashed and tangled, and he was reassured. What day was it? Night, rather. He didn't know. Next issue of the *Crier* probably due. Or overdue. He'd rerun an old one. Remember when. What did it matter, always the same news anyway, they'd probably not even notice. Well, the new brides would. The newly promoted and the newly bereaved, damn their black relentless souls, their pride of names. And there was the one-man mayoral race, heading into its silly season now with Pioneers Day just around the corner, and pool hours to be announced, Little League box scores, the repaving of Sixth Street to report. Now Ellsworth saw the abused writer above his sink, the unappreciated one, the one forced to hack out his miserable worldly pittance at the expense of his art, a more tragic character than the suffering one, though not as appealing. He gave the abused writer a sympathetic nod, the suffering one an ironic smile, turned to his old painted kitchen table whereon his gathering opus lay, and saw in an instant that the Model had vanished. This was the meaning of the dream of raging fire, and the panic it had stirred in the Artist's heart. Had he really wished to destroy it all? Just because she'd—because she wasn't—because he can't find her? But she might still be here, after all, just hiding, playing a game, as in the old days. There were old days? He hadn't thought about them, but probably there were. Now the Artist rolls over on his back, there at the bank of the dark glittering river where he's flung himself, and he sweeps the wet hair out of his face, gazes up through the branches of his forest at the vast and vaulted sky above, where all is nameless and nothing is. His fate without her. Perhaps she's vanished to remind him that there *were* old days, that there is an ancient bond between them that he, in his intransigent pursuit of beauty, has tended to forget, or ignore, and that he must recover these lost connections, these buried feelings, if he is to plumb his true creative depths. That's assuming the child left freely, of course, and on her own. He holds his breath and listens for the Stalker's vile laughter. His insinuating wheeze, his sinister steps, any sign would do. Silence. A terrible emptiness all around. He seems to remember now her desperate cries, muffled by a ruthless hand clapped to her tender mouth, her bare limbs flailing through the undergrowth. What then? Well, he must rescue her! His art depends on it! The Artist lies sprawled on his back by the rippling stream under the scattered stars, considering the heroics that face him on the morrow and contemplating meanwhile, as he prepares to drift off for a bit so as to refresh himself for the coming ordeal, the unspeakable things the blackhearted Stalker is no doubt doing now with and to the captured child. Ah! No! The villain . . . !

Who, in this town and on this night, might by most be held to be Maynard II, alias the Nerd, he whose unremitting acrimony concealed a single kernel of burning love like a kidney stone that would not pass, and who, presently, found himself reliving old days and bitter bonds, unearthing rages best left buried. He was back in law school terrified again by exams he could never pass, his head thick with torts and writs and penal codes, which, as he did, suffered from cruel aliases and so were better known as tarts and half-writs and penile codes. Beyond the open bathroom door of their barren student rooms, his wife of the moment was in the red tub on her knees, sucking off some guy whose face was hidden by a flounce of shower curtain. Even with her mouth full, she was telling the asshole (who was it? the jock she was jazzing across the hall? big bad John? his law professor? the cunt-crazy kid out at the country club? the anonymous buttocks she clutched told him nothing) all about Maynard's failings as a lover: "His sperm tastes like toe-cheese," she said. The words in the law book he was studying kept blurring and changing before his eyes, but he did make out "jus naturale," which (the guy in the tub was either coming or vilely laughing) he suddenly understood clearly for the first time. Right! So when Daphne started to reveal his secret love—"You know who the Mange's really got the hots for? You'll never believe this!"—he rose up and turned on the heat, he really let the bitch have it, with pleasure watched her sizzle and pop (the guy was gone like he was never there), bouncing about in the charred tub (scorched the red paint right off the fucking thing) as though hot-wired. He felt powerful and pressed up against the ceiling in exhilaration as he fired away, then left her flopping helplessly there below in her dark bathwater stew and flew out the window, stretching his limbs joyfully as he soared above the empty streets and sidewalks of his mean little town, now groveling contritely at his feet. He saw or heard (or was somehow aware of, as though she might be the town itself) Veronica crying ("What are *you* doing here?" he seemed to hear her gasp or maybe scream), and that reminded him that the reason he was out here was because he was searching for their runaway son. The little smartass: he'd tan his cocky hide, but good! Maynard spied the patch of woods at the edge of town, crotched between the highway and the road to the airport, and losing altitude, went looking there.

Oddly, his absent son, wherever he was (strange place), was at that same moment, if not exactly flying, at least getting about in some manner different from walking, more like swimming maybe, only not through water but through something like thick warm air. He felt, though unencumbered by those clumsy suits, like an astronaut on a space walk. Little, as his family called him so as to mark one Maynard from another, was a long way from where he'd started on his trip, and nowhere to go but on, having no idea, if he did try to turn back, where "back" might be, nor any desire to do so. Here down below, no mean empty streets, no patch of woods nor country club, just, wherever he looked: People. Doing it. A sea, a tumultuous sea, of people, of naked people, all coupled up and going at it, in all the ways Fish had shown him in those books from his father's library, and in lots more ways besides. Wow! There must be thousands of them! Millions! No one that Little knew down there, or knew for sure. They *sort* of looked like people from his hometown, but they sort of didn't, too. The heavy air was resonant with a distant thumping music like the kind made by an organ and heard in church, but more insistent, as though egging on the people below. It was like a giant noisy mall with just one thing for sale. Why, sure, this must be hell, Little thought, and he noticed then something like a whiff of brimstone in the air, or else eggs gone off. And so what was he doing here? Was he just making a discovery or did he have a job to do? Little felt privileged, afloat above this panorama of fornicating bodies (that Bible stuff now suddenly made real and vivid in his expanding mind), but he felt left out, too. As though he were reading about it instead of really living it, something between him and what was going on down there not unlike tracing paper or maybe more like plastic wrap. His own cool maybe. "Cool is cool," Fish once told him rather mysteriously, "but too cool, Turtle, and you miss it all." Even if that missed "all" was hell, which maybe—hell, that is—was not so awful after all. So, wait, Little/Turtle had wanted to know when Fish told him that, was *God* too cool and, so, you know, also out of touch? Was *that* it? Fish didn't think so. Not a fornicator either, of course, how could He be? More like a pud puller, Fish had said and grinned, and both had flushed, then ducked the unsent bolt and laughed. Little wished his best friend Fish were with him now, he'd know what next to do. Lots of Fish-like types down below, but none he seemed to know or who knew him, though most were too far gone in what was either infernal torment or else the rapture (that word he'd got from the preacher's books, now dazzlingly illustrated) to see past their noses (yes, they all had very noticeable noses, bobbing in the air to the organ beat like birds' beaks at the feeder) even if they did know him. Which gave him, who wished to do but wished first to see before he did, encouragement: if he did get closer for a better look they'd hardly notice, so what the heck. He could almost hear it, like a divine command: let it happen. And so, like his father airborne in some other realm, through the pungent throbbing element, Little drifted down.

Though Little Maynard, aka Turtle, could not know it, his best pal Fish, having let it happen, had now, in consequential deep chagrin (he too wished for a friend nearby), confined himself to his own room, unwilling to leave it even to eat or watch a baseball game on TV, his sisters giggling and pointing whenever he had to step out to duck into the toilet ("Where can you see the full moon in broad daylight?" Jen called out, probably a joke she'd heard out at the mall), much worse, he knew, awaiting him outside the house, so fuck it, fuck them all. His father, made privy to the scene his tearful bare-arsed child had made climbing up on the car dealer's roof to get his jeans down (he'd drawn a crowd, including a busload of summer campers from Lennox's own church, stopped in the street to take in the glowing spectacle), had at last this evening been able to invade his son's dark unkempt retreat, and now knew more than he wished to know. Behind the boy's humiliation: dire events afoot. Or seemingly so. Lenny knew the woman rather too well, one of the first people he'd gotten to know here, and he doubted there was anything she was incapable of. Should he speak to the authorities or warn old Stu? Probably. But not really in Lenny's nature. And so he stretched out beside his sleeping Trixie, restless in her new discomfort, and letting slumber draw him nigh, as with ease it always did, he played with the images his son's story had provoked, searching for his Sunday sermon. The clothing of nakedness, Adam's need to, e.g. Not in modesty: what did the dumb animals care who watched or even know of what they saw? But to symbolize the putting on of manhood. Of humanhood. No, too easy, ho-hum, they'd tune him out. To close an era, then. Not of innocence but of dumb abjectness. To dress is to speak. To assert dominion, self-dominion. And the pain of that, the terror, the loss of the father and all that. Okay, but to be naked is also to be without guile. Another view, so to speak, of those turned cheeks. Thus, Jesus naked, whipped, and naked on the cross. Could he do that? No: over the top. And too many would see the legend writ there where nailed up: DAPHNE AND STU: BEST DEAL IN TOWN. Jesus, too, was ridiculed of course. KING OF THE JEWS: just another piece of bumper sticker kitsch, meant to amuse while committing murder. And was it that? Or about to be? His son was understandably agitated, he seemed literally to be choking as he spat it all out, and the poor boy was desperate to bend the world's burning gaze away from himself, point at anyone or anything in his agony, so who could say for sure? Ah well. "Suffer little children to come unto me," said Jesus, "with their pants down." Lenny laughed. Jesus, that great consoler, knew how to take the sting out. World-weary, though, you could see it in his face. Same old stories, always sad, over and over, stacked in the blood and reshuffled through time, the human comedy so-called, no way out. So, what was the answer? "Love," said Jesus (another joke maybe, but maybe not) and, putting his arm around Lenny, led him over to where the disciples were gathered, drinking beer and singing bawdy party songs. There were some women, too, dressed in togas and singing along, John's wife among them, whom he could hear but couldn't see, and his own wife Trixie, silent but in full view, full-bellied, dancing. "Our little Salome," said Jesus at his side, if it was still Jesus (more like John), "always good for a little head." Which indeed she was giving, without losing a beat, the singing disciples having clambered up on tables and stools and raised their robes, Lennox thinking, at least she won't get pregnant that way, though of course she already was. There were three clear knocks at the door. "Hey, Knucksie," the disciples called, hustling Trixie out of sight. "Fresh blood! Bring the suckers in!" Right, his old job, how did it go? "Who is it knocks at the door of the hallowéd temple of brotherhood?" Something like that. "A lowly neophyte, master, begging he be granted entry, that he might pledge himself to grow in wisdom and in love!" "Enter in due reverence, neophyte, upon your hands and knees!" It was his son Philip, Lennox saw, who was to be initiated. They were alone on a barren hillside, overlooking the little town below. He could see the civic center, the golf course, the airport, the malls, the disciples in a distant faceless cluster at the hill's foot. In his hands he held a wooden paddle bearing the fraternity coat of arms, and he felt old and betrayed by the callous ways of the world, misused, unfit for the tasks imposed upon him. Who was he to be so tested by God or by John or by anyone else? Who was he, easygoing Lenny, to play the patriarch? It wasn't fair. His son knelt at a stone altar, charred with the fires of picnickers or maybe bums or gypsies, and he pitied him. "Don't worry, son," he said. "We're only characters in an old story." "It's okay, Dad," Philip whispered from his position of mortification across the altar. "Let it happen."

There was a hollow knock at the master bedroom door in the house of the BEST DEAL IN TOWN, but the knocker entered without opening the door and not on her hands and knees, maybe not even on her feet, spectral as she was, her wet hair plastered darkly to her luminous skull and her eyes literally ablaze with a raging fire within. Her thin mouth gaped like a puppet's and something like a windy sigh emerged and the whole bedroom turned ice-cold. Brrr. Never could keep her damned mouth shut, that woman. Perhaps it was just a drunken dream, Stu's maybe, or else Daphne's, or maybe somehow they were sharing the same shivery nightmare, or thought they were, hoped they were, how could you live with such a thing in the real world? Have to cut back on the joyjuice. Starting tomorrow, swear on the blue book. Though Winnie had never been short on self-expression, she had nothing to say on this occasion or others like them (too many of late), no need to, just her cold breath was nag enough, her fiery eyes were. The only voice in the room was old Stu's, itself a sepulchral wheeze, broken up by snorts and hacks and toneless drowsy mumbles: "Oh, I do remember, Win, you old howler, remember it like yesterday—done you wrong, I know, and myself little enough good as well, though I did appreciate the silence after and, old head-blown junker that I was, felt souped up for a time. After all them years rustin' on the blocks, shit, but it felt good. But what would you know about that, eh, Win? Born out of your time, you were. You could whip a drayhorse, but didn't know an ignition switch from a handbrake, you had me runnin' on no cylinders at all, I was due for a trade-in, damn your lamps—stop that! you'll just smoke up your chimney! I told you I remember, how could I forget? Leaky old brainpan's got more holes in it than a shot muffler, can't deny it, but I can't burn that night out of it, hard as I try. So, sure, I'm sorry. Sorry I looked back, for one thing. Damn near spoiled the good times. And of course, the joyride couldn't last, beautiful as it was, too many potholes like always, I knew I'd throw a rod sooner or later and wind up in the crusher, but, hell, who don't? It's your time on the road that counts, not the boneyard you end up in, right? Ah, that stirred the embers, didn't it? Can't wait, can you, you old boat? So how'm I gonna get it, whaddaya got in store? Eh, Win? What's it gonna cost me?" "Maybe if we'd offer her a drink," Daphne said, or seemed to say (it was only a dream, wasn't it?), and the flames in Winnie's eye sockets blazed up again, her hissing exhalation frosted the room. "It's you, li'l darlin'," Stu rumbled (in his sleep, or in hers). "That's what the old bird's tryin' to say. And behind you . . . I can see . . . someone else . . ."

So could red-eyed Gordon. He wished he was dreaming but he was not. He was in his darkroom, crying in his acid-stained sleeves. He hadn't made an amateur mistake like this since he took up photography, and now, just now—! Outside his darkroom door, his wife Pauline was crying, too, he could hear her, a kind of dumb doggy whimpering. He'd forgotten to bring her any new clothes, except for the nightshirt which had had to be ripped at the neck and did not even cover her hips, and she was hungry (she was always hungry), nothing open until morning, but her problems seemed inconsequential compared to his own. How was it possible? Gordon had rushed home from the mall, trembling with excitement (nearly went right through the Main Street light, gave a giggly wave to the police chief as he hit the brakes that must have looked downright maniacal), and after splitting the new nightshirt hauling it impatiently over Pauline's big weepy head and punching open their last ham for her, which she'd wolfed down nearly as soon as he'd wrestled it out of the can, he'd made straight for the darkroom, promising Pauline that as soon as he'd finished his first set of prints—"This is it, Pauline! The greatest artistic achievement of my life!"—he'd go out to the steak house on the highway and bring her back a quadruple Surf 'n' Turf special with extra potatoes and a whole Dutch apple pie for dessert. "With chocolate-marshmallow icecream and butterscotch sauce!" And then: the terrible discovery. Which he'd refused to accept. Of course he'd seen the dark muddled appearance of the negatives as soon as they'd come out of the developer, but no. Out of the question. Under the enlarger he'd seen it, too, and as the prints accumulated their emergent shadows in the acid bath, but not until, in his frenzy, he'd begun the third set of prints had Gordon finally come to acknowledge the impossible truth: he had somehow reused film on which he had taken pictures of Pauline standing in the tub. What was that used film doing in his camera bag? This had never happened before, and Gordon did not see how it could have happened now. But he could no longer deny it. The evidence of his unpardonable folly hung from nylon lines in the soupy red light above his head like freshly polished guillotine blades. On all of them, Pauline's vast expanses of flesh, that flesh itself washed out and spectral, now bore spectral double impressions of another person who, so faint were the features, could be any person, the subject's legendary radiance contributing to the evaporation of her image. In one double exposure, slightly less burned out than the others, perhaps because of the darkness of the cubicle he was aiming at or because there was a large patch of Pauline's wet pubic hair in the original shot, he seemed to be able to make out John's wife's back, the linen tunic over her head and arms raised, and he worked desperately on that photo through several prints, isolating the area from shoulders to hips and carefully filtering out the hairy background, or foreground, which looked like a kind of beaded gauze curtain, but all he ended up with was something that looked more vegetable than human. The double exposures, had they been planned out, using Pauline's monumental flanks, for example, as a shaped screen on which to cast the image of John's wife striding through diaphanous clouds, etc., might have been beautiful, but opening the shutter fully twice over as he'd done had erased all the detail, all sense of a tactile surface, ruined, ruined, his chance of a lifetime. Gordon sat slumped in despair against the old metal high-stool in there, hot tears streaming down his cheeks, listening to the wistful whining of his poor grotesque wife curled up outside the door, and remembering something the woman at the library, the wife of the druggist, had once told him when he was still a young man and all afire with his highminded artistic ideals. Integrity, discipline, dedication, talent, faith in yourself, these are all very good things, Gordon, she'd said, and certainly you cannot be an artist without them, but they will not be enough. There's something else needed, too, something much less easy to name or define. Call it, well, a mystery. *The* mystery. From which, at this moment, Gordon felt utterly closed out.

Rex also felt closed out, but not from any supposed mystery (though he would have agreed with Kate: the musicians he loved called it soul), rather just from the piece he wanted. The keys he'd stolen when he'd blown off the job out here at the airport had got him into the main building all right, but John had apparently changed the lock on the door to his private office, the suspicious bastard.

The room, Rex remembered, had big steel-framed industrial windows that looked out on the loading ramps and runways but didn't open. This cheapshit door would be easy to force, of course, or just to punch a hole in, but he couldn't do that. His idea was to remove one of the rifles in the gun case, unnoticed, then return it the same way before anyone knew it was missing, no prints on it but John's. Kill two birds, as they say, revenge the tune in Rex's head even more than murder. He'd left Nevada sleeping fitfully, told her he was feeling edgy, had to go for a jog, back soon. She'd mentioned earlier that John was out of town for a couple of days, this was the moment. Would the sonuvabitch then, the evidence all against him, really take the rap in a town he owned? Nah, but it might at least cause the arrogant cocksucker a little discomfort, and cost him a night or two of sleep wondering who the fuck it was who could walk freely around inside his pants like that. So how was he going to get in to the goddamned place? Well, try turning the handle, numbnuts: wide open. Hah. It had been a while since Rex had worked out here, and he'd only been in John's office a couple of times, but the big windows let in enough light from the parking and loading areas outside for him to make his way easily across to the big glass case that housed some of John's famous gun collection. These keys worked. Smooth as silk. He had the glass doors open and his gloved hand on the piece of hardware he wanted when he realized there was someone else in the room. Sitting in the padded swivel chair behind John's desk. Might be John of course. But probably wasn't. Ice tinked softly against glass like chopsticks on a deadened cymbal: a lonely drinker. In the dark. Not John's style. Rex was playing all this in his head with his hand on the rifle, just above the stock. He took the rifle down out of the case, turned, and aimed it at the figure behind the desk. "Turn on the light, mister," he said. If it was John, of course, he was dead. The rifle probably wasn't even loaded. "And don't try anything funny." He heard the ice again as the guy took a drink, set the glass down with a sigh, then reached forward and turned the little switch on the desk lamp. It was John's sideman, the one Nevada described as a babyfucking psycho. Dressed in what looked like designer jungle fatigues. Was he waiting here for John? "Planning to kill someone?" the guy asked, his voice slurring slightly, and took up his drink again. "I heard someone prowling around," Rex said, taking in the scene. "Thought I'd better arm myself just in case. So, what's your story?" "Short on other options in this greasy little pit stop, my friend, I'm getting pleasantly fried, how about yourself?" Rex lowered the rifle, sat back against a butt-high filing cabinet, lit up. "I recognize you now.

The hotshot in the sports jet. John's buddy." "His partner. Help yourself." He gestured vaguely toward the bottle, staring at Rex's gloved hands, seemingly amused. There was a picture of John's wife and kids on the desk, an ashtray, the bottle, the brass lamp. And something else: handcuffs and a horse crop. "Don't drink on the job. But you should let people know when you're going to hang out here, General. Surprising nervous types like me can get you messed up." "Work here, do you?" "Part-time." "No shit." Rex had the feeling he was not fooling this sneering wiseass with his jive and began to wonder if he'd have to waste him. Somehow he didn't think so. It was like he was too cool to give a shit about anything, murder included. About that, he now said, as though tuning in to Rex's head: "Ever kill anybody?" "No." "Thought about it, though, I bet." "Maybe." "Sure you have. Natural as sex. We'd all kill if we could get away with it. Always somebody we'd like to have out of the way. Who's in your way?" "Fat dudes. Like you." The guy smiled, peered up at him over his whiskey glass, his face spookily half-lit by by the green-shaded desk lamp, his smirk luminous, his eyes, though gleaming, set in deep shadows. "How about John?" Rex was taken aback, took a quick drag on his butt. This cat was truly weird. Outside. "What about him?" "Well, he's certainly rich. Big man, John. What do you think? Would you like to kill him?" Rex knew his hesitation had given him away, so he said: "Yeah, I think I'll go look for him now, get it over with. Hang around here much longer and I'll take out the wrong dumb motherfucker." He pushed off from the filing cabinet, strolled to the door, rifle in hand, flicked his cigarette out into the corridor, then turned back. "If you need anything, pops, look for me down at the night watchman's crib by the main hangar." "Sure. You bet. So long, killer."

Big rich John, pit-stopping Bruce's lifelong pal and partner, was at that moment, give or take a time zone or two, stretched out under a lean handsome woman on a slowly rotating circular bed in her own bachelor digs, very fanciful and high-tech, up the coast from L.A. where they'd met earlier that day, though not for the first time. The woman collected Victorian children's book art, it was all over her walls like a giant composite comicstrip, imaginative and sensuous and richly hued, color gradations as fine as hairs and all now in vibrant flowing motion, as though stirred by a fairy wind. Everything was in motion: the lights, the furniture, the undulating music which seemed somehow more visible than audible. In short, John was stoned, enjoying a magic carpet moment with a powerful young sorceress, wild and beautiful. Life was. He said that. Wild and beautiful. She, pegged to him, riding him like the golden knight on her wall, both hands at the pommel, kneading balls, clit, and thighs, digging in their pubic hair as though searching for buried treasure, agreed. He felt very peaceful, letting the bouncing cheeks of her solid little ass slap his cupped hands like juggled fruit, feeling a world away from ejaculation, yet racing along at cliff's edge at the same time, ready to tip at any moment, but that moment still his to choose. And meanwhile, everything, *everything* was as though organically fused and doing a delicious full-spectrum color dance for his fiberless optic-wired head alone. This shit lasted forever, he knew, but he was in good company and prepared to squander a few of his life's hours, his long life's hours, it was like a time between times. He had just bought a national trucking firm to go with his air cargo operations, his money was on the right horse in the convulsive communications and entertainment industry, thanks in part to his fiery rider, and he was headed back home to his own annual Pioneers Day barbecue to announce plans to build a racetrack on a rundown farm he'd picked up at auction. For some reason, her sexual energy maybe, this woman reminded him of Marie-Claire, though of course not so mad—in fact, this woman was not mad at all, she knew exactly what she was doing, even spaced out on acid she did. John did not share Bruce's regressive appetite for shy little girls, the fantasy fuck of eternal playboys who cannot grow up; John was turned on only by smart mature strong-willed women with lives, power, talents, wealth of their own. And if they lacked any of that he provided it for them, as best he could. Not for their sake. For his. It made the sex better. What about your wife? What? The woman had stopped bouncing for a moment and had settled back into his broad hands, doing a slow twist around his cock. Does she ever do this? Sure, everybody does. He couldn't remember when last, though. Couldn't even remember if he saw her the last time he was home. Must have. This feels very fucking good, he said. It'll get better, sweet prince, she laughed. He saw now why he thought of Marie-Claire: her teeth. When the woman smiled, she displayed Marie-Claire's pebbly little rows of white babyteeth. But whereas Marie-Claire's smile suggested a catastrophic vulnerability, this woman's was more sensuously calculating, witchy in a way, not unlike the mirrored smile of Snow White's stepmother, probably on the wall behind her though seeming to hover in the air just over her shoulder. He told her so and she grinned again, her eyes gleaming, her auburn hair coiling around her perspiring face wild as the wild Medea's now sliding into view, and told him about a pornographic cartoon she'd seen about Snow White and the Seven Dwarfs, all the time wriggling her hips round and round. The whole cottage got into it, humping away, shooting jism out its chimneys, and with all those dwarfs involved, of course, that girl got it every which way up every hole she had, gave me a lot of funny ideas. Not about dwarfs and princes, I hope. She laughed and, tightening up, twisted harder. I remember the first fuckfilm I ever saw, he said, fingering her circling anus. She gasped as he worked his finger in and grabbed at his nipples as though to brace herself. Saw it on a big screen. Friend of mine in town set it up, his father owned the moviehouse, the Palace, the old Palace Theater. The Palace, she repeated, her eyes squeezed shut. He thought his were, too, but he saw everything, and more besides. *Home Movies*, the film was called, I think. A smalltown couple with two kids, a girl and boy, have the neighbors in to look at their holiday movies. The neighbors sit around with their knees together, oohing and ahing politely, but what they're seeing of course are all sex scenes, mostly incest in all the ways you could imagine with a few naked campers and gullible hitchhikers thrown in. The woman on top of him, still clawing at the flesh around his nipples, was pumping back and forth vigorously now, her eyes closed, biting her bottom lip with her row of little teeth. As he went on describing the movie, not really wanting to, but as though spellbound by his own voice, which seemed to be booming out of the quadraphonic speakers in the corners, he found himself at some point telling her instead about the last time he'd been up at the cabin with Bruce, together balling three women at once, two of them a mother and daughter. Nevada had apparently set it up, or some of it (the third woman might have been a scheduling mistake), but she wasn't there. At one point when they were all in a sweaty tangle, Bruce had cast a poignantly sorrowful look at John over the ass of the woman on his face, then lifted one hand off her quivering butt and given John a brief high five, John slapping back, thinking nothing of it at the time, but worried about it since. What the hell was Bruce trying to say? Beats me, the woman groaned. But what about the neighbors? The family raped them, he gasped, and they had an orgy or something, but the strange thing was seeing that film in the Palace. The cliff, he realized, was crumbling at his feet. Or thereabouts. It was like a fucking cathedral, that moviehouse, a golden-domed two-decker with a lot of ornate detail, red plush seats, a lobby like a hotel's, we'd all gone there with our parents to see the classics, the original *Snow White*, for example, it was like a part of history, something bigger than all of us, and suddenly, there we were—*whoof!* God! *Great!* Awesome! the woman rocking away on him whimpered, her head thrown back now (his view was of her slender white throat, arched chin, dilating nostrils, which seemed to be merging with the dancing overhead lights and swirling ceiling), her raspberry-tipped chest wet and heaving, her sleek belly rippling like the sails on Sinbad's ship, listing beside the bed. He was asea on Sinbad's sea, storm-tossed yet satin-pillowed, spume-blowing nigh at hand. But wha-whatever happened to—*gasp!*—that fantastic theater? The Palace? It was in the way, he wheezed. I tore it down. The woman jerked forward, her burnished hair whipping the air, her vagina convulsing. Oh Jesus! she laughed. Whoo! You fucking bastard! I think I'm coming! Pink labial folds had burgeoned around the mouth of the rabbit hole Alice was falling down, the wet red sides of the hole itself throbbing in constrictive waves like the vagina that clasped his cock, and Daphne sprouting laurel leaves while Apollo grabbed at her vanishing ass—there they came! pop! pop! pop!—was like the onset of some stupendous mythical orgasm. He felt like he was coming and not coming at the same time, and then, as she cried out, or the music did, or he did, the cry all around them like a lightning flash, there was a great quaking as though the Big One had hit, and in his balls at least, it had. John, shuddering blissfully as his loins turned explosively inside out, was intensely happy. Not as in ever after, but the genuine article. Right now. Life, goddamn it, if you lived it, really fucking lived it, was very very good.

The old Palace Theater that John suddenly erased from view one day was being, as time passed, erased from the communal memory as well, there was already a whole new generation in town for whom it was only a legend, remote as the fall of Rome, which had sometimes been witnessed there. John's daughter Clarissa was just a toddler when the Palace came tumbling down, all movies were for her and her friends linked to the magic of the sunswept malls, and there were scores of people who had moved here since then who supposed that the bank and office buildings in that block had been there forever. Ask Kevin the golf pro out at the country club about the Palace, for example, and though he'd been in town for more than a decade and saw at least one movie every week, he would probably suppose it was a form of smalltown self-mockery of the sort he'd heard so much of here, or maybe a gibing way to refer to someone else's fancy roost. Contrarily, his predecessor, a married man, had, while attending a predemolition festival there of big-screen epics, got blown in the back row, just under the projection booth, by the orthodontist's daughter whom he later eloped with and whose own legend as a wild thing had itself achieved, in this town anyway, epic proportions. Both of them were long since gone, though, taking their memories with them. Floyd and Edna had also moved to town that year that Kevin came and so had never known the famous moviehouse, witnessing only the blocklong pile of rubble just up the street from the hardware store that Floyd managed, the rubble itself disappearing before they'd even got used to this new place and so by now forgotten as well. They'd even arrived too late for the auction of the appurtenances and decorations of the Palace and its near-neighbor, the even more famous Pioneer Hotel, though Edna did find at a junk dealer's a pretty plaster of Paris statue from the moviehouse of a girl turning into a tree that she bought for the backyard for only three dollars on account of one arm was broken, but Floyd made her put it away in the basement because he said it was pagan and sinful, Floyd having become a (mostly) strict born-again Christian since coming here, even though, because of his new business position, they went to the rich folks' church where the born-again notion was not very popular. The preacher at that church and his family had also come here after the downtown renovations and so knew nothing of all those old buildings that had once dominated the business center, though the reverend had once, tuning in to the memories of others and borrowing from archive photos published in *The Town Crier*, used the old Palace Theater in one of his sermons, his topic being the ephemerality of man's brief gaudy show on earth compared to the simple grandeur of God's theater of eternity, something like that, few could remember it afterwards any better than they could remember most of the movies they'd seen in the Palace. He did stir some tender memories, however, so his sermon, even if it didn't make much sense, was, for some in his congregation, erotically stimulating, a fact that might have aroused old Floyd's wrath, had he known of it, but not Reverend Lenny's: God is love. And vice versa. The crippled lady at the pharmacy had come to town about the same time as the preacher and so had never been inside the Palace either, but her husband Cornell had rarely missed a movie there that he'd been allowed by the ratings to see, and his sister and brothers too had spent some of the most significant moments of their childhood and adolescence inside its ornate high-domed interior, their parents being themselves faithful customers, but one of Corny's brothers was dead, the other had put on a dress and left town forever, and poor Corny himself either had no memories remaining or had no words with which to express them. Of the four children, only Columbia might have provided a significant recollection or two about the fantasy structure that was once the very heart of this community, though what she probably remembered best was the popcorn popper and candy counter.

Town chronicler Ellsworth, determined to preserve some record of that great secular temple, which he had disdained as a youth but toward which he now felt increasingly sentimental (he used to take Barnaby's little girl there on Saturday afternoons, they saw *Bambi* together), had, long before he'd "turned darkly inward" as his friend Gordon put it and become so reclusive, pressed at least a dozen people in town to write an "I Remember" column about the old Palace Theater, all of them agreeing with embarrassed laughter that there were sure a lot of stories they could tell about that place, but none so far had. Most, when asked, said they were "still thinking about it," though Columbia's and Cornell's father Oxford, having little else to do these days except mind the grandchildren now that Gretchen had taken over the pharmacy, had managed to compose a number of discontinuous fragments and lacked only a theme that would unite them, a kind of bonding agent, as it were, which, the more he thought about it, was turning out to be his dead wife Kate. That half-blind Oxford should be the old moviehouse's memoirist was ironic, of course, since he knew nothing of its fabulous decor except by hearsay and had witnessed its spectacles through a myopic haze; even the stirring posters in the lobby he had had to examine with his nose pressed against them, unstirred by what he could not wholly see. But courting options were few when carless Oxford courted Kate, carless not just because of his disability (Kate could drive and when, rarely, they could, she did) but because gas was being rationed in those days and tires could not always be replaced, and that being so, the Palace Theater was about the best they had to hand by foot, other than the library where Kate worked, which served them for some of their more private moments, especially conversations of the intimate sort. Though she never went to university, Kate was a great reader, the reader Oxford always wished to be but could not for the terrible weariness it cost him, Kate often reading to him in those courting days, and after marriage, too, when work and children gave them time alone, and so every invitation to the Palace was accompanied by his apology, Kate insisting in return that she loved the movies, and learned from them, too, much as she preferred to read. "To imagine something is to create it in our heads when it is not there before our senses, and that's what we do when we read," she said one night as they walked out of the Palace after watching the newsreel twice (there was war footage and Kate's brother was headed for the European theater, as it was called, soon after would die there, not centerstage, but lost in the chorus as it were, unbilled and overlooked in the reviews). "I would rather imagine something than see it, and there is something wrong with that, I suppose. It's why librarians are thought to be such eccentrics. But sometimes I think that seeing is only a kind of imagining and an impoverished and unreliable one at that, even though our eyes probably lie less than words do, or can do. We like film because we feel like it's connecting us immediately somehow with the real world and with no words in between, or anyway no words you have to listen to. Turning on the image directly turns off the imagination maybe, but we are given an existential assurance about the world and ourselves in it, even if illusory and superficial, that books can never give us." Moments like that made Oxford adore her and want to hug her, and sometimes he did, so his memories of the Palace Theater were in effect bound up in the same kind of romantic sentiments and vague nostalgic impressions that everyone else had. Without any real reason, except that he was next to his wise Kate, his arm around her in the dark, sharing in some manner the unfolding play of light and shadows up above their heads (for Oxford's sake, they always sat down front), Oxford would break into tears, not just during their courting years but in all the years thereafter as well until, Kate herself dying, the old Palace disappeared; they went almost weekly to the movies back then, sometimes with the children or with friends like Alf and Harriet, often just the two of them together, even after television became all the rage and they were the only people in the theater past adolescence. Kate even liked to go to the commercial genre movies, the westerns and romances, the gangster movies, thrillers, screwball comedies, because she said it was like going in for a tune-up: they reset the basic patterns. Coming out of a monster movie one night, a movie Oxford loathed for its antirationalist advocacy of faith in antiquated belief-systems as a means of problem solving and its depiction of scientists as either villains or victims of their own unfortunate capacity to reason, Kate, responding, said: "That's one way of looking at it. Folk art is always afraid of the new, which science represents, and that's part of the fear of monsters. But it's scary for everybody to imagine getting turned into something entirely different from what we think we are, even if we don't much like what we are, just as it would frighten us to have the world we live in change its basic rules in incomprehensible ways all of a sudden. Start spinning in the other way or something. Monster movies are not about the resolutions, that's just tacked on to make them palatable. They're about the problem." She paused and turned back to gaze up at the old Palace Theater. The marquee lights were off, and the heavyset young man who ran the theater was up on a ladder changing the titles for the following day. The next movie, as previewed, was about a dangerous and seemingly indestructible criminal who enters a peaceful community and terrorizes it, called *The Intruder*, or something like that. Probably a man of reason who makes all the wrong moves in that movie, too. "We like to think, even when we're being reasonable, Oxford, that there are fixed boundaries—to our bodies, our essential being, our homes and families, our towns and nations—it's how we know or think we know we have a self. But maybe it's all a mad delusion, maybe there are no boundaries and no selves either, our conscious life just a way of hiding the real truth from us because, simply, it's too much to live with. We have to stuff it back down in the pit where the creepies live, if we want to function at all, even if functioning, as we call it, is possibly the craziest thing we do. Art, even bad art like Hollywood horror movies, puts us in touch with that truth by breaking down the boundaries for a moment, producing monsters we secretly know to be more real than the good citizens who eventually subdue them." "So what's to save us from the abysmal monsters within," Oxford sighed, "if faith's not on and function we must?" She turned toward him with a smile, a smile he could not quite see but knew was there. "Irony," she said, and took his arm to lead him down the dimly lamplit street. "And love. Which is also ironic."

Ah, the old Palace Theater, loved too by Dutch, that heavyset fellow whom Oxford saw up a ladder one night. He was standing, not far from the popcorn machine, in the grand lobby of the famous old moviehouse, breaking his own no-smoking rules and nodding at acquaintances amid the sellout crowd passing thickly through to the auditorium, John and his wife and kids among them, he was amused to note. A coup: Dutch had managed to book *The Back Room*, a rare underground flick using amateur talent, for its first-ever viewing on the big screen: "Where the Movies Are Still the Movies," as the faded lobby banner said. In the projection booth, he found the film already strung up on the projector, surprised to see it was on thirty-five-mil instead of eight- or sixteen-, though how could he have shown it if it wasn't? He'd watched the thing a thousand times, but he still wasn't sure what he'd see when he started it up. Ah, yeah, that's right: the old Getaway. But tarted up by Hollywood, hardly recognizable: glass panes on the windows instead of chair seats, a brass bed in place of the old sprung leatherette sofa, an electric lamp over the table in the middle—though the pennants, panties, and tattered calendar pinups on the walls looked genuine enough. The door opened, a real door with moldings and panels, not the tabletop John had mounted there, and the crowd pushed in, the same crowd he'd just seen in the lobby. They looked confused, turning round and round, taking the place in but not knowing what to do with it. Dutch could tell them, but not without spoiling the film. In fact, he realized now, he was part of the film, the projection room where he sat being separated from the cabin by a glass panel, a two-way mirror maybe since the others didn't seem to see him, though he could see them and himself, too, if it was himself and not just an actor playing himself. Or vice versa, whatever that meant—Dutch by now was sharing the confusion of the others. He was there in the room with them, wandering around, feeling lost, maybe he didn't know this film so well after all, and holding on to his dick as though if he let go of it he might lose it altogether—and, now that he thought about it, maybe that *was* how this movie came out, the shock ending, it was what made it so famous in the underground, wasn't it? He looked around for John, but he saw that there was no one here he knew. He was frightened now and wished he'd never booked this film. He tried to find some way out, but the crowd was too thick and there was a strange damp chill in the air. At last he spied old Stu the car dealer, sitting at the bar, and made his way over to him, still holding on. Something he had to tell him, couldn't think what, a joke he'd heard maybe, but at least it was someone familiar, he might find a way out of this movie before it was too late after all. But when Stu turned toward him he saw that his face flesh was moldy and dropping off the bone and his eye sockets were empty, just dark hollows: oh shit! that's it! *these people were all dead!* Dutch shrank back in terror and awoke in the dark. Where the fuck was he? His groin was wet: had he peed himself? No, beer, he'd spilled his beer. He was in the Back Room, sitting sprawled out in his velvety movie seat, salvaged from the Palace demolition, he could feel it under him, his pants down around his thighs and also wet from spilled beer, his limp dick, too, which he was still holding as if he were fishing with it, the lights out in the room at the other side of the mirror. Jesus, must have been some show, whoever it was, he couldn't remember, put him straight to sleep. He could hear soft snoring, couldn't tell the sex of it, thought it might be a woman. He wanted to get up, reel it in, pull his soggy pants on, go to bed. But he couldn't move. Too goddamned tired or something. Lead in his ass. Then, suddenly, the lights in the next room popped on, so startling him he nearly cried out. There were five or six guys in the room, all dressed in dark suits. One of them came over to the mirror to comb his hair, peering intently into it as though trying to see beyond it. Dutch, feeling looked at, pulled his pants up. I probably ought to give this shit up, he thought. The guy turned away (who was he? Dutch felt like he knew him), someone opened the door, and John's wife came in, dressed like a bride. They peeled the wedding gown off her, which was all she was wearing, and laid her out on the bed, her legs spread. Dutch was hard again (this was something different!) and, pumping away, he leaned forward to see what he could see. Oddly, not much. It was like there was something wrong with the camera, a water bubble on the lens or something—or on the mirror: he wasn't sure where he was anymore—but the less he could see, the more excited he got. He stood, his pants dropping to his ankles, trying to get a better angle, but the bubble moved where he moved. Didn't matter, the cream was rising, the lid was about to blow! But then the guys all turned toward him. The woman—was it still John's wife? he couldn't tell—curled a finger and beckoned him. There was no mirror. Dutch wanted to run but couldn't move, he was rooted to his dropped pants. The guys in the dark suits walked stiffly toward him with black grins on their horror-movie faces and he woke up again. In the dark as before. Still fishing with his dick, everything wet down there, etc. Didn't know where he was. Or if he was really awake this time or still asleep, or, whichever, what was going to happen next. Except that he had no intention of moving a muscle until it got light again. Probably going to be a long fucking night. But he'd sit tight, wherever he was, hold the hand he had.

The night was going to be a long one for Ellsworth, too, nor did he have a hand to hold, that was just the problem, empty-handed before the abyss was what he was. He'd made something out of nothing before, but did he have the strength to do so now, at this hellish hour, his spirit so depleted? After dozing and waking, dozing and waking more times than he could count, he'd stumbled down out of what he called his garret over the printing plant and *Crier* offices, intending to go home and fix himself something warm to eat, microwave a frozen soup or something, he was making himself ill with his obsessive work habits (pity the cafe across the street wasn't open twenty-four hours, this town just wasn't civilized enough for writers), when he had finally realized, pausing at the foot of the creaky old stairs to gaze blearily at the local wall calendar printed in the back shop each year for Trevor to provide to his clients at Christmastime, that the next issue of *The Town Crier* was indeed due out on the morrow, or later today as the case might be and undoubtably was, and he had not even started to put it together. For a long time, he didn't know how long, he was still half asleep, he just leaned there, unmoving, in front of the calendar, thinking the unthinkable: that, for the first time in over twenty-three years, he might skip an issue, or even (the one thought seemed to follow inevitably upon the other) cease publishing altogether. After his forest fire nightmare, shared as it happened with the Artist, Ellsworth had tried to put himself back to sleep with fantasies (the Artist's) of rescuing the captive Model from the nefarious Stalker once he was rested up enough to undertake it. But what was the Stalker doing to her? He had to imagine the Stalker's fantasies before he could imagine the Artist's, and this he found both more exciting and more disturbing, especially since the Model did not seem as upset about her treatment as he did. He or the Artist, he wasn't sure now. Half asleep or half awake, it all tended to get blurred and come and go in odd ways, such that at one point he found himself dreaming about the time, or else remembering it, that he took Gordon and Pauline to the movies, this was when he was still trying to recapture the bohemian life, hoping to blend art, friendship, and free love in one exemplary contemporary relationship, perhaps even a legendary one, and Gordon pushed Pauline ahead of him into the row of seats and followed her in, leaving Ellsworth stuck on the outside; only in his dream, if that's what it was, instead of Pauline it was a little girl and Gordon was still between them. Was he drawing her picture? What was he doing? When he shook off this confused and irritating image, he discovered that there was another buried beneath it, something he had in some way been envisioning all along: the devastated forest, stripped bare and charred to the roots, as far as you could see, no sign of life except for the Artist, alone and broken in the terrible black-stumped desolation, a man with nothing more to live for, more dead than alive, weeping silently as Ellsworth was weeping. Enough. (She was gone! Not a trace!) Time to take a break. This month's town photo, the one at which he was now so bleakly staring here at the foot of the stairs, a photo taken by Gordon like all of the others in the calendar, was of some Pioneers Day parade of the past, John's wife in a frontier costume waving distantly from an open convertible, as she did every year when she was not waving from a float. Must have been taken fairly recently, given the car models, but she looked like a child in the photograph. The child Ellsworth had once big-brothered. He knew that she was a faithful reader of the *Crier* and that if it did not appear she would be disappointed. Whenever duty called, as it was doing now, often as not it bore her cadences like an echo. "Tell me a story . . ." He checked the piles of unopened mail in the front office, hoping for hard copy, and there was some, but not enough. School was out, the high schoolers he'd come to depend on so heavily had other things to do, and even the contribution from the ministerial association was missing. There was an anonymous "I Remember" submission that he couldn't use, all names deleted, about a "prominent local businessman" who had made "an innocent young kid" pregnant and forced a "fetal murder" upon her that had cast "a hopeless black cloud" over her whole life, which did not seem to have been a short one. Some rather dreary photos in the weekly packet from Gordon: a tulip bed in bloom, an unidentified pole-vaulter going over the bar, a wide-angle shot of young people in the food court of some mall, John's daughter among them, a men's-club luncheon meeting, vacant tennis courts with puddles of standing water, a group of leached-out old people at the nursing home, also looking vacant. Ellsworth wondered if the author of the "I Remember" love story was among them. Gordon seemed to be raiding his archives, too. He hadn't even photographed the street repairs out front. But Ellsworth couldn't fault him, he himself had not gathered the usual local sports and club news, called the police station, courthouse, hospital, checked with John and other community newsmakers, interviewed the lone mayoral candidate, had not even, until now, sorted his week's mail—in short, Ellsworth had done none of the ordinary things necessary for putting out a responsible newspaper, he had no one but himself (and the Stalker) to blame. Too late now, though. Nothing to do but follow Gordon's lead and load up with thefts from the past. He went through the old bound issues of the *Crier,* checking the June editions, every five years back, for in-this-month items, struck on the heroic death in battle fifteen years ago of the son of the local pharmacist, a death that had shaken Ellsworth in ways quite different from the rest of the community, triggering the commencement of his loss of faith in the very notion of keeping a human chronicle, an abandoned line in his work-in-progress once marking the moment. He remembered asking himself: Who was this young man, so loved, it seemed, by all in town (though Ellsworth hardly knew him), and what his untold, now untellable, story? Fragments he had, a few witnesses, personal tributes: all surfaces. Concealments of a sort. What did it signify that Yale's real story, like those of countless others, was lost forever, replaced by a ceremonious invention? Or did it matter? Was that what all stories were, all lives? Yale had been a child here. There were Little League box scores. Boy Scout rosters. There were cast lists of school plays and class photos. John's wife was in them, too, they were classmates. They went to movies together. This was not in the obit folder, but Ellsworth had seen them in the lobby of the Palace when he first came back to town. Shocked him at the time. How did that fit? The Palace lobby alone was so full of crossed trajectories it made your head spin. And the Eastern university, the French girl, the distant war that killed him, suddenly the whole world was crowding into this sad little town, his file cabinet couldn't hold it all, his mind couldn't. So he catalogued dates and achievements and listed the bereaved and quoted the official military report and announced the memorial service and scribbled a "30" at the bottom and, pretending he had not been defeated, closed the drawer, telephoned the hospital to see who'd been born that day. Since then: hundreds of editions, thousands of spurious stories, as though trying to paper over the flux, believing in none of it, but faithfully doing his duty as though there were a point to it. The image of the Artist in the charred forest came back to mind, and he knew that, inappropriate though it was for the novel (the Model would be found, he'd see to that), it was true for him. To beat back the crowding despair (hopeless black clouds piling up everywhere), he decided to reach back to a happier time, some three years before Yale's death: the wedding. Not just to cheer himself up, but to reconnect with a more purposeful self, one who might see him through this dark night's desperate task. He dragged the tall volume, more fingered than most, down from the shelf, opened it to his big photo spread the week after the nuptials: already he was feeling better. A few hundred words on some remember-when theme, he supposed, together with four or five photos, a couple of ads (if they hadn't come in, he'd give them away), and another page was history, even if history it wasn't quite. Might even find some unused wedding snaps in the archives, if they were still orderly enough to find anything in them at all. Or, better: a look back at the old Pioneer Hotel. A couple of postcard views, mug shots of past owners, mixed with Rotary, Kiwanis, and BPW meetings held there, that convention of regional state highway commissioners that had changed the map, highschool team dinners, birthday parties and weddings, John's included, Gordon's moving portrait of the door left standing when all the rest came down. A good story for Pioneers Day and all that. The hopeless clouds were breaking up. He could do this. Then he noticed, for the first time, that in the group photo of the rehearsal dinner in the Pioneer Hotel banquet room the night before John's wedding there was a young man in the front row with his fly agape, his white underwear, hopefully underwear, plainly showing through. Ellsworth had used and reused this photo countless times—how had he not seen this before—!? There was a typo in the caption he'd missed, too, "weekend festivities" actually reading "weakened festivities," though that kind of a slip was more understandable, rare as it was. No, wait, it wasn't "weakened," it was "weakneed." As was, double-*k*'d, Ellsworth. He slumped into a chair. What was happening?

A question much like the one the young man in the photo with the open fly asked when someone in a tracksuit thrust a rifle into his hands and said: "This way. Come on. She's in the ravine." Before Beans could get an answer to the inquiry he then posed, however, that rough gent was gone like he never was. Beans joined the hunting party creeping through the trees ahead of him for fear of getting shot at by mistake if he didn't, but stayed to the rear, out of the flicking beams of their flashlights, which were like death rays to his throbbing head. A squat cop in sweaty shirtsleeves and suspenders and an old guy with a long snout led them. Toward what, Beans could not guess or even imagine, but he understood that it was very big. Crikey. Step out to take an innocent piss, and look what happens. Beans had awakened, still clutching his Swiss Army knife, in a closed-up Country Tavern, eerily empty, illuminated faintly by a bluish light filtering through the grimy windows, his face pasted to the table (must have passed out in spilled beer), his head cracking at the seams, and his bladder set to burst. The pornflicks were off, the jukebox dark. He'd pushed himself to his feet, feeling stiff and achey, pocketed the knife, picked up a fallen drumstick near his feet, and given the cymbals a sharp crack just to break the ponderous silence, scared himself doing it and sent a painful rip through what would be his brain if he had any. Dust had risen from the cymbals like a visible form of clatter, there was dust and dirt everywhere, stamped-on butts and food wrappers, bottles lying about in the gloom like spent artillery shells, unemptied ashtrays and dirty glasses, a veritable shithole. Beans thought about brother John entering on the morrow into the wedded life and wondered about the nature of this transformation: did it really bring an end to such joys as these? He shuffled creakily through the slough of disport to the door (tried the switch, the lights were dead) and stepped out into the moonless night. A few heavy mechanical hulks lay strewn about in the lot and ditch as though after a stockcar race, and there was roadkill at his feet, but across the way in yonder copse, he could see lights dancing in the branches, other trucks and cars pulled up on the side of the road. So, he was not alone in the world, after all, as he had feared. Not hoped? Was it human company at last, then, that misanthropic Beans sought? No, something far more precious at this hour, whichever hour it was: a hitch, a ride, a lift for heart and body, back in to the hotel where he might shed these fulsome rags and pillow his suffering head. First, however, he turned back and lifted his stream against the smutty flyblown windows of the Country Tavern, bringing the promise of light where heretofore there was none, as was always his virtuous wont. It was a record-setting pee, pity old Brains wasn't there to time it, yet another momentous historical event that would escape the world's capricious attention, and when he was done the lights in the woods he'd noticed earlier were gone. He crossed over, passing between the parked vehicles—a sporty lot, on the whole, models he'd not seen before, though on the wee side—and heard their voices deep within, saw a distant nervous glimmering like that of fireflies. He thought of curling up in a truckbed until they returned, but there was lightning behind the tavern and an unpleasant chill in the night air and uncurling later might prove an agony worse than the nocturnal nature stroll that was its present alternative. Beans walked into the woods. He was wondering how he might introduce himself if these were not members of the wedding party, but no introductions seemed necessary when he caught up with them, he was armed without a welcoming word, merely a brief instruction: "This way." All right. Sure. Distantly, he caught a glimpse in the shadows of someone who looked like he'd just escaped a mummy's-revenge horror movie: Beans, trailing at the rear, closed ranks. Was this a test? He was reminded of the fraternity scavenger hunt he went on as a pledge. That ordeal ended with a beer blast. He hoped no such revels were part of tonight's program. He also hoped the rifle wasn't loaded. Beans was the sort of fellow, he knew this all too well, who tended, no matter who or what he might be aiming at, to shoot his own foot off, and then be thankful after that was the worst he'd done. "We've lost her," someone said. This was good news. But then a cantankerous old buzzard in cuffs and leg irons and wearing a ballcap backwards spat through gaps in his teeth and, nodding his head at something down in the gully, said: "Nah. There's her scat. Still steamin'." "How do you know it's hers?" a younger burrheaded guy in yellow golf pants and a windbreaker of some kind wanted to know; Beans perceived immediately this whinging fellow had as much appetite for this exercise as he did and could be a useful ally. "By the size of it, buckethead," said the old geezer flatly, and spat again. "Anyway," said the stubby cop, "if he don't know, who does?" This seemed to satisfy everybody unfortunately, and they all moved on, following their prey's evacuations, pressing deeper into the treacherous undergrowth. Beans tagged along, having no choice, the way back by now beyond recall. His head was splitting. A puke loomed on the near horizon. Speaking metaphorically of course out here in the pitch-dark forest, as in: just around the corner. He sidled up to the burr-headed guy in the glow-in-the-dark arse-bags, who was now sneaking a suck from a hip flask, and said: "Some picnic, hunh?" The guy winced, offered him the hip flask, Beans took a swig without thinking, felt his stomach turn over when it hit. "I forgot," he said, handing it back. "I'm a teetotaler." "Yeah, me too." And then they saw it. Her. Shit. Beans set his rifle down against a tree and backed off. He was at the wrong fucking party. He'd find his own way out of here.

Nocturnal nature strolls had been part of Alf's insomniac routine ever since Harriet's death nearly a decade and a half ago, though, if still nocturnal, largely deprived of nature now that the old city park was gone, he missed it sorely. The new civic center, if only tolerable by day, was a downright blight by night, a pale dead thing heaped up hugely in the murky half-light that hung around it like a disease. A "sleeping giant," someone called it, though it reminded Alf more of certain lethal structures he'd seen during the war. He avoided it when he could, preferring the suspended stillness of dormant Main Street or the older prewar sections of town like the one in which he lived, though sometimes habit drew him back to where the old park had once lain waiting for him with its amusing wooden bandstand and its meandering paths lit by amber postlamps, welcoming as sleep itself. Used to walk with Harriet there in the evening, back when walking in the park was still something one did in a town like this, and after her death, while it was still there, he liked to wander in it at night, alone, feeling, not her presence, but the calm that used to accompany him when they strolled there together, which, sex apart, Alf took to be all he'd ever know of love, and maybe all there was to know. Alf believed hysteria to be the only reasonable response to the human condition, love, or whatever it was he was calling love, its unreasonable antidote which let you sleep at night (what wouldn't let him sleep tonight, for all the drinking he'd done, the humorless TV sitcom reruns he'd surrendered to when he got back from the club, was a memory of some kind, it seemed to lurk at the end of one of his fingers, like the imprint of a switch that had to be toggled: as he passed under an intersection streetlamp, he stared at it, trying to see what it saw, but all he could make out was something like the pad of his own finger, softly mirrored: a compress? the bulb of an eyedropper?). Not that he'd forgotten that lean, vivacious, wisecracking, freckle-nosed nurse he'd met in the field hospital while taking some poor forgotten matchmaker's shattered leg off, still gave him pleasure to think of her and the way she grinned at him back then, but that part of love he knew to be even more of an illusion than the soporific part, a kind of instinctive response to buried genetic coding, as most forms of pleasure were, and usually brief as appetite and its slaking, repeatable but not sustainable. Of course . . . there were, as Oxford would say, the grandchildren . . . Alf smiled to himself, ambling along there in the dim-lit dark, enjoying momentarily the joke he was in, was in a sense the butt of, or *a* butt, one among the multitudes, hearing Harriet say, looking up from one of her novels, You think too goddamn much, Alf, it's going to give you nosebleed. Ellsworth, he saw, was working late again, his printshop windows all ablaze, the man himself pacing around inside, unkempt and frenetic, a scene Alf had witnessed walking past here in the wee hours before, usually about once a week. Another way to provoke a peaceful sleep, one that used to work for him: set yourself a task, no matter how pointless, and complete it. How much of the lives people thought they were living here were in fact invented by Ellsworth and his weekly (most called it "weakly") *Town Crier?* Well, somebody had to do it, else they'd all be left without identities, no matter how spurious. His own included. Alf had always thought of his doctoring as somehow intrinsically meaningful, but given his perspective on life as a kind of horror show not meant to be consciously witnessed, it probably made less sense even than Ellsworth's obsessive scribbling. Around the corner, the photographer's lights were on, too: a busy night. Perhaps his wife was unwell and keeping him up, some sort of organic or possibly glandular disorder that Gordon had mentioned nervously to him a couple of days ago outside the Sixth Street Cafe. Behaving a bit strangely of late, that fellow, more strangely than usual, there was talk about him out at the club tonight, in and around the burlesque misadventures of the minister's son (who had an acne problem Alf was treating, as well as the worst case of athlete's foot he'd ever seen), some of it funny, some less so. Maybe his wife's illness had something to do with it. The woman seemed unwilling to come see Alf, he should probably visit them one day soon. If he could find the time. Alf had stopped taking on new patients years ago, but the ones he still had, aging as he was aging, had more problems than they used to, and he could not easily refuse their many offspring (John's daughter had just been in to seen him, for example, birth control pills she'd wanted, he'd said no, she wasn't old enough, she'd thrown a tantrum and said he was out of touch, he'd agreed, let her have them), if anything his workload was getting worse. People he used to see once a year, he now saw every week. Gave up house calls a decade or so after the war, except for invalids and people in nursing homes—which, more and more, his patients now were. Poor old Barnaby, for example (the civic center, though a block and a half down the street he was crossing, had just made its dreary presence felt: Barnaby had built the park that it displaced), who'd told him when he'd stopped in at the retirement center to see him a day or two ago that he'd been having problems with Audrey lately, she'd changed his pills or something, it was hard to understand half of what he was saying, the words tumbling like chunky gravel out of the side of his mouth. Earlier, Alf would have gently reminded his old friend that his wife had passed away some years ago; now he merely said he'd talk to her about it, see what he could do, and Barnaby just shook his old grizzled head and pulled on his ear and said it wouldn't do any good, her damned mind was set. The town was full of the ghosts of dead wives these days: out at the club tonight, old Stu had heaved his arm around Alf, leaned boozily against him, and rumbled into his near ear that Winnie was back, bedeviling him like she always used to do, he had to have a sleeping pill strong enough to stop the old girl from pestering him to death, can you help me, Doc? Alf had smiled but it hadn't seemed to be a joke: old Stu's damp red eyes were full of pain. Drop by, he'd said, I'll see what I can do. "Nothin' in your pocket? No? Shit, Doc, then I'm in deep trouble . . ." And then, for an alarming moment, the old doc feared he might be in deep trouble, too. He was just passing an unlighted alleyway (he'd been thinking: that memory at the tip of his finger: could it be of a tumor?), when he noticed there was someone skulking about in the shadows. It flashed to his mind what a dangerous place the world had become, he was a damned fool, people didn't walk alone at night anymore, could he yell loud enough that Ellsworth or Gordon or someone would hear him, but then he saw who it was: Oxford's odd boy Cornell. He was scrabbling about in there, feeling the walls, trying the doors, peering through the darkened windows. The family pharmacy backed onto this alley, a couple of doors down. "Corny? Are you all right?" The boy froze, pressed up in a tight little crouch against the small concrete loading platform at the back of the corner five-and-ten. A child still, though he'd fathered eight, at least eight, no doubt more to come, no sign of it stopping. "Hey, Corny, didn't mean to take you by surprise. It's just old Doc here, son. Come here a minute." Corny hesitated, then abruptly obliged to the extent of taking up a position against a telephone pole a few feet away, moving toward it in his usual herky-jerky way, then slouching against it as though he'd never been elsewhere. His wispy blond hair, oddly luminous in the darkened alley, fluttered down over his heart-shaped face like dry weeds, giving him the appearance of a startled rodent peeking out from its nest in the straw. "Couldn't sleep for some damn reason, so I was out taking a walk. Glad to find some company. How are you doing, Corny?" Corny shrugged: "Same old shit," he said in a voice that was little more than a hiss. Alf smiled, approached him slowly, hands in pockets. "Listen, what are you looking for?" Cornell tensed, but stayed where he was. "You want to tell me, son? I saw you hunting about there. Maybe I can help." Cornell looked doubtful, shrugged again, looked away, his skittish eyes scanning the alleyway. Alf thought: John's wife! Was that it? He glanced at his finger, startled by his insight: was it possible? "What?" he asked, hearing Cornell mutter something under his breath. He leaned closer to the strange boy. "The door," whispered Cornell.

Cornell didn't think the old fart would help him, and he didn't. He said to come see him at his office. Sure, man. See you around. Like many in town, Cornell was plagued by an elemental question about life, only his was not so much "Why am I here?" as "How did I get here?" He used to live here, back when his family was still all together, and then, for a time which he thought was going to be forever, he didn't, and then suddenly he did again. The first part was the best part, being taken around by his big brothers, playing with his sister, being read to by his mom, and his dad still liked him then, even if he was always on his case about hanging around the house too much, playing with games and toys, you're a big fellow now. Then he went away. It was his dad's idea. His brother had got killed and now Cornell got sent away with his brother's girlfriend. Who was nice to him at first and even let him take her clothes off, he could see why his brother liked her, but who then did a terrible thing. And Cornell had to admit that he probably didn't make the coolest move when he saw what she'd done, he could hear his dad chewing him out for not using his old noodle, why don't you grow up, Corny, and all that: he ran. Not smart but he was scared. He didn't know anyone in that faraway place. He didn't even know how to speak the stupid language they spoke, though he'd had a year of it in high school, it was all slurred when they talked it, like they were trying to hide what they were really saying. They were unpleasant to him and he was afraid they might blame him somehow for what had happened to Marie-Claire. So he ran, and the more he ran, the more scared he got. He'd left all his clothes and things behind, all he had was a little bit of money and the bottle of wine. He pulled his shirt over his head when he passed the wine shop where he'd bought it. There was something about "Love" on the label, he was afraid it might give him away, so he got rid of it in a street bin, or what he hoped was a street bin, it might have been a mailbox. He spied the big church he could see the top of from up in Marie-Claire's flat, the one on all the posters, and headed for it, but suddenly there were a lot of police everywhere, so, in a panic, he turned and ran the other way. It was late, after nine o'clock, but the streets were lit up like the downtown back home at Christmastime and full of scowling people with cigarettes hanging in their mouths. He tried to stop running, he was just drawing attention to himself, but he couldn't, he kept breaking into nervous little trots, stopping, running again, everyone was looking at him, and there were police here, too. Then he saw a sign with some steps down into a hole under the street, and though he didn't know what the sign meant in French, from what he could remember of his high-school Latin, he felt he would be safe there, so he ducked down the stairs. There was some kind of underground railroad at the bottom. He bought himself a ticket (should he give a tip? he didn't know, but just to be safe, he did) and for a while he rode around, trying to think what he should do next. He didn't know how long this went on but someone in a uniform woke him up when he fell asleep once and he had to get off. He pretended to leave the place where the trains came and went but he didn't. He snuck down one of the tunnels. It was dark and smelled bad and he was afraid, but he was even more afraid to go back up on the streets again. There were little pockets in the walls he could squeeze into when the trains came by, which they did less and less. He found a tunnel that had no tracks and he went down it, a shortcut to other tracks, he figured, but he never found them. One tunnel led to another and he got completely lost. There were people living down there, he discovered, they were like half-dead and slept in newspapers and plastic bags and they spoke the same language as the people on top but they didn't seem as bad somehow. None of them at least were police, he was pretty sure. He pretended to be deaf and dumb and they gave him something to eat sort of like tough baby chickens in a soup that smelled like bad breath, but he was hungry and ate it. Time passed like this, he didn't know how much, seemed like forever, but he couldn't tell because there weren't days and nights down there, and his watch was gone, must have lost it, or maybe he gave it to somebody, until eventually he began to forget why he was down there and started looking for a way out. He had always avoided the tunnels that stank the most, but now he thought those must be the sewers and maybe he could get out that way. So he held his nose and plunged in. He was right, but it was pretty sickening. By the time he saw some metal stairs leading up into the roof, he was a soaking mess and feeling dizzy from trying to hold his breath all the time. He thought he'd have to crawl out a hole when he got to the top, but instead he found a door up there. He opened it, and stepped out, the light blinding him at first; he held his hands over his eyes and peeped out through his fingers: didn't seem to be anyone around. He glimpsed a shady place and crept over to it, huddling there behind a trashcan until he could get used to the daylight and figure out where he was and what to do next. And that was when he noticed that the sign on the trashcan read KEEP OUR TOWN BEAUTIFUL. He *could* read it, this was not French. He peeked around the side of the can. Some things seemed different, but he recognized where he was. He was in the alleyway behind his father's drugstore. He felt like crying, he was so happy. He ran in to say hello to everybody and an ugly old woman with thick glasses and a clubfoot started yelling at him, saying he smelled like rotten fish. She closed the place down, banging about furiously on her clubfoot, dragged him back out into the alley and into the old pharmacy delivery van, and took him home (it *was* his home, but it was like she owned it and it was full of crying babies) and gave him a bath. There was nothing fun about this bath, she was very rough with him, though the usual happened a couple of times when she touched him there, and she smacked him for it. It turned out he was married to her and all those kids were his. Of course, by now he figured he was only dreaming and went along with everything the way you do in a dream, it was anyway better than a French sewer, which was where he supposed he really was and where he'd be again when he woke up. Only he never did. Or at least he hadn't so far. Was this normal? That's what he would have asked old Doc, if he'd got the chance. That bossy crippled lady who said she was his wife wouldn't listen either. She only boxed his ears when he tried to tell her about it and sent him out to play pinball machines or video games, which were maybe the dream's most interesting new things. His mom would have listened but she wasn't in this dream. But what if it wasn't a dream? He went back out in the alley and looked for the door he'd come through, but he couldn't find it. If only he'd been paying more attention when he stepped out. He didn't want to go back down there, he just wanted to know where it was so he could show it to that woman who wouldn't let go of his ear (her name was Gretchen), and get his mixed-up life sorted out.

That woman whose name was Gretchen lay in Lumby's bed longer than usual that night, clearly troubled, and not just because they'd broken the plastic penis while trying out some new positions Gretchen had found in a marital manual which were a bit beyond their athletic abilities. They had both pretty much worn themselves out playing with all those things and now they were in a more reflective mood. And what was troubling Gretchen, as she said, was her marriage. Well, it would trouble anyone, that was what Lumby replied, unable to come up with anything more humorous, feeling too contented and exhausted and also a little bit sore here and there, and having heard Gretchen's complaints about her mentally defective brother Cornell many times before. Tonight, though, Gretchen seemed to have something else on her mind, and Lumby waited, half-dozing, for her to spit it out. They could hear one of the children crying, a nightmare or a wet bed or something, but they could also hear Granddad shuffling down the hall to take care of it. We haven't had any more babies for over three years now, Gretchen said, not since the second twins, and Columbia, who felt that the eight that came the first five or six years were already eight too many, much as she enjoyed playing Auntie Lum, said she thought that was because of the IUD which she'd helped her put in, but Gretchen said no, she took it out almost the same day, it made her too twitchy, like it was all the time humming or buzzing or something. But what I mean, she went on, is he keeps avoiding me all the time, oh, I know, Cornell's not exactly what you'd call an attentive husband—but, well, in a way that's just the point, he used to pay me no mind at all except when I crawled into his bed, and then for only a second or two, which was enough for me, given the mess his pajamas and linens are always in, but now whenever I go over to his bed, he either pulls the sheet over his head, or else he jumps up and runs out, and during the day he won't even stay in the same room with me or let me give him his baths any more, and you know what kind of baths he gives himself. Lumby still couldn't see where all this was going, and she was starting to drift off, dreaming awake, sort of, about playing doctor with her little brother (she had to play nurse in just a few hours, she should try to get some sleep), and he asking her what she heard when she put her stethoscope to his weewee, she replying music because she'd once heard it called an organ. But then she woke up again, because what she heard Gretchen say was, I think there's another woman. Corny? Columbia felt like laughing, but was careful and didn't. Come on, Gretchen, who'd have the little pest? I don't know, maybe someone before he met me? Before he met you, the only girls he knew were in comicbooks. Except for Marie-Claire. Who scared the pants off him. Do you think she did? Gretchen asked. You know, get the pants off him? Are you kidding? Lumby said. She was Yale's girlfriend. Do you think she'd go for a basket case like Corny? I did, said Gretchen simply, and Lumby, sorry now she'd put it that way, realized that there was a real problem here. Her sister-in-law was truly and helplessly in the grip of the green-eyed monster, and if she was jealous even of a dead girl, making jokes would not release her. So instead she said: I'll keep an eye on the little dimwit for a few days and let you know what I think. That seemed to make things better for Gretchen somehow and she snuggled up against Lumby as though in loving gratitude and when, in anticipation of her father's wake-up knock, dawn cast its dim glow through the curtains like a movie on a screen, Gretchen, smiling in her sleep, was still there beside her.

The dawn movie on Veronica's screen was more like a horror flick, or the fluttering tails of one, it was still ripping through her consciousness, shredding her sleep, leaving her too shocked and exhausted even to pry open her eyelids, which were mucky from crying all night. Everything was mucky, her whole body felt covered in slime from the awful thing. It seemed so real! She'd come across it while cleaning house, or dreaming that she was cleaning house. It was hunched down in the dirty place behind the refrigerator, where sometimes she was frightened by mice. She pulled out the ironing board and there it was with its large eyeless head like a cowled mendicant and bent shriveled limbs with little clawlike hands and feet. Veronica knew immediately who it was, of course: "What are *you* doing here?!" she'd screamed, holding the folded ironing board in front of her like a shield. No reply, just a wet raspy breathing as it huddled there in the dim niche, all curled up, throbbing faintly. Her first impulse was to throw the ironing board at it, but she was too terrified to move, her limbs were like stones, her heart, too, and she felt something hurting down deep behind her navel somewhere. She wished Maynard were home to shoot it (where *was* he?), but at the same time she was relieved he hadn't seen it. Not yet anyway. He'd been in such a rage of late, this thing could make him dangerous. Yes, she had to get rid of it before he came back, but how? She realized that this was a question she had asked before, in real life, and all the guilt and pain of that came rushing back and made her scream again: "*No! I didn't mean it!*" The thing in the corner cocked its high-domed head like it was trying to hear through the puckery hole in the side of it. Snot dripped from its nose and when it breathed it made a bubbly sound as if it were breathing underwater. She heaved the ironing board up against the space between the wall and the refrigerator so it couldn't escape and went scrambling for the phone to call the doctor at his home. He wasn't in; she left a message on his answering machine, still screaming, she couldn't stop herself. She was afraid to go back to the kitchen, she needed help, she couldn't face this alone. Help came. Ringing the door chimes. A miracle! "*Yes! I'm coming!*" she screamed. It was what's-her-name, John's wife. She used to be one of her best friends, probably still was, she told her all about it. About what was behind the refrigerator, about where it came from and how she got her bottom smacked in the motel shower after, about everything. Even about how she celebrated what would have been Second John's birthday every year. "*He would have been seventeen in March!*" she cried. "*The same age I was that night at the drive-in!*" The drive-in? She told her about that, too, it all came shrieking out, high-pitched and delirious, like something had burst inside, even Ronnie didn't know what she was saying half the time. "*I was so scared!*" John's wife was very understanding. She said she was there to help. On behalf of the PTA, she said. Okay. Ronnie began to calm down. But she was still screaming. "*Come, look! It's horrible!*" She ran into the kitchen to show her, but it wasn't there any more. The ironing board had been pushed aside and there was a gleaming viscous trail from the refrigerator to the head of the basement stairs. "*Oh no!*" It was lying in a squishy heap on the concrete floor at the foot of the stairs. But it was still breathing. Sort of. John's wife explained that it would be all right, its bones were too soft to break. This was not a consolation. Veronica wanted to smash it with something and put it out in the garbage, but instead she had to help John's wife carry the slippery mess back up the stairs between them. Yeuck! It was oozing gunk and it got all over her. John's wife wrapped it in a sheet (had she taken it off the bed upstairs? was that where Maynard was?) and together they took it out to a supermarket shopping cart John's wife seemed to have brought along for the purpose. The swaddled creature's wet strangled wheezing was terrifying and pitiable at the same time. Veronica felt like crying she was so sorry for it, but she also felt like throwing up. Then John's wife told her something very important, so important Veronica stopped crying and carrying on and just watched, stunned, as the woman disappeared down the street, pushing the shopping cart with Ronnie's unborn son in it. But when she woke, she could not remember what it was John's wife had said. She lay there with her eyes closed, listening to Maynard's bubbly wheezing beside her, trying to remember. It was so important! Something about—uh-oh. Wait a minute. Bubbly wheezing? Maynard—? Oh no . . . ! It can't end this way! she thought confusedly, trying to go back to sleep, or else to wake up again. She could hear the thing snorting and whuffing as it cuddled closer, blindly reaching out its slimy monkey's paw. Oh my god! Was it trying to suck her breast—?! She screamed and, her eyes still glued shut, leapt from the bed.

Barnaby's eyes were wide open. He had never been more lucid. It often happened this way at the dewy end of a night. The two halves of his cracked brain slid together like train cars coupling, and he could see clearly, if only for a short time, about as long as it took the dew to rise, what a fucked-up old ruin he was. In these dawn moments he had no confusions, understood everything: how Audrey, dying too soon, had undone him utterly with her bastardized will, how John had pushed him to the edge, then over, imprisoning him here in this cheap pre-cremation motel after the stroke, how his beloved daughter, literally all he had left in this world, had drifted away from him, probably blaming him for everything that had happened, how even his old friend Alf had lost interest (and, hell, who wouldn't?), patronizing him at best and leaving him pretty much in the hands of that dotty old lady who liked to pretend she was Audrey. Alf at least took his side on the civic center controversy, even if he supposed Barnaby wasn't listening when he talked to him about it, and, living in one of Barnaby's houses, praised his craft in his dour taciturn way: "You built things to last, Barn. Trouble is, that scares people. Nowadays, they need things around them that wear out faster than they do." Sanctuaries of the family, that was what Barnaby was building—solid foundations, rational structures you could trust, tasteful neighborly details, a principle of restraint and comfort and proportion throughout—but people didn't have families in the old way anymore. If they ever did. Just an illusion maybe, a mere veneer. Look at his own. A damned catastrophe and heart irreparably broken after. Figuring out the real world made you want to kill yourself—in fact, come to think of it, he'd meant to, he had rescued his old handgun for the purpose, holstering it under his armpit so he wouldn't forget where it was, but it wasn't there anymore. John's sponge-brained mother must have hidden it; maybe her son had told her to. He was as good as dead anyway, why not prolong the agony? Watch the old boy twitch and wobble, have a few laughs. So why hadn't he shot himself when he had the gun in hand? Because he'd wanted to explain himself to his daughter before he died. Warn her about what was happening. Tell her how much he loved her. He no longer believed he was able to do that. Even in these sounder moments, the words that came out were not the ones he was thinking. Dying was about all he was able to do now, and that wouldn't be easy. Barnaby had come to understand that dying was not acquiescence to something inevitable, quite the contrary—life was what was passive. The body could go on forever, or nearly; to die it had to be instructed. This was the function of what men called spirit, nihilism was after all man's truest instinct, this was the ultimate message of his acids: turn it off. His own self-destruct switch had been flicked, the instructions had been passed, but the circuits had shorted out. At this rate of staticky disintegration it could take forever. So where the hell had that stupid old woman hidden the goddamned thing? Probably in the bottom of the laundry basket, said his daughter. Right. Good idea. The laundry basket. He sidled, dragging his dead leg, toward the bathroom door. This was hard work. He felt like he was struggling against strange impersonal forces. Like the sort that ran the town now. Used to be one big family. No longer. What John had done, in effect, was take the roof off. Neighbors and strangers were the same thing. Locks on all the doors now. Burglar alarm systems. Even though no one stayed home. He poked around, found a shirt he'd been looking for. Here all the time. Not why he'd come in here, though. He struggled to pee and dribbled on his bedroom slippers. Just a trickle, didn't really need to go. So that wasn't it either. His medicine maybe. He fumbled with the cap on the plastic vial. When it finally popped off, everything spilled into the sink and on the floor. To hell with it. Wouldn't kill him to do without until Audrey came, and if it did, he'd have done himself a favor. Where was the old bag anyway? It was getting light outside. The birds were going at it. Was his daughter just here? Had he been able to tell her anything? Why was there all this dirty laundry all over the floor?

The early light of day found Barnaby's lawyer and fellow plotter Maynard in the woods at the edge of town, kicking irritably through the dew-drenched undergrowth. He didn't remember coming out here; rage must have brought him. The birds had their dawn chorus cranked up full throttle, the shrieking little shit-factories—he wished he had his gun along to shut the fuckers up. He must have dressed in the dark: red-and-orange golf shirt with the green monogrammed pocket now containing the house keys, chafing his left nipple, the shirt tucked into black pinstripe suit pants belted high over his pot, tennis shoes without socks. In the past when he'd stormed away on sleepless nights, Veronica had sometimes locked him out. She could never explain herself afterwards. Maybe she wanted him to hit her, needing the attention. She often hit him back or threw stuff at him. It was about their only way of talking to each other; the rest was mostly just senseless screaming. The only thing in his pants pockets was the ancient garter, always with him, frayed and limp from so much fondling over the years. Maynard fondled it now. It was dark in here and damp, but beyond the leaves a pale violet light was spreading across the sky like a morbid stain. It was probably going to be what some would call a beautiful morning. Maynard hacked up a gob and spat contemptuously. Beauty. Only humans in their egomaniacal perversity could dream up such a sick idea. Warped everything. One night out at the club he'd heard old Alf argue that intimations of beauty were nothing more than the old pleasure/pain principle in operation, and Maynard could go along with that but not with the association of beauty with pleasure. He came on a patch of wild bluebells poking up in the dim light, stepped on them. That's it, he told himself. Fuck everything. Christ! He loathed—bitterly, deeply, and intimately—this town and everyone in it, loathed his wealth, his career, his family, his past, his future, life itself. What would have happened, he often wondered, had he not been born a Maynard between Maynards? What if he had been free to leave town for good when he left high school as so many did? As apparently his brat of a son had done, a Maynard or no? Same thing probably. And (he twisted the garter around his fingers) fleeing this shithole was just not on, not for him, not for the moony lovesick Nerd. Whom he loathed above all others. Ahead of him, like secret writing in the dark forest, loomed a stand of young birch trees, ghostly in the dawn glow, inviting his admiration. He turned away in disgust, found himself at the edge of a small thorny ravine. Recognized it. A grin spread painfully across his bristly face, couldn't stop it. The little guttersnipe's baptism that wretched night had been his as well. In commemoration of the sickening occasion, he took his prick out to pee and was just letting go when his true love came riding by on her bicycle, dressed in her white tennis costume. She waved and smiled, but he could not wave back, both hands busy trying to stop what he was doing and get covered up without pissing all over himself. And then (he was beardy and rumpled, unwashed, smelled bad, was dressed for the circus with his widdling weenie on view, no wonder she didn't stop) she was gone. He staggered down through the ravine and up to the road, thought he could see her pedaling around the turn just up ahead, a flash of pure white like a bird in flight, and hitching up his pin-striped pants, Maynard II went stumbling after.

The daughter of the lady cyclist glimpsed by the rumpled lawyer at the edge of Settler's Woods was getting married. It was a modern wedding. The bride was dressed in a string bikini, high heels, and a bridal veil that opened and closed like a shower curtain. It was not clear who the groom was, but Clarissa's father was there, looking pleased as punch, and chiding Granny Opal for not being with it, the old stick. Jennifer, who had been kept awake all night by the wanderings in and out of her bedroom by her spacey sleepwalking big-bellied mother, was glad her best friend was getting married and so wouldn't be mad about getting left out of the day's coming adventures. Which she could not quite imagine but which filled her with a kind of apprehensive delight, like the first time she had to jump off the high diving board, knowing she'd love it if she didn't kill herself. Her dad was there that time. He didn't do anything, he didn't hold her hand or jump with her or even say anything, he just stood down there smiling up at her in that easy way he had, and she knew it would be all right. Nevada had a smile like that and now it was Nevada Jen trusted to see her through whatever was coming next. She could hardly wait, she was so in love she ached all over, but she was scared, too, and Nevada's smile seemed to say: Stay cool, don't worry, it's okay. Jump. Nevada was at the wedding, too. She was arranging the flowers. Heaps and heaps of them, so piled up that people disappeared in and out of them. It looked like fun, sort of like playing house in leaf piles, but when Jennifer started to follow her sister Zoe into a particularly inviting hole to roll around, Nevada, smiling her serene smile, steered her away and up toward the altar where the wedding was to take place. Jen's mother, who was no longer pregnant, was up there playing the organ (dressed only in her underwear, good grief, Mom as usual), and her father was trying to get her brother Philip to come out from behind the pulpit where he was hiding. Philip was up to some kind of mischief back there, and her father was getting exasperated. "It's beginning!" he shouted. But it wasn't. Almost everyone in town was there, wandering about in a completely disorderly fashion like at a very crowded cocktail party. It'll never happen, Jennifer thought, laughing. They're just pretending. It was funny and she kept laughing, almost like someone was tickling her. But there was also something dangerous about it all. Clarissa had stained her lips with real blood as though to try to warn Jennifer about something, something she couldn't tell her out loud, and when Jennifer, trying to be cool and friendly, asked, "So, who's the lucky guy?," Clarissa's eyes flashed with anger and something like panic. "Hey, sorry," Jen said (the church seemed to have darkened: had they started the ceremony?), and she noticed now the little tattoo just below and to one side of Clarissa's navel. It was of a semiautomatic weapon, its black barrel pointed down into the bikini, butt toward the hipbone. This had several meanings, she knew, like "PULL MY TRIGGER" and "DO IT AND DIE," which was the name of a hot movie out at the mall, but it also seemed to have a secret message, meant for Jennifer alone. There was a little flame at the tip of the gun barrel like a licking tongue and two words by the handle she couldn't quite see. It was, she realized, a cry for help. Clarissa was going to die! Or someone was! Jennifer went looking for Nevada but apparently she'd done her decorating job and left. Her dad was gone, too, and the music had turned metallic and heavy, like a funeral march performed by a rock band, not at all the sort of thing her mother played. Old Hoot, the hardware store man, was in the pulpit, looking straight at her and shouting out in his loud nasal whine about the fires of hell, which sounded more like the farce of hail. But in fact it was getting hot in here. Jennifer understood now why Clarissa had been wearing a bikini, it made sense. The flowers had wilted and were beginning to rot, it was suffocating. There was a spotlight on her and the relentless music was driving her up the wall. Then the man in the pulpit shouted out something really weird: "Cut off her hair!" he cried. What—? Jennifer sat up, sweating, with the sun in her face and music blasting out of her brother's room, remembering now the words she'd seen on the tattoo under Clarissa's navel: "BUTT OUT." She smiled to herself, pushing her tangled hair out of her face, wiping her neck and chest with her nightshirt. Her father was right. It was beginning.

It was the phone that made Otis sit up that morning: Snuffy had pulled him out of the line and put him in as quarterback in a tough game, and his throwing arm had gone dead on him just as he got the snap and the opposing team was coming at him: he couldn't get rid of the ball, he couldn't even get his arm above his waist, his linemen had faded from sight as though they didn't exist, he was going to get killed. He came to with his arm gone to sleep from snoozing on top of it there at his desk. It was Pauline. He stood and did a couple of quick knee-bends, pumping his arm to get the tingling out, telling Pauline, yeah, yeah, speak slower. He hadn't been sleeping well at night lately, too many worries, and so found himself occasionally nodding off like this at the station, making his workday a bit blurry at times. There were a lot of things about the town that weren't sitting just right with Otis these days, but what was worrying him most was John's wife. More than once now, he'd found her car, unlocked and the keys inside, parked far from home—in the empty supermarket lot late one night, for example, once behind the church, last night right in front of the station—and, his neck tingling in a funny way, had had to run it home for her. It was unusual and just the sort of irregularity that made Otis nervous, more so because it had to do with her. When John got back later today, he'd try to talk to him about it. Otis couldn't understand what Pauline was saying, he was too groggy and she was very agitated, so he excused himself brusquely and set the phone down on the desk, went over to the cooler to splash his face with a handful of ice water. The thing that was most nightmarish about that football game was the crowd. The bench itself was empty, just a kind of cold wind blowing down it, even old Snuffy had left or else had gone to sit in the stands—where no one was cheering, it was very dark and moody up there, more like they were a crowd at a funeral. Or an execution (he remembered thinking, if only *she* were here, everything would be all right, but she wasn't and he was up the spout). The field was dark, too. He could see those goons coming but he couldn't see their faces. He wiped his own face with his handkerchief, blew his nose, and picked up the phone. Pauline said she had to see him, something awful was happening, there was no one else she could turn to, Gordon was gone, he had to come right away. The urgency of Pauline's appeal, as though she just couldn't wait for it, excited Otis, but the idea of seeing her alone again also made him feel uneasy. Last time was not so good, it was like he couldn't get it up as big around her anymore or else she was getting loose with age or something, and he'd thought at the time that maybe their long romance was finally over. When the shoe don't fit no more, as the old song goes . . . Though they could still be friends. Old shoe friends. But he could hear her crying on the other end so he said, okay, hang in, he'd be over in a jiff. "And bring a bag of doughnuts," she begged. He supposed the problem had to do with her husband, the station had been getting several phone complaints about Gordon of late, that flake finally losing it maybe, so what met Otis at the studio, though he thought he was ready for anything, caught him completely by surprise. He pushed in with the doughnuts, ringing the little bells, called out, heard Pauline's whimpering reply in the next room where Gordon shot his portraits. Otis noticed there was a scatter of unopened mail on the floor that had come through the door slot; Gordon didn't seem to be paying much attention to business. Curtains were drawn, the place looked closed down, though he remembered seeing lights when he had passed by here on his rounds last night. Ellsworth had been up all night, too, maybe Gordon had had to get some work finished for the *Crier*. And maybe not. Otis parted the bead curtains and stepped back into the portrait studio, thinking he'd probably better check out Gordon's newest batch of photos, there might be something to all those complaints, and what he saw, squatting on her haunches there on the little stage like a carnival exhibit, was Pauline, wild-haired and sobbing, wrapped in nothing but a bedsheet, and big as a mountain. Even squatting, she was eye-level with Otis. Otis couldn't think what to say. He tipped his cap back and scratched his head. If that don't beat all—! Her teary eyes spied the sack of half a dozen doughnuts and, from the look that crossed her big red face, he figured he'd better give them to her right away, though he had thought they were going to share them. They vanished in six bites and she looked like she might eat the sack as well. And then she *did* eat the sack. "Oh, Otis," she bawled with her mouth full of chewed paper. "What's happening to me?" He didn't know. He had the idea, though, that those blown-up photos of her private parts might have something to do with it and he thought maybe he ought to examine them again. Just in the line of duty. He lifted one edge of the sheet to have a look (kept his other hand resting on his hip holster, didn't know why, but it was like he was scouting out strange territory and had to be ready for anything): she was one huge woman. Not fat, just huge. Her flexed knees were big as football helmets, her colossal butt like a pair of boulders. Still soft, though. And they bounced when he jiggled them like they always did. His walkie-talkie buzzed, interrupting his inspection. The station had just got another complaint about that kinky photographer, he'd been caught hanging out in women's changing rooms out at the mall again, what should they do? Otis told them to send a squad car out to pick him up and hold him down at the station until he got back. "Might be a while," he said. Pauline was still sniveling, using a corner of the sheet to wipe her nose, but she'd calmed down considerably, and now watched him with the hopeful wet eyes of a good old birddog waiting to be told what to do. So he told her: "Now, let's go see them photos again. You won't need the sheet."

Many—Dutch, for example, or Waldo, Nevada, Bruce, or Daphne—would have dismissed these photographs that Otis was now so intently examining (later, he would take them with him as "material evidence," though evidence of what he could not say) as mere pornography, butt and beaver shots intended to arouse the scopophile, disparaging perhaps the model, whose shape was generous and skin not without blemish, even while admiring the technical quality of the image, some—Bruce in particular—admiring as well the perversity of the image-taker, a profession Bruce likened favorably unto the sadist's. Others, too—Trevor, Marge, Lorraine, Floyd—would have found these photographs perverse or worse, a cruel theft of sorts, a violent dispossession of the other, and wretched of purpose, but Ellsworth, with an understanding bred of lifelong friendship, would have perceived their profound lyrical intent and artistic integrity—and did in fact, for he had viewed them and most others in Gordon's private albums, kept unaware of one series only, that which now had undone (his own undoing) the photographer and plunged him into such despair as well as trouble with the law. For this was a man, Ellsworth would have said, who loved less flesh than form, more pattern of light and dark than what tales or implied excitements those patterns might bespeak, one who sought to penetrate the visible contours of the restless world, ceaselessly dissolved by time, to capture the hidden image beyond, the elusive mystery masked by surface flux, and the name he gave that which he pursued was Beauty. When Ellsworth, for whom movement was all and the stasis that his friend coveted was not Beauty but Death, or both at best, complained about "the easy accident of an opened lens," Gordon had insisted that "accident," as he called it, was in fact the essential creative gift, defending his photographs in terms of found objects and aleatory music, about which he knew only what Ellsworth himself had told him when he came back, showing off a bit, from the outside world. To prove it, he gave Ellsworth a camera and told him to go take a hundred photos or so (Ellsworth was bored after a dozen) and they would judge them after as works of art, and of course none stood up as Gordon's did, though Ellsworth was personally fond of a picture he took at a young war hero's tomb during a visit by his family there with the French girl who later committed suicide (this little exercise happened a long time ago), simply because there was so much story concealed in it, however ill-managed the shot, and another of three middle-aged women, grinning stupidly at him, seated together on a park bench in the old city park (now vanished), only one of whom, themselves at the time in mourning for a lost friend, was still alive today, an innocent image of love and grief, emotionally enhanced by overexposure and poor focus. He published both (with byline) in *The Town Crier*, but took no other, for his friend was right, he was no photographer, nor a visual artist of any kind, appreciative of the real thing though he could be, and moreover he came to understand, in more than just a metaphoric sense, that things as well as people actively showed themselves to the photographer because of his gifts, country roads stretching out to display their longing to him, vistas unpeopling themselves to reveal their troubled depths, houses fluttering their starched lace curtains at him like flirtatious lashes, light entering their wide porches to open them into a broad friendly smile, their flower-bordered cement walks reaching out to the front sidewalk like firm proffered handshakes or decorated cleavage. Sometimes. Sometimes there was a darkness, withdrawal, implicit rebuff, threat. Gordon shot the town, Ellsworth often thought, as if it were a strange dream enacted, a dream dreamt by the dead in which the living were condemned to mythic servitude, Gordon as artist not their liberator but the revealer of their common condition which might yet lead to liberation if they would but look closely enough, something his own Artist once said in another way (a line now lost, or rather, perverted by the Stalker, in the novel's sudden turnings) with respect to the mythology of the pose. For Ellsworth, much as he admired his friend's talent and respected his quest, no single photo, no single painting or artifact of any sort, no matter how magisterial, could equal any of these things, however modest their quality, when linked together in telling pattern, and for that he often loved the photos Gordon himself most disdained. The family portraits, for example, trite compositions when singly seen, utterly trivial, artificial, and repetitive, but bearing in their austere and staged formality the power of tragedy when seen in temporal sequence, a record of loss and joined resistance to loss. If Gordon prized most that photo of laundry hung out to dry, crisp and stiff in the cold, or this of pale luminous buttocks, all detail burned away except at the perfect fork, or that of a gleaming black coffin held aloft in an overcast sky by four ropy hands as white as bone, Ellsworth loved more his own fat photo archives with their gas stations and orators and sliding Little Leaguers and humpback bridges and trailer parks and Rotary club meetings and pet graves in backyards and Bermuda-shorted duffers and candy-poled barbershops and dancing highschoolers and gingerbreaded bandstands and beaming trophy bearers all ajumble, like a million stories waiting to be told and a million more with every shuffle of the pack. He could appreciate Gordon's fascination with an empty mall parking lot as a mysterious space, as though nothing had given birth to itself, but he got much more out of it in context with other photos of that mall at other times and of other malls besides. Here a photo of a since-dismantled fountain from an early mall in town, its cement belly adorned with scrawled graffiti (all that rich local culture, lost forever!), there one of the glittery escalator at the inauguration of the new highway mall, the six-screen cinema ads and opening day sales as oracular backdrop, both set beside this one of the steamy food court, filled with the downy young like chicks in an incubator, at yet another mall (though the viewer might commingle them), each enriched with faces and fashions and all the passing foolishness of their times, and add to these another of the bus station soda fountain and pinball machines, once locus of the courting rites of the young now no longer young, and yet another of the abandoned Night Sky Drive-In movie theater, sacrificed to the highway which gave birth to the newest mall, showing its desolation of spirit by the grass and weeds sprouting through the cracks in the cement ramps, the sagging fences, leaning screen, marred by the stones and bottles thrown at it, and then a worker standing in rubble, guiding a beam aloft, and a tennis-costumed woman and her leather-jacketed children in that parking lot before seen so deserted, now filled with gleaming vehicles of the latest models, and a stark empty-windowed downtown dime store closing down forever, and so the story grows: of the town, and of the viewer, and of the photographer, too.

As they dragged the distraught photographer out of the fancy women's-wear shop at the mall, his eyes filmy and unfocused and his knees giving way beneath him, what he kept blubbering over and over was: "It doesn't matter, I didn't have any film in the camera anyway," a fact that seemed to be causing him more dismay than his arrest. They paraded the poor bewildered man down the corridor, through the busy cafe area, past the table where Opal sat alone, and on down the next corridor as though to prolong what perhaps they perceived as an entertainment for the shoppers, and from the grins she could see on people's faces that was probably how it was taken. The young were openly laughing, pointing, making jokes. Opal was not entertained. Her own spirits were too low, her confidence in her own grip on the proprieties too shaken, to take pleasure in the humiliation of any fellow creature, especially one so harmless as the photographer, who was a bit idiosyncratic maybe, but a decent citizen and a loving son. Opal had known from church the man's mother, a saint in her way, her husband killed on one or another of those beaches during the big war (Mitch had played his part on the home front in that one, as had her son in the lesser ones since then, for which she was grateful), the woman widowed so young and all but penniless with a son to raise, then in turn dutifully and tenderly cared for by that son when her own health and mind failed her, a fate that Opal hoped she would herself escape, but confident that her own son would be no less caring if such a calamity befell her. And what would her son say about her present troubles? He would not be patient with them. Mother, he would say, let that addled old man be, there's nothing you can do for him, just watch over my wife and children when I cannot, I'm depending on you. And now she'd let him down on all counts and, moreover, behaved in ways he would not believe, nor could she still, though she knew she had. The girls were gone, she'd looked everywhere, it was all her fault, she'd stayed too long, but she'd called and they weren't home either, no one was except the cleaning lady, and now she could do nothing but sit in this rancid public parlor, feeling utterly estranged, surrounded by misbehaving children and that indecent racket they called music, waiting, hopefully yet fearfully, for her charges' safe return. She had brought Clarissa and her friend Jennifer to the mall this morning, as she had often done, though much earlier than usual, and she knew by their twittery excitement that something was up (those thin little shorts they had on didn't even cover their behinds and they were wearing their belly buttons out like brooches) and she should stay, but her visits to the retirement center had become more than mere duty or habit, rather something like a compulsion, something she had to do more for herself than for that stricken old man, who had become, in fact, not so much a family friend as an adversary. And one of a very peculiar sort. It had begun simply as a way of coping with the awkwardness of Barnaby's befuddled mind, humoring him in his confusions rather than forever correcting him, a sort of kindness, really, and therapeutic, too—he seemed to speak more clearly than before—that was how she had thought of it when she'd started taking Audrey's part in Barnaby's imaginary dialogues. These were not genteel or affectionate conversations: Barnaby was an angry man, and Audrey, he was convinced, had with malice done him wrong. Opal was equally convinced that Barnaby was misjudging her, her mistakes, if any, innocent (John *was* a charmer), and besides the dead should be allowed to lie in peace, so she took it upon herself to defend a woman toward whom in life she'd never really felt a fondness, at first in her own voice and then, when that only seemed to stir up Barnaby's rage, in Audrey's. Audrey had been so different from Opal—vivacious, brassy, self-assured, dynamic, daring, proud—that what most amazed Opal was the ease with which she assumed her role, standing toe-to-toe with the irascible old fellow, silencing his pigheaded bluster finally with the force of her own irrefutable logic, her doughty good sense, exhibiting then her own anger at his mistrust, backing him up until he fell into a chair, apologizing: "But . . . Aud, I've felt . . . such pain . . ." "I know." Then he'd lean his poor damaged head into her bosom or onto her shoulder and rest there a while, she stroking his age-freckled pate gently, consoling him as best she could, until he forgot and it all started up again. She took to cleaning up his room for him, straightening the bed, sorting his laundry, scolding him for bad habits ("Don't walk around with your robe gaping like that, do you think people enjoy looking at an ugly old coot like you in his underwear?" "Too much trouble, tying and untying it, Aud, slows me down when I have to go to the bathroom . . ."), even helping him with his baths because he said he hated the bath lady who treated him like he was three years old. "She's right, you are three years old, now stop picking at yourself like that and lean forward, let's get this over with." "Wish I could, Aud. Get it over with, I mean." "You stop talking like that, you old buzzard! Who would I have to fight with if you quit on me?" Which did remind her to take the gun out of the little raggedy holster in his bathrobe while he was in the tub and hide it at the bottom of his laundry basket. Sometimes she prepared some food for him or cleaned his refrigerator or microwave, read old newspapers to him, gave him his medicines, clipped his toenails. "Now, Aud, we've got to do something about that damned will." "It's been done. I don't want to hear another word about it. Give me the other foot." He'd been especially difficult today, spilling his medicine, dirtying the bathroom, throwing his dirty clothes about, refusing his bath, getting in a rage about a "dawzer," whatever that was, even trying to strike her with his cane, but she took the cane away from him, pushed him down into his rocker, cooled his heels with a smart dressing-down, and then, when he'd lapsed into a more melancholic mood, gave him a haircut. She noticed he was eyeing the scissors, so she teased him for a while, setting them down where he could almost reach them but not quite, then quite casually popping them in her handbag when she got ready to go. Sometimes, leaving Barnaby's little apartment, a funny feeling would pass over her, as though she had to remember to be Opal again and might not be if she forgot, just a fleeting sensation, but enough to make her shiver. Today, though, the funny feeling, after what she saw in the main lobby, had not gone away, the shivering hadn't. Passing by the visitors' logbook, she had glanced to see if she had remembered to sign in and was startled to see Audrey's name written there.

More than once. But in Opal's own handwriting. She felt confused and somehow threatened, almost as though there were a hand at her throat, and she reached for the pen to do something, but there were other people in the lobby, coming and going, she had to leave it. And she'd lost all track of time, she'd been gone too long from the girls, Clarissa so irresponsible of late, she had her father's bold independent ways, but not always his good judgment, and that dangerous mall crowd—Opal was suddenly afraid, for the girls, for herself, for her whole family, and dazed and panicky, she went scurrying back, hunched over the steering wheel as though trying to push the car instead of drive it, arriving finally, still shaken, but more and more her old self, her old dowdy steadfast inept and timorous self, to find her fears confirmed, the girls nowhere in sight, and nothing to do after an anxious search and a call home, an embarrassed inquiry or two (where *were* those scamps? they'd hear it from Granny Opal when they got back!), but sit and wait. In this glossy marketplace her son had made, though certainly not for her (she was not eating or drinking anything, people wanted her table, the busboys were giving her impatient looks, but she would not, could not really, move), a setting that seemed to demonstrate something her friend Kate once told her, sitting in the city park and speaking then about the most recent achievements in outer space: "When the edge *becomes* the center, Opal," she'd said, "then the center becomes the void."

Where were those two scamps? They were up in the air with Bruce and Nevada, not quite in outer space, but, as Clarissa put it: "Far out!" It had started as an ordinary highspeed joyride, but Clarissa had insisted Bruce put his sports jet through all its tricks, and so they'd climbed and rolled and looped and dived and then skimmed the whole next county in about ten seconds flat! It was unreal! Uncle Bruce and Nevada sat together up front, and it was easy to see how much in love they were, the way they couldn't stop touching each other, Nevada especially—Bruce, who was dressed in silky soft army clothes, acted cool like he always did, but Nevada seemed crazy in love, and she and Jen were getting excited, just watching them. Uncle Bruce said you had to be careful, speed was a kind of addiction, "an escape from meat," as a woman he once knew liked to say, she was so hooked on it, she came all apart each time she put her feet back on the ground again, she seemed constantly to be fluttering and spinning then like those little plastic whirligigs until she could get back up in motion again, just watching her in a closed room made you dizzy. "Was that Marie-Claire?" Clarissa asked, and Uncle Bruce smiled (sadly, she thought) and said: "Well, yes, I guess it was." "But if you do get addicted," Jen asked, "how do you stop?" "You learn its opposite," said Bruce, almost as though he'd expected her question. "A sort of counter-addiction." "Woo, sounds real Zen," Jennifer said, making Bruce and Nevada laugh, though Clarissa knew it was just something she'd got from her mother. Bruce took them on a series of rolls then that made the earth whip round and round about them like he had it on a string. "Wowee! This is awesome!" shrieked Clarissa, and Jen agreed but said she was a little woozy. "Oh Jen!" Clarissa complained. "Don't grinch us out! This is fun! More, Uncle Bruce!" "Well, if Jennifer's not feeling well," said Nevada, suddenly very concerned, and Uncle Bruce eased up. "How are you doing, kid?" "I'm all right," said Jen, though she didn't sound like it. Was this a trick? They seemed to pay her a lot more attention now. "Maybe you'd like to work the controls," Bruce suggested, and Clarissa jumped up and said "Oh yes!" and beat her to it; from the greenish look on Jen's face, she was probably doing her a favor. "Daddy always lets me fly his plane, sitting on his lap," she lied—her father was pretty strict about the rules, though he did promise to teach her someday—and she popped herself on Bruce's silky lap as though she knew exactly what to do, and, more or less, she did, she'd been watching closely and she was a fast learner. She felt very cool and, though she didn't attempt anything crazy, she didn't just fly in a straight line either. Meanwhile, she was very much aware of where her bottom was and, though she had never thought of it as a tactile organ before, she used it now as a kind of fat clumsy cartoon hand, very thinly gloved, and as she put the plane through its swoops and turns, she squeezed and pinched and scooted back and forth, until Uncle Bruce said he thought that was enough, they'd better get Jennifer back on the ground again, and he seemed a little ticked off, but he did give her a friendly smack and then left his hand there as he lifted her off his silky lap, she pretending she was having too much fun flying to stop, almost like she was already getting an addiction, so as to keep his hand pressed there as long as possible, but then she made a mistake and turned them upside-down when she didn't mean to and that ended it. But her bottom was still tingling with the dreamy memory of what it had been holding on to when Nevada dropped them off at the mall and they found Granny Opal all alone at a table inside, looking like she was not having the best time of her life. So she and Jen bought her a cherry mush and diet colas with lemon slices for themselves and explained that Uncle Bruce came by and gave them a drive in a super new rig he was trying out, it was really neat, and they elaborated on that to make it sound real, but they didn't really have to, she didn't even seem to notice they'd been gone, and then she told them about the photographer getting arrested and, though she didn't tell it very well, she and Jen laughed at everything Granny Opal said and that seemed to cheer her up and she even ate some of her cherry mush.

When from his second-floor office window in the bank building Trevor saw the rubber-kneed photographer being taken into custody down at the police station, he who had never known delight (this thought had remained with him, steady as pulse) suddenly experienced, like a brief foretaste of that which eluded him, a strange mixture of anguish and exhilaration, both emotions arising from the same realization: He had done this! He who had changed so little had, irreversibly, changed a man's life, and maybe the lives of everyone in this town! Of course, Gordon had helped, but this scene transpiring in the street below was, in a real sense, Trevor's own doing, his own, as it were, personal work of art. And his burden: Gordon seemed all but lifeless, as though his spirit had fled, and Trevor's own heart sank when he saw the state the man was in. Trevor had, on returning yesterday from the spectacle at the mall, determined to end his mad clandestine pursuit of the photographer, but at the same time he had tried to understand what it was he had really been doing. He had been, in some sense, seeking after truth, yes, but of what kind? And to what end? He recalled an economics theory professor he had back at university who held that the central principle of all human interaction was simple raw power, he laced all his lectures with reminders that economics, history, life itself could not be understood without remembering that. He said it was the basis not merely of community order, but also of religious faith, science, and the search for truth, and of course of love, friendship, marriage, and family. There were jokes about the man's home life and some pointed out he didn't have tenure yet so no wonder his brain was a bit maggoty on the topic and it was popular to dismiss his lectures by saying that what little power *those* had was got by jacking directly into Machiavelli (an obscene image was often used to express this), but Trevor found the argument compelling and wondered often at his own powerlessness, which the accretion of knowledge by itself did not seem to overcome. His fascination with the professor came to an end when someone posed the question of the disinterested artist: his answer was along the same lines, but far less convincing, dismissing disinterest as though it were a silly myth, suddenly broadening his definition of power to include things other than the manipulation of other people, and refusing arbitrarily ("Let me teach you something about power," he joked) to take any more questions on the subject. And now Gordon had, in effect, posed the question again. That question, or its answer, seemed to touch on this matter of delight, as had Gordon himself in an interview published a few years ago in *The Town Crier* (Trevor had clipped this interview, kept it in his office desk drawer, second down on the right, he was looking at it now): When asked why it was he had taken up the photographic profession, he'd replied, the profession to make a living, the vocation to devote himself to art. But then why not one of the fine arts, painting or sculpture? He was a poor man, his options were few; but his goal remained the same: the pursuit of beauty. But of what use, the interviewer had pressed on, playing the devil's advocate, is beauty? None at all, the photographer had responded. Nor is there any use for the ecstasy that accompanies its contemplation . . . Had Gordon known such ecstasy? Trevor did not know, but he did believe that Gordon had chosen a life that made access to that sensation possible, even if it might mean you sometimes ended up running around in pink nightshirts and arousing the displeasure of the police. You could see intimations of it when Gordon worked: it was as though he were unaware of his own being in the world, transforming himself into a mere prism through which the beauty of the world might pass. This intensity: it was something Trevor felt he could never achieve, except perhaps through someone like Gordon, though he had not, when he'd begun this pursuit, foreseen his own active role in shaping its direction. At the time, he was simply fascinated with Gordon's own covert pursuit of John's wife—and that was another thing, John's wife. Had anyone besides himself noticed that she seemed to be vanishing, not as when someone leaves town, but as an image might fade from a photographic print? If so, they were not mentioning it, and Trevor himself was reluctant to bring it up and risk looking the fool, but his old problem of being unable to register her features after seeing them had worsened: he could no longer register them *while* seeing them. He'd tried to come to some understanding of this by locating and replotting her point on his actuarial graphs, but her point had vanished, too, and he began to wonder if perhaps her disappearance might not have something to do with Gordon's photographs of her, as though he might, so to speak, be stealing her image. Or was he, aware as Trevor was of her vanishing, trying to preserve it? His pursuit of Gordon had therefore acquired the additional motive—essentially altruistic, but not without its own links to power, beauty, delight—of watching over John's wife, or at least of trying to understand what was happening to her, and it now occurred to him that the key to that understanding, and perhaps to his entire quest, might well lie in the photographs Gordon had taken of her. Was this the moment, with Gordon under arrest, to have a look at them? He put the interview away, checked his tie, blew on his hat and donned it. He might have accomplished more than he thought with those phone calls! Hastily, he dropped down to the police station to inquire about his friend whom he had seen in some distress, did he need any help, and was told he was only being held until the chief got back, it was no big deal, he'd be home by suppertime. He thanked them, exchanging pleasantries, and left, trying to move without undue haste, but heading straight for the studio; just as he drew near, however, the chief of police came backing out of it, his gray shirt dark with sweat, some books or albums under one arm, keys out to lock the door, so Trevor made an abrupt right turn and took a hopefully casual-seeming stroll around the block, cutting through an alley to shorten the circuit, getting lost briefly (it was as though they'd turned the block around on him—he was overexcited), his own back perspiring by the time he had finally returned. He peered into a display window (toys: perhaps he had a nephew) that reflected the street, having observed the way they did it on TV, and when he'd caught his breath and it seemed safe, he straightened his hat, dropped over (if anyone asked, he was ordering up a photo for Marge's surprise mayoral campaign, to be announced today), and rang the bell. What would he tell Gordon's wife? That he'd been taken on as her husband's legal aide perhaps, she was pretty simple, probably didn't know an accountant from an attorney, and under the circumstances she would no doubt appreciate any help at all. Just investigating the allegations, ma'am, and I thought it might be a good idea to look at a few photos. No answer. He rang again. Maybe she was down at the station, another break, he tried the door though he knew it was locked, he'd have the place to himself if he could just get in, but he'd have to hurry. There must be other doors. He'd try at the back. But whoa, inspector, walk, don't run. And stop giggling.

The announcement of Marge's candidacy for mayor did not, after all, appear as scheduled, inasmuch as its vehicle, *The Town Crier*, for the first time in its long history, did not itself appear on its scheduled day, and though most people in town did not even notice this until it was pointed out to them, Marge certainly did. She went immediately to the *Crier* offices to complain, but found them closed and dark, nor could she rouse anyone when she banged on the door, though she was sure Ellsworth was in there somewhere. She called Trevor from a payphone in the Sixth Street Cafe across the street (Oxford, sitting in there with two of his grandchildren, said he hadn't seen him today, but then he couldn't see her either, so what did that prove?) to ask him what she should do, but got only his answering machine. Everywhere she looked, there were giant posters pasted up with her would-be opponent's goonish mug on them, and she felt ganged up on. What she needed was a friend, but Lorraine had been so evasive of late, Marge decided just to go over to her house and confront her directly: was she on her side or not? When Lorraine came to the door, she looked startled and confused, but she invited Marge in, in her clumsy way (Marge was thinking: even if she's with me, is this sloppy awkward woman a useful ally or a liability?), and Marge, in spite of her momentary doubts (already she was thinking: if she's with me, she's beautiful, but she wondered still why she seemed so standoffish), was so grateful to see a friend in this moment of crisis that she wanted to give her a hug and only held back because so many contrary emotions were flickering across Lorraine's face (the trouble with this woman is that she's never grown up, Marge was thinking, somewhat contemptuously, she's a silly cow who just lets the world run over her) and she was afraid of doing something (but she's nevertheless the smartest woman in this town of dummies, Marge herself excepted, and she has to struggle against so much more than Marge does, starting with the lout she's married to, she deserves nothing less than the unconditional love and admiration which she is now feeling for her) that might confuse her all the more. The poor woman seemed about to cry. Was she ill, Marge wondered? "Well, yes and no," Lorraine said, her voice quavering. "Yes and no what?" "It's sort of like an illness." "What is?" It's odd, Marge was thinking, it's almost like she was reading my mind. "It's not really like reading, it's more like, well, just listening." "What? You hear everything I'm thinking?" "A lot anyway. It comes and goes. And not just you. Everybody." Though Lorraine was starting to cry, Marge suddenly felt like the vulnerable one: how do you turn this thing in the head off so you don't give everything away? "You can't. I can't either. It's very tiring. You were wondering why I've been avoiding you lately." "Because you didn't want to know what I was thinking?" "Are you reading my mind now?" "No, just guessing." "I was afraid to find out what you really—well, you know, that you might—and now you're wondering if I've always been doing this or if it just started up." "Something like that." "It began one night out at the club. That night John's wife got the drink spilled down her front—" "I remember. I was there." She recalled how silly Trevor had got that night, staring at those wet breasts. "He wasn't the only one." No. But this was terrible! "You don't know the half of it, Marge, it's a living nightmare!" gasped Lorraine, dabbing at her eyes with her blouse tails. "I'm sorry," she added, responding to something unflattering that Marge was thinking, and tucking in her blouse, went into the kitchen, returning with a box of tissues. She blew her nose and said: "Oh, Marge, I've so needed someone to talk to!" Marge, who was not one to express her feelings aloud, was therefore relieved that the genuine warmth she was feeling toward her friend Lorraine at this moment did not need further expression, and instead she said, having just thought of it again: "Lorraine, I came to tell you, I'm running for mayor." "Really?!" exclaimed Lorraine, her face lighting up with the surprise of it, with the surprise of *being* surprised. "That's wonderful! I had no idea!"

Marge had been right. Ellsworth had been in the *Crier* offices when she knocked, still was. Or, rather, he was on the floor above them in what he liked to call, as a struggling artist, his garret, but which was today just his old dusty workroom above the shop. He'd been dozing fitfully on the cot, exhausted but too disturbed to sleep. He had not, for the first time since he undertook the task, kept today the record, he knew that, but the record he *had* kept all these years, or thought he'd kept, was now, he'd found, dissolving on him, as though to teach him what he had always known—that words were not, as he liked to pretend, the stubborn monitors of time, adamant and fixed as number, but were time's recombinatory toys and about as hard as water—and so to taunt him with the futility of his record-keeping mission. Or so it seemed last night: he allowed he was not well, his tired mind too lost to imaginary realms to keep its grip on real ones as firmly as a good reporter's must. Specimen: the caption he had written for the famous cake-in-the-face wedding photo so many years ago, which, when in his most panicky moment last night he'd looked, had seemed to read: "MAID OF HONOR NOURISHES WEDDING GHOST"—but which had resolved itself to "GUEST" once more when, merely, he had rubbed his eyes and taken a deep breath. In short: the word had not lost its stability, his perception of it had. Was this a consolation? That, in effect, this book—the Stalker!—was driving him mad? Not much of one, nor was the less hazardous notion, which he could not quite believe, that what the word had faithfully kept he had simply remembered wrongly: the bride's dress, for example, or the year the Pioneer Hotel came down. Dates were dates, places places, and that special wedding section was too well thumbed for him to find himself reading, for the first time, a paragraph deep in the story that began: "On the night before the exchange of vows, the groom bade farewell to the solitary life at a well-rounded entertainment provided by his many staunch friends . . ." Ellsworthian, no doubt, he could not deny it, but he knew he had not written it, or if he had he had not printed it, and if he had he no longer knew what he had done his whole life long. A possibility, of course; another: that he'd somehow nightmared himself into such an hallucinatory state last night that in his fevered eyes, no boundaries were secure. He'd half-reasoned so, half of reason being all he'd left to work with, and so, as history melted and mutated before him, he'd shaken his head, slapped his cheeks, stomped about the room, and looked again, often to good effect. What finally defeated him, however, and deprived this day the town of its weekly self-portrait was what he found in the celebrated photo of John and his bride dashing for the limousine under a shower of rice. This photo was one of his favorites, for it seemed to capture in its communal seed-burst gaiety the great promise of that historic occasion—only now the unanimity of that good cheer was marred by a single solemn face, staring ominously out through the cloud of falling rice, straight at the camera, and when Ellsworth saw that face he knew in an instant who it was: the Stalker! He was sure of it, even though he didn't really know what the Stalker looked like. And as Ellsworth in dismay stared back, the Stalker's eyes seemed to widen and his cheeks to tremble (though perhaps it was only Ellsworth's hands trembling) as if suppressing laughter: Ellsworth fled. And up here remained in full retreat, thinking, somewhat foggily: the book must go. The burning of the forest was not a nightmare, it was a kind of prescription. He rose from the cot, feeling shaky, stared gloomily at the heaps of manuscript pages scattered about the room: on chairs, the table, in shelves, on the floor. A great devastation loomed; probably he should eat something before he commenced it. He picked up a sheet off a nearby chair, read: Art emerges, not from what is seen, but from the longing for what is not seen. Did he write this? He didn't remember. Who said it? The Artist, consoling himself now for his loss? No, he was inconsolable. But not really the sardonic Stalker's style. Then—? Good grief! The Model!

Hunger was making Pauline shaky, too, and though devastation was not on her mind (it never was, not even back when Daddy Duwayne tried to implant it there), something approximating it was already taking place in the studio as she blundered about desperately, looking for something to eat, knowing, even as she squeezed painfully through doorways and knocked things over in her clumsiness, that there was nothing to be found. When Otis left with the albums, he had promised to order up a dozen pizzas for her, but they hadn't arrived and she really couldn't wait much longer. She tried to call him again, but found it hard to work the little dials on Gordon's old-fashioned rotary phones (had to turn them like bottle caps) and kept getting wrong numbers and busy signals. Putting two and two together was not what Pauline did best, but as she pressed her bulk through the doorway to check the downstairs refrigerator one more time (empty of course; on her last fruitful pass, she had found a withered lemon stuck to the back of the vegetable drawer by its own rot: she'd brushed it off on her thigh and eaten it whole like a piece of candy), it suddenly came to her with the force of a blow to the head, the sort of blow she was constantly giving herself now whenever she moved, that she was still growing and if she didn't get out of here soon, she'd be trapped inside this building—already she couldn't get up and down the stairs—and that would mean (two plus two) she'd probably starve to death. Even if they let her husband out of jail, Pauline knew she couldn't count on him, he was so caught up in his work these days. But if she went outside, what would she wear? The one bedsheet she had wrapped around her was flimsier than underwear, and the other bedsheets and blankets were upstairs out of reach. She remembered the dusty old burgundy backdrop curtains in the portrait studio, and she squeezed back in there to (woops!—*crash!*—sorry about that) take them down, hoping Gordon wouldn't be too mad about her borrowing them. She couldn't get her big fingers around a safety pin, much less a needle, so, her stomach rumbling volcanically all the while she worked, she fashioned a kind of loose simple cloak (good old highschool home ec!) and stapled it together with the stapler from the front-shop counter. Reaching through the bead curtains for it, she decided to take them along, too: "for dressing up," as she thought of it, though mostly it was to belt the loose flaps in place. Leaving by the front door with bells jingling did not seem like a good idea, and anyway Otis had locked it when he left and the little catch would be too fidgety for her fingers to work from the inside. But the back door was too small, even sideways she kept getting snagged on something. Of course, it would help if the screen door weren't there. How do these little hinge gizmos work? Never mind, it was off. Still couldn't get through, though. She took off her new cloak and beads, lay down on her side and pushed her legs out into the alley and then (ouch!)

her bottom, got up on her hands and knees and, jiggling back and forth, worked her top part out, dragging her new clothes with her. As she was still wiggling her shoulders through, she peeked through her flopping breasts and legs and saw a man watching her from across the alleyway, one hand clapped over an eye as though he were taking an eye test. She recognized him: Gordon's insurance salesman. He couldn't seem to stop staring, though the look on his face was different from most she'd suffered all her life. More like he was having a heart attack or had eaten something he shouldn't have. Well, who could blame him, she probably was a sight. Pauline, being an incurious sort, did not stop to wonder what the man was doing there, nor why he didn't at least come over and give her a helping hand, she figured most people would be put off, seeing her like this, and they would anyway suppose she was big enough to take care of herself. She pulled the cloak on over her head again and tied it with the beads, then went over to apologize to him and ask him where she might find something to eat—quickly!—but he just fell back into the rubbish there, still holding his eye and stammering something about his wife and the mayor. Well, too bad, but she had problems of her own, so, her growling stomach replying for her, she left him sitting there and made her way, knees bent and head ducked so as to cause as little alarm as possible, down the alley toward the Sixth Street Cafe.

Where Alf at the time was taking his midmorning coffee break, hunched over in front of the dusty plateglass window with his old friend Oxford and Oxford's two youngest grandchildren, a pair of twins, not yet four, who had their father's heart-shaped face and wispy blond hair but who, under their granddad's patient tutelage, were already reading and doing their numbers. "It was like he felt he was locked out or something, and didn't know how to get back in," Alf said, gazing wearily out on the asphalt street which seemed to be sweating in the morning glare. He had been trying to describe his nighttime encounter with Oxford's peculiar son Cornell in the back alley, but Oxford, fascinated by his grandchildren, excitedly filling in their dot-to-dot books at the table next to them ("It's a lady! With a pointy hat on!"), seemed to be only half listening. The street was eerily empty. Civic center or no, the downtown was going to hell. The newspaper office across the street looked shut for the duration. No paper so far this week and no sign there'd ever be one again. Alf rubbed his eyes, wondered if he ought to look in on Ellsworth, make sure he was all right. "Still not sleeping well, I take it." "No." "Alcohol's a clumsy sedative, Alf. Flurazepam's better." "Tried it." "Methaqualones? There are some good ones out now." "Hard on the liver." "Especially when mixed with scotch, I suppose. You know, now that you mention it, Kate once said something amusing to me about doors. It was not long before she died, at the time they tore down the Pioneer Hotel. It was a sturdy old thing, that hotel, not unlike an ancient warrior, as Kate said, hard to bring to his knees." "Mmm. Harriet and I stayed in that old warrior for a week or so when we came back after the war. From the smell, we must have been booked into the armpit." "So John finally had to use dynamite—" "I remember. It was like a goddamn bomb had hit." Brought it all back. Couldn't sleep for a week after. It was the week when missing Harriet hit him hardest. "And when the dust cleared, all that was left standing was the big front door, completely intact, columns, architrave, and all. Majestic. Inviting. But opening onto nothing." Alf remembered that standing door, remembered identifying with it in some way, but the memory seemed to be in black and white, so he didn't know whether it was from actually seeing the thing itself or from the photo of it in the newspaper. If Alf had been asked, he would have said he never read the local rag, but now that it had not come out, he realized he was badly missing the silly thing. "'Mostly we build walls,' Kate said then, 'to separate the inner from the outer, the private from the public, the sacrosanct from the common, the known from the unknown. Doors are put in the walls to ceremonialize the crossing from one into another, which is sometimes a fulfillment and a delight and sometimes a frightening transgression.'" Oxford glanced over at his grandchildren. "Like in the story of the three little pigs: a ritual transgression of the sanctity of the home that takes place at the doorway." "Always thought that was an oedipal fantasy," Alf said, signaling for a coffee refill. Should get back. The preacher's wife would be there by now. And there was that hysterical message on his answering machine this morning: "Help! That thing you took out! It's back!" No clue who it was who'd called. "You know, the home as womb with Big Bad Daddy outside, trying to blow his way in." "Maybe. Same thing. The door as a 'magical threshold,' as Kate called it, promising access to some mystery beyond or within. And what John had done, she said, was strip the door of all illusions, reminding us that all magic was nothing but sleight of hand, and thresholds were mere artifices in the middle of nowhere." Oxford smiled wistfully, glancing over at his busy grandchildren. "And maybe you're right about the three little pigs, Alf. Maybe poor Corny is just missing his mom." John was back. Alf saw him emerge from the hardware store next door with a look on his face that said he'd either just fired old Floyd or given him a raise, with John you couldn't tell which. Alf, glancing at his finger, remembered there was something he needed to talk over with John (what was worse, it seemed to be growing), but just then the waitress came over to say that he had an urgent phonecall. It was his nurse. An emergency. A man struck blind. Come quickly, she begged, the poor man was beside himself.

Nurse Lumby's quaint expression, used figuratively to describe her hysterical patient (to whom, on the doctor's orders, she was now administering a mild sedative, with some pleasure, by injection), would have been understood more literally by her brother Cornell who had become more and more convinced that there was not one of him but two. It was as though there were a parenthetical Corny inside the outward one (or containing it), or as if he were carrying a shadow around that did not always move as he moved, and from time to time he would spin around to see if he could catch the shadow out, or if not the shadow, then, in whatever form, that other self. He had to be careful not to do this when the woman called Gretchen was around, because she cut him off from his video games whenever she caught him at it (this morning, for example: he thought he felt something, like—what?—like a tap on his shoulder, he spun around—and there she was, scowling at him through her bottle-glass lenses; she clumped over like a movie monster, pulled the plug on the one drugstore machine that still worked, slapped his head when he tried to protest) on the grounds that the games were making him battier than he already was, though from his perspective, if not from his shadow's (he couldn't speak for that other self who seemed, incredibly, to be married to that peg-legged freak and to be the father of more children by her than he could count, never mind learn their names), she was the one who was crazy. Sometimes the whole world seemed crazy, but this did not worry Cornell, his mother always said that most right thoughts were, when first thought, thoughts of one lonely person—most crazy thoughts, too, of course—but the point was, it was cool to be different. Which he was, really was, and she always said she loved him because of it. Now, deprived of his only compensatory pleasure in this upside-down world (or was it inside out?), Corny curled up in a niche behind the drugstore publication racks and thumbed gloomily through the magazines, exploding in his pants whenever he glimpsed plump bosoms or inviting nests of pubic hair or even sometimes just pictures of round juicy things with creases in them, but otherwise inconsolably bored and depressed. A bummer, man, it truly was. Life, everything. Maybe later, when fish-eyes wasn't looking, he'd steal a pocketful of coins and the keys to the store van and sneak out to the mall arcade, in spite of the ridicule he often suffered out there from the teen-meanies—the zit-snits, as he used to call them in at least one of his lives. He was staring dejectedly at a picture of a nun, dressed only in her wimple and white stockings, being ogled by a priest hiding behind a cathedral gargoyle (it was the hideous gargoyle that most fascinated Cornell even as he popped off at the sight of the nun's naked bottom with the thorned heart of Jesus tattooed on one cheek: when would this nightmare end, he wondered?), in a photo feature called "Les Girls de Paris," when a woman standing near the racks peered over his shoulder and asked him if he was planning to travel to France this summer. He recognized her. Though she was married and rich and famous now, he remembered her mostly as Yale's girlfriend in high school. He used to follow them around, especially in the house or at the movies, to see what they did together. What they did was hold hands a lot, though once Yale kissed her, and that was the first time that thing happened in Corny's pants when he wasn't asleep or at least in bed. Her remark now might have been meant as a joke, but she didn't appear to be making fun. She seemed more like his mother when he brought stuff home from school, like, you know, really interested, and when he mumbled he could never go back there, she asked him why, and he (he was afraid the woman with the stubby leg would come over and tell him to keep his wackiness to himself, but she didn't even seem to be listening) told her all about it. What door? she asked when he'd finished. So he led her out into the alley and took her, step-by-step, through his midnight searches, though everything looked different in the daytime. More ordinary. A plain old dirty alley, that's all it was, it was embarrassing, man. He began to see himself as Gretchen saw him—a pathetic loony with messy pants—and he was sorry now he'd brought the lady out here. But then, in a dark place out of the sun, he saw the trash cans again: KEEP OUR TOWN BEAUTIFUL, they said. And he knew, if he turned around (why were his knees shaking? why was he hesitating? what was he afraid of?), the door would be there. But when, screwing up his courage, he did, it wasn't. Nor was the lady. What *was* there was a great huge womanish thing hunkered down behind a pickup (she was so big she was only half hidden by it), snorting and whuffing like a wild animal as she pawed ravenously through the garbage of the Sixth Street Cafe. She looked up at him (or down, really) through her uncombed hair, a blob of meringue on her nose and wilted lettuce leaves hanging off her lower lip. His heart skipped a beat. But not from fear. "Corny?" she whispered. "Is that you?"

The old Ford pickup Pauline was crouching behind belonged to the hardware store on the corner, a family enterprise operated by John, run by his father, grandfather, and great-grandfather before him, and before that John's great-great-grandfather, the famous pioneer horse-trough maker who first set up shop here where, on the rolling prairie, there was then no corner, thus, as though drawing an X on the ground, creating it and all that followed, or in some such mythic language had Ellsworth once put it in a popular *Town Crier* article years ago about "Dreamers and Builders." The historic two-story brick structure was one of the few downtown businesses left intact, more or less intact, from the old days, though not the old days of the great-great-grandfather. Why had John spared it and so little else? Some said that it showed a sentimental streak in John, others that he'd cynically set out to enhance its value by destroying its more beautiful competitors; most, though, thought he just hadn't got around to it yet. For the past dozen years or so, John had entrusted the day-to-day management of the old family business to an out-of-towner named Floyd, a former trucker and traveling salesman who happened to be passing through when the manager's position was vacant. Floyd was not a hunter or a golfer, was not a social drinker, and had not flown nor would he ever, but he was a good bowler and his past life had afforded him opportunities to play a lot of cards (he had earned John's respect as a bridge partner), to read the Bible through and through, and to pick up several manual skills of the sort taught in such places, which he had used to good effect since coming to town. And the store he managed, in spite of the competition of the malls, most of it created by John himself, had managed always to show a small profit from year to year, a tribute to Floyd's nuts-and-bolts know-how and his tenacity. So while Alf, next door at the Sixth Street Cafe, might have surmised that John, emerging from the hardware store with that icy grin on his face, had just fired old Floyd (good riddance if he did, he was an irascible old sonuvabitch, and something of a religious kook, nobody liked him), the truth was that John, who knew how to use the talent he found, had just promoted Floyd out of the hardware store at last, doubled his salary, and put him in charge locally of the new national trucking line he had acquired on his most recent business trip out West, a company he intended to link, as he explained to Floyd, with his air cargo operations. Which was why the hardware store manager, more emotional than most in town supposed, could now be found down on his white-overalled knees in the do-it-yourself section, next to the wind chimes and redwood twin-lounge kits, giving tearful and vehement thanks to his divinity: Redemption! Sweet Jesus! It was really possible! All his dark and tortured past seemed to fade away like a dissolving nightmare and he bellowed out his rapturous joy (the highschool kid who worked for him, alarmed by his employer's hysterical rant, ducked out the back door: whoo, Old Hoot's gone off the deep end again, time for a joint) as God's grace descended upon him like light filling a room or water a bucket—Praise the Lord! He was saved! Saved at last! And, so saved, once-covetous Floyd, gripped by a love of the world now sublime and pure, coveted no more.

The man whose wife Floyd had once in sin but, now redeemed, no longer coveted felt himself, back in his old hometown after invigorating westward journeys, on something of a mission. The town (he had not been paying enough attention to it and it was important to him) seemed idled, confused, unfocused—"sunk in the doldrums," as his mother would say—its communal pulse slowed, its eyes glazed over, and John, charging purposefully through it, was bringing it back to life again. At the airport when he'd landed (the last ten miles and final descent had seemed much longer than usual, he was probably trail-wearier than he thought, but he shook it off), he'd found his manager and town's future mayor dozing, snorting resonantly through his sausagey nose, and unable to say, when abruptly awakened with a boot to his shins, whether he'd seen Bruce or not, though Bruce's private jet was parked there. To get Snuffy up and running again, John had taken him on a brisk tour of the warehouse sheds, asking him to figure out where they were going to house the local headquarters of the national trucking firm he'd just bought and to get estimates on any new loading bays and access roads they'd have to build; when he left him, on the phone to his crew and barking out orders in his trademark no-crap rhetoric, the old coach's eyes had brightened and the familiar fire had returned. In town, John stopped in at his bank offices (a teller whose child had developed bone cancer squeezed his hands and thanked him for helping to bump her up on the priority list for an urgently needed marrow transplant, which she said had gone well, and everyone in the bank seemed to straighten up an inch or two and flash a smile as he passed through) to check his mail, sign checks, return calls (Nevada said: "We have to talk . . ."), send out a couple dozen faxes, order up flowers for his wife and call the caterers to make sure everything was ready for his Pioneers Day barbecue: "Whatever we did last year, you better increase it by about twenty percent. It's going to be a big one." At home, he got Clarissa who, sounding radiant and cheerful, clearly shared his good mood; she said she just *loved* Granny Opal and she'd leave a note for Mom that he'd called. Yes, she thought Uncle Bruce was probably in town. He phoned his mother to thank her for all her help with the children and for visiting poor old Barnaby so regularly ("Anything I can do for him?" "No! No, he's—he's fine!"), then called Kevin out at the club to tell him to get his clubs ready, he'd be out shortly after lunch. When asked, he told Kevin to go ahead and hire someone for the club shop, he'd sort it out with the board later. "Also, start thinking about a food-services manager who's able and willing to fill in at the bar, Kev. You need more time out on the course to keep your competitive edge." "Great! I'll get started on that today, John!" He had decided to accept outstanding offers, modest though they were, on some of the assets Barnaby had acquired in his failed takeover bid so as to help cover the purchase of the trucking firm and to provide cash for the development of the racetrack, so he dropped by Trevor's office to get the paperwork started, but he wasn't in. Off to lunch maybe. Not a bad idea, but John wasn't hungry. He'd talk Kev into throwing together one of his classic hot beef-and-pepper heroes out at the club when he got there. Which he hoped would be soon: he felt a string of birdies coming on, lined up on his scorecard like fucking turtledoves on a clothesline. He dropped down to the chamber of commerce, back in their old quarters after finding their new civic center offices too damp and noisy, to see how the parade committee was coming along (lagging behind as usual, maybe more than usual, his visit serving as a wake-up call), picked up a map of this year's route, told them about the latest new business he was bringing to town, dropped hints about the racetrack. They seemed upset that this week's town newspaper had not appeared, not yet anyway, with all the Pioneers Day announcements and advertisements (it was almost like they'd begun to believe the goddamned holiday would not occur unless the paper announced it), and he assured them he would drop by Ellsworth's shop to check it out. "Will, uh, will your wife be in the parade this year, John?" "Sure, why wouldn't she be?" On his way over to the hardware store where he had a surprise to spring on old Floyd, he saw Lenny helping heavy-bellied Trixie out of their car in front of Alf's antiquated medical facility. The only doctor still with downtown offices, the building itself a decrepit fossil like its occupier, ready for the wrecking ball. He'd offered Alf a good price to move to one of the new medical centers but Alf said he was too old to change kennels, he'd die soon enough, and John, though he'd joked to the contrary, allowed that was probably so. The minister and his wife waved and John waved back as he crossed over to the old family store. His cranky tough-as-nails manager in there collapsed unabashedly into tears when he told him he was putting him in charge of the central operations of the new trucking line and raising his salary by half again with additional bonuses based on traffic, after which the old cracker broke into either prayer or joyful cussing, John couldn't be sure which. He paused at the door on the way out: about time to rethink this ancient relic, what his father liked to call the family's public badge of honor, though he often winked when he said it. So what, then? A watering hole for the out-of-town racetrack crowd maybe? Souvenir shop? Museum? Or: all three at once. Why not? A slowly rotating bar, say, in the middle of a cyclorama of the age of the pioneers (he knew just who to hire as a technical consultant), old weapons, clothes, and implements on display, and some coin-operated interactive video machines for exploring the daily life of the prairie settlers. In virtual reality maybe: walk around in their vanished lives. Unspeakably dreary when lived, an entertainment when revisited. He already had a piece of the new high-tech action, he could put it to practical use right here at home. Probably have to buy up the cafe next door for floor space, eat up some of the alley, but it could be a big money-spinner, bring traffic in off the highway, too: he'd have them, so to speak, all drinking out of great-great-grandpop's famous horse trough again. He called out to old Alf, just shuffling back to work across the street, reminding him about the barbecue (Alf nodded, asked him to give him a call later, John said he'd see him out at the club), then popped his head in the door of the Sixth Street Cafe to remind Oxford of the same thing. "Pioneers Day! Already? Çan't be—!" "I'm afraid it is, Oxford. Time flies!" "But—" "House flies!" shouted one of the children and they both giggled. "And bring the grandkids!" He left the old pharmacist, nose down to the table, muttering to himself and trying to read the dial of his wristwatch through his thick lenses, and crossed over in the direction of city hall and the police station, nearly getting run down twice, first by the pharmacy van reeling out of the alleyway with witless Cornell hunched over the wheel, then by his cousin Maynard's black sedan, which came barreling around the opposite corner, tires squealing, driven by a wild-haired stony-eyed Veronica who looked like she'd just fallen out of bed. Had she been trying to hit him? John grinned his clenched-teeth grin, brushed his sleeve. He had a surprise in store for her fucked-up hubby, too, one that should cheer him up. He was planning to offer his abused cuz the chance to run the new racetrack (best to have someone in the legal profession in the front office, he figured), assuming of course that Mange was ready to make the right sort of investment in the enterprise, but he was saving this announcement (have to make sure they were invited, struck as they were from the official lists: he made a mental note) for the barbecue.

Where Veronica was headed (she wasn't trying to run John down, she didn't even see him, she'd have flattened anything in her path, blind with terror as she was, and the source of it just behind her like hot breath on her neck) was the doctor's office: she burst in screaming something about John having come back, or *some* John, as though there might be several of them, she had him in the trunk of her car, she claimed, he was all covered with a wet sticky stuff, you've got to come see, I don't know what to do with the thing, help me for god's sake, she was totally incoherent, the poor woman, still in her housecoat and pajamas, and, like the insurance man before her, she had to be sedated—*urgently,* the doctor snapped, a kind of unpleasant rage overtaking him as it sometimes did on busy days, though restraining this one needed his help, so completely out of control was she. "There, there, Veronica, *easy* now . . ." Columbia, trying to be soothingly understanding while punching her with the needle, said she was really sorry about her son, and the woman shrieked out: "How did *you* know—?!" "Well, I think everyone—" "*Everyone—?!* Oh my *god!*" "You haven't heard a thing since he ran away?" "Ran away? What—? Oh, *that* son! No, no, I guess I forgot, sorry, I'm so confused . . ." Columbia, too, popping the needle out past the cotton swab, was feeling a bit woozy from it all, this whole town was going around the bend and dragging her with it, really, it was too much. The waiting room had been filling up all morning and the phone ringing itself off the wall with people suffering from nothing worse than apparitions or odd premonitions, with itchy children who wouldn't keep their clothes on and tired parents needing pep pills and people who just couldn't remember what day it was and wondered if they'd come down with Alzheimer's. She'd chased most of them away on the false grounds that the doctor was in surgery all day (in reality he was in one of his bitter-old-man days, drifting off groggily for coffee just when things were at their worst), but some were too desperate and hysterical to be put off so easily, the insurance man, for example, who had been struck partly blind and kept blubbering something crazy about a giant woman and a dead child ("It was my fault! I was the one!"), and who was now lying in his underpants, one hand clapped to his dead eye, on the examining table in the room where the doctor performed small surgeries, like removing boils, adenoids, or ingrown toenails. He was still attached to the electrocardiograph suction cups, she hadn't had time to disconnect him, but anyway they kept him from thrashing about. Columbia had a policy with this man, her sister-in-law as beneficiary, she knew him well, and he'd always been such a reserved gentleman, so composed, it was a shock to see him in such a state. "Hello? No, the doctor can't come now, he's got a waiting room full of sick people, you'll have to come here if you want to see him. But if it can wait until tomorrow, I'd suggest—all right, all right, I'm not deaf, I was just trying to help, there's a long line but, if you must, come ahead!" The only one out there who had a scheduled appointment was the minister's pregnant wife, fortunately a patient woman who was somehow able to smile benignly through all the pandemonium, in spite of the enormous weight she was carrying around, bigger than she was it almost seemed, while one lunatic after another came piling in, demanding the doctor's immediate attention, which on this day was in short supply, even for real emergencies. One being the lawyer's maniac wife, who had finally succeeded in dragging the doctor down to the street to look in the trunk of her car, threatening to throw herself out the window if he didn't, and they didn't doubt it. On top of it all, the only person in town whom Lumby felt she could count on was consumed by an insane jealousy and had been on the phone to her every fifteen minutes, in and around all the other calls, wanting to know if she'd been keeping an eye on her shifty brother as she'd promised, she couldn't find him anywhere. While the doctor was gone, the minister's wife suddenly started singing at the top of her voice, then stiffened up and skidded out of her chair onto the floor. She lay there on her back, limbs asprawl, obscenely exposed, her thin cotton dress rucked up over her naked body, eyes open but staring at nothing, a strange smile on her cracked lips, out of which a kind of whispery hum emerged as though from the back of her throat or below that even. Lumby tore off a few yards of paper sheeting from an examining room table and tossed it over her (the phone was ringing again), though most eyes in the room were on, not the poor woman's private parts, but that great sleek quivering mound that rose high above her with a protruding navel on top like the knotted end of a balloon or the fuse of a bomb. The doctor returned just as Lumby was hanging up (this day was going to be endless, already it seemed like it ought to be over and it had hardly begun), holding his dripping hands out in front of him, barely glancing at the woman on the floor or those around her as he stumbled through, headed irritably for the restroom: "Nothing in the damned thing of course, just some mucous gunk like oily snot all over the floor! Remind me to take next week off!" Whereupon Gretchen phoned again in a panic: "Corny's run off! With another woman! You said you'd watch him! You *promised!*" "What do you mean, run off?" "He's stolen the van! And all the money from the store! And now the police are coming! Please! *Help* me!" The humming in the waiting room had risen to a wild whimpering whine, the sort that sometimes escaped Gretchen during their games together, and people were banging on the reception window, complaining about it. "And, Lumby?" "Yes?" "Lumby, who's Pauline?" "Pauline?" "It's his heart!" someone was shouting from the waiting room. They were carrying in an unshaven man in pinstriped pants and a gaudy summer shirt who seemed to be foaming at the mouth. She recognized him: the lawyer married to the hysterical woman with something nasty in the trunk of her car. "Get him out of here!" she cried. "Take him to the hospital!" She was nearly screaming. The phone started to ring again, she'd hardly put it down. The doctor came out of the restroom, scrubbing his hands with a paper towel, wanting to know why the hell that man was still attached to the EKG, and Columbia replied flatly, brooking no objection: "I have to make a run to the pharmacy." Enough was enough, she was out of there, pressing through the madhouse of the waiting room, so dense with commotion and distress (behind her, the phone was pitilessly sending forth its demented appeal) it was like tearing through layers of unspooled gauze.

"Hello, honey—? Me again. Hey, where the hell *are* you? I ask, nobody seems to know. I hope at least you're listening to your messages. I need somebody to *talk* to, sweetie, things are so weird now, you're the last best friend I've got, and all I get's your damned answering machine. And, believe me, I mean *batshit* weird—like, Winnie's back? Living with us? I know, I know, there's the old guilt trip crap, and I drink too much, we both do, and mostly it's Stu who sees her or thinks he does, what's left of his red hair standing right up on end, just like in the comic strips, but I saw her one night, too, when Stu woke me up with his goddamned country-boy snoring. Standing there, right at the foot of the bed, all lit up, big as life and twice as mean. And you know what I thought of when I saw her? It probably made her mad, but I couldn't help it. You remember Harvie, you know, Yale's brother, the one we called Hard Yard and King Dong? The one who's carrying that monstrous thing around in girls' panties now? Well, maybe you never saw it, goody-goody that you were, but it was not only long as your arm, it had a very peculiar color, or rather lack of color, pale and waxen from the root all the way to the end of it like all the blood had got sucked out, and faintly peachy in tone the way they paint up dead bodies, very spooky, at least in the dark. I never saw it in daylight. Maybe they were shining a light through it, I can't remember. But even when it was soft, which I guess was most of the time, the end of it was a kind of see-through blue like it was bruised somewhere deep below the surface, the opening of it just a gray metallic slit—it looked like it had been stapled at the tip. Well, that's what Winnie's mouth looked like, a thin gray staple in her bluish face, and the rest of her, too: opaque like Harvie's cock and waxy and sort of glowing from inside but pale and bloodless except for her eyes which were red-hot, just like Stu had said they were. Made me laugh, sort of, what I was thinking, but she scared the shit out of me, too. Almost literally—I mean, I was loose for a week, and I'm still not back to anything regular. Which is why I've been thinking about calling the whole thing off. What whole thing? You see why I need to talk to you? What's the matter, honey? Are you ticked off at me because of what the useless asshole I'm married to did to you out at the club that night? Listen, forget it. Forget *him*. Remember that photo he keeps on his desk, the one from your wedding party? Well, just between you and me, old Stu-pot's about to get a whop in the chops with another fucking piece of cake. Just desserts, as you might say, and none too soon either. How do I know? Amazing Grace told me, honey. Beats tea leaves any day. Jesus, I can't believe I've let that limp-noodled hayseed sonuvabitch rob me of a whole damned decade of my life—my *best* decade—how did it happen? Life's funny sometimes. Funny like a toothache's funny, I mean. Over all those lost years, I'd almost forgotten what real fucking was like. Maybe I never knew, not until Rexboy came along. Not even John—well, you know, I shouldn't even have mentioned it—but, wham bam, ma'm, and all that, and anyway it's been ages, I'm sure you knew, and I'm sorry if you didn't, but oh well . . . Anyway, Rex is different. He's there for me all the time. He says he's in love. That's hard to believe, but what the hell, I believe it. And now all I can think of is hard dick, *his* hard dick, I'm thinking about it right now, I'm—ah!—excuse me, honey, I—ah! oh . . . ! Whoo . . . Hang on, sweetie. Be right back . . . Hello? You there? No . . . ? Sometimes I almost think you're only . . . But where was I? Oh yeah, hard dick. How could I forget? Remember that knock-knock joke we used to tell as kids? Knock knock. Who's there? Wilma. Wilma who? Will ma fingers do until . . . Well, I'm here to tell you they won't do. But, t.s., baby, as my lover man would say, they'll have to: he's turned off the spigot, stopcocked the mains. Only until after the barbecue at your house. But that seems like forever. He wants to keep a low profile, he said. Hell, I said, you *better* keep it, your low profile's the one I like best. It's all yours, he said. After the barbecue. I can't wait. Literally. I'm so fucking horny, honey, I can't think straight. But happy, too, happy and horny, I can't tell you how happy I am. But also confused. Worried. Mixed up. Scared. What are we doing? I don't know what's right and wrong anymore. The fucking I'm getting is so powerful, so real, everything else is just a dream, and in a dream what's right and wrong, right? Somebody dies, who cares? It's just a dream anyway. Speaking of which. Had a weird one last night. I think. Sort of last night. Rex and I had been having it off out at the motel on his midafternoon break—what Rex calls his tea break: *t* for tail—and we'd decided to go into the Getaway for a drink, we were both parched, drained of *all* our bodily fluids, I mean tears, too, it was our farewell fuck until, well, until later, and I was very emotional on top of being so randy I could hardly walk without leaving a snail trail between my legs. We didn't bother to dress, I pulled on my raincoat, Rex his overalls, we planned on coming back to the room. But the bar when we got there was different. It was more like that old clubhouse that the senior boys built when we were in high school, you know, the place where I lost my cherry. Dutch, who was Dutch just like he is now, said that the old cabin, which had once been just where the new bar is now, had grown back overnight, there was nothing he could do. The place was full of sniggering nerds in baseball caps and pimpled burrheaded nosepickers wearing letter sweaters, which was how I knew I was in a nightmare. A couple of girls in white dresses with their black- and lime-colored underwear showing through were sitting at a table, chewing gum with their mouths open. A guy in pegged pants and a Hawaiian shirt came by, leaned over and kissed one of them, and when he raised up he was chewing her gum. I felt like I knew these characters but I didn't know them. Rex was gone. I understood this. This was some other time and he wasn't around yet. Somebody was playing 'Are You Lonesome Tonight?' on the jukebox, and I said that's a laugh, and some guy with a ducktail and leather jacket over a tee shirt said what is, hot pants? He sat down next to me and then a bunch of other guys did, too, and they started playing around, undoing the buttons on my raincoat, popping my tits out and laughing at them, shoving their hands inside to grab at the rest of me, I was beginning to get scared, not only of them, but of myself, too. I hated what these little shits were doing, but I was too damned excited to make them stop. That was when you came along. In a ponytail and a cashmere sweater and pleated skirt and honest-to-god bobby sox. You smiled and sat down and put your books on the table and the guys all apologized and left. You'd just saved my fat ass, I don't know how you did it, it was like a miracle, but, what can I say, I didn't feel all that appreciative. There was somebody I wanted but I couldn't remember who. I thought it might be John, but then he came in with Ronnie in her cheerleading rig with her bare tum ballooning out between the sweater and little skirt for everyone to see and admire. I started telling you about the time I put itching powder on her tampon just before the Homecoming float parade when she was your Maid of Honor—do you remember how she jumped around up there? you probably thought Ronnie was just trying to steal the show—but you weren't there any more. I realized those guys must have come back and dragged you over to the filthy old cot they had in there. I could hear the springs going somewhere out of sight. I knew you needed me now, more than ever, but instead of coming over to help, I pulled the raincoat around me and walked out the door. On the way I passed Ronnie, and I said, I'm sorry about your missing kid. No problem, she said, sneering down her beak at me, always more where he came from. The smart-ass. All right. So, here comes the really freaky part, honey. Like I promised. It was dark outside, I knew Rex was gone, the car keys were in my raincoat pocket, so I got in the car and drove home, had a couple of shots of gin, said nighty-night to a snoring Stu, fell asleep, and woke up here at home this morning, still in my raincoat. So, tell me. When did I leave the motel room? Have I left it yet? Did I say goodbye to Rex if I did? Are you listening . . . ? Where *am* I, sweetie? What time is it? What *day* is it? And why, feeling so good, do I feel so bad? Honey . . . ?"

Ronnie's missing kid had also long since lost, though no loss by him was felt, all sense of time and place, such coordinates being of little consequence to him in this dimensionless paradise wherein now, in joy, he drifted. He was in—he understood the meaning of this mysterious word now and he would not forget it—he was in ecstasy, pleasured in the mind and in the heart and in the body tip to toe. His journey to this blessed condition had been long and not without its false turnings, lured first as he'd been to other enticements, other anticipations. Foremost: fulfillment of all the implicit promises of those books that Fish had shown him, their images of enchanted couplings spread out below him in a panorama of such congested diversity as to dizzy the mind, even while prickling the weenie, drawing him downward, the better, he'd imagined, to see, and then, if he could, to do. But the view had not improved as, through an ever denser medium, he'd descended, and in some ways it had lost its clarity, as when a book is brought too close to the nose, becoming blurred and grainy and distorted. An effect, he'd supposed, of the strange atmosphere which, once passed through, would vanish like a mist, the way that the mind clears when full knowing is achieved, and he'd understood then, or had thought he understood, that he had seen all that could be seen by eye alone and that one must now do to see what was as yet unseen. Okay. I get it. So: ready or not . . . He'd braced himself for this manly test and, letting his clothes go as had seemed to be their own desire, he had thrust valiantly against that which was keeping him out, but try as he might, he had not been able to progress, feeling as he sometimes felt in bed at night, pressing against his sheets and pillows, barred from some unimaginable delights just beyond his ken. Then, as he'd pushed and fumbled, groping for flesh and contour where there were none to be found, he'd come upon a tiny rift in what he'd suddenly realized was something more like a movie screen, containing all these images but only as an illusion on its vast curved surface: he'd thrust one hand into the small gap and then the other, there'd been a soft crisp ripping sound as of discovery, and the scrim had suddenly split apart like drawn curtains, vanishing into the distance and carrying all those busy fornicators with it, leaving Little afloat in a luminous infinity decorated with brilliant-hued galaxies in the way that a Christmas tree might be hung with colored lights. Bright blue and scarlet comets and golden falling stars, and emerald, flashed across the depths like sensuous writing and there was an intensely beautiful murmur in the air as of hidden angel choirs that seemed not so much to strike upon his eardrums as to caress them and the rest of him as well. The colors of this spectacular cosmos did not remain constant, but slid through hue's inexhaustible spectrum as if color were a kind of liquid, washing through it in tidal floods, and he felt intimately stroked, within and without, by these chromatic ebbs and flows. Delicate aromas floated upon the ether like edible fog in celestial icecream flavors, entering him through all his orifices, and he felt his body stretch out like modeling clay as though to offer more territory for their invasion. As the gentle murmur rose to a rhythmic hum, embracing him all over and penetrating him to the core with its rich hydraulic beat, he ceased to wonder where he was and instead surrendered to a bliss he knew to be—so many meanings this voyage had revealed to him!—beatitude itself. He was—his mind knew this, his heart felt it to be so, and his body, fondled by sound and color and fragrance as though these things were animate beings, ardently attentive upon his person, responded by raising his stiffened weenie like a quivering flagpole—in the land of glory. It was going to happen! It was really going to happen! No! It was *already* happening! He gazed down upon his resplendent weenie—no, not a weenie, but a *penis*—no, not a penis, but a prick, a dick, a what? a *cock!*—which now, so had he grown, seemed half a universe away, its bold head haloed by its own dazzling radiance and vibrating in the cosmic wind like a crawling thing's antenna. It seemed to be trying to uproot itself—he could *see* the roots which were spreading their green tentacles through the tropical heat of his vast glowing body, as though reaching for securer moorings in anticipation of the brewing storm—and he felt a desperate and delicious tugging, not only in his thighs and bowels, but throughout his trembling frame, in his head and chest and even in his fingers and his toes. And then, as the kaleidoscopic colors burned in hotter hue and the air grew redolently spicy and the angelic chorus gave way to piercing trumpets, his whole body suddenly shrank into itself and then gloriously exploded, scattering itself majestically throughout the throbbing cosmic space to form vibrant new constellations in all of heaven's hues, scintillant as sugar crystals, and Turtle, overpowered, overjoyed, at one with the universe and with himself, suffering still the honied aftershocks, gratefully wept, thinking: Wow. Cool. I like it.

The body as a cosmic, or at least an outsized presence and, when grasped entire, potential source of revelation, was also the subject of Otis's sober (more or less sober) study, when abruptly interrupted by the arrival of John striding into his office at the police station with that team captain's bearing of his and asking what was going on. "Material evidence," Otis said, hurriedly shuffling the photos into a drawer. "Odd case. Has me stumped. I'm glad you're back, John." And he was, too, but wished he'd been announced, unable yet to stand to take John's hand. It was the phone that rescued him. "Hasn't stopped," he said, leaning around to pick it up. Another call about the traffic lights, all out of sync. And who switched the street signs at Third and Main? "Some kid's prank," he growled, rising. "We're working on it." He hung up, ordered all calls put on hold, and John, shaking his hand, asked then about the photographer, offering to pay his bond and find him legal help; Otis said there was none to pay, he was letting the man out soon, and legal help was not the sort that sad fruitcake needed. He filled John in on what had been happening out at the mall and apparently at the swimming pool, too, maybe right out there on Main Street, they had a real problem here. He didn't tell John about the ruined photos of Pauline he'd seen hanging in the basement darkroom, because he didn't understand them himself. Like the man was losing his touch or something, and it might be pushing him over the edge? No, too simple and it didn't explain Pauline. Might just be something artsy he was trying that Otis didn't understand—or it might be more sinister than that. John wondered aloud about the newspaper that hadn't come out yet this week, and Otis said he didn't know what was wrong over there but planned to check it out when he got a moment free. Which wasn't going to be right away, the calls were coming in about one every three minutes; he told John about them, disguising his own misgivings by saying it was probably just the kids let out of school with nothing better to do than mischief, and John, laughing, agreed. John did make Otis feel better just by being here, as though his mere presence in town were somehow a calming force, jurisprudential in nature, decreeing order and the common good. Otis told him so in his own gruff words ("This town needs you, John, you should stay home more!"), and when asked, agreed to tear up the overdue parking tickets (also two for drunk driving) of some of John's visiting business associates on the grounds that the fines might get in the way of much larger investments here. Sure, why not, made sense. Hard to collect them anyway. He was glad to hear about the trucking firm, less happy about the racetrack, though he didn't say so. Together, they went over the planned safety and security procedures of the parade route, which ended as usual with patriotic and political speeches in the civic center parking lot, where local churches, clubs, and merchants would be setting up the stalls that had replaced the old Pioneers Day fair since the city park had disappeared. Otis explained how he intended to have the cars off the parade route streets the night before, then went on to mention, a bit hesitantly, that, speaking of cars left on the street, he'd found one of John's abandoned late at night a couple of times while he was gone, and had had to take it home for him. John thanked him, adding: "She's getting a bit too big for her britches, that girl, I'll have to talk to her. Let me know if it happens again." That's right, it could have been the kid, that made sense, too, as with most everything John had to say, and Otis let it go at that, but he didn't think this was the answer to what he felt more like an eerie taunt. They were releasing Gordon just as John was leaving and Otis could see by the wince of consternation that John had instantly grasped how disturbed the man was, his round face flushed and his eyes damp and inwardly focused, his mouth partway agape. "If there's anything my wife or I can do for you—?" John offered, startling the photographer, who seemed to see him now for the first time: he turned pale and began to tremble, then spun about and left without a word. "Better go with him," Otis told the officer who'd brought him through. "Make sure he gets home okay. And check on his wife." John had left while this was going on, saying he'd be out at the club if he wanted him, so Otis added: "And don't be surprised by what you see." More phonecalls then, stacked up on hold ("There's been some kinda robbery over to the drugstore, Otis, I've sent a couple guys over to check it out . . .") while John had paid his courtesy call, among them the sullen motel-keeper out by Settler's Woods, reporting the bold daylight theft of sheets and food. "Right out the back door. A whole damned truckload, Otis. I think it was that dipshit kid from the drugstore." Oh oh. Before he could get through to the photographer's studio, his officer called in on his cellular phone: "It's a mess over here, Otis. She's broke out and took the back door with her."

By the time John reached the club, Kevin had his irons newly polished, woods lightly waxed, their "Club Champion" mittens laundered, all grips gently textured with fine resin-dusted ebony paper (Kevin's own secret treatment), the bag's leather bits rubbed down with boot oil, and stocked with all new tees and golf balls, scorecard, sharpened pencils, and a couple of deeply dimpled, slightly heavier putting balls that Kevin had been experimenting with and which John, too, had taken a liking to. John was in one of his better moods and Kevin felt uneasy about disturbing it, so he held back most of the main news of the past couple of days, telling John only about the job interviews he was conducting and the story everybody was telling about the preacher's kid on the car dealer's roof, including Waldo's version about polishing the shingles. John laughed generously and asked if his wife had been out. "Uh, not sure," Kevin said, turning away. Wrong question. "Might have seen her out on the back nine." John accepted that with a shrug, asked him to whip him up a beef-and-pepper while he was changing and Kevin had to tell him that the kitchen had been stripped bare this morning by thieves, the best he could offer him was peanuts or olives from the bar. John's big smile faded and he glared at Kevin for a moment as though blaming him for the theft of his lunch. "Well, goddamn it, Kev, have you called Otis?" "Sure," he lied, though it was only a white lie because he planned to, as soon as he could figure out what to tell Otis that he'd believe. "What is this, some fucking third-world country? Who the hell would steal food nowadays? Christ! Call Waldo at the mall and tell him to grab up a bunch of tacos out there, take the rest of the day off, and meet me in half an hour at the fourth tee." Kevin could have laid on an answer to John's question had he waited for one, but he was relieved not to have to, not yet. He had earlier spied the little piss-yellow van weaving up the groundsmen's private access road, kicking up dust and gravel, and he'd gone trotting out to chase it away, but what he'd seen as he came up over the rise near the dogleg at the fifteenth had brought him up short: a gigantic woman in a red cape was squatting at the edge of the rough down there, taking a dump. She'd looked familiar, but Kevin hadn't been able to place her, not in those proportions, she'd made the trees look like saplings, the van a toy. She was with a skinny little wimp less than half her size, and they were both staring up at him like he was the weird thing on display. He'd yelled at them to get the hell out, this was private property, and he shook his fist at them, but he didn't go on down there. The woman had wiped herself with a big white bath towel, which she'd dropped on the fairway after using, and then had crawled back into the van, unable after several tries to get her humungous bod in any way but butt first, pulling her head with its thick bird's nest of black hair in after, and off they'd gone. Curiosity had got the better of Kevin, and he'd gone on down to take a look at what she'd left there (he'd kicked the filthy towel into the rough, let somebody else bring the damned thing in), and while he was studying the amazing pile, he'd heard someone ask him if he needed any help. It was John's wife, dressed in her bright blue-and-violet Bermuda shorts with the matching top, the one that left her midriff bare, just climbing down off her electric golf cart at the edge of the fairway. "No, no!" he'd exclaimed, stepping hurriedly out of the high grass and weeds. "Just, you know, making my, uh, whaddaya call 'em, rounds . . ." She'd asked him then, showing him her seven-iron, if she was using the right club for her lie. He'd recommended the five and had found it for her in her bag. Her irons had seemed tarnished or smeared with something ugly and, oddly, she'd seemed to be playing without a putter. "Hey, bring me your clubs when you come in and I'll clean them up for you." She'd smiled, glancing over his shoulder into the rough, and he'd left her then, not looking back, knowing damn well if he did so she wouldn't be there, humping it straight back to the clubhouse, where he'd discovered he had been cleaned out, right down to the mustard and ketchup pots, and not at all sure what he'd seen and not seen.

They were rocketing through town at what seemed to Pauline like roller-coaster speed, Corny hunched over the wheel of the old pharmacy van and jerking about as though he were playing an old pinball machine, or one of those new beeping and quacking games with the TV screens she'd seen out at the mall, her view out the windows from her scrunched-up position in the back not unlike those colorfully violent screens, full of racing objects streaking by and suggestions of mass mayhem at the edges. Rarely as many as half the van's wheels were touching the ground at the same time, the shockless old vehicle hitting bottom with every serious contact, the wheels scrubbing the frame with each screeching turn; if Corny wasn't hitting the things that flashed past, he was surely taking the skin off them. It was a scary ride, and painful, too, as her body slapped the sides and her head banged against the metal roof with every swerve and bump, but squeezed in there with all the tools and supplies and other junk, something big and hard wrapped in a tarpaulin had got jammed between her thighs and Pauline was riding it with the kind of abstract gratification she'd not known since she gave up bicycles. In truth, under the circumstances (what demands her body was making!), she appreciated Corny's crazy speed and, even more, his amazing food-gathering ingenuity, which frequently, given his techniques, necessitated the sort of quick exit he always made anyway, Pauline being more afraid of death by starvation than of any mere car crash which, with her new size, seemed somehow less able to do her much harm. She felt, in short, she was more likely to dent than to be dented. A lot of the stuff in the back of the van had been hastily dumped out in the alleyway so she could squeeze in when Corny had first swung the old beat-up yellow van around, and he'd promised, looking over his shoulder anxiously, hair in his face and his wispy little moustache twitching, to get rid of more once they got underway—and he'd done so, they'd been leaving a trail of debris wherever they'd gone, clearing the van to give her more breathing—and eating—space, though the more room he created for her, the more she seemed to need. She knew she wouldn't be able to stay in here forever, but at least she was free and being fed and maybe together they could find a safe place she could get in and out of, that was what she'd asked of him, and Corny, always the silent type, had nodded his agreement. Corny had seemed desperate to get out of the alley where he'd found her as soon as possible, shoving her in as soon as he'd cleared some space and then tearing out of there, wheels spinning, like a cat with its tail on fire (one of Daddy Duwayne's favorite pastimes when he was in a good mood), leading Pauline to assume that Corny had probably borrowed the van without the owner knowing it was being borrowed, an aspect of this adventure that took her back to her highschool days and added to the nostalgic pleasure she was getting from the rough lump of tarp and metal between her legs and from being unexpectedly reunited with this strange little boy from her past, the only person in the world who had ever said to her: "I love you." Unless her mother had before she could remember, if she ever really had one. Pauline had never forgotten that touching but bewildering moment, even though Corny had seemed to, had seemed to forget over the years he ever knew her. Nothing strange in that. None of the boys she was friendly with back then acknowledged her now, and even Otis was a different Otis from the one who used to take her out parking in his panel truck, a smelly old thing with a corrugated floor not unlike this tin box she was rattling around in now, and he such a sweet softie back then, a harder man now. They all seemed embarrassed about that past they shared with her, which always gave her such pleasure when she thought about it, at best pretending to know her only as the town photographer's wife and helper, as though, becoming that, the rest of her history had been miraculously erased from the town's memory. But maybe Corny hadn't been pretending. When she'd called out to him, he'd seemed suddenly to wake up, as though from a deep coma, and to see her there for the first time since before he went on his graduation trip to Paris. And he hadn't hesitated. He'd come over behind the Ford pickup to let her pull the trigger on his twiggy little cock-and-load zinger three or four times in a row (not an easy thing to do without hurting him with her new treetrunk thighs and truncheon fingers: his testicle—she remembered how he loved to have her hold it as he spilled his seed—was like a seed itself, a wee little shotgun pellet, when she took it between giant thumb and forefinger), then, pulling up his pants, had dashed off to get the van and, hardly before she knew it, their wild ride had begun. They'd raided dumpsters and garbage cans, private refrigerators (starting with his own at home), restaurant kitchens and bakeries, supermarkets, butcher shops. He'd hit the malls, motels, the golf club (where, gratefully, she'd been able to use the bathroom), fastfood joints, and all-you-can-eat buffets. Some of it he'd paid for, most apparently not, for they were always on the run. But he actually caught up with her appetite, and soon they were emptying out more things from the van and stocking it with food and other supplies, such as the laundry sacks full of sheets and towels he stole from the motel, from which she might fashion a new garment now that she was outgrowing her burgundy cloak with the bead trim. There was a lucky haul at a highway steak house, where four black plastic bags of fresh garbage lay waiting for them, but they couldn't fit them in, just splitting them when they tried, sowing her and the van with pungent refuse, and they knew then they'd have to find a place for her to hide while Corny went foraging on his own. But where?

Reverend Lenny had seen the pharmacy van careening past in front of the doctor's office, just before Beatrice's friend Veronica came squealing around the corner from the other direction, jumping the curb as she hit the brakes and the parking meter, more or less at the same time, crumpling one fender and popping the back trunk ajar. She flung the door open and dashed pell-mell into the building in wild-eyed alarm as though something were chasing her, whereupon, closing her door and trunk for her, Lennox had begun to rethink the central theme of next Sunday's sermon, which, though not yet fully fleshed out, had to do with the miracle of motherhood, an ancient Christian topic of great inspiration and solace. Rethinking it because, to tell the truth (he had just stepped out to the street from the bedlam of the doctor's waiting room where his miracle-stunned wife sat glassy-eyed and estranged, benumbed by her prodigious burden), there was also something eerily unsettling about reproduction's uncanny power over the reproducer, as though God were in the gamete not the gamers, His eye on, not the sparrow, but the sparrow's sperm, not the rueful soul, but the ruthless seed. As the police passed by with the downcast photographer, about whom dreadful rumors now circulated, he had thought of his own past trials with the law and with his loins, and of those of his children now, Philip and Jennifer, with little Zoe no doubt soon to follow, and the unborn unnamed child as well, ensnared, as all within the animate world, in pleasure's cruel deceptions, condemned as all to suffer love's remorseless punishments. His sermon, he realized, was not to be a message of good cheer, God bless Mom and all that, but rather one provoking somber meditation upon the enigma of life itself. When, in all sincerity, we ask, "Who am I?," is there an I to be asking and is it an impertinence, mere tools of purposes not our own, to assume so much as an attribute of who-ness? In short, what can we be sure of beyond the middle term of that inquiry, the is-ness of our immediate presence in the world, an is-ness which itself knows no person nor belongs to one? Across the street, the old pharmacist whose van he'd just seen roaring past emerged from the cafe with two of his blond-haired grandchildren and was greeted there in the bright midday sunlight by John's mother, holding the hand of her little grandson Mikey, and Lennox's sudden affliction of the heart was in some manner assuaged, this genial clasp across the generations somehow ameliorating the essential tragedy at the core, to which, momentarily, he had been a witness but for which he need not be a servile messenger, and at the same time providing him a consolatory homespun image for a sermon which had threatened to become a bit doleful, not a great idea in the summertime when attendance was anyway never at its best. Alf came down then with Veronica, his head bobbing lugubriously, to look at something in the trunk of her car (he seemed appalled, she horrified, but as far as Lenny could see there was nothing there), then the doctor, holding up his hands from which some dirty ooze dripped, shook his old gray head in disgust, rolled his eyes at Lenny as though begging for mercy, and returned to his office, while the hysterical woman, pointing at something in the street, left the car and went running back in the direction she'd originally come from, and Lenny thought: Without an I as God-given, we have to invent one with our thoughts, our passions, our actions, or ones we think of as "ours," and this we offer up somewhat desperately as our humanity, though, alas, no one may be receiving, no one watching. Well, I am watching, Lenny thought, and I will testify to the nobility of their self-creations and the righteousness of their desires, and thus, in spite of everything, will celebrate motherhood after all. A rusty old pickup pulled up and two men unloaded a man from the back, incongruously dressed in pinstriped suit pants and a golf shirt. It was Veronica's husband. "Is that my car—?!" he gasped faintly as they carted him inside. For wasn't survival within the dark inscrutable heart of paradox (he was staring into the junk-laden rusted-out back end of the pickup as though the awesome mystery he was contemplating might be physically visible there) miracle enough? And wasn't motherhood's essence the perpetuation, in blind hope and wistful joy, of that impossible paradox, of that unquenchable faith in life's invisible but ultimately discoverable meaning? Yes, he had his sermon! Lenny was halfway home before he remembered that he had left his wife back in the doctor's office, so he turned back, hoping he wouldn't forget the best lines, and when he pulled up to the curb the nurse was just coming out the door, looking outraged about something, her face flushed and eyes wincing in the sunlight. "You'd better go in there," she snapped. "Your wife's making a spectacle of herself!" And then she charged off down the street, her fat back squared, in fury and disgust. Inside, Beatrice lay swaddled in wide loops of paper on the floor, ecstatically entranced, serenading the world with one of her otherworldly hums, her outlandish belly rising above her as though it were something that had fallen upon her, pinning her there. He decided to take her home and visit the doctor another day, enlisting the help of the two good Samaritans from the pickup truck in getting her out to his car. It wasn't easy. The paper swaddling came unwound, tripping them up, and Trixie was into one of her more energetic trips, tossing and twisting as though in the grip of wild cosmic forces, her pink belly bobbing in the sunlight like a buoy afloat on a violent sea. "Looks like she's about to pop," grunted one of his helpers, gazing uneasily into the very source of the mystery that was the intended subject of Lenny's sermon, and the one supporting her bucking rump groaned: "Whoof! What's she got in there, cannonballs?" An ambulance came whining up while Lenny, one arm locked in his wife's armpits, was struggling with the door, and the driver jumped out to join them. "Is this the one? I thought we was to pick up an older dude with palpitations." "Nah, he's inside, mac. But give us a hand, for chrissake, before we drop her and crack her open!" She sang to him from the backseat all the way home, going silent only at the moment he pulled into the driveway, when he heard her say, quite distinctly: "But where, then, is the center?" "What?" he asked, turning round, but she was sound asleep. Not a bad line, though: he could use it. He left her there and went inside to draft his sermon, thinking: it's in life's quiet moments when the truth most clearly resounds. This enlightening stillness did not last, however: his little daughter Zoe, apparently left all alone in the manse, shattered it with her hysterical wailing as she came running down the stairs into his arms. "Daddy!" she sobbed. "I'm so scared!" "It's all right, honey. We're home now. Where's Jennifer?" "I—I don't know!" Her little chest was heaving, her eyes swimming, she could hardly speak so choked up with terror was she. "Calm down, sweetheart, there's nothing to be afraid of now." "Daddy!" she blubbered, gasping for breath and hugging him close. "There's a . . . there's a great big monster lady in the church!"

While the preacher was searching for the Christian answer, or indeed any answer at all, to the dilemma posed by the unexpected encampment of the photographer's monumental wife and all her attendant bags of garbage and heaped linens in the middle of what many in town held to be God's house, or one of them anyway, old Stu the car dealer, butt of so many off-color jokes of late, was cutting a sweet deal with the son of the town's leading pharmacist: they were taking his advice at last and turning in their antique van for a real delivery truck, big enough for heavy furniture removal, yet easy to hop around town in and no need for a special driver's license, Stu's only worry being whether, according to his calculations about car sales and life expectancy, he was about to sell one vehicle too many. Hadn't old Win been flashing him the red light? He sent Cornell off on a test-drive while he thought about that and paid a visit to the gin bottle just to keep his mind clear and his morals clean. He saw his young mechanic taking a quick look-see at a possible transmission problem under an aging station wagon, which was being held up by a hastily placed hydraulic jack, thinking it probably wouldn't need all that much to accidentally kick the jack out, but he wasn't sure he could heave his freight all the way over there without a breakdown, and if he tried and blew it he'd probably rather have a fleet of station wagons land on him than that rough and randy boy with a blown gasket. Who knew the kid would never return from the test-drive, he was stealing the fucking thing, any asshole could see that, and feeling like a kind of partner in this scene already, Rex nearly rolled out from under the wagon to quash the stupid deal, but held back, thinking: fuck it, I'll collect the thing when the spread is mine, and punch the little shit's eyes out while I'm at it. Whose wife had similar intentions and indeed, having got wind of the possibility that her hated rival might have been offered sanctuary at the church, was already on the way over there, armed with her own tubular steel walking stick, swearing she would beat both their brains out, and that damned preacher's, too, her sister-in-law Columbia clinging to her arm and begging her not to let jealousy endanger their familial harmony and to ignore her deranged halfwit of a brother who didn't know what he was doing. But who did know, full well, and who was racing back to the church now to pull Pauline out of there before she got too big for the double doors, figuring this truck would do them till they got out of town if they *could* get out of town, and after that they'd have to play it by ear—or, rather, by rear, which was the biggest part of her and pretty much set the conditions of their flight. Not just getting it in and out of things, but also having to fill it up and empty it out so often, it wasn't easy to keep moving. Which Otis knew and set his tactics by, figuring sooner or later, so long as he kept them encircled, they'd have to stop running and turn themselves in, a residual affection toward his old friend from the trailer camp with whom he'd shared so much making him want to bring this chase (it was a chase now, no avoiding that, too much had been stolen, those two seemed to have no respect at all for private property) to a peaceful conclusion, though, under the circumstances, he couldn't quite imagine what it would be. She'd have to be kept somewhere, that much was clear, and given her new dimensions, they'd never be able to wrestle her into captivity, she'd have to be coaxed into it voluntarily. Otis had to hope the affection he felt toward her was mutual and persuasive enough, doubting that her increasingly moony husband (Otis was reminded of some of his shellshocked buddies from the war) could manage it or would even take the responsibility or be able to imagine it as his own. Probably true, for Gordon was utterly absorbed now in his own artistic crisis, unable even to load his camera or change a lens without dropping it, it was as though all his gifts and skills had fled or been stolen away, and he felt like a pianist with severed hands or a scholar overtaken by senility's dreadful erasures. Moreover, Pauline, in her departure and against her nature (but of course she was changing), had seemed to take determined revenge upon his studio, the place had been wrecked and much seemed to be missing (had others been here?), and Gordon, in his distress and confusion, felt that his own sanity—and, more importantly, his art—depended upon a minimal restoration of order. Yet this, too, like the principal subject of his lifelong quest, eluded him, it was as though some essential pattern had been broken, some code forgotten, and all he could do in the end, after turning round and round, picking things up and putting them down, was sit and stare in bewilderment at randomly shuffled piles of photographs gathered up from the floor, searching out her image. Which seemed always to be blurred or partially blocked or oddly cropped or fading from the print he held. He came across a good one of her in a Pioneers Day parade from a few years back, but though the image was crisp and bright, it was as though she were in disguise. Still, he set it aside to examine more closely, along with one taken more recently at the dedication ceremonies for the new civic center, in which, during the keynote address by John's father, she was leaning toward her own stricken father who was being honored on this occasion (he looked like halves of two different people clumsily patched together, not a pretty sight), whispering something to him behind her program. Gordon could see only part of her face, of course, and that none too clearly, but her knees under the hem of her skirt as she pivoted toward her father, one slightly higher than the other, were in provocatively sharp focus and, indeed, dominated the photograph. He knew he had, somewhere, from years back, a shot of her in a gently thoughtful mood, seated in the second row (there were only two) of a Literary Society meeting at the public library, on a night when Ellsworth read from his one-character novel-then-in-progress, *The Artist's Ordeal,* which Gordon thought sounded more like an essay than a story, and said so ("How can you have a story with just one character?") when Ellsworth asked him his opinion, causing a brief hiatus in their friendship (Ellsworth called him a fatuous provincial illiterate); but the photo that turned up in the pile he was sifting through had been taken at the back of the room, over her shoulder, and she was simply a shadowy presence—though the light on her cheek like a tiny luminous parenthesis made him catch his breath when he discovered it—foregrounding the writer and the plump bespectacled librarian who had introduced him, a woman who had once told Gordon: "Photography is a kind of magic, plucking images out of the flux like phantom rabbits. In the real world, Gordon, the thing we reach for is already something else when we grasp it; the photograph exists in the real world and shares in its mutability, but the image on the photograph belongs to the imaginary world, which is the world of death and never changes." And then she'd smiled. Perhaps the best picture in his lap was one taken in front of the altar at the famous wedding nearly two decades ago, in which she was just lifting her veil to bestow the nuptial kiss upon her newly plighted spouse, while the minister and the four proud parents looked on, a photo that seemed to capture in its charm and freshness and simplicity the very theme of the entire series and thus of his life's work: the unveiling of the mystery, gesture stilled and made incarnate, possessed, the hidden radiantly revealed.

When Barnaby gave the bride away that day, he confusedly answered for the groom as well: "I do!" At the reception banquet later on, during one of the many rounds of toasts, his wife Audrey, now dead these seven-some years, recalled that at their own wedding back before the war, when asked by the preacher "Do you take this woman," Barnaby had tipped his head forward and asked: "Do I take *what—?*" "Well," she added when the laughter subsided, "at least he didn't say 'which' or ask how much!" But even when the father of the groom put his own two bits in, asking around his dead cigar whether it was true that on their wedding night Barnaby had taken the bed apart to show her how it was made and couldn't get it back together again for want of the proper tool, Barnaby smiled through it all, feeling good about himself and about his life's work, which, he felt, had reached a new level of grace and maturity: he was at his peak and enjoying it. And he was pleased, too, with his handsome new son-in-law and junior partner in the expanding family construction business, in spite of the boy's unearned cockiness and the irony that he was Mitch's son. The war that Barnaby had served in had been like a wall that had fallen between then and now, dividing one world from another in time as it was now divided in space, such that few present that day remembered or chose to remember that Mitch and Barnaby had once been rivals for Audrey's hand, a grasshopper-and-ant story with Mitch the gregarious wisecracking ladies' man, Barnaby the quiet but manly fellow with his nose pressed dutifully to the grindstone. While Mitch was up at State, playing the field with aggressive gusto, learning the rhumba and the shag, tooling around in Packards and LaSalles (once, until with a toot on he tried to drive it up a tree, he and the bank owned a flashy Cord convertible with a powerful V-8 engine and front-wheel drive which would do well over a hundred on a straight stretch, his ever-ready makeout special), mixing football and beer blasts with fraternity bull sessions, high-stakes bridge, and blanket parties, and cracking his econ and history books only when he had to (not often, the fraternity was usually able to steal the exams in advance), self-taught Barnaby was back home in the middle of a lingering Depression, turning the struggling family lumberyard into a successful construction company and honing, in deadly seriousness, his builder's skills and vision. Barnaby was already constructing solid family homes of indisputable quality, testing out his innovative marriage of streamlined neoclassical designs with traditional American values of comfort and space, while Mitch was still swallowing goldfish and beetles and fondling his way drunkenly through Sorority Row. Barnaby owned a used Model A (in decent condition, though on dirt roads it was an embarrassment) which he drove when taking Audrey out on a date on those rare occasions when she was in town, otherwise he got around in the old lumberyard truck. No one gave young Barnaby (he was already, not yet thirty, known around town as Barnaby the Builder) much of a shot with Audrey, they all figured she'd end up with Mitch sooner or later, or some well-heeled party guy like him, wild as she was back then. It was said that, on a dare during a weekend fraternity party up at State while she was still in high school, Audrey had danced a fan dance, stark staring, just like at the World's Fair. Mitch was there. Barnaby wasn't. She had an hourglass figure back then, wore skintight molded dresses, mostly black, with pointy uplift bras and lots of gaudy costume jewelry, painted her lips and nails in matching carmine red, told naughty jokes with a gravelly voice, chain-smoked with intentionally provocative gestures. She was the first girl in town to wear a strapless gown to the senior prom and was known as a hot smoocher, fast and dangerous. Yet this was the young woman who, on the eve of the war, against everyone's expectations, put on a white Victorian bridal dress and married in solemn ceremony old-shoe-common Barnaby the Builder, and who became, after the war anyway when everything settled down, his steadfast companion and business manager and caring and committed mother of their beloved daughter.

Women, people would say (some of them), who can figure them? Not that that ended the rivalry between Barnaby and Mitch; perhaps it had never ended, even after the marriage of their children. Barnaby had been an old-fashioned prairie isolationist before the war, Mitch an outspoken interventionist (after all, there was money to be made), but Barnaby served throughout its duration as an officer in the Army Corps of Engineers, often on the front line and in both theaters, while Mitch managed to be classified 4-F and, through defense contracts and speculation, became one of the richest and most powerful men in the state. Though he married, Mitch went on living the life he'd always lived, and so, some said, did Audrey, as though, snazzy in her narrow-waisted, wide-shouldered suits and her hair swept up in the latest fashion, rehearsing for war widowhood. But Barnaby, whatever he might have suspected was going on back home, never regretted his war years, and in fact it was while moving along just behind the front in the Old World, witnessing all those devastated villages and thinking about their reconstruction, what he would keep and what take down and what changes he would like to impose, that he came upon his concept of "town planning," an utterly original thought that continued to excite him even after he discovered it had been thought of by others, centuries back—you could even get a degree in it up at the university. It didn't matter, his mind was on fire with it, and when, as a lieutenant colonel soon to receive his final promotion (he would be the town's most distinguished returning war hero), he was granted a six-week furlough before transfer to the Pacific theater, he spent most of it walking his little town, block by block, going over survey maps at the registrar's office, plotting out his intended transformations once the war was over, even getting the city, through Mitch's connections, to purchase some of the land he wanted, and, only incidentally, as it were, but as an immediate consequence of the powerful creative energies that possessed him, impregnating Audrey, who gave birth to their daughter about three months before his release and return.

Despite their rivalry and the social distance they generally kept from one another, even after they became in-laws, Barnaby and Mitch enjoyed a symbiotic relationship that helped make both their dreams come true, Mitch enriching himself on investments without which Barnaby could not have realized his vision for the town. Mitch's political influence helped, too: his uncle by marriage was the mayor when the war ended, and his wife's brother in time succeeded him, and what her kin couldn't manage, money usually could. Thus when Barnaby, home on leave, told Mitch about his plans to develop the town around a new city park, the old one being a mere square block in front of City Hall and surrounded by business, making expansion of it impractical, Mitch set about buying up some of the rundown properties Barnaby had pointed out to him, surprising the owners with his generous offers, but knowing full well that the city, through Opal's relatives, would pay him twice that when the park was built. And did. And he even got the old park in a tradeoff when they ran out of money, the most valuable piece of undeveloped real estate in town, demonstrating his generosity and public spirit (for which he was widely applauded) by moving the bandstand, statue of the Old Pioneer, and historic flagpole to the new park at his own expense, setting the statue on a new rugged stone plinth. The reshaping of the town around the new park was a phenomenal achievement. Only a war hero could have pulled it off. The whole community was reoriented, away from the dwindling creek and long-gone early settlements (even the Old Pioneer's gaze was turned), toward its slummier back side which was totally erased and refashioned in Barnaby's image, upgraded almost overnight into the most desirable properties in town, though Barnaby, taking only his construction earnings, owned none of it. Which Mitch thought was, frankly, pretty stupid. Mitch's personal ethic, which he shared with most in town, was that the world, the only one around, the one they all lived and competed in, was a business world where wealth was synonymous with virtue and poverty was either a case of genetic bad luck (which was what charity was for) or of criminal weakness of character (poorhouses and jails). Mitch knew how to read this business world at a glance and act without hesitation (wherein lay his virtue), and he knew that within his own environs and generation the true saints would be in real estate and banking, quick-witted speculators, alert and well-connected, having, as it were, God's ear. Grandpop's old hardware store may have suited his own times (though Grandpop himself was a wise investor), but was now a mere symbolic relic, a sentimental image of his family's proud historic role in the settling of this great nation, often mentioned in Pioneers Day speeches and newspaper articles, and worth keeping for that reason alone. If Audrey confounded everyone by settling down and marrying Barnaby, however, it was nothing to the surprise the townsfolk experienced when, within a year, rakish Mitch took to wife his business partner Maynard's younger sister, plain straitlaced Opal. Well, it just goes to show, people said, that being about all they could say in the face of such a marvel, most predicting that Mitch, having married on the rebound from Audrey, would soon be chafing at the bit. The truth was, though, that Opal suited Mitch just fine: seducing innocents always did give him a charge, and then, after the pleasures of the conquest and the birth of a worthy heir, he was left free to live his life as he wished to live it, no bit to chafe him. And was Audrey ever part of that unchafed life? Who could say? Just how far Mitch ever got with Audrey was anybody's guess, Barnaby's included, but that Audrey developed such an intense affection, evident to all, for Mitch's dashing young son surprised no one. With her daughter's engagement and marriage to this bold handsome boy, Audrey seemed literally to experience a second blossoming; she became once more the life of the party, bright-eyed and vivacious, recovering as if a wand had been waved her lost youth, until it vanished suddenly one year and she was gone like the smoke, so moodily glamorous in its day, that killed her.

At the dedication ceremonies for the new civic center, built by John and named for his father-in-law, now retired, the honoree's venerable colleague and one-time rival, standing under the inspiring statue of the Old Pioneer, which now rose up six feet higher than before thanks to an imposing new pedestal donated to the city by his son's company, declared in his public eulogy that the structure they were dedicating today, one of the most magnificent ever seen out here on this great prairie, represented all the noble values that he for whom it was being named stood for: pioneering contemporary design combined with old-fashioned comfort and functionality, technical expertise at the service of communal harmony and the good life and traditional family values. Mitch cited the retractable sunroof over the swimming pool as a tribute to Barnaby's own architectural innovations, and likened it to the eyelid of a sleeping giant opening onto the heavens, an image suggested to him, he said, by his granddaughter who was sitting on the platform with him. She was applauded. Mitch took the occasion to lament the absence of Barnaby's dear departed wife, whose heart was always young and whose irrepressible love of life and beauty was somehow embodied in this graceful structure, and the dead wife was also applauded. Mitch went on to say that the civic center symbolized a coming together of the entire community and a revitalization of its heart and nerve center, which had been allowed to deteriorate, putting the health of the entire town at risk, adding that Barnaby himself (who, jaw hanging open, was watching all of this with one cocked eye, the other, heavily lidded, seeming to have something else on its mind) had often spoken of his desire for just such a complex. On a more personal note, he told about the time that he and Barnaby worked together to create, virtually out of nothing, the old city park, on whose former grounds they all now stood, Barnaby confiding to him then his secret vision. "One day, Mitch, he told me, something important will happen here on this piece of land, something that will bring all our townsfolk together in fellowship and prosperity, and meanwhile we have to protect it, keep it green and free from careless development and out-of-town speculators until that day when its true homegrown purpose will be made manifest. And now, today, my friends, his dream has come true!" Marge, obliged to be present that afternoon, but experiencing nauseating waves of helpless rage and loathing, could agree with only one thing John's unregenerate father said all day, and that was that not even the Old Pioneer settled this land all by himself: it required concerted action by many people to achieve great changes. In fact it became part of her mayoral platform call for radical electoral reform, as outlined in her unpublished position paper, and something she used while canvassing the very neighborhoods that Barnaby had once created and laid out: only by working together could they bring down the corrupt and ruthless oligarchy (sometimes, depending on her audience, she said "patriarchy") that ruled this town for its own profit. But after walking her butt off all day, trying to arouse grassroots enthusiasm for her "Rout Out the Rip-Offs" campaign, all she had were the three votes she'd started with, and she wasn't completely sure of the other two. It was a nice day (too nice: she had chosen an austere business suit with a long skirt for this historic occasion, and she was sweating like a pig), most people seemed to be off picnicking or holidaying, and those who weren't just stared at her in alarm like she was something from outer space, most of them slamming the door in her face while she was still explaining who she was. This wasn't going to be easy. But then, exhausted and depressed yet as determined as ever, Marge conceived of a bold maneuver: she would go straight to John and solicit his public support for her candidacy. Not only would he have to admit that she was right on all the key issues, but more importantly, inasmuch as all tyrants, she knew, liked to preserve the illusion of democracy, then in truth, a truth he could be made to see, he needed her, even if only, from his perspective, as token opposition. Moreover, she thought, striding into John's broad-lawned neighborhood now as though to the first tee, feeling upbeat about this campaign once more (what a coup this could be!), he might even perceive, at last, the longterm wisdom of establishing some sort of practical political partnership with her, one based on mutual respect and frank exchange, thereby putting his great creative resources to more admirable ends.

Like all polar opposites, they were two of a kind, a rare kind, persons of courage and integrity and boundless energy (in Marge's mind, as she wove through all the cars parked out in front of John's house as though negotiating the sandtraps at the twelfth green, and bounced up the front steps, she could see herself and John, crossing paths in all the air terminals and power centers of the world, acknowledging one another with an understanding nod and a smile—she was nodding, she was smiling—as they went about their complementary tasks for the betterment of all mankind): together they could do anything. John met her at the door in jeans and boots and a suede vest over his bare chest, a couple of bottles in his hand, and told her she didn't need to knock, come on in, then turned his back on her and walked away, which threw her into some confusion and made her forget her opening sally. Nevertheless, Marge followed him on into the kitchen which was full of caterers and big metal boxes full of food, laying out her argument, or at least what she could remember of it that didn't sound too silly in the rather stupefying circumstances of the crowded and busy kitchen, and somehow managed to get the point across that she was running for office and wanted his support. "Sure, Marge," he said, setting the bottles down impatiently, and he reached in his pocket, pulled out his wallet, and gave her a dollar bill. "Now, come on, this goddamn thing's bigger than ever this year and I seem to be short of help, I have to get the drinks around." "What?" He glanced back at her from the screen door, as if seeing her for the first time. She stood there in her unseasonal suit, sweat running down her spine, her hair hanging in damp strings around her face, still holding the dollar bill out as if it were a ticket to something. "What goddamn thing?" "Hey. For Christ's sake, Marge, Happy Pioneers Day. If you need a shower, help yourself. And while you're at it, change the towels for me in the bathrooms and I'll give you another dollar."

As his principal employer, kicking the monogrammed screen door open, came out on the back deck with bottles in his hands, Trevor, sporting his new black eyepatch, which had provoked considerable comment amongst the guests this afternoon, caught a one-eyed glimpse of his wife Marge standing in the kitchen in her business suit, looking drawn and defeated. No doubt John had been cruel to her once again. Yet she did seem always to bring it upon herself as though it were part of her exercise regimen, testing her virtue by stripping for a lecher, so to speak. Trevor tittered into his glass of iced gin, his third of the day, the doctor having told him a good snort now and then might be good for his circulation, preventive medicine against the sort of problem he was having.

Traumatic neurosis was, Trevor believed, the technical term for it, but when he'd tried to explain to Alf what he now believed to be the true cause, heretofore repressed, of the first episode all those years ago, the doctor, harassed by a waiting room packed with distraught and clamorous patients—*im*-patients, more like it—had only half listened to his stammering confession, then had brushed it aside as poppycock, saying, as he wrote out a prescription, that as far as he was concerned all bodily disorders were ultimately electrochemical and should be treated as such, in kind. "As the main switching station of the central nervous system, the brain has too goddamned much to do to be able to handle all the incoming traffic and has to throw a lot of it out arbitrarily or shunt it off onto unused sidetracks. It makes mistakes, there are mixups, accidents, sometimes catastrophic wrecks, and then panic sets in. What we can try to do is correct the mistakes, clean up after the accidents, and by oiling the machinery, as we like to say, calm the panic. The rest, Trev, is just sentimental quackery." After fitting him with his eyepatch today, Alf, grumbling that he was rusting up and suffering from catastrophic overload himself, had abruptly closed his office, shouting out over the protests of the other patients that if they didn't leave now he'd lock them in until after the holidays, and then he'd offered Trevor a ride to the party. Party? The barbecue. Oh yes. So much had happened, he'd nearly forgotten. It was today, then? Before leaving downtown, Alf had stopped by the newspaper office to see if he could rouse the editor, but no luck. The editor had a life policy with Trevor and, having no heirs, had a complicated and whimsical list of beneficiaries (Trevor remembered the names and sums for each), including the library Literary Society, which no longer existed. He'd have to drop by soon and get the policy updated, at which time he would suggest a modest increase. This was the sort of knowledge Trevor carried around, the names and numbers that, boringly, filled his life and prevented him from living it. On the rest of the drive to John's house, staring out the rolled-down car window with his one eye, Trevor had tried intently to *see* the town, to really *see* it, as perhaps the photographer saw it, without all the technicalities and computations and what in his business nowadays they called data processing that always blocked his view, concentrating now on its shapes (which were two-dimensional but somehow therefore more compelling as, flatly, they slid past one another), its summery hues and vivid midday contrasts of light and shade, the way most things flowed into everything else as though it was all of a piece, and yet the way certain objects stood apart, as though in a different dimension, displaying their peculiar contingency, a gleaming sky-blue tricycle in a shadowy front yard, for example, a porch swing rocking slightly in front of a broken window, a long-limbed dog sniffing at a dark wet trail that seemed smeared across Trevor's flat framed view like an oil slick or gradeschool mucilage, a gleaming black funeral van parked incongruously in front of a gaily painted fire hydrant with a beer bottle perched on top. But it was no use. Even as he attempted, in effect, to control the incoming traffic and fill up the switchyard with enduring sensual evidence that he was *here*, in the *world*, that this was truly his life, his own singular and inimitable life, that was rolling by, never to roll by again, he realized he was still calculating, still beclouding his vision, halved as it now was (and if he wasn't careful, he might lose the other one), with abstractions and doubts and sophistries, and that the life he was passing through would never really be lived, would never really be his own, he was not in the control tower but tied to the tracks, he hadn't seen a thing, couldn't recall it if he had. Even in his scrupulous surveillance of the photographer, which he now regretted, innocent as it was, or as he'd meant it to be, he had seen, and yet not seen. His wife's friend Lorraine and her odious husband had arrived at the barbecue about the same time he had, he already drunk and noisy and slapping backsides (Trevor's own got a swat in passing: "Hey, Triv, you ole pirate, bottoms up!"), she looking a bit more haggard than usual and, usually a beer drinker, moving straight in on the hard stuff, filling a tall beer glass with bourbon. Trevor had been, idly, wondering why as she went lumbering by on her way to the gazebo in the rose garden, evidently headed out there to get besotted all alone, and what she'd said, pointing to her head, was: "I'm trying to turn it off." "That's funny," he'd replied without even thinking, "I'm trying to turn it on." She'd paused for a moment to smile at that and he'd had the strange feeling that she understood him perfectly, might indeed be the only person in the world who did or ever could. And then she was gone, replaced by the banker and his wife, who wanted to know if he'd heard about the arrest of the photographer for exposing himself at the mall and about his wife who had left him and was said to be on some sort of wild crime spree. "They say she's got big as a barn and has run off with the drugstore simpleton!" Trevor could add a pertinent tidbit or two, but it gave him a headache just thinking about what he'd done and what he'd seen, or thought he had (when was that?), and his good eye began to throb, so he tsk-tsked along with them, then excused himself ("Doctor's orders, heh heh!") to go fill up his gin glass again. When his wife Marge came out, she handed him a dollar bill and asked him to keep it for her but not to spend it, she had in mind making somebody eat it. She didn't even seem to notice his eyepatch, she was in such a blind rage. And she looked drained, big wet patches in her armpits, her long face creased and sagging as though suddenly aged by a dozen years, fatigue attacking her like her appetites did, or like her enthusiasms did on better days, full frontally and without mercy. Lorraine came in from the rose garden and, after a moment during which she refilled her glass, she said: "But isn't that blackmail, Marge?" "No, Lorraine," Marge said grimly, "it's politics." Trevor didn't know what they were talking about, but supposed it was bad news, and wondered if it was Lorraine who had put his wife up to this harebrained idea of running for mayor, but Lorraine glowered at him and said: "Are you kidding?" He topped up his glass, plunked in a cube, and went over to the grill where John, looking burly in his vest and jeans, his bronzed chest exhibiting a rich crop of curly white hair (Trevor was wondering about John's wife: had no one else noticed?), was directing the caterers in broiling hamburgers, hotdogs, chops, and small steaks. Young Kevin, the burr-headed manager of the country club, had good-naturedly donned an oilcloth apron over his silvery blue golf shirt and lemon-colored pants to lend John a hand, and the busty gum-smacking blonde he'd brought ("Both she and the shirt are from our new line at the pro shop!" he'd grinned on introducing her) now turned to Trevor and said: "Hey! Cool! Eyepatches are so sexy! How did you lose it?" "Lose it?" "Your eye, silly!" "Ah, the first time?" "Sure, the first time. How many times can you lose an eye?" He hesitated. But she was gazing up at him with such sweet abandon, he found it was contagious. He smiled. "Oh, well, I killed someone." "Yeah? No kidding! On purpose?" "Not exactly. Sort of. The possibility just presented itself and, not really thinking, I took it." "Wow! That's so romantic!" she sighed, and leaned against him, pulling a string of gum out from between her teeth and putting it back in again. Kevin, turning the meat on the grill with plastic-handled tongs, winked at him over his shoulder. Next, he thought, I will tell her about my career as a, well, a private eye. "Why is it always other people who have the groovy lives?"

Sweet abandon: perhaps it *was* contagious, certainly many of the crowd gathering in John's backyard seemed to be catching it, or perhaps they were reaching for it as a defense against their doubts and trepidations, which mostly went unexpressed, Lorraine's included, though it fell to her to be their reluctant collector and sorter, not easy, given the way people's thoughts darted about so frivolously, especially when they'd had a couple. Or maybe it was the couple she'd had, and the couple after that, that had dimmed her cataloguing faculties, making it hard for her to screen out the static, which back in college was just a metaphor for academic bullshit, but now was real and made her head ache with its relentless buzz and crackle, worse when raw desire arose, as it always did at these come-and-get-it blowouts, and clotted the swarm of half-thoughts reaching her with its dense wet colors, making her head feel like it was filling up with hot soup as it all poured in. One disclosure that separated out was that, of those who'd noticed, none seemed surprised that John's wife was not here, or was seemingly not here (there were two schools of thought, as in two schools of fish), nor for that matter was she herself surprised, though she could not account for this other than by way of the tautology that, were John's wife here, things would be different, but they couldn't be different because this was the real world and this was how things were, so she couldn't be here. At the same time, none who'd noticed seemed to want to talk about it, or even to think about it, as though that tautology about the world might not hold if they did so, and instead they opted more or less unanimously for sweet abandon, or abandon certainly, sweet if could be. Similarly—but differently (what did John think? she didn't know, she'd been steering clear of him after what Marge had asked of her)—there was the annual Pioneers Day parade and the local fair and soapbox oratory that traditionally followed on, which people *were* talking about, trading impressions of what they said they'd seen or heard, but which nobody was *thinking* about, or, rather, what thoughts they had came *after* what they said or what some other said. Lorraine heard so much of this chatter with all its visions and revisions that she, too, began to imagine the parade and fair, such that when the banker's wife said she thought there were fewer pioneer costumes this year than last, Lorraine said, quite firmly: "No, there were more." "Yes," said the banker's wife, "I think you are right." Alf was standing there with them, his gray head bobbing out in front of him as though measuring a pulse rate, and what seemed most on his mind was a huge tumescence the size of a beach ball on the end of his finger or which his finger was palpating, though in fact the bony thing, twitching slightly as if with palsy, was encircling a sweating glass of cold whiskey. This seaside image gave way to something more like a ship in a bottle, though there was a slimy visceral quality about the squirming ship, as Beatrice, the preacher's wife, waddled by in her red boots, looking like one of those bass drummers in a marching band, trying to keep her gargantuan belly from dragging through the grass. The loopy little pothead couldn't put three words together in her noodle without getting one of them upside-down, but she did bring a little music into Lorraine's own noise-bruised head as she passed, and for that she was grateful: a kind of sweet choral humming like a movie version of a band of angels. Sensuous, but not soupy: its ethereal tints more like light filtered through stained-glass windows. It was very nice, and Lorraine wondered if anyone here over fifteen had a joint, she could use a radical change of frequency. "We should get that poor girl a wheelbarrow," she remarked after Trixie'd staggered on, and the banker's wife said, "Yes, that's a good idea, perhaps John has one," and then went on to say, gazing dreamily about her (they were all standing there in a blazing sunlight, so ebullient it seemed almost unreal), how much she appreciated these long days of summer. Alf growled that this one seemed just a little longer than usual, and she agreed with that, too. "That's how it is when you're having a wonderful time." Many thought as Alf did and as the banker's wife said she did, but Lorraine overheard others marveling to themselves about how time flies and the way the day had just sort of rushed up on them, as though it couldn't wait to get started, for fear of—what? No theories out there, though Lorraine's own personal explanation for it was that she always collapsed into these timeless states when school was out, if it weren't for Sundays and the midweekly newspaper she'd never know when anything was. And now the newspaper apparently was no more, maybe Sundays soon would follow, it might be bliss, if you could handle the surprises. At least she was luckier than poor Marge and had dressed appropriately for the day, her two boys having assisted her in this by heading out the door with some of her clean white linen in their grubby little paws. "Hey, where do you guys think you're going with my sheets?" "To Mikey's house. It's for a play!" "To Mikey's house?" She'd heard them thinking then about how slow and stupid she was: Really dumb, man, out of it! How did we get a mom like this? "Mo-om, you know! It's the barbecue!" "Sure, I know that," she'd lied. "But Mikey can provide his own props." "He doesn't want plops, Mom. He wants sheets!" Okay, okay, she'd let them go, she couldn't stand to listen any longer to what the little buttbrains were thinking. So she'd changed into her backyard frolic rags and was just pulling the door shut when Waldo came back from the golf course looking baffled, an expression that suited him. "Nobody out there!" he'd exclaimed, shaking his corked head. "Even the bar was closed!" "They're all over at John's." "John's?" So she'd waited for him, and now he was over by the hotdog crematorium checking out Miss Sweet Abandon herself, pawing doggily at her dishabille, Trevor's weak kidneys having temporarily lost him post position. Another half dozen gathering around the little gum-popper as well, admiring the rips in her cut-off cutoffs: Lorraine, drifting by on her way to the bourbon bottle, realized that the head-soup she'd been complaining about was really more like pooled drool. She poured and backstroked out of it, but more hormonic blushes invaded her head, now of a thinner bluish sort like ink and commingled with thesauric musings that brought back to mind her old freshman composition courses: she turned around and saw Beatrice's husband Lennox with a big lump on his head, looking dazed, just stepping out on the deck behind her, and she knew at a glance his was another vote for the where-the-hell-did-this-day-come-from party.

Ecclesiastical sanctuary, a practice made famous in the Middle Ages but with roots deep in the pagan past, which is to say, in those preliterate times when all of man's most sacred precepts were forged, was a principle in which Lennox (now blinking in the sunlight, feeling wistful and blue, on John's back deck) had long had an academic interest—in fact, he'd once written a paper on the subject back in his college days, or at least had helped to write one with a fraternity brother, the theme being that the concept of a sacred place could survive only as an ineffectual metaphor in a free market economy where everything was up for sale, metaphors included—and a time-honored custom he had, moreover, in his own more dissolute and renegade era, vehemently espoused on the grounds of Christian charity and canon law (and also of Anarchy, yay! and Down with the pigs!), but until now he had never had to face the dilemma as a churchman of granting it or denying it in the real world. But there she was, camped in his church, a half-naked woman several times larger than himself, begging him to let her stay, at least until her boyfriend got back, and not to tell the police. And also did he have anything for her to eat, like for example a couple of turkeys, no need to cook them, just so long as they were defrosted? So what was he to do? Sure, providing sanctuary would be the Christian way to go, God's love and all that, but on the other hand there were no, well, facilities for her here and his church was already a pigsty, full of garbage, dirty sheets, and other stuff he didn't even want to look at too closely. Nevertheless, he was about to disregard all that and grant her request, when she reached up to loosen the beads around her upper torso and, with an explosive pop, put an elbow through a stained-glass window high over his head, whereupon he decided, God's love be damned, she'd have to go. But then it occurred to him that with very few changes in his sermon-in-progress (the mother's womb as the ultimate sanctuary, the notion of the high altar as a man-made center for a centerless world and thus a sacred refuge for all sufferers, and so on), he could make dramatic use of this creature, perhaps bring her on as a surprise boffo at the end, wake the congregation up with a kind of visual representation of the impossible paradox, or one of them anyway, he'd find an appropriate name for it, why not? Let it happen. But then her boyfriend came back, all out of breath, saying he'd found a real truck for her and they had to get out of here right away, *she* was coming! In the end, it was a good thing, because even the church's big double doorway was already too small for her, it took a lot of pushing and squeezing (Lenny was reminded of the job he had back in highschool, packing icecream into pint and quart boxes) to get her through it and she was in tears most of the time, especially when she snagged her beads and broke them all. Lenny was contemplating the deplorable state of his and God's showcase and classroom after they'd gone, wondering who he could get to clean it up for him, maybe John could send some of his workers over or else order up a crew of garbage collectors from city hall, when the crippled lady from the downtown drugstore came thumping in, crunching scattered beads under her orthopedic boot, banging her metal walking stick on the floor and demanding to know where that jezebel was who had stolen her husband away. Lenny, foolishly, tried to explain the principle of sanctuary to a woman who was clearly not in the mood for a lecture of any kind, and, calling him a pimp and a home-wrecker and an accomplice of thieves and adulterers, she attacked him with the steel cane. The nurse who had followed her in tried to restrain her, but had to duck her slashing backswings, so Lenny, to defend himself, dove in under the weapon, throwing the startled woman to the floor where her glasses went flying, and proceeded to wrestle with her for possession of the walking stick. "How dare you strike a physically handicapped blind lady!" the nurse screamed and threw herself on him, biting and punching and kneeing him in the stomach. This freed up the crippled woman long enough for her to grab up her steel cudgel and, swinging blindly, to crack Lennox across the skull with it. When he came to he was in the arms of John's wife, who was holding a cold compress to his forehead. She said she had just been passing by and wondered why all the doors were open and came in and found him here. She asked him how long he'd been lying here, but he didn't know. He explained what had happened or what he thought had happened, and she said he was only doing his Christian duty and personally she was proud of him. Her hands were very soft and tender, and he lay there longer than he needed to. They got into a conversation about religion and sanctuary, which she asked him to explain to her, and then about life in general, what it all means, and so on, and meanwhile, with her help, he got to his feet and brushed himself off and offered to walk with her wherever she was going (she was going home) and to carry her packages, assuring her when she asked that, yes, he was going to have something of a lump there, but he was all right and he needed the fresh air. On the way to her house, he found himself telling her his life story with all its ups and downs, everything from his breeze through high school in the laps of his teachers, through his university days as a struggling religious studies major and chaplain of her husband's fraternity, not excluding an account of the notorious Greek toga party at which Beatrice was introduced to the fraternity life, and then the rather unorthodox early years of their consequent marriage, leading to his abortive career as a college professor (he was made responsible for another person's bad trip, a theme he had touched on in one of his sermons on the pastor's burden, she recalled), and finally to his arrival in this town, all of it justifiably cast as rites of passage in his lifelong quest for meaning, by which time they had arrived at her house, and they walked on in. There seemed to be a lot of people toward the back of the house, but she ignored them, fascinated with his story, and asking him if now he was happy here, she started up the stairs. He admitted, following her with the packages, that he suffered a certain lingering discomfort, as he felt himself to be a free spirit entrapped in ever-narrowing circumstances and, moreover, there were things in a past shared with her husband and others that could not be erased, though he was certainly not a person to hold a grudge. Also he had to confess to a certain feeling of hypocrisy as a Christian pastor, for which he had few gifts and even less conviction, believing man's condition to be more desperate than that assumed by the Christian faith, or any other faith for that matter; he'd once been a scholar, or a sort of scholar, of them all, and without exception they all offered consolations that were not such. By now they were in the master bedroom and she was taking off her linen jacket and her shoes, and she asked him if that was the meaning that he had found in his quest. He replied indirectly, setting her packages down meanwhile and unbuttoning his shirt, by saying that only shortly before she'd found him he'd been thinking about the terrible littleness and aloneness of man in the vast indifferent cosmos. Is there anyone else out there in the universe like us, he asked, as she reached under her linen dress to pull down her pantyhose, or are we, all of us, nature's tragic freaks?

His disquisition had excited him, almost unbearably, and it was a great relief to get his pants and shorts down, though he'd forgotten to take off his shoes and had to sit down on a chair to do that. In terms of cosmic time and space, after all, we are not even visible, he went on, kicking free of the entanglement at his feet and peeling off his socks, just ephemeral creatures rising from and fading into the dust of our insignificant planet. She was on the other side of the bed in her one-piece dress, removing her earrings. He'd tried to catch a glimpse of her legs when the pantyhose came off, but there had seemed to be nothing underneath them. Nothing at all. But she smiled at him, a smile full of admiration and of, yes, well, of faith in him, and emboldened, he said to her: Even history loses its meaning, you see, its consolations vanishing like those of religion. We don't matter as individuals, as a community or a nation, or even as a life form. He stood, proudly yet humbly, in all his earthly glory. We are meaningful, he said gently, only in our nowness and to each other. Her face flushed with admiration and surrender and she lifted her dress up over her head and she was gone. John came in then and asked him what he was doing in his bedroom with his clothes off. "God knows," was all that Lenny could think to say. John went over and picked up the puddle of clothes on the floor and tossed them in a hamper. "Well, you're missing the party. Get dressed and come on down. And bring the resurrection and the life with you, Reverend," he added, pointing. "There are plenty of desperate pioneers down there eager to receive the holy spirit."

The Reverend's oldest son Philip, often called Fish, and known also, to a certain beloved but unloving party, as the Creep, the possible—no, probable—circumstances of whose conception his father had just detailed during the recounting of his life story, was badly in need of a pal. His father's narrative had been loosely based upon the heroic quest motif, and this motif, had he known of it, might have served his son as well as a way of understanding his own present ordeal, since being the butt of a popular joke was something he shared with many of those household names of the ancient past, most of whom were at least granted the company of a boon companion upon whom they could unload their woes when fate was knocking them around. But Fish's best buddy had run away and, really, there was no one else, the only other person to whom he might turn for sympathy holding him in withering and unremitting contempt. She would be at the barbecue of course, it was at her house, but he was afraid to go there and take the heat. "Aw, go on, superstar!" his sister Jen had taunted. "You're famous! Or anyhow your ugly duff is! You can open up a booth out in the gazebo:

cut a flap in the seat of your pants and charge a buck a peek, two bucks to pop a pimple, you'll make a fortune!" Of course, Jennifer was trying to keep him at home, she didn't want him to see Clarissa today, she was afraid he'd tell. What he'd overheard. On the extension phone. And he would. Rejected as a lover, maybe he could at least become a trusted friend, and if that meant ratting on his sister, hey, easiest thing in the world. It would be less easy to explain to Clarissa what had really happened in the car dealer's house, but Fish wanted to talk about that, too. With somebody. He could see what everybody was laughing about, but they didn't know the real story, it wasn't just a joke. He'd finally decided to call up the police and tell them what he knew, but when he'd refused to tell them who he was, the policeman had shouted at him, "We've had enough of this crap! Get off the line, sonny, or we'll trace this call and have you arrested!" When he hung up, he felt he had to get out of the manse. Just in case they *did* trace the call. Not much hope, but he went over to Turtle's house anyway. Turtle's mom peeked out at him when he rang the bell, her eyes buggy like she was watching a horror movie, then she whipped the door open and yanked him inside by his shirt collar. She was always very nervous and bossy, but today she was out of control. She was still in her housecoat, her face was pale and wrinkled without any makeup on, and her hair was sticking out in all directions like something had scared her and made it all stand on end. "I really can't stay," Fish apologized, his voice squeaking a bit. "I was just wondering if maybe your son came back, but—" "He's behind the refrigerator again!" she cried, sounding more like a squawking bird. "He is—?" "You've got to help me!" She dragged him toward the kitchen. He tried to hold back, but she really had her claws in him. "Maybe I could just come back a little later—" She pushed him in ahead of her, then shrank back, chewing her nails in the doorway, waiting to see what he'd do. The kitchen was a crazy scene, the floor smeared all over with some kind of sticky gunk, pots and pans flung everywhere, and half the furniture in the house piled up against the space between the refrigerator and the wall. "He's back there! Please! Get him out of here!" "Uh, I don't know, maybe your husband—" "My husband? My husband? He'd kill me if he knew!" Fish had no idea why this might be so, but certainly Turtle's dad could be pretty nasty if his dander was up, which it often was. A man on a short fuse. "If I only knew where his father was!" "Who?" "It's *his* fault! *He* should have to get rid of it!" All this talk about husbands and fathers seemed pretty mixed up, but Fish agreed with her: "Yes'm, that's right. He's probably at the barbecue." "Barbecue—?" "You know,

Pioneers Day, over at—" "Oh my God! Is that *today—?!*" And she was out of there, the front door banging open and her feet, still in bedroom slippers, slapping down off the porch. The house was suddenly very quiet. Fish hesitated. He could hear something moving behind the barricade, or thought he could. "Turtle? Is that you?" Nothing. "Turtle—?" Just a kind of squishy sound. Whoo. Time to go, man. He unstuck his shoes from the floor and took off, and as he reached the street a truck pulled up and the driver leaned out and asked: "Anybody home here?" "Nah. Everybody in this house is out to lunch!" He saw that the guy, that video games freak from the drugstore, was going in anyway, so he turned around and shouted: "Hey, while you're in there, take the pet for a walk! Behind the fridge!" Fish longed to see Clarissa more than ever now and, determined to tough it out, he headed toward her house, come on, chicken, let it happen, but he lost his nerve a block later and turned homeward. Life was a bummer, it really was, no pun intended. You are what you get born with. Period. You don't like it? Tough titty. And as for women, well, they weren't at all like he'd thought they were, his father's books didn't show half of it. The manse was empty when he got back, everyone else at the barbecue. Except Jen, away on plans of her own. Nothing to do but beat off, Fish thought glumly, heading for his father's library. The phone rang. A hollow unsettling sound in the echoey manse, but he let it ring. Then he thought it might be Clarissa trying to find out where Jen was, so he picked it up. "Hello, Philip?" Not Clarissa, but he knew who. He'd heard her voice earlier: silky yet firm with just a touch of a soft chummy twang. He figured it belonged to the woman he'd seen sitting with Jen and Clarissa sometimes at the mall. "Hey, this is a friend of your sister's." "I know." "Your sister's in a bit of trouble, Philip, and I need your help." "I don't think so," he said. No more older women, that was one of his new rules, not even to say hello and goodbye. "Clarissa needs your help, too, Philip. Believe me." "Well, but, I was just about to, uh—" "Are you alone?" "Sure, everybody's gone to the—" "Stay right there, Philip. This is important. I'm coming over."

Turtle's father, the nasty man with the short fuse, who Fish supposed must be at John's barbecue like everybody else in town except himself, was in fact back in Settler's Woods again, pawing frantically through the weeds and litter, in fruitless search for that which, now lost, he held—except for the leg it came from—most dear in the world, his dander up all right, but directed wholly against his own criminally negligent self: how could he possibly have let it, when for almost twenty years it had never been, out of his grasp? He'd awakened in the hospital, not knowing where he was at first, plugged up to various devices, remembering only a kind of dream he'd had about walking in the woods and seeing John's wife bicycling by in her tennis clothes. Had she fallen? Or had he fallen? Had he used the frayed garter as a bandage of sorts? He couldn't recall, but (he was off the cot and searching desperately through his pants pockets) he definitely no longer had his most precious possession. But where—?! How—?! In a panic (he'd felt like screaming!) he'd hauled on the pinstripe suit pants, tucked in his golf shirt, pulled his tennis shoes on over bare feet, and, head ducked, had bulled his way down the pale corridors and out of the building, responding to no one when they shouted at him: let the sonuvabitches try to stop him, it was *his* fucking heart, he had his rights! The hospital was on the edge of town, not far from the highway and the woods (it was not a dream, he'd been there, he was sure of it), it was a doable walk, or jog, rather, he was on the move, piecing together, as he galumphed along, what remained in his loss-stunned memory of his earlier trek out here: the ravine, right, he'd been taking a piss at the fucking ravine! So he started there, kicking through the thorny underbrush, poking around in the damp leaves and suffering all over again the terrible chagrin he'd felt when, all aglow, she cycled by. It had to be here! But it wasn't. He retraced his steps, working his way inch by inch from the ravine back to the first place he could remember being and then again back to the ravine. Nothing. Nothing at all. Oh shit. It was gone. Gone—! But what the hell had he been doing out here in the first place? That's right, he'd been hunting for his truant son, he'd nearly forgotten about him, the irresponsible little sonuvabitch, it was his fault this had happened. He was furious with him, but at the same time he loved him of course and he realized that, down deep, he'd been missing his boy sorely all the while. It was what had been keeping him up nights. That and, well, some other things. He wanted to blister the kid's backside for running off, bringing this catastrophe upon him, but he wanted to hug him, too, and be hugged by him, and to teach him what the world was like (goddamn it, you don't just go running off into it, son) and to protect him from the worst of it, his only child, next of the Maynards. Well, maybe he was right to go. Escape the fucking curse. Which he, Maynard II, could not, could never. With an aching heart (yes, it was damaged all right, irreparably), he sank to his knees near where he'd peed, or had started to before she passed by, and began turning the leaves over one by one, tugging away the thornier plants, tossing aside the sticks and twigs, the beer cans and cigarette butts, scratching at the ground around, feeling (pinstriped trousers notwithstanding) like some sort of prehistoric man squatting miserably in the dawn of time, trying to understand by touch alone who and what the unfathomable Other was. And what he touched was hard and stony but smooth in the way that bone was smooth and was indeed bone, and as he dug the earth away around it, he saw that it was a skull. His son's? He shuddered and tears came to his eyes and he forgave the boy with all his heart and he dug deeper and discovered that there was a big hole in the middle where the nose should be, as though . . . He really didn't want to know any more. He covered it up hastily and stood, looking around him, his hand scrabbling about in his empty pocket. He thought he saw something moving and the heavy silence was broken suddenly by some violent thrashing about deep in the woods like some huge wild animal was loose—and it sounded like it was coming closer!

Mitch, driving in from the airport in one of John's cars, picked him up on the road out there as he came stumbling breathlessly out of the trees just past the humpback bridge, looking more like beast than man, teeth bared, eyes beady, and jowls dark, and dressed up like a circus animal. John's punishment had been hard on the poor fellow. Mitch was glad it was over, for his nephew's sake. In truth, Mitch had rather admired the daring of Barnaby's and Maynard's attempted raid, and he supposed that John, who always relished a bruising battle, especially when he won, probably did, too, though he couldn't say so. When Mitch pulled over and shoved the door open, Maynard shrank back in terror and threw his hands up in front of his face. Whew, the sonuvabitch was really in bad shape. "It's all right, son," Mitch said, leaning across the passenger seat toward him and extending his hand. "It's just me, your uncle Mitch. Come on, get in." Maynard hesitated, then seemed to collect himself. "Sorry," he said, the glittery panic in his eyes fading to a dull stare. "I'm—I've not been feeling well." He shook Mitch's hand briefly (no more than a second or two, but Mitch could feel the trembling) and, head ducked, dropped heavily into the seat, pulled the door to, and after a nervous glance over his shoulders into the woods, sat slumped there, stubbly fat chin on his chest, gloomily contemplating his muddy knees. When Mitch, relighting his cigar from the car lighter, asked him if he'd spoken to John lately, he got a barked "No!," making it clear John had not yet sprung his surprise on him. Maybe his son had changed his mind. More likely he'd just been too busy. "It's high time you did," Mitch said, but got no response. Probably he had taken too many hits and was wary. Or maybe there was something else. As they rolled on into town, Mitch asked him if everything was all right at home. "I mean, you know, your wife's been a bit funny lately." Completely off her trolley, more like it, the crazy twat. "She been giving you trouble?" "No, it's not that." Maynard seemed to be struggling for some way to talk about it, whatever it was. His clothes were a mess and he smelled pretty funky but he could clean up at John's. A full and immediate rehab was in order and, by the looks of it, it shouldn't wait another day. "It's just that I lost something. Something important. And—" "Oh yeah. Your son, you mean." "What?" His nephew peered dimly up at him for a moment, then looked back down at his filthy hands, dangling limply between his knees, turning them palms up as though there might be messages scrawled there. Christ, he was an ugly bastard. "That's right. We haven't heard a thing." "That's tough," Mitch said. "Only son and all, I know how you feel." He knew better than to ask about his brother-in-law, Maynard's old man, who was going gaga. Pretty depressing. All of us headed that way. Don't think about it. So instead Mitch told him about the hippies who'd camped out in the old hangar out at the airport. "Left a helluva mess. Fucking garbage everywhere. The crews out there never saw them, just some kid in a truck the manager took a pop at as he tore out of there, but they must have been a whole damn gypsy caravan. Where in God's name do these people come from?" When he'd asked the mechanic who'd shown him into the hangar where the manager was now and what he was doing about it, he'd replied: "You mean Snuffy? I don't know, ain't he the mayor now?" So now Mitch asked: "What do you think of the new mayor?" Maynard didn't know there was one. His nephew was silent for a time, reading his hands, and then he raised his head and looked around him and said: "How long has this day been going on?" Jesus, no answer to that one. Mitch, chewing his cigar, shook his head and said: "Looks like the whole damned town's here." The street outside John's house was parked bumper-to-bumper and the drive was full too, so Mitch pulled into the space in front of the drive, leaving the keys in the ignition. Maynard seemed alarmed that Mitch wanted him to join the party, but Mitch insisted that he and his wife had been invited, his son had told him so personally, and that in fact John, he knew, had a surprise in store for him, something great, let's go see him now. "You know John. A rough customer in a brawl, but never one to hold a grudge, and in the end he always sticks with family." When Maynard held back, Mitch bit down on his cigar and told him this was his chance to get his life back in order and he shouldn't fuck it up. He should also pay more attention in the future to his dress and to his personal hygiene, goddamn it, but today it didn't much matter, this was an informal party, so let's hit the head for a quick wash and shave and get with the pioneer spirit. Or spirits. "God knows I could use a stiff one and so could you. So, come on, son! Move your butt!"

Needing a stiff one was but one of many such remarks that passed for wit or wisdom at John's annual Pioneers Day barbecues, that particular mot (as Ellsworth, absent today, would say) repeated at this one, with a wink and a wistful grin, by Waldo, the paint-and-wallpaper man, in cordial conversation with the gum-snapper his wife called Sweet Abandon, and no doubt employed by others this day as well; there were only so many such lines in town and they had to be shared around. "I know what you mean," most would say, returning the wink, though Sweet Abandon, perhaps, so young, still not adept at what Kate the late lamented librarian used to call the community codes, did not. What she said, popping a bubble, was: "No shit. Listen, you got any blow on you?" Waldo's grin vanished for a moment, then spread easily across his flexible jowls again. "I can get some," he said. This willingness to be of service to one another, for whatever reason, was characteristic of most of the guests in John's congested backyard: this was a friendly town, and for all that it had grown in the last decade or two, still a town, just as in the days of the pioneers, where most people knew each other and even knew what their jobs and hobbies were and where they went to church, and where common courtesy, without frills, was the daily norm. "Can I help?" "Let me refresh that for you. What's your poison?" "Drop by the shop tomorrow, I've got just what you need." "Listen, what I need, nobody's got." "I know what you mean." Humor, courteous neighborliness, now and then a gentle ribbing, these were forms of local discourse that were at the same time declarations of affection and togetherness. Thus, there was no malice intended, or at least very little, when Maynard stepped out on the deck in the smiling company of John's cigar-chewing father, indicating that his long painful exile was over, and was applauded by everybody in the backyard for having the best costume at the party: a golf shirt tucked in tailor-made business pants with muddy knees, the pioneer's dream. When the preacher's wife passed by the barbecue grill, holding her tummy up in front of her with both hands, one of her husband's parishioners, wielding tongs like forceps, called out: "I've heard of a bun in the oven, Beatrice, but that one takes the cake!" and others, playing joke-tag, one of the town's favorite pastimes, especially at parties and during happy hour (what old Stu, also not yet here today, liked to call "Can You Tup

This?"), added: "Maybe somebody forgot to set the timer," and "If it's the pastor's wife, it must be a hot cross bun," and "Looks more like a baker's dozen!"— "Or else a dozen bakers!" someone laughed—and none of these remarks were meant in any disparaging or disrespectful way, or to call into question the Reverend's paternity or to suggest inadequate precautions taken, not seriously anyway, but all were at heart expressions of sympathy and sodality, and were taken as such by those at whom they were directed, except for this or that individual with a fragile ego or an underdeveloped sense of humor. These persons, whose lives, though proud, were lonelier than most, set apart as they were even at amiable gatherings like John's backyard barbecues, were often as not dubbed by the townsfolk with accordant nicknames—and though they did not always appreciate them as such, these were also a form of inclusion and friendship, a kind of community embrace of its unembraceables—like the Nerd or Old Hoot or Mad Marge. Who now, having abandoned her mayoral campaign (the general opinion seemed to be that John's flunky was already the mayor, she must have missed something), and being overdressed for this vacuous lawn party which mocked the day it supposedly celebrated (pioneers didn't *have* lawns!), decided it was time to butt out and cool off with a round of golf. But she lacked both car and partner. She knew where her car was, parked many blocks away where she'd been canvassing with her clubs in the back, but where the hell, now that she needed her, was Lollie? The banker's wife explained, in what was probably an expurgated quote, that Lorraine had left in somewhat of a tizzy, saying that when she came back, look out, there'd be the dickens to pay. Marge's husband Trevor, sporting his new black eyepatch like a codpiece (Lorraine had used the image earlier and, annoyingly enough, it was true) and tipsier than Marge had ever seen him, also refused to leave with her when she asked, wanting to know why she always tried to spoil it whenever he was having a little fun. "What—?! You call this fun—?!" Feeling betrayed and furious with them both, Marge stormed away, shouting out her disapproval of the ecological insanity of all this wasteful suburban sprawl and arrogant overconsumption as she went ("Happy Profiteers Day!" she yelled), no doubt eliciting, somewhere amongst the revelers, yet another repetition of "There's someone who could use a stiff one." "I know what you mean."

Mad Marge may have needed a bad-humor cure on this day, the Nerd as well, but not the man they called Old Hoot, the former hardware store manager, now managing director–elect of John's new nationwide trucking and air cargo operations, who was in such a euphoric state he looked like he might explode. The broad smile on his craggy face was almost scarier than his scowl, so unfamiliar was it (there were two teeth missing, one on each side, that no one in town had ever noticed before), but certainly none could match him for the heartfelt fervor and spirit of joyful thanksgiving with which he was celebrating this traditional day of the pioneers; he was everyone else's therapy, a stiff one personified, and most, when they saw him, broke into broad smiles, too. A rough customer, old Floyd, folks generally thought, but hardworking and loyal, and John was now repaying that loyalty. As he always did. So no one, or almost no one, begrudged him his sudden good luck. Spiffily dressed in a new summer suit with two-toned shoes, checked shirt, and silver bootlace tie, a new moustache shadowing his lip, Floyd was himself feeling very much like a pioneer, having breached some impossible frontier and finding himself moving now into exciting new unexplored territory (genuine respectability, for starters), and he did not hesitate to let people know that he was, by the grace of God, a man reborn, his mind cleansed of all impure thoughts and his repentant heart forever devoted to this town which had raised him up from the depths of hell. When John passed by, bare-chested in his cowboy duds, Floyd raised a toast to his benefactor, thanking him for having faith in him, unworthy as he was, when most of the world did not, and asking God's blessings upon him and all his enterprises, and John, with a faint smile, raised his can of beer in return and said simply that he considered Floyd the right man for the job. Floyd flushed and smiled and tears sprang to the corners of his eyes. "And God bless your good wife!" he added, somewhat stifling the general cheer, though no one could say exactly why. Perhaps it was because Floyd's own wife Edna had not yet arrived, arousing some curiosity, and perplexing Floyd, too, as he said when asked. "She went buying for the new house, as I recollect. Probably just got carried away." Not like Edna, of course, a cautious shopper to say the least, but the astonishing news had made her a bit giddy and it was true that she had gone buying, as Floyd said, and with the promised new house in mind: one, she imagined, with old trees in the yard and a big picture window and carpet on the stairs instead of rubber mats and a toilet that really worked proper, or maybe even more than one. "I cain't believe it, Floyd," she'd said, steadying herself against the kitchen sink when he told her, "but I do, I sincerely *do* believe it!" Because she could see it in his face. And so, she had gone out to the big mall on the highway where she rarely ventured so as to look for something sufficient to mark this mighty change in their lives (she could almost hear her stepmother telling her: "Edna, go fetch me a sign!") and what she'd finally chosen, it being too early to pick out curtains or wallpapers, carpets or cabinets, since they hadn't even gone house hunting yet, was a beautiful table lamp with a porcelain dog for a base, all curled up like it was asleep, and a red shade above it with a pretty silver border around the top and bottom, plus a red velvet cloth, the same color as the shade, for it to rest on. She'd deliberated for a long time because it was so expensive, and when she finally plunked down her credit card she felt a twinge of guilt, but she was sure in her heart that it was just the right thing and that she would love that dog for all her life. As she was wheeling it out to her car in a shopping basket, she ran into John's wife, dressed in a lovely pioneer costume with bonnet, full skirts, and apron, who paused to admire Edna's purchase. How nice, she said, the way the lampshade matched the little cloth, and she showed Edna the throw rug she had just bought which also had some of the same red in it, as well as colors which were similar to the silver stripe and the porcelain dog, especially the painted collar with golden studs around the dog's neck. It was just amazing how they went together, she said, and she insisted Edna must have it. Edna protested of course, it was strictly something she never did, but John's wife said Edna would be doing her a favor to take it, she'd picked it up by mistake but didn't really want it, honest, and it would go so well with Edna's new house when she had one, and certainly it *was* very beautiful and it really *did* go perfectly with the lamp and when John's wife told her it was a prayer rug and that she wanted her to have it as a housewarming gift, how could she refuse? It seemed like God's will. So Edna rolled it up and put it in her shopping basket with the lamp and the cloth, telling John's wife she didn't know how to thank her, John's wife saying there was really no need to, it was truly a pleasure, have a good day, and then she was gone. Edna pushed her shopping basket out into the parking lot, still very happy but worrying already about how she was going to explain all this seeming extravagance to Floyd, and, as she opened up her car trunk, she was arrested for shoplifting.

"No, I know after all the fights he's got into up there he ain't due for parole till the other side of doomsday," Otis was barking into the phone as they brought Edna in for booking, "but I got me a goddamn crisis here, Bert, and if that hellacious butthole can help me I gotta get him down here and toot sweet, you hear?" He clapped his hand over the mouthpiece, leaned toward the hardware man's sad dowdy wife. He saw she'd been crying. "Just set down there a minute, ma'am. We'll try to figure out what happened, soon as I get off this call." He glanced at the Oriental carpet his officer was showing him. Didn't see too many of those around here. "Don't worry, Bert, I'll keep the sonuvabitch collared, you'll get him back in one piece, mean as when you mailed him. Okay, call me back. But don't let me down!" What a day. Seemed like a week. Crazy things happening. Those two on the run, tearing up jack. People lost in front of their own houses. Or acting weird, like the photographer. Or the lawyer's wife. Picked her up in her nightgown; running around on the streets, absolutely out of her onion. She'd bashed her car into a downtown parking meter and abandoned it and was now about as coherent as a headless chicken. Wouldn't go home. "No, no, that *thing's* there!" she'd screamed. But he'd shipped her back in a squad car anyway and called the hospital where her husband was a patient. He'd checked himself out. So to speak. Anyway he was gone, nobody knew where. This restlessness: it was what most bugged Otis. He wanted to yell at everyone to stop where they were and just hold it for five minutes. And now this lady, who'd never given anybody any trouble in all her life, trying to steal a damned rug, which didn't even look all that new, it just didn't make sense. When he asked her why she did it, she said: "I can only say I never stole it, nor nothing else, in my whole born life. It was, well, give to me by a certain person." Otis didn't believe her, but something about the way she said it made the back of his neck tingle. He rang up the merchant in question and turned to one of his officers who was on the same bowling team with the woman's husband: "See if you can find Old Hoot." "He's prob'ly over to John's, Otis." "John's?" "You know, at the barbecue." Otis, phone tucked between chin and shoulder, shuffled through the papers piled up on his desk, but he couldn't find his calendar. "How come *that's* going on when I got all these other problems?" The merchant, having heard John's name mentioned, said he'd call back, and Otis told the woman to make herself comfortable until her husband got here, and did she want a cup of coffee? No answer, she was crying again. Meanwhile, phonecalls were stacked up dozens deep. A lot of them about Pauline: "Otis, I just seen something you won't believe!" "I know, it's a bit unusual, but we got it under control." Sure we do. Like hell. She and the drugstore loony were on a wild crime spree and it seemed like there was nothing Otis could do to stop it. Reports would come in, Otis would chase them, see the filthy remains of their passage, but they'd be long gone. Sometimes he'd run into Cornell's wife and sister out there and they'd berate him or get in his way or trample over the evidence; he warned them he'd book them both as accessories, but the drugstore lady had a way with her steel crutch that made it hard to reason with her. And a lot of the calls and what he found when he got there were clearly Corny's own diversionary tactics—he was crazy maybe, but he was wily. Like those jungle weasels who'd earned Otis his Purple Heart. Sometimes it seemed almost like there were two of him. Some of the complaints were real: the stolen truck from the Ford lot, their temporary encampment out in the old airport hangar, thefts from motels and restaurants and private homes. But they didn't add up to anything that helped him track them down. Which was why he had his call in upstate. Maybe he should be asking for the National Guard instead of Duwayne, but Otis hated to have any truck with outsiders: the town should solve its own problems, he believed that. His officers phoned in from the lawyer's house: "Hey, Otis, this place has been ransacked. Big mess in the kitchen. Really ugly. That broad took off screaming as soon as she seen it. Should we pick her up again?" "Naw, let her go and get back down here soon as you can, we got more urgent things to worry us!" And he wasn't talking about shoplifting, which was frankly the least of his problems. The suspect's husband arrived in a blurred fit of rage, bewilderment, indignation, and sheer panic, spouting Biblical bombast, but Otis told him to calm down, there was probably a simple explanation, and by the way, congratulations on the new promotion, he'd heard about it from John. That helped. Floyd wiped his brow with a blue bandanna and said, thanks, he was real pleased, God be praised, and asked his wife whatever did she want such an ugly rug for anyway, she knew how he hated things with patterns on them in the house. "I didn't want it, Floyd. It just, well, sort of turned up in my basket." Floyd started ranting to her about the slippery road to perdition and made her get down on her knees to pray with him, which she meekly did, but then the merchant out at the mall called and said, given the parties involved, he'd just take the rug back and wouldn't press charges, so Otis told them both to get up and go back to the party and try not to let it happen again. "God bless you, we won't," said Floyd solemnly, adjusting his silver bolo and buttoning his suit jacket as he rose. He was not a big man, but he was standing tall today, radiant and full of himself. He took his wife's arm. "For as Jesus says, we must enter by the narrow gate, though the way be hard and those what find it is few. And if a person will not stop sinning, he is better out of the world than in it." He drew himself up, stroked the fresh fuzz on his lip, and with a smug, almost beatific smile (Otis was reminded of paintings of martyred saints in his old catechism manual), turned to leave. "Say, hold on a minute, Floyd, that reminds me," Otis called out just as he reached the door. He fumbled through the loose stacks of phone messages. "Was you ever in Santa Fe?" Floyd looked like somebody had suddenly stuck him with a pin, just between the eyebrows, and he shrank about half a foot. "Santa Fe—?" he rasped. "Santa Fe what?" "No, that's okay, I didn't think you was." "But—!" "Go on now, I'll see you directly over to the barbecue." "Otis? Call from upstate. They're sendin' Duwayne down here in a prison van with a coupla escorts. And Bert says to tell you, if you lose the vicious cocksucker, you'll be takin' his damned place!"

Yea, though those who find it are few, entering through the narrow gate the hard way (never let him down yet) was Waldo's most sacred intention and imminent prospect. As soon as he cleared out the tinhorn competition: going off to get the goods had lost him his place in line. No hurry, this make was a lock, enjoy a bit of the day's festivities. He already had a buzz on, having sampled the merchandise, and felt very much in control of his own destiny. And hers. He chatted with Kevin at the grill while munching a steak-burger and admiring, over Kev's shoulder, the cheeks of her little pink ass, plumped out under the ragged hems of her cutoff shorts and dazzlingly aglow in the sunshine like painted fruit. A few clumsy greenhorns around her, a teller and a shopclerk or two, the poor kid looked bored out of her gourd, seemingly amused most by old gin-soaked one-eyed Trivial Trev who could hardly keep his balance, drunk as Waldo'd ever seen him. Kevin, wearing one of the new line of pro shop shirts today as advertisement, said he was surprised that old Floyd had gotten the big transport job instead of Waldo, and Waldo said he was surprised, too, and for a minute the buzz faded and his prick went limp, but then he laughed and said that interior decorating was more in his line, if you know what I mean. Kevin laughed and said he did, leaning in to turn the dogs and burgers, and just then the little bimbo with the juicy bumbo glanced up: Waldo patted his pocket and winked, and she smiled, lifting tittering red-faced Trev's hand off her overflowing bubby where it seemed to have fallen from out of the sky as if by accident. Waldo wiped the mustard off his mouth, asked Kevin to hold back one of those new shirts for him—"A big red one, stud!"—and walked over to ask Trevor if it was true that it was a hen that had pecked his eye out. Trev's mood darkened and he tried to reply in kind, probably meaning to ask if Waldo's ears had got that big because his wife was always pulling him around by them, as Waldo himself would have done, but what came out in a wet loose-lipped slur was "'Syour ear big 'ike 'at f'm getting it pulled off alla time?" "Well," Waldo was able to drawl, staggering Triv with a clap to the shoulder, "pulling it off is one way to make it bigger, old son, but when you grow up I'll show you a better one," and Sassy Buns grinned and popped a bubble and said: "Why can't you old guys talk like normal people? Come on, really, how did you lose it?" "Y'wood'n b'lieve me'f I tole you," Trevor said, lifting his chin, his good eye rolling about haphazardly in its socket. He spread his arms out as far as he could reach, pitching gin at passersby. "It wuzzat big!" "What was?" He flushed and burped, wiped the drool. "You know." He might have been trying to grin wickedly or he might have been about to throw up, it was hard to tell. "That!" he squeaked and reached round and grabbed the girl's fanny, then keeled straight over on his face, dragging her shorts partway down as he fell. Those around her whistled and laughed and she said, snapping her rags back in place and pulling her feet out from under the fallen body: "I thought this was where the nice people were!" Waldo patted his pocket. "Some are nicer than others, pet. Ready for a cee-break?" "Yeah," she said, with a gum-cracking glance Kev's way. She blew a kiss at his back. "Let's go get it on." He'd called Dutch, it was all set, but one problem: his old beat-up wagon was gone. Lollie must have taken it. But hadn't he just seen her a few minutes ago? Damn. Waldo figured he'd have to hit up John, risk losing momentum, maybe worse, but then he spied one of his good brother's chariots—his famous blazing saddle—blocking the driveway, checked: the keys were inside. This was indeed a beautiful day. Even if he hadn't gotten the promotion he so richly deserved. "Here we are," he said, popping the doors open with a slow triumphant wink. "Wow! Cool!" He could tell the kid was really impressed by the way her unharnessed tits bounced when she hopped in and stroked the leather seats. "Okay, baby," he growled, "get ready to fly!"

Clarissa had been ready all afternoon. Hadn't he promised? All she had on was a cut-off tee shirt, sandals, and her thinnest shorts, no underpants, just in case she got back on his lap again. No, not in case, but when. She'd told him she really got off on flying with the world above her head and she wanted to do that on her own and he'd smiled that tragic smile that made her feel so creamy and said next time she could. Sometimes, she'd said, she felt like she wanted to fly straight into the sun, and he said sometimes he felt that way, too. She remembered his hand lingering on her bottom as he lifted her off his lap: it was like a delicious dream and made her want to put her own hands between her legs. And his. But so far no Uncle Bruce. What was more ominous: no Jen either. When she'd asked Jen's father, he'd said he didn't know where she was, he'd thought she'd come here with her mom. But he was very vague and tried to change the subject and asked about her own mother and Clarissa was pretty sure he knew more than he was telling her. Jen's mother, of course, was not merely vague, she was completely out of the human loop, and when Clarissa asked her where Jen was, she hiked up her disgustingly huge tummy with both hands and replied in her little singsong voice that we are all in the universe and the universe is in all of us. Great, thanks a lot. The Creep had not shown up, but after what had happened, no one expected him to. As for his little sister Zoe, she was as big a help as her mother. She said she'd heard Jennifer talking on the telephone to a girl. "That was me, dummy, *I* was talking to her on the telephone, but *then* what?" "I dunno. I think she took a bath." Clarissa got angry and tried to press Zoe for something serious, but the little crybaby just puckered up and ran to her mother. It was very frustrating. When, in a casual way, she asked about Uncle Bruce while helping her father carry food and stuff out to the backyard, he'd paused to glance, unsmiling, at her costume (she was wearing as much as he was, wasn't she?), then had said that as far as he knew Bruce was in town so he'd probably turn up sooner or later, here, princess, take this pepper mill and cold six-pack out to the guys at the grill. Out there, they were emptying the water from an ice bucket on the face of an old man with an eyepatch lying on the ground, her daddy's spooky accountant. They were all laughing so he probably wasn't dead. Old Hoot 'n' Holler, her Sunday School teacher, was praying over him just the same, while his wife stood by in her usual pathetic daze, looking like she'd swallowed something she shouldn't have. Then her Aunt Ronnie, who wasn't exactly her aunt, turned up in nothing but her wrinkled nightgown, completely wigged out, and when her husband tried to reason with her she started screaming bloody murder like he was trying to kill her or something. Boy, marriage, it was really great. Clarissa's dad took charge, as he always did, and led the crazy woman upstairs, but why, she wondered, did he even *have* goony friends like these? Clarissa turned around and bumped into her granddad who gave her a boozy hug before she could duck it and asked her if she knew where her granny was. Clarissa said if she wasn't here she was probably visiting Grampa Barn at the rest home. A plane flew over but it wasn't his, it wasn't even a jet. She was so mad she felt like hitting something, so when the banker's wife asked her if she had enjoyed the parade today, she snapped back that parades were for little kids and mental retards. "You may be right," the lady smiled. "Certainly they do have a lot of fun at them." It was hopeless. She went inside and called the manse again but nobody answered. Her stupid little brother was wrapping a couple of his nerdy buddies up in sheets, no doubt for one of his sicko plays. They looked like cocoons with their heads hooded and just their hands and feet sticking out. She gave one of them a kick with the side of her sandaled foot and asked him if he could feel it. He could. He was bawling. The other one asked her not to kick him, but she did anyway. "Gotta be fair," she said. Then her Aunt Ronnie came down the stairs on her father's arm, dressed in one of her mom's linen dresses, which didn't quite fit, and looking trembly and wild-eyed, and when she saw the boys in their sheets she freaked out again. "Now there's *two* of them!" she screamed and went running out through the kitchen, where there was suddenly a very loud clatter. Her father scowled darkly at all of them on his way through, and Clarissa said: "Now see what you've done, Mikey, you little idiot!" But he didn't care, he never did. Still no answer at the manse. She listened to it burping away for a long time, her rage rising with every ring. If Jen had betrayed her, she'd kill her. She suddenly felt terribly lonely, her chest tight like she was about to have a heart attack. She wished she could find Nevada, but she didn't know how, had never asked. She was the only person besides her dad she could still trust. She hated to have people see her cry, but if she was going to start, Nevada was the person she wanted to be with. She was the only one who'd understand.

Clarissa's understanding friend could hear the phone ringing when she arrived at the manse, but she told Philip, gripping his arm, not to answer it. He flushed and said he didn't mean to. Without letting go of his arm, Nevada said: "Your sister's gone, Philip." "Yeah, I know, she's up in the air with Clarissa's Uncle Bruce." She gazed at him gravely and, somewhat sheepishly, he looked away. She could see how Rex must have had fun with him, but he wasn't an ugly kid, just scrawny and awkward with a bit of an overbite a beard would hide and a pimply complexion he'd probably outgrow. If he bulked up a bit, he might almost pass for cute, and later she would tell him that and change his life. For now, she said: "It's worse than that, Philip. Listen, do you have anything to drink around here?" "Uh, well, my dad . . . in his library . . ." "Okay," and still clinging to his bony arm while that damned phone kept ringing, she shrank toward him as though needing his support, letting her hand tremble just a little, and his body quivered in return. He reminded her of somebody, something in his brow or eyes, an old adolescent boyfriend maybe, or some guy who'd kissed her at church camp. She'd taken this on as a job she had to do, but she began to think she might have fun as well. It had been a while since she'd had one of these to play with. "Let's go there. We can talk." Once, when she was young and her parents were still trying to get it together, she'd been sent to live for a while with grandparents who were very religious in a gospelly oldtimey way, and for a time Nevada had been taken in, hook, line, and sinker, by the whole Jesus scene, down the aisle, soul to Christ, and all that, so it gave her a special kick now, even though his dad's study looked more like a prof's than a preacher's, to be seducing a green-ass kid in a place like this. Before she let go of him so he could get the drinks, she pulled him close and whispered in his ear: "I don't think she's coming back, Philip. Ever." She pressed her cheek against his scraggy pecs to hear his heart banging away as if he'd just been through a massive workout, and Philip, clumsily, put his hand on her back, then took it away. She withdrew, turning her face aside as though she might be crying, and went over to examine his father's books while he got the bottles out. "There's some brandy and, uh—" "Great. Just a couple of fingers. No ice." Keep it simple. "I feel so shaky." Jen had told her about the sex manuals, so she looked for them, all the while telling Philip how much she cared for his sister and how upset she was about what might be happening, dropping hints that Bruce was her lover and had made her do this (Philip had overheard their conversation, after all, something she had to worm her way past), and so she also felt betrayed and vulnerable and, well, just a bit heartbroken. When Jennifer had told her about her brother listening in, Nevada had asked in barely concealed alarm if he was going to tell her parents: "No, he's going to tell Clarissa." And of course Clarissa would be pissed off and probably run to her father and then they'd all be up shit creek. So, yes, she'd assured Jennifer, shepherding her to her tryst, she'd figure out some way to keep Philip home from the party. "Trust me." Though now she had different ideas. The poor boy, she knew, had an unrequited crush on John's snotty daughter and she'd have to get around to Clarissa sooner or later, that was after all why she'd said she was coming over here, and anyway she'd be useful: Nevada had a note in her purse that Philip would have to deliver soon, and Clarissa would be the bait. But not yet. There was still some time to kill. And a novice dong to blitz: she might as well enjoy this. "I've been so worried," she said softly. She'd found the book she wanted, picked out a good page. "I feel somehow calmer . . . with you, Philip . . . in a place like this." Philip was pouring brandy out self-consciously, his back to her, so she stepped up behind him and laid the book open in front of him, wrapped her arms tenderly around his chest, and murmured, her jaw gently massaging his meager traps and dorsals: "This is some kind of church, Philip! I think I've, you know, seen the light! How do I join, lover?" She let her hand slide down over his fly, while the other crawled under his shirt. "Like they say," she whispered, stretching up to lick at his ear while unzipping him, "if you can't save the soul, at least bless the body."

While Philip, on this annual Pioneers Day, was finding adventure, not by leaving home, but by returning to it, an ironic experience that must have been shared by many of those forgotten stay-at-homes the oldtime pioneers left behind in the glorious past, his missing sister Jennifer had, earlier in the day, embarked upon the more traditional course to fresh discovery, launching herself irrevocably (Nevada was right, she would never return) into the unknown, feeling herself literally uprooted as she rose into the air inside the magic chariot (as she thought of it, for it *did* all feel like a fairytale, thrilling and enchanting, but not quite real) that was taking her, princess of the moment, to the royal ball. Though she had no clear idea as to what that ball might be like, Jennifer was not afraid and chose to let herself be surprised, letting her thoughts drift instead to what it was she was leaving behind—willingly of course, but sadly, too, and with nothing but an overnight bag—even as it shrank away below her. Her parents had come here when she was not even five years old and the only thing she remembered from that seemingly infinite time before then was a sudden happiness after great unhappiness, like when (like now!) an impossible wish comes true. And also a favorite Red Riding Hood doll she once had with all its clothes gone except for the hood (whatever happened to it?) and holding Zoe as a newborn baby. All the rest of her remembered life had transpired in that little town down below which now looked like a model village for a train set or a Christmas department store toy town. She could see the shopping mall where she and Clarissa had spent so many funny and exciting times together, and, silly as it looked from up here (it was like an ant farm she'd once had—she'd always called it her "ant theater"—which she'd spent long hours staring at and which had led her to write a line in her diary that said: "If you can't help doing it, then you might as well make a show out of it!"), she knew she was going to miss it, just as she'd miss her family and especially her dad and her new brother or sister she'd never know and also school and the swimming pool (she could see that, too, like a bright blue postage stamp on her little postcard town) and her own bedroom and her father's church and Sunday School, and above all her friend

Clarissa, who would be hurt and would absolutely hate her for what she was doing, but hopefully not forever, because she just couldn't help it, and she thought that Clarissa, more than anyone in the world, would understand, since it was Clarissa who had first talked to her about how when you wanted something badly enough nothing else made sense, no matter how crazy your wanting was, back when Jennifer had never known that kind of wanting nor could even quite imagine it, though she'd tried, since Clarissa had made it sound so interesting. The title of an X-rated movie at the mall which they never saw had finally summed it up for them: "Helpless Victims of Desire." That's what she now was, one of those. "I'll never go to my senior prom," she said out loud, and then she asked to circle the town once again before they flew away forever. As she picked out the places she knew, she realized that they were all associated with some memory or other, such that her life, which was lived in time, and so was here and then, as quickly, not here (when had they taken off? it seemed like a century ago! no, more like: once upon a time . . .), had somehow got imbedded in all those places down there, so that the town was, well, not her life itself, but a kind of map of her life, and of course the lives of everybody who lived there, all laid on top of each other. And so, though from up here it looked like something you might see in a geography book, a fixed and geometrical something you could pinpoint in space and anchor yourself by, it was not a real place at all, you couldn't *have* pinpoints in infinity, after all, didn't one of her teachers tell her that? That was just an illusion, the sort of illusion she was now leaving behind, escaping, in her fairytale fashion, the fairytale of her childhood. The only thing real was right now. And then again (her heart was banging away like crazy): right now. "Okay," she said, feeling a bit woozy from staring down at the turning town (it was like being on a fairground ride, and it reminded her of those magical fairs they used to have down there in the city park when they first moved to town, and how excited she always was before they all went, the whole family was, her mom and dad, too, and how one night she got sick on a scary ride that whipped and spun her about like suddenly the world was broken and wouldn't stop no matter how much she screamed); she leaned back in her seat with her eyes closed, searching for the right words for saying goodbye, which, when found, she spoke, calmed by them, with a dreamy smile: "Let it happen."

Oldtimers would argue that the Pioneers Day fairs that so excited Jennifer were merely dim imitations of the great fairs before the war, back when Pioneers Day was the town's most wonderful event of the year after Christmas, and even better in some ways, because Christmas was a family holiday spent in wintry weather behind closed doors, whereas Pioneers Day was a sunny celebration of civic pride during which everyone in town got together: at the parade, at the political rallies where candidates outdid one another with promises of even greater Pioneers Days in the future, at picnics and ball games and swimming parties, and above all at the great fairs which ran all day for three days and three nights, and which had everything from livestock judging and church raffles and booths selling local home-canned and home-baked foods, caramel apples and cotton candy, through the usual penny arcades, funhouses, and freak exhibits, to awe-inspiring carnival rides straight from the World's Fair and famous musical acts down from the big city. The austerity of the war years reduced all that to a local fair, highlighted by the occasional visiting movie or radio star selling war bonds, and after the war they never really recovered their old glory, though so long as the city park existed they continued to be held and the townsfolk, especially the young, continued to enjoy them when they weren't off on vacation. Pauline, who was forbidden by Daddy Duwayne to attend them, sinks of iniquity that they were, never missed a one and in time even had a booth of her own, so to speak, sometimes back of the carnival company trucks, sometimes under the wooden bandstand, sometimes just behind a bush, it didn't take long, and she almost always got a present. One night she was lingering near a shooting gallery where the boys always gathered, when John showed up with his pretty young wife, and she watched, fascinated, while he shot at the little mechanical ducks wobbling creakily on a rotating chain at the back of the gallery. He never missed and once two ducks fell over at the same time, though maybe the gallery operator was just being friendly and made it happen. He won a beautiful stuffed teddy bear with bright button eyes and a big red ribbon around its neck and he gave it to his wife, who already had an armful of such prizes. She turned and saw Pauline staring and, with that lovely smile for which she'd been famous since her Homecoming Queen days, she gave it to her. Pauline glanced up at John to see if it was okay, and for a fleeting moment she saw that magical prince with hair alight of a year before, but then as quickly he was just the handsome young man who owned the hardware store and he had turned away with his wife and they were gone. Pauline, still clutching the teddy bear, saw then that some moments transcended ordinary time and could not be sustained or repeated or even in any way approximated again, though that was obviously what all these holidays were trying to do; they could only be experienced at the moment they happened or not at all, and then, afterwards, they might be remembered or they might not, but it didn't matter, they just were what they were. Nevertheless, though it really *didn't* matter, she was feeling happy in a sad but peaceful sort of way, so she decided to close shop for the evening and, hugging her teddy bear, to go home to the trailer. Where she was met by a red-eyed ranting Daddy Duwayne, who made her crawl around naked on her hands and knees like the animal he said she was, whipping her as she circled round him for going to the fair and doing whatever it was she did to get the teddy bear. Then he nailed the bear up over the old TV from the junkyard and, while assaulting the gates of hell from behind with his rod of wrath, he blasted it to smithereens with his shotgun. Afterwards, he cut off the shredded body and left the eyeless head nailed up like a hunting trophy. It was still up there when she and Otis visited the trailer and it was one of her daddy's crimes she reenacted for him, or that they acted out together, several times in fact, it was one of his favorites, though Otis only pretended to shoot his pistol, instead shouting out "Bang! Bang! Bang!" in his funny wheezing voice, which she always thought was because he buttoned his shirt collar too tight around his throat. Dear Otis. They'd been such good friends, and for so long. Not anymore. He'd been chasing them all over town, blocking their escape routes with patrol cars, putting armed guards up around restaurant kitchens and collecting the garbage bags before they could get to them, it was a desperate situation. They couldn't sneak out of town unseen in that big circussy truck Corny had borrowed, and everywhere they'd gone they'd been recognized and teased or chased away and even shot at. Finally, there was no place left except Settler's Woods, where they'd come after first leaving a trail of false clues leading out of town on a back road. Corny could not hide the truck, and she didn't really fit in it anymore anyway, so he'd decided to unload their supplies in the woods and return the truck to the Ford garage and try to trade it back in for his old van, which was all he needed for picking up groceries. So now Pauline was all alone and, big as she was, a bit scared. The trees were too close together, she couldn't move without bringing down limbs and branches and making huge crashing noises, and now that her red cloak barely reached her armpits and didn't cover her front at all, she was getting scratched all over. Corny had told her to keep out of sight, but, even when she scrunched down, she could see over most of the scrubby trees out here, and so, she supposed, she could just as easily, if anybody wanted to look, *be* seen. And there was another thing. Why she needed Corny. She'd never been a great thinker. But now (as if her head were imitating her bowels) she was becoming less of one.

It was Pioneers Day and the Ford-Mercury garage that was Cornell's destination was officially closed, but by chance—or perhaps not by chance, more by quizzical design, the sort of design, for example, that governs the formal structure of a joke—its venerable owner and his young mechanic, the latter chauffeuring at his own insistence, were also headed out there in the old tow truck, though by the main road which Cornell was no longer free to travel. The ostensible purpose, being duly acted out by both as if it were the real one, was the theft of the very truck which Cornell, though they didn't know this nor would much have cared if they had known, was now returning. Along the route, which was a sunny well-used thoroughfare, Stu spied several people, some clients, mostly fellow duffers and elbow-benders—whom he might have hollered out to, but they'd have only smiled and hollered back and gone their way, even if he'd have shouted something like "Help, police!" or "I'm being murdered!" which everybody would have supposed was just a punchline to another of his dumb jokes. Which, truth to tell, it would have been, dumbest of the lot. He and Daphne had just been staggering blindly toward the door with John's annual barbecue vaguely in mind when Rex appeared there as if out of nowhere. Stu was momentarily startled but he was not surprised. He'd been expecting this moment ever since Winnie started turning up at the foot of the bed at night, and today his little darlin', uncommonly sober of late, had been uncommonly drunk since breakfast. Which, in shared apprehension, had sent Stu to the pump, and so both their engines were pretty well flooded by the time Rex made his sudden appearance at the door, dressed in his sweatsuit, to tell Stu they had to go out to the lot because a truck had been stolen, Daphne would have to go on to the party alone. It don't matter, Stu declared magnanimously, waving his hand about, plenty more where that one came from. Rex protested that it did matter and they'd have to get going right now. They played out this no-it-don't, yes-it-does routine for a turn or two, and it reminded Stu of a famous old wedding-night joke, but Rex didn't want to hear it and Daphne complained she already had. Stu said, all right, go ahead on out, son, I'll drop Daph off at the barbecue and meet you out there. Why are you always patronizing me, I can get there by myself, said his little peach among the lemons, hitting the doorjamb with the side of her face as she tried to lurch out past Rex. The blow seemed to have turned her around because she marched away straight into the dining room and hit something else, then came back into the hallway, yowling and cussing like the old girl who got her tit caught in a wringer and wanting to know why the hell he was being such an irresponsible asshole, my god, this young fellow, who was only trying to be of help, was more interested in his business than *he* was, and of course that was genuinely true, as Stu had to admit, and did. Stu asked Rex then if he'd heard the one about the old boy who goes to the doctor because his dingus has gone soft and he can't get it up anymore and he wants the doc to do something about it. The doc takes one look and tells him—goddamn you, you old fart, turn it off and get outa here! Daphne screamed, you're driving me crazy!—tells him that his job is to cure the sick, not—*oh stop it! stop it!*—raise the dead. Rex grinned at that and said that's a good one all right, come on now, let's haul ass, and meanwhile, as though by accident, flashed a handgun from his sweatshirt pocket which he'd probably stolen from the garage. It seemed to Stu like there could be other things he might be doing on behalf of his own well-being, but he wasn't doing them, he was walking a docile path toward the tow truck, Rex just behind him, pointing him aright when, like a leashed hounddog sniffing the flower patches, he tended to stray. He aimed for the driver's seat, but Rex pushed him roughly away and said he was too fucking drunk, he'd drive. Stu couldn't get up on the high seat by himself, Rex had to help, pitching him up there like he was made of straw. That boy had a bit of gristle on him. Also he had a rifle. Stu had glimpsed it in the back while getting tossed in. Plan on doin' some shootin', do you? Stu asked when they started up. His young mechanic grinned a wicked grin and said he thought maybe together they'd go after that guy who stole the truck. That got a hollow cackle out of old Winnie, ever the backseat driver, who was now hovering, Stu felt, just behind his shoulder, her fiery eyes all lit up with diabolical delight, even though this wrecker didn't have a backseat. Stu told her to can it and Rex said can what? and Stu, running on automatic, crooned: Can it be true / that you / have someone new / left me alone / and feelin' blue, and Rex growled: Jesus, nothing I hate worse than somebody wrecking a good song, Winnie's hot laughter all the time singeing Stu's ear. Stu kept thinking, all the way out to the car lot, about jumping out of the car or twisting the wheel out of Rex's hands or grabbing the handgun or in some other way escaping his fate, but like that old boy who wanted his sex drive lowered, thinking about it was about all he could do about it.

Meanwhile, Stu's little darlin' was staggering out onto John's back deck, one of the last to arrive, telling everyone she saw, whether they asked or not, what

Rex had told her to say: that Stu had something he had to do out at the car lot before coming, one of his trucks had been stolen or something, he'd follow soon. Sounded rehearsed because it was rehearsed, people didn't seem convinced, she was getting nervous or else was already nervous, hard as she was trying not to be, trying not to appear plastered, too, with even less success, though a courtesy call paid to the host's gin bottle helped. Hair of the dug, as old Stu called it. "Why in God's name doesn't somebody stop it?" she asked out loud, but no one paid her the least attention, nor did she really want them to, her cold feet outvoted by her hot—what? One of that old rube's worst and truest jokes. She could use a friend, though, dammit, but when she asked, John said he didn't know, she was probably inside somewhere. Someone said: "She was beautiful in the parade today." "Parade?" John was duded out like a cowtown sheriff which made Daphne feel uneasy, so, as appealing as his naked armpits were, she moved away. Her face hurt, must have hit something with it, though when people asked if she'd fallen off a barstool again, Daphne said she didn't fall, she was pushed. That was funny enough but it might not have been the right thing to say, so she added that Stu had something he had to do out at the car lot, one of his trucks was stolen or something, he'd follow soon. No shit, some guy with big ears said flatly, staring right through her, though it was hard to tell whether he saw too much or nothing at all, wasted as she was. Daphne had driven here in a fog, mostly down the middle of the street, pinching herself to keep from passing out altogether. She'd wanted to call the whole thing off somehow, but she no longer knew exactly what the whole thing was, it was all very weird—like she was in a bubble and the rest of the world wasn't happening anymore. She'd creased a few car doors and crunched a fender or two trying to park in the crowded street out front, but never mind, insurance would pay for it. More business for the lot. Which was where Stu was, she said. One of his trucks. What? Stolen, he'd follow soon. Or something. Really? a woman asked. Daphne tried to focus on her, couldn't. It might have been the banker's wife: the lady was worried about the rising crime rate. What was happening? she wanted to know, but Daphne couldn't tell her. Couldn't tell her her own goddamned name, if she'd been asked, luckily wasn't. The preacher's wife, who was rolling by just then, holding her stupendous belly up with both hands, said what she was worried about was the depletion of the ozone level and also that she might have her baby any minute now. Her husband smiled vaguely and said things aren't always what they seem. He was gazing at Ronnie who, eyes popping, was crowbarred into a dress that fit her about as well as her old cheerleading costume used to, the bony cunt. She was even jitterier than Daphne was, and when John's little boy came out of the house wearing one of his father's white shirts like a jacket, its tails trailing in the grass, and with a homemade stethoscope around his neck, she screamed out: "*That nasty little twerp, what does he know about human suffering—?!*" Normally, her husband, Daphne's ex, would have popped her one at that point, but the Mange, wearing dirty suit pants belted high over a golf shirt, seemed somewhat out of touch, one hand in his pocket, playing with himself, his eyes focused on his feet. Mikey came over and stuck a felt heart on Daphne's ribs, just below her breast, and stabbed it with his stethoscope. Yipes! Everyone was watching and laughing, so Daphne, sweating, told him her heart was full, honey, but her bladder was even fuller, she'd go get him a sample, and she wobbled away, feeling her backside severely scrutinized, but confident she was giving nothing away. Inside, however, she nearly lost it: there was Winnie's ghost! Oh my god! No, *two* of them! "*Get out of here, you crabby old bitch!*" she'd screamed. But it wasn't her, neither of them were, it was just Lollie's brats tangled up in sheets. She wanted to strangle the little jerks, but they were already crying and Daphne was determined to remain cool and unruffled, a sober friend of the family whose husband would be along soon, something he had to do before coming. A truck had been stolen. She told the two boys that and it seemed to settle them down. Didn't do much for her, she was still feeling haunted and oppressed by a nameless dread, but she had a long relaxing pee and felt better. But when, after peeling off the felt heart (it was black), she stepped out of the toilet, there was the preacher's kid staring at her in horror as though he'd been watching her through the door, the expression on his bloodless face exactly the same as when Rex grabbed him by the scruff and carried him out of her bedroom. Big booted John came striding in from the kitchen, handsome and hairy, read a note that the boy, never taking his eyes off Daphne, handed him, then gave the poor kid a sudden sock in the snoot that sent him crashing into the next room if not into the next world, and charged up the stairs, taking them three at a time. Oddly, this bit of action cheered Daphne up. She felt less exposed somehow, this boy had taken the punch that might have been thrown at her, so, pumped up with motherly gratitude or whatever, she reeled in there with a damp washrag to console the little sweetie and wipe up the blood and snot.

Philip, however (he was Philip now, and a man, after the convulsive revelations in the manse), was not consoled nor was to be consoled, nor could he, in spite of his newly achieved maturity and all his manly will, turn off the blubbering while that murderous old bag swabbed at his face, which seemed to have a big aching hole right in the middle where his nose should be, and asked him what was in the note that made John so mad. "I don't know!" he sobbed (he couldn't stop sobbing, it was humiliating). "It was only about my sister!" She wanted to know what about his sister and who had sent the note, but he wouldn't tell her, he'd never tell anybody. But then Clarissa came storming in and kicked him in the ribs and demanded to know what awful thing he'd done that made her dad hit him and where was his damned sister anyway? "She's gone. With your uncle Bruce." That made her kick him and hit him all the harder—"I don't believe you, asshole!" she screamed—she even landed blows between his legs and on his face where her dad had punched him, even though people were trying to hold her back. "*I* didn't do it!" he whined, curled up on the floor, too stunned to stand. "Nevada did!" That at least brought a momentary end to her frenzy, though he felt he'd betrayed a sacred and intimate trust. "Nevada—? How do you know Nevada?" "She gave me the note," he said, leaving out the details. Which were the best part. "She wanted me to lie to you about it!" "Hey, isn't that the kid who mooned the world off old Stu's roof?" someone laughed. "Aha! Is that why Daphne beat it outa here?" "She the one who popped him?" "No, John's daughter done it." Clarissa said again that she didn't believe him, but he could tell, looking up at her through his tears past the throbbing mass between them ("Whew, he's got him a honker now like our new mayor," someone said, and someone else suggested they'd better get the doctor), that she did. Her face looked as punched in as his own. She was straddling him like a warrior, and Philip saw that she was naked under her shorts and she was beautiful inside there, and he knew that, though he'd thought he'd outgrown her with all that had happened to him today, he was mistaken, he still had the hots for her something awesome. "I didn't want to come here. I only did it for you," he confessed. "Shut up, Creep! You make me sick," she snarled bitterly, and she might have started kicking him again, she was really steamed, but then her dad came in with his flight jacket pulled on over his leather vest and said: "I don't see Mom right now, Clarissa. Take over here until she turns up." "Is it Jen, Dad? Is she—?" He nodded briefly, looked down at Philip and said to stay away from that sleazy little shit, and was gone. She looked suddenly soft and vulnerable, terribly hurt, trying not to cry, and Philip wanted desperately to reach up and pat her neat little butt, just in sympathy, as a loving friend, but he knew she'd probably break his arm if he tried. Especially after what her dad said. Anyway, it hurt too much to move. The baggy-eyed old doctor shuffled in with a drink in his hand and squatted down creakily beside him, poking about in a perfunctory way. "Hey, maybe you oughta let John's boy fix him up, Alf! He looks more like you than you do!" "Lemme tell ya, the kid's got the same touchy-feely ways, too!" "He's hilarious!" "Yeah, I loved it when he pulled his rectal thermometer gag on Old Hoot! That dumb cracker jumped a mile!" "Careful! Floyd's a big man now!" "Looks like it's broken, son," the doctor declared wearily, and hauled himself to his feet. "I'll go get my bag." Clarissa's dad was in the room again, very riled up, something about all his missing cars. "Where the hell's the Porsch?" "Grampa Mitch must have taken it," Clarissa said. "He went to pick up Granny Opal." "But the Lincoln's gone, too!" "I don't know, Dad." "Damn it, I've got to get out to the airport!" The doctor dragged some keys out of a pocket which seemed to reach to his knee and tossed them to him. "It's the old—" "I know it. Thanks, Alf. I'll have someone run it back in." So, what was in that note? Philip could tell by the way Clarissa's dad was acting that it must have been important, but why did he hit him like that? His mind blown by all the things Nevada was doing, dazzlingly naked there in his father's dusty library, Philip hadn't been paying enough attention to what she was saying. She'd given him a hickey on his neck to remember her by, thanks a lot, but now he had this broken nose as well. Grown-ups were really weird. And also a little scary. Zoe came in wearing a white shirt that reached to her shoes and a folded paper hat with a red cross felt-tipped on it, and he told her to go get Mom or Dad, he had something to tell them about Jenny. "Mommy's not feeling good right now, she's got a bad tummy and she's lying down on a picnic table, and Daddy's writing his sermon, and I'm not Zoe anyway, I'm a midwipe."

Philip's friend Turtle, who perhaps would once more have to be called Maynard III now that Philip was no longer Fish, was also learning something about suffering as a sequel to celestial bliss. His amazing adventures, begun in some long ago time now forgotten, were, he realized, coming to an end in the very immediate present. And it wasn't the happy end that he'd imagined. No, forget bliss, boy, forget beatitude, forget the land of glory, Little was back in hell again: his dimensionless paradise now had very serious dimensions, the Christmas tree lights were going out, the hidden angel choirs were screaming bloody murder, and what the sensuous writing of all those tidal floods of color, now mostly a horrible red, were saying was: get your butt *outa* here, man! And that was what he was trying to do, kicking and punching, but it was getting too cramped to swing and there seemed to be less and less of any place to go! All those vibrant new constellations in all of heaven's hues which his exploding weenie had helped to make had suddenly started to clot together like they were magnetized and they were bulking up and closing in on him, crowding him for space. Once intimately stroked by all those chromatic ebbs and flows, he now felt intimately pummeled by them. It was awful. The kaleidoscopic colors were burning his flesh, especially the tender bits, a stench like tangible fog was suffocating him through all his orifices, and his malleable body, once majestically stretched out over the whole ecstatic universe, was now getting squashed down into a miserable wet lump. He struck out with all his might at the rubbery walls contracting around him, but it was like punching an old beanbag chair. It was getting dark and hot, he could hardly breathe, and he was afraid that this might be the terrible apocalypse, sinners beware, that Old Hoot 'n' Holler was always on about. Our Father which art in heaven, Little began to pray, but he couldn't remember the next line, he was too choked up, all he could think of was forgive us this day our hallowed bread which didn't sound right, so he just shouted out: "Please, God! Mom! Dad! *Help!*" Couldn't even hear himself. It was like he was underwater or something. It was pitch-dark now, he couldn't see his knees in front of his nose, which was where it felt like they were, but he had the definite impression, as a clammy hand clawed at his face, then snatched him by the hair, that he wasn't alone. There was somebody else in here with him!

Mikey's grand rabbit-from-the-hat finale was, by general consensus, the best act he'd ever done, though for many present it was the first they'd ever seen, for, as Oxford had noted, this sunny backyard pack-up was dense with strangers, strangers to him at any rate, most of whom when asked had said they worked for John. Of course, Oxford had been out of touch with the town since Gretchen took over the drugstore, the community had grown up around him while he'd been fascinated with the growth of his own little family, eight of whom were with him today. Somewhere. They had learned early how to escape the narrow circle of their grandfather's myopia, finding him again only when they needed him, and in principle, if sometimes with a doubting heart, he approved of this independence. The three who stayed closest to him were the ones who, alas, had inherited his and their mother's disability, one fate his own four children had escaped, if other fates had, also alas, ensnared them. It was the curiosity of these three, their little hands tugging at his, that had drawn them all close to Mikey's, well, hat, so to speak: the lady on the table. She had something between her legs, they wanted to see it, could he lift them up? Mikey meanwhile was being rewarded with well-earned applause and laughter for his uncanny imitation of Oxford's old friend Alf with his bent-backed slouch and his drooping lower lip where a cigarette always used to hang until Harriet's cancer when he gave the habit up, and capturing exactly the way Alf's bony gray head seemed to fall forward off his shoulders as though spring-loaded, bobbing to a heartlike beat. Not everyone here knew Alf, but fingers pointed and smiles broke out when he shambled out onto the back deck with some fellow peeking out past a faceful of bandage, Lennox and Beatrice's boy maybe, hard to tell from here. Earlier, Alf had talked with Oxford briefly about Beatrice's interesting condition, saying it seemed premature but he thought she was about ready to pop, if in fact she was really pregnant, then went on, in the confidential manner they'd fallen into over their decades together as doctor and druggist, to describe other recent cases that were puzzling him ("Trevor seems to be under the strange delusion, you know, that somewhere in the past he might have killed somebody . . ."), foremost his own sensation of something like a soft insistent pressure at the tip of his finger—he'd lifted his finger, the one, Oxford knew, that Alf used to palpate the inner recesses, to let Oxford examine it through his thick spectacles and certainly the pad was spread flat, but, as he was a spatulate-fingered man, they all looked much the same—which Alf believed to be the physical manifestation of a half-remembered missed diagnosis: "A tumor, I think. But the sonuvabitch keeps growing." He stared at it in some wonderment. "It's bigger than a goddamned melon now, Oxford, that blimp of a belly over there couldn't contain it." "Give Eric a call, see what he thinks." "He'd think I was senile." Mikey had also picked up on Alf's obsession with his finger in his own ingenuous way, miming the frantic effort to get something off it that wouldn't go away, scrubbing it on his clothes, on other people's clothes, shaking it, sucking it and spitting, shooting it with a toy pistol, finally pretending to hack it off, put the severed bit on a skewer, cook it over the coals until it caught on fire, douse it in Alf's own glass of whiskey, then, with a beaming smile of success, head still bobbing like an old turkey's, put it back on again, holding it up, only a bit smudged, for all to see. Then, with Beatrice's little daughter Zoe trailing along as a nurse with a pillowed tummy (no doubt Oxford's own daughter Columbia was this parody's target, she out on some wild-goose chase after her mindless brother this afternoon, best Oxford could tell from her weepy telephone calls from all over town), Mikey slouched over to the minister's wife, twisting and groaning on the picnic table, and threw a wrinkled sheet over her, Oxford pulling his grandchild out from between her legs just before the tenting fell. Beatrice was beginning to pitch and yell as the spasms hit and Oxford wondered if he should interfere, but he supposed that Alf, nearby, knew best—"No, let him go ahead," Alf laughed, "he's doing a good job!"—and instead allowed the woman to grab his hand and squeeze it, his grandchildren clambering up on the bench for a closer look, the other five by now having joined them, along with dozens of other children pressing round, adults, too, drawn by the spectacle and Beatrice's wild yelps. Mikey pulled on a pair of yellow rubber dishwashing gloves and, lower lip adroop, probed beneath the bouncing sheet. Beatrice reared up off the table suddenly, crying out in alarm, and—*schluuu-POP!*—out came Maynard and Veronica's long-lost runaway son, yanked by his hair, wet and naked and sputtering helplessly as one rescued from drowning. Everyone whooped and cheered. "That was really cute," someone behind Oxford giggled. "How'd he do that?" Little Maynard gulped, blinked, looked at the crowds around him, and crawled back under the sheet to look for something. While his sparkling bare behind was in the air, Mikey gave it a newborn's smack and then all the other children, shrieking with laughter and fighting each other for position, had a turn. The grown-ups would probably have joined in, but the boy was already out of there and down off the table, frantically hauling on the soggy clothes he had just retrieved, while everyone laughed and applauded John's comical son. Everyone except little Maynard's parents. His father strode over and boxed his boy's ears soundly—"Jeez, Dad, what did *I* do—?!" the child whimpered as his father swatted him again, then dragged him away, still pulling his pants up, Beatrice letting go of Oxford's hand at last and rising up on one elbow to gasp: "He didn't mean any harm!"—while his mother Veronica, hysterical until now, just collapsed wearily into a lawn chair, splitting either the chair or the zipper on her dress or both, and said: "Oh, hell, I don't care." Beatrice cried out and arched her back again, and her daughter Zoe, her nurse's cap hanging down over one eye now and tummy pillow fallen between her knees, waddled anxiously over to grab Alf's hand and pull him back to the table, where Lennox was also waiting now, and that was how Adam was born, but not before Oxford, his memory triggered perhaps by the sudden descent of twilight (time to get the grandchildren home and into bed), recalled something Kate had once written for Ellsworth's newspaper on the theme of the imagination vis-à-vis the real world, which was always changing, she observed, while the imagination, our defense against the abyssal truth of the subconscious, tried to hold it still. In real life, which she called "crepuscular" ("We are born into a dying of the light. . ."), everything we try to grasp is already something else; art, she wrote, floods itself with light, or with darkness, which is another kind of light, so as to shield us from the dusky terrors of the flux and feed the appetite for hope. She was speaking about the movies actually, especially the black-and-white ones—this was around the time when films "in living color" were coming to dominate the Palace Theater programs—and how, with their "real" yet chiaroscuro images, they confused art and reality, absorbing them into one another, each, in consequence, destroying each, which, she said, was what made them "beautiful." Ellsworth added a disclaimer, saying that the views expressed by the author were not necessarily those of the editor, and that he himself believed the only terror that life held was its enduring dullness, which art and the imagination gratefully relieved.

The Stalker has returned but without the Model. The Artist has not foreseen this, no one has. There is an inadmissible question that seems to rise like mist around the Artist's ankles, and then, pulling his heart down with it, to sink again. The forest has not been burned, but it has been charred here and there, as though scarred by the Artist's pain. It is not resignation he feels so much as emotional exhaustion. The jaded expression on the Stalker's face suggests that he has depleted himself with cruel pleasures, a suggestion he does nothing to deny. "Ah yes," he sighs, touching a dirty fingertip to the nipple of a childish breast in a drawing lying at the Artist's feet, then tracing a sinuous line down across her navel, over her pale little belly, twisted in anguish, and into the hidden crevice between her clenched thighs, "a pure delight!" The Artist wishes, not merely to smash his face in for this vile profanation, but utterly to destroy him, to eradicate the depraved monster from the face of the earth, but grief has sapped his strength and will, and he feels that it is he who is being slowly but inexorably erased. Like the rock beside the riverbank on which she once had knelt: vanished now, as though dissolved into the stream, itself diminished to a trickle like drying tears, ever more diminishing.

"I know what you have done," he says bitterly, indicating with disdain all the drawings scattered loosely on the barren ground about him. "You see, I have imagined it all." The Stalker studies the drawings with an undisguised admiration that borders upon awe. "An extraordinary likeness!" he exclaims, picking up a drawing of himself, reared high in wild-eyed revel behind the Model's upraised buttocks, his hands tightening the studded chains around her throat as he slakes his savage appetite, and he holds the drawing up before his face as though gazing into a mirror. "It is as though you have violated the border between art and reality!" "Art neither contemplates nor intrudes upon the real," the Artist replies dispiritedly. "It *is* the real, upon which all else intrudes." The Stalker shuffles through the drawings, spreading them about, selecting this one, then that one, for closer scrutiny. "Yes, you have seen everything," he acknowledges, stroking the Model's outflung thigh in a particularly barbarous sketch as though to ease her terrible pain, or to recall it. He tosses the drawing aside. "And you have seen nothing." The Artist has feared just this rebuke. He is a sensitive and decent man, he knows, and no doubt there are depths of depravity his imagination, which in his pride he likes to think of as boundless, cannot plumb. "In truth," sighs the Stalker, "I do not know where she is, nor have I seen her since she left you." "But you both disappeared at the same—!" "I was searching for her. Perhaps to do with her as you have fancied. But to no avail. She's gone." The Artist, stunned by this revelation, if it is one and not just another cruel deception, stares down at his drawings, which he believed to be passionate and intransigent pursuits of imaginative truth when he made them, but which now seem little more than feverish bunglings of a corrupt and pornographic soul, cartoons from hell. "All I found was this," the Stalker says, reaching into a ragged shirt pocket and handing the Artist a scrap of paper which he recognizes as a corner torn from one of his own drawings. On it is written: "Art's true source is not in the seen, but in the longing for the not-seen." In her handwriting, of course, the naive evenly looped script of an innocent child. The Artist's hands are trembling. "Do you think she might come back?" "It seems like a farewell message," says the Stalker. "It is, I suppose, her way of continuing as your Model." He smiles wistfully. "A lot less fun, though, isn't it?" The Artist stands, feeling a bit shaky. How much time has passed? When he looks around, the Stalker has gone. He is alone in his darkening forest. He leaves his materials and drawings behind and steps into it, as a way of stepping out of it: what has a center must somewhere have an edge.

What makes a man step out of himself and into some no-man's-land of the spirit? What is it that turns the healthy courting of danger within the rules of the game—games like mountain climbing, say, or skydiving or war—into a self-annihilating urge to dissolve the borders of the game itself and defy its rules as one might defy gravity or number or the passage of time? John did not understand this urge but he knew what it felt like, having found himself, more than once in his life and often as not in Bruce's company, poised on that frontier and tugged toward its fatal breaching. It had the aura of a joke, a final joke shared between friends, and as that larger self they created between them laughingly dared to assail the edges, so they each dared, too, feeling a part of something that compelled them to deny their lesser mortal selves. Admittedly, he got a passing buzz out of it. But John, unlike his city friend, had played too many team sports to be seduced by these commonplace delusions of the almighty group self, nor did he suppose that concerted derring-do would give them any sort of magical freedom from the inexorable laws of the game, as Bruce in his restless transgressions sometimes seemed to. In fact, John loved the rules, for he was, as always, team captain, and the rules empowered him and defined the limits by which he tested himself and moved and judged others. John's game was life, Bruce's death, but he understood that Bruce therefore lived closer to the truth than he did, was in reality another side of *himself,* one he could not finally bring himself to embrace, except by proxy in the person of his nihilistic friend. And now, as though to taunt John for his pussyfooting ways in the face of the Great Fucking Mystery, as Bruce would say, the walls that Bruce had assaulted with his abduction of Knucksie's little girl were in effect the very ones between them, or at least those built by John: his community and (if Nevada was to be trusted, as of course she wasn't) his own family. Nevada's note had said that Bruce, who seemed "very violent, very suicidal," had apparently used the girl's big brother Philip as go-between to lure both Jennifer and Clarissa to the airport. She thought he was headed up to the cabin and that he had something "very ugly" in mind. "I think he's checking out and trying to take the world with him." She'd found out about the plot too late to save Jennifer, but she'd managed to "distract" (her quotes) the kid from his Clarissa mission and get false word to Bruce that the boy had chickened out so that he'd leave with only half his prey. The meaning of that wistful high five that Bruce had given him during their two-on-three the last time they were together up at the cabin was transparent to him now: So long, buddy. Catch me if you can. The dark-souled sonuvabitch.

John loved him, but he wasn't sure, as he rolled down the runway and lifted up into the gathering twilight, a rifle in the seat beside him (not the one he wanted, which for some reason seemed to be missing), if he was headed up there to rescue Bruce from himself or to kill him. Light filled the plane as he rose into it, but the land below, as he banked to the north, was cast in shadow and the unlit town looked small and vulnerable, lost on the vast prairie, diminishing, as though it might not be there when he returned.

It had been a beautiful day, one that, it seemed, could go on forever, so it was almost a surprise when all of a sudden the light began to fade and twilight fell. Out at the edge of town, Mitch popped the Lincoln's lights on as he pulled into the parking lot at the retirement home (didn't want to hit one of these old dodderers wandering around, they'd sue your ass off), thinking about retirement himself, but not here, one reason being he wouldn't mind getting away from some of the old ladies in town who once were not so old. Aging with your wife was one thing, seeing what your old loves turned into really took the starch out, something his son didn't seem to mind so much, having perhaps more starch to start with. Other car lights were coming on around town as well: Lorraine's on her way back to the party, for example; Nevada's as, disappointed, she pulled away from the airport; Cornell's on the back road to the Ford-Mercury garage. Stu wanted to turn the light on in the office out there, but Rex said no. Waldo, snuggled into his lovenest, as he liked to call it, also preferred the lights off, the invading dimness adding a kind of melancholy beauty to this simple little room where he felt more at home than in his own home. Sassy Buns said it was like nowhere, man, like some piece of sterile shit they'd sent into orbit and then forgot about, but her shoes and shirt were off and her sudden anger when he'd made the mistake of calling her Sassy Buns to her face ("You got some kinda sick buttocks fetish, old man?" she'd snapped, and Waldo had had to admit: "Yeah, haw! I sure do . . .") had subsided and he had the impression she was enjoying the luxury nose powder he'd procured for her. Until she said: "Phew, what's this shit been cut with, bathroom cleanser?" Waldo had paid top dollar and was sure of his source, she was just giving him a hard time. As he would do for her, sweet thing, in turn. Dutch was not behind the two-way mirror watching them for once: to hell with all that. In fact he was thinking of closing down the Back Room, his days and nights were getting too mixed up. He'd woken up in his office when the staff came in to tell him about the thefts of food and linens. He didn't remember having fallen asleep in the office, but he was glad he was there instead of someplace else. He'd checked out the losses, called Otis. He'd thought that was this morning, just a little while ago, but now the sun had suddenly gone down and Otis and a couple of his cops were in his front office, taking down the numbers. He decided he'd also lay off the beer for a few days. After he finished the one in his hand. Otis was trying to recruit him for some kind of posse he was getting up, but Dutch said he planned to stay right here, stand guard over what was left. Otis gave him a two-way radio to use in case the two thieves showed up again and asked him who brought John's Porsche out here? Dutch didn't know. "Has it been parked out there awhile?" "Can't say." Otis was used to running John's cars home of late and he had to go there anyway. As usual, the keys were in the ignition, so he sent the others to pick up Duwayne at the jail and meet him at John's while he checked out the golf course and the airport in the Porsche, following other leads. He was not happy about the onset of darkness. Made the hunt harder. But he couldn't wait until tomorrow, Corny and Pauline had become a serious threat to the community and they had to be stopped now. The country club looked shut down and empty as he swung by, enjoying the machine he was in, though in fact Marge was out there on her own, caught out by the sudden twilight while cutting through a dogleg on the back nine and unable to find her ball on the other side of it for a moment even though it was in the middle of the fairway. She knew she should quit, but she was still blowing off steam, running her aborted mayoral campaign from hole to hole as if from issue to issue. Her golf shoes had been in the car trunk with her clubs, but with the clubhouse closed, she'd been forced to play in her business suit, which made her feel like she was clapped in irons and greatly stifled her drives. She could sense the terrible weariness of the long day overtaking her and felt about to drop, but there were only a couple of holes to go and she had to walk them to reach her car anyway. There was no one else out here, so she unbuttoned her blouse and rolled her skirt up around her waist and, loosened up now, took her frustrations out on her approach shot. Which was a beauty. Lofted up out of sight, then falling down through the dusk onto the middle of the green and rolling backwards toward the hole. Seemed to disappear. Hey! Had she holed out? Beautiful!

Meanwhile, back at the center of the dying day's doings in John's backyard, where the garden lights were coming on, the guests were reluctantly preparing to make their farewells, lingering for a last drink or maybe a couple, perhaps one more of those juicy quarter-pounders, said to have been ground from the flanks of blue-ribbon winners at the last 4-H Fair upstate, or else a final handful of crunchy liqueur-filled chocolates, imported direct from Switzerland, or even both at the same time, in the same bun, why not—any macaroni salad left?—Pioneers Day only happens once a year. This was what Lorraine saw when she returned with Waldo's shotgun, loaded with buckshot, in her fist: a lot of drunks falling goofily about in the gathering dark with their jaws snapping. How long had she been gone? Off-key party songs were erupting here and there, yips and shouts, loose laughter like belches, the birds and crickets, slow off the mark, now making up for lost time in raucous chorus behind it all. Reverend Lenny and a deflated Trixie were cradling a newborn, still red in the face, under a bug light on the back deck, surrounded by oohers and ahers, Daphne among them, telling everyone Stu had something to do at the garage, he'd be here soon; Lorraine heard the same thing twice like an echo: it was a recital, the woman desperately clinging to the only thing she could remember, her mind otherwise murky as a sump pit. The shotgun got a certain amount of attention as she passed through the crowds, but as far as Lorraine could tell not many people even knew who she was. Out in the pot-scented rose garden, where children were chasing lightning bugs, John's daughter, in a seething rage, was snorting something through a straw; the girl's furious thoughts were incoherent, but Lorraine empathized with their import: insult, betrayal, murder on her mind. "Sure, be glad to give you a lift," some guy standing in the flower beds said as Lorraine drifted past, "how's this?" "Woops! There went my drink!" "Ha ha! Wait here, I'll bring you a new one." "Just a little one!" "Don't worry, honey, it's all he's got!" No one tending the glowing barbecue pit, where meat burned quietly. Caterers were collecting empty pans and dishes, picking up some of the rubbish in black plastic bags. Lorraine found an abandoned whiskey glass and downed its contents. Yeuck. Stale and watery with a butt at the bottom. Still a shot or two at the bottom of one of the bottles: she finished that off, too, sucking from the neck. Nearby, Veronica sat slumped in a lawnchair, still as a stone. The image in her head was fetal and slimy and its name was Second John. The image seemed locked there like a fixed exhibit in an empty room, and Lorraine understood that head was badly damaged. Takes one to know one, she said with a shudder, and rubbed her aching brow with her free hand. She climbed up past the Holy Family, kicking a couple of beercans aside (Daphne was saying: "Something he had to do out at the car lot . . ."), and went into the kitchen, where Marge's one-eyed Trevor was huddled miserably over a hot cup of coffee, his sick hangover making Lorraine's hurt head hurt the more. Kevin was in the hallway, leaning against the john door, hustling a bank teller with a sad story. No Sweet Abandon, all tattered and torn. No Waldo either. Lorraine didn't need to tune in to get the rest of the story. She knew where they were.

Thus, John's annual Pioneers Day barbecue drew, somewhat abruptly, toward a close, for some a pleasure, others not, some lives changed by it, most merely in some small wise spent, a few wishing it could go on forever, others that it had never happened, or, having happened, that it could be forgotten, of all wishes wished, the one most likely to be granted; but first, while many were still finishing their last, or nearly last, drink, police chief Otis arrived, raised his bullhorn, and addressed the remaining guests in John's backyard.

He said: "Folks, sorry to butt in here when you're having a good time, but this town's got a serious problem and I need your help!" There was applause, and Edna clapped, too, because Floyd did. But were the others applauding the police officer or the problem? It seemed a touch wild out here and she wished she was back home, just her old simple home with the running toilet, forget grand ambitions. Like her stepmother always said: Edna, sometimes the worse thing can happen to you is getting your dreams come true. "If you haven't been home today," the burly police officer hollered through his bullhorn, "you probably been robbed!" Oh dear. That got everybody's attention. At least the new porcelain lamp was safe in the trunk of the car, though she didn't know if she ever really wanted to see it again. The officer went on to tot up all the crimes that the giant lady and the mental boy from the drugstore had committed, and she could see by the tall list why he hadn't wanted to bother about a mix-up with one little secondhand rug. His voice, which sounded like an old radio broadcast, seemed to be coming out of the night sky. It had got dark almost as soon as he'd begun to talk and now you couldn't hardly see his face, it was like a curtain had dropped. "People around town are reporting dented cars and broke doors and windows and shingles knocked off roofs," his voice said. "They've used a airport hangar like a latrine, there's a church been desecrated and busted up, she's almost completely indecent and scaring little kids, and everywhere she goes she's leaving a filthy trail of slime and garbage!" "If *I* was completely indecent," some lady squawked in a high voice, "I'd scare *everybody!*" The people around her laughed and said "I know what you mean," but if it was a joke, Edna didn't get it. But then she was not in a humorous mood. She felt ashamed and confused and responsible for the change that had come over Floyd ever since leaving the police station. She and Floyd were standing talking to the bank president and his wife, he having taken a sudden new interest in Floyd what with his promotion, and what his wife said now was: "You work so hard to make a decent life for yourself and then these irresponsible ruffians come along and try to take it away from you, it just doesn't seem fair!" "No," said Edna, "it don't rightly," and the policeman with the bullhorn said: "And now she's got so big she's disrupting traffic and bringing down phone lines and TV antennas!" Fortunately the lady's husband was so drunk he didn't notice how Floyd, who'd been so friendly and fairly popping his britches with big money talk before, had pretty much shrunk back into his old squint-eyed meanness, untrusting and shutmouth, except when he had something to recite from the Bible, and moresoever since the police turned up. The sour old Floyd was not so good at impressing bankers maybe, but Edna knew how to talk to the old one better than the new smiley one who scared her with his noisy swoll-up ways, and so she told him now plain out that she never took that rug, that John's wife give it to her and just went away and left her stuck in all that trouble, and where *was* she anyhow, and Floyd, finally listening to her, said what the hell are these buggers trying to do to us, you think? The police chief meanwhile was introducing the new mayor who got up and declared that this was a tough ballgame, but they all had to hunker down and dig in and get ready for a butt-kicking bone-crunching free fight. "We gotta get our back off the mat!" he shouted through the bullhorn. "That's one big piece a meat out there and she's playin' hardball with us, so now it's our job to team up and take her out! Together, neighbors, we can do it!" Floyd said: "We'll be goin' now." "We should oughta say goodbye and thank you," Edna said, but she wasn't sure who to, except maybe the little boy. "It don't matter," Floyd said. "Come on."

While his old coach and math teacher, who was now the mayor, however that had happened, was winding up the crowd in his punchy lockerroom style, telling them about the shoot-out at the old airport hangar and how the bandits nearly ran him down, Otis, given the first moment he'd had in what seemed like weeks just to catch his breath and think, posed the question to himself: What had he set in motion here? What was the final objective of these troops he was lining up? Would Pauline, as Snuffy's rhetoric and even his own as he thought back on it seemed to imply, have to be, well, taken out? This had not been his original game plan. He'd set out just to bring Pauline home and turn her over to people who knew more about how to deal with her problem. If only she hadn't broke out and teamed up with that dimwit from the drugstore. Of course she had to get out, she was hungry: Otis remembered how she had demolished that bag of doughnuts and wished now he'd brought her a couple hundred bags more. Though that wouldn't have been enough either, she was one ravenous lady. Her husband should have done something, damn it, all of this could have been prevented. But, that's right, he had been under arrest. Or, rather, he'd been a temporary guest of the police department. So things happened. Too many things, really, for Otis to be able to manage them all, one crisis piling up on another, civic order collapsing around his ears, and then all those crimes they committed, seemed like he was getting a call a minute, they were running him ragged, and so, next thing he knew, here he was in John's backyard forming up an armed posse to go out and hunt both of them down. He glanced over toward the cruiser in the drive where Pauline's daddy sat, manacled, in the backseat, grinning out at him under his ballcap. He spat through the gap in his teeth, dirtying the inside of the cruiser window. The incorrigible bastard. A menace to society. And not just mean and crazy but no doubt a cold-blooded murderer as well. If he were genuinely serious about justice, Otis should've tried to find out years ago about that "dead sister" Pauline had chillingly described during their investigative sessions out at the trailer, and whatever it was had happened to her missing momma. So he was taking a big risk getting Duwayne released to him like this, the sonuvabitch was dangerous even when locked up in a padded cell and he still harbored a homicidal grudge against Otis, blew a gob straight in his face first time he saw him today, then just grinned when Otis cocked his arm to throw the punch he couldn't throw. But Pauline had often told Otis about all the times she'd tried to run away and how Daddy Duwayne always tracked her down and dragged her home to the trailer again, and Otis was running out of options. She had to be stopped, whatever that meant, and wherever she was. Still, he was having his doubts. Otis desperately wished John hadn't taken off. He'd know what to do, as he always did. Otis had come here, not just because this was where most everyone in town he could count on could be found, but more because he needed John to lead this thing and see that it came out right. But no John, no anyone except the two kids, even John's parents had checked out. Otis had brought the abandoned Porsche here and had had to give John's daughter the keys, uneasy as that made him feel, and what she'd said was that her father had got called away on an emergency. A friend of hers was in trouble. A *former* friend, she'd added and turned away. And now he didn't see her anywhere or the little boy either. A lot of people had left, even while he and Snuffy were speaking to them, and he found himself feeling a bit like a sheriff in one of those old oaters, come here like a fool to appeal to the cowardly cabbageheads in the town saloon. Of course he would not, like those forsaken sheriffs, have to face Pauline all alone, Otis knew that; on the contrary, the problem would be to keep the drunks, zanies, curiosity seekers, and hell-raisers away, which was mostly what he saw out there in the darkness now. Maybe he ought to postpone all this until morning when John got back. Hell, he didn't even know where he was going to take his squad once he'd picked them. But then he got a call on his cellular phone from the Country Tavern out by Settler's Woods: "They's some humungous animal out here, Otis, looks a lot like a nekkid woman, and she just stomped the bejesus outa old Shag, he's flatter'n a day-old pancake! And I can't even find Chester, she musta et him!" Now it was murder. And he knew where they had to go. He took the bullhorn back.

She didn't mean to. It was a dark moonless night and she was hungry and that boy with the automatic zinger had not come back and she could not remember where he had hid their food. She saw lights and heard music and crept over there. Well, crept. It felt to her like creeping but she did break a few trees and accidentally tipped a car into the ditch. She could smell cooked meat and beer and so she went poking around in the garbage cans at the back and that was where she stepped on something. Just made a little squeak. She figured it was better not to look. There wasn't much to eat but what there was she quickly put away, eating straight from the tipped-up cans. Everything tasted pretty good, even the plastic bags, though she cut her mouth when she bit into the bottles. There was something else sniffing around back there so she ate that, too. Then some people came out and started making a fuss and she remembered that she was supposed to keep out of sight so nobody would know where they were. It was probably too late, but it was dark so she thought she might be able to slip away unnoticed, and she might have, too, if they hadn't had all those cars and trucks in her way. They made quite a racket so it was obvious to everyone which way she was going. Still, no one seemed to want to follow her, and in fact most of them were running to their cars and going home, if their cars still worked, so while they were busy at that she burrowed deeper into the woods and found a dark place that was scratchy but warm where she could snuggle down and wait for her friend to return. But no sooner had she got settled than she realized she had to go to the bathroom again, that was the trouble with all this eating, so she crawled over to the big ditch she'd used before and did her business there, then found her way back into her secret place, keeping her head down all the while, scuffing up the brush behind her so they couldn't follow her tracks. She didn't know why she had to do this, but she knew it was important. Her friend, whose name she could not quite remember, had said so. Why had he not come back? She did not know that either, but she never doubted that he would. Unless he'd had an accident or had got caught himself by whoever it was that was chasing them. It was mostly her fault they were being chased, because of how big she was. There were many things she did not remember now, but she knew she had not always been this big. Exactly why it bothered everybody so much, she couldn't be sure, but she guessed it was just something they weren't used to and that got on their nerves. She could appreciate how they felt because she wasn't used to it either, and didn't know if she ever would be. She missed things like beds and those white things—bathtubs—too much. But maybe, after she'd forgotten them, like everything else, she'd stop missing them and things would be all right. She curled up in a nest of wrinkled sheets she'd earlier worn like someone in her old life used to call, as he tore them off her, her "seventh veil," and there half dozed with one eye open, her ears and nose alert, listening for footfalls or men talking, her empty stomach gnawing at her again, and wishing her friend would come back soon and show her where their hidden food was. It was awfully late. Where was he anyway?

At the door. And through it. Found at last, when least expected, nor where he'd have thought to look. All the way out here, slipping through back streets and unmarked roads in the borrowed truck, Cornell had been thinking about his escape from Yale's girlfriend's apartment after, well, after what had happened to her, and how his whole life since then seemed like a single thread: through those scary streets, down into the ground below, then through that dark stinking maze of tunnels and sewers, up the metal stairs, out the door at the top, into a life with that clubfooted lady that was, somehow, already underway, then out again to find the one true friend he had in the world, and now once more on the run, but aboveground and with something important to do and no longer all alone. That thread of his life, he sensed (he remembered Marie-Claire's horrible final message: maybe what she'd meant to say was THINK!), was now being knotted, he didn't know how, but it was all coming round full circle, and he was suddenly sure he would find at last the door that he'd been looking for, solving the mystery of his life and freeing himself from the sensation of there being not just one of him but two. That second Corny, the mixed-up married one, shaken off for awhile, was back with him now, not so much riding in the seat beside him or in the truckbed behind as actually sharing the driver's seat and interfering with his moves, even if he was trying to help, as he sometimes did on hairy turns or in heavy traffic with his video games reflexes, but more often determined, it seemed, to lead him astray in some random rerouting of his intentions: he had to be single-minded about this business and simply could not. What he had to do now, if the other Corny would only let him, was return this cumbrous truck and pick up his old van, make a quick grocery run, then meet his friend in the woods, which was where he now imagined he might discover that elusive door (something about the smell of the place had stirred a faded memory and excited that imagining) through which they could make their escape before the crazy people in this town caught up with them. The last place they'd tried to hide was an unused hangar out at the airport and that had worked for a little while, poor Pauline could even stand up and walk around a little, but they'd hardly settled in when they'd been surprised by four or five very mean guys, including one of Corny's former high school teachers, who'd actually shot at them with a gun. Holy cow! Corny had had to floorboard it out of there, right through the lot of them and crashing out the half-opened door, and, with all the roads out of town cut off by police cars, there was nowhere big enough left to go but Settler's Woods. Not perfect. Once inside there was no easy exit, and it was risky to be so near the highway and strip, though the motel was useful for food and clean sheets, which Pauline wore like diapers now that her red cloak hardly came below her armpits. The Country Tavern was close by as well, and there was a mall Corny could reach by foot. So, after finding a safe place to hide Pauline and the truckload of food (it didn't look like a place where a door might be, but that was where the sensation struck him, gazing up at his friend as she squatted to offer him her finger between his legs—zowie!—that he was at least getting warm), he left a few false garbage clues to send the police chasing and then took the back roads to the Ford garage, skirting danger as best he could whenever the second Corny wasn't making him take wrong turns—as he did too often, turning the trip out into a maze. Corny was worried, hopping down out of the truck at the car lot, about all the time he'd lost: he'd left Pauline in the woods in blazing midday sunshine, and already it was pitch-dark! He found the old van, but locked up: the keys must be in the office. Which, fortunately, though everything appeared closed down for the night, was unlocked. He turned the handle and crossed the threshold and that was when it came to him that the door he'd been looking for all this time was the one he'd just stepped through.

Across town in the retirement home built by John, Barnaby stepped through his bathroom door, dragging his leaden leg behind him, staggered over to the laundry basket, and tipped it over. "God, Barnaby!" Audrey snapped, from her seat on the toilet, "can't you give a woman a little privacy?" "Too old for that, Aud. I just thought of something." "Well, that's a novelty," she said sarcastically, but she seemed uneasy, watching him as he struggled to tip the hamper upside down. Not a simple trick for a crippled puddinghead. But he managed it and, sure enough, the old handgun he'd been looking for all this time clattered out onto the tiled floor. She leapt up off the pot, but she was hobbled by her lacy drawers (Audrey always was one for fancy underthings), so for once he was able to beat her to it simply by falling on top of it. Not sure how he was going to get up again, but he had the gun and it was pointed, however unsteadily, from under his chin, up at her. "Now sit back down there," he said. "We're gonna have a little talk about that rewrote will." She plopped back in place looking a bit deflated as he pushed up onto his elbows and knees, waving the gun more or less in her direction and reminding her that he was a mite shaky so she shouldn't get adventurous. "I thought I'd moved it from there," she sighed, staring at all the dirty laundry scattered across the floor. "I must have forgotten." Using the tub and lavatory, he was able to haul himself to his feet, but not without the gun going off, sending a bullet ricocheting out of the washbasin, off the medicine cabinet mirror, and into the ceiling, and provoking a squawk from Audrey, who jumped a foot off the stool, then snapped: "You damned fool! You want to kill somebody? You can't undo what's already been done!" In some remote subdivision of his devastated brain he knew that was true, but in the front war-room lobes behind his eyes, from which heavily fortified enclosure he was organizing this do-or-die operation, there remained a stubborn hope for victory. "We can try," he said heroically, and accidentally fired off a shot through the window. Audrey winced and ducked but stoically kept her seat. "You're a crazy old buzzard who ought to be locked up," she said. She was really boiling. "It's a good thing John's running the company, or we'd all be ruined. I'm *glad* I changed that will!" "Why do you favor that coldhearted boy, Aud?" he asked, trading anger for anger. "On account of he reminds you of your old beau?" "Oh brother! Why don't you stick that peashooter up your backside, lamebrain, and leave us all in peace?" "Hey, tell me, love of my life, I've always wondered, did you ever have a tumble with that ruthless whoremonger?" "Well, what can I say, Barn? Mitch was once a handsome man, and he had a charming way with the ladies. Which is more than can be said for present company!" The doorbell rang. "That's likely the police," Audrey said, reaching for the toilet paper. "They probably want to know why you've been shooting at the neighbors." The bell rang again and someone banged on the door with his fist. "All right! All right! I'm coming!" he shouted, though he knew that was not what it sounded like to others. Audrey was the only one who understood him now, so it was just as well he hadn't knocked her off, he might need her to get him out of trouble. He limped out, trying unsuccessfully to holster his weapon in the sock sewn into the armpit of his robe, and as he opened the door, shot the carpet. There was Mitch with a dead wet cigar in his mouth. "Don't shoot, Sheriff, I'll marry your daughter!" Mitch said, and took the gun away from him, looked it over skeptically. He glanced past Barnaby's shoulder and added: "You all right, hon?" She came running over and fell into Mitch's arms, and he gave her a big hug. "I've been so frightened, Mitch!" Mitch backed out with that two-timing woman under his arm, the little silver gun pointed at Barnaby's kneecaps. The sonuvabitch was stealing his damned wife, right from under his nose, but Barnaby wasn't surprised, they'd taken everything else. Wouldn't have been surprised if he'd shot him either. Wished he had. He was really all alone now. Couldn't even do himself in. He shut down the war room and his daughter came in and closed the door. "Where have you been?" he croaked. "I've *needed* you!" He was crying, he couldn't help it. She put her finger to her lips and shushed him and led him over to his bed to tuck him in. "It's all right," she said. "I'm here now."

Wife theft of course was an old joke, as old as wives, but as Stu would say if he had any spit left to say with, it's not the theft but how you steal it. Rex, now tucking his old boss and rival in for the long night out at the Ford-Mercury car lot, using methods more direct, less consoling than those Barnaby presently enjoyed, had figured all the angles and knew nothing could go wrong now from here to the tagline. Rex had had a lot of jobs in his life—stockboy, fridge and TV repairman, taxi driver, deliveryman, mechanic, gigolo—but for this gig he'd cut his chops killing pigs for bacon-makers. Probably the spot in his life, short though the run was, that had given him the most satisfaction. Not all that easy on the old olfactories, but at least at the end of the day you felt you'd accomplished something. Which was how he felt now, cooled out at last after an edgy time. Rex had been noodling along without direction for too long, trying to think his way through every move, every bar, like a goddamned greenhorn, but now that he was onstage at last he found himself relaxing into his own sense of time, on top of the beat and ready for his break when it came, knowing that it would all happen as it had to happen so long as he kept to the score. At the same time, he was able to let in a lot more space, to stretch it out just for the pleasure of it, to enjoy, in a word, the telling, and for openers, there was Stu's record collection which the old jughead beamed out over the lot most days and which sorely offended Rex, twangy whining country and western shit for the most part. He ordered Stu to take them out of their jackets and hold them for him while, one by one, he dug deep raw X's into them with a screwdriver. The old shitkicker, sneezing explosively, gave it his best attention, probably hoping that was the worst that was going to happen to him, and when Rex spared a couple of classic rockabilly discs Stu's eyes lit up there in the dimness and a grin twitched on his loose lips. "Reminds me of the one about the old boy," he wheezed, "who was chawin' tobacca in church one day when the preacher's missus come in and—" Rex poked the barrel of the rifle into his flapping jaws, chipping a couple of crooked teeth, told the dumbfuck to chaw on that awhile, and then laid out for him his plans for a long creamy set with his own fat missus, now waiting for him back at Stu's crib. Not too long a set: he loathed the boozy bitch and her big spongy ass, but he didn't say so. One lick at a time. He emptied the chamber of the garage handgun and gave it to Stu to hold while he still sweated fingerprints, planning to reload it afterwards and fire off a couple of rounds, turn the old yuck into a heroic defender of the fort, if a dead one. Okay, time for the main theme: stay inside, follow the chart, and take it out. At the last second, the old used-car shark tried to pull the cornball someone-behind-you dodge—"Winnie—?" he gasped—but Rex only grinned and, straightahead, no frills, completed his closing rip. But when he turned around, there in the shadows: there *was* someone! He panicked for a moment, thinking: setup! But wait: wasn't that the thin streak of piss who stole the truck? Perfect! He eased up, feeling the beat again. Not the tag expected, but he could play it. You're all right, my man, if you just keep listening.

There was something very big lurking at the shadowy edge of the woods out back and the reformed motelkeeper, holding down the fort but still far too sober to play the hero, heaved his beercan at it, then ducked inside and locked all the doors and windows and pulled the blinds and, rubbing his sore arm (used to be able to throw a ball as far as most guys could hit one—now he probably couldn't get it back to the pitcher), went back to the bar for another beer. Or more than one, some resolutions would have to wait. "Otis? Are you there? Can you hear me? Otis?" Nothing but static. At first he'd thought it might just be squirrels or raccoons rooting around in the garbage and he'd gone out back to shoo them away. But then he'd heard a branch come down and could swear he saw something peeking out at him over the treetops, and what might have been a flexed knee sticking out, catching the parking lot light, at least ten feet off the ground. Shit. "Otis, do you read me? This is Dutch! I got a major problem here!" Fucking useless. The fat-necked sonuvabitch was probably home in bed. Or playing poker somewhere with Dutch's bartender and the rest of the staff that he'd volunteered away, leaving Dutch alone on the front line and the whole damned motel to run. Luckily it was all but empty tonight, most of John's barbecue guests staying out at their new hotel on the interstate, the barbecue itself having sucked up the Getaway's ordinary evening trade, but that was no real consolation, Dutch could use some company. He thought about rousting out Waldo and his milky-breasted bimbo, but supposed they'd both be bombed out of their minds by now and more trouble to him than help. He turned on the TV over the bar and watched a baseball game for a while and, after an inning or two and a few more beers, began to doubt what he thought he'd seen and was even glad he hadn't got ahold of Otis and his boys after all and dragged them over here, they might have thought he was off his rocker, and what was worse, they might have been right. Dutch had not been sleeping well and sometimes it felt like he wasn't sleeping at all, even in the middle of what had to be nightmares. He knew what his problem was. Oh, not too much pud pulling: hell, if anything, keeping his hand on his rod and his mind on both kept all three out of worse, an old sportsman's dictum. No, it was that mirror. *That* dicked him. It was living too close for too long to that borderline between what was real and what, like a movie, for example, even if made out of real stuff, wasn't. And it wasn't really a line so much as a kind of thin film, and when it dissolved: well, you were fucked, buddy. "I got the bad, bad Back Room Blues!" he growled to the tune of an advertising jingle between innings on the TV, and poured himself another beer. So he was closing it down. He should probably dismantle it altogether, but he thought he might need it again some day more desperate than this one, or John might for other ends. Dutch was tempted, feeling so lonely, to take in one last farewell performance, but beefy old Waldo looked out of his depth tonight so it could be a pretty depressing show. Like watching sick carp in an oily pond.

Stick with the baseball. That's what he was thinking (top of the eighth, tying run on first, nobody out) when Waldo's harpy of a spouse came rocketing in, stuck a shotgun up his nose, and demanded the key to her husband's room. Dutch gave it to her, figuring on maybe giving Waldo a warning call, but she spun around at the door, swinging the gun his way, and yelled: "Don't even *think* about it, fatso!" Whereupon Dutch decided this drear night might have something to offer after all and went back to his old movie seat to watch the action.

Thanks to the daylong rumors and sightings, Otis's stirring twilight speech in John's backyard, and the fleeing Country Tavern patrons surging back into town, news about the big thing in the woods was getting around. In fact, as always happened, people were seeing big things everywhere, and Otis had to field a lot of nuisance calls, as when someone called to say the big thing had got into their basement and blown all the fuses, please help for god's sake, while others claimed to have seen it hiding behind the darkened mall or in the deep end of the civic center swimming pool or under the humpback bridge, and everywhere it went, people said, it was leaving a mucky smear. There was even a report that the stolen truck had been seen heading north out of town without a driver and with two big feet sticking out the back. Shackled in the backseat of the patrol car, Duwayne cackled at all these calls coming in and said it sounded like the great Whore of Babylon had this fiendish sinkhole of iniquity by its diabolicals and wouldn't let go till the Day of Rupture come to kick ass and send them all to hell and perdition, praise the Rod of Wrath and His Holy Spirits, go git me a drink, Otis. In spite of Duwayne's crazed running commentary, Otis took all the callers seriously and had their stories checked out, as he always did, but he had his own sights set now on Settler's Woods. He'd been narrowing their escape options all day and he knew that was where they'd have to go. Before leaving the barbecue, he got the doctors present to put the hospital on alert, deputized a dozen or so of the younger fellows, sending those without weapons of their own to the airport with Mayor Snuffy who had the keys to John's gun cabinet, and told the others to meet up out at the Country Tavern in an hour's time. He talked with old Oxford about his simple son's shenanigans and the deep trouble he was in right now, and then fended off as best he could Oxford's clubfooted daughter-in-law, who came bobbing violently out of the night and attacked him again with her steel crutch, this time for partying it up instead of keeping the public order as he was paid to do. When she found out he was recruiting for an armed posse to try to capture the two bandits, she insisted on being deputized in spite of her obvious disabilities, which included being blind as a bat. He told her it was against the law to use relatives of the accused, though he didn't know whether it was or not, but in any case it didn't snuff her wick, she got more fired up than ever. He figured, for her own safety, he ought to lock her up for the night, but he didn't know which of his men would be willing to take her on and he was not keen to. Finally, Oxford's heavyset daughter, who had the most influence on her, was able to persuade her to back off, though Otis supposed he'd see them both again before the night was over. He tried to reach the motelkeeper out on the highway next to the woods to warn him that the two they were looking for might be in his neighborhood, but he got no answer. The Country Tavern, having taken casualties, seemed to have shut down as well. This was it then. He could feel it, like atmosphere: Last quarter. Last big play, game on the line. Before he could break away to join Mayor Snuffy and the boys at the airport, though, old Stu's wife grabbed his arm. She said she thought Stu was about to get hurt, hurt really bad, he should get out to the car lot as soon as possible and try to stop it, but when he impatiently asked, stop what? she couldn't say. Almost too drunk to stand. "Hell, I don't know, honey, just something he, you know, had to do before coming."

Well, she'd tried. She could do no more. One story ending, another revving up. Her life seemed full of them. She used to be the nice girl next door, back when the idea of excitement was a school field trip to a dairy farm; now she was not so nice but it was more interesting. So was she. Obviously. She ached to be home in bed, but not alone. Had to time it right. Alibi and all that. So she lingered, killing time and bottle dregs, keeping up her hellos and excuses, so all could say: I remember Daphne. More and more, not hellos but goodbyes: the joint was emptying out. The fuzz had wrecked the party. She watched as the preacher and his otherworldly wife packed up their new baby and cuddled it off into the night, thinking that, hell, she wasn't too old to get one of those things. That hunk could make her a beauty that'd knock the pants off all the other babies in town. But what would she do with it after she got it? Hard to imagine. Reverend Lenny's older boy, with his nose broken and face in plaster, had not seemed all that ecstatic about the new arrival. Or arrivals: that act was pretty funny, even if young what's-his-name, pencil-peter, he of his father's Our Fathering vocation, didn't think so. He'd fled the scene his mommy'd made, either in chagrin or else to go gawk at the famous desperados with the rest of the tourists. Maynard's repopped brat, star of Mikey's magic show, had seemingly taken off, too, though his parents were still here. Twat of Twit and Twat was sleeping with her eyes open down by the barbecue pit (poor thing, she'd got so ugly it was heartbreaking); Twit, as Daphne discovered when she went for a pee, was in the master bedroom fondling someone's panties. Guess whose. The Mange still had the hots for her after all these years. Daphne might have gone in there and taunted the snarfing sleazebag, as was her wont, but she saw that he was crying and figured the shitheel had suffered enough humiliation for one night, let him be, especially since she was in such a celebrative mood, or should be. Wasn't she? What was wrong? Why these flashes of the blues? Well. She was at heart a good woman who wished everyone could live forever. She didn't want one story to have to cancel another. Something like that. And also, give him credit, she'd miss the jokes. Of course, there were compensations, one big one in particular, but she'd been without it for a while, would be at least a night longer, and badly hooked, she was hurting: didn't junkies get the blues? So she wanted her steady fix but she wanted it to be painless. Had it already happened? It was a pity one had to live all these stories in tandem instead of all at the same time. Why couldn't life be spread out like memory was, with past and present all interwoven and dissolving into one another, so you could drift from story to story whenever the mood struck and no one really hurt by it? Instead: out of the old and into the new. Get ready to gasp and cry. Could she do it? Could and would. She looked around but found no one who belonged here to say goodnight to except little Mikey, who was busy rehearsing a new number with a little girl who looked like the youngest of Lenny and Trixie. They must have forgot her. Mikey was staggering around clumsily with his hand in the underpants of a Raggedy Ann doll, and the little girl was coming after him with some kind of plastic space cannon, firing table tennis balls. Who was that supposed to be?

She burst into the room, shotgun at her shoulder, slapped the lights on, and shouted: "Okay, asshole, say your prayers!" But the room was empty. Should have known better than to read a corkhead's mind. Or maybe Dutch tipped them off after all. Probably. Room looked used. But the bed, though indented here and there, was still made. Lorraine sniffed the air. A certain sweaty aura maybe, but no clues. Had she really intended to shoot him? Or just scare the pants off him? Most likely, if his pants had already been off, to shoot him. She looked under the pillows and found a packet of fancy imported rubbers. Unopened. She pocketed them as evidence. Evidence of what? Thwarted intentions. Ditto, the girlie magazine in the wastebasket, the toothbrush in the bathroom. Though she didn't recognize it. The tub was dry, but one of the hand-towels had been used and tossed on the floor. There was a glass that had had whiskey in it. What kind? No idea. In the little plastic wastebasket by the stool, there was a thick wad of chewed gum. She left it. Some evidence she didn't need. The inside bathroom wall, she saw, could be rolled back, half of it sliding into the other half, making the bathroom in effect part of the bedroom. Cute. This was a real little lovenest. Overheads with dimmers, adult video channel on the TV, an abundance of directional lamps, mirrors, speakers, soft polymorphous furniture, odd suggestive knickknacks. Maybe there were always condoms under the pillows, porno mags "left" in the bins. But, wait. What did she mean, "suggestive"? Well, just that: objects that at first glance meant nothing to her at all, when looked at individually, seemed, almost literally, to suggest another use, inevitably sexy. For example, a little twist of silken cords with knots at the ends, like something cut from old-fashioned curtains and sprayed on a tabletop as a decoration: pretty, she thought, until another thought reached her, as though from the cords themselves: a whip. A chest of drawers drew her attention next, the bottom drawer: in it she found a vibrator. She'd never had one, never even seen one, but she knew, as if it were telling her so, that was what it was. She turned it on (she knew where to turn it on!), just to check the batteries. Well, why not? She kicked off her shoes, hauled down her slacks and panties, then thought it might be a good idea to wash it first. While she was soaping it up in the bathroom, she had the peculiar sensation of observing her own broad sagging backside; not used to bathrooms with open walls, made her self-conscious, she clearly wasn't meant for the erotic life. You're an ugly old cow, she heard herself saying, but what the hell, live it up! She had a sudden hunch, opened the medicine cabinet, found a jar of skin lotion, and understood its purpose immediately, took it back to the bed with her, where the shotgun lay like a discarded lover. She lathered the vibrator with the lotion and watched herself in the mirror as she inserted it and turned it on. Wow! Pretty good! She lay back on the bed, raised her feet, and let her rip. It was weird, but the whole room seemed to be encouraging her, and what she was thinking as she came was, yeah, terrific, the power of visual metaphor! When it was over, it wasn't over. She still felt restless. She washed the vibrator and put it back, but she didn't feel like putting her pants on. It was weird, but it was like the room was talking to her. And what it seemed to be saying was: how about the shotgun? That would be something different. It had a little ridge at the top of the barrel for sighting and it felt good to rub that against her clitoris. It was already pretty oily, but she applied a little more lotion and worked it in. How deep can it go? she seemed to be asking herself. How big a one can you handle? She pushed it in, watching herself in the mirror, inch in, half inch out, inch in, imagining the stud who would be hung with something like this. Whoo, this was even better than the vibrator, slower but reaching deeper, just the madness of it was turning her on, and she could feel an orgasm coming unlike any she'd ever known, oh fuck, she whimpered, and the whole room seemed to be feeling it, too, it was like she was fucking the room as she shoved the shotgun in, or the room was fucking her, deeper and deeper, it was savage and delicious, and the thought came to her as though out of nowhere, this is it, it's never going to get any better, go for it, take all of it you can, then blast away! Yes, yes, she was gasping, and she reached for the trigger, but as she did so she caught a glimpse of herself in the mirror, and, even as she was coming, what she saw instead of a scene of pure ecstasy was her own ugly puss, puffy with rut, her fat misshapen ass and flabby thighs, and something very alien stabbing her vagina. She whipped it out, mortified and angry, and blasted away her mirrored image, registering, just before she pulled the trigger, a sudden wild panic in her image she didn't feel in herself.

Was that Waldo's toothbrush that Lorraine found in the motel bathroom? It was. Also the traces of whiskey in the water glass, the half-full (always the optimist) flask from which it came now tucked in his back pocket. But had Dutch called to warn him? He had not. Their decampment in the old station wagon parked out front had been the bright idea of the gum-smacking charmer in the raggedy cutoffs whom his shotgun-toting spouse had nicknamed Sweet Abandon and whom Waldo, but only to himself, called Sassy Buns. She it was who'd lured him out here to the darkened country club this moonless night because she said her biggest fantasy was to get balled on one of those velvety golf greens, or maybe on all eighteen, a hole at a time, how many corks you got to pop, Pop? Haw. He wasn't sure yet he'd get to pop one. She was something of a mystery, hard to figure. When he'd poked his finger in one of the gaps in her shorts back at the motel, making some good-natured crack about holing out with a clean stroke, she'd leapt off the bed, yelling: "Hey, I came for the high, man! What are you, some kind of sex maniac?" "Naw, only when I'm awake," he'd said with a sad grin, and she'd laughed at that and snapped her gum and picked her shirt up off the floor, her handsome bare tits, dusted with spilled coke which he'd hoped to snort directly therefrom, bouncing freely, and said: "This dump sucks, come on, let's split!" When he'd told her he was disappointed, he'd sort of hoped to get laid, she'd said, all right, no problem, and told him about her fantasy which had to do with an early sex experience with a caddy. Or did she say, her daddy? Never mind, here they were, approaching the first green, and he felt in good form even if wick dipping in the wild was not his wont. "What's par for this hole?" she asked. "Four," he said. "With a good drive and a bit of luck you can be on the green in two." As a rule, he counted himself lucky if he was on in five with nothing worse than a pair of putts to go. But if he was going to have to go the round, he wanted to keep his strokes to a minimum. "Have you ever noticed," she said, "how the first holes on golf courses are always the easiest and most inviting? It's like the first stages of puberty when it's all just a lark. Only after you've left the clubhouse far behind do you realize, led on by the easy openers, what you've got yourself into." Waldo paused and unscrewed the cap of his hip flask, took a hit, and contemplated this pale half-naked waif skipping down the fairway in the darkness before him. She wasn't exactly what she'd seemed. "Do you sometimes wish you'd stayed back in the clubhouse?" he called out. She turned around. He could just barely see her nipples, black pinpoints on her narrow chest. He couldn't tell if she was smiling or not. "Oh no. But sometimes I wish the people I was out on the course with had a better sense of how the game was played." He supposed that was a dig, like many he'd heard before, but what he said, trying to revive her fantasy and his plainer hopes (he hadn't been around one of this sort in a long while and he wasn't sure he could handle it), was, "I know what you mean, baby, a big driver might separate the pro from the duffer, but the game's won or lost around the greens." "What separates the pro from the duffer," she said, "is knowing how to change your stroke when the old stroke fails. And how to find your balls again when they're lost in the rough." She laughed, sounding more like her old sassy self, and added: "Drop your pants." "Hunh?" "Come on, old man, you wanted it so bad, let's get to it!" She stripped off her own shorts, kicked them away. "Your lie!" She was beautiful but he couldn't see much: a kind of ghostly cartoon cutout with two dots on the chest and a black patch down in the middle. Instead of green and hole, though, he was thinking sandtrap. Nevertheless, he worked his shoes off, moved the flask to his breast pocket, lowered his pants and drawers, and stepped out of them. He didn't know if she could see how things stood with him, but if she could she had to be impressed. "Okay," she laughed, "catch me if you can!" And she turned those saucy cheeks by which he'd christened her and was off and running down the open fairway. Not too fast. More like a glowing hop, skip, and, if he ever caught her, a jump. She looked like a flitting moth, rare and tender and just aching to be pinned, as they used to say back in the old chapter room, and with his trusty one-eyed scout pointing the way, Brother Waldo, yawhawing boldly in the hollow night, went galumphing after.

One-eyed Trevor, home alone and still monstrously hungover, his bloodshot good eye nearly as blind as his bad, sat huddled over his actuarial charts, searching for some sort of reassuring pattern, a set of probabilities he could count on, but it was like trying to read underwater. Nothing stood still, everything flowed into everything else, it was making him nauseated, or rather, more nauseated than he already was. When Alf dropped him off on his way to the hospital, the first thing he'd done was wolf down half a box of brown sugar, he didn't know why, it just tasted good. Then he'd swallowed some aspirin and antacids with cold coffee and rinsed out with mouthwash and sat down with his volatile actuarial charts to wait for Marge to come home. That image of the fluttering moth that had occurred to Waldo would have applied as well to Trevor's headachy experience of the points on his charts: not only John's wife's now (he couldn't even find hers), they were all dancing capriciously all over the charts, sometimes flying right off the page, other times sinking like stones or bloating like spilled ink. He tried to trace his way, step-by-step, back to the source of his despair, and though it hurt him to think at all, never mind in any systematic way, it seemed to him that the root cause of it all was his clandestine pursuit of the photographer's clandestine pursuit of John's wife. A whimsical and innocent game at first, it had become an unconscionable obsession, having little to do with pursued or pursuer, but all to do with himself. The buried treasure he had sought to uncover was his own sick soul. It was horrible. He could hardly bear to sit in the same room with himself. Where was Marge now that he needed her? Marge—? The question finally penetrated his miserable self-absorption. She'd left the barbecue early, begged him to go with her, he'd been in no mood to caddy for her while she worked off her temper, had scornfully refused. She was obviously in pain. How could he have been so insensitive? And where was she now? It was the middle of the night! Good heavens! *Something must have happened!* He was suddenly on his feet, wobbly as he was, and out the door. Trevor hated driving by night even more than by day, but he had no choice, he had to find Marge. His sudden anxiety made him tremble so, he could hardly get the key into the ignition, but at the same time he felt energized, strong (maybe it was the brown sugar), and ready for come what may. He headed straight for the country club, hunched over the wheel, to see if her car was still there, and come what did, before he reached the turn-in, was that girl from the barbecue who'd been excited by his eyepatch. She was standing on the road that ran alongside the course with her shirt over her shoulder, a bundle under her arm, and her thumb out, radiantly aglow in the beams of his headlamps. The excitement her excitement had engendered had long since left him along with his barbecue supper, but she was, as he was, alone in the night, so what could he do? Though it gave him a strange feeling, as if he were being willed by his action, not willing it, he swerved to a stop to let her in. "Hey, look who's here!" she laughed. "My knight in the shining eyepatch!" She kissed him on his cheek, her bare breast brushing his arm, and the car stalled, then he flooded it. "So what're you doing out here, big time? I was afraid for a minute you were going to run me down! Have you been following me?" "Oh no, no! I, uh—my wife! She hasn't come home and—!" "Your wife? You didn't tell me you were married—well, but what does it matter, right?" She popped her gum and gave his thigh a squeeze. "Anyway, you won't find anybody in their right mind out here, man. Nothing but chiggers and spiders and gross crawly things. It's the pits!" She brushed off her breasts, her legs, peered inside the waistband of her raggedy shorts, an expression on her face of mild annoyance, or else (it was familiar somehow) of placid consent. "Some old drunk dragged me out here and tried to rape me—you know, the make-out-or-get-out kind—I had to run away. It was awful! I don't know *what* I'd have done if you hadn't come along!" She snuggled closer, stuck her gum under the dashboard, laid her head on his shoulder. "Hey, I don't mind if you were following me," she murmured. "Really. I'm flattered that a cool guy like you would even be interested." She reached up and nibbled at his ear. He had the strange sensation that she was reminding him of something he'd forgotten. Or that she was correcting a flaw in his computations: something certainly was shifting. "I've got the key to a motel room in this bozo's pants," she whispered. "Wanna go?" "Well, I, uh, never . . ." "You don't like me—?" "Oh no, I *do!* But—" "Don't worry, then. I know how to show a guy a good time, honest, just give me a chance." Her tongue was in his ear and her hand inside his shirt. Her bare leg crossed his thighs and nudged between them like an eraser scrubbing away an error. "But what?" she breathed. "Tell me, killer. You never what?"

He hesitated, closing his good eye. "I have never," he confessed softly, feeling everything come round for him at last (perhaps he *had* followed her out here!), "I have never . . . known delight . . ."

As for John's erstwhile troubleshooter, who had so known but who had always, successful businesswoman that she was, given more than she had received, the gumpopping hitchhiker's disparaging judgment upon the local country club applied equally to this whole pig's ear of a town, Nevada having come round to Bruce's bitter take on his friend's backwater fiefdom: a living nightmare. It was, the pits, a house of horrors. Where the hideous crawly things were the deadbeats who lived here. Nobody in their right mind, like the lady said. Nevada rolled along through the creepy half-lit streets, empty but for a stray dog or two, a car crossing several blocks up, a distant siren. She felt like she was touring the land of the dead or a wax museum after hours. Remote shimmerings of heat lightning stirred memories of her white-whiskered granddad's apocalyptic fantasies. It was time for her to blow this sick scene once and for all before it fucked her mind completely, which was what she was going to tell Rex when she saw him. She'd like him to come along, meal ticket on her, but if not, not. She'd gone out to his motel, nobody in, though his car was there. Out jogging maybe. She'd made herself at home, put on some music to beat back the silence, worked out a bit with his weights, but in the end the emptiness had spooked her, so she'd hit the road again, looking for lights. Downtown was dead, she cruised the strips, feeling oddly panicky whenever the darkness welled up around her. Her hotel out on the interstate was full of John's friends, down for the holiday, even her own suite was being used, couldn't go there without getting sucked into bad shit. She drifted past the malls, where the young were buzzing around restlessly like flies on dung, having no one to take their anger out on except each other. There were a few cars dragracing in the mostly empty parking lots, tires squealing. She heard a bottle break hollowly: the sound of her own empty fantasies gone bust, she thought. But what could she have done? She'd got caught between two old pals, playing rough. She'd grabbed what she could while she could and now it was time to turn the page. She had met John out at the airport after sending him the note, supposing she'd be invited along, but after he'd got out of her what he wanted, he'd told her in effect to go fuck herself, looking down his broken nose at her like a lord at his dirty kitchenmaid. Something he had to do himself, he'd said. He'd seemed suspicious: did he know about the signed agreements Bruce was leaving behind for her? Well, what if he did, fuck-all he could do about it, they'd be partners now in effect, and if he didn't like it he could shove it up his royal wazoo. That was how Nevada had put it to herself, glaring at his back as he'd crawled up into the cabin, but she'd been crying when he took off without her. Like that old bluesy song Rex so loved: Goodbye, good times . . . The tears had dried now but she was still feeling wasted and strung out, so she decided to make a pit stop at an all-night drugstore where she had a friendly connection. Just as she was pulling in, though, that steely black Porsche she knew so well went rocketing past, horn blaring and brights ablaze, announcing: look out, buttheads! this is an emergency! John? He'd found them? Her heart was in her throat as she leapt back in her car. What now—?!

No, Clarissa: going nowhere, anywhere, ready for come what may, as she'd been ready all day, or so she'd thought, for come what didn't. Betrayed! Not just by two-faced Jennifer, but by Bruce and Nevada, too! Those *shits!* She could never forgive either of them. Her only real friends! Or so they'd seemed: she'd been suckered yet again by her infantile trust of others. When was she going to grow up? She spun up onto the interstate and, burning rubber as she accelerated, went barreling down the open highway in her daddy's blazing saddle, as he called it, daring anyone or anything to get in her way. She watched the speedometer rise past 140, but she felt like she was sitting still, not moving at all. Signs, cars and trucks, light poles whipped past as though under their own power: it was the sensation she used to get on merry-go-rounds and rollercoasters, the world going into a wild spin while she sat anchored at the center of stillness. She slowed and a sense of her own motion came back to her. A bird caromed off the windshield, startling her, and she cut her speed even more, took the next exit ramp, looped around, and headed back toward town, see who's hanging at the mall, a rock station at full blast, fanfaring her coming. She wanted to hit somebody or rape them or tear their eyes out or something, she didn't know what she wanted. She found the usual crowd. More of them outside than in, that kind of night. The Porsche impressed them. They passed around some grass cut with angel dust or smack or both, a vague blend of pass-me-downs, that did nothing to soften the implacable fury that gripped her mortified heart. A couple of the girls had stripped off their tops, and Clarissa did, too. A guy with his shirt off said, "Let's walk through the mall like this and see if they throw us out," and she told him to fuck off. Kid stuff. Mall-rat Mickey Mouse. She'd always loved this mall, ever since her dad brought her here on her seventh birthday, just after he'd built it. A day in her memory when the sun shone as though for her alone. It was magic and it was hers. Now the magic had suddenly left it, like when somebody dies and leaves nothing but a cold clammy body. These scuzzy candy-butts were spoiling it. When a girl asked where Jen was, Clarissa snapped: "She's dead, man. Gone. Forget her." "Really—?!" They wanted to know more, but Clarissa had nothing to add. These assholes were getting on her nerves. She felt surrounded by flesh-eating aliens and it was making her want to throw up. Even the light was weird. As often in moments like this, when she felt completely alone in a scumbag world, Clarissa asked herself, what would Marie-Claire do next? Her destiny: whatever it was, let it come. The guys started pressing her to give them a ride, suggesting in their dork-brained way that they wanted more than one kind, so she said: "Okay, show me what you got, I only go with the biggest." "Got?" "In your pants, stupid. Haul it out. Let's measure up." The girls were giggling with their heads down like they'd just seen someone poop themselves. "Lay them out on the hood there, if you can find them. The longest gets a ride he won't forget." A couple of the bigger boys unzipped, but the others started backing off, the wimps. One of them asked if she even had her license yet, and she heard someone say she was so ripped a ride with her was like a one-way ticket to nowhere. The class nerd mooned her, his mashed-potato ass being the only joke he knew, but not close enough for her to stub her roach out on it. So she flicked it in its general direction, gave them all the finger, and gunned it out of there, tires screaming in her behalf.

The class nerd was not alone in assisting the heavens on this moonless night, others including Clarissa's father's Assistant Vice President in Charge of Sales and his clairaudient but troubled helpmeet, as well as the motelkeeper, her father's old battery mate, who'd caught it (his destiny) but good, and at this moment lay mooning the indifferent world in the very room serially occupied so recently by the other two, though now it was his alone. He had just knocked the telephone over and was groping for it with his left hand, finding it oddly elusive even though he knew just where it was. As he knew where everything was, it was all quite clear to him, Dutch felt perfectly sound, composed and carefree, a bit bored if anything, and he seriously considered simply locking up for the night and sorting things out in the morning. At the same time he knew he was dying. He could see himself lying there in the shattered glass, fatally wounded, fumbling for a fallen phone which, when dragged to his ear, turned out to be dead. Poor bastard, he mused. Pity he had to check out in such undignified circumstances. Of course, Dutch thought (always thinking), he could still use the two-way radio the police chief had given him. If—big if—he could reach his back pocket, now somewhere down around his ankles. Which were miles away in some other room. He could hear someone frantically rattling the door. Probably Waldo's old lady wanting back in to get her pants back. Could he go over and open it up for her? He couldn't, right though he was about it being underclad Lorraine. She'd fled the room in abject terror (her impression was of someone exploding bloodily right through the mirror), then had thought better of it, but the door had snapped shut behind her and locked her out. She shook it and shouldered it and kicked it, but no dice. And no help from within. She raced for her car, tugging her shirt down as she ran, feeling dreadfully exposed, but the old wagon wasn't there! Someone must have stolen it! Oh my God! She ducked into the scraggly bushes at the edge of the lot; her thighs were wet and it felt like someone with icy breath was breathing on them. No one around, though, or she'd know it. She did pick up something like a fuzzy overview as if from a low-flying plane (she glanced up into the empty sky), but it didn't seem quite human, whatever it was, her own imagination maybe, all atingle as it was, as was her bare ass also. She was crouched there, drying her thighs and tears with her shirttails and meditating on the awesome vicissitudes of death, wisdom, and paradox (her destined lot), when it occurred to her that there might be a spare room key at the reception desk. So she crept around to the front, braced herself, leapt into full view from the highway, and threw herself at the double glass doors. But they were locked, too. The scurrilous sonuvabitch must have shut up shop before waddling off to his peepshow. She tried to force them, but felt her backside light up from the passing traffic like a billboard, heard sirens not far away, had to beat a quick retreat. Thus, on opposite edges of the town, both Lorraine and her maiden-chasing spouse found themselves this night in paired plight, let loose in the wild without prospects and in nothing but their shirts, her corkhead hubby, all forlorn, now slashing around in the rough somewhere on the back nine at the country club. He'd been taken in. Not for the first time. He had a gift for it. She whom his wife called one thing, he another, having lured him out here and in here, had, sassily, abandoned him, her pale will-o'-the-wisp buns dancing elusively through the underbrush ahead of him the last sweet glimpse he'd had of light itself. All dark since. Couldn't see his hand in front of, his nose before. Where was he? No idea. Hopelessly lost and getting eaten alive by mosquitos, Waldo was consoled only by his pocket flask, which, though drained dry, he sucked on like a pacifier, in the same way that his wife, when distressed, as now, found solace in nibbling the polish off her nails, or their friend the motelkeeper, who had so recently hosted them both, in scratching his balls. When he, like Adam, had 'em.

Inconsolable Floyd had also been had, he knew that, no matter what his hopes. The former hardware store manager, recently promoted, though no golfer, had spent most of his life in the rough and, after being granted a glimpse of the green, was getting kicked back into it as sure as candy turned to shit. Far from mooning the world (Floyd was a private man whom even Edna rarely saw in a state of nature), he was still wearing his fancy new beige business suit, checked shirt, and two-toned shoes, though the knees and elbows of the suit were stained, the shirt unbuttoned, bootlace tie hanging loose, shoes caked with beery mud. He knew he'd overprided himself and, first thing he'd got home, in penance for his sins of vanity and presumption, he'd shaved the fuzz off his upper lip, and then he'd knelt to pray; but no prayer came out, a curse more like. It was all gone. He was still clutching at the impossible dream John had put in his battered old head, thinking it might somehow still come out all right, but he knew in his gut it wouldn't. Couldn't. Which just wasn't rightful. He'd sincerely tried, Floyd had. He'd spent a dozen years as a rich man's ass-kissing flunky, treated no better than a blesséd pinboy, teaching God's word to the spoiled brats of the town, playing all the stupid games they played, and now, with the sudden resurfacing of a past he no longer recognized as his own (his eye was on eternal salvation, the Risen Son, God's grace and bounty, not some hairless tattooed pussy in Santa Fe, for Christ's sake), it was as though these dozen years had never happened, or had happened in a dream. Predestination: you had to take it seriously. He packed a couple of bags and told Edna, who sat slumped on the old sofa looking like something found at the back of the fridge, an unwrapped porcelain lamp in a box at her feet, not to worry none but he might have to go off on a business trip soon, though he didn't know how soon or for how long. Meanwhile, though, he did require a new car, and maybe right away, so he rang up old Stu, hoping it wasn't too late; but it was his fat profligate wife who answered, mumbling boozily over and over that Stu had something he had to do out at the garage, one of his trucks had been stole or something, he'd be here soon. Finally nothing for it but to shoot out there, just in case, though Floyd figured Stu was probably shacked up somewheres, for which, though on principle he disapproved, Floyd couldn't blame him. No big surprise, then, to find the place dark. Completely. Even the all-night floods over the car lot were out, the only light coming from the distant flickering of heat lightning on the western horizon. Under the circumstances, Floyd reckoned, borrowing a car might be better than buying one, Stu would understand, and if everything worked out okay he'd bring it back later in the week. So he tried the office door, found it open, pushed on in, and stove his toe on something that turned out to be old Stu hisself. Uh-oh. Just rolled a gutter ball. No time to look for keys to a new model—he could hear the distant wail of approaching sirens—but Stu did have a handgun in his fist that he no longer needed, so Floyd took that and tore ass out of there.

All this business with guns. Columbia disapproved. Guns were important to the nation, you never saw a pioneer without one, but, though it was almost unpatriotic to say so, those wild romantic days were over. You didn't have to shoot Indians anymore, if they did bad things you could just electrocute them. It was one thing she'd learned from her father: people kill, not guns, granted, but guns make it too easy, maybe even too much fun. If it weren't for guns, poor Yale would be with them still, though that was war and maybe it wasn't a fair argument. She used it, though, just the same, in her desperate effort to dissuade her overheated sister-in-law from arming herself and taking the law into her own hands. Lumby was exhausted and just couldn't take much more. It had been a very long day, or week, or whatever it was, she'd lost all track. Her white uniform was filthy and patchy with sweat, her hair damp and stringy, her feet were sore, and she couldn't remember when she'd bathed last, or even washed properly. And all because of her cretinous little brother, who definitely wasn't worth it, but you couldn't tell Gretchen that. How could she love such a dumb jerk so? Well, maybe she didn't, but she loved something, and Corny stood for it, so it was the same as loving him. For Lumby it was much easier, she loved Gretchen plain and simple, and so stuck by her no matter what craziness her jealousy got her into, though there had been times in this punishing odyssey when her mind, dragged down by a protesting body, had loved less than her heart did. The pattern had been the same, over and over: her strenuous attempts to restrain her sister-in-law thwarted sooner or later by Gretchen throwing herself, blind and lame, into the fray, leaving Lumby to extricate her and defend her from counterattacks, often at great hazard to her own vulnerable person. None of which Gretchen, in her madness, seemed to appreciate. She probably couldn't even *see* the blows that Lumby took on her behalf, but even if she did or could infer them, it didn't seem to matter to her: all she cared about was getting Corny back. And, clearly, she would kill to do that. So, when Gretchen had been rejected as a volunteer for the police posse (what a relief!) and had decided therefore to arm herself (oh no!) with Harvie's old hunting rifle and/or Yale's army revolver, both kept in the pharmacy storeroom because her father refused to have them in the house where the children were, Lumby had feared the worst: Gretchen, myopic and rabid as she was, might shoot at anything that moved, including the mayor and the police chief, and Corny was too stupid to stay out of the crossfire, all those children would be left fatherless, whether or not they noticed the change, and once the bullets started to fly they might all get killed. Guns were like that. It was almost too terrible to contemplate. Since Gretchen wouldn't listen to her and she had run out of arguments, Lumby's only recourse was somehow—though she hadn't the least idea how the wicked gizmos worked—to sabotage them, even if that made Gretchen mad at her for a time. So, though ready to drop, Columbia dogged Gretchen's heels, prepared to do whatever she had to do to save all their lives, or at least the life of the one she loved. But as they approached the drugstore, Columbia saw that there were lights on and told Gretchen so: a break-in! She tried to hold Gretchen back but that woman, once set on a course, could not be stayed: she clumped heavily right on down the street, through the door, and up to the video game machine where Cornell was hunched forward, nose to the screen, his head looking a bit squashed in but otherwise her useless dimwit brother, same as ever (to collapsing Columbia he was a beautiful sight), slapped him fiercely about the ears and shoulders, and hauled him away, asking Lumby to close up the store for her, she was taking her wayward husband home and locking him in his room for a week as punishment for all the grief he'd caused them, chasing after a shameless jezebel like that. He didn't resist, though he seemed to have no idea what she was talking about, which was to say, numskull Corny as usual. Columbia pushed the door shut behind them, double-locked, turned off the lights, and, finger still on the switch, fell asleep in her tracks there where she stood.

Columbia's view of guns as wicked gizmos was not shared by the town police chief, but he did not romanticize them either, nor did he even use them for sport, and he wished, as Oxford and his daughter did, that there were fewer of them around. For Otis, guns were merely tools of his trade, deterrents against disorder, protectors of life, liberty, and property, and necessary weapons in the eternal struggle between Good and Evil. When he thought of the Good, he thought of the Virgin and her terrible vulnerability, the image that had made a soldier and lawman of him, and on his way out to the airport to meet with Mayor Snuffy and the boys, Otis had the officer behind the wheel stop by the church so he could drop in to ask the Virgin for strength and guidance. She told him he had a long hard night ahead of him (he already knew that) and asked him if his heart was pure. He said he thought it was but those photographs bothered him somewhat. She reminded him that he had taken them as material evidence and that examining them was therefore part of his sworn duty, but that if he was improperly aroused by them he should think of her and her great suffering and of her loneliness. Otis was kneeling before her and she seemed to place her soft hand on the back of his neck for a healing moment, which he understood without understanding, likewise this whole tender conversation with something made of—what? plaster of Paris probably, or the stuff they made dolls out of. The cold shiny feet of which he reverentially kissed, and then, Pauline's monumental thighs crowding into his thoughts like a kind of mental avalanche, he hastily crossed himself and withdrew. Back in the squad car, Pauline's Daddy Duwayne, manacled in the backseat beside him, cackled wheezily and asked what it felt like to give communion to all seven scarlet-tongued heads of the Great Whore of Babylon at once, and Otis whacked him up the head with the flat side of his revolver, knocking his baseball hat off as his ugly nut bounced against the window, which was another use of his occupational tool. It was the providing of such tools to those members of the newly deputized posse who had no weapons of their own that was the purpose of meeting at the airport before the general rendezvous at the Country Tavern: the mayor, who until recently had worked there, had the keys to John's gun cabinet and permission to use the arms at any time for the defense of the municipal air facility, of which the hunting down of the two bandits, who for a time had trespassed illegally on airport property, was considered an extension. When they pulled in, they found the young mechanic from the Ford-Mercury garage already there, though in the dark, fumbling with the locked door and startled by their arrival, as though he thought they might be the bandits catching him from behind. A case of mistaken identity, everybody was a bit jumpy, they laughed it off. "Ah, there it is, I been looking for it," Snuffy said, taking the mechanic's rifle, then handing it back. "You might as well keep it, son. You're gonna need it. Now, let's get this goddamned ballgame underway." The mayor led the way in with his key ring; passed out the weapons; then, cranking up into his old half-time mode, said that nobody'd ever handed nothing on a platter to this town, they didn't have no mountains or oceans, lakes or gold mines or rivers, everything that was here had got made by oldtime hustle and grit and teamwork, and the job this team had to do tonight was take out a couple of dangerous elements that threatened a quality of life here which had required more than a century to knock into shape. So everybody should stay on their toes and knuckle down and brace up for a long, hard, and bruising night. We gotta dig in and pop them suckers, boys, he said, before they pop us! There ain't no runners-up when it's do or die! Otis informed them that the two killers were holed out in Settler's Woods back of the motel and they were all going to join up now with the others at the Country Tavern, where he'd lay out the strategy for the rest of the search. Some of them wanted to know just how big Pauline really was, so Otis asked the young golf pro, who'd had a good look, to give them all a description of what he'd seen, but since it had to do with Pauline taking a stupendous crap and that fellow was something of a joker who liked to act out his stories, Otis had to turn him off (he was just lowering his pansy-yellow pants) before his hunting party turned into some other kind. His recruits were a bunch of cockeyed goofballs for the most part, Otis knew that, he shouldn't be putting guns in the hands of any of them, except for his own boys, his old coach, the garage mechanic maybe (he sure as hell wished John was here), but what could he do? Like his old commanding officer used to say: A man can't choose his own emergencies.

A lesson that Trevor the accountant was learning, for though he had no one to blame but himself for where he was (this irrational pursuit of a phantom called delight, he must be mad!), what he discovered there was not of his doing, nor could he have foreseen it. His emergency was this: finding himself, a respected middle-aged accountant, married, alone in a motel room with a young girl in raggedy shorts whose name he didn't even know and, lying on the floor in his own blood, a wounded man, more or less naked and possibly dead, a gun on the bed and clothing scattered about, ambulance and police cars pulling up outside, sirens screaming. "Gosh, I'm so scared!" gasped the girl, dropping what she was carrying and throwing herself into Trevor's arms, the bare arms around his neck frightening him nearly as much as the body on the floor or the red and blue lights flashing against the window blinds. "Thank goodness I'm with someone who knows what to do in situations like this!" Trevor's knees had turned to butter, his brains too, and he had to bite his cheeks to keep from crying. "You're so cool, man! Just grinning like that!" The police were hammering on the door. "Hey! Who's in there? What's going on? Open up!" "Don't let them know I'm here!" the girl cried, and grabbing up an armful of clothing again, she ducked into the bathroom, blowing him a last-second kiss, just as the door exploded inward and men in white jackets, others in gray and blue, some with their pistols drawn, came crashing into the room. "There he is!" The butter melted and he sank to the floor, but was soon hauled, roughly, to his feet again. "Shoot him if he moves!" "That your shotgun, killer?" "No!" he whimpered, as something hard and pointy bruised his ribs. "*Ow!*" His bladder gave way and a wet warmth spread to his knees. "It's—it's all a mistake! She—!" "She—? She, who?" "Wait a minute. Ain't that John's business manager?" "Trevor—?! What the hell are you doing here?" "I-I'm not, I don't, it's not what it—*a client!*" he gasped, churning up the head butter. "What—?!" "He, you know, a p-policy! Insurance! I, uh, I had to—!" "You're tellin' me you're here to service a fucking insurance policy—?!" "I hope for old Dutch's sake it's a good one," grunted one of the ambulance men lifting the motelkeeper onto a stretcher. "The poor bastard's had the best part of him blown clean away!" "Yeah, pretty much tore his right hand off, too!" "Is he alive?" "Barely. He's lost buckets." "Lucky he had that two-way radio Otis give him, what with all the phonelines around here took out." "Hey, this broken glass is weird! Look! One side's like a mirror, but the other—" "Hold on, whose purple pants are these? These fruitbags yours, buddy?" "*No!*" "Anything in the pockets?" "Some golf tees. Keys. A pack of rubbers. No, wait! A billfold! Well, I'll be goddamned!" "Who is it?" "These here are old Waldo's pants!" "Jesus, you think he left without them?" "If he did, he shouldn't be hard to find." "Shit, John's not gonna like this!" "No, but just the same we'll have to get a warrant out." "Yeah, well, later. We're due over at the Tavern. Otis will be pissed if we don't hustle our butts over there." "What about all this shit?" "Grab it up and bring it along!" "Trevor, we oughta lock you up but we don't have time. So, you go home and stay outa trouble now, goddamn it, and we'll talk to you tomorrow, you hear?" He nodded bleakly, feeling the nausea rise again, and then he was alone in his wet pants on a bloodstained floor littered with broken mirror fragments, staring into the messy darkness of the little room beyond, which seemed to be reflecting his own dark messiness within. Alone, but not for long. Marge's friend Lorraine poked her head around the door, then jumped inside and slapped the door shut with her hips. *"Don't look!"* she shrieked, and only then did it register on him that she was wearing nothing but a shirt, tails tugged down between her thighs with both hands. She glanced around wildly, then loped leggily into the bathroom, high-stepping through the broken glass. *"No! Stop!"* he cried, but too late. Would this folly never end? He stumbled over, abashed, to explain what was beyond explanation, but when he looked there was no one in there but red-faced Lorraine, tying a towel on and screaming at him that he was a sick voyeuristic pervert, get the hell out! What was worse, she was right. She threw a toilet plunger at him and everything went black. Had he gone blind in the other eye as well? If so, so be it. Trevor had seen about all he ever wanted to see.

The Artist? The Model? Both gone, like vision itself: mere memories, and so illusions. His desire to see has cost him his sight. Blind in both eyes, and so pitiable, he gropes, utterly alone, through the pitch-black night in a forest he cannot even be sure *is* a forest, only his memory and his reason suggest this to him. That ever-deceptive memory. That foolish reason that led him into this doomed project in the first place. Who was he to use another to try to see into himself? Who was he to intrude upon Art's sacred domain? Of course, if Art, as the Model suggested, is not the contemplation of beauty, but the encounter with its absence, then he should, encountering absence in its utmost purity, be in ecstasy, but he is not. Black on black is a metaphor, perhaps even a beautiful one, but it is not Art. But why blind? You may well ask. Probably it's an allegorical blindness, curable only by allegorical means. No, I'm sick of all that. Then my fate is sealed, and your commitment to allegory is complete. Nonsense. Why can't I simply restore your sight? There, you see? you have it back. No, sadly, I do not. Some things you can do, some you cannot. I don't understand. Nor I: we are both intruders here. Tell me, then, what you in your blindness see. I see the fire raging through the forest. I thought I knew what it meant, but now I don't. There was a fire, then? There might have been. If so, I think it expressed the terror of a world devoid of Art. Or of the void of Art? Who can say? What vanished was the Real. No, its mere Model: the Real remains, as you yourself, blind within it, must surely know. All I know is the unseen fire's power to consume all in its path. In that respect it's much like time, and so may represent a simpler terror. Against which Art stands. So you say; show me it. Alas, I lack the gift to do so, though I believe it to be so, and have had a glimpse, I think: There was a stone once, in the stream . . . But now it too is gone, the stream as well perhaps. What then can you do for me, left sightless and alone in this bleak forest, torched by your own uncertainties? Can you lead me out? Of course: give me your hand. Here: it is your own. Ah. Yes. As I feared. We cannot leave here then. No. The endless night to which you are condemned is mine as well? It is.

Waldo, so condemned, or so it seemed, and as blind as Ellsworth's Stalker (couldn't see a fucking thing), crashed ponderously through the thorny undergrowth, not in hopes of escaping it, but in desperate flight from the mosquitos that swarmed upon him whenever he stood still. "*When the going gets tough,*" he cried out into the empty black night, as he staggered through what felt like the gnarled claws of old hags, grasping vindictively at the offending flesh he now so liberally offered them, "*the roughs get rougher!*" But was Waldo, thus clawed and bit, repentant? No, if those radiant buns should reappear, he'd chase them all over again, but not to do them harm, oh no, prince of a fellow that he was, his heart was big and full of love, and life, so short, was sweet or else was wasted. Waldo paused to suck at the empty flask and the mosquitos whined around him. Had he heard something? Yes, a distant growling roar, not unlike a power mower. Hah! Kevin always said he liked to do the fairways at night! Rescue was at hand! Waldo plunged toward the sound like a castaway striding through heavy surf toward an unseen shore, and in due time stepped out upon a fairway. Ah! His bare toes reveled in the grassy carpet, giving him a pleasure comparable to a good massage, or the relief one's buttocks felt when a paddling ended, fond memory of the fraternal past. He followed the sound of the motor down the fairway, toward which green he had no idea, nor had he any preference, confident old Kev would have a bottle out here with him, good scout that he was, and wondering only why he saw no light. Naught but a remote flicker of heat lightning in the west like a reminder that not all lands were lightless. But then was Kevin mowing in the dark? He was not, nor was it Kevin. It was (Waldo padded softly upon the spongy green, leaned close to make out the horsey bare-legged creature sprawled athwart the hole) old Mad Marge snoring! Christ, what a cannonade! Poor Triv had to live with that? Marge lay upon her back, limbs outflung, still clutching a seven-iron in one fist, jaw slack and vibrating with her resounding snores, her blouse open and skirt rolled up around her waist, flag tossed aside, the ball in the hole between her powerful thighs as though she'd shat it there. Imagining remarks to some such effect that he might mockingly make (and others that she might make to mock in turn his unadorned and inert condition, but what the hell, company was company), he gave her a firm barefooted kick in the side of her rump, but she didn't even lose a beat in her steady drum-fire barrage, nor did successive kicks do the trick: Sleeping Beauty was utterly elsewhere, her big-boned bod abandoned. Well, well. He drew a putter out of her dropped bag, a pair of balls as well, which he tossed down at the edge of the green, facing her open fork, faintly illumined by the occasional glimmerings from the west. "*Fore!*" he hollered into the hollow night and crisply stroked the first: he could hear it as it whispered across the green, rattled around in her thighs like a roulette ball, and dropped—*k-plunk!*—into the hole. The second made a clocking sound, then bounced back out again like a pinball ejected from a scoring dimple. He went over to pick it up and to pluck the two from out the hole. His hand brushed her pantied crotch while reaching in and felt something rippling behind the cloth like a scurrying mouse. Curious, he pushed to one side the narrow strip of reinforced fabric and lost his fingers to wet fleshy lips that hotly sucked them in. Hey! Wow! Everything was on the move in there! That sucker was alive! And still she thundered on, lost to this world and to all others, her sonorous concert interrupted only when, with effort, he popped his ruminated fingers out. "John—?" she gasped. Waldo, reprising his famous Long John impersonation, rumbled: "Yeah, baby, I love ya," and his Sarge Marge phobia momentarily overcome and putter cast aside, he leaned forward to work his wedgie in where his trailblazing fingers had gone before. Her raking snores returned as though to sanction his—*yowee!*—brave endeavors. From which no quick retreat: her limbs snapped round him and—*woops!*—clapped him to his task! Love: oh shit, it's—*hang on!*—a real adventure!

Love as an adventure was not one of the subtopics of Reverend Lenny's sermon-in-progress, but perhaps only because he had not yet thought of it, for love in the larger sense, he'd decided, watching his wife Trixie feed the new baby by candlelight (the power had gone out, not just in the manse, the whole block seemed dark), was to be its central theme. The love of one's fellows and maternal and marital love and love as the ultimate sanctuary and love as a miracle and as the true source of all meaning, or at least such as we're granted in this paradox-ridden universe of ours, bereft of certainties as it was. In the expression

"I love you," neither subject nor object could be identified or be proven to exist, only the verb was beyond dispute, the only indispensable verb in the language perhaps, centering all others. The event that had brought all his scattered thoughts to focus was the birth, in a spectacle of birth, of his spectacular son. Were there comic aspects to his abrupt arrival on this lonely planet? Well, so much the better, for such was the nature of the human condition within which it participated, Lenny's theme embracing as well the cosmic joke of love. "But where, then, is the center?" Beatrice had mysteriously asked earlier (she did not now remember this and he but barely did; fortunately, as he was doing now, he'd taken notes), and the answer was: in love as incarnated in their little Adam, so named by Beatrice in awe, not shared by Lennox, of his conception, which she associated with a fugue by Bach. "It was like all the organ pipes had got stuffed up inside me, one by one," she said, "each one resonating with its own special pitch and tone, filling me up with such ecstatic music I almost couldn't stand it!" Mind, spirit, and body as a musical instrument, love as the well-struck chord: he took a note by the flickering candle (it felt like the world had emptied itself out, even his other children had been swallowed up by the night, and only they three remained, huddled around the last of the light like the nucleus of a new adventure: yes, he was thinking now about the adventure of love), while Beatrice, giving breast, quietly chatted away. "Look at his pretty little mouth, Lenny, how it curls around my nipple, he's not just sucking at it, he's licking it, nosing it, playing with it, such a sexy little baby! All the time I was carrying him I had the feeling inside me, not of a baby, but of a passionate lover, one who'd found all the places that made me hot but from the inside out: my nipples would suddenly get hard, my throat would flush, my thighs would drip, and all my senses would turn inward and I wouldn't know where I was! Once he got the hiccups, and I nearly died from pleasure! Where did he come from, Lenny, this strange little boy?" Lenny didn't know, didn't care. Things happened. That was not what mattered. What mattered was the message that was being transmitted, a message that was always the same and never the same message twice, easily read, yet impossible to decipher, though the attempt to do so was his life's work and privilege. "Maybe," he said, "he came from the desire to resist the indifference of the universe. Maybe we still haven't settled down, Trixie. Maybe we're still on the run, still rebelling." "Oh dear," she sighed, and hugged the baby. "I hope not."

Mother love, to be celebrated in Lennox's forthcoming Sunday sermon, was also what roused Veronica at last from her backyard stupor and sent her out alone into the dark unfriendly night in search of her, well, her son, so to speak, her bad-penny Second John: slimy, hideous, mindless, but pathetic, too, utterly helpless, needing her, his only mom, how could she have wanted to hit him with an ironing board? Everyone at the party had been complaining about the slime trail, most of them blaming it on the monster woman, so even at night it was easy to find and then to follow, not from east to west but from dry to wet. Some streetlamps still burned but most were out and she walked through patches of absolute darkness where the power seemed to have failed with only the slime trail itself, faintly phosphorescent, to show her the way. It led eventually into a noisy bar, one she'd never been in before, a saloon more like, with a big bar made out of railway ties, the only thing vaguely familiar, and sawdust on the wooden floor and gaslamps hanging over wooden tables where loud drinking men played cards and broke into brawls and vulgar songs and laughter. She saw him in a corner, on the floor, still swaddled and hooded loosely in the dirty sheet he'd been wrapped in, the little mendicant with the big head and shriveled limbs, her boy, sort of, her Second John. The men were teasing him, flicking their ash and flinging their beer dregs at him, spitting on him, kicking him, and ridiculing in despicable ways his tendency to suck at anything that neared his hooded face. Veronica braced herself (why did this remind her of some of her most awful moments in high school?), then marched over to stand between them and her son, remembering only after she'd got there and they'd all rudely reminded her with roars of laughter that the borrowed linen dress she was wearing was split up the back. She scolded them in a high-pitched voice she could not quite control for being cruel to a handicapped person who could not defend himself and who wasn't even a child yet. This sent them all into howls of finger-pointing laughter, spilling their beer and tipping tables over. "You all ought to be ashamed of yourselves!" she shouted, and knelt to give the poor thing, wet and squishy though she knew he was, a motherly hug, feeling herself poke out the back of the dress as she squatted, giving them all something fresh to whoop about. "You're nothing but a bunch of bullies!" she cried. "That's tellin' 'em, Ma!" Second John exclaimed, suddenly tossing back the cowl, as though peeling off a disguise. He stood before them, just a head above her doubled knees, bald and diapered and smoking a big black cigar. She gasped. "Why, you're the—!" He spat and laughed and whipped a pistol out of his diapers and shot the hats off three or four of the men, all of whom were now diving for cover, then slapped Veronica on her exposed backside and, waving his pistol about, said: "You're a real pal, Ma! Whaddaya say we sow a few wild oats here and teach these bums a lesson in family values?" "I-I don't want any violence—!" she begged. "Who's talking about violence?" he laughed. The bartender in his white shirt with sleeve garters rose up behind the bar with a twelve-gauge shotgun, Ronnie screamed, her son blew the gun out of his hands and then blasted away a row of bottles over the quaking barkeep's head. "All I want's a little tit!" "What—?!" "Ma, I'm your little baby!" "But I-I don't have any milk!" she gasped. "That's okay, I'm not hungry, I just need a little comfort," he said with a sly affectionate grin, tonguing the cigar from one side of his mouth to the other. He reached inside her linen dress and popped a bare breast out. "You've kept me waiting, Ma! All these years! It wasn't fair!" "Darling, please—!" She felt sorry for him and what had happened, but much as she loved him, she wished he'd put her breast back. She seemed unable to do it herself or even to rise from her vulnerable squat, it was like she was paralyzed with shame and remorse. "They tell me the old man comes here from time to time on the arm of one floozy or another," he whispered, "and next time we'll be waiting for him, right, Ma? Blam, blam, blam!" He popped the other one out. Such a strong-willed child. It was not easy being a mother. In a far corner some men started laughing and singing "The Little Milkmaid" and her son whirled and shot the overhanging lamp off its chain, sending it crashing to their table with a fiery explosion like a fireworks display. "Hey, wow! That's neat!" Second John exclaimed around his tattered wet cigar and shot another lamp down, and then another, jumping up and down and shouting with childish glee. "This is fun, Ma!" Just a little boy at heart, though he scared her with the games he played. He paused, peered inside his diapers. "Uh-oh. Help, Ma! It's number two, I think."

Accustomed to the games Bruce played and prepared for the worst though John (the first one) was, he was still taken aback by the scene that confronted him up at the cabin when he finally arrived. The worst that he'd prepared for? That he'd find them dead. Nevada had suggested that Bruce could be thinking about "checking out," and might take the kid with him. She'd also held off telling him about Bruce's departure with Lenny's child until he'd had a several-hour head start and in his new jet to boot, so whatever John found up there, he figured, would have to be old news. Unless it was all just an elaborate scheme, using a preacher's daughter as bait, to mock John's smalltown proprieties and lure him out of secular duty into holy play, a lesson Bruce never tired of trying to teach him. "At heart a religious man," Bruce called him in his farewell note, "who sometimes lost his way." Farewell? Yes. No bodies maybe, but John had no reason to suppose they were still alive, and Bruce's final instructions gave him every reason to suppose that they were not or soon would not be. Why had he come up here then? To try to stop it, to save his friend from himself and so save a friendship he did not want to lose. John had been guilty of few futile gestures in his life, but this was one of them. Bruce's plane was nowhere to be seen when he flew in, but the cabin, ablaze with florid light in the dark night (his landing beacon), was as though inhabited by a menacing presence, and John entered it with his cocked rifle gripped in both hands, by now supposing that Bruce had the rifle that was missing from his gun case. The cabin had been transformed into a kind of hothouse, brimming with flowers, piles and piles of them, heaped up so high one had to crawl through special wickerwork tunnels to move from place to place. It was like a kid's back-garden fantasy house, except that there were niches along the way with pornographic photographs mounted in them, lit from behind, some little more than marriage manual posturings, others more exotic and violent. John himself was in one of them, that bastard. How'd he get that shot? Here and there: a shoe, a sock, a ribbon. In a mirrored niche, a pair of panties, a spot of dark blood in a bed of white petals. It was all a bit suffocating and John was glad to leave the flowers behind and emerge at last in the main bedroom, which felt like an amphitheater after the claustrophobic tunnels. He was less glad about what he found there: ropes tied around the bedposts, cuffs, whips, including ragged twists of thorny long-stemmed roses and a horse crop, blood-soaked sheets and towels, here and there other stains, more excremental. A flayed summer dress, once white, lay in grisly shreds on the floor and, in a corner, like a proxy for its former owner, a little overnight bag, lifelessly agape, its contents spilled out and crushed underfoot. On the chest of drawers: a sheaf of documents with Bruce's personal cover note, anticipating John's arrival, though perhaps in Nevada's company and not so soon, for it spoke at length about the revised handwritten will, attached, and accompanying power of attorney forms and notarized instructions to be used as authority while the will, for probable lack of a corpus delicti, was contested. All of which clearly enriched their busy little troubleshooter. There was even an envelope of cash for Nevada which, Bruce suggested, should best be laundered before using. "Cleanliness is next to godliness," he wrote, continuing the religious theme introduced in the opening lines: "As a religious man, dear John, you will appreciate what you see here as a sacramental act of extreme devotion and exaltation, and will accept it as guide and precept on your own irresolute route to sainthood. Many years ago, on the eve of your disappointing compromise with the profane world, in that wayside chapel known as the Country Tavern, you effected my own conversion, doubting Thomas that I was, by announcing that what was about to follow was in reality a church service in a holy sanctuary, and indeed it was, one of many such revelations I've been granted in your company. I have ever since been the voice of one crying in the wilderness, calling you back to your true vocation, your existence in nonexistence, your authentic life beyond the edge." The nihilistic wiseass was insufferable, but the "Goodbye, John" at the end still hurt. John scanned the documents: many of Bruce's women were rewarded but Jennifer was not, so probably bad news. Not much he could do about it. Nor about this place either. Finished. Should just burn it down, but he was too practical a man for that, he'd have to put it up for sale. Needed a good purging first, though, and John had a lot of tensions to work off, so he built a fire out in the incinerator, starting with the bedding, clothing, photos, overnight bag, and Bruce's revised will. The flowers and all the rest would follow. He figured he'd be done in time to get home by dawn.

Which was not soon enough for Otis, now gathering his troops together in the lot outside what Bruce called "that wayside chapel." The chief was into crunch time and could use his old team captain to help call the plays, but he could wait no longer. The town had been stripped out, power and phone lines were down, there'd been killings, and from the attacks along the periphery of Settler's Woods—the motelkeeper had been shot, for example—he figured Pauline was getting dangerously hungry. The parking lot of the closed-down Country Tavern looked like a goddamned wrecking yard where she'd stumbled through on her last foray. Of course it often looked that way, junkers being the vehicle of no choice among the Tavern regulars, a lost lot mostly, from the wrong side of town. Otis's side of town. He'd hung out here himself in the old days. The Tavern was popular with the school football team in the off-season, being a place they didn't ask your age, a good hole for poker nights and stag parties and beery rough-and-tumble. A lot of famous events had happened out here, but they were not the sort of stories that ever made it into *The Town Crier*. Then came the army, and what furlough time Otis got he spent here, especially after his old man blew his head off. He was wounded in the war, discharged, came home depressed, took a job helping to build the new highway, and the Tavern became more like home than home. Drank too much. Got into too many fights. Might have got into worse, but John changed all that. Talked him into joining the police force. Built him up as a town hero and the promotions came along fast and steady with John behind him. He'd declared his true love out here on a tabletop and now John had helped him find its true expression. So Otis reduced his Tavern time to football afternoons and when he got married that stopped, too, coming out only when called out. Not often. Mostly having to do with what the regulars called tourists. Their own problems, they sorted out themselves. Some of these guys had, unbidden, joined his posse, drunkenly vowing revenge for the loss of Shag and Chester; Otis told them to go on home (they just smiled) and ordered up an ambulance for the victims. "You sure you want an ambulance, Otis?" one of his officers asked. "There'll have to be an autopsy." "But they're—" "Don't argue with me, goddamn it! Just do as you're told!" He was very edgy, he knew that, couldn't help it. He felt betrayed somehow. Otis hadn't really thought about it until tonight, but the fact was, Pauline had been his best friend, the only real friend he had, and now, though it wasn't exactly her fault, she was ruining it, threatening to turn his whole life since his Country Tavern days upside down, just by being who she was, forcing him to destroy what he loved to save what he loved. She made him feel like the wickedness he was up against was himself. What was worse, a lot of these other guys out here, he'd discovered, felt much the same way he did, only less guilty about it, and that burned him all the more. He'd heard someone waxing sentimental about knowing Pauline from the old Pioneers Day fairs, and before he could stop himself he'd drawn his revolver. Jesus. If he'd been able to see the prick, he might have greased him. Calm down. Remember the Blessed Virgin. He raised his bullhorn. "Okay, we got no time to lose. This is what we're gonna do." Pauline was dangerous, but Otis wanted to resolve the crisis without calling out the National Guard, though he knew he'd have to move fast or the problem would, literally, get too big for them. His tactics were simple: encircle and patrol the periphery with his own boys to try to cut off the escape routes, lead the deputized posse into the center himself, along with the mayor. "What do we do when we find them, Otis?" "Arrest them." That was the official line. In truth, although he didn't want to harm her, he didn't know what he'd do with Pauline if she did surrender. "We gonna rassle them freaks to the ground, are we?" "From what you been sayin', ain't that sorta like tryin' to bring a tree to its knees?"

"Nobody said this'd be easy," Mayor Snuffy yelled out. "Remember, to shoot a takedown, you can always win with a tough ride, but you gotta be aggressive!" "Sure, coach, you take the lady, I'll take the other one." "Maybe if we all stood there with our dicks out, she'd just go down—" "Shut up!" Otis barked. Someone asked who the prisoner was, so Otis, in a biting rage, flashed a light on his ugly mug and introduced them all to Pauline's old man, explaining tersely that he was here because he knew how to track and handle her. Duwayne, his ballcap on backwards, spat disdainfully through the gaps in his teeth, rattled his chains, and hollered out that the terrible Day of Rupture was upon them and there wouldn't be no handling to it, just a lot of blood and tears and gnashing of teeth, Otis cutting off his wind with a rifle butt to the solar plexus and warning him he wouldn't have any teeth to gnash with if he didn't shut his goddamned trap. "Easy, Otis," someone said, and he nearly hit him, too. He passed out flashlights and ammunition, asked the young car mechanic who was soberer than most to stay to the rear to cover their ass, ran radio and weapons checks, tossed his jacket in the patrol car: it was a close, sticky night. Must be a storm brewing. "Listen, have you talked this out with old Gordon?" someone asked. "What's *he* got to do with it?" he snapped. But then he thought better of it. "Send a car to pick him up," he muttered glumly. He stared into the ominous darkness of Settler's Woods. Maybe he should have called out the Guard. Could have used a few choppers with heat-seeking missiles in his arsenal instead of this bunch of bleary-eyed clowns: already a couple of the rifles had gone off accidentally out there in the darkness. For Otis, at times like these, horseplay was a felony. "Okay, men, this is it," he said through his bullhorn. "Let's go." But before they could cross over, the last of his squad cars rolled up with the news that the owner of the Ford-Mercury garage had been shot dead in his own office. "Goddamn it, I don't have time to deal with that shit now!" Otis cried, feeling like someone had just thrown him an infuriating block out of nowhere. "What did they kill him with?" the mayor wanted to know. "One of those," said the officer, pointing at the mechanic's rifle. "Musta happened about the time we was at John's place." "That's the bad news, Otis. The good news is the simpleton's back home again. Big Pauline's in there all on her lonesome."

Of the many famous but unreported events that had taken place in Otis's old stamping ground over the years, not least was the legendary stag party on the eve of John's wedding, the night Bruce was first introduced to this "wayside chapel"—as were all of John's other fraternity brothers, down from the uninursery (as Brains would say) for the grand occasion, among them doleful Brother Beans, he of the inimical wit, contest-winning wind instrument, and Swiss Army knife. Which he was still gripping in his fist when he awoke from a thumping nightmare, a gift no doubt of his thumping hangover, his face in sticky spilled beer and bladder ready to erupt. He'd been out hunting somewhere. In the nightmare, that is. Something gross. He'd had the uncomfortable feeling, he remembered, that he was around spooks of some kind. The Freudian content was inescapable, but Beans escaped it, a knack he had: nothing that entered his head stayed there for long, it was hello and goodbye. Time now, having helloed himself shitfaced, to say goodbye to the moribund Country Tavern. There were a few bodies around, but none Beans knew. Lights, music, movies, bar, all shut down. Beans considered giving the cymbals a crack, just to see if these dead might rise again, but decided his raw brain, which seemed to have got outside his skull somehow, couldn't take it, nor did he relish commerce with any he might thus return, no doubt embittered, to the living. He staggered through the butts and bottles and other detritus of the prenuptial joys to the door and on out into the moonlight, worrying about the long sick walk to town and the critical decision he would have to make ere he set off: to wit, which fucking direction was it? First, though, weewee time. Beans was often deemed an impractical man, but not true. Now, for instance, he used his pee to hose down the dust-caked windows of the Country Tavern, yet another of his good deeds that history would fail to record, wondering as he did so about the peculiar feeling of déjà vu that came over him. Something to do with the absent Brains, his old pal, now greener pastured: faint recall no doubt of one of many such early-morning makings of water (not made really, just, like all of life, borrowed and passed on) they had, after immemorial nocturnal adventures, shared. Out on the lonely road, cranking the throbbing blob on his neck to one side, then the other, he discovered through his pain, just down the way a piece, an old battered pickup parked aslant on the shoulder, and he thought he could make out voices in the woods. He was not alone in the world after all! He picked his way over into the trees where, yes, he could hear heavy thrashing about and grunts and curses, the tenor of which led the ever-rash Beans to a rare exercise of caution before declaring himself: he watched from behind a tree as two men struggled toward a ravine with, what? a body? Yes, a body. Well. The walk to town—run, rather—would probably do him good. But now he worried that they might hear him as he made his characteristically graceless exit and marry the witness's fate to that of their victim, now tossed rudely in the ditch, so he crouched down and, seriously ill but sobering up fast, waited for them to finish their business and take their leave. Their business included pummeling and kicking the body and then pissing on it. "Clean the whore up," one of them tittered: Beans recognized him as Brother John's scowly cousin, the other one being the sullen fat boy who'd organized the stag party. They both looked blitzed out of their skulls. The fat boy asked the other one how much he'd put in, and he said about thirty, forty dollars. "Here, you've just doubled your money," said the fat boy. He tossed something down on the body, a single bill perhaps, pocketed the rest, and the two of them staggered out of there, hooting and snorting and singing "Roll Your Leg Over." Beans waited until he'd heard the doors slam and the old truck grind and rattle away, then crept over into the ravine to examine the body. Naked but for a few wet tangled rags, ghostly white and motionless, but still warm. He put an ear to her breast and heard a beat: so, still alive. In a manner of speaking, for, though her eyes were open, she clearly couldn't see him and she was limp as a rag doll. Just a little kid in dirty school socks with a five-dollar bill resting on her damp tum like a fallen leaf or a sale price tag. Familiar in some odd way, though he was sure he'd never seen her before. Somebody in the movies maybe. He was equally sure he'd never seen the old gent in the leather jacket and ballcap standing beside him with a shotgun either, though he was also weirdly familiar. Like somebody you might meet in a nightmare. "What you been doin' to my little girl, you iniquitous transgressin' sonuvabitch?" From his knees, Beans whispered: "I, uh, I heard noises and came over. Sir." "Great Gawdamighty, Behold my accusséd affliction!" roared his interlocutor and poked the gun up Beans's tender nose. He could feel the puke rising. "Her defilement's in her putrid skirts, her temple's been desecrated all to frickin' hell!" Beans held up his hand asking to be excused, wishing badly he could have the old dream back. He'd been too hasty about waking up. "This unholy shit-soaked abombination has gotta be smited, Lord! Amen! It's time to bring down the final reckonin'!"

She could hear his nasal squawk in the darkness, calling down eternal hellfire and dangnation on all around him, a voice that belonged to her old life though she could not name it, knew only that she feared and hated it, yet loved it, too, in some sad painful way. There were other voices and a distant flickering of lights in the trees like insects in grass. They had passed close by, gone on, were coming back again. Her little friend who'd been helping her all day had vanished into the night and she was alone and hungry and afraid. There was more food somewhere but she couldn't find it, she'd torn up the forest looking for it, until the men arrived and sent her scurrying for shelter. Now she squatted there in the scratchy darkness, trembling, waiting for she knew not what, nor knowing just what she'd do when the waiting ended. As his voice drew near, she remembered that he used to tie her up and yell at her and do bad things to her, though what he did exactly was less clear than how much it hurt and where, and how she couldn't get away no matter how she tried. And he was kind to her sometimes, too, if she did the things he liked, and sometimes he cried and hugged her and called her his little baby, though this was bad because he always got angry afterwards and hurt her all the more. She closed her eyes and sniffed the air and picked up the odor of his old leather jacket, worn and often wet, which smelled like just-turned cider, and there were other smells as well, those of tobacco and body lotions and breaths soured by drinking, and the acrid smells of the sweat of men she might have known (she could almost taste them on her tongue), others strange to her, and the smells, too, of fear and excitement and confused desire, and when she opened her eyes they were standing all together down in the trees, shining their little lights on her, hushed it seemed by what they saw. Most of them had weapons, pointed at her, and bunched together like that, they looked like a single glittering animal with quills erect. A burly little fellow who was familiar to her stepped forward and shouted up at her through a thing in front of his face: "Pauline! We don't aim to harm you none! It ain't your fault, but you been seriously outa line here and you got the whole town shook up!" When he said her name, it brought back something about who she was, and she looked down between her legs and scratched herself there. This got the other voices going again and focused all the lights. "Now stop that, Pauline! Listen to me! You come along peaceful-like and we'll figure out some way to take care of you and get you covered up proper and find you something to eat!" She was still afraid but his voice through that thing soothed her like something on the radio and she thought he might help her like her other friend did and she reached down toward him. He yelped and fell backwards, trying to get away, and there was a bang and then another one and something pinched her in the arm and suddenly there were more bangs and pinches and light beams flying in all directions and all those little men falling and scurrying away like they had wasps in their pants. The burly one jumped up and cried out: "No! Don't shoot, goddamn it! Hold your fire!" Several of them had run off, but those who'd stayed picked themselves up and chittered and laughed nervously and hid behind trees to watch. There was a very funky smell all around her now and she knew they were afraid and there was nothing she could do to make them less afraid. It was then that the one whose squawky voice she had first recognized hopped forward with his hands and feet stuck together and came right up and stood by her knee with a rifle he'd picked up off the ground and shouted out that was enough, he'd send any sinner here to hell and beyond who tried to hurt his little girl. "We ain't fixing to hurt anyone, Duwayne," said the burly one, coming forward. "You done your bit. Now get your ass back here before it gets shot off!" She picked the chubby little fellow up and put him in her lap so the one with the rifle wouldn't shoot him. All the others went scrambling away again and there were more bangs and shouts: "You okay, Otis—?!" "Christ-amighty, what do we do now—?!" "Nothing!" he yelled back, hanging onto her tummy wrinkles. "Don't shoot! It's all right! Just gimme a minute to think!" "It ain't all right, you miserable hind tit of the goddang Prince of Darkness! The time of the tribulation is at hand!" Ah. She remembered that. And the wide gate and the narrow gate, and the rod of wrath that always got stuck into both of them. And something else: that this was the one who'd done something bad to her mother and sister. She'd nearly forgotten that, but it came back to her now clear as a picture in a storybook when everything else in her head was slipping away. She lifted him up to have a better look. "No, I never," he protested. "I done a lotta sinful shit in my time, Pauline, mostly on accounta demon drink, but I never done that." He was wriggling around in her fist, so she squeezed a little harder, while cuddling the other one close against her tummy. "Now hold on, Pauline! Your momma killt your sister with her kitchen shears, and she was gonna git you, too, that whorish old gash had the devil in her, so I, you know, brought an end to her persecutions before she could do her wickedest." An end? "Well, we got company here, Pauline. Let's say I chased her diabolical hellhole off the premises and she ain't been beholden since. Hey! Wait a minute! The wicked hosts is them down there! Smite *them,* not me! Not your own daddy! Pauline—?! *Stop!*"

Rex, though invited to the party, missed all this, his odor not among those that Pauline sniffed out, nor would she have recognized it had it been, for he was not of this place. He of those mighty pecs, traps, and dorsals that Nevada so admired was at the moment jogging toward the road out to his motel, mission accomplished (not of this place, not yet, but soon), not exactly as he'd scored it, but close enough that the original tune could still be heard. He'd been surprised when the scrawny dweeb who'd stolen the truck turned up in old Stu's office out of nowhere like that, but he'd struck him a quick blow with the rifle butt that had caved his wispy-haired conk in like an overripe melon. Okay, so forget the old vendetta against John, my man, play the changes, improvise: put the rifle in the dingaling's hands and let Stu shoot him with the pistol, the perfect crime. He'd pulled the door closed, arranged both bodies, turned to load Stu's handgun, and when he'd turned back the door was still closed but the dingaling was gone. The next thing he'd heard: a van driving away. Hey, more to think about, but no sweat, back to the main theme. The head. Get John. He'd been tempted to speed things up with a car off the lot, why not, the place was half his now, he could take a new Connie for a spin, for example, but, no, play it like it's written, man, save the joyrides for your fat tomorrows. More problems at the airport where he'd intended to return the murder weapon to John's gun cabinet, but this time found the office door locked. He was just resolving that when the police showed up with some drunken tourists, and he thought for a bad moment he might have to waste all these people, few of whom seemed armed, but none friendly. Not a pretty thought, but life was like that sometimes. When the ancient bumpkin with the long snout reached for his rifle, he figured he'd have to be the first to go, but then it leaked through to his hyped-up nut that these yo-yos thought he was on their side. So he was. Cool, man. What's your story? They had to go shoot a woman. Sounded like a dead moose hunt to Rex, not his scene, but he went along with them until he could find a chance to break away. The redneck copper made it easy for him by posting him as a rearguard tailgunner, the only witnesses to his stealthy withdrawal being the preacher's kid and some buddy, sitting by themselves in a ditch he was cutting through on his way out of the woods. He recognized the little dumbfuck more by his sudden panic than by his plastered-up face, which looked like a hockey mask glowing faintly in the dark. By now he'd shed the ax, so Rex just grinned as he loped past and chanted out an "Our Father," his retreat marred only by the shit he had to slop through at the bottom of the ditch. Speaking of slopping in shit, he had a score to settle with old Daph next time he saw her: the bitch had lost her nerve, her tip-off meaning the body'd been found much too soon to suit him. But not tonight, she could sweat this one out on her own. Tonight, after this long run: a good shower, a joint, some jazz, and then, never know, Nevada might drop by, they could celebrate their latest business successes together. A pair of real tycoons, they were. A Porsche came bombing up from behind, roared past, making his sweats flap, then screeched to a spitting fishtailing halt a few hundred yards ahead. Rex knew this wet dream machine. He'd had to bathe and pamper it for John when he worked out at the airport, and had had a run or two in it himself at times when John was up balling some bird in the sky, being careful to set the speedometer back and top up from the airport tanks afterwards, John being touchy about people playing with his toys. So what did the abusive shit want now? Too late to switch tracks; Rex trotted up to the car, ready to punch him out if it came to that, and John's barebreasted daughter opened the door and stepped out and asked him, leaning back and stroking her crotch, if he wanted a ride. It was like Christmas: his alibi, his shot at John, and a hot lick or two to top off the night, all handed to him gift-wrapped. The kid was fried to a crisp, her eyes like stones: her pinpoint-nippled tits showed more expression. Sure, baby, he said. What kind of ride can you give me? Get ready to fly, mister, she said. But, first, off with the sweats. Off—? Take them off! They stink, I don't want them in the car! Come on! Is there nothing but blushing wimps around here? She whipped off her own shorts as a challenge and flung them over the hood into the weeds beyond, glared at him for a moment while he took in the lightning-illuminated sights, then she popped back in the driver's seat and slammed the door. You coming or not, ace? Wouldn't miss it for anything. He kicked off his shit-stained runners, peeled his socks away, stripped off the sweats, the jockstrap. Took his time about it. She watched him all the while but he wasn't sure she could actually see anything, so ripped was she. He wasn't hard but didn't want to be. That's pretty good, she said. You do that in front of a mirror every day? The little ball-buster. Every day, all day, he said, just waiting for you to come along. He dropped his bare ass onto the soft leather. You blow a pretty mean horn for such a scrawny little snotnose. Let's see if you know shit about driving this mother. She hit the floorboard and they spun out of there, popping gravel, hit fifty at the first crossing, were doing better than eighty when she ran the first light. She had a lean adolescent shape with a prominent ass, a little slack, sinewy thighs, breasts like small muffins, was probably still a cherry; should be fun, he figured, in a fragile kiddiefuck sort of way. She stayed on the back roads, not all paved, doing over a hundred on straights and not much less on turns, took intersections without a slowdown, left the ground more than once, then hit rock bottom, never taking her bare foot off the pedal. Okay, mister, she said. Eat me. Sure thing, doll, but that wheel cramps my table manners. I got a— *Now!* she demanded, lifting her left foot off the brake pedal and up on the seat, knee against the door. Get to it, asshole, or get out! He figured this was not the moment to slap the little mink and so instead worked his fingers into her pussy, trying to open up a groove, but it was tight as a green walnut down there. This was going to be like blowing a stoppered sweet potato. As he leaned down to search out a mouthpiece with his tongue, he glimpsed something looming up ahead of them in the road. It was that old humpback bridge out by the selfsame woods he'd just departed, coming at them out of the heavy night at a hundred and fifty miles an hour. "*Now!*" she yelled, and jammed his head down under the wheel between her trembling thighs.

When the murderer came jogging through the ditch in Settler's Woods, Fish—or Philip, rather—was just telling Turtle that he'd finally grown out of being hung up on Clarissa and that now that his sister had taken off, he'd soon be leaving, too, which Turtle was sorry to hear. "Why can't you at least stay until I finish school, so I can go, too?" The breaking up of an old friendship was a hard thing. Though maybe it was already over. Fish, who didn't want to be called Fish anymore, wouldn't even talk to Turtle at the barbecue at first and said he was disgusting and stank like something dead and made him sick. Fish had finally got over his crummy mood and apologized, saying mostly he was just upset about the new baby, but every time Turtle tried to tell him about the amazing things he'd seen, about all the fornicators and the splitting movie screen and the beautiful colors and what happened when his weenie exploded, Fish told him to shut up, he really didn't want to hear about it, and anyway it was stupid and boring, and asked him instead: "What made your old man so mad? Why did he hit you?" "He said it was all my fault, I'd made him lose something." "Lose what?" "He wouldn't say." The police had come to Clarissa's house then and asked for volunteers to hunt a monster lady and Fish had volunteered and then so had Turtle, but the police told them they were too young, go home and go to bed, which got Fish mad again. "I've done more stuff today than those dickheads have done in a lifetime," he said mysteriously, scowling around the bandage in the middle of his face. "Let's go out there anyhow." That suited Turtle. His old man had promised him a good tanning, so he was in no hurry to go home. On the way out, passing under a streetlamp, Fish showed him the hickey on his neck that an older woman had given him that day and told him then all about what had happened in his father's library. "You mean you fornicated her?" "I didn't fornicate her, man, I fucked her! Lots of times!" "Yeah, really? Is that different?" "Sure. It's not what you do, but how you feel about it while you're doing it." He told him about the game the woman had played with him, seeing who could think of the most names for the things she pointed to in the pictures in his father's books. "She said talking dirty made her hot. Proper words like fornication and penis and vagina didn't even count. She always won, of course. But, boy, I really learned a lot!" "Yeah, me too. One thing I saw—" "I said shut up about all that!" "Yeah, sorry, Fish, I keep forgetting." "And don't call me Fish!" "Right." "You know what else she said? She said I had a prong like a Tex-Mex chilidog! She said fucking with me was like dipping a jalapeño pepper in a pot of hot sauce!" "Wow! That's great! Was it?" "Sort of. Better even." They'd reached the meeting place just in time and had hovered at the edge while the police chief gave all the orders and then led everybody into the woods, bellowing through his bullhorn: "We'll all stay together now!" But they didn't. He and Fish peeled off at the ravine because Fish said he saw a man with a gun who was a murderer and who might want to kill him. "Why?" "Because I know he's a murderer. And I fucked his old lady." Fish was full of surprises. Turtle had missed a lot while he was gone. It was nice and quiet in the ravine, and Fish was in the middle of explaining about wet thighs ("I don't know, they just sweat or something, it's messy but it's great!"), he was full of conversation now, so they stayed there to talk awhile. "It was the first time my athlete's feet didn't itch." Turtle sat down on a round stone and, while trying to make himself comfortable, found a sort of wristband and put it on. "Kind of frilly, isn't it? Looks more like something a girl would wear." "I don't care." It was weird talking to Fish in the dark because the white bandage around his nose was like his whole face, only a midget face, it even had little dents and shadows that looked like eyes and a mouth, so Turtle kept talking to the bandage eyes instead of the real ones. "Do you smell something funny here?" Turtle asked. "You know, something like a toilet?" "Are you kidding? I can't smell *any*-thing!" Turtle asked him why Clarissa's father had hit him, and Fish said he didn't have the foggiest idea, it was the biggest surprise he ever got, but it had sort of cured him of ever being interested in Clarissa again. Which was when that man came running past and Fish jumped up like he was going to run away and whispered that was the one, that was the murderer, even though he was reciting the Lord's Prayer and cried out to Jesus Christ from the bottom of the ditch. When he was gone, Fish sat down again and said that praying didn't mean he was religious, in fact just the opposite, that scum was really an atheist and a blasphemer. Turtle tried to get Fish to talk about doing it to the man's wife, but Fish suddenly didn't want to talk about sex anymore. So instead they talked about religion, Turtle asking him what blasphemy was. "It's like swearing, or when you make fun of religion." "You mean, like when we say, 'Our Father which fart in heaven, hollow by Thy name?'" "Like that." "What happens if you do blasphemy?" "You go to hell forever and ever." "Wow, maybe we better stop." "But I don't believe it. I don't believe there is a hell." "You don't?" "I don't know what I believe anymore. I don't think I believe anything. Nevada said religion was for wimps." "Nevada?" "The woman I was telling you about. She made me read the Bible out loud, putting dirty words in place of the ordinary ones while she gave me head. It was maybe the most religious experience I ever had." "While she what?" But before Fish could answer, they heard yelling and gunshots and then people running their way, so they jumped up and started to run, too. When they reached the road into town, they stayed at the edge of the woods so they wouldn't be seen, though Turtle didn't know exactly what the secret was about. He heard the crackle of fireworks and then a spooky noise like a far-off howl and he glanced up in the sky and saw a surprising thing. "Wow! Look!" How did he *do* that?! "Shut up! Here comes a car!" "No, look! Up there!" He had his hands together and his feet and he was pumping wildly like he was riding a pogo stick. Was that the trick? "There's a guy flying!" There was a far-off ripple of lightning just as his ballcap flew off. "Yeah, sure, but come on, duck down before they see you!" "No, really!" But the flying man was already gone and Fish was dragging him down into the bushes as a car shot past on the road. "What are we hiding for? Why can't we just ask them for a ride?" "Don't be such a dumb jerk! Those old farts are completely out of control! They'll shoot at anything that moves!"

When Big Pauline shifted her hips, taking out a grove of trees, and pitched her old man out into the night like a football, all hell broke loose inside Settler's Woods. Otis slithered down out of her crotch and dove for cover as the entire posse, what was left of it, opened fire, shooting wildly but probably hitting more often than not a target hard to miss. Kevin did not even take aim, firing haphazardly over his shoulder as he scrambled away, but he was sure he drilled her more than once, hearing the bullets go *thuck, thuck, thuck* into the soft wall of her flesh. All together they must have hit her with hundreds of rounds, but she hardly changed position except for lifting an arm in front of her face and swiveling a few degrees to take the low-flying bullets in her butt. Most of the flashlights had been abandoned and lay in the weeds now like glowworms, but even in the darkness Big Pauline was easy to see, a huge lowering silhouette, bigger than the trees, faintly illuminated from time to time by distant sheet lightning. In one such flickering, Kevin, reloading, saw that one of her eyes was bleeding like she was crying black tears and her flank appeared to be peppered with zits. She seemed more puzzled and hurt than angry and reminded Kevin of some deer he'd shot before they'd died, and of his own mortality. Well, he shuddered, life, death, it was a great fucking mystery, probably never to be fathomed; he aimed at her wounded eye. It had not been a good day for Kevin, if a day was all it had been, starting with Pauline and her partner cleaning out the clubhouse kitchen after she took that monumental dump in the rough at the fifteenth. She was big then, bigger now. John had lightened his heart with the offer to let him hire a new salesperson for the club shop, but after he'd unexpectedly found the perfect chick, who'd turned up like out of the blue, she'd been snatched away from under his nose while he was, in gratitude, boy-scouting at John's barbecue grill. And then he'd realized, too late, that John wasn't even around to appreciate his good deeds. He'd done a lot of drinking after that, maybe before as well, and now, in these dark damp woods, he was paying the price, his mind blistered and belly churning, kept on his feet and continent by a medicinal hip flask filled with twenty-year-old malt from John's party, an emergency measure he hoped would serve him until he could get back to his rooms at the club and let it all blow. The gunfire had died down a bit: maybe she was dead but just hadn't toppled. But then she let out a pathetic wail, oddly soft and girlish, and they all started firing away again. She swept her hand and took out the tops of half a dozen trees overhead as though swatting at bees, and that prompted a deeper retreat for most. Kevin felt too miserable to move, remaining huddled behind his topped tree and wishing somewhere behind his awesome nausea he were wearing something less luminous than yellow golf pants. Someone yelled at him, Otis maybe, to pull back, he was in the line of fire, so he got up on his hands and knees and began to crawl woozily to the rear, when he felt himself embraced all round by something soft and rubbery and warm and lifted through the air. "Don't shoot!" he could hear someone shout. "She's got Kevin!" "Holy shit!" "Look out!" "She's going to eat him!" It was like being on a fast elevator: his stomach got left behind as the rest of him rose above the trees. His yellow pants had probably had it. With one finger she flicked the rifle out of his hand and he figured that hand wouldn't be worth much for a good while. Up close he could see that her near eye was pretty much gone and her cheek on that side was pocked and bloody. The occasional glimmerings of lightning lit up her white teeth, clenched in a grimace, and the ghostly white of her good eye. She opened her mouth and there was a distant rumble of thunder and more shots were fired. Kevin ducked and she shielded him with her body, turning him upside down, and up came the barbecue. Down, rather. Woof! Out it came! From both ends! Gross! With her free hand she uprooted a tree and swung it like a club through the woods below. There were screams and shouts and someone yelled: "Pull back! Pull back!" Beyond his retching and gut explosions, he could hear them scuttering away, some groaning and shouting for help. He was being held up again in front of her face. He was all alone now and all cleaned out. Felt a little better, not much. More appreciative of his present fix, which made him feel worse. Hand hurt like hell. He could see through his tears that there was a sad inquisitive look on her face, but he was at a loss for words. What could he say to such a woman? "You've got a good natural swing," was what came out. "Really." This made no sense. But what did? It was always his best line and at least it gave her pause. Her grimace faded and her full lips spread into something like a melancholy smile. She licked her lips with a tongue that looked like the backside of a walrus. Her teeth lit up, her eye, there was more thunder: not just summer heat lightning, a storm was on the way. Would that he might live to weather it. If she was going to take a bite, he wasn't sure which end he'd rather she started with. Either way, it was probably the end of his golfing career. Her smile faded. She lifted her nose, sniffed, and a frown crossed her broad brow: yes, no doubt about it, Kevin noticed it, too, there was the smell beyond his own smells of woodsmoke in the air.

Where there's smoke, there's fire, and Clarissa, soaring aloft into unknown realms, could see below a great burning ring of fire, and could feel it, too, the car red-hot beneath her seat, the scorching heat searing her, but as though from inside out, and between her legs a hammer blow, bone crunching bone, that popped the wheel from out her grasp and sent her father's splendid machine bouncing up, as if undriven, from the road, yawing and rolling like an unruddered ship as it rose up into the black night. Take it easy, Clarissa, slow and steady, she seemed to hear her father say, giving her her driving lessons. Foot off the clutch, both hands on the wheel, and ease up on the gas, don't try to set the world on fire, a car's a tool, goddamn it, not a trip. Keep your wits about you! Real power is power you've not yet unleashed, so feel it all but use only what you need. Oh Daddy! I'm sorry! I won't do it again! But it was too late for that, she could not turn back, could not get off the dreadful trajectory that, rashly, ruinously, she'd launched herself upon, and in the grip of blinding panic she rose and spun, while the forest burst into flames below as though ignited by her own wild fury's folly. She'd hit the bridge with bare foot to the floor, thinking what? to rise where Bruce and Jen had gone? Some foolishness in her mind-blown rage, meant to avenge the insult of their snub, and that was when, as the axle bounced and the frame struck sparks and the steep ascent began, the hammer blow was struck and she lost her grip on the suddenly treacherous wheel, the car careening madly as it left the road. And as she overturned and the night sky reeled and the woodland burned below her, she felt a fire blaze up within as though a lightning bolt had struck her where she sat—and suddenly, spinning, she was thrown free (and, hey, buckle up, her father always said, because you never know) and for a moment hung in space, the wild whirl stilled, then down she plummeted, headlong, like a shooting star, falling and falling, landing at last in the little creek below the bridge which received her fall and cooled her burning body as pain engulfed her and her breath left her and her eyes went dark.

As Clarissa in mad careen rose and plummeted, so Waldo, too, riding high, bounced and reared and soared and plunged, but was not thrown, belted in by thighs of steel, and having passed, as love's brave adventurer, from curiosity and carnal desire through wonderment and awe and deep alarm to mortal funk and finally sheer exhaustion, he slept now even as he pitched and rolled, his stentorian snores chorusing those of his wildly bucking mount, this the raucous concert that greeted Lorraine and Trevor upon their arrival at the seventeenth hole, drowning out the remote rumble of threatening thunder, and that left them, for the moment, standing there at the edge of the torn-up green in stupefied amaze. Just before the lights went out in the motel bathroom, Lorraine had picked up on Trevor's anguish and, dressed by darkness, asked: "Who did you think was in here, Trevor?" He hadn't answered, but the impression she'd got looked a lot like Sweet Abandon, and the mystery of the switched pants no longer was one. She'd knotted the bath towel around her waist and led her erstwhile best friend's half-blind husband out to his car ("You see, it's all right, Trevor, just a local power failure . . ."), asking that he drive her to the place where he'd picked up the girl, he muttering, "What girl?," but meekly taking her there just the same, the choral snore then bringing them the rest of the way to the edge of the shaved green whereon these sleeping beauties tirelessly jounced and tumbled. "They're like some kind of perpetual-motion machine," Lorraine said at last, breaking the spellbound silence between her and Trevor, and loosening the towel, sat down on the bench next to the ball-washing pump and the tee to the final hole, her mind less on revenge (certain justifiable cruelties did occur to her) than on trying to find a language adequate to describe the performance being played out before her. But dimly lit: that helped, no squalid detail, please, the broader strokes will do. One such stroke now lifted the entwined duet beyond the cusp of green and down they rolled, losing not a beat as, snoring on, they rose and fell beneath each other, landing in that undulant turf below where Lorraine commonly fluffed her shots, her rakehell hubby back on top once more, flapping loosely in Marge's tenacious clasp, the milky pallor of his broad rump phosphorescing rhythmically in the steady pulsing from the sky. A storm was brewing, and just over the horizon, it seemed to her: something was on fire. She flexed her shoulder, still sore from the shotgun recoil. "You wish to know delight and here you've been sleeping beside it all these years," she said, and Trevor started: "What—?! How—how did you know?" he gasped. "I guessed," she lied. "Should we wake them up?" he asked. "If," she said, knowing full well he didn't think so, "you think you can." The accountant, weighing up the options, sighed ruefully, came over to sit on the bench beside her, his black-patched eye the one she saw. "Why do we even get married?" he asked, a rhetorical question, she knew, but she answered it just the same: "It's an art form, making something out of nothing." The bouncing lovers had fallen into a sand-trap and were now kicking up a sandstorm that partially concealed them from view, carrying the turbulence around with them as they shifted, motors roaring, about the pit. "There is something fast and furious and beautiful about the sudden casual encounter, you know, like yours with Sweet Abandon. There's the feeling of—" "Who?" "That girl from the barbecue." "Oh. But I didn't—" "I know." But it *was* beautiful, he was thinking, or nearly was, or might have been. "Yes, there's a feeling of being free from story, or at least of your own sad hopeless tale—if there's a story at all in the one-off quickie, it is cosmic and essentially electrochemical and you are not a 'character,' only an action." "Yes, I see that," he said, and she saw that he did. It's like a waking wet dream. Did she think that or did he? It was hard to tell, for his thoughts, she saw, were interlaced with hers now with the same sort of rhythmic intimacy that conjoined their more athletic mates, now out of the sandpit and noisily churning up the watertrap nearby; she didn't even need to tell him that prolonged affairs and marriages were forms of storytelling and thus of human artifice, tender but droll attempts to impose meaning on the lonely, empty, and all but intolerable cosmos. She laid her hand on his lap. "Your pants are wet." "I—it was—!" "I understand." She did and knew he knew she did, her hand still where she'd laid it. In the watertrap the froth was rising like ferment around the pounding bodies, all tinted now with the ocherous tones of a wet sky burnished by the distant fire. Something big was burning over there. The broken rhythms of the snoring couple convulsing at the water's edge told Lorraine that the break of dawn, however stormy, was not far off, the night, not yet, but soon, would end, the shades disperse, a thought her one-eyed companion on the bench was having, too. She squeezed. "Why don't you take them off and hang them over a limb to dry?" Because, she started to say but heard his own like thought penetrate hers: "Accountants can be artists, too," he added. "I'm sure. Here. You can put my towel under them if you like."

Settler's Woods was burning. The fire, roaring its hollow inanimate roar as it licked at the black sky, seemed to stroke the lightning out of the night as it stormed inward from all sides toward the center, where a deep darkness also reigned. A great conflagration, unlike any this place had known since Barnaby's lumberyard went up just after the war. The glow of it could be seen all the way across town, as far as the golf club and no doubt beyond. Indeed, on a night so dark and overcast, with the power out, the whole town seemed gilded by it, and many of those not asleep were soon drawn to the source of so eerie a spectacle, some dressed only in raincoats pulled on over pajamas, these gathering sightseers adding to the worries of the beleaguered police chief and mayor and the forces of law and order they'd assembled there, all of whom were now encircling the blazing woods, weapons poised to shoot whatever might come raging out through the billowing smoke and flames. That big thing was in there somewhere, ringed about now by a circle of fire, that was what might come out, that was what people were waiting to see: Big Pauline. The word was, she was wounded and dangerous. People should clear the area. Of course, they pressed closer. How big was she? There were rumbles of thunder in the air, and some of the armed men said that might be her, walking around in there. She could kick a car like a football, they said. There were rumors she had eaten people alive.

"She picked her own father up and threw him so far outa here he ain't been seen since!" She was once a woman, known to many in the crowd, intimately to more than a few, and as a woman, was wed to the town photographer, surely soon to be a widower and so to be pitied, and indeed he was pitiable, standing there at the fire's edge in a fat gap-mouthed stupor, his bulging lashless eyes blankly reflecting the flames, looking, without his familiar camera and bagful of lenses, as though he'd left his wits somewhere as well. He seemed to be the only person present who did not know why he was here. The police chief wished, frankly, he'd not had the man brought out, dazed and clumsy and unreliable as he was, useless to him and a likely casualty if things got worse, and they showed no signs of getting better. The tossing of his prisoner, for whose well-being he was responsible (how was he going to explain all this to Bert and the boys upstate?), was the act of terror that had convinced him finally that this creature who was once his friend had to be destroyed. Before that, he'd been clinging, while clinging to the soft ridge of flesh just below her navel, to the hope that they might somehow find a peaceful resolution to a public crisis that had, increasingly, become a personal crisis of his own: not just that as a prisoner of sorts, he was in the line of fire and could get killed (he was not afraid, he had been through all that in his days as an expendable grunt in a deeper, darker woods, and what was a football lineman but a body in the line of fire?), but more that he was being forced to choose, loving both, between order and the embodiment, not to put too fine a word on it, of its contrary. Forcibly snuggled up against her warm rumbling belly during her interrogation of her father, he'd gazed up at the tender monument of her overhanging breast, rimmed with a pale radiance whenever lightning rippled, and felt himself at the edge of some fundamental revelation and some fundamental change, as though . . . as though he might . . . But then she'd cocked her arm and spread her legs to pitch the old goat, and his brief visionary moment over almost before it had begun, he'd fallen out of her relaxed grip and slithered down through her dense jungly bush, barely escaping being flattened as, hurling herself forward to complete her throw, she'd slapped her thighs together just as he'd dropped between them. The mayor and the deputized posse had opened fire to cover his escape as he scrambled out from beneath the beetling mass of her squatting haunches, limping from his fall, and she'd groaned and lashed out at her tormentors, tearing up the space around her and sending them all scattering in frantic retreat. All but the young golf club manager who, slow to react, had got snatched up by her, whether as hostage or provender, it was hard to tell from down in the trees. His capture had restricted them to shooting at her bottom half only, which only added to her rage without bringing her down, her savage counterblows forcing them into ever deeper withdrawal, dragging their wounded with them. It was the mayor who had finally suggested they burn her out. "No choice," he'd said, and most had agreed. The police chief had objected, but he'd lost his bullhorn, and could be heard by only a few and those few had little sympathy with his dithering. They were all frightened and exhausted and nothing else had worked. "But what about the guy in the banana pants?" "He's dead, man. She ate him." And so they'd spread out and encircled Settler's Woods with gas cans and torches and, on a signal passed by honking horns, had set the fire that now raged, sending flames soaring into the sky and drawing townsfolk to its edges by the hundreds, more arriving every minute with blankets and coffee thermoses and instant cameras in spite of ominous signs of an approaching thunderstorm and repeated police warnings that everyone should return home immediately or face possible arrest. Some scoffed at the extravagant accounts and said they doubted any such creature was in there, but others said she was in there all right, they'd seen her, plucking trees like Brussels sprouts and eating people whole, chucking them into her jaws like breakfast sausages. There was a sudden clap of thunder, and the skeptics in the crowd wisecracked about that ("I suppose she just let one!"), but an old boy from the Country Tavern, showing them his fresh scratches and bruises and torn shirt, said it was no joke, that was one mean fucking mother in there, and he gave them all a chilling account of what had happened to poor old Shag and Chester earlier in the evening. "Damned right, flat as a doormat, I shit you not!" A woman in a checkered nightshirt and anorak, sipping coffee, wondered aloud where John was, wasn't this the night of his Pioneers Day barbecue, and someone said hadn't he been killed in that terrible accident at the humpback bridge they'd passed coming out here, and, no, argued another, that must have been someone else, John had flown upstate to call out the National Guard. Others said they'd heard his daughter had been abducted and possibly his wife as well, and there were reports that the motel at the edge of the Woods was on fire and its owner shot, that babies had been stolen from their cribs to feed the monster lady and that churches had been desecrated, and that the owner of the Ford-Mercury garage and his wife had been brutally murdered in their own home or else in an ambush out at the car lot. "They say the manager of the hardware store might have done it." "I'd heard it was the simpleton who was helping Big Pauline." Thus, at the edge of the burning forest, the wild rumors spread like the fire itself, now closing in on the dark center of the woods and setting the air in there madly awhirl. Suddenly, there was a blinding light and a terrific explosion as a thunderbolt came smashing down as though sucked into the woods' core and people were knocked to the ground or fell over one another and everyone pulled back, even the police and their deputies. They'd all heard it: something like a haunting baleful wail, or maybe it was just the whine of the whirlwind at the center of the great ring of fire, but now the storm began in earnest and the lightning crashed about them and the sudden hurricane-force gales whipped up the forest flames, and sparks flew in all directions. "It's gonna get outa hand!" someone shouted, and indeed little wildfires were starting up everywhere and people's clothes and hair were getting singed as they tried to escape the burning shower and there were fears the sudden violent winds might drive the fire into town. "Oh my God! I left my kids home sleeping!" "Damn it, Otis! I told you this was a bad idea!" But then the rain began to fall, great lashing torrents of it, upending people as they ran toward their cars, turning the ground underfoot almost instantly into a river of mud through which they slipped and splashed and crawled on all fours, the incessant flashes of lightning cracking around them like celestial whips, herding them, soaked and terrorized, homeward to their dark empty beds.

Outside the saloon a storm was raging, echoing the turbulence within as Veronica, changing Second John's dirty diapers on a wooden cardtable, got set upon by all the barroom rowdies offended by her little boy's childish antics with his pistol. They were both sprayed with beer and pelted with cigar butts and peanut shells and candy wrappers and lashed with a thunderous barrage of uncouth insults, mostly having to do with the contents of his diaper but some calling his origins into question and others deriding her exposed backside, which she couldn't help. It wasn't fair. "If I had an ass like that, I'd sell advertising space!" "The last time I saw an ass like that, it was pulling a plow!" That didn't stop them from attacking it, she could feel them crowding up behind to make painful use of it as Maynard so often did, and she certainly didn't like it, but what could she do, she had both hands full and open safety pins in her mouth and her baby was crying: "I been caught with my diapers down, Ma! You gotta hold them off any way you can!" The few gas lamps he hadn't shot down were swinging on their chains as though buffeted within by the storm without, sending shadows flying about like wheeling bats, and tables and chairs were crashing as the men clambered forward, their vile threats and humorless laughter like a hot beery breath on the back of her neck. Though she shielded her son from the worst of it, they were both being drenched in buckets of beer, her backside their last line of defense, all too easily breached. There was nothing to do finally but pick the baby up, dirty bottom or no, and make a run for it. But she could find no way out. All the exits were blocked. The men surrounded them, brandishing hard penises and baring their tobacco-stained teeth as they closed in. The saloon seemed on fire from the dancing light of the swinging lamps. "We're done for, Ma!" Second John cried, clinging painfully to her breasts. "Do something!" He was slippery and getting heavy, she almost couldn't hold him, and the smoke from his cigar was making her nose sting and her eyes water. Then, just as she was about to collapse from exhaustion and despair, First John's wife came in with a fresh diaper, made the men put their penises back and return to their tables, settled the lamps down, took the baby's cigar away and threw it into a cuspidor, cleaned his bottom, gave him a change, and wrapped him up in a towel the barman gave her. "Come on, now, let's send him back where he came from," she smiled, and led Veronica out the door to a windy railway platform, where a train was just pulling in through the thunderstorm. "I didn't know the train still came through here," Ronnie said, putting her breasts back inside. "You have to know where to find it." Her friend handed the baby to the conductor, who tossed it behind him, and the train pulled out, seeming to pull the storm away with it as it went, and Ronnie started to cry. "It's all right now," her old classmate said gently, helping her up out of the lawnchair. "It's letting up. You can go home now." "I'm sorry," she sniffled. "I'm afraid I split the seat . . ." "It's not your fault. It's been left out too many times in the rain." "No, I meant—" "Here, you're completely soaked, poor thing. I've brought you your nightgown, which is dry at least." She took off the ruined linen dress and dried herself with the towel offered her and pulled on the nightgown and thanked her hostess for the lovely party, begging her pardon for having stayed so late, then stumbled out by way of the darkened driveway and headed wearily home through the wet streets in the lightless early dawn.

Though there was no sign in the sky that the black stormy night had ended, Barnaby, sitting alone by his window watching the wet orange glow that had taken his daughter away get swallowed up in the darkness, knew by his own knowing that dawn had arrived. All night, she'd been at his bedside, listening to his bitter tale of duplicity and betrayal, but then the glow had appeared which, even in his crackbrain confusions, he knew to be a fire, though he'd thought it was his own house burning, the one they'd all lived in when she was a little girl and Audrey was young and beautiful. He'd worried aloud about Audrey's safety, her life might be in danger, and his daughter had said, yes, she'd better go see, but not to worry, she'd be back soon, get some rest. "Be careful!" he'd rasped as she left, though he couldn't be sure she'd heard him. "I love you!" Had it really been his daughter? Maybe, maybe not. In retrospect, she'd looked a little like the resident nurse, at least when she departed, if not when she arrived. He'd staggered to his chair by the rain-lashed window to watch the lightning explode and the rain whip past like crashing tides and the fire slowly die and to wait for his daughter's return, though now he no longer expected her. What a night. He was a crazy old buzzard, like the lady said. Thought he could change what could not be changed, a delusion he shared with builders the world over. He'd found the gun he'd intended for saner purposes and shot up the place, lucky not to have killed someone. Or unlucky. Though he now knew that the woman who had left with Mitch last night was not Audrey, he still felt deceived, certain now that the heart of the woman whose hand he'd won had never been won at all. That silly woman who'd pretended to be her knew more than she knew. Audrey, too, had only pretended to be Audrey, or at least the Audrey who'd lived with him. The knowledge saddened him and added to the sorrow and emptiness that engulfed him in these rare dawn moments of lucidity, but he knew it was more his fault than hers. He the builder who had not built well. That house deserved to burn. The only light on the horizon, now gone, too. He imagined the charred ruins: his hopes. His daughter wandering through them, grieving: his legacy. He wandered there, too—tottered and shambled, rather, all grace vanished—and he tried to speak to her but could not. Though he could almost reach out and touch her, there was a distance between them that could not be bridged, as between past and present, or between part and whole. He shuffled through a door, thinking about his burning lumberyard. The waste, the waste! He looked at his image in a mirror and was not surprised to find it broken up into ill-fitting fragments. He had more than two eyes, which accounted for his lack of focus, a mouth whose parts did not all join up. Of course, it was the mirror that was broken, though it cast back a truer image than when it was whole. He leaned forward, bracing himself on the sink. It was crunched in the middle with cracks radiating outwards like a spiderweb. Had he tried to drive a nail in it? Or had Audrey?

Across town, Audrey—or Opal, rather: that dangerous game was over—had also, as though in mirror image of that broken man, been sitting sleeplessly by the window, watching the glow of the fire fade in the sudden crashing downpour, the downpour itself slowing fading as though dying with the fire. It was dawn, but a dawn that shed no light. The only light shed had been shed within and that in the blackest depths of the night when that old fool, who was her annoying husband and also an old family friend she hardly knew, started shooting at her while she was sitting on the toilet. As Audrey, she knew then that, as Opal, she had been her disappointed husband's second choice, not merely when he'd married her, but for all the years thereafter while Audrey was still alive. Had she and Mitch consummated their affair? Even as Audrey, whose memories of her past romances were suspiciously dim, she could not be sure, although, as Opal, she was certain they had had a fling of some kind even if nothing came of it, Audrey being, for all her harsh banter, something of a tease and more insecure than Opal had ever supposed. But it didn't matter what they'd actually done. Audrey had married Barnaby, perhaps to avenge an imagined wrong, or a real wrong, for Mitch had always shamelessly played the field (he had?), and Mitch had replied in kind, their marriages a private dialogue between them, their partners little more than analogues of spite. So shattering had this revelation been, so complex and disturbing her feelings about it, she'd not even been able at first to rise from the stool when Mitch turned up at Barnaby's door. For, as Audrey, she now loved Mitch in a way that, as Opal, she never could nor ever would, while, as Opal, she resented his intrusion upon this revelatory drama, still unfolding, and at the same time was grateful to him for his timely rescue from a crazed old man. With whom, however, she now felt a deep bond not unlike that of an understanding lover, or at least the best of friends, and for whom she feared more than for her would-be rescuer when the gun went off. Which startled her and made her jump up off the seat, for, as Opal, she was embarrassed to be caught so compromised, even though she somehow felt it was she who was catching Mitch with Audrey, who wished to be caught in dishabille, so to speak, by an impetuous lover whom she would rebuke even as he burst in and laid eyes upon her, refusing his advances in spite of the gallantry for which Opal was so grateful, while gazing directly in his eyes as she slowly pulled her panties on, letting him know clearly what it was she was refusing him, even as Opal pulled them on with modest haste, too flustered even to remember to flush. All of which made her start to cry, whether as Opal or Audrey, she wasn't sure, and when she opened the bathroom door and saw them both standing there, her husbands, or her lovers, one of them with a gun in his hand, the other one tottering as though he'd been shot, it was all so mixed up that she was suddenly terror-stricken, and all atremble, ran over to embrace one of them, but she didn't know which until Mitch opened up his arms ("You all right, hon?") and then, thank goodness, she had no choice. Mitch had wanted to call the police, but she'd dissuaded him, saying, since no one was hurt, they should let John handle it, and she'd begged him to take her home (to Opal's home), she couldn't bear to see another soul tonight, if he wanted to go back to the party he could go without her if he liked, and then, looking as though she'd just rebuffed him (who had he thought she was?), he'd done just that, or gone somewhere, at dawn gone still.

Maynard's fright was of a similar order: confusion, exposure, and imminent danger. When he'd awoken he'd not known where he was. He was in a darkened bedroom, not his own, fully dressed, even to his shoes, and curled up around the backside of a sleeping woman, his hands cupping a soft smooth bottom under a silken nightie's hem, his face in her loosened hair. His wife's? No. Then—? This sweetness . . . His whole body had gone rigid as though suffering a seizure when the truth hit him, and he'd nearly swallowed his tongue stifling the cry that rose to his throat. He'd lain there in a kind of ecstasy of terror, not knowing what to do, but not wanting to let go of the greatest joy he'd ever had in life, had literally in his grasp. That bottom! Hers! The piece of silk between his cheek and pillow, dampened by his tears, had then been freshly dampened, but now by tears of incredulous bliss, his hands suddenly aware of their being in the world in a way no part of him had ever been before. He'd longed to press beyond where now he touched, but had been afraid to break a spell that held him as much as her in thrall. She'd stirred slightly, and Maynard had felt a fury at his chest that it would not stop heaving, and at the noisome breath he breathed and at the scratchy beard that roughed his cheeks, the clothes that walled him off from her, the odors of his unwashed body which rose now to thwart all hopes of declaring, even by the gentlest gesture, the desperate love that so consumed him and made him tremble, head to foot, this trembling angering and frightening him as well. He prayed to let this moment last forever, but it couldn't, he knew, no moment could, something had to happen and something did: a car pulled into the drive below, startling him so, he jerked his hands away, and then, the damage done, no way to put them back. Nor had he time or liberty: he heard the car door slam and knew he was a dead man if John should catch him here. He slipped out of the bed (she sighed and rolled over, making his stuttering heart race the faster, his stomach turn) and crept from the room, trying desperately not to fart until he reached the hall, and succeeding only so far as the door. "John—?" she murmured sleepily. John was coming in the door downstairs, which one, the back? The side door by the drive? Maynard had forgotten the precious garment soaked by his lovesick tears, but too late now. He heard steps below and ducked into a room where a child with two heads stared at him from under a blanket on the floor. "Nighty-night," he whispered, terribly confused, and again his gut betrayed him, making the two heads giggle and whisper. This was worrying. He slipped out, listened from the head of the stairs: John was in the kitchen opening the refrigerator door, popping a beercan, shushing the dogs. That's right, the dogs, he had forgotten about the dogs. What could he do? Crawl out a window and jump from the roof? Hide in a closet with all his gases until John had slept and gone again? Cut his throat? Finally, what in a blind funk he did was take off his shoes and, muffling the stuttering put-put from his treacherous behind as best he could, he'd tiptoed barefoot down the stairs, through the hall, past dining room and living room, and on out the front door into the soggy dawn. It worked! Or nearly. John called out from inside the house just as he reached the front sidewalk and knelt to put his shoes back on: "Call me later on today, Maynard! I've got a proposition!"

"John—?" "Yes." "Something terrible! Clarissa—!" "I know. I saw the woods smoldering when I flew over and stopped off there. They told me." "I was with her until now. She was so brave—" "So they tell me. She was pretty well sedated by the time I got there." He set his tumbler of whiskey beside her earrings on the night table, sat down on the edge of the bed to work his boots off. "She'll be in traction awhile and have a sexy scar or two, but she'll be okay." "What-what's all that?" "Some flowers for you." "Oh. That's very nice, John. It was sweet of you to remember." "I dropped some off at the hospital, too. A lot of people got hurt at the fire. Did you know Dutch got shot?" "I'd heard." He stripped off his leather vest and jeans, his shorts, tossed aside the panties lying on his pillow, and stretched out beside his sleepy wife to finish off his whiskey. Remember what? Had he missed their anniversary? "When I find out how she got the keys to the Porsche, somebody's going to eat them." "There was some man with her." "I know. A guy who used to work for me." "They say she was—" "My guess is they both were." He'd been found in sweats, but the pants were on backwards. "It was just lucky your secretary was driving past." "Yes, luck or something." "She pulled Clarissa out of the creek and gave her the kiss of life. The doctor said she would have died." Flying back, he'd traced out the series of Nevada's double crosses, of himself, of Bruce, of everyone, Lenny's boy included. He'd concluded that Clarissa never was a target, not of Bruce anyway, and so he'd probably punched Jennifer's brother for the wrong reason, though the kid no doubt deserved it for something all the same. And now, it was just too convenient that Nevada was at the wreck at almost the same time it happened. Had Clarissa been a target after all? Was that why he'd been lured out of town? "Is Bruce all right?" his wife murmured. "I don't know. I don't think so." "I'm very sorry, dear." Sleepily, she curled into his outstretched arm. "It was all just a joke to him," he said, setting his glass down, and rolling over between her thighs. She lifted her knees, adjusting to his weight, hooking one foot atop his butt. "A joke?" "Life. His problem was, he couldn't wait for the punchline." Watching his town seem to sink away and vanish into the shadowy earth as he lifted away on his wild Bruce chase, he'd felt that something was being taken away from him, something valuable he could not afford to lose, though he could not quite name it, and the feeling had stayed with him all through the night, even as he labored to cleanse the cabin of all evidence of that ruthless overweening motherfucker's violations, indeed of his very existence (had the puffed-up asshole greased himself? good riddance!), an inner purging matching the outer one, and that feeling of some impending but ineffable loss had pursued him until his return at dawn when once again his town had risen up out of the misty soil below him, its resurrection signaled by the dying flames and smoke from Settler's Woods, sent up like a beacon in the disintegrating night as the violent storm which he'd had to skirt sheathed its weapons and withdrew. She kissed his shoulder as he rolled away, picked up his glass again. Loose Bruce was gone, like a joke when it's been told, and like a joke, once heard, you really didn't want to hear it again. But . . . "I feel like some part of me has died," he admitted. "Oh, that reminds me," she said with a sleepy yawn. "Stu's dead." "Stu?" "He was killed. And they ruined all his old records." "But wasn't he here at the barbecue?" "He never turned up. I tried to call Daphne, but her phone was off the hook." Why did that old jughead's death make him think of Marie-Claire? John didn't know, but now he knew what had been missing up at the cabin, that feeling of unnameable loss that he couldn't put his finger on. Bruce had taken away with him Marie-Claire's slashed canvas.

The funeral for old Stu, held two days later, was a memorable event whereat it was proved that one could indeed enjoy an old joke twice, and twice again. The church lawn, before and after the brief memorial service, was filled with a great congregation of ordinary townsfolk, young and old, all recalling jokes the old car dealer had told them, as well as amusing anecdotes about his life, which in retrospect seemed funnier than when he was alive, and though most had shared in these events, especially the older generation, and so had heard all the stories before, the sudden violent death ("Talk about your punchlines," someone said, and another added: "It's like the one he liked to tell about the guy who took a leak at the power plant . . .") of the town's favorite raconteur had, just as suddenly, made them all new again: there was a lot of laughter out on the church lawn that day, sighs and tears, too, and expressions of alarm that such a thing could happen in this town, but even more laughter, and everyone agreed, they don't build 'em like ole Stu any more, that old boy was a vintage model. There were a lot of flowers in the church, as though to provoke the corpse into a resuscitative sneezing fit, but the service itself was a soberer affair, mainly out of respect to the widow, who seemed to have lost her sense of humor and was taking it all pretty hard. She'd obviously been hitting the bottle and looked haggard and distraught, and when John brought her into the church during the singing of "Amazing Grace," she stumbled and nearly fell and those near her heard her hiss: "Stop that, damn you! Go away and leave me alone!" Who was "you"? Most knew. It was what she'd told the police: it didn't matter who'd pulled the trigger, it was that old ghoul's fault. The police had their own more mundane theories. No one had as yet been charged, but the manager of the downtown hardware store, who'd skipped town in dramatic fashion after the killing, was the prime suspect. Rumors of a violent past, a prison record, a falling-out with Stu over a lemon he'd been sold, money troubles. The general view in town was that Floyd might have done it, might not have, but nobody liked him anyway. Under the circumstances, it was something of a surprise when the fugitive's wife turned up at the funeral and timidly took a seat in the back pew. She sat alone, others shying away as though they might catch something if they got too close, until John's wife came in, no doubt straight from the hospital, and sat down beside her and took her hand in hers for a moment, which startled her at first, but then she calmed down. As always, a healing presence, John's wife, and the pew soon filled up, people acknowledging that the poor woman was only trying to do the Christian thing and had herself been effectively widowed by the tragedy. As the preacher, whose own daughter was missing and feared dead, reminded them, the point of many of the deceased's favorite jokes was that things were not always what they seemed and there was often a consoling surprise at the end, and he asked them to pray, in these times that tried the human spirit, for strength and guidance, recalling for many of the mourners, perhaps on purpose for he'd heard it told many times at his own expense, old Stu's story about the young preacher and the old widow on their wedding night: "You just take care of the strength, Reverend, and leave the rest to me."

Ellsworth, reporting in the revived *Town Crier* on the funeral of the popular owner of the Ford-Mercury dealership, whose life had come to such a cruel and senseless end, took note of the minister's tribute to the dear departed's renowned sense of humor, which had provided so much strength and consolation for others in the community in the past, adding, in his own words, that death may carry away the person, but the stories, like rocks dropped in a stream, remain. This relative immortality of the stories vis-à-vis their actors and tellers had been much on Ellsworth's mind of late as he emerged from what he thought of as his "long dark night of the soul" to engage with the human world once more, this world of rock-hard stories and transient lives to which, as chronicler, he'd been so long devoted, but which, in his absence, had passed without report, a delinquency he deeply regretted and said so in the double issue that marked the *Crier*'s return, promising to fill in all the missing news items by way of "I Remember" columns from his readers, which he solicited in his apology and also in person wherever he went, at the car dealer's funeral, for example. He reported on that funeral, and on the annual Pioneers Day parade (for which he found few reliable witnesses, but his files were full of suitable archival material), and on the burning of Settler's Woods, which he'd observed at a distance from his own second-floor window (a shocking moment as light bloomed suddenly in the impenetrable night: where *was* he—?!), and the casualties ensuing therefrom, including the town photographer's wife, who was also his professional assistant, a tragedy of immense proportions, which was all he would say about it, and on the deplorable accident at the humpback bridge (in a separate editorial he appealed, once again, for the removal of that perilous structure), and in short, on all the old news that he could gather in, catching up as best he could on all the deaths and births, the marriages and engagements, burglaries, accidents, operations, golden anniversaries, arrests, birthdays, Little League and bowling team scores, church attendance figures. What he couldn't report on was where he'd been exactly or how long he'd been there, for, returning as though from another dimension as the fire rose and fell on the horizon and the terrible thunderstorm crackled and boomed around him, he did not know himself. Something had passed, but it hadn't felt like time, and in a place that was more than a place and yet no place at all. After the storm had exhausted itself, he had, as though compelled, gone out to Settler's Woods to gaze, aghast, upon a charred and misty dreamscape which seemed to have sprung directly from the dark abyss of his own imagination. He'd remembered something Kate the librarian had once said to him about this seeming interplay of art and life: the formal resonances between them, she'd said, suggest that both are organic human enterprises, so we shouldn't be surprised when they sometimes seem to live inside each other. But he *was* surprised, and had felt dreadfully empowered and hopelessly vulnerable at the same time, and not just a little disoriented by his recent adventures. He had half expected to find the Stalker wandering there, blind and reproachful, but had discovered instead his old friend Gordon, standing alone in the mud at the edge of the smoldering woods, soaked through and staring blankly into the black wet heart of the devastation. "Are you all right?" he asked. Gordon, unshaven, hands in his pockets, continued to stare straight ahead. "The stillness . . . ," he said. There *was* a deep quiet all about. Of course the birds had fled. There were, here and there, a few deep green patches spared by the fire, but most of the treetops and foliage had been burned out, leaving only the blackened trunks and naked branches like scorched arms reaching up out of the earth in anguished horror. Nothing moved except the gray wisps of smoke snaking upward through the dripping branches. "It's over," Ellsworth said, with a finality that surprised even himself, and his friend somberly nodded.

It was the stillness that also most struck Columbia when she awoke in the first wet pallor of that dawn, still standing by the glass door of the drugstore, staring out on the empty downtown streets as though she'd never shut her eyes all night. She had, though, had slept at least, eyes open or closed, for she'd dreamt that she'd been caught out in those very streets in the storm with no clothes on (she was hunting for her pajamas, which someone, Corny maybe, had mischievously hidden out there), and was being chased by the doctor with one of Gretchen's plastic penises and a scalpel, crying: "Nurse! Nurse! It's time for your pharmaceuticals!" It was still raining when the dream faded and she found herself awake, but the storm was letting up, the thunder rumbling now in the far distance and a pale light rising as though from off the streaming pavement. Her legs, as they'd been in the dream, were like fat lumps of lead, she could hardly move them, so she leaned there a moment, shifting her hips slightly to restore the circulation, and while she was doing that she saw a curious thing which made her think she might still be dreaming: two people in nothing but their shirts staggering barefoot down the slippery street in the rain, holding each other up with hands clapped round on naked hips. A sight to see, even for persons in the medical profession, there was probably even a statute against it, but there was not much they could do about it. They had helped Trevor load log-sawing Marge into his car just before the storm hit, then had dashed away through the whipping gales and lightning flashes to pick up their old stationwagon, parked by the clubhouse, forgetting, having got so used to going about as they were, that they had no pockets—Waldo, yawhawing, slapped his beefy thighs—and thus no keys. They'd had a good laugh about that and, rather than break the car door and sleep under a leaky roof with more problems on the morrow, had decided to walk on home, dressed in the storm. And had had a good time doing it, pausing from time to time to rest their tender feet, and play around a bit like kids in the crashing rain, Waldo having awakened on the edge of the green in Lorraine's arms, completely mystified, but in a jolly and appreciative mood, saying it was the best he'd ever had and he wanted more of it; it was like the old days, football weekends and beach parties and monkey business in the bushes behind the sorority house. They were met at their front door by the police who said they wanted Waldo to come with them immediately, as soon as he got some trousers on, his purple pair being presently, they reported with a knowing smirk, in police custody. The guy he'd shot, they said, was not expected to pull through, and they had to get Waldo out to the hospital while the fellow was still alive and could identify him. "Haw," said Waldo in utter amazement. In a way, it was good they were there because they also lacked their house keys and the police helped them break in. Did they really think Waldo had done it? Lorraine couldn't tell. She couldn't tell what Waldo was thinking either nor what the cops thought about her bare ass which they were staring at as if it were a major clue to some ghastly crime, or perhaps the crime itself, and that gave her such a tremendous sense of relief that she lay down on the floor while Waldo was still pulling his pants on and fell sound asleep. What Waldo was thinking about was how simple life was but how you could never figure it out, a paradoxical verity underscored by his visit to the hospital bedside of his old bud Dutch who was said to be barely hanging on. "He's lost a lot of blood. And other things." They had Waldo's missing golf pants there and his old shotgun, and when he asked where they'd found them, they said out at the motel before it burned down and had he been in such-and-such a room last night? "I mighta been. But how did the goddamn gun get there?" Dutch, who'd already told these yo-yos when they dragged the sniveling accountant in that he'd shot himself, stirred himself enough to growl: "You loaned it to me." "Oh yeah, right," Waldo said. "I did—?" The meathead. "Hey, Dutchie! What're they talking about, burned down? What the hell happened to you, old man?" Fuck off, Dutch said, or might have said, and as Otis's cowboys took the boob next door to visit the guy they were now calling Pee Patch ("Haw! Who?"), Dutch sank back into the drugged stupor which, he supposed, was all the rest he'd know of life, and all he wanted to know. It was like he'd told John when he'd dropped by with an armload of flowers not long after his wife had been in: the last picture show was over, he was ready for the fade-out. John and his wife had been out to visit their daughter, also in the hospital for some reason. In intensive care, they told him. Sounded serious. And was. When she woke up, full of a dull leaden pain all through her body, her mother was sitting beside her. "Mom! Where have you *been—?!*" she cried, and realized there might not be any sound coming out. But her mother heard her somehow: "Right here beside you, sweetheart, all the time." She thought she heard her go on to say she was a murderous little shit and her dad was thoroughly pissed off at her for what she'd done, but saw that it wasn't her mother then but Nevada. Or else her dad, it was all a blur, who said, no, he wasn't angry and told her to hang tough when she broke into dry tears (she could move nothing, nothing at all), adding that he loved her, though by then she'd probably passed out again. When John asked Alf what her chances were, Alf said she was a strong healthy youngster and she should pull through, but it would be painful and would take a while. There wasn't much she hadn't mashed or torn or broken, she'd need some repairs, now and later on, and might end up with a permanent brace. Which was what he'd told her mother as well before he sent her home to get some rest, longing for the same prescription. It had been one crisis after another, and Alf was dead tired, but then he was always dead tired at dawn, and he'd been buoyed up through the interminable night by the lifting of a great weight off his shoulders, or, rather, off his finger: that polypous lump, which in his imagination had grown larger than the body which he'd supposed contained it, clumsying him dangerously in the emergency room and making it difficult for him even to do up his fly, had suddenly vanished as lightly as did the night give way to dawn. About that same time, Clarissa's mother had entered the intensive care center, looking worried but well, a welcome sight, and he had known then that everything would be all right, and confidently told her so, though he had no clear medical reason for saying so. She'd stayed on, watching over her daughter, while he'd attended the succession of traumatized patients who came rolling in on gurneys like floats in a nightmarish parade, and he'd felt watched over as well, more sure of himself than at any time since the war when he had Harriet at his side, and indeed he'd had the sensation that beautiful young nurse was next to him the whole night through, a remarkable experience he intended to tell Oxford about the next time they met for coffee, though he could have told him on his way home, because Oxford was already up, feeding the youngest ones and getting them dressed, coaching the older ones in their breakfast preparations and telling them all about the games they'd play together that day. One of the triplets had been awake all night with a tummyache, so he'd been up when Gretchen proudly brought his errant son home like a trophy from a hunt, and had been able to help her bandage up poor Corny's head. "He must have taken a wallop from that big home-wrecking jezebel," she'd explained, blushing happily as she pushed her spectacles up on her nose. "Maybe it will teach him a lesson." Oxford had slept little, waking ahead of the children, worried about Columbia who'd never in her life stayed out so late, but she came home at dawn, a bit surly, saying she'd got caught out by the storm and had had to spend the night in the drugstore, and had Gretchen come out of her bedroom yet? Oxford said she hadn't, and indeed, except to attend to basic human necessities, she didn't come out for a whole week, and Oxford had to fill in for her down at the drugstore and watch the eight grandchildren, too, which in truth he enjoyed, and neither he nor anyone else was surprised when a beaming Gretchen finally came bobbing out into the kitchen one morning and, perched jauntily on her short leg, announced that she was almost surely expecting again. Which depressed Columbia no end, even though she had seen it coming, and made her want to complete her degree and become a registered nurse so that she could take a job up in the city and leave this cruel town forever.

By the time Gretchen emerged with the glad tidings and resumed her oversight of the downtown drugstore, the broken hardware store window around the corner had been replaced, the power had been restored out by Settler's Woods and the phonelines repaired, most of the storm and fire damage had been assessed and insurance claims submitted, *The Town Crier* had reappeared, letting everyone know what had been happening recently (John's wife contributed a touching column on "The Kiss of Life"), work had begun on removing the old humpback bridge, John having generously offered to do it at cost, the city council had met to discuss his proposal for clearing the burned-out woods for residential and commercial development, John's daughter and the older man who'd hitched a ride with her that night were both out of intensive care and most of the others, like Pee Patch, as they were calling him, for whom Otis had felt personally responsible, were out of the hospital altogether and back to work, the motelkeeper being the most notable exception. It was still touch and go for old Dutch, and, as part of the annual blood drive chaired by John's wife, all who were of the right blood type had been up to give the old fisherman a transfusion, Otis included, but the unhappy man had shown few signs of improving, or wanting to. The Ford-Mercury garage had not yet reopened, but there were rumors the widow might be considering marriage to the company mechanic injured in the wreck at the humpback bridge, or what was left of him anyway, a move generally perceived, since he was the only one people trusted out there, as both practical and charitable. The murder itself was still officially unsolved, but Otis had launched a nationwide search for the hardware store manager and ex-jailbird who had disappeared the night of the crime, dramatically signing his departure. At first, when they'd discovered the shattered display window, they'd supposed the store had been broken into overnight, but the door had not been forced and little seemed to be missing: a cash register handgun, a couple of tools, maybe some loose change. But then they'd found the bowling ball with the crimson fingerholes which had been thrown through the window with such force it had torn through the display partition behind and ended up down an aisle near the back of the store. When Old Hoot went, he went. The same could be said for Pauline's old man, who was Otis's biggest worry. That vicious psycho hadn't been seen since the night of the fire, and the people upstate wanted to know how he'd got out of Otis's custody. They didn't buy the story he told them, which was nevertheless mostly true. It seemed impossible the old ranter could have survived that toss, but though the search was widening, no body had as yet been found. The joke was (Otis didn't find it funny), he was still in orbit. "I reckon you ain't seen the last of him," Bert told him on the phone. "You're the one who sent him up, ain't you? Duwayne don't forget things like that." Bert, browned off over the loss of his prisoner, might only have been putting the needle in, but he had Otis looking back over his shoulder from time to time, just the same. Otis, whose sense of humor had been badly dented, had got something of a reputation since the fire at Settler's Woods for being moody and explosively ill-tempered, not the easiest guy to work for. When, on the morning after the fire, the officer charged with ordering up autopsies on the two Country Tavern victims had confessed he'd not followed through on that one, Otis, enraged, had threatened to dock the man a month's pay and take his badge away from him, managing only a faint unamused smile amidst the general laughter when the officer explained that "Aw, hell, Chief, Shag was just a yeller mongrel dog they kept out there, and I don't know about Chester, but that was probably the name of that ole three-legged beer-drinkin' alley cat out back." Though he was maybe the best lawman the town had ever had, there was talk about his retiring from the force, especially with the threat of official charges being pressed against him for allowing Duwayne to get away and the insurance investigations into the source of the fire that had destroyed the motel and other property, for which Mayor Snuffy had chewed him out, saying, dammit, he'd let the team down. It didn't help that John, who could usually ease problems like these, was furious with him for giving Clarissa the Porsche keys: "Bad fucking judgment, Otis." It was, he knew it, he was unable even to think clearly anymore, and he had a permanent limp now and he was no longer certain he knew what "keeping order" meant and, well, he'd lost his best friend, so was it any wonder he'd taken to spending a lot of time locked up in his office or alone in church, and had even, hard man that he was, been seen crying from time to time, especially on his visits out to the new landfill near the airport?

Of course, there were those who insisted that Big Pauline was still alive and running around wild and naked somewhere, that Otis's claim to have trapped and killed her in the fire and then buried her remains in the recently dug landfill was just a police cover-up of a failed operation, flawed from the outset by exaggeration and incompetence, that more likely she'd just snuck off in the storm with her infamous father (there'd been any number of sightings), or else had peed her way out before the storm even hit, a theory generated by the admittedly delirious account of the country club golf pro, when he was rescued shortly before dawn by what remained of the police posse after the firestorm had chased most of them away. Kevin had been thought dead, possibly eaten alive, so they were surprised to come upon him in a swampy, foul-smelling, but unburnt grove in the depths of Settler's Woods, overcome by smoke and all but unconscious, but still alive and rambling on incoherently about the way that Big Pauline had saved his heinie, an amazing story that earned him the nickname of Pee Patch for some time thereafter, later shortened to Patch, which was easier to live with once he was behind the bar at the club once more. By that time the story, in all its retellings, had begun to lose its original contours, which he himself did not remember, having to rely entirely on what the police told him he'd said when they'd found him, and had begun to resemble one of old Stu's shaggy dog jokes, may the old champ of the nineteenth hole rest in peace. When he'd first come around in the hospital, still in a state of shock, his lungs scarred, his bandaged hand known to have at least seventeen fractures, and his head and gut wracked by a hangover of titanic proportions, Kevin had had the impression of an angelic presence at the foot of his bed and he'd thought that maybe he'd died. But then he'd seen it was only John's wife, and then John himself had come in later with some flowers. After that: a continuous parade of country clubbers, dropping by with booze and food to hear his stories, he was something of a legend, or rather, more like a cartoon character in a dirty comicbook, but never mind, it was fun lying there, recounting his strange adventures on that dark night, as told to him by his rescuers, like old movie reruns. "What a night that must have been!" they'd laugh and slap their knees. His hand healed but he was never again able to take a proper grip on a golf club, which brought an end to his career out on the pro circuit and changed his teaching habits somewhat, though his lessons out at the club when he got back were as popular as ever.

Lessons that Imogen took when she and Garth moved here, weekend golf being de rigueur in this town, where not much else ever happened. Tennis, swimming, bowling, workout gyms with weight machines, even squash courts and a baseball stadium were available, but John's crowd, the men anyway, were all golfers. Golfers and drinkers. Imogen was convinced that the reason John took

Garth out of small arms contracting and distribution and brought him to town to run the racetrack and related enterprises after John's cousin got sent to prison was because Garth had beat him over eighteen holes one day down in New Orleans and John wanted to get him up here where he could have another shot at him. In fact, her husband hadn't won a round since, learning something out there on the links about John's fierce competitiveness, his powers of concentration, his stubborn quiet force, though he'd done well enough to earn John's respect and friendship. She and Garth had bought a home in a new development called Settler's Woods across from the playground in Peapatch Park, which was either where the original pioneer, whose statue lorded over the place, had his vegetable garden or else where his wife grew sweetpeas and other flowers; this town was full of hokey stories like that. It was a friendly place, though, easy to settle into and made easier by John's wife, who was certainly the person to know around here. She threw a big welcoming party for them, introduced them to all their friends and everyone at the church, proposed them for memberships at the country club, took Imogen shopping, helped her enroll her two girls by a previous marriage in the local schools and invited both children to her son's birthday party, connected them to doctors, dentists, insurance agents, and bank managers, coaxed Imogen into joining the church choir and took her to her first PTA meeting (Imogen was immediately elected treasurer), and had her over for bridge nights when the men were out of town. Which was fairly often. John had inherited from a former partner some swampland in Florida and they often went off there for what they called business meetings and to do a little deep-sea fishing and sailing. Whatever else they did, Garth didn't say, and Imogen didn't ask. Garth could sometimes be a bit scary. Instead, whenever he was away, she amused herself as best she could, which included taking golf lessons out at the club from Patch, a middle-aging man with a damaged hand, possibly a war wound, a randy sense of humor, and an intimate teaching style that included cuddling up from the rear and reaching around to help with the grip and backswing, which took Imogen back to her days of dry-humping at highschool dances. Patch would plant one foot on the outside of her front foot to hold it in place, then push at her back foot with his other one, his knee between hers, thigh bumping the cheeks of her ass apart, his calloused hands stroking hers around the stiff leathery thing in her grip, proxy for the chunkier one bumping at her butt. Patch was not exactly her type (John was), but was attractive enough in a meaty sort of way, so finally, when he proposed it, she gazed down at their four intertangled feet shuffling in the grass below them and said, Okay, but my husband will kill you if he finds out. Patch just chuckled wickedly in her hair. So what the hell. Can't say he wasn't warned.

John's suburban development of Settler's Woods where Garth and Imogen later lived provoked the usual knee-jerk protest from Marge, who accused the mayor and his police of doing John's work for him by torching the woods on purpose, then clearing it for him at the city's expense, but most noticed that Mad Marge's heart no longer seemed in it. John, as Garth was to discover on the golf course, was tenacious and hell to beat, so maybe she'd finally just given up, her strong will worn down at last by a will yet stronger. Which John was famous for, along with his cool daring, his unbending loyalty, his attention to detail, his appetites, his broken nose, his generosity, his killer instincts, his love of the bruising battle. To which list he would add, though others might demur (Maynard, for example, in spite of all that John had done for him to get his sentence reduced and take care of his family in his absence), his compassion. Edna was one who would agree that he was a compassionate man, even though she'd not been directly told who'd paid off her mortgage when Floyd disappeared from town, and Dutch was another, a survivor in spite of himself, who'd been well compensated by John for the loss of his motel and distracted finally from his other deprivations by their codevelopment of Getaway Stadium, a new ballpark and sports facility built on the site of the old motel, originally for summer youth programs and Little League baseball, but large enough that they were eventually able to lure to town a minor league farm club, one that Dutch, owning a piece of it, later helped to run. Nevada, the popular aerobics instructor who took over the new health club at the expanded civic center, would never have described her former boss as a compassionate man (no such thing, she would have said), but she knew him to be flexible in his negotiations and not without feelings: like Otis, John had lost his best friend, and though he never mentioned it, Nevada knew he was hurting. Maybe it was the only serious loss that fortunate man had ever suffered, and as there was nothing he could do about it, his grief, like hers, could be ignored but never wholly assuaged, though his basic principle—"Caring too much for another is a bad investment"—helped. "Everyone and everything's expendable, including yourself," he liked to say. "The important thing is to keep your eye on the game." An expression his wife had never heard, though she had heard him instruct her to keep her eye on the ball. Did she believe him to be a compassionate person? Who could say? She was never asked the question nor ever volunteered an opinion, though she herself was judged to be, as Ellsworth put it in an article on her many charitable activities following the devastating fire at Settler's Woods, "the very paragon of compassion, grace, and civic virtue," a woman loved by all no less than John was by all esteemed.

When Ellsworth dropped by Gordon's studio to ask for a recent photo of John and his wife to accompany the article and to schedule a shoot of the charred and spectral woods, where bulldozers were already rumbling in like robotic predators, eating up the historical moment, he found his friend much changed. Gordon was suddenly an old grizzled fat man, stooped and broken like the ancient humpback bridge they were tearing down out there, and Ellsworth wondered if he himself seemed as changed in Gordon's eyes. The shutdown photo shop was a shambles. Ellsworth had never thought of Pauline as much of a housekeeper or business manager, but her absence was clearly being felt. Photographs and curling negatives littered the floor, albums lay open on chairs and countertops, the bead curtains had been torn away, the portrait studio was a wreck, and there was dust and clutter everywhere, yet Gordon, poking lugubriously about, seemed hardly to notice. His sagging jowls were covered by a dirty gray stubble and his eyes were filmy and unfocused. Ellsworth commiserated with him on his bereavement, remarked that his place looked about as chaotic as his own *Crier* offices ("storm-tossed" was the word that came to mind), and expressed his indignation at Gordon's unjust treatment at the hands of the police, which he said he intended to write an editorial about. "Artists are always misunderstood." "Jail," Gordon said dully. "I'd never been there. But I recognized it. It had the smell of death in it. It was my own darkroom." He picked up a photo from a pile, studied it, set it down again. Ellsworth saw that it was a picture of John's wife in the Pioneers Day parade, one he might use, but that Gordon had been looking at it upside down. "I felt terribly wise and terribly stupid at the same time. And very much alone. I kept hoping you might come by." "I'm sorry. I only just found out. At the time, I was, well, somewhere else. Some time else. It was, I don't know, like I was locked into a certain day, if that was what it was, one I thought would never end." Ellsworth meant to say no more, but realized that what he'd just said made no sense. "I was writing a novel." Gordon seemed surprised by this and a glimmer of his old self returned. "You mean *The Artist's Ordeal*? Is it finished?" He hesitated. "I don't know. I think so. But I can't find it." He'd returned from the grim desolation of smoldering Settler's Woods to the grimmer desolation of his own offices, shocked afresh by what had met him there. His shelves and file drawers were all spilled out and he'd evidently ripped up the sole remaining archival copies of the precious wedding issues, among many others. Perhaps, he'd thought, he was mistaken about the importance of the official chronicler to the keeping of the communal memory, but he'd shaken off his doubts and set about putting his and the town's lives back together again. He'd just been pasting up the scraps as best he could when, around noon, she came in. While sitting all night at the hospital bedside of her child, she'd composed a little essay for his paper on "The Kiss of Life," she'd said, looking up at him as she used to look up at him when they were children, adding with an apologetic smile that she hoped it was not too badly written. Suddenly, he'd wished to hold her hand and read to her as he used to do, this time from his own work, and she'd seemed pleased when he'd suggested it. But when he'd gone looking for the novel, it wasn't there. Only traces. A sheet or two. Scrawled notes. A few mad ravings tossed helter-skelter. "I guess I burned it after all." He glanced again at the photograph on the top of the pile, but saw now that it was of Gordon's dying mother. Gordon must have shuffled them about. The old lady seemed to be staring accusingly up at him, her flesh sunken, toothless mouth agape. A shriveled breast scissored between her gnarled fingers. In his novel, he had written about "the unspeakable things" the Stalker was doing with the Model, but, no, wrong, everything was speakable. "What did you want from her?" Gordon asked suddenly. He'd picked up a soupy grayish photo that seemed to have no image on it at all. "Her?" "You know." "I-I'm not sure." His friend's sorrowful gaze dropped to the murky photograph. "Nor I."

The return of *The Town Crier* was greeted by the usual disparaging wisecracks, but even its severest critics were relieved to find it each week on their front porches again. Things had been happening during its absence, but now it was as though they were *really* happening, and even those events that had gone unreported had been rescued from oblivion by Ellsworth's reconstruction of them, in the same way that the more ancient past had been recovered through his innovative "I Remember" columns. A popular former town librarian, who had passed on some years back, had written in an "I Remember" contribution of her own that "Memory is all we have to keep time from taking everything away from us," and not only did most townsfolk agree with her, but many had that column clipped and pinned up somewhere or tucked in a cookbook or the Bible so they wouldn't forget it. For Marge, the weekly newspaper was less significant as history (she had her scorecards for that, sharing her husband's respect for numbers as about all the history one could count on) than as a bully pulpit, she having been a frequent contributor to its letters page, though less so now than in the past. Had she lost her crusading zeal? Had John finally worn her down? Not exactly. For dreamless Marge had had at last a dream. Where she'd had it, she wasn't sure. She remembered being out on the darkening golf course, feeling very tired, and stumbling toward the seventeenth green, which looked very soft and cushy. She'd just holed out and the last thing she recalled was bending over to look in the hole for her ball. Then she woke up at home. But in between . . . She'd tried to tell Lollie about it, but though she'd had to listen to countless dreams from Lorraine over the years, her friend had refused to listen to the only one Marge had ever had. "I was dancing with . . . somebody," she'd said. "Then suddenly it was more than dancing." "I don't want to hear about it, Marge!" Was Lorraine reading her mind? No, that was over and even her memory of what she'd heard had dimmed. Lorraine was just being selfish. The dream had begun in the basement of John's fraternity house where Marge learned that she'd just been elected. They prodded her forward and, because the issue was zoning problems, she took off her clothes or maybe they were already off for the same reason. Likewise her partner, who told her it was time to start straddling the issue, and that was when the slamdance began. Body contact, he grunted bruisingly. I love it! Though it was the only dream Marge had ever had, the amazing thing was, she was still having it, though most of the preliminaries had long since dropped away. No complaints. It was a pretty good dream, even if there was not much to tell anymore, were there anyone to tell it to. Certainly not to Trevor who was too tired even to talk most of the time and who got terribly flustered whenever she even mentioned the bed, not to speak of sleep and dreams. So, in effect, she'd been subverted from within, knew it, didn't care: dancing John could do what he liked, or almost. When she learned of John's plans to develop Settler's Woods after the fire, she had written to *The Town Crier* about it, accusing the city of sinister collusion, but her letter had appeared the same week that they dug up some old human remains out there, including a skull with the middle of the face missing, Ellsworth heading the story, "Grisly Find in Settler's

Woods," and flaunting his rhetoric in an editorial on the need to clean up that dangerous area, so her message did not get through. No matter. Back to beddy-bye. To speak in the philosophizing manner. Besides, Settler's Woods was one of John's most graceful developments and popular with the community. He preserved most of the surviving trees, mature timber enhancing property value these days, carved the area into interesting odd-shaped lots following the old creek bed (Marge and Trevor bought one), and built a pretty little park with a children's playground around a small grove in the center that had somehow escaped the fire, John thus, ironically, becoming celebrated, like his fondly remembered father-in-law before him, as a builder of city parks.

Opal was proud of her son and loved the park he built, wishing her grandchildren were still small so she could bring them to it, as she used to take them to the old one and her own little boy before them. Oh so long ago. The statue of the Old Pioneer had been rescued from the civic center parking lot and given a nice new pedestal and, though you had to crane your neck to look up at it, it was like having an old lost friend back home again. She missed the old bandstand and the performances there and the family picnics and the summertime speeches her handsome brother used to give, but her husband Mitch, at her urging, had donated a dozen benches in memory of members of the family and old political friends, and they were not as comfortable as the old ones perhaps, but they made her very happy. She liked to sit in them, half dozing in the sun, and watch the children play, letting the past wash over her like a loving embrace, and she often found herself being asked to mind this one or that one for a moment while their mothers dashed off on errands, something she was pleased to do, for it made her feel wanted again. It was so much nicer than the malls, which had no trees or benches at all and no neighborliness either, whatever Kate might say. One day, she found herself sitting on one of the roomier contoured benches of the old city park with that dear friend and with Harriet, too, one on each side. It seemed that Audrey had recently died and they were talking about this, Opal understanding that her friends were really congratulating her on the Audrey inside her having died, since if they were still alive Audrey must be, too. Nonsense! snorted Harriet, and Kate said that, yes, life was, that was what made it so sad. And so beautiful. They saw the young stringy-haired newspaper editor coming their way with a camera, looking sheepish, and Opal exclaimed: All this has happened before! Kate smiled and said, Yes, no doubt, probably everything has. Harriet smiled her own ironic smile and said that the one thing she had no doubts about was that nothing ever happened twice. Opal realized that this conundrum her friends had posed on either side of her and the distinctive smiles on their two lovely faces there in the dappled sunlight were the last things she would see or know before she died, and she felt a pang of grief, and a pang of love.

Ah well, grief, love, sometimes it was hard to tell them apart, so profoundly bound up in one another were they, for no mortal love was free from death nor death's grief from a grievous love of self. When Yale was killed in the war, Oxford, though paralyzed with a sudden despair that dropped him to his knees, realized that he'd been suffering the loss of his beloved son from the day he was born, and that he'd cherished that suffering. In her suicide note three years later, his cancer-stricken wife Kate wrote: "Why we turn against reason, Oxford, is because it tells us we can never have the one deathless thing we most desire and that all our lesser loves must end in sorrow. It's almost unreasonable to be reasonable. I love you, Oxford, but can express this now only by inflicting grief upon you, which, alas, I find I would do with pleasure. And so I deny my love and mourn only myself. My own grief satisfies me and, as you are no longer loved—indeed, you no longer even exist for me—you are freed from all mournful thought of me, who certainly does not exist, unless grieving gives you joy." He'd thought it a cruel letter at the time, but had come to understand that wise Kate had loved him with a rare transcendental love and had found a way, while dying, to express it, and then the tears had come afresh, self-pitying tears, of course, at what he'd lost. For Kate's friend Harriet, who'd died a couple of years earlier, tears were nothing but a sales hook for the entertainment racket, though she'd happily shed plenty over books and in the movies, if seldom in life. "Meat's meat," she always said dismissively. "It has its needs, but you can't take them seriously," and her husband Alf, whose hands were daily busied by needful flesh, agreed—until he held her trembling hands in his ("Hey, do you remember when . . . ?" he'd murmured awkwardly) and felt the life go out and knew then that what he'd loved, though rooted in the self, was not the self. Over the years since then, Alf had found some consolation in the healing of others, or at least in the easing of pain, his own included, bourbon being his usual self-prescription, just as Oxford had consoled himself with his multitudinous grandchildren (at least two more now on the way), the two men meeting most mornings for coffee in the Sixth Street Cafe to exchange thoughts on such topics as love and grief and also the news of the day, which on this particular occasion had to do with the building of the new racetrack ("Coming Soon: The Sport of Kings!" was the headline in the *Crier*), the old bones found out at Settler's Woods which Alf had been asked to examine, the return of Alf's nephew, a highschool classmate of John's, to run John's new international transport firm, recent rumors about the hardware store next door, closed since Old Hoot fled town (there was a business associate of John's visiting from the West Coast this week, she said to be a high-tech hotshot), the surprise marriage announcement of old Stu's widow, and the decision of Oxford's daughter, who was also Alf's nurse, to go back to school and complete her degree, which Alf, generously, offered to help pay for. John's wife, walking her dogs, passed by the cafe window just then, reminding Alf to tell Oxford about the strange sensation he'd had at the tip of his finger and how it had vanished, but before he could get to it, Trevor the insurance agent came limping in and joined them briefly with a cup of soup which he spooned up hastily with quaking hands, and then as quickly got up to go. There were dark bags under his eye and eyepatch and what looked like bruises on his face and neck. "Are you all right, Trevor?" Alf asked. "I-I'm not sleeping well." "I'll give you a prescription." "No. It won't help." He ducked his head, tugging at the cuffs of his linen suit. "It's all right," he said. He squinted at them with his good eye, then leaned closer. "It's a lucky life to have known delight," he whispered, his soft lips quivering. "Isn't it?" "He's suffering from delusions," Alf explained when Trevor left, as though that explained anything at all.

"Oh, I know, honey, I was just kidding myself, it was a big mistake, but he said he loved me and that big booger between his legs was as hard as brass and all mine, so how could I help it? I'm basically a nice person, you know that, but it was all I could think about, it was driving me crazy and I did crazy things. I still think about it, all the time, but now I have to help him find it. It's awful, but what can I do? He owns half the garage, I can't get out of it, I can only hope to hell the pathetic sonuvabitch falls out of his bed and dies. That fitness freak you're so crazy about who gave him the kiss of life can kiss my ass, goddamn her. Why couldn't she leave well enough alone? Isn't that Brucieboy's girlfriend? If so, I wish to hell he'd come back and claim her. She knows Rex from somewhere and keeps butting in, watching over him like he's her kid brother or something, it really gets my goat. The chilly bitch says she doesn't trust me, and when he comes home from the hospital, I'm afraid she's going to move in on us. Do you think she's trying to get a piece of the action? Probably, hunh? What a mess. And he's so *mean* to me! Honest to God, it's the worst thing that's happened to me since back during my first marriage when I was playing around and got that infected lovebite on the ass. You remember? Thought I'd die. Why the hell was Rex driving John's car anyway? Oh, I don't blame your daughter, poor thing, she's suffered enough. No, it was Winnie's fault, I'm sure of it. The old ghoul was just getting her own back out at the humpback bridge where she bought it herself. I'm glad they're tearing the fucking thing down, scares the pants off me every time I have to drive over it. Winnie's nailed old Stu, and me, too, in her witchy way, sticking me with this murderous basket case, maybe the old battleax'll go away now and leave me alone. What's worse, I have to admit, honey, I miss old Stu. His hillbilly music, his dumb jokes, his sneezing and farting, all of it. And I don't have anyone to get swacked with now. It's so boring tying one on alone! At least you're back, sugar. I'm so glad, I was lost without you! I've got so much to—hey, did I tell you? I ran into Colt again. Why didn't you warn me John was bringing him back here? It was terrible. He didn't even recognize me. When I told him who I was, the dickhead just stared at me and said, No shit. Really! It was disgust at first sight. I couldn't blame him. I'm such an ugly old bag now, who'd want to recognize me, even if they did? Looking in a mirror makes me puke. It's all over, it really is. Oh God, I'm crying and I can't stop! The good times are gone, sweetie! I'll never know hard dick again! I'm so scared! How am I going to get through the rest of it?"

Nevada, whom Daphne called a chilly bitch, had a more professional attitude toward hard dick perhaps than did the likes of sentimental heart-on-her-sleeve Daphne, but it was not as callous a one as those who'd enjoyed her services might have supposed. For Nevada, hard dick was a monument which she helped raise, sometimes merely by what she revealed or concealed, a kind of magical sleight of body, other times more dynamically, using her orifices and appendages like an artist's tools, making something happen out of nothing—though of course it wasn't nothing, that was just the point: monuments were never the thing itself, merely an emblem of and tribute to it. All her life, at least since she'd given up oldtime religion, Nevada had believed fundamentally in hard dick—something to hold onto in a time of trouble, she often said to Rex, a mighty rock in a weary land—and in the mystery behind it, something not visible on the surface, part human, part cosmic, which it was her task and fortune to help reveal, or at least to invoke. To erect. Which made her something of a priestess, she knew, a responsibility she took seriously (pleasure, she took seriously, too, most else besides; Nevada was at heart, contrary to the popular perception, a serious woman), keeping herself fit with a rigorous training program and staying alert to the nuances of the vocation. Now, with Rex's accident, it was not that her faith had been shaken, but that it had deepened, drawing her beyond the iconic and the monumental into the subtler paradoxes of soft-dick love. Or such, at any rate, was the consequence of her decision to stay on here in a small prairie town she loathed with all her heart to be near to and care for the only thing human she'd ever connected to in this world since her old granny cashed in. And he needed her. The fat lady was trying to renege on their contract and might even be dangerous, and John, fearing a major lawsuit, was as usual taking the offensive and might hit Rex with everything from statutory rape to murder to force him to cut a deal. John blamed Nevada for the trouble Clarissa had got into and for what had happened to Bruce and Jennifer as well, both assumed dead, saying that as far as he was concerned she was an accessory to kidnap and murder, but he also owed her a favor for dragging his bloody child out of the creek and saving her life, for dressing both of them before the ambulance came in the clothes she'd found scattered by the roadside while tailing them (until she found the shorts, she'd thought she was following John), and for getting Rex to agree, conditionally, to say that he'd been the one driving. Nevada had expected a substantial payoff from Bruce for setting him up with his farewell cherrypop, he'd even talked about making her a full business partner of John's, presumably by way of a final will, it was the main reason she'd wanted to go up to the cabin with John that night, but she wasn't surprised that she'd been double-crossed. By Bruce or John or both. All she got handed by John was a wad of dark-stained bills tagged, *For the pimp.* Was that blood, or had Bruce wiped his ass on them? She handed them back. Suspicious by nature, she didn't trust them anyway. When she asked John pointblank if there was a will, he said there might have been, but it wasn't worth much, was it, if there was no body. And that was exactly how much she learned from John about what he'd found up there, though he did have effective operational control of a lot of Bruce's properties and investments after that. What Nevada asked for, standing there in her bloody clothes in the hospital room that grim dawn, knowing she was beaten, beaten badly, was a permanent job in or near town so as to be near Rex. John gazed at her thoughtfully, then at crushed and unconscious Rex, putting things together. We can work it out, he said, and later he sold her the new health club franchise at the expanded civic center for a dollar where she gave aerobic and weight-training classes and he transferred a couple of investments into her name which were probably hers anyway, and in time they even became something like friends, though they never got it on again, nor did she wish to. Not now. Maybe later when his own dick went soft.

One day, long before that happened, when John had to make a trip up to the state capital for a meeting his father had arranged with members of the state gaming commission, Nevada said she knew someone up there John should visit. She was a professional, but she'd buy him his ticket and it would be worth his time. John doubted this and distrusted Nevada still, but took the phone number along. Before leaving, he stopped by the police station to talk with the troubled chief and suggest a career change, but learned that Otis had left for Settler's Woods where they might have found their missing prisoner at last. Not so. "These have been here some while," Otis said, kicking at the bones. Bulldozers, clearing the charred stumps, had turned them up at the edge of a ravine. Otis was disappointed and worried, looking edgily over his shoulder, and so was receptive to John's proposal. He said he'd think on it and let him know when John got back. John, in turn, was sobered by the bones, and realized he'd not yet shaken off the emotional garbage of Bruce's suicidal betrayal. Something in him still wanted the old days back, but the loss of his old friend, he knew, was permanent. The miserable asshole was either dead, which was highly likely, or, if John ever ran into him again, he'd have to kill him. Grief for John was an appetite like any other and, a man of many appetites, John believed in feeding one with another. Thus it was that the idea of an exotic fuck in the old style appealed to him as both wake and exorcism, so after the meeting, which did not go well (luckily, he'd made sure that nothing was in his own name), he called and booked an hour before dinner, figuring he could return later if she was good and he wanted a nightcap. He expected her to surprise him and she did. Not the sex. She was young, skilled, limber, thoughtful, even contemplative, better with her vagina than her mouth (she'd had a good teacher), but, except for her expressionless mask and Goldilocks wig, conventional. She fucked by the numbers, almost as though out of a manual. Probably the most exciting thing about her was her aura of terrible vulnerability: she was, whore or no, intensely virginal. She was literally trembling as he entered her. But that wasn't the surprise either.

When Clarissa got out of traction and was able to travel, albeit with a back and neck brace and crutches, she went up to the capital for the first of the plastic surgery her father had scheduled (nothing but the best, as always), and, though she did not know her father had preceded her nor ever found out, Clarissa also paid a visit, arranged by Nevada on the promise that it was a secret between them, to her old friend Jennifer. It was a cold wintry day, and Jen's flat was dark and chilly. The living room and bedroom looked like shutdown movie sets, very posh and with lots of soft beautiful fabrics, even on the walls, but they sat at a plain wooden table in the dismal little kitchen at the back, Jen in a droopy housecoat and close-cropped hair, drinking Diet Cokes together. It was an awkward meeting, around noontime, before Jen's working day began, and although, thanks to Nevada, each knew a lot about what had happened to the other, they found it hard to start talking about it. It wasn't that Jen was unhappy, really, but she was different. Or something was different between them. For one thing, Jen had taken up smoking. But more than that. She seemed thinner, more hollow cheeked, still pretty in an angular sort of way, but older, her faded complexion showing traces of creamed-off makeup. Clarissa had suggested in her phonecall that they meet for a taco or a hamburger somewhere, but Jen said she never went out anymore, so now Clarissa asked her why not, and she said she just didn't like it out there, it was too confusing, a big meaningless blur. "In here, I know what's what," she said, turning her Coke glass round and round in its own sweat ring on the table. Clarissa filled Jennifer in on all the family news ("The Creep came to see me every day . . .") and told her how Nevada pulled her out of the wreck and gave her the kiss of life, and Jennifer, stubbing out her cigarette in the jar lid that served as an ashtray and lighting up another, said that she and Nevada were lovers now. "Sort of. It's more like being sisters maybe, but it's what we have that's steady. The men just come and go." Clarissa was shocked but tried not to show it. Jen asked her why Rex was in her car that night and Clarissa told her. "I was really pissed off that you'd gone off with Bruce alone. I got stoned and went completely out of my skull." "Probably they were just trying to protect you. It wasn't very nice. I think maybe he meant to kill me and changed his mind." She stood up, cigarette dangling in the corner of her mouth, and dropped her housecoat and Clarissa, blinking, saw slanted light on scarred flesh, and then Jen was sitting again, the housecoat wrapped around her. "It was beautiful, though. The whole cabin was full of flowers. It was like a dream I'd had." Clarissa, trying to stay cool, said: "Well, my scars are worse, and there was nothing beautiful about it." Jennifer nodded, stubbed her butt out in the heaped jar lid. "I'm awfully sorry." "Except for one moment maybe, when I felt wildly free. But I can only vaguely remember it." Clarissa went to use the bathroom, Jen helping her as far as the door, and when she came back she asked about the ruined painting hanging in there. "Marie-Claire did it. It was the only thing he gave me afterwards. A kind of souvenir. While he had me strapped down, he said he believed Marie-Claire had found a kind of final ecstasy through pure form before she died, and he wanted to use me the same way she had used her canvas. It was pretty scary." They both agreed that Bruce was a totally screwed-up guy, though Jennifer said she still loved him, even if he was dead. Maybe that was what was different about her. When Clarissa got up to go, Jen started to cry. She apologized, and what she said, wiping her eyes on her housecoat sleeve, was: "I can never fall in love again." "Who knows?" Clarissa said, leaning on her crutches. She was feeling strangely jealous of Jennifer, and she was ashamed of it. "Anyway, Jen, once was better than nothing."

Like sister, like brother. Jennifer's brother Philip, too, carried the torch for a lost love well past all hope of reciprocation and past even his desire for it. Years later, married and with children of his own, teaching at a small college not unlike the one his father taught at when Philip was in kindergarten, enjoying an affair with a young biology colleague (hey, let it happen) and popular with the students of both sexes (his philosophy, taught him in his father's own study by the beautiful schemer who changed his life: if you can't send the soul to heaven, lover, at least, hallowed be thy kingly come, send the body . . .), he still suffered a kind of wistful flush whenever Clarissa came to mind or was brought to mind by news from home sent by Zoe. As when she first got elected to the state legislature, for example: he could hardly recognize her from the newspaper photo, but what he saw when he stared at that strong handsome woman standing by her private jet in her business suit was the vulnerable little teenager in her hospital bed, utterly locked up in casts and braces, but fiery-eyed and taunting him still, even as she asked a favor of him, demanded it, rather, an image that provoked in him an almost unbearable longing which, as an educated man, he supposed was at heart a longing for a lost innocence. Got the hots, as he and Turtle used to say, but the hots he got these days were not for sex but for the wonderful all-consuming glow that used to accompany its anticipation while it itself was still largely unknown, a glow he could only experience secondhand now by way of the occasional undergraduate or, glimmeringly, by reliving his passion for Clarissa. His friend Maynard had also gone the grad school route in time and had even visited Philip's college when Philip managed to get him short-listed during a search in what passed for a philosophy department there, but Maynard was too weird even for this lot. He lectured from his thesis-in-progress which espoused the theory that the big bang theory of an exploding and contracting universe was nothing more than a residual memory from the womb—but nothing less either, for who was to say that we did not, in each of our cells, reenact the entire history of the universe? That might have gone down without a blink had he not defended his thesis with a wild mix of evangelical religious metaphors and research based largely on his ritual visits to porn parlors, Maynard being evidently another trying to recapture a lost delight, but about as crazy as his poor mother who, last time Philip saw her, screamed every time someone opened a door or she had to turn a corner. Of course, loopy as his own folks were, Philip was not really one to talk. Maynard's embittered father, who had whipped the boy for things as insignificant as a dirty wristband found in the woods or a childish question about angels and orgasms, did a bit of prison time eventually, caught out in some irregularities at the racetrack, and since Philip was off to college by then, Maynard was taken in by his own folks and given Philip's old room. Which always made Philip feel uneasy in a way he could not quite pin down, though Maynard became more like family to him than his own family did, except for Zoe. Philip had drifted away from his parents over the years, or they from him, never did get used to baby Adam, who always seemed a bit scary to him, nor ever saw Jennifer again, though he knew she was alive somewhere because Clarissa told him so. He'd gone to visit his love every day after the accident while she was in the hospital, enduring her bitter invective, responding abjectly to her least demand, mostly in silence, never once professing his love, nor replying in kind to her humiliating ridicule, often with an audience of other friends about. Then one day, when no one else was around and she seemed particularly angry and restless inside all her bindings and apparatuses, Clarissa asked him to reach under her bedclothes and jerk her off, not being able to use her hands was driving her crazy, come on, Creep, make yourself useful. And so, breathless with terror and excitement, his eye on her braced hips and rigid cast-locked elbows, his broken nose tingling inside its own plaster mask, he slid his damp trembling hand into that tender crevice he had so long coveted and, with his finger up her at last, felt all thought dissolve into pure sensation, like a hot brain bath, what his mother would have called beatitude or an ecstasy attack, a sensation which lingered in the memory to this day, though he no longer remembered what his finger felt, if in fact, stunned as he was, it felt anything at all. Her own pleasure engulfed him and he came in his own pants, not knowing how it happened. Okay, I owe you one, Creep, she said afterwards. Now get lost. Never did collect. Never hoped to. Dreamt of it, though. All the days of his life.

Otis owed one to the Virgin and she did collect. After retiring from the police force and before taking over the management and security operations of the municipal airport, a vacancy created by the election of Mayor Snuffy, Otis went on the religious retreat he had solemnly promised her, withdrawing from friends, family, and all worldly obligations to a small rustic cabin at the edge of a summer camp run by the church. Except for attending Mass in the little chapel in the woods, he kept himself apart from the children and the staff and the other people on retreat, eating alone, reading the literature provided, taking long silent walks, praying and meditating and reflecting upon the cross and images of the Virgin and of Pauline. These latter he kept out of sight nor did he even mention them in the confessional, for, though he had the Virgin's own permission to study them and attached no sinfulness to them, others might not have understood that his interest in these little paper blowups of the creases and dimples and hairy bits of naked flesh was not prurient but contemplative: Otis, in short, thumbing through the photos, was seeking something like the mystical hot brain bath that had benchmarked the emotional life of young Fish. That fateful night in the woods in Pauline's lap, pressed up under the tender overhang of her monumental breast, illumined only by the stuttering radiance of the turbulent skies, Otis had felt himself as close to a true religious experience as he'd ever known, but one interrupted by his sudden untimely and painful fall between her thighs (he could remember, as he hit the ground, glancing up in panic at her massive craglike buns for fear she might sit down before he could get to his feet and scramble out of there), and his desire now was to recapture that visionary moment just before, wherein, as he now recalled, his whole life as Officer Otis the guardian warrior had been revealed as a mockery, a self-delusion: what did his lifelong obsession with order and disorder have to do with this turbulent, radiant, and tender world which knew, at heart, no such distinction? Oh ye of little faith! her belly had seemed to murmur into his pressed ear. What measures you take to conceal the truth from view! Yes, he had been ready at last to shed all artifice—to be a man merely of the here and now was to be a man closed out from eternity!—and to embrace, if it could be said to be embraceable, the legendary abyss, which seemed to lie just beyond the warm undulant flesh to which, before he fell, he clung. But then, suddenly, he was on the ground again and, with gunfire crackling, it was back to business as usual. Except he was dead tired, hadn't slept for what seemed like weeks, so the rest of that night was like a walking nightmare—the madness of the fire, the exhausting storm, her weight, the confusion, the mud at the landfill, his terrible weariness—and he remembered little of it, dependent upon these photos to bring it back to mind. Which they did but dimly, referring, like most criminal evidence, more to themselves than to anything else. But then, one twilit evening, he was staring, his thoughts elsewhere, at a shot apparently taken in the rain, or perhaps in the bath, and he suddenly seemed to see behind Pauline's twinkling pubes a faint second image peeking through: a pure white presence, like a tunic, flowing beside its ghostly twin as though shadowed by its own reflection. What? He peered closer. No. Nothing more. A photographic flaw perhaps. No, wait! There, up by the appendectomy scar: a gaze—*that* gaze! He gasped and fell to his knees, felt a tingling on the back of his neck. It was she! The Virgin! A miracle!

Gordon, the town photographer who had taken the photos that so engaged the attention of the former police chief on his religious retreat, received in time an unexpected bequest when Trevor the insurance agent suddenly fell victim to time's ceaseless violence and wasted away and died. There was no explanation in the will, only the proviso that it be used to further the legatee's artistic endeavors. Not quite a miracle perhaps, but certainly a surprise. In an article in *The Town Crier,* editor Ellsworth praised the deceased for his generous support of the arts in the community and pointed out that the recipient of his beneficence, recently widowered, had devoted his life to serious artistic endeavors, both public and private, which had heretofore gone largely unrecognized. When interviewed, the photographer was reported to have said that he hoped to accomplish a complete study of the town, exploring it exhaustively, block by block, to unlock its elusive secrets and reveal its hidden surfaces. What Gordon really told Ellsworth was that he was through with photography, there was nothing left to see worth seeing, it was his inclination to return now to drawing and painting, and to portraiture in particular, which he proceeded to do, though with the help of photography, copying directly from his studio shots and sometimes, for variety, from photos taken out on the streets, or even from magazines. A bit mechanical maybe, but everyone seemed to love them and to think of him thereafter as the town artist. Ellsworth objected privately (Gordon, gazing at him as one might at a prospective model, was shocked to notice how gray his thin stringy hair had become, how deep the bags beneath his eyes, and wondered where those photos were he took when they were young), but without conviction, for he himself, shrugging his shoulders when asked what had happened to *The Artist's Ordeal,* had launched a new novel about his grandfather, an itinerant printer who had made his living passing through villages such as this one, producing commercial handbills and selling how-to-do-it and children's books, and who here met a widow who wrote poetry for weddings and funerals and married her and settled down. He would *not* call it *The Artist and His Muse,* he said when Gordon suggested it. Something more like: *I Remember: The Story of My Grandfather.* Gordon offered to provide illustrations for it. The studio reopened, but by appointment only. Disenchanted with his former pursuits, Gordon no longer sold or developed film, accepted news photo assignments for the *Crier,* added to or even refiled his backshop collections (though many of the prints were useful to him in his new career), nor took school, club, wedding, anniversary, team, or any other personal, social, or group photos away from the shop, but he did put up new hangings and reactivate his old studio, the portraits taken there often serving as the basis for his higher artistic aspirations, and thus he continued to contribute to the town's pictorial history, if not so extensively as before.

By coincidence, on the day of Trevor's funeral, Floyd called home. He wouldn't say where he was. On the road somewhere down South. He had another truck which he'd got from a guy who suddenly didn't want it anymore. And now a hitchhiker he'd picked up had just offered him a job running drugs up from the border with it. "You gonna do that?" "Heck, no. The sonuvabitch'll pay dear for even askin'." "Don't do nothin' wrong, Floyd." "No. Where was you all day? I rung up earlier." "To a funeral. You recall that feller we bought our house insurance from? He died." Edna pressed her skirt down across her knees.

"When you comin' back, Floyd?" "Not for a time, I reckon. Who's John got in the store?" "It's shut down. I hear tell it's gonna be a museum." "Always was one. Did he find him some sucker yet to run his truckin' racket?" "Looks like it. Some feller from outa town who useta live here oncet. His wife seems nice, she was at the funeral today. They say she used to be on TV. Anyways that's what they wrote in the newspaper." "What did they write about me in the newspaper?" "Nary a word. Was you expectin' to be famous?" "You know what I mean. What did they say when Stu got killt? Who'd they say done it?" "They never did." "It wasn't me, Edna. I swear on the Bible. I never touched old Stu." "Who said you did?" "There's some thinkin' it." She really didn't want to talk about all this. It was making her cry again. It was awful all the questions she had to answer when he left, all the things they told her. "Are you keepin' warm, Floyd?" "Here where I am, keepin' warm ain't a problem. What's a problem is I don't have no money to send you. Not yet." "It's okay. I'm gonna have a job soon at the new pioneer museum." "It ain't okay. But nothin' I can do. If I get some, though, I'll drop it off with your half sister like always." "I reckon she'll be about as happy about that as she ever was." "Just so she don't turn me in. Did you talk to the bank about the mortgage?" "Yes." Charity ticked Floyd off so, she figured it best not to tell him the rest. "It's okay for now." "How's it okay?" "Just okay. Oh, a funny thing, Floyd. John's wife come by not long after you went off. She brung me that little rug. You remember? She said she heard they'd been some mix-up and she was sorry and wanted me to have it." "That damn rug!" "I told her I didn't want it, thank you. I wouldn't let her leave it. Finally, I just shut the door on her." "You done right! Who does she think she is, anyhow? Uh-oh. Listen, I gotta go now, Edna." Edna felt a sudden chill. It was like a cold wind had got inside her. What it was was a thought, plain and simple: Floyd wasn't coming back. Not ever. It was like he'd died. All she'd have would be this voice. Maybe. "I'll call again soon as I can. I miss you, Edna. You take care now, you hear?" "You, too," she said back, her voice trembling, but by then the line was dead.

The forest had vanished. It was as though a door had closed. She searched for it but the landscape had changed. Wherever she walked, it was ever more desolate, as though it were dying from within. Like a failure of the imagination, she thought, having been taught to think this way.

Her friend and teacher, too: gone, as if he'd never existed. She'd only meant to lead him out of the forest before it destroyed him, just as she'd said in the note she left behind, but as usual, he must have misread it, and now all she had left was his voice in her head, his fancy declarations about art and nature and truth and beauty and all that, his barked commands and the cruel criticisms that made her cry, his stormy impatience with failure, the groans that wracked him as he ripped up his drawings of her when he despaired of ever approximating his unattainable ideal. She loved him, perhaps simply because she had no other to love, but she learned not to say so for it made him distant and moody and caused his drawings to smudge and the paint to run on the canvas. To love and be loved was not what she was given to do. She might rather not do what she did, be what she was, but there seemed little choice, it was as though it were somehow her destiny and her due to pose forever, kneeling on a rock at the edge of a flowing river, that he might enact his noble pursuit and its attendant tragedy. But where now was that river? Where was that rock? And where the forest that framed them? Could she find it and resume her place, it might restore him to his and to his famous ordeal, but as she roamed the world in search of it, a forest seemed less and less likely. That which had created and sustained the forest had vanished with the forest's vanishing. Now a cold wind blew, from which no cover. In the old days, he'd sometimes read to her, holding her hand, and she often dreamt now in her bleak wanderings of a fairytale rescue like those in the stories she'd heard then and heard now in his voice only, but her waking life knew no such dreams, for all those stories, she knew, had died when the forest died. A fire? She seemed to remember one, but perhaps it was not so dramatic as that. More like rot at the roots maybe. A withering away, a withdrawal, a subsidence, much as a fading memory sinks away and is gradually lost to recall, so too this forest so lost to sight one doubted that it ever was. But though astray and abandoned, she persisted in her search in spite of all that had happened, tracing and retracing her steps, for she was sure of it: there *was* a forest and she was there and a man was there. Once . . .